*ELEPHANT
AND
CASTLE*

Books by R. C. Hutchinson

THE ANSWERING GLORY

THE UNFORGOTTEN PRISONER

ONE LIGHT BURNING

SHINING SCABBARD

TESTAMENT

THE FIRE AND THE WOOD

INTERIM

ELEPHANT AND CASTLE

ELEPHANT AND CASTLE

A RECONSTRUCTION

by

R. C. Hutchinson

RINEHART & COMPANY, INC.

NEW YORK   TORONTO

COPYRIGHT, 1949, BY R. C. HUTCHINSON

PRINTED IN THE UNITED STATES OF AMERICA

BY H. WOLFF, NEW YORK

ALL RIGHTS RESERVED

For M. M. from M and R

People in This Book

ARMOREL CEPINNIER. (Sometimes called 'Rellie,' 'Susie,' or 'Sue.')
Her aunts, EDITH and GEORGINA CEPINNIER. ('Edie' and 'Georgie.')
Her grandmother, GERTRUDE CEPINNIER.
Her sister, CHRISTINE ('Chrissy'), married to EVERARD LISKE.
Her cousin, RAYMOND. (Sometimes revealed as the narrator.)
Her mother, IRENE.

>*Deceased Persons mentioned:*
>Her great-grandmother, DOROTHEA TRUGGETT.
>Her grandfather, LAWRENCE CEPINNIER.
>Her father, ARTHUR CEPINNIER.

Her former fiance, Captain GORDON AQUILLARD.
Her friend 'DUFFY' (Dorothy Elwin, afterwards Mrs Filliard).
ELIZABETH KINFOWELL (friend of Duffy).

GIAN ARDREE. ('Toughie.')
His parents, SIMON and MARIA ARDREE.
His sister ROSIE, married to ED HUGG.
MR OLLEROYD, lodger with the Ardrees.

TREVON GRIST, Warden of Hollysian House Boys' Club.
Sergeant FLOCK, Instructor and Factotum at the Club.
'SLIMEY', Carpenter at the Club.

DAISE EMPIRE
Her parents, CHARLIE and MATILDA EMPIRE.

Armorel's daughter, ANTONIA ('Tonie').
Her son, GORDON.
Elizabeth's son, MICHAEL.

MR CUDDISH, Stipendiary Magistrate (later Mr Justice Cuddish) at the Damien Street Magistrate's Court.
MR HOUSENCROFT, Solicitor
MR CLEWARD, Solicitor
SIR WALTER DIBEL, M.P. } London personages.
COLONEL DEWIP, Deputy Governor of Spenwick Prison.
NURSE WIMPLE, at the Old Brompton Hospital.
ORMISON
THE FIDGLEY BROTHERS
TERENCE HUBBITT } Boys at the Club.
'NIBBLEY' TOMS
MRS INCH, an elderly woman of no fixed abode.
MR TIM HEALD, owner of Begbie's Store in Mickett Lane.
JAMES ARDREE, brother of Simon.
DAPHNE STEABEN (afterwards Mrs Scobaird), school friend of Armorel.
CAPTAIN ROGER DESTERIN, friend of Irene Cepinnier. } Guests at Armorel's wedding.
FREDERICK HUTCHINSON, cousin of Armorel.
HENRY KINFOWELL, husband of Elizabeth.
MISS EXCEL, proprietress of the North View Private Hotel.
MR AND MRS CUPWIN
Their children, EILEEN and DESIREE CUPWIN.
MISS ST ESTWYN
MR AND MRS ASKELL } Guests at the North View Hotel.
MISS GESWICK
MR BISHOP
IZZY BROOKS
LOFTY CHIFFOP } Friends of Simon Ardree.

For a list of other people who appear in this book, see page 657.

Cellarer's.
E.C. 4.

7 May 1939

My Dear Hutchinson,

The man who told you that I "knew something about the Mickett Lane affair" was exaggerating. My acquaintance with the business was so brief and fragmentary as to be almost negligible.

For many years now my professional concern has been with less murky goings-on. I report flotations, mergers, a bankruptcy or two, things which would not interest you at all (but which have more meaning than the man in the street commonly supposes). I chanced on the Mickett Lane distress through the accident of being in the neighbourhood when it happened. I had been interviewing Jaslin, the margarine king, who for some reason known only to himself kept a hide-out in that district, and when I was putting my story through to Webb he switched me over to Shagan, the assistant news editor, who through twenty-seven Fleet Street years has retained for every murder that comes along a naïve and boyish appetite which I find rather endearing. He had got wind, in the way he does, of the Mickett Lane killing, and as news was slack and most of the crime team were up in Cheshire nosing round the Macclesfield nonsense he asked if I would nip round and get an early cut at it. I could not say No to the old darling and I went.

There was the usual crowd in the street, staring at the windows. I suppose they hoped to see an angel appear and carry the departed up into heaven. The cop doing sentry at the door was a man I had got to know in my novitiate, our relationship had been cordial and financial, I let it be known that I was principal of the Funerals Branch of the

Board of Trade and he let me in (which cost Shagan two quid). On the whole I wished he hadn't. Anyone who wants to study the interior architecture of Mickett Lane can do so without fear of being jostled by me. The Scene of the Crime was a bedroom upstairs. They had drawn the curtains, and there was one electric bulb burning over the bed, but the curtains let in quite a lot of daylight, giving the room the neither-the-one-damned-thing-nor-the-other appearance which you get in an empty theatre with the stage set and the curtain up. There was a smell of disuse and disinfectants, with a lingering stink of face-powder. At my age I am not, I hope, sensitive to what the half-baked call "atmosphere", but I found the cheapness of the whole set-up quite disagreeable. There were two or three seedy little men in smart three-guinea suits doing exactly what they do in whodunits, taking photographs with micro-cameras and making measurements, one fellow with a cigarette stuck to his lip was calling out the figures just as a tailor does. No one took any notice of me, and I had the impression that if I'd started to intone the burial service in a high, childish treble or to unleash a brace of bloodhounds from my brief-case they still wouldn't have taken any notice. It was that sort of scene, by Tchehov out of Madame Tussaud. There was a rheumy-eyed old man who I suppose was the police doctor examining the body. So feeling that I ought to give Shagan his money's worth I examined it too. The medical was kind enough to point out the wounds in the throat, which I could perfectly well have seen for myself. A wheezy old bore in love with footling technicalities.

It was less exciting than any butcher's shop, but slightly more distasteful because of the faked twilight and the soaked bedclothes—blood soaking into brown earth was somehow never quite so unpleasing to look at. This, I suppose, denotes some atavistic squeamishness in my make-up, since the object under examination did nothing to set my thoughts to pity or anything of that kind—it had far less semblance to a living human body than a stone image, and later on, when I saw a photograph of the woman alive, I could not see the smallest resemblance. What was rather curious, though, was that from this white mask, partly hidden by matted hair, I was able to derive the certainty that she had once possessed some beauty. Had she been a woman of ordinary prettiness there would have been nothing left to show. I also remember noticing the night-dress, which had Venetian rose point at the top. That and the face seemed to go together, and I thought it a pity that lace of such perfect workmanship had been ruined by staining. The tecs, who are always as resourceful as sailors, had got in a bottle of something to ease their labours and they good-naturedly offered me a noggin, but the teacup had not been washed properly and I didn't want it.

So Shagan really got precious little for my pains. Jimmie Cobarl, who covers all the higher-class slayings, took over the story and did his best to put a mystery angle on it—there was that rather corny business, you remember, about the two sets of fingerprints on the handle of the knife. But that of course petered out in a few days, as I guessed it would. Betty Shepworth (I think it was) had a shot at re-hashing it for our Sabbath by-blow with a sob-stuff angle, and that went over like cotton wool falling into a drain—there just wasn't any sob angle as far as I could see. We can turn up the throb column in question in our office file if you like. But it was a bum story, anyway.

I'm sorry I can't tell you more. If you're still interested, you might visit a pub called the Old Richmond—go to Elephant and Castle Station and anyone will direct you. The barman there—mention my name—knew something about the people concerned, and could probably put you on to others who knew a lot more; but I'm afraid you won't get much. The fact is that the parties involved were evidently very ordinary and very dull parties. The crime was a vulgar crime, inspired by some commonplace motive, which except for the protagonists had no meaning at all.

Let me know if you're ever in town.

              Yours,
              Charles P. F.

PART ONE

I

*T*HE FACTS will be stated and you shall make your own judgements.

In the strictest sense, it is impossible to give facts uncoloured by opinion. When a man says "We had dirty weather" you know that he disliked it; another would have said "It was fresh and exhilarating, though there was a good deal of rain." No one can relate all the circumstances, and those which a man selects, deliberately or not, will owe their inclusion at least a little to his prejudices, as well as to his habits in observation and memory. But remember, too, that your own prejudices operate all the time. Whatever comes to your mind comes through your own screen of intricate associations: the memory of something said in a schoolmaster's sarcastic voice; the loneliness of a foreign city; a soldier's kindness in a railway carriage when the first light was revealing frosted fields; defections and disillusionments. The phrase "What I should have done . . ." marks, as a rule, a misunderstanding of the nature of things. The largest mistake about truth is to imagine that it is simple.

"But there aren't any taxis about," she said. "Besides, I like going on trams."

But there was no petulance, there was hardly wilfulness in her voice, which was always grave and mellow. Her smile gave the words a gentleness. Indeed, all her movements were gentle, and seemed to be an extension of her body's grace. And besides, Aunt Georgie thought, one must allow for all that the poor child had been through.

For the moment there was no tram either. The No. 35 which was coming down St George's Road had pulled up with a jerk at the end of Colnbrook Street. A drayman was in difficulty with his horses and the tram, by stopping short, gave him the chance to get himself straight. It's always the same, the tram-driver said to himself, directly you get south of the river you're in among bunglers. But he was sentimental about horse traffic, for the London he had grown up in was the London of the early eighties and at forty-two, with four years of muck and fright behind you and with only the converging rails in front, you see your childhood in gentle hues.

Georgina said, "Aunt Edie will wonder why we've been so long."

"She'll think we've been killed in an accident," Armorel answered gently, half-turning to survey the length of Contessa Street with a tourist's curiosity. "She'll say that the ways of Providence are past finding out but you can rely on Providence to do what's best for us all."

"Oh dear!" Aunt Georgie said.

A small Morris van turned into the street and pulled up a few yards down on the right, its new green varnish a flash of gaiety in the street's dull tones. At Marshall Gardens the tram had been stopped once more.

I suppose, Aunt Georgie thought, for a moment following her niece's gaze along the slovenly side-street, I suppose Edith would say that people who live in such places have done something to deserve it, even if it's just a secret sin that only God knows about; and then, vexed with the way her mind referred all such problems to Edith, It's possible, she thought, that really they like it because of not having to worry about clothes. And this, thought Armorel, surveying the pinched houses, the iron roof of Dibdin's cooperage, rusted enamel plates on the tobacco shop, is what you get from laissez-faire. Yet there were trees delicate in winter nakedness against a pool of glass-green sky between the school and a signal-box; the hard light of a February morning came more gently upon damp pavements through the brown cloud which a train had left on the viaduct, and before the soot-stained bricks where the road went out of sight a child, wheeling a home-made barrow, wore a coat of brilliant blue. Raggedly, enfeebled by the grinding of the main road traffic, a trickle of *The Arcadians* came from a piano-organ beyond the turn.

To those who lived in Bowler's Tithe, Contessa Street (which has been rubble since, and the rubble cleared away) was merely a channel, the place where you started running if you heard the tram; in summer a tank of stuffy heat, scented with glue, in cold weather a funnel for damp and bullying gusts loaded with the smell of railway. It had fallen into dullness, Lizzie Bentlock thought, gazing from the upstairs window at the green van and the workmen going home to dinner; the Trims had gone, and Macdonald and his daughter, there was no one left to make the street what it had been in her day. To Daisy in the blue coat the street was cosmos: the place where the trams went by, to hound and crush all children as she had learned, was merely a rampart of dim sights and noises within which the habitable world was laid.

So while it lasted it had more than a name, than mere identity, this passage-way, this space in which the builders had spawned a few drab specimens of their art. It had its privacy. The sounds were chiefly an overflow from the main road, the moan and shudder of trams, a tidal monotone of engines; from the main road it took a few ingredients of its breath, the smell of tar and lubricant, of old, damp furniture, of a taproom opened in the morning: but the noise which returned with dear familiarity to a man back from Flanders was that of machine saws in the cooperage; the reek of frying fat came from Ted Olsen's, while the yard belonging to Blake's upholstery gave nostalgically the scent of dung and rain-soaked hay. In all the busy hours people were drawn in from the main road in the way that a few animals from a driven herd will turn at any gateway: railwaymen on their way to the Sanctuary Sidings, pedlars and high-heeled girls, the Bowler's Tithe people who seemed to exist as ballast for the trams. It was earlier in the day that women with dropped-over shoes and hessian bags would call to each other across the road or wave to a window as they paddled round to the shops; Contessa Street's own people; and in the evenings, when it was light, both path and roadway were possessed by the Contessa children, so that a passer-by could feel himself an intruder. On Sundays, in a gap between the trains, you heard from right across the river the City's bells.

From the brewery the 'A' shift came by twos and threes on bicycles and passing the women on the kerb the younger ones did look at Armorel's legs, of which, in the gray silk stockings, even the knees had grace. A youth twisting his machine with reckless skill through the moving mesh of traffic, bending it into the calmer street with one foot on the ground, called "Lost y' Rolls, sweetie?" and she gave an answering smile. But the smile was of no use to him, it had no coyness, nothing that he looked for. Her face was no use either, though he could recognize in its shape and colour what old gents admired in dark pictures at the back of an art-shop window; like her carriage and her clothes it belonged to rarer tables, not meant for honest hunger.

Aunt Georgie said fearfully: "I still don't see why you wanted to come to this place at all. There are plenty of dressmakers who do alterations in ordinary parts of London. Miss Hawker shortened that coat for Christine, she really did it very neatly."

"Well, I liked this woman's advertisement. It was honest. It was the only one in the column which hadn't got 'Christian' or 'Gentlewoman' jabbed into it."

Hardly aware of Aunt Georgie, whose chatter she could answer without stirring the muscles of her mind, she watched the men on bicycles and the last-minute shoppers with a faint, friendly smile. For a few moments the sun had broken clear; and the hum and chatter of the highway, conglomerate odours quickened by the cut of winter, came upon her sadness like the noise and breath of sea. 'There is a world elsewhere!' To eyes grown used to the laburnum trees of Cromer's Ride, to Hilda Abbess's tennis-courts and drowsing cedars, this movement and this hardness gave the semblance of a battlefield. These who passed, she thought, who could not spend a shilling till they had made it, were concerned with livelihood, not the mere decorations of living; they did not act a part, they were in possession of reality because they were a portion of reality themselves. The dwindling tattoo of a goods train gave room again to the high whine of the saws; "Did you see that bleeding loco?" a man in the roadway said, "I was firing that sort back in 1910," and the signal on the viaduct rose again and somewhere beyond the schools a tug was hooting. Noticing how Georgina winced when a boy whose face was covered with impetigo hobbled past them, she thought, That's how you get when you've surrendered to the sheltered life; a few more years of Cromer's Ride, and I should be the same. It was hard to imagine her own mind yielding to environment as Georgina's had. But the events of last October, the disgrace and misery, might seem in the end to have been a salutary warning. Her failures, as she saw them at this moment, had been in a formal dance which one could call Young Ladyhood, performed on a narrow and tritely decorated stage. There was a world elsewhere; and finding this other world about her, with its straitness and its live confusion, This, she thought, is an arena where the minuettists would stumble and be crushed, and where a swordsman finds himself at ease.

The lugubrious jingle of the distant organ petered away. A window shot up, a strident voice bawled suddenly, "That's right, Mrs Ardree, don't you take any neck from him!" and broke into gusty laughter.

"Rellie, quick, here's the tram now! Be careful, there's a lorry coming!"

"One minute," Armorel said, "there's something happening."

Another of them! the tram-driver thought. The elderly woman he had seen from fifty yards away shook her umbrella at him as if she were Boadicea defying all the Roman legions, made a stiff-jointed rush to the platform, realized that something was missing and bolted back to the pavement. As a matter of routine the lorry-driver, coming up on the tram's near side, stood hard on his brake and saved her life.

"Rellie, what are you doing?"

The tram moaned on towards Camberwell Green.

"I'm sorry, Georgie darling. But I want to see what's going on."

The man who had driven up in the green van had entered the tobacconist's (where they also sold baking powder, dog biscuits, writing pads, the *Westminster Gazette* and sometimes brussels sprouts) and performed Stage One of his mission, which was merely to demand the overdue payments. In accordance with the rubric of his instruction-book he then stood back while an ounce of humbugs was sold to a fat small girl. When the shop was clear he performed Stage Two.

"Well then," he said, "my employers much regret that they are obliged to act in accordance with the terms of the contract—Paragraph 17—of which you have your own copy. Since payments are now seven weeks overdue, the ownership of the apparatus reverts to Ingeniomatics Limited."

A good, quick get-away was the main thing. The weighing-machine was itself some seventeen pounds in weight. He put his arms right across the counter, got a good grip and held it in to his stomach. "Good-morning!" he said with flat politeness.

The woman running the shop behaved as these women generally did. She had babbled about "just another week," about money coming in soon, about the first two payments having been made right on the dot. The 'Employers much regret' speech, made as the Instructions enjoined 'in a firm, clear, authoritative but not hostile voice,' had left her bemused. He was out on the pavement before she had really tumbled to what was happening.

But then she acted quickly; much more quickly than he would have expected, for she was a short and heavy-breasted woman of advancing middle age, with eyes which looked as if she was short of sleep. She jerked up the flap of the counter, dashed after him and grabbed his arm, shouting "Tsat belong to me! Tief 'n' robber! Two pound I pay—belong to me!"

From the other side of the street a raucous voice shouted, "That's right, Mrs Ardree, don't you take any neck from him!"

The salesman took no notice. He moved on towards the back of the van. But when the woman suddenly caught hold of his hair he did what almost any man carrying an awkward burden and thus attacked would have done: he moved his shoulder so as to give her a jab with his elbow. The blow, shallow as it was, may have hurt her. Her reply was to tug viciously at his hair, and this made him drop the machine. The machine, falling, struck the woman a glancing blow on the hip and she, screaming like the damned, collapsed on to the kerb.

This, in the shortness of time which always seems a miracle in London, brought a policeman; actually he was on duty at the crossroads less than sixty yards away, he was a man of long service and his professional reflexes were good. But before he reached the site of the trouble another performer had appeared. This was a youth of eighteen coming home to the shop for his dinner. He had seen the sharp jab which the salesman had given to the woman (who was his mother), he had seen her fall. She was now in a heap on the pavement, very slightly bruised, groaning piteously and talking gibberish at the same time, while the salesman stood beside her, flummoxed, with the thought uppermost that this was going to cost him the job he had been so lucky to get. The weighing-machine was upside down and broken in the gutter. The scuffle which followed, witnessed with enthusiasm by old Mrs Bentlock, with amusement or interest by several passers-by, was a squalid affair lasting less than a minute; for the way an English street-row goes is generally humourless and untheatrical. The boy, Gian Ardree, went swiftly but quietly up to the salesman, as if he were going to ask him the time, and then struck him with great force just in front of his ear. The salesman hit back savagely, with some effect. The two got into a clinch, much as heavyweight boxers do, and before the policeman had reached the spot the man was lying on his back, the boy kneeling on his chest and jabbing at his face. By this time Maria Ardree was on her feet again; and when the constable, with a gruff "Come on now, that's enough of that!" started to haul the boy off by the collar she attacked him viciously from the flank, forcing him to turn and catch hold of her arms. At this point the boy must have been confused, and there seems no reason to doubt the sincerity of his later statement, "All I could see was that some bloke was going for Mum." It was not surprising, then, that he in his turn, as soon as he was on his feet, whipped round and went for the policeman, with such ferocity that in an instant the policeman was down on his bottom, half-stunned and with blood all over his mouth and chin. But the boy was not content with this. In that moment when the policeman was helpless he struck him again, so that the man went over like a sawn tree, his head crashing against the front spring of the van, his elbow on the surface of the road, where, a second afterwards, he was lying face-downwards and unconscious.

The bystanders now took a hand: the English do not care, as a rule, to have their policemen murdered in the street, and the second, unnecessary blow had not been overlooked by the brewery men, who were accustomed to consider fighting with some discrimination. A pair of them got hold of the boy and held him. The constable was carried into a house on the other side of the street and a cyclist was sent off for assistance. In a very short time an ambulance came, and two more policemen.

It is perhaps of interest that the salesman, temporarily deprived of his good sense by the shock and pummelling he had suffered, tried to carry the weighing-machine back into the shop, as if that would cancel out his own part in the affair; and that Maria Ardree, in appearance fully returned to her sober faculties, ordered him with elaborate righteousness to take it away and bring her another one in good repair. This seemed to be the only aspect of the proceedings in which she had retained her interest.

The boy, when a policeman led him away, was in sorry case. He was a creature short in the legs but elsewhere big in body, with great breadth of shoulder, and his large head, tightly capped by black and rather curly hair, was built with a rough distinction: the grey eyes large and heavily browed, gibbous cheekbones thickly lapelled with down, an austere finality in the shaping of the channelled over-lip, of the spare cheeks and jaw. His hair, now, was full of dirt, there was dirt as well as blood spreading from his forehead all down one side of his face, which for the rest had turned to an unhealthy white, and on to his yellow muffler. His shirt was torn diagonally from the shoulder, letting most of his hairy chest and his stomach show bare, a triangle torn from his trouser-leg hung below one raw and bleeding knee. He walked with his left leg dragging crookedly, as if it wanted to go a way of its own; in another context its behaviour would have been amusing. A muscle behind that knee was torn, and one had said the boy must be in agony; but his face showed no awareness of pain, or anger now, or shame or defiance. The look in his eyes was one of detached interest, as if the main road which he was approaching had just the value of novelty for him. Passing the women who stood at the corner he did turn his eyes for a moment: the girl's head with its crest of copper foam was uncovered and the dove-blue coat she wore, which would have passed without notice in Bruton Street, was not unnoticeable here. In that glance he may have received some impression of her slenderness and the delicacy of her skin; he can hardly have seen how nobly the eyes were made, the depth of their smoke-blue colouring; and then, as if this image was not worth a busy man's attention, his gaze went back to the barber's pole on the other side of the road. Very soon a police car arrived from Damien Street and took him away.

"Where are you going now?" Aunt Georgie called in agony, as Armorel started to walk along Contessa Street.

"I must find out what it was all about. I want to know who that boy is and what they're going to do with him."

2

*I*T WAS thought wiser to say nothing about the incident to my cousin Gertrude, who of late had heard as much about Armorel's waywardness as an old lady could reasonably be asked to bear with. (But she got wind of it and had the whole story fitted together in a few days.) Edith, of course, was on to it at once. Georgina, determined in her kindness to protect the child, answered her sister's questions with a clumsy evasion; and evasion worked on Edith as linseed on draghounds. In truth Georgina, when cornered, rather enjoyed the narration. "Of course really, Edie, it wasn't what you would call a street-fight at all. It was just one man walloping another man. Or rather one man walloping two men, and a woman walloping them all, as far as I could see. Of course I had no idea what the time was. And you know it really was rather funny, Rellie standing there—of course poor darling she didn't realize how wicked it all was—Rellie twisting up her gloves and saying under her breath, 'You silly woman, you idiot, you're kicking the wrong man.' Of course I was quite helpless, I was holding the bag with the new hat in it, as well as my umbrella."

"Is it very amusing," Edith inquired, "when some blackguard attacks a policeman and knocks him senseless? Do you think Armorel's father would have liked her to see a man behaving like a wild beast—a man made in God's own image—and to treat the whole thing like a peepshow?"

"Well, you know, Edie, poor Arthur did always like a bit of excitement himself."

"Yes," Edith said, like winter settling upon the countryside, "and I suppose Armorel's mother may have spoken those very words this time three years ago."

So Armorel got another lecture. From Aunt Edith. Gertrude, loaded with more than seventy years' experience of human caprice, was too tired to lecture anybody; perhaps too wise to lecture her granddaughter, for in Armorel she recognized a Truggett in all except appearance, and she had known so many Truggetts. She was one herself; a Truggett manquée, as she once told me, having tumbled into marriage with the son of a Warwickshire landowner and so into the sheltered waters of maternity.

She did not often leave the house at this time. She wrote letters to old friends in her clear and beautiful Victorian hand, and gave a great part of her time to wood carving, which had been her hobby since childhood. Like many old women she had the fame of being formidable and bitter-tongued; but this reputation, spread euphemistically by her daughters, was partly based on her special behaviour to them. Edith and Georgina, as she saw them, were wholly Cepinniers (without the Cepinnier good looks); only Arthur had been a Truggett in his fibre and intelligence, in his ardent dissatisfactions. In truth, Gertrude's acerbity was superficial; it betrayed a continuous irritation with Edith, and the need of every old woman for some attitude, like helplessness or ambient disapproval, to wear as a moral shawl against the gusts of autumn. When you took her away from the day-to-day affairs of

Cromer's Ride she could talk with a quiet independence, and with as much good sense as many more pretentious intellects. You found that the staunch Protestantism which her relations alternately feared and smiled at hung on a framework which was rational and humane; and upon other subjects she was always slightly 'advanced,' though the advancement may partly have been designed to irritate Edith. There was, I think, one source of bitterness in her life: a lingering jealousy of her mother's fame. I doubt if she ever had the qualities for wearing Dorothea Truggett's mantle: the mental range, the incessant ardour; but I am sure that she herself believed so, and felt that only the protectiveness of a too-loving husband had prevented her. "But what do they really do," she once asked quite pettishly, "these women who gabble to me about their districts and their committees!" And then she added, with peculiar mournfulness, "Oh well, I've done nothing either, I suppose. And the years have all gone by."

I knew the Cepinniers first when they lived at Standle Minster, in Dorset, and I have a very early memory of being taken there by my mother to see Dorothea Truggett in her last years: her last months, I suppose, since her life and mine had overlapped for barely four years when she died at the age of ninety-one. I remember quite clearly the matched greys in the carriage which was sent to meet us at Blandford, and the mere in the Park, which for some reason I imagined then to be the Sea of Galilee. The rest is clouded and fragmentary, but my mind has kept a definite picture of Dorothea herself, sitting bolt upright in the high-backed wicker chair which was afterwards for many years in the drawing-room at Cromer's Ride. I am not sure if I identified her as a human being at all, because I had not been acquainted with a human being who kept so perfectly still; she seemed rather to be a life-sized doll, made with peculiar skill to smile and to speak. For she did speak to me, in what sounded like a man's voice. (Her daughter Gertrude's voice, in later years, became very much the same.) It is on record that I asked her, with the forthrightness of infancy, if she was an angel; and that she answered, "Mr Disraeli said I was a witch, and ought to be burnt alive." (Surely an unwise thing to say to a child; but it made not even an aural impression on me.)

It is difficult to know whether that encounter left me with any memory of her features. I think it did, but I cannot tell certainly how far the picture I see now, quite sharply and in three dimensions, comes from a child's candid eyes and how far from Sargent's portrait in the Walker Art Gallery which was painted in the same or the previous year. That portrait, reproduced as a frontispiece to Sarah Goodwin's *Four Famous Quakers,* is before me now, and I am almost ready to say "Yes, this is exactly how I saw her." The smallness of her mouth surprises me, as I believe it surprised me then. It must have been unusually tiny. And I find it almost impossible to imagine that mouth shouting Scripture into Lord John Russell's carriage, while two policemen struggled with her at a corner of Parliament Square, 'in a voice that could be heard on the Embankment.' The story that once, when staying with the Percys, she pulled a bishop out of bed to roar in his ear "When wilt thou learn that God is Love!" is probably an invention. But the Middlesbrough Riot is history: and when a thousand ironworkers swarmed along Corporation Street with sticks and rails, yelling for the blood of the wretched Puckroft, it was that same exquisite mouth, crying "Friends, I declare you shall not lay your hands on one of Christ's children!" which silenced and at length dispersed them. Her skin, if Sargent's brush and my memory are faithful, was far less wrinkled than that of most aged women, and so clear in texture that one would suppose it had been diligently cared for throughout her life. No one, seeing that face, would guess that she had brought up her family, from choice, in a four-roomed weaver's cottage; that before producing her great treatise on Conditions in Coalmines she had worked for eighteen months at the coalface; and had lived and laboured, herself a very sick woman, in the Santa Lucia quarter of Naples through the terrible autumn of '84. Only the eyes, I think, must have told a perceptive stranger what kind of woman she was. Sargent himself said that he had failed with them, and yet when I first saw the original painting they held me fascinated with their depth and flame. Those eyes make me see a little of what Miss Goodwin meant by her remark: "There was in her love something which I can only describe as ferocity . . . Men whom she had merely rebuked, and in no easy terms, loved her no less than those who were clothed and fed by her inexhaustible generosity. She, for her part, gave her love to all as freely, almost fanatically, as she gave her mind's and body's labour. But her love transcended the huge field of her sympathy; her fellow men could not alone absorb its fulness and its violence . . ."

It must have been a little hard for Lawrence Cepinnier to have so exceptional a mother-in-law under his roof for seven or eight years:

one may admire the Winged Victory beyond measure without wishing to have it in one's parlour, a lodestar for tourists. He was a white-moustached old Wykehamist who lived in an aura of inoffensiveness, an amateur of rural crafts and personalities, one who vaguely hoped that all the transitions of life would be as gently managed as the colours of a Barbizon landscape. To such a man Dorothea Truggett's volcanic presence, her contempt for the luxurious, the abruptness of her obiter dicta, must have felt like a clatter of applause between the movements of a symphony. Yet his grief for her loss was even greater than her children's and he wore himself to illness in trying to trace and maintain the many channels of her generosity. (That was an activity which cost him money as well as care; for Dorothea's possessions, when she died, were valued at £230, with a personalty of £87. 15s.) Rather pathetically he relinquished, soon after her death, certain small luxuries for which she had reproved or rather—I think—teased him: he no longer had his glass of madeira at mid-morning, no longer paid his annual visit to Parsloes Park. His own trotters were disposed of; and two or three of his most valued pictures went to Sotheby's at the same time. ("I think she looks a sweet woman," Dorothea had said about one of them, "and if thou art certain, Lawrie dear, that she and the young man are actually married then I suppose no one could complain. But I do think on Sundays she ought to have something stuck over just that portion— even Eve had that.") That sale, however, may have been merely to raise money: a part of the timber in the Park had been sold some time before.

There was not much at Cromer's Ride to remind you of Lawrence's personality. One could have felt it, perhaps, when Gertrude first moved there, when Streatham was not yet a mere suburb and the tall windows of the dining-room gave a view of Surrey hills. With houses on each side, and a string of reach-me-down villas beyond the garden wall, it became a place that he could not have lived in and remained the man we had known. He needed some generosity of space, where the elements of an ordered landscape could merge into each other: the trim box-hedges of a rose garden, close-mown lawns falling to the meadowland like a starched apron on a skirt of serge; a sash of mist hanging across the mere and the heavy green of Whipper Coppice against the distant blue-green of Earl Godwin's Camp.

7, Cromer's Ride (as Gertrude's house became) had been built without a downstairs lavatory. Neither in the single bathroom, cluttered with shelves and cupboards, nor in any bedroom was there a convenient mirror for shaving. These were the kinds of things it lacked, and most of all it lacked fresh air and light. She did not care for draughts, Gertrude said. The air, as she required, stood still: air, one would have said, which the builders had originally trapped there: heavy, stale, and bearing pertinaciously throughout the years the reputable odours of a provincial drapery store.

"I think it's exactly right for you, Mother," Arthur had said. "So much cosier than Standle Minster, as well as being so much cheaper to run."

"And your own room, Arthur darling, is it perfectly comfortable?"

"Mother dear, I'm certain that if King Edward came to stay with you he wouldn't ask for anything better."

After all, he was never there for more than three or four days, for in the earlier years of his marriage Irene couldn't bear him to be longer away from home: Armorel and Christine would never go to sleep quickly, she said, if their daddy hadn't been in to say good-night.

And perhaps he was more at home at Cromer's Ride than in any other part of his world. Not that his mind could canter there, but at least it could trot in the ordered and familiar avenues, and the shyness in which he was gripped as tightly as some are held by arthritis was unlocked in a house where everyone had made their final opinion of him years before. At his own home he had that feeling of release in the nursery whenever he had the children to himself; but that was seldom, because Irene preferred to share his meetings with them: within a minute or two she would always be there, leaning against the rocking horse, wearing her impartial smile, saying, "No, Arthur darling, Rellie isn't old enough for that . . . We don't really know if the Bible stories are true, do we! I don't think Rellie ought to listen to what we don't know is true." At Cromer's Ride Edie would badger him about his clothes, insisting that he would do better in business if he went to a West End tailor; "And you know, Chubby, Irene is really quite clever about her clothes, and you don't want her to feel that her husband's dowdy." But he had only to look pathetic and say that he hadn't at the moment any clothes smart enough for visiting a West End tailor. And there was O'Connor to be kissed and to slap his trousers in return, "You know I won't have such impudence, Master Arthur!" and Georgie to be teased about the affair with Mr Gretton.

"I saw him only the other day, Georgie, and he looked quite haggard. He said, 'Cepinnier, how is that beautiful girl, your sister?'"

"So you told him, I hope, that Edie was in excellent health. Yes, Chubby, you know perfectly well it was Edie he was after."

"Georgie my darling, it was a wife he wanted, not a mount."

"Chubby, hush!"

"You don't think that any human voice could possibly penetrate the partitions of this mausoleum!"

"Oh, you won't say anything to Mama against the house, will you? Mama would die if she heard anything against it from you."

"Our mother, Georgie, is a woman of tolerably robust constitution. Any criticism from her only son would undoubtedly put strain upon her heart, but not necessarily a fatal strain."

He never left any mark upon the house. There were photographs of him in Gertrude's room, a demure small Arthur in velvet, an Arthur turned to stone with his bride on his arm, but that was all: the guncase under the sideboard had belonged to Lawrence, the Rowlandsons to Lawrence's father. Even when he was there his presence scarcely altered the house's emanations. If he wanted to smoke he used the garden. The room he slept in was always tidy, the bedclothes turned back in the morning, his night-shirt folded. Whenever he went upstairs this slight, fair-bearded man, who had bloodied a Foreign Secretary's nose in the dining-room of the Athenaeum, would change into house slippers as the nurse at Standle Minster had taught him.

"Really," Edith said, "you'd hardly know that we had a man in the house."

"Then what," asked her mother, "is the point of having one!"

But Gertrude could take a certain pride in his behaviour when they had women visitors at afternoon tea, for these 'poor suburban petticoats', as she called them, would candidly envy her his perfection. Certainly he had brought his afternoon manners to the level of a craft: his eyes were so sharp for empty tea-cups, his movements so unobtrusive, his eyes proclaimed such pleasure in female conversation. A certain roughness of opinion which he occasionally betrayed in the morning-room (and which Gertrude, in truth, provoked) would never reveal itself here. If the ladies had heard some story of young Mr Cepinnier's dangerous radicalism they disbelieved it as soon as they talked to him. "Ah, no," he would say, "I've got no head for politics. I simply vote as my wife tells me . . . Exactly! Why, when we have a dramatist of Mr Pinero's calibre, should we send for our plays to Norway!" And he would move the screens without being asked, and when O'Connor carried out the tray he would hold the door for her with a courtesy which reminded Edith, oddly and touchingly, of their father.

These were not merely party manners. When the visitors had gone he remained at his mother's disposal, thoughtful and circumspect. She did not have to ask him to get her spectacles—he had noticed that the case was not on the mantelpiece. He knew that with the Truggett economy which Standle Minster had never destroyed she liked to use the last of the daylight. He realized that Edith with her long back and her rheumatism was best in the Knole chair. These attentions were valued by women who, living always together, could not in reason trouble very much about each other's smaller comforts. But they valued his conversation still more.

Sometimes, when their mother went to bed early, the 'children' would play three-handed whist, of which Gertrude formally maintained an elegiac disapproval. But this happened rarely. Now that the girls could no longer be ordered to bed the three women darkly competed for the pleasure of having Arthur a last few minutes by himself: Gertrude always hoping for a breath of masculine worldliness, and perhaps an argument, Georgina for a little teasing, the easy comradeship and sweet absurdities of their nursery days. The loser in this three-cornered struggle was generally Edith, who had to find time for the new, elaborate procedure of her devotions. Success mattered least to her. She would have liked, of course, to confide in him: on her belief that Georgie was still young enough to hope for a bridegroom (if only she would take more trouble with her hair); about how difficult Mama had become, treating O'Connor as her personal maid and interfering with the housekeeping, which by agreement was now Edith's province; but she knew that she could never find voice or words for what she most wanted to say—how tenderly and fiercely she loved him, how she wanted him not to despise her for her failures, how hard it was for a woman to know and fulfil her duty.

For himself, he seemed indifferent which of them captured him; and for the lucky one he would allow his mood to reflect the colour of hers. So for his mother he would rouse himself to flame against Mr Chamberlain, with Edith he was serious and attentive. For Georgie he had gentle gaiety or silence as her face appeared to bid him; and to her, guardedly, he would sometimes speak a little of his own interests, of his loathing for the underwriter's trade, of friends who had dropped him or whom he had dropped. But those subjects he would allow to fall away like sand through the fingers, he would say "But, Georgie, you don't deserve to be bored with such foolish affairs. It's only stupid and feeble people who lose their detachment, who get hurt and angry as I do. Directly you get ill-tempered you prove that you're as much a moral dwarf as all the others . . ."

She liked to talk to him about his children, knowing that he adored them. But here, here only, she found in him the shyness with which his ordinary friends were so familiar. "Yes, I should say that Armorel is a pretty child. But how is a man to know? Of course everyone flatters her looks to please me, and one's own aesthetic sense is quite unreliable."

"You'll bring them to see us soon?" she often asked. "It would be so lovely."

"Yes, sometime, I suppose. But Irene thinks they're too young to be away from home without her."

"But there's plenty of room for Irene as well."

"I know. But you see, there are difficulties in looking after children in someone else's house. I mean, you want them to keep to their home routine, and you don't want to be a nuisance."

She realized it was useless to press him. How well she knew that attitude of his, the little fingers linked and the thumbs stuck up, his mouth closely smiling at what anyone else would have thought to be an amusing memory, while his eyes gazed sleepily into the fire.

"Then Mahomet will have to go to the mountain. I'll come and stay with you, as soon as I've finished helping Edie with her Waifs and Strays bazaar."

"Yes, Georgie, I'll get Irene to invite you. But it may be a little time. She's changing the rooms round, she's making a new nursery next to her own sewing room. It's rather—well, you know, she likes to make visitors comfortable, and she can't do it when there's something else on her mind."

She told him one evening that Armorel was her favorite. "Of course Chrissie is very sweet too. She's so demure, so confident. She seems to live in a dignified little world of her own. But I can't forget the smile that Rellie gave me the very first time I saw her. Exactly as if she'd known me years before and as if she'd been longing for me to come back."

"Yes," he said. "Yes, she sometimes smiles like that now."

He was in one of his silent moods, and she let the silence enwrap them. All the house was quiet except for the clocks and for Edie coughing. He was sitting on the floor beside her chair, he took her hand and went over it as a doctor might, as in childhood he had played with his mother's hand, feeling the veins, remotely smiling. She would have liked to follow his thoughts, but she knew that he was grown-up now, and that when a man swims out into that stream the best that a woman can do is to stay close by for his return. John Truggett's clock in the morning-room struck the half-hour.

"You know," he said, "I wonder and wonder why God lets us make children in that accidental way."

"But, Chubby, we don't make them!"

"You see a girl," he said, as if she had not spoken, "and you seem to need her. Or is it that you feel she needs something from you?—protection?—I don't know what it is. So a marriage is arranged, as they say in the *Morning Post,* and you sleep in the same bed, and then there are children. There's not really any more plan behind it than that."

She said, while he still played with her hand, "But isn't that a lovely and beautiful thing to happen?"

"Sometimes I think it is a damnable thing to happen."

Presently he said: "I've one grudge against you, Georgie. Being brought up with you, I always imagined that boys and girls weren't so fearfully different, and I got the idea that men and women weren't either. I mean, we always had much the same ideas, we didn't tell fibs and we didn't sneak on each other. We both meant the same thing when we talked about being fair. We had our secrets, and our jealousies and all that, but we didn't cheat. Not even on April Fool's Day—we had our rules and we stuck to them. So did poor old Edie, she never cheated either. And another rule was that when you were hurt you didn't cry more than you absolutely had to. So of course I got the idea that all women were like that, brave and loyal, and honest in the way they think about things. I suppose that's what they call naïveté."

"But most of them are like that. Surely they are."

"Some of them are bitches," he said. (It startled her, that word, which he pronounced with a quiet fury entirely new to her. She had heard it first from the doorway of a cottage she was passing, and Nurse Violet had wheeled her fearfully away, with sinister warnings.) "Everything they do or say is part of some scheming, because that's the only way their minds work. Their minds are so twisted up that truth can't find its way inside." And letting go her hand, and tightening his fist so that the knuckles whitened, he uttered like pistol shots two more words which she had never heard at all.

The house could absorb such a disturbance in its rhythm and quietness. At night nothing got past its outer walls, one heard only the strange hiss and gurgle of the water pipes, the tedious industry of clocks, sometimes a prolonged coughing from Edith's room. That spasm of Arthur's violence, Georgina's sobbing in her pillow that night, were washed over by the succeeding tides, losing their outline, remembered only as people say "There, along that path, just by the gate, that was where I once fell over and cut my knee."

His letters were just the same. He wrote to them all, to Gertrude every week as he had done from Framlingham, to each of the girls every month. The letters were never without a kind message from Irene, there was usually something gay about the children; and to Georgina he often wrote at length about their new frocks and accomplishments, Christine's odd sayings, the grave report which Armorel had given him of her first day at a kindergarten school.

He had been tired that night, Georgina thought; something was on his mind, there might have been some little quarrel. Yet the memory of the evening stayed when she had long forgotten most of his actual words: the memory of his tightened fist, the sunken fire's light on his grey, locked profile. It rose when they first heard the dreadful news about Irene; it came back still more vividly with the letter telling them that he was missing since the second Battle of the Aisne.

And naturally Armorel re-awoke the memory. When she first came to live at Cromer's Ride she reminded them all of his gentleness. Her voice and movements were so graceful, she took such pains to do nothing which would upset her aunts' or her grandmother's routine. She lacked, of course, the gossamer thread of gaiety which had been a part of her father's charm; her smile was never quite without sadness, her laughter had a note of unreality. But that, they agreed, was only to be expected; and they would not have wished to have a boisterous girl in the house, or even a girl like Christine, who made the most extraordinary remarks, and who talked of her anomalous husband in a way that was positively zoological, without understanding (they hoped) a quarter of what she said. It was only rarely that Armorel fell into what Georgina thought of as 'Chubby's serious mood'; and it never happened when anyone except Georgina herself was present, for when Gertrude or Edith was about there was that small tension in the air which forbade the wandering of thoughts. It happened when the child was tired; when a little party of Edith's friends had sat for a long time discussing church matters which must have been above her head, or when Edith herself had been querulous and impatient. And it was always likely to happen on those rare occasions when a letter came from Irene. Georgina would find her without book or sewing in a room falling into darkness, her lovely body completely still, as if the spirit had deserted it, her eyes lethargic. It was the mouth, then, that recalled Arthur: the lips folded away, the muscles of the jaw so tightly caught that they trembled, as those of some patients, brave only by volition, when an abscess below the finger-nail is being lanced. Then, if she spoke, it was in a voice less carefully held than the one she used every day; and she would say, perhaps, "My mother's written to ask me for Daddy's new address. I should have thought the motor-racing man could have got it for her from the War Office. But of course I must send it at once—she used to to talk to me so much about good manners." And then, perhaps, there would be a kind of laughter; leaving Georgina able only to murmur some triviality and go away.

A day or two after the tram-stop episode she was inclined to that mood. Georgina saw it coming on.

"Aunt Georgie, you know I promised Aunt Edie I would help her on Monday with the handbills for the Austrian Relief concert. Do you think she would let me off? There's something else I want to do. Georgie, darling, could you be a dear and ask her—she may think it's all right if it comes from you."

This was too much for Georgina's courage: she had done her full share as buffer in the last few days, and Edie's present temper was far from reliable, with old O'Connor in one of her most awkward moods. "I'm sorry, Rellie, no, you must ask her yourself."

By an error of judgement she arrived in the drawing-room that afternoon, just before tea, when the interview was under way; and as Edith had caught sight of her she could not quietly escape.

"But you see," Edith was saying patiently, "you did make me a definite promise, and I've made a promise to Mrs Nowell. That's what I'm concerned about. People who are—well—worse off than we are don't seem to bother about promises nowadays. It's probably owing to the War. That's why I feel it's so important for people like ourselves to carry out our undertakings to the letter. And you still haven't told me what it is you want to do."

Armorel was perched with her palms on the keyboard cover of the piano, her young breasts thrusting in the marocain dress, her pretty knees crossed over. She was smiling, as if Edith had just paid her a little compliment. She said peacefully:

"It's something rather private. I'm afraid another day wouldn't do."

"Of course, Rellie, I don't in the least want to poke into your secrets. Only naturally, as you're living here, we like to have some idea where you are. I mean, is it to see friends?"

"Aunt Edie, darling" (she still spoke very softly), "you know I'm going to be twenty-one in a few months' time. And I have got a younger sister who's married already."

Edith said hesitantly: "Well, I'll have a word with Mrs Nowell and see if she can possibly find someone else. Only I shall expect you—"

"I'm terribly sorry, Aunt Edie, but I've quite definitely decided to use that day as I want to."

This was a moment when a third woman would have put in a few tactful words to set things right, had her wits moved fast enough; Georgina's moved like shire horses at the end of a day's ploughing. Edith said with terrible quietness:

"Rellie, don't you think that's rather ill-mannered!"

There was just a moment before the gentle-voiced answer came:

"Well, the way I look at it, Aunt Edie, is that your treatment of me is just one long course of damned impertinence."

Another moment passed.

"Rellie, where have you picked up that word?"

"I've heard Daddy use it, for one. And he was as good a Christian as you are, since that's what seems to count."

"What word?" asked Gertrude, coming in for her tea.

" 'Damned,' Grannie."

"Well, he never used it in here. You must go out into the garden if you want to use words like that. Over by the rhododendrons. I hope O'Connor's made the tea a bit stronger today—yesterday it tasted like rusty pipes."

Armorel made her apology, as Arthur might have done, in a graceful note slipped into Edith's room. Early on the Monday morning, having borrowed a pound from Georgie, she set out for the Damien Street Police Court. From what Ardree's mother had told her, she was convinced that the boy was not really vicious. She believed that a few words from her might make all the difference to the result of the case, and she was determined to say them.

3

"AND YOU HAVEN'T SEEN your husband since last September? You've no idea where he is?"

"No, how should I know!"

"The N.S.P.C.C. inspector says you told him that your neighbour, Mrs Brim, was always in the ground floor room in the evenings when you were out—"

"Well, she was most nights."

"Yes, but on that Tuesday evening—Tuesday the twenty-second—did you go to see whether she was in before you went off to the cinema?"

"Well, what would be the good! I don't go to the cinema to amuse myself, same as what you do. I've told you, I get my living there, I got to get my living somehow. I can't tell the manager I can't come that evening because Mrs Brim's gone to see her sister. Can I now?"

But the girl was not asking for anyone's sympathy. Her white face was passionless, her thin, small mouth was as hard as Galba's. She had refused the offer of a chair and stood as rigidly as a soldier, looking straight across the Court. The baby, asleep with his chin on her narrow shoulder, had brought up his last feed, leaving a cascade of mess down her smart, thin frock. With her mouth shut like a pair of pincers she waited with the patience of machinery for the smug to answer that one.

The little tired man under the grandiloquent canopy suddenly moved his head.

"Mrs Scherwinsky, I want to ask you a question. How often do you give your baby a bath?"

"I do him Fridays. When I get back from the Rex. I never missed once since I had him."

A smile touched the mouth of a woman standing by the door. Sickening superiority, Armorel thought. There was no majesty here, dignity only of a provincial kind. The room could have been the conventicle of one of the straitest sects, or a place where concert parties rehearsed. It was the young man now who asked the questions, the man with his dark clothes sharply creased and the voice of slopping milk a little turned. And by what right did he, who could never have gone hungry to feed a child, let alone borne one, ask these questions putrid with innuendo! The tired manikin, the celebrated Mr Cuddish, she supposed, had dropped into his previous posture, forearms on the desk, hands clasped, his head with its oversized dome supported by one thumb propped into the underlip. She watched him intently. His eyes, half-closed, were frozen like a dead man's, staring to some uncertain point beyond the witness-box, his body so still it was hard to believe that he was breathing.

People came in and whispered and went out again. The woman Scherwinsky was led away, her place was taken by one who might have been her grandmother and who argued with His Worship in terms of equality as with a familiar chess opponent, before accepting with royal complacence his usual figure of ten shillings. The rest of the drunks were put through quickly.

They had not much chance, she thought, these wayfarers who stumbled in to fight on their opponents' pitch, bewildered amateurs with the practised hands surrounding them. The Court's simplicity was only a snare; they were listening, these officials with bored and homely faces, they had heard the tale a thousand times before and they knew exactly where a gentle tap would buckle it. Belonging to neither side she was lonely. The policeman glanced now and then in her direction, her eyes went down the flowing taper of her own legs to the fan-shaped over-buckles of her shoes and she wished again that she had dressed more shabbily.

"Gian Ardree!"

A movement somewhere behind her, a sharp intake of breath, made her turn to look that way, along a row of worshippers at a service they didn't quite understand. And there at the end was Mrs Ardree, sitting between two men: perhaps she had been there all the time. One of the men was whispering, the pug-faced one with a knitted tie which had drifted from its moorings; she did not seem to hear him, and having bestowed on her his thin, professional smile he moved over to the other side of the Court.

The tracks through the powder on Mrs Ardree's cheeks were evidence that she had wept profusely, but now she was moderately composed: her lips moved busily, as if in a dumb show of lecturing, her puzzled eyes went every way like a six-month baby's, but her head remained completely still, couched, a little on one side, in her rolling breast and shoulders as a chop lies in a dish of mashed potato. She would not answer Armorel's friendly smile; she might not have seen it, much less have recognized the young lady who had come into the shop, that complicated day, to ask her questions; neither did she answer the scrag-haired man who leaned sideways to murmur something in her ear. There was in the stillness of her body, lagged in dusty velveteen and yellowing lace, the mien of a foreign princess on show, drilled to quiescence and the utterance of a few gracious phrases. With her teapot shape and the violent blue of her dress, her stertorous breathing and the volume of eau-de-cologne which drifted from her half across the Court, she seemed a little out of drawing. The stage was catholic, it could absorb a great variety of feature and of costume within its tessellation. The person of Maria Ardree was not absorbed.

" . . . and nothing but the truth. On Friday the twentieth of this month at 1.10 p.m. I was on station duty at Damien Street police station. I was ordered to proceed to Contessa Street, following on information re disorder in that street. I arrived in Contessa Street at 1.22 p.m. . . . I then measured the distance between the kerbstone and the blood on the carriage-way, which I found to be two feet eight inches—"

"You mean, measuring on a line going at right angles from the kerb?"

"Yes, Your Worship."

"To the centre of the pool of blood?"

"Yes, Your Worship. I then examined the mudguard of the vehicle already mentioned . . ."

Precise and colourless, the pattern of impartiality, the voice came like the market news from a tape machine. Mr Cuddish was a waxwork again, the bleached face of the clerk was the face of an aged croupier. Yet no one seemed more detached than the squat youth in the dock, whose eyes, turning with curiosity about the Court, never once rested on the witness. Seeing him in profile, she thought he looked older than when he had limped past her in Contessa Street. Older and less barbaric, for his face was clean, his hair had been cut and his great shoulders fitted (much too tightly) into a jacket of shiny serge. But not less formidable. With the flatness of its planes, the narrow fit of flesh to bone, you could imagine this the face of a mountaineer, perhaps of an espada; except for the drifting eyes which, as she saw them now, had the gentle, fumbling scholarship of a chimpanzee's.

It was the police surgeon talking now. ". . . also abrasions in the left leg and left forearm . . . comminuted fracture of the right humerus with nerve involvement and impacted fracture of the right forearm . . . Unconsciousness lasted 68 hours . . . possibility of compression . . ."

Mr Cuddish stirred like a vane in a whiff of wind.

"Can you give any opinion on how long it will take to heal these injuries?"

"You mean, sir, the injuries to the arm? It's not possible to be certain at this stage. I can only say that at present it appears to me rather unlikely that the constable will recover the full use of the right arm."

"Now, with regard to the head injury. Am I right in supposing that when an injury such as you have described occurs it's possible for serious nervous disorders to occur at a later period in the patient's life?"

"That is so."

"And he is a man of what age?"

The surgeon hesitated. Close to Armorel's seat a small woman with her thin hair in a tight bun half-rose to her feet. She said in a little voice, the cultured voice of a parlourmaid in an old-fashioned house:

"Forty-six, sir. And a fine father. I beg your pardon, sir. Only he's my husband."

There was a moment's stillness while this raw interpolation echoed against the room's impersonality. Then Mr Cuddish continued to address the witness.

"Now, I want to know this. These injuries that you've described—can they, in your opinion, have been caused by the constable falling first against the side of a stationary motor car and then on to the road?"

"Yes, it's feasible that they were caused in that way—he is a heavy man—fourteen stone, I should say. Perhaps I ought to add that normally one would not expect to find anything like such serious injuries resulting from such a fall."

"Now, supposing that the constable had been standing on a mattress—the kind of thing they have in a gymnasium—and he had been struck by another man: could the same injuries have been caused?"

"No, most emphatically not."

"Not even if an extremely powerful man had struck him?"

"No, sir. Definitely not."

And now, she thought, Mr Cuddish is enjoying it. It was part of the essential infancy in males that they gloated over technicalities, especially those of fighting and wounds. As if it could matter! The man had been seriously injured, the boy here had struck him, there was nothing in dispute. Her gaze turned to the dock again. She wished she were nearer, and to the front of him, to see if there were cruelty in his curious eyes; for that, she thought, is what really matters, and that is what I could tell a hundred times more certainly than these men who do not even trouble to look at him. The woman who had interrupted sat perfectly still again. Poor thing: but what was she here for, did she hanker for revenge, was she so simple as to imagine that Ardree had attacked her husband with deliberate malice, or that it would benefit her one farthing to punish him! It belongs to the dark ages, she thought, as a new witness and then another went into the box; it comes from the crude morality of the barbarian legislator Moses, whose tribal bombast is served up to English children as transcendental wisdom: this notion of righting one man's injury by seizing the nearest human cause of it, proving him wrong by diagrams and clapping him in the stocks. With her hand curiously trembling she took a sheet of paper from her bag; wrote, "I am willing to give evidence as to character of Accused. Armorel Cepinnier"; addressed it to "Solicitor for Defence, case of G. Ardree" and passed it to the man on her right.

The pug-faced man was earning his fee. He had let the constable and the surgeon go unheckled—no use wasting time with the old hands —but the witnesses who followed, men damp and vibrating with stage fright, were dainty subjects for his gladiatorial art.

"You say you did not throw the machine at Mrs Ardree? But the machine was in your hands? And you made a movement with your hands—a vigorous movement, I think you agreed it was? And the next moment the machine was striking Mrs Ardree? Oh, it fell!—you're quite sure it didn't walk across to her and hit her of its own accord?

". . . You admit that you struck the accused several times? Yes yes, I know you told the Court it was in self-defence. You 'struck out blindly' —I think that was the phrase you used? And yet you say you *know* you never hit the constable? Perhaps you can tell the Court *how* you know you never hit the constable? . . ."

And at each reply he smiled, sticking his little yellow teeth into his upper lip, gazed up to the ceiling, nodded slowly, and then glanced quickly round the Court. 'Ladies and gentlemen,' his eyes and his gestures said, 'it may astonish you that the world should contain a fool and a liar of this calibre, but to me the spectacle is so commonplace that I find it merely tedious. As a matter of interest I shall exhibit for you just a few more specimens of this moron's duplicity.' The note had reached him, but he only put it in his pocket. He sniffed, raised the collar of his coat and re-fitted it, indicating a certain weary distaste for the task of tearing the prosecution case to shreds.

The youth Ardree remained aloof. You could not have guessed that all this questioning had anything to do with him.

When the first of his own witnesses was called, the pug-nosed man became a new personality. The sneer disappeared as if it had been wiped off with a sponge, the tension of all his gestures collapsed, his very clothes seemed to alter, fitting his limbs more kindly. The battle, his expression proclaimed, was over. It only remained for him, Mr Josiah Hosencroft, solicitor, of 29 Cressport Street, to show how all this horrible misunderstanding had occurred and to demonstrate the Court's ardent sympathy with the sufferers. Slowly, with an awkward dignity, Mrs Ardree went into the box, moving as if under the management of tugs. She smiled shyly to her son, stumbled through the Oath and then waited stoically, as it appeared, for a giant grapple to descend and carry her off to the Lambeth Incinerator. "You," said the Clerk, "are Mrs Maria Ardree, the wife of Simon Ardree? And you are the proprietress of a general store in Contessa Street, Lambeth?" Mr Hosencroft gazed about the Court benevolently, as one realizing that a child must sometimes have his way.

The man like a lorikeet rose and said sharply: "This witness has been in court all the time, Your Worship." Mr Hosencroft swelled to a mountain of innocence, for a minute and a half the two men fought like cocks in a Limehouse main. ". . . In the circumstances you may proceed with this witness," Mr Cuddish said, "but any other witnesses you intend to call must immediately leave the Court"; and the man who had sat beside Mrs Ardree was hustled out.

"And now, Mrs Ardree!" Mr Hosencroft said paternally. His head went a little to one side, his fat small hands drooped outwards, he enclosed the whole Court in his philanthropy. This was the bonne bouche of the day, the prize for which, reluctantly, he had kept the Court waiting so long: this spectacle of human innocence, of womanly virtue, long traduced and scorned, emerging at last in radiant purity for all the world to see. "And now, Mrs Ardree, I'd like you, if you will, to tell the Court just exactly what *did* happen on that Friday."

The smile, the ducal courtesy which flowed out to her from his eyes, his hands, his waistcoat, should have moved Mount Etna to acquiescence. Maria Ardree was dumb. She did not look frightened now, or even sorrowful. She had congealed to a piece of masonry, oblivious, impervious, a rotund, spilt-over body only technically alive.

"Come now, Mrs Ardree!" Mr Hosencroft said.

That was like the last thrust of a rod, freeing a choked conduit. Mrs Ardree said abruptly, but not ill-naturedly:

"All of sem are liaren tieves." She drew a whistling breath. "I ask him very clear, what happen if machine is wrong, what happen if I have no money every goddam week? You are all right jussasame, Mrs Ardree—he sait sat—sissis where you sign sepaper, see? you have one copy, I have one copy. One pountown, see? Nex week, one pountown. Nex week, where issa money? Money? I laugh! You ask Mr Olleroyd, I sait, I tell him to ask Mr Olleroyd where issa pountown! Machine?—no goodatall! I tellimtsat. I tellim I weightsababy of Mrs Lewis, I put on tsirteen poun—allseman give me wissa machine—sebaby go down zump, semachine bite at his toe and he screech. So! she say—Mrs Lewis—So! my baby is two yearen sree monce, ant he weigh no moresen tsirteen poun!! Fugh! (Mrs Lewis sisis.) So I tellseman he can take off semachine, but I will first have my two pountown. Wassiser good of semachine if all sebabies weigh tsirteen poun, no minder whatsayweigh! Mr Olleroyd, you see Mr Osencroft, sir, he have a long time whenset is no work for a fur-nailer, so sen he give me no money. So you see, Mr Osencroft, sir—"

The clerk said with kindness, "Now listen, Mrs Ardree, you mustn't waste time telling us all sorts of things. All we want is your account of the struggle in which the constable was injured. What do you remember about that?"

Maria nodded.

"My son, sare, my son Gian!"

"Yes?"

"He see sat sepoliss is attack. So he try to knock a hell from seman sat attack sepoliss. My son vayr, vayr strong man. He bring back his arm, he swingse arm, *zump!*—seman turn away, searm hitse poliss—*zump!*—sepoliss fallonse road. All broke."

From that statement nothing would shift her. She embroidered, she re-modelled. At every opening, and even where no opening seemed to exist, she strayed again into the lush pastures of her experience, her earlier life, the life of her family, the misfortunes of Mr Olleroyd. But when they brought her back she had her story essentially the same: her son had fought to protect the constable, the blow had miscarried and fallen upon the constable himself. Her energy increased, and having reached its highest frequency it never slackened. It solidified her body—her gigantic bosom, the cabriole arms, the great pouches which formed her face and neck—as the inrushing air hardens a cycle tyre. The whole mass vibrated, she struck at the air, she fired her sentences like bullets, her alarming gusts of laughter cracked against the courtroom's sombre decency like the taunts of street boys scrawled on churchyard walls. The display was prodigious, the embellishment grotesque. But not for an instant comic. For, as Armorel could see, it was not a performance at all. Her facts were so far at variance from what the other witnesses had soberly affirmed that no one in his senses could accept them. Yet she, Maria, was believing every word she said. And she was fighting. You presently forgot the foreigner, you forgot the woman, you saw only the soldier. Mr Hosencroft was out of it, she neither had nor wanted anyone to help. She knew that all these pale and flat-tongued people were against her, she saw they had steered her son into their gin, she was going to face the pack of them with her own clean sword and carve a path for his escape.

". . . I tell you, Mr Worshipen sirs, if my Gian would have *kill* sepoliss, if Gian would have kill *all* sepoliss, he do it because he is braven kine, because he lov sepoliss sesamas he lover sismosser! Tsat issa truce, and you *knowit* satsatissa truce!"

The lorikeet said: "No questions!"

"Thank you, Mrs Ardree. I think that is all we want."

The witness called next was the man who had sat on Mrs Ardree's right and who looked like a horse-coper got up for a wedding. The way he lumbered into the box suggested that someone had promised him a good view which he was ready to take on trial; and having read the Oath as if it were a mildly entertaining newspaper paragraph he slowly scanned the horizon, twisting his long neck like a tortoise's, frowning and smiling without prejudice at nothing in particular. You had said from his appearance that a middle stage in his development had been left out. His narrow head, with hair like moorland swept by fire, belonged to a man in the later forties; the high forehead yellow pocked, skin tightly stretched on the long nose and long upper lip, a dappled, smoky lichen on scraped cheeks and broken chin; but the lanky body was a boy's who has grown too fast, the large and clumsy hands moved with the independence of a boy's. His clothes might have been designed to stress that incongruity: his starched collar, much too big for the scraggy neck, rode up at the back, leaving the tie behind; the black coat, very long in the body, left inches of his wrists quite bare; and his waistcoat, adorned with a gold watch-chain and with coffee stains, had nuzzled up against his hollow chest so that his brace buttons, dragging at their anchors, were revealed beneath. He seemed a patient man. You could not tell from his moist grey eyes if he were happy or sad.

". . . name is Simon Ardree and you are occupied as a 'theatre specialist'?"

"Well, I don't know that I could rightly say. You see, sir, in these times it's a matter of putting your hands to what comes along. Now Mr Vincent, who I get work from now—"

"Well, we'll take that as we've got it down here. Your name at any rate is Simon Ardree?"

Simon Ardree reconsidered the question, and then said seriously, in his overgrown Merseyside voice:

"That's what they always told me."

The clerk glanced at Mr Hosencroft. Mr Hosencroft, rising with dignity and taking a new manner from its hook, said as one initiate to another, "I think that what you tell the Court, Mr Ardree—just very simply in your own words—I think it may put the whole of this matter in its proper light."

"That's right!" Simon Ardree said. For a few moments he went on looking about the room, as if his speech must be written somewhere on the walls. Then, shrugging his shoulders, he said confidentially to Mr Hosencroft "Well, it's like what she says. Only she can't get her words right, not even after all these years, she's never done any book work as you might say, she don't seem to get her tongue round some of the words. Well, it's like what she said, this Olleroyd, you see, he gets all behindhand because he can't get work, the fur trade being in the state it is, and the wholesalers what send my wife the stuff for the shop they won't send so much as a packet of salt until they've got the money for the last lot. Well, this machine, you see, Maria never did ought to have taken it, the same as I said to her myself."

"Were you present," the clerk asked abruptly, "when the incident in Contessa Street took place?"

"No, I was over at theatre. That would be three miles, going the way the bus goes. Well, two and half, say. Make it two and three-quarter miles, and that would be as near as you'd want."

"Well, then—"

"But when I come home she tell me what went on. That was a proper mix-up, the way it looks to me. As my wife said, the boy there couldn't have done more nor less, with that man half-murdering his mum on the pavement. That's not right. I reckon I'd have found the money for that machine—"

"Now listen! The Court doesn't want to know what your wife told you. We've had all that from Mrs Ardree herself. If you've no evidence to give from your own direct knowledge then you're merely wasting the Court's time."

"Sure! And mine!" Simon Ardree said, and shrugged his shoulders again, and stepped out of the box. But upon an afterthought he turned back, and in the voice of one who has run far with urgent tidings he addressed the top of the Magistrate's head.

"I'll just say this—if you'll pardon my speaking, sir. I know this lad better than what you do, and there's not a grain of vice inside him. Quick in his temper he may be. And with nobody but his mum to keep a hold on him as you might say, all through the war, that was, and a good part of the time before that—well, a lad don't rightly learn to keep a hold on himself. I tell you, sir, I'm his father, and taking him from the inside, as you might say, I know there's nought only good in my son."

He bit his lip. You could see there was something more he wanted to say, but the words would not muster. So his mouth broke open in an imbecile grin, he shrugged his shoulders once more and once more turned away.

And now he was utterly dejected, one far stupider than Armorel could have read it from the set of his body, from his forlorn, evasive eyes. True, his mouth smiled again as Maria ostentatiously welcomed him back to his seat. But he sat down with his great hands perched like spiders on his knees and stared at the floor between them: a man to whom Canaan had been shown and denied.

The clerk turned to Hosencroft, "Do you wish to call the defendant?" and for a moment Hosencroft seemed to lose his assurance. He stared suspiciously at the opposing solicitor and then at the defendant himself.

Gian Ardree shifted slightly and suddenly spoke: "I never meant to hurt him, or nobody."

"Now listen," said Hosencroft. "Do you want to go into the box and give evidence?"

"I don't see no point," Gian Ardree said.

It took a few moments for Hosencroft to assume his full forensic stature. Then, with the dignity of Portia, he turned to the Court. "That is my case."

The stir which Armorel expected did not occur. There was no whispered consultation or fluttering of papers, no adjournment, no expectancy. Only a second or two of silence passed, and Mr Cuddish said:

"I find this case proved. Is there anything known about this defendant?"

A policeman went into the box and delivered a recitation.

"There is one previous conviction. At the Lambeth Juvenile Court on the 28 October 1915 he was bound over for twelve months on a charge of malicious damage. He attended the Sand Street Elementary School until the age of 14, when he became employed as a baker's delivery boy. At the age of 16 he obtained employment as a jet washing hand at the Hibbage Lane depot of the East Southwark Traction Company, and was in that employment up to the date of his arrest. I have—"

Mr Hosencroft said suddenly, and with startling violence:

"*'Up to the date of his arrest'!* Are you in a position to tell the Court on what grounds my client has been dismissed from his employment?"

"I didn't say he had been dismissed."

"In fact, he has not been dismissed?"

"Not as far as I am aware."

"Your Worship, I must protest against this evidence. This witness, who is an experienced witness, uses a phrase which clearly implies—"

"I think we can leave that," Mr Cuddish said. "We're all quite clear now that the defendant has not been dismissed from his employment."

Without an instant's pause Hosencroft pounced on the witness again.

"Are we to understand, in fact, that you have received no information of any kind from the employers you mention? Nothing about character? . . . Oh, you *have* information as to character?"

"I was going to say, when I was interrupted—"

"Oh, you were *going* to say! Yes yes, let's hear what you were *going* to say!"

"I was going to say the employers have stated in writing that the defendant's work and character have been satisfactory."

"Ah, now I see! First of all you told us that my client was employed *up to* the date of his arrest. Then you admitted that he was never dismissed from his employment. Now you most fortunately remember that the employers have made a written statement about the defendant's character. And you say that the character given is 'satisfactory'."

"Yes."

"You're quite certain that that was exactly the term used?"

The witness glanced at his transcript.

"The term used is 'entirely satisfactory'."

Hosencroft struck the table before him with resounding force.

"So—*at last* we come to the truth of the matter! You now admit that the defendant was *not* dismissed from his employment, and having searched in the rather cloudy recesses of your memory you recall, and you are good enough to inform the Court, that so far from dismissing my client his employers have gone to the trouble of making a *written* statement to show without—any—reservation—whatever—that his work and his character—*and* his character—has always been entirely satisfactory. *Entirely* satisfactory! Your Worship, I refrain from making any comment on the manner in which this witness has given his evidence. If Your Worship pleases, I propose to call evidence as to character of a less—well, shall I say, of a wholly impartial and reliable kind."

There was no longer a trace of defeat in the expression of Hosencroft. He was an artist who did not much care whether the audience liked the play so long as he was satisfied with the intrinsic merit of his own performance. He was satisfied now: you saw it in his face, in the new deliberation of his movements. He had thrown the powers of evil into confusion by his able musketry, he had marshalled his own forces with that calm ability which, however often he tasted it, never quite lost its relish. He wriggled luxuriously in his clothes, as one enjoying a hot bath. He stroked his neck, gathering the loose flesh forward, and his hands went slowly down to his pocket. A crumpled piece of paper came out, he glanced at it and leaned over to speak to the clerk.

It was for Armorel a moment of freezing terror. She had watched the crude, ill-balanced play in growing distaste. And now, because of her impulsive action, it seemed that she was to walk on the shoddy stage herself, a junior member of Hosencroft's troupe, with only the shred of a line to speak. But the name called was not her own. It was Trevon Grist.

And here at last, she thought fleetingly, is someone able to restore the balance; for the low voice of Grist revealed the dearer sort of schooling. But when he had said a few sentences she realized that he belonged to the multitude of the merely well-intentioned. He was a large shambling man in the thirties; the kind, by his physique and the rough casting of his head, who walks by himself through Austria and Greece, with Donne and Hopkins in a worn rucksack. He was described as a club warden, and his personality would doubtless make some impression in a village hall or with a pair of male friends in an A.B.C. Here he was useless. He had known the accused, he said cautiously, some three years ago; to be more exact, he had last been in frequent contact with him three and a half years ago, when the boy was fifteen. Well, no, he couldn't say that he had known him intimately. Of course he regarded every member of the Club as his personal friend; but whereas there were some boys that he knew very well, others were not the kind who gave much of their confidence to an older man. He did remember that young Ardree had always struck him as a decent and honest boy. Rough, yes. Inclined to be quick-tempered—but that was common among boys of that age, in some respects it might almost be called a healthy sign. Indeed, he thought—though here he had to rely on memory, and he dealt with a great number of boys—that Ardree was one of those who would always take the side of a boy feebler than the rest . . . Speaking on oath, he would not like to say exactly when Ardree had last attended the Club, but it would be in June or July 1916. At fifteen or so it was quite usual for boys to drift away from the Club, they considered themselves grown men at that age and they had new interests—there were no girls in the Club. And so on and so forth. It was all impressions, half-memories, a stream of vagueness. One small and sensible lie, "I always considered Ardree one of the best boys in my club," might have been of some use. It would never come. This woolgathering giant was one so terrified of a useful lie that he would leave truth stranded.

Now that the moments of intense relief were over she returned to a deeper malaise. She knew positively to which side she belonged. She was sorry, deeply sorry, for the injured policeman and his wife. But sentiment should never be allowed to cloud one's moral vision as, she supposed, it was clouding the vision of nearly everyone in this room. An act of violence had been done and here was the young man who had done it: that was clear enough. But no one seemed to be inquiring coolly and percipiently why he had acted in that way. His own statement, taken in the police station when he must still have been in high agitation, was recorded in the stilted phrase which made all such statements virtually meaningless. His defenders against the peril in which the charge had placed him were a pair of middle-aged children, almost inarticulate, and now this fumbling Laodicean. What use to talk of justice when the reality, seen closely, had such a pattern as this!

"No," the witness was saying, "I can't say I've ever turned a boy out of the Club . . . No, I've never refused one admittance because of his reputation. After all," he continued awkwardly, "I'm not so particularly virtuous myself. I've got a temper, I lash out sometimes."

She had still a chance to act. No one could stop her making the few steps across the Court to say in Hosencroft's ear, "I have some important evidence. It may make all the difference." That would be partly true. She had, in fact, very little to go on, but at least she could say her piece a hundred times better than the Ardree parents. Her brain was working swiftly now, she had almost completed the two or three sentences which would force these lethargic people to see the incident as Gian Ardree must be seeing it. Only the initial courage was wanted, enough of resolution to cross the paltry space between her and the solicitor. And already her feet, moving in advance of her will, had shifted. In an instant she would have risen and been on her way.

Something stopped her. Not lack of will, some other part of will, so distinct that it might have come from outside: the whispered voice, perhaps, of Cepinniers long forgotten, people who knew their status, who avoided display. It was over, anyway. She knew with misery that she would not gather fresh momentum.

And the case was virtually finished. The clerk was passing papers up to Mr Cuddish, officials were stirring. They were close to the kill.

Mr Cuddish started reading the documents; but not, apparently, with much attention. His expression was that of a schoolboy at his desk, the filmed eyes on the text-book a mere screen for the inward eyes roving by sunlit streams. Perhaps a quarter of a minute passed, not more; in which there was no sign that the wheels of his reason moved at all. A frown, or the momentary closing of those opaque eyes, might have satisfied the girl intently watching him that he brought to his duty more than the perfunctory skill of a booking clerk. There was no such sign. He was a pink and drowsy little man, his only thought—she imagined—was of getting back to his club.

Less than a quarter of a minute, and he had begun to speak. His voice, a little high, tinged with a legal preciosity, was kept to the pitch of conversation: the voice of an elderly schoolma'am announcing changes in the time-table to the senior monitress.

"You have been brought before me on a very serious charge, that of assaulting and injuring an officer which the public (that means all of us) employ for their protection. If the officer had died from his injuries, which might have happened, the charge would have been still more serious: in that respect you are fortunate. As it is, you have inflicted serious harm on an innocent fellow-being. That is a wrong which you cannot now put right. Neither can I. But it is my business to see that the police, in the discharge of their duty, have all the protection which the law can give them. Which means that people who wantonly attack them must be punished. Three years ago you were brought before a Juvenile Court for being a nuisance, and you were bound over. That appears to have taught you nothing. The evidence which the Court has heard proves beyond any reasonable doubt that you attacked the constable with the most callous savagery. You are nearly nineteen years old—no longer a child—and you have got to learn that society will not tolerate this kind of hooliganism. You will go to prison for three months."

There was a small, curtailed cry, such as a rabbit makes when a keeper kills it. That came from Maria Ardree. The face of Gian scarcely altered: there was only a momentary tightening of his jaw, the small grimace of a climber who on reaching one ledge finds a steeper pitch in front. One curious thing he did, as they were leading him away. He turned right round and stared woodenly at the injured constable's wife, and seemed as if he would take a step towards her. But the policeman prevented that, and Gian was led from the room.

The Court began emptying. Armorel stayed in her seat, bending over her bag so that little of her face should be seen.

4

*M*ERELY TO steer away from Cromer's Ride she got on a bus going westward; and sat there as in a private room, lace-curtained by her thoughts. The pain of defeat had to be worked out as men walk off their stiffness, and her mind rehearsed now with laborious perfection the part she had failed to play. Through the shape of 'Phosferine' and a man's felt hat she could see herself in the box, she could hear her own voice, very quiet but distinct; serious, self-reliant, the antithesis of all the stolid and the fumbling voices which had come before.

"It was absolutely plain, from where I stood, that the Accused was in complete confusion. His mother was lying on the pavement, and the only idea in his mind was that he must protect her . . . I had a long conversation with Mrs Ardree, and by making allowance for the natural excitement in which I found her I was able to form an unbiassed picture of the character of her son. I am absolutely satisfied that he is normally a young man of excellent character and very quiet behaviour, devoted to his parents . . ."

And a new scene came as a lantern-slide comes on the screen, first doubled with the slide before and then left plain: the Chinese screens in the drawing-room, the Landseer engravings; and through the petulant horns and the cough of gears she was listening to Aunt Edie's sensible and shaded voice:

"Yes, but, Rellie, it does seem a pity not to make use of your relations. I mean, if your father were at home he would naturally ask this Captain Aquillard to meet him somewhere. They'd get to know about each other, in the way men do. After all, if you go into business partnership with someone you do find out something about him first, and marriage is a far closer partnership than any business. I'm sure Grandmother would be delighted to have him here for a weekend, say. Before we let anything be put in the papers . . ." And Edie's voice again, still quiet and sensible, so sensible, but with a deathly chill in it:

"Listen, dear, I think it's better that you should read Cousin Harold's letter for yourself. I don't want you to think I'm reading more into it than what he actually says." (This time Aunt Edie's own room, with the October morning sun on its hideous bedstead and austere grey walls; Edie sitting by the dressing-table, trying to be natural and friendly; Cousin Harold's plunging script in violet ink on sheet after sheet of Brooks's notepaper.) ". . . You see what I mean, Rellie? 'Unstable'—well, a great many men have become unstable through their war experiences. That's something which might be put right. But you see what he says on the next page—what he got from Captain Aquillard's own commanding officer. 'Aquillard had said that in his view the fact that she was a married woman was immaterial.' You know, a responsible senior officer doesn't make up a story like that. And if you marry a man who holds that view of marriage . . ."

The bus groped forward a yard at a time and then stood shuddering in the tangle of Bridge Street. The silk-hatted messenger who stared straight at her face, a dray-horse flinching from its bit, the chaste exuberance of Barry's clock-tower were only a film across the high-backed sofa in the Plumes at Beaconsfield where Gordon Aquillard sat and fiddled with a pair of trouser-clips.

"Yes, it's a pity—I wanted to tell you in my own way, so that you'd understand." (She must try to capture it once again, as those who have no head for heights are drawn to high towers, the dreamlike sensation when he said those words, the feeling that she watched herself as well as him.) "You see, the facts don't speak for themselves—facts never do." (The smile at the side of his mouth, while his eyes stayed pitiful, as if he were curious to see how she would suffer from a pain familiar to him.) "The facts are that I was in love with a woman, and that she was married to someone else. We had a child . . . Yes, we are still friends, though not in the same way." Then Grandmother's voice across the velvet table-cloth, as crisp and final as the magistrate's this morning. "My dear child, to behave very stupidly at twenty is like having measles at ten. It takes a little longer to get over, that's all."

And this evening, she thought, as the tumbled current moved again and drew them into Whitehall, this evening I'll be in the little chair—'Dorothea's chair'—with the child's nightgown that has to be hemmed for the Rotherhithe Mission; Aunt Edith will be talking about Mrs Nowell's concert, and the way poor Mrs Nowell wears herself out. Later, perhaps, if Grandmother went to bed early, there would be a cosy half-hour with Georgina. Georgina with her kind eyes would ask for the history of the day, the glow of her sympathy was not to be resisted, and drop by drop the story would trickle out. ". . . No, Aunt Georgie, I did nothing at all, I sat still like a perfect little lady. Of course I meant to say something. But I just hadn't got the nerve to walk across to that mouldy little lawyer . . ." In time Georgie would pass it on, since concealment was as little in her nature as falsehood. There would be meaning looks, perhaps nothing else, criss-crossing over the dining-room table, and in Gertrude's room Gertrude would say masterfully, "My dear Edie, the child must have these escapades. All young people go through patches of sentimentality." Of course, in theory it would be easy enough to lie to Georgie; and another person could have made the lie a protective scab under which in time the wound itself would heal. But at Hilda Abbess's she had lived five years in the north light shed by women hand-picked for integrity; and she was Arthur Cepinnier's child.

Then, just then, as the bus swept past the Horse Guards, she knew that this must not be a second failure. The first would not matter in the end, it belonged to a farandole as extraneous to the march of life as Cromer's Ride itself. But this morning she had found herself voiceless among the voices of hunger and conflict; and if she finally yielded to that impotence no battlefield remained, she was cast as permanent spectator. No! Today's defeat was secret and not final. The man was not dead. She had seen him caught in a senseless man-made engine, watched dumbly as they hustled him away, to what a charnel house she could sufficiently imagine. That much was over, and the evil she might have prevented would be so much harder to undo. She had no plan. But she felt, beyond her angry resolution, a power of understanding quick and hard enough to overhaul the mischief of a random justice. *Are baffled to fight better* . . . She was committed now. There would be no discharge in this war and no soft campaigning. That was as she wished, and she did not believe that one who kept his face towards a single, high objective could be beaten in the end.

Filled up again with well-pressed coats and tidy umbrellas the bus had become intolerable in its prosperous complacence. As it curved into Cockspur Street she shoved her way to the platform and jumped down.

She had thought of having lunch at a place she knew in Wardour

Street, but the need of someone to talk to had grown urgent and from that came automatically the idea of Duffy Elwin's flat. She crossed over to a call-box and rang Duffy's number.

The decision had been made in a moment: it proved, she thought as she waited for Duffy's voice, that a page had been turned. For nearly six months now she had avoided everything to do with the School of Economics, including the friends she had made there (for since Gordon had given up his lectureship the whole story of him and her was as private as Trafalgar Square). A week ago, Duffy's flat was the last place she would have thought of visiting. That was where she had met him first of all. It was in Duffy's sitting-room, that incredible August evening (with Duffy rushing out to fulfil some tactful engagement) that he had talked in his gently cynical way about Goethe's debt to Winckelmann; had stopped abruptly to say in an unnatural voice while he stared at her shoes, "You know, I've always been so damnably unhappy"; had seized her hands and covered them, her neck and then her mouth, with almost brutal kisses. It had seemed impossible in these last months that she could bear to sit in that room again; but now, as if this day's march had brought her to a new crest, she felt she could look back on the bitter months with a semblance of detachment. There was another country on this side.

The charivari of the telephone gave place to Duffy's racing, schoolgirl voice:

"But, my dear man, I like to lie down in my bath! How can I lie down if great enormous blobs of red-hot water keep thudding on to my chest? Hullo! hullo!"

Armorel said: "Listen, Duffy, I'm in town, just for today. I'd love to see you. Could you give me a bite of lunch. Or would it not—"

"Darling," said Duffy in agony, "do hang on one tiny moment, I've got a ghastly man here, I mean I've got an awfully sweet man here to do the ghastly geyser, he's accusing me of stealing his spanner—what?—oh, I wondered what I was sitting on, could you keep it somewhere else, do you think? Lunch? Darling, lunch would be superb. Oh . . . Oh, there is just one thing—"

"Now, Duffy, be honest! If you're going out somewhere, or if you're short of food—"

"Darling, there's mountains of food. The whole place is oozing with it. There's only just one tiny bother—No, listen, if I ring straight away I can catch her just before she leaves the hospital."

"Catch who, Duffy?"

"Elizabeth." There was a pause at last. Then, "Oh, I suppose you didn't know, it's such ages since I wrote. Elizabeth's living with me at present just for a few weeks. You see, Henry's gone abroad somewhere and she's let her own flat and she wants to be somewhere near poor little Michael while he's in hospital."

"But which Elizabeth?"

"Well, that's what I meant to tell you. It's—it's Elizabeth Kinfowell."

For a moment the line brought nothing but harassed breathing and when Armorel had said "Oh . . ." another silence followed.

"You know about her?" Duffy asked at length.

"No—should I?"

"What? No, no, of course not. Only—only her husband's slightly famous and that sort of thing. But listen, darling, I'll ring off now and get on to her straight away. No, of course not—no, it isn't that—darling, I'd simply never forgive you if you didn't come."

Armorel went to Strand Station and took a ticket to Belsize Park.

There was a moment, as she walked up Paisley Gardens, when the newborn courage left her. On so many evenings this had been their rendezvous. Often he would come out first, bringing notes to work on for the following morning, and when she had thirsted through the stuffy day for the hour of this walk from the station it was here, just here by the fire hydrant, that she had been able to see his narrow head as he sat in Duffy's bay window. A whistle, and he would turn and wave; in a few seconds he was striding out to her, disguising his limp, smiling with his thin mouth closed as if they two had hatched a plot of superb originality; and here, in the middle of the street, they would embrace as unashamedly as if a forest sheltered them. To see this death-mask of her happiness was to feel the jag of physical pain, an oily smoke in the nose and lungs. She would have turned, even then, and gone back to the station; but Duffy had seen her, Duffy was leaning far out and calling to the several million citizens of London:

"Darling, I think the latch is down, and I can't come down, everything's in a ghastly crisis, but you'll find Mrs Chean's key hidden in the same old place—you know, in the bottom of the drain pipe. Don't touch the door, it's been painted. Oh, hell, I knew that would happen!"

That, too, brought back Gordon's smile, and Gordon's felted voice, "Duffy, of course, is specifically designed by nature to be the mother of five gigantic boys, who will grow into brigadier-generals and place the posts of Empire further out." But there was no escape now. And with Duffy you did not need to guard yourself: you could weep, and she would only rummage for aspirin and face-powder; you could go raving mad and jump on the mantelpiece, and she would nod sympathetically and hunt you out a volume of Jung.

She was standing at the top of the stairs, holding a sauce boat and a pair of crimson pyjamas. She whispered—and the whisper came down the stairs like the ferocious ventilation of underground stations:

"My dear, it's too awful for the poor darling, his wife's in hospital, or gaol or somewhere, and there's only his prehistoric mother to look after both the infants, and one of them's cutting a tooth. How could anyone concentrate on other people's geysers with all that going tearing round one's subconscious! Listen, darling—do come in, darling, you look lovely, what a perfectly heavenly colour, that coat—listen, I couldn't get through to Elizabeth, so she may be coming and she may not. (Do you mind holding this—yes, it is hot.) I'm so terribly sorry. Only it's the imbecile girl on the hospital switchboard, she would keep putting me through to the surgical ward."

Armorel said, taking off her hat, "But does it matter? Will she be frightfully shocked at finding you've got such plebeian friends?"

"Darling, don't be so silly—of course not—she's perfectly used to it by now. No, it's only I thought it would be so much nicer to be all by ourselves, there's such a lot I want to hear all about. Would it be an awful bore just to look at the potatoes—the poor darling's cut his hand on the safety tap and I was just half-way through bandaging it when you came."

The worst was over now. The room's separate features were the same, the grubby chintzes and the hand-painted mirror stuck with invitations, Nash's *Inverness Copse* hemmed in by lacrosse groups, Duffy's half-finished essays and half-darned stockings over everything; but the midday light from a gelid sky showed every outline hard as in a child's drawing, the evening magic had all gone. She found, standing over the gas-cooker while Duffy flew back and forth like a bagatelle ball, that she could refer to him in an easy voice.

"You know, I rather wish Gordon had been there this morning. I feel he'd have got up and said something, or at least it would have been a comfort to have someone seeing the whole business the way I saw it. Such a mockery it was—going into everything except what really mattered. And a sort of awful middle-class calm over everything, as if they were doing an experiment in chemistry."

Duffy went out to pay the boy from the stationer's. "I know," she said, returning. "All law-courts are like that. David Egerton told me about it once—you know, he was reading law before he changed over to botany. He said the lawyers all get together beforehand in the vestry or wherever it is and they just decide exactly which way the thing's going to go. So everything that happens in court is just façade. Darling, do you think that fish is good enough to offer some to the gas-man?"

"I'm not going to let the business rest where it is," Armorel said, when the gas-man's portion had been taken to him. "I was feeble this morning, because I didn't know my way about. I'm going to get hold of a solicitor and see what can be done."

Remembering suddenly that she had promised to turn off Mrs Chean's oven, Duffy flew downstairs. She said, when she came back, "Rellie, dear, you're absolutely certain the young man's worth helping?"

"I'm quite certain that I'm not going to see an act of injustice done right under my nose and do nothing about it."

But she doubted if Duffy, still fastened in this ante-room of life, would entirely understand.

The gas-fitter went at last, with a tin of Ovaltine for his wife: either the geyser would be all right, he said, or it would just go bust and settle the whole argument. A man with asthma took away the laundry, an exasperated voice on the telephone was told that this was not the Public Library, they left the washing-up and took their cocoa over by the window. She thought, with a momentary grief, If Gordon had never come this would still have been my own life: the aureole of friends, the rush to get essays done in time, the delicious, protracted pauses. But across the intervening distance—and how large it seemed, far larger now than the separation from Hilda Abbess's—the pattern had lost its pertinence, like the dress you wore in an old photograph.

Duffy, running level with her thoughts, said: "You've quite decided not to start again? You could re-register, couldn't you, and take the finals next year. You know that Gordon's in America at present? He won't be back before June—he said that definitely in his last letter.

He's not sure if he'll come then. He's got an option of going on there for another year."

"Oh, you still correspond?"

"Well, yes, he sends me snippets of news, you know, every now and then. He likes to hear a bit about people we both know. I couldn't refuse him that, could I?"

"Of course not."

"It would be such fun if you came back. Everyone's forgotten about that business, you wouldn't find them being sympathetic and tiresome. And I mean, after all, everyone's supposed to have an affair, or whatever you call it, unless they're like me with a face like what you buy for mouse-traps. No, I don't mean that with you it was just that sort of affair."

Bunched in the wicker chair, holding her cigarette like a taper, she surveyed Armorel through its smoke with all except the malice of envy. Here was perfection: the ripeness and the innocence, a body moulded faultlessly to wrestle or to float in the air; eyes where the eager light held steady as October sunshine, a warmth, a gentle and unconscious grace in the gestures of head and hands, in the way the lips and tongue moved, forging instantly the smile which the grave voice was to carry. She did not want that loveliness for herself, because she could not imagine such possession: she was content to warm herself beside it, like the aged people whom you see hunched motionless before a Leonardo.

She asked abruptly: "Shall I tell him I've seen you when I write? Or would you rather I didn't?"

"I'd rather not," Armorel said.

"You feel—sort-of—final about that?"

"Yes, Duffy, quite final. I can't—I can't get on with people who don't tell me things. It's all right if they do tell me, but not otherwise. I suppose that sounds like nonsense to anyone else."

"No. No, it doesn't."

The latest of Gordon's letters was in the bag under her chair, and the thought of letting Armorel read it—even of making her read it—came like a nudge on the arm. But she held herself against the impulse, wondering if this were the time. Then there were confident footsteps along the pavement, and the spring of the front gate whined.

Armorel, looking over Duffy's shoulder, caught sight of a slender black coat, of a white face. A woman was coming up the steps.

"She's come back after all!" Duffy said. In one moment she was all alive again—from her voice it might have been the bailiffs arriving—and the next had taken her half-way to the door. "I must tell her about that whatyoucallit!" she said over her shoulder and was off downstairs.

Armorel could not hear what Duffy said in the hall. But she heard the answer, in a voice where pleasure seemed to break through tiredness, "Oh, but I'd like to meet her very much!"

That weariness was in Elizabeth Kinfowell's face when she came into the room; but for a moment only, as she glanced mechanically at the mantelpiece for a letter, and then stood still, unfastening her coat, letting the thoughts she had travelled with drain away. When her eyes came round to Armorel she smiled as if in recognition. ". . . so much about you!" she said gently. And Armorel answered as if the smile were familiar, for it had that nature, it was not from a shallow sowing. There are people whom you know to be often ill, though they rarely speak of it. They slip away sometimes; and no one sees them in the early hours of morning when they walk up and down the bedroom, when they sprawl with a pillow clutched against the face and listen to the clock ticking. In daytime it shows only in the eyes, in a moment when they are taken off their guard. Elizabeth had that in her eyes before she smiled; and her face, which Lotto could have painted, had the whiteness of faces kept away from daylight.

"No, thank-you, Duffy, I had lunch on my way. No, Michael's not much better—I think I'll move him as soon as I can and look after him myself. The nurses have all been reading books on the Approach to the Child, they're rather horrifying."

She was middle-aged, by a girl's standards: with the grey strands in her hair she might be thirty-seven, Armorel thought (giving her nine years too many); and though she sat on the floor with her back against the wall she remained their centre-piece. In part, because of her stillness. She did not smoke. None of her movements was hurried or needless and her hands, folded round her knees, never moved while she talked. Her body had not the fullness of motherhood, but she was a finished work; you could not imagine that there were experiences left to deepen her maturity.

". . . all morning in a police court?—you poor dear! I loathe law courts of any kind. Were you giving evidence or something?"

Armorel said: "Well, no, I thought I might have to, but in the end I didn't."

She had been through the whole story with Duffy: for this different listener she told it differently, with less excitement, with (she felt) greater sophistication.

". . . Of course, it wasn't really my business—I only just happened to have seen the alleged assault. But knowing what I do about the boy—I'm quite sure the mother was sincere in what she told me—I can't possibly leave things where they are. I'm going to fight that sentence, if it takes me all my life . . ."

Sitting on the arm of a chair, Duffy exulted in this meeting which she had done her best to prevent. She collected humans for their own sake, and here were two of her dearest acquisitions, each the rarest of its kind, placed in her cabinet side by side. To watch and listen to either was for Duffy a continuous happiness; and now, she thought, the virtue of each was enhanced by the other's. They were alike in grace of person and of speech, they shared an electricity of spirit which brought every stranger within its field; yet they differed as dramatically as spring and autumn, and she could fancy as her contented eyes ranged over them that she saw at once a single plant in different stages of its growth, here eager to thrust against the weather, here strong in its acceptance.

"Yes," Armorel was saying, looking a little towards the window, "I gave up the course when I was only half-way through. I wanted to be doing something a bit more practical. And then my relations with one of the lecturers had got rather complex—Duffy may have told you. It wasn't doing his work any good. Nor mine."

And Elizabeth, as Duffy anxiously watched her, said undramatically, "I suppose that's altogether past repair?"

"I shouldn't want it repaired," Armorel said.

It was characteristic, Duffy thought, that Elizabeth's eyes were tied to a fly's movement across the window frame as she said without emphasis: "They do make things terribly difficult, don't they! Are you doing a job now? What sort of thing are you after?"

"I'm not quite sure. I definitely don't want to go missionizing. I should hate to be one of those women who preach and patronize. If it wasn't such a drawn-out business I'd go in for law—that's a good jumping-off ground. By the way, do you know any solicitors? I shall have to get someone to act for me in this Ardree business—on the legal side, I mean."

"Tell me," Elizabeth said, "how much do you know about this youth? Well, perhaps I should mind my own business. But it's rather the crux of the whole affair, isn't it? I mean, as I understand it, the line you mean to take is that the magistrate awarded a penalty without paying any real attention to the young man's character."

"And then," said Duffy, "there was this business of his being bound over two or three years before."

Armorel said: "Oh, in all probability that meant nothing at all." She was not entirely ready, just now, to take a helping of Duffy's wisdom. "I imagine children are generally brought to the juvenile courts simply because their parents are too busy or too lazy to curb their high spirits. They're like the incompetent nursemaid who always calls in Mama."

Elizabeth nodded. "Yes. Only you really want to have some concrete evidence that it was a case of that sort. I mean, these lawyers, they're the most terribly finicky people to deal with. They always put on a most tender bedside manner and they say, 'The difficulty is that the Judge simply won't take any notice of what you thought he thought'! At least, all the ones I've ever dealt with talk like that."

Her sadness showed most when she was smiling. A second stream of thoughts was flowing, for a moment she looked tired again. Armorel, won by her tiredness, said patiently:

"But I don't see how I'm to find out about that earlier case until I've got a lawyer to help me. Surely that's his part of the business."

Elizabeth shut her eyes. "It's in the Lambeth part of the world, isn't it? Duffy, who was that man who used to appeal in the *Spectator,* the man who ran some settlement or something? A rather odd name— Grind, Terence Grind, something like that."

"I know who you mean." Following her own routine, Duffy made a tourniquet of her handkerchief and all but broke the joint of her thumb. "Grist!" she said triumphantly. "Trevon Grist. He once gave a lecture somewhere, and Eileen Arbathage was to have gone, only she got flu."

Armorel looked up.

"Oh, but that's the man who was in court this morning. I'd forgotten his name but I remember now. Yes, Trevon Grist. Oh, my dears, he's a hopeless creature. He was supposed to be speaking up for Gian, and all he said was that he couldn't remember anything about him. Or that was practically all. Oh, he really made me angry."

"But do you think," Duffy said, "he may be the sort of person who just goes all groggy in a court? Some people do."

"At least it's possible," Elizabeth said thoughtfully, "that he knows more than he was able to say in court, for one reason or another."

Already Duffy was away to the bathroom. She was a creature always ravenous for action, and by action she meant the frantic movement of her tennis-ball body. "I know the telephone book's in here somewhere," she called back. "That ghastly man was having his fish on it."

"You know, I really do think it would be worth seeing if we could get anything out of this man," Elizabeth said; and the 'we' was grateful to Armorel's ears. "I mean, if only because he's on the spot. At the moment we know practically nothing about Ardree at all."

"I know quite a lot," Armorel said, but without hostility. "It's not just what his mother told me. The moment I saw his face I knew that he wasn't just a hooligan. Though I'm not sure that it would stop me, if he was. I mean, it's not the nice, well-behaved people who want looking after. There are plenty of people like my aunts to look after them."

"It was right under the bath," said Duffy, who appeared to have been there too. "I suppose he put it there to be tidy. Really, men are not quite sane, are they! . . . 'G' . . . 'G' . . . 'G' . . ."

"What I feel," Elizabeth said, "is that you can't know too much about people. The reason I'm always in such a mess is that I never keep that rule, I merely pass it on to others. There was a waiter who stole my handbag once, the management were going to hand him over to the police but I begged him off. I thought he was rather a pathetic little man, a half-caste of some sort. And then just at the time he would have been in gaol he knocked an old woman down and broke both her legs. She happened to be the wife of the mutessarif and they hanged him."

"But surely one doesn't get anywhere if one guards against that sort of thing. You've got to trust your own judgement."

"Well—as long as you can."

"Always!"

Duffy asked: "Does 'R' come before 'Q'? No, I've got it, 'Grist, T.' that must be the one. The address is 'Hollysian House, Burke's Wharf, S.E. 1.' That's all—it doesn't say anything about him." She was already on her way to the telephone. "I'll get him, shall I?"

Elizabeth said: "Well, it might be worth—"

"No!" Armorel said quickly. "I shouldn't know what to say. It's frightful explaining who you are on a telephone."

"Exchange?" said Duffy from the bathroom. "Oh, I was going to ask you for a number in Lambeth, but I don't think we want it now . . . Oh, what a rude young woman!"

"I know just what you mean," Elizabeth said to Armorel. "Only it might be worth your taking down the address, in case you think of seeing him any time."

"Wait—I've masses of paper," Duffy said. "Here, tear some out of this, it's only my notes on the Theory of Wages and I never take any because I never can understand the man. No, listen—let's all go and see Mr Grist."

"My dear!" said Elizabeth. "Three females in a covey!"

"It won't damage him permanently. No, wait. What is today? But it *is* Monday!"

"Should it not be?"

"But today's the last of Mr Kelby's Gurney Memorial Lectures!" She was making calculations from her wrist-watch, she had to subtract eight minutes for each three hours since winding. "But if it was twenty-past twelve at one o'clock," she said distressfully, "it must be at least ten-past three now. And you can't get to the Victoria and Albert in under half-an-hour."

"But, Duffy, why go at all? You said the earlier ones were so frightfully dull."

"I know—that's why I must. The poor darling's such an elephantine bore that practically no one turns up." She had begun to grab for bags and books, her unusual hat was recovered from beneath the cushion on which Armorel was sitting. "Darlings, could you possibly forgive me? If this watch is gaining as much as it should do I might not be late until I'm nearly half-way there. If I'd started eight minutes ago I'd be less late than I was last time. By this watch, I mean. Rellie darling, do stay just where you are—do you mind frightfully if Elizabeth gives you your tea?—I think the caddy must be on my bed, I was making a cup for the gas-man and I wanted to look up a quotation in Malachi."

Elizabeth said: "Go—bless you! Leave me to poison her."

"Go on!" said Armorel. "Run! I'll come and see you again."

From the window they watched her standing irresolutely on the pavement, still clutching her hat, looking vaguely about her as if something must be missing, a Newfoundland dog or her clothes. They heard her say, aloud, "But, my dear, what a dreadful thing to have done!" Then she was off like a mole in liquor, and as she tore round the bend they could hear her calling, "Stop! Oh, you beastly driver, do stop!"

Elizabeth put a kettle on the gas-stove and sat down again.

"Let's be comfortable for another quarter of an hour, then I'll make some tea, and then we might go and see if we can get anything out of this man, don't you think?"

Armorel considered this. She said:

"I think I shall go. But I really don't see why you should bother to come."

"Would you rather I didn't?"

"Oh, I'd love you to. Only it seemes absurd that you should trouble."

In truth, she was in two minds. The Ardree affair belonged to her alone, she wanted to be in action, quickly and by herself. And yet there was temptation to keep Elizabeth as long as she could. For here was rarity, and here was a warmth she could not resist, because it came from the burning of old timbers. Her rebellion against all the presumptions of seniority would not operate against this woman who wore her beauty like a scar.

It seemed as if Elizabeth caught her thoughts. "I wish we were the same age," she said. She was looking at Armorel's hands, which had the grace of a child's hands rather than a woman's. "Just because I was born a few years earlier, everything I say sounds pompous. We can't quarrel on equal terms."

"But do we want to quarrel?"

"We've got to. You see, I'm against the whole of this Ardree business. I feel it in my bones that he's not worth it. That's really why I want to go with you, I want to hear what Grist says about him, and if it's bad, as I think it will be, I mean to rub it in. I want to stop you having any more unhappiness. And of course that's about the greatest insult one woman can throw at another."

Armorel said: "I don't see that. But then, I know you're wrong about Gian Ardree. How could your guesses be more right than what I've heard and seen?" And she in her turn wished that their ages were the same; it would have helped to fight this thing out on her own level. She said with all her gentleness: "I can't think why you should worry about it making me unhappy. It's terribly kind . . ."

Elizabeth looked at her eyes. She said in the voice of every day: "I do know about Gordon Aquillard. Of course Duffy told me. Well, you'd realize—Duffy's affection for all of us is not a thing she can keep in pigeon-holes."

They could laugh then. And Armorel said in a voice which felt admirably free from emotion: "It was Duffy who introduced us, of course. Here. He used to sit where you're sitting now."

"I know."

"However, that's history."

"Is it? I don't feel, myself, that anything's ever past and done with. The past re-creates itself, one way or another. Sometimes we can influence the re-creation."

"I don't think I understand."

"I am no philosopher," Elizabeth said. "I'll make the tea—no, you sit still!—and then I suggest we go and see this Mr Grist."

5

*I*N THE largest room of Hollysian House Boys' Club, where the high, whitewashed walls were hung with railway posters and with coloured prints of the Florentines, an elderly man without one hair on his head was tugging at a pair of parallel bars.

"Well, if he's anywhere Mr Grist would be in the library," he replied to Elizabeth. "He hasn't got no sort of proper office, get me." He was looking morosely at the bars and then at the rope above them. He wore a running vest and a pair of loose serge trousers, he appeared to have been planed and finished off with emery paper, you felt he could only be entirely happy when pulling up trees. "Same thing every night," he said, "the moment I go down to see to the boiler the little perishers get hold of these bars and shove them under the rope so they can swing right across on to the box-horse. Well, that's all right if you know what you're up to, get me. And if you don't, well, they'll just break all their little ruddy necks."

"Perhaps we could find Mr Grist," Elizabeth said, "if you would tell us where the library is."

"It's this ruddy floor's the cause of all the trouble," the sergeant said. "If you was to get at that other end, both of you, and just give him a tug, when I say 'When', then I could lift him up out of this hole he's got stuck in." Automatically the women took up the position he gave them. "Mr Grist, he's not all that gone on having visitors," he said. "Leastwise, not lady visitors, get me. Now when I say 'Heave!' you just heave, only mind your toes. Not before I say. Now then—heave!"

"Perhaps you could have a word with him," Elizabeth said after heaving, "and tell him it's something rather specially important we want to see him about. It's about a boy who's in trouble."

"Now that will surprise him!" he said succinctly; and then, turning abruptly, he marched to a door at the far end of the room, struck it violently and went inside. Over the plywood partition they heard him say:

"Coupla tarts . . . say that one of the lads've got 'em into trouble, get me . . ."

And they heard Trevon Grist say softly: "Oh, hell take all these bloody women!"

But he received them with an overall of politeness clutched about his hostility. In the way of a man unused to women he put them side by side on a pair of hard folding-chairs and stood opposite them, leaning against a spray of crude, signed photographs, holding his lapels, only looking at them in furtive glances. At this second view Armorel found him larger in presence: the light came from behind him, his large, blond eyebrows like wire entanglements looked as if they had been taken out from the sparse hair on his skull.

"I was in the Damien Street Court this morning," she told him, "when the case of Gian Ardree was being heard. I don't suppose you saw me."

"No," he said, as if she were trying to sell him something. "No, I didn't."

"It was rather an unsatisfactory case, wasn't it!" she said.

"In what sense?"

"Well, I mean, no real attempt was made to find out what sort of man they were dealing with. He might have been a thorough young hooligan, or he might have been a decent youth with a bit of a temper who just didn't realize the power of his own fists—the magistrate hardly seemed to consider the question at all. And since Ardree had got no one but a pack of clowns to support him he was bound to show in a worse light than he should have. That seemed perfectly obvious to me."

"And to Cuddish," Grist said. "Cuddish is very far from being a fool, you know. He has these people coming in front of him all day long, he doesn't miss a great deal. Makes mistakes, of course, but then—"

"You don't think that a man's character ought to be taken into account before he's punished?"

"Character? Well, yes, if we know what we mean by 'character'." He looked about the room despairingly, like an honest sportsman surrounded by bird-lovers. "These young chaps," he said fumbling, "they're odd. They're neither the one damned thing nor the other. They're not children, so you can't treat 'em like children. Only they behave like that."

The interview was dying from anaemia. Elizabeth made an effort to revive it. She said in her low voice, with something of a man's inflexions:

"The point is this: we feel that something might be done to help this boy, and we thought you might give us some guidance. You may have records from the time when he used to come here—something to give us an idea what sort of young man he really is."

"Records?" he said, as if she had used a foreign word. "I don't keep anything very much, you know. One hasn't got clerks and that sort of thing." He was smiling faintly, apparently at some old recollection. He shambled over to the far end of the long, untidy room and unlocked the home-made cupboard there. "1915, wasn't it?" he said as he rummaged; and at length, "Yes, Ardee, G., I've got something about it. Nothing to go on, really—facts are never anything to go on, there's nothing less important than facts. I mean, facts as one generally knows them." It was still Elizabeth to whom he spoke; reading the paper he had found he went back and stood on her free side, with his hand on the back of her chair. " 'October '15, run in for smashing shop-window. Apparently three others concerned, with A as ringleader, but others got away. Reason given by A: rudeness of shopkeeper to his mother. Query manifestation of Latin temperament, though A predominantly English type.' That's all I put down at the time. You see, one gets scores of incidents like that, it would be hopeless trying to keep a complete dossier."

"So you really can't help us at all?" Elizabeth asked with patience.

"Well, really, I'm afraid not." He took the paper and locked it in the cupboard again, unconsciously lit the cigarette which he had been putting in and out of his pocket. "You know, really," he said to Elizabeth, "it's the sort of thing one does better to keep clear of. When these fellows get to the police court stage they're most fearfully tricky to handle. They don't see things the way you do. Someone gets a bit sympathetic and they take that as flattery—a great many of them. It's natural in a way. If one's pride gets damaged one looks round for something to straighten it out again. And if the treatment feels nice you may think it's worth having more trouble to get more treatment—especially if the treatment wears a skirt, if you don't mind my saying so. To be perfectly frank, I'd keep these lads a thousand miles away from women, except their own sort of woman. They know where they are with them." It was getting dark in the room. He suddenly shouted: "Flock! Kick up a light at this end—brace up!" The sergeant called back "Sir!" and the naked bulb dangling over the trestle-table put the room into garish light. "You'd like some tea or something," Grist said. "Flock!"

Elizabeth had got up. "No, thank-you, we've had tea. You've got a wonderful collection of books—do people send them to you?"

He turned away from her and looked disparagingly along the shelves which filled the whole of one wall. "I brought most of them from Wantage," he said. "I've got to keep them somewhere. The boys read some of them—peculiar, the things they do read. It's the Henty stuff that no one touches—they've got a sharp nose for anything healthy and they avoid it like the Black Death."

"You live here all the time?" Elizabeth asked.

"Yes—it's a very good place to live, you get no one interfering with you. And I get the best view in London."

He beckoned and she went to stand beside him at the window, which looked through a comb of masts and gear to the misted river, the glow of a locomotive's cabin moving near Blackfriars Bridge into the City's crenellated darkness. "I agree," she said. But while he still looked out, biting his lip as if with some peculiar excitement, she turned a little to watch his profile. The electric light showed him poorly shaved and his soft collar dirty. His blue suit was worn like a sack, and all the power in his head and hands, in the fine and angry mouth, was spoilt by the little, nervous movements which overran his body like an intermittent ague. "Of course," he said towards the river, "none of my perishing customers think this is worth looking at. Their idea of a view is something with a rosy-cheeked girl right in the middle of it." Then he turned to face them again, smiling a little grimly.

He said: "If I get to know anything more about Ardree—anything of any interest—I'll let you know. I can't promise more than that. If you'll give me your address?"

Elizabeth had automatically given him her card before she said: "But it's Miss Cepinnier who wants the information most."

He said as he wrote down Armorel's address: "I have warned you, haven't I? You find very often that these fellows don't like an outsider butting in. They dislike people who don't understand their point of view, and if you want to understand that you've got to give your whole life to it." At last he was looking at Armorel, impersonally, like a student of zoology. But a moment afterwards he was speaking to Elizabeth once again, "You follow what I mean, don't you?" and as his eyes examined hers his mouth wriggled into its curious, rather painful smile. "You see, at all costs I've got to protect my lads against designing females . . . Well, I wish you'd tell me how to pick out the non-designing ones."

The building was coming to life with the clatter of boots and the cannoning of brittle voices on the walls of the gymnasium with the pectoral bark of Sergeant Flock, "Now you just come away out of that to commence with, you perishing Higginson, I've told you a score of times, get me!" "We seem to be opening shop," Grist said with a note of disdain, perhaps of regret. But the echoing noises only emphasized the pervading chill and bareness, it was never a place where the gentler kind of intercourse could advance. He led them with gloomy embarrassment to the top of the stairs.

The sense of physical exhaustion had returned before Armorel was back at Cromer's Ride. She got in with a key borrowed from Georgie, collected some biscuits from the kitchen and went straight to bed.

In the first, shallow sleep she was at Damien Street again. She had reached the witness-box at last, Mr Cuddish surveyed her coldly with Elizabeth smiling mysteriously beside him, all the faces stared at her with frozen menace while she tried to speak and no words would come. She looked in desperate appeal towards Elizabeth and Elizabeth's face turned into Hosencroft's, it came towards her bodiless and she woke crying out with fear.

A part of her mind stayed somnolent, so that the sharp, intaglio pictures were wrongly grouped. It was across the Court, now, that Trevon Grist spoke to her, it was he who stopped her from giving evidence. "I agree with Cuddish," he kept saying, with his glance straying towards her body but always avoiding her eyes, "Cuddish and I know how to deal with a man like this, we don't want any interference, we want to keep all females a thousand miles away." And because she knew that those were not his exact words she struggled feverishly, turning one way and the other till the pillow fell off the bed, to get them right. She ached for Gordon to come and help her: Gordon who could remember word by word some passage in a book he had read only once, who could have got hold of Grist and made shrewd fun of him and pinned him down; and once, from a spell of tears, she spoke aloud in her quiet, sensible voice, "Gordon darling, do tell me what he was saying, I can't remember, I can't decide whether he really meant anything until I know exactly what he said." Then she remembered that Gordon was four thousand miles away, that only Elizabeth had been there.

And Elizabeth, distillation of beauty and understanding, the warmth of life breathing in steady pulse from the lineaments of deathly illness, Elizabeth was only an insoluble complication.

A single day is nothing: that one as it receded would fall to the level of the rest and its train of small humiliations might vanish with it. In a few weeks the court-room would be blurred, Grist would be only a name. And could not Elizabeth, friend of a friend, the chance companion of a few disagreeable hours, be lost in that oblivion as well? Yes, if Armorel could wish it. But she wanted at least a different kind of parting, one where they stood level in fortitude and understanding, equal in each other's esteem. Was that worth waiting and labouring for? Only if Elizabeth herself were worth it: and that was decided not by reason, not by the value a mere collector would set on her eyes and voice, on the heat and power compressed within a vessel so slenderly wrought. It was settled by a need too simple for resolution, the desire to worship a flame, the hunger to be accepted but first to accept.

With the night passing as prairie drifts across carriage windows, she had lost the day's objective: someone she had noticed in captivity, a man to whose rescue she had pledged herself, but whose name and features now eluded her grasp. It was Elizabeth who continually perplexed her search, always the name and Spartan purpose that she hunted for were only just beyond earshot when Elizabeth's lithe voice flowed in to thrust them further away. She knew that the voice could be stilled if her will demanded it. But in the grinding solitude she was frightened to lose its sweetness; ever, ever to leave this tenderness which kept her from the austere journey.

6

*B*UT IN THE MORNING, though her head ached, her mind was clear. In a letter written three days afterwards, asking her cousin Raymond to advance some money, she said:

> I have made up my mind on this business, and I shan't alter it. I can't expect you, as a man, to understand my feelings—or rather my thoughts, because this is a question of thinking rather than feeling. I suppose the ordinary, 'sensible' view would be that one small act of injustice doesn't really matter. That's what I can't agree with. If I made excuses and let one incident like this go past I should gradually find myself taking others in the same way until I stopped feeling that injustice in general was anything to worry about. If, on the other hand, I go to war on this one case I shall at least demonstrate to a number of people who have power over the lives of others that their actions are watched and that there is always the possibility of trouble when they make slipshod and callous decisions. It may seem to you that I am making a fuss over

something trivial, but I am absolutely certain it isn't that. Three months in prison may not sound anything much, but with a young man with deep feelings like Gian Ardree it's going to affect the whole of his life. I know that from intuition—and I refuse to believe that intuition is something to be pooh-poohed. After all, it's generally admitted that people's real character is too subtle a thing for one's mind to understand properly, so if intuition won't help you to understand it, what will?

I don't care what this is going to cost me, in money or anything else. . . .

She had already been to Cleward and Staiforce in Sackville Street, where she had insisted on seeing Mr Stephen Cleward himself. Mr Cleward was likely to be out most of the morning, the clerk said. Very well, she would wait most of the morning. Mr Cleward, when at last she was shown into his office, had the merit of not being paternal. He listened without interrupting, his hands folded on the table, his eyes occasionally rising to her face. Well, to begin with, he said, it would be mere folly to appeal against the verdict: from what she had told him, the fact that the accused man had deliberately struck the constable was not open to argument. But it might be possible to appeal against sentence. Candidly, he did not advise it. It would be a costly business, involving a great deal of preliminary inquiry, and it was extremely unlikely to be successful. However, if she was determined to go through with it he would get into touch with the solicitor who had defended at Damien Street, ask for his minutes of the case and start to explore the ground from there.

"It looks to me, as I see it at present, as if there's only one possible ground on which an appeal could be lodged—the mitigating circumstance that the constable appears to have struck the boy's mother, or at any rate handled her roughly, just before the boy attacked him. It may be possible to argue that that fact received insufficient attention . . . Character? No, it's generally very hard to get anywhere with arguments relating to character—character is something that can't be assessed, you will realize that there never was a murderer in court who hadn't been kind to his aged aunt and rescued half a dozen tabby cats from drowning . . . You say that your own memory of the whole incident was perfectly clear? You were about how far away?"

"Oh, quite close."

"About ten yards?"

"Oh, more than that. Perhaps thirty or forty yards."

"But you distinctly saw the constable strike the woman?"

"No, I shouldn't say that he struck her. He grabbed her and gave her a sort of shake."

"I see . . . Now, can you tell me whether this young man is likely to consent to the appeal?"

"Oh, I should think so. But that doesn't really matter—I'm going to put up the money myself—"

"Yes, but actually it does matter. It's impossible to lodge an appeal unless the defendant has signified his consent."

"But there would surely be some way of getting over a technicality like that. Isn't that what lawyers are for?"

"No," he said gravely, "it isn't the business of lawyers to evade the law. People think that, but it isn't so."

"Then do you mean that everything's got to be held up until that point has been settled?"

No, the preparation of the case could go forward in the meantime. And, after all, it need not take very long to communicate with the governor of the prison, who would take steps to ascertain Ardree's wishes in the matter. No, there was nothing to be gained by Armorel going to the prison herself, it was very much better to follow the recognized procedure. No, really, at the present stage there was nothing more that she could do.

Except to write a date and an address on his pad he had hardly moved throughout the interview: he waited now, embarrassingly motionless, for anything further she might wish to say.

"I do want you to realize," she said, "how very important this is to me. I've no personal interest in the young man—it's for a different reason altogether. There's nothing private or feminine about it, it's a matter of one's public responsibilities."

Yes, of course, Mr Cleward entirely understood that. There would be no unnecessary delay in putting the matter in train.

Two days later she was in town again, in Whitehall Crescent, where Sir Walter Dibel received her with kindness. Yes, he had been intending to write and ask if there were any news of her father. She must not give up hope. Arthur Cepinnier was the sort of man who did not die, he was *sui generis*, he was too rare a being for the world to lose. It was a time of hopefulness, was it not—the crocuses would be showing before very long in the Embankment Gardens. Was she fond of gardens? Ah, to him gardens were everything, every year he longed more intensely to turn his back for ever on London and devote himself to his half-dozen acres at Maresfield. He hoped she would visit him and Lucia there sometime.

". . . Yes, I'm certain you've done the right thing in putting the whole business into the hands of a first-rate solicitor—oh, yes, Cleward has a very high reputation . . . Ah, no, you see, so long as the case is *sub judice* one can't make any movement through a parliamentary channel. If you do decide in the end to try and get the matter ventilated, then I think your proper course would be to go to your own member. Who would that be, now—yes, of course, Dickie Spears. Oh, you couldn't have anyone better than that—he's a most human creature, I don't know anyone who takes more pains over people's little personal problems . . . I'll tell you what—you might see if you can get an interview with Rupert Ingoyne. No, I don't know him personally, but the London magistracy is rather up his street . . ."

This London was full of vacuum-operated doors and of secretaries, guarding on either side from public freedom and from private safety a limbo of oil-cloth and inquiry windows, unhomely smells and presentation calendars, a silence like the silences of warfare, underlined by a distant chatter of keys, broken by strident bells and voices siphoning from doors that swung and shut again. The phrases with their standard intonations were soon familiar, 'I couldn't rightly say when he *would* be in.' 'He never sees nobody after dinner,' 'Perhaps if you was to write a letter first of all!' She endured this outlawry, because she had learnt from the experienced that every campaign is nine parts boredom. She was polite and guarded, sensible, ruthlessly tenacious. With the male watch-dogs she behaved as courteously as with their owners, refusing the more comfortable chairs they wanted to sacrifice to her, willing to do everything except get out of the building. Even with the women secretaries she was nicely mannered, "Yes, I understand perfectly, I can imagine what a job it is to keep him free from interruptions," her voice always gentle and persuasive, only her eyes hinting, with a shade which they could appreciate, that all the secretaries on earth would never deflect her from her purpose. The fruits were small: Mr Praed would give her a personal introduction to Mr Macdonald, who was on the committee of the Weston Steward Legal Aid Association, Mr Grievish would write a letter to Colonel Finnestall: but the seeds were being thickly sown, some must fall at last on fertile ground, she could not believe that there was no reward for an unwearying resolution.

On the Friday evening, returning to Cromer's Ride exhausted from the day's pilgrimage, she found a letter in a foolscap envelope: an island of chaste typewriting enclosed by gigantic margins:

> We are advised by the Spenwick Prison Authority that the prisoner Gian Ardree withholds his consent from the filing of an appeal against the sentence awarded at the Damien Street Court on the 9th instant.
>
> We regret that we are therefore unable to act further in the fulfilment of your instructions.

On each of these evenings when she came home late some dinner had been kept hot for her. The gas-stove in the dining-room must not be lit again, since gas had become one of Edie's favourite economies: so O'Connor with the countenance of mutiny brought a tray to the drawing-room. It was not a comfortable hour. The elder women sewed while she ate and talked spasmodically of their overlapping worlds; in a nervous fashion, like players at forfeits, the aunts asked her questions.

"I suppose it's still quite difficult in town to find a taxi?" "I suppose you see a lot of idleness, with men being demobilized—are there many signs of discontent?"

For them it was not easy, since their niece's actual occupation in London could not be discussed at all.

In one afternoon of bitter warfare, conducted with pale, taut faces and in voices hardly above a whisper, Aunt Edith and Armorel had reached an understanding; and the understanding was wholly in Armorel's favour. In future she might come and go as she pleased, and she was not required to state her business: the only stipulations were that she should not be away for the night without special sanction and that she should not 'become in any way involved' (which phrase they both sufficiently understood).

What other result could Edith have achieved, in those days of enfranchisement, against an opponent who within her aura of gentleness had become as granite-willed as a Protestant martyr? What weapons had she to use, now that the force of her own will, gathered in her white lips and the grey, unwavering purpose of her eyes, was met by one which did not even flinch before it? Incapable of empty menace, she could not threaten to make her brother's child homeless. The little money Armorel had was her own, and a girl of twenty could not be sent to bed for disobedience. There was a means by which she could have found out all she wanted—might even have won herself the chance to interfere. A few simple sentences were all she needed: 'Darling Rellie, I'd do anything in the world for your happiness. I see my baby brother in you, and that makes you more precious to me than anything I possess.' But she was an Englishwoman born in '65, and for her, the betrayal of an intimate emotion was more impossible than physical immodesty. She could only say, in that livid interview which had left her with a whole day's torturing headache, "Yes, I know you did exactly what you wanted when you were a student. And do you honestly think the result was a success?"

The dust which the battle had stirred hung in a still cloud, in a region so sequestered the climate had no wind lively enough to disturb it. Poor Georgie, in those days, was often in her own room and on her knees, letting the burden of her distress flow out in tears, longing for the skill to turn her thoughts into prayer. Then she would sponge her face, and creep to the top of the stairs, hoping to get down to the morning-room without meeting Edie on the way; and somehow it happened again and again that Edie emerged just then from the kitchen passage, and immediately glanced upward.

"Is there something you want, Georgie? Are you feeling all right?"

In such a passage their mother took no part. But as usual, she knew more than they supposed; more, indeed, than they knew themselves. To a cousin of a younger generation she wrote at that time:

> My dear ridiculous Edith is again in conflict with Arthur's child. How I wish these people would come to blows, or at least shout at each other with good Protestant curses—I find Edie's sulks so monotonous. It appears that Armorel has fallen in love again, which Edith finds shockingly unnatural, never having had any dealings with livestock. This time the fortunate gentleman is unfortunate enough to be serving a term of imprisonment for housebreaking, or some kindred indiscretion. (My information comes from Walter Guestward, a tedious person on whom Arthur used to lavish his wayward charity, and whose handwriting would disgrace a board-school child.) My granddaughter is hotly occupied in extricating him from this predicament; she argues, I presume, that if iron bars do not a prison make they are at least an intolerable obstacle to courtship; and she is so sanguine as to imagine that this

straightforward reasoning can be impressed upon those members of your Sex who have the general ordering of our lives and conduct. I see no use in interference. For myself—if a disintegrating memory still serves—I was never inspired to a *grande passion* by any member of the burgling fraternity; but I belong in age to a vanished century, in spirit—as far as I can judge—to an extinct millennium. It may be that the New Age of which they speak in the newspapers, and which seems to be coming upon us like dandelions in the spring, is to find its generative force in an alliance of the ornamental with the criminal classes. At any rate it appears to me quite useless for my dear Edith to prowl round the entanglement like a pussy-cat outside a fish-shop on early closing day. I did my best to make her see the folly of such tactics when Armorel was in pursuit of an adulterous tutor. Do you, by the way, happen to know whether she is persecuting anyone to lend her money? . . .

The house, large as it was for the needs of five women, kept them too close to each other; its very quietness was a growing irritant. Had they been separated for a while, even by the breadth of an English county, the genius of their earliest friendship might have flowered again: the days of tobogganing at Standle, the joyous evening of Gertrude's return from London, when the girls had stayed up till midnight to see their mother put on her Presentation dress and waltz all round the drawing-room, those memories, tinted with warm and lively colourings, were covered now by the insidious growth of many seasons, and with them the graciousness which they engendered was lost. Remotely, affection remained. Not seldom, each would have revealed it. But like the paralysis which falls on men before photographers a curtain of inveterate reserve came down upon the kindness they would have shown.

And what can it mean to Edith, Georgina thought, this wild behaviour of Rellie's!—nothing, except inconvenience, and a slight on her ludicrous self-esteem as virtual mistress of the house, the controller of everyone's comings and goings! To Georgina it meant so much more than that. She had believed that her friendship with Armorel was slowly deepening. The child had been someone to talk to, a personality of new, delicious fragrance, and willing at times, as their acquaintance ripened, to reveal her private thoughts with a freedom she would never show to the others. That phase was over now and perhaps it would never return. Armorel showed her no less sweetness; had increased, perhaps, in thoughtfulness of behaviour, in quickness to pay little attentions to the comfort of them all and especially to hers. But if Georgina gave some innocent lead—"Is everything going on all right, Rellie?"—the girl would flutter into safety like a robin upon a careless movement of its tamer. "Oh, yes, Aunt Georgie—yes, I've nearly finished the little coat I'm knitting for Christine's baby."

Late on the evening when Armorel received the long envelope (the envelope which Edith had vainly held up against the light, while Georgina watched her through the keyhole), she slipped along in her dressing-gown to her niece's room.

"Rellie—may I come in? Oh, I'm sorry, I didn't really want to disturb you—I just thought that O'Connor might have forgotten your hot-water bottle. She does forget sometimes, she doesn't really think about her work."

She stood unhappily just inside the door, which she had not the courage to close behind her, and blinked towards the lamp by which Armorel was reading. The child had surely grown thinner, she thought, seeing her in her night-dress; thinner and almost haggard with fatigue.

Armorel said: "Georgie darling, you'll get cold! It was sweet of you to think about the bottle."

But Georgina could not simply melt away, leaving to the winter of loneliness this perfect blossom which seemed to droop from lack of sun. The sight of such weariness, a face so numbed with disappointment, suddenly broke the fetters of her timidity.

"Oh, Rellie—Rellie darling, I was going to say—couldn't you have a day at home tomorrow? Or perhaps we could go into the country—I can walk quite well if I put on my old shoes—we might find somewhere to have tea. I wouldn't gabble all the time. You're looking so dreadfully tired."

Armorel slipped down from the bed and kissed her. "Georgie darling, you're so awfully kind!" The voice was a little husky, but perfectly in control. "But I'm not really tired at all. And tomorrow I've got a job to do. It's frightfully urgent. Georgie, I'm so awfully sorry! Only I've got to get on with this business, I can't let anything stand in my way."

The waiting-room again; the worn oil-cloth, the chairs placed as a child sets out his dominoes, the chocolate dado; and this time the high sash-window looked on to a stiff pattern of vegetable plots and asphalt paths, a barracoon of iron-roofed huts and chimneys. The smell, forbiddingly, was that of school.

The deputy governor, the deputy governor's personal assistant said, saw visitors only by appointment; an appointment could be applied for through an officer of the Prisons Division of a grade not lower than assistant principal. "I have a letter from Sir Rupert Ingoyne," she told him frigidly, holding that verbal accuracy will justify all ambiguous implications. Knowing Ingoyne as the kind which beams on everything it sees and then falls into a passion about notice boards or swill-bins, the personal assistant let her stay.

And at ten to two, with her stomach chattering from hunger, she was led through a grid of passages to an austerely handsome sitting-room.

A little, compact man in a light-grey suit, with a bow tie which carried on the colour of his brilliant eyes, put her into a chair with archaic courtesy.

". . . Since half-past ten!" he said with distress. "My dear young lady, I can hardly bear to think of your looking at such a view for all that time. I'll tell you a secret—I'm biding my time. One day I hope to have all that nonsense swept right away. I shall have a pond in the centre, with water-lilies; a semicircle of borders on this side, always blazing with flowers—especially tulips in the season, there is no other flower with quite the perfection of the tulip—and at the far end sweet-peas, with a screen of rambler roses behind. That will do something to hide those horrible laundries and things. I don't know if the clients will really like it—I think they may. Now tell me, of what service may I be to you?"

His eyes remained upon her face, he nodded attentively all the time she was telling him her business. But she could not help imagining that the image which really occupied those kindly, eager eyes was made up of tonsured lawns, of statuettes and fountains, aubretia leaking from the cracks in crazy paving. "My point is," she concluded, "that in all probability Ardree did not in the least understand the question when it was put to him. For example, he may very well have thought that the appeal would cost him or his parents a great deal of money, and that would naturally have made him refuse. I suppose it was some kind of warden who saw him, and one can't expect a man like that to have any special skill in explaining a legal matter. I imagine he just said 'Do you want to appeal or don't you?' And he may even have said 'It'll save a lot of bother if you say No.' "

Colonel Dewip waited for some time before he answered. His eyes, at last, were straying surreptitiously towards the window. It was the curse of both Adam and Eve, she thought once more, that Adam was made a gardener.

"But in fact," he said, "I saw Ardree myself. I had quite a long talk with him—he was sitting where you are now. I liked him. He agreed with me about tulips."

"Yes, but about the appeal!" she said swiftly. "I'm quite certain that when I see him myself I shall be able to put the whole thing in a different light. I can make it clear that I'm going to bear the entire cost myself—"

"But—if I may interrupt—you're not allowed to see him." And now, almost with relief, she caught sight of the official in him, the man—the thing—she had to fight, in all these offices, beneath all these urbane exteriors. "The regulations about interviewing prisoners are very precise," he said, "and on the whole—I may say—remarkably sensible."

His voice was still pleasantly pitched, he still wore his courtly smile. But now she perceived the tensity in the structure of his mouth and chin.

She said: "Yes, but surely regulations have to be interpreted in a rational way—"

"—I agree!—" he said.

"—and isn't the whole idea of putting highly qualified people in a position like yours just so that they can cut through red tape according to their own judgement?"

"I think you've slightly over-simplified the question," he answered. "However, I don't want to waste your time discussing generalities. The essential fact is this: in my judgement it would be very improper, and very harmful, for you or anyone else to try to influence Gian Ardree towards altering his decision. The issue was made entirely clear to him. He was given ample time to consider it. He has now made up his mind, and it might make him very unhappy if someone pretending to better judgement tried to make him alter it."

"Unhappy?" she repeated. "I can't believe that anyone can be happy by just submitting to things."

"That's not exactly what I mean," he said. He looked for a mo-

67

ment or two into the palms of his hands, as if they carried notes for a speech. "You know, there's one element in the mentality of certain delinquents that a great many people overlook—the delinquent's own moral sense. His conscience, if you care for old-fashioned words. One minute, may I finish, please! Nearly everyone who's ever sentenced in a court of law feels a sense of outrage to begin with. A great many go on feeling it for the rest of their lives, and those provide society with one broad species of problem. But there are some who gradually come round to admitting the rightness of the sentence, or at any rate that there was some rightness in it, and those people quite often want to go through with the punishment. They know they've done something wrong, and they want to expiate it. Now you may think that's very naïve and out-of-date—you may even call it atavistic. And yet, you know, the more I see of human beings the more I doubt whether those labels help us much. But perhaps I'm being rather obscure?"

"But of course not!" she said, and smiled. All her manners were equal to his. "But I don't think I ought to take up any more of your time."

Throughout the interview she had sat straight up in her chair, collected, attentive, with her skirt carefully smoothed over her knees. She stood up now.

"I really only wanted to ask you the one question," she said, "—whether you would allow me to see Ardree or whether I should have to apply to the Home Office first."

He nodded. "I think I've answered that."

"It was very kind of you to see me," she said.

"I hope we shall meet again," he answered.

"I think perhaps we may, at a later stage."

Back in the Sidcup Road, where the morning's drizzle was turning into rain, she remembered seeing a tea-shop a little way down and started walking towards it. In the minute that followed she was very close to final defeat. If Gian Ardree cared so little for his own cause, there was practically nothing to be said for continuing the struggle. She had made her protest. It was manifest that she could do no more.

It was perhaps the noise of the street which interfered with that decision, perhaps a breath of wind which carried a smell of railway into the street's locked, moistened air. For an instant only she was back at the corner of Contessa Street; for an instant in some dream of a few nights back, where the face of Ardree had stared at her piteously from the angry shadows, and she had called in answer, "I won't let them harm you!" In the courtroom she had known exactly where her loyalty should lie: not with the ones commanding the puppet show but with those who were fastened to the strings. And now, when all that people seemed to want of her was to accept their kindness, to gaze at charming views from cosy chairs, that loyalty could almost be dismissed as an illusion. Yes; and in that fashion, at such a moment as this, causes were lost. This was the place where so many had steered off into safer waters, to be praised for easy, creditable sailings; and where a few, regarding safety as less endurable than the whip of north-east gales, had shoved the tiller the other way.

She was opposite the tea-shop now. She did not cross. A bus was approaching, townward, and she stopped it. An hour later she stood in a wide passage, with the clamour of Whitehall traffic dulled by the rain driving on the high windows. Yes, her business was extremely urgent. No, she had no appointment, she had come straight from Colonel Dewip, with whom she had been in conference all morning. No, she had business elsewhere tomorrow. Yes, she was perfectly prepared to wait.

7

*T*HAT AFTERNOON, Elizabeth Kinfowell sat in the waiting room of the Old Brompton Hospital, continuing a letter to Gordon Acquillard:

'The doctors say that Michael is making satisfactory progress,' Elizabeth had written, 'but oh it's so terribly slow! If only I could have him with me all the time—but he's not well enough to be moved yet, and I comfort myself by saying that it may be better for him to be in the hospital. He is in the public ward so that he can see other children—I think that's better than his being in a room of his own, with no one about but nurses. I spend as much time with him as they will allow. But a hospital staff is not easy to get on with. Of course the poor dears are terribly overworked, and leading that sort of life they develop—most of them—a rather stylized attitude towards other human beings. I think they are perfectly right—you can only keep on top of a job like theirs by cultivating a wholly professional outlook. But sometimes when they talk as if they *owned* Michael, and when they go on and on in a haloed-martyrish way about all the trouble his irregularities give them, I do feel a childish and disgraceful longing to seize them by their natty little white collars and bellow into their faces, "Yes, and it took me eleven hours to get him into the world, and that wasn't such tremendous fun either!" '

Those last sentences would have to come out: it was needless and perhaps harmful to say anything about the eleven hours. In any case the words were barely legible, for she had written them as the train was going over the points at Swindon.

It seemed as if this letter would never be finished: there were so few opportunities for concentration. Daytime was crowded and full of complications: the hospital put her outside its doors at intervals convenient to itself, and in those intervals she had to deal with Henry's requests (which were tantamount to orders) at breakneck speed. Henry wanted her to see old St Pirouell, to get hold of Edward Manaton and persuade him that Henry still maintained an eager interest in the affairs of the Boettger group. A long letter sent her in haste to Shropshire: Henry had decided to return early next month, bringing the Nicholedds with him, and he wanted Easterhatch got ready, with the Winchester Room arranged for Hilda Nicholedd, who would be enchanted by the view of the Welsh hills. A telegram followed, reaching her only when she got back to London: Henry had changed his plans, he was going on to Rapallo with the Nicholedds. . . . And more than ever, now, she felt the moral obligation to see that Henry's wishes were fulfilled.

'I think you would like to know,' she wrote, 'that I have met Armorel. She came to have lunch with Duffy, so of course we were introduced. She is a very, very sweet girl, so young and lovely, and yet with such character. I instantly fell in love with her myself.'

That sentence too would want altering—as it stood it might suddenly kindle memories which would pain him. But the most difficult part was to come. She had to tell him that, in her coolest judgement, his return to England would only lead to the bitterness of a fresh disappointment. She wanted to persuade him that this opinion had no taint of prejudice, that it was absolute and final; yet in making the judgement as hard as a concrete wall she still wanted to lessen its hurtfulness. The task would have been easy were she ready to show a tenderness of her own; but such an intonation would instantly make him distrustful, it might even recall him to a more remote unhappiness. She went to the window to shake her pen into the courtyard, and started writing again.

'I want to explain, though it isn't easy, exactly what I think her feelings about you have been and are now. You must remember, first of all, that she is very young—though mature in some ways—and has always been with people who accept certain moral laws with complete simplicity, people who don't recognize such things as white lies and cannot conceive the idea of a "good" person hiding the truth from someone who is supposed to have all their love and confidence. When a girl with that sort of background stumbles upon a different attitude—and actually finds it in the very man she worships—she suffers a shock far greater than—'

The smell of carbolic suddenly increased, and there was Nurse Wimple in the doorway, immaculately white, selling the hospital's efficiency with the steady smile which radiated from her rather large premolar teeth.

"His Lordship is ready for you now, Mrs Kinfowell!"

"Oh, Nurse, how awfully sweet of you to come and tell me!"

"Only this morning I don't think you ought to stay too long," Nurse Wimple said, steaming ahead along the corridor. "You see Mrs Kinfowell, these wee preciouses do get so worked up over visitors, and then that means such a terrible business trying to settle them down again. I didn't realize yesterday you were staying quite so long—I was seeing about something in the other ward—Sister was just a wee bit waxy. You don't mind my just mentioning that, do you, Mrs Kinfowell? Sweet little kiddie, isn't he! Highly strung, of course—perhaps he's got a daddy who's highly strung? You can always tell when they're highly strung, you know. They want a lot of looking after when they're highly strung, you know, Mrs Kinfowell. He's like you to look at, isn't he?"

"I'm afraid it's terribly exacting work for you," Elizabeth said, "dealing with such a very small person."

"Well, of course it is when they're highly strung. But you know, Mrs Kinfowell, I've always been gone on kiddies. I don't mind how much I do. Now you will be careful you don't do anything and get our little Lordship excited, won't you, Mrs Kinfowell!"

He lay hotly more across the bed than along it, his eyes closed, a little pool of dribble on the pillow. Elizabeth sat down noiselessly, not touching the crumpled hand which lay stretched out towards her. In these visits it was often the best moment, this when he first saw her there. She would not hurry it.

"I expect His Lordship's having a little sleepybyes," Nurse Wimple whispered across two beds, and Michael opened his eyes.

He was puzzled for a moment, and then the smile came. Gratefully, Elizabeth put the hot small hand to rest on top of hers, and his fingers started feeling for her rings. With that he seemed to be content for a time and she stayed quite still, smiling, although she was in a position where her pelvic weakness gave her pain. Only when he began to move his head, murmuring a little, did she lean over to raise his shoulders and shift the pillows.

"Perhaps Nursie had better see to that!" Nurse Wimple said, darting from the other side of the ward. "You've got to be careful how you move them, you know, Mrs Kinfowell, when they're like that. That's where the training comes in, you see. His Lordship wouldn't like it," she said to Michael, "if he got back all the horrid pain again, would he now! Lovely smile, he's got, hasn't he, Mrs Kinfowell! Funny —he always smiles like that for me!"

"It's so kind of you!" Elizabeth said.

And indeed the girl's hands were perfectly skilled, for he lay in comfort now, only wriggling his stomach now and then, and murmuring a little, in response to some pain which must come from within. He stayed wide awake, no longer smiling, but with his brown eyes following any small movement that Elizabeth made. He had his father's mouth. And in his meditative regard she could imagine she saw a mind already reasoning; so that, when the nurse had gone, she found herself speaking to him with her lips: "Better now! Getting better all the time! Mummy will take you home soon—Mummy's never far away!" instinctively expecting him to make some kind of answer. Once or twice, in that hour, he did speak, a little: a single word each time. But the words were shapeless, they died as the flame of a match dies in the wind, and the small mouth, collapsing, was left for a time with a tiny crease in the upper lip. Only she would have noticed that, recognizing the crease which would show in his father's lip when the exact word had failed to come.

The pain he suffered was perhaps very slight (and trivial compared with hers, for the bed and the chair she sat on were at awkward levels); and his suffering would not have hurt her so intensely could she have told him how it came, have talked to him of a happier time ahead. Better, she thought, if she had seen in the quietly following eyes only a consciousness too dull for any understanding; but these patient eyes were not an animal's, beyond the irises' reflection of the ward's high window she seemed to see a stirring like distant smoke in an autumn haze. In that mysterious landscape she imagined she saw fragile thoughts moving as her own moved, however unskilfully; she could even suppose a mind which said "I know I am your son." This was the essential misery of all these hours, when she sat smiling and sometimes stroking his thin, bare arm with the tips of her fingers, when the crackling starch and a ceaseless flurry of competence up and down the ward reminded her that she was a trespasser: to see this other mind so close, to feel so fiercely the right of possession, and yet to have no ground where his understanding could accompany her own.

He stretched his chin as a man does when his patience is overloaded. He moved his shoulder restlessly, and she leaned across to arrange the blanket in a shallow bridge which would relieve him of its weight. He sighed then, and his curiosity seemed to increase. He raised his head, his left hand slid towards her, but his right hand like a prudish escort came out to draw it back. With a struggle he kept his head up for several seconds before it tumbled back into the pillow. He cried a little then, but the sobs quietened as if a door had been pressed upon them, as if he were ashamed of crying. "Michael!" she whispered, "precious Michael—are you blaming me for giving you life?" and forgetting in one moment that the nurses were never far away she took his hand, she gently opened it and filled it with her kisses. Michael watched her patiently, and afterwards his solemn contemplative eyes fell to the tear she had left on his arm.

Nurse Wimple was wafted to the bedside like the quick and healthy winds of October. "There's a call for you, Mrs Kinfowell—they've put it through to Sister's room." She swooped on the blanket and remoulded it round Michael's shoulder. "Oh, you bad bag of sixpences—how did you get your naughty blanket all like that! . . . You know your way to Sister's room, don't you, Mrs Kinfowell?"

Elizabeth knew it. This had happened before.

"Oh, Mrs Kinfowell," Sister Edds said over her shoulder, "perhaps you'd tell your friends that the hospital isn't supposed to take calls for patients' visitors. The rule applies to rich and poor alike," she added.

"I really am most terribly sorry, Sister." She took the receiver. "Duffy darling," she said, "I'm awfully sorry, but I must tell you—unless it's something terribly important you're not really allowed—"

"But, darling, it is! Something really frightful has happened!" and there was in Duffy's voice an anguish which made Elizabeth picture her surrounded at that very moment by leaping redskins.

"Darling, I am so sorry!" Elizabeth said. "Did you leave the scones in the oven too long?"

"It's worse than that! It's a man. He came and wanted to see you. I said you were out."

"Duffy, how drastic! What sort of man?"

"My dear, a ghastly man. He had on a sort of blue suit, and one of those hats made of—you know—"

"Felt?"

"Yes—but listen, the really frightful thing is this, he wanted to know where you'd gone to."

"Yes?"

"And I wasn't thinking, and on the spur of the moment I told him."

"And what did he say?"

"He said, 'Oh, that bloody plague-house—I avoid those places as much as I can!'"

"Well?"

"I thought you ought just to know."

"Well, that's terribly kind of you, Duffy. Only another time—perhaps not actually telephone. You see, it has to come to the Sister's room, and she's so kind, only she's terribly overworked and she's got such a load of responsibility. . . . Thank you so much, dear, for ringing."

At the door of the ward Nurse Wimple was standing like a varnished Cerberus. "We can't see His Lordship just for a wee while, Mrs Kinfowell. His Lordship's having one of his little busy times. You know the way to the waiting-room, don't you, Mrs Kinfowell?"

Elizabeth did know.

With a sense of frustration she started to work on her letter again. No, it would not do. She tore off the sheet and began a fresh one.

Duffy says that in your letter to her you talk of coming back in June, although the job is interesting and lucrative and might go on for another year. Well, now that I've talked to Armorel you may like to have my views—and I do want you to believe that they're absolutely honest.

There were heavy footsteps in the corridor, and upon the hospital's many muted noises there broke a man's loud and petulant voice: "I tell you I have *not* come to see a patient! I've come to see a woman who *is* seeing a patient. I don't care one hoot in hell about your blasted regulations." The door swung, and Elizabeth realized what Duffy had meant about the hat. Here it was, on the head of Trevon Grist.

"Ah yes," he said, as if he were making an arrest, "you're the one I want. You won't remember me, my name's Grist. You came to see me with a person called Miss Cepinnier."

"But of course I remember. Won't you sit down?"

"This Miss Cepinnier," he said, continuing to stand, "I don't know anything about her—I take it you do?"

"Well, she's the friend of a friend."

"Oh, is that all?"

"And a very sweet girl. Not a very happy one."

"Oh—why not?"

"Well, for one thing her father's missing."

"Ah, that improves matters. I mean—I always think people aren't much use until something fairly unpleasant has happened to them. I don't suppose you'll understand."

"I do, as a matter of fact. Won't you smoke?"

"You see," he continued, mechanically accepting the cigarette and lighting it, "I will not have a lot of sentimental curio-hunters flapping round my boys. They're too good for it. People don't realize—they see them lounging about the place and spitting on the pavements, they think they're just a lot of uncouth children. They're not. In some ways they're about three times as adult as the Kensington article—and often a damn sight more virtuous. They cheat and they tell fibs, because that's the way one keeps alive, down at their level. But they do things for people, they've got an automatic kindness, it doesn't have to be pumped up or even rewarded."

She interrupted: "But listen, I don't think Armorel had any intention of flapping around. She only wanted—"

"Armorel?"

"—Miss Cepinnier—she merely wanted to get Ardree's case re-heard. She felt he'd been very harshly punished and she wanted that put right."

He nodded grimly.

"Yes, evidently, by what Cuddish tells me—the beak who put him in jug. Friend of mine, Cuddish. She's been sending him letters which could get her into prison herself."

"Oh. I didn't know that."

"Luckily for her, he's a better-tempered bloke than I am." He sat down at last, not on the chair but on a table covered with medical journals. "Look, this is Cuddish's idea, not mine. He came to see me about it last night. What he said—roughly—was that if Miss Whatshername thinks Ardee's an injured innocent she'd better do something practical—not just go about blackguarding other people like himself."

Elizabeth said: "Something practical—such as?"

"Well, you probably realize—or you may not—that with these delinquents everything depends on what happens to them when they come out of the clink. My job as a rule is to get 'em back into the Club, then there's some hope of getting 'em civilized, one way or another. Old Flock does most of it. Well, Cuddish wants to improve on that. He thinks that with a bloke like Ardree a woman might do more than a man can. If she's the sort that'll put her mind to it. He thinks we want a woman stuck in somewhere in the Club. Personally I think he's cracked, but he happens to be one of the Trustees. And incidentally a hell of a good bloke."

"Tell me," Elizabeth said, "have you found out anything more about Ardree since we saw you?"

"I've been to the place where he works," he answered, staring gloomily at his boots. "They've nothing against him there, except that he's not too friendly with the other blokes. They used to chip him about being a dago—because of his mother, you see—and he wouldn't stand for it. Gave one man a hell of a hiding, and then it stopped. Does his work all right." His eyes followed the smoke of his cigarette as if the subject of Ardree bored him. Then, suddenly, he faced her again. "You, what do you think of this crazy notion of Cuddish's?"

"That's not a very simple question."

She was trying to rein her galloping thoughts, thoughts which always dragged towards Gordon. Few men could be less like Gordon physically than the sulky giant who stood now, with his back against the window-sill, challenging her with his faintly insolent eyes:

The taut, sprung body of Gordon Aquillard had always seemed too slender to contain his nervous violence, and here was one which had swelled without resistance until the play of nervous forces, lost in its immensity, could agitate only the small slack muscles of its surface. Yet what Elizabeth saw was their kinship, their friendliness, their common insufficiency. "People fail because of their dependence," Gordon had once told her (sitting on the tail-board of the waggon, staring angrily at the rocks above them). "Saul of Tarsus brought Christianity to Europe," he had said (kneeling on the floor in Duffy's sitting-room, sharpening a pencil into the fireplace), "because he never let himself be sidetracked into intense relationships." And now this Trevon Grist, with his mission to protect the boys of Lambeth from interfering ladies, here was this seedy pedagogue gyrating awkwardly about the Ardree bush when all the time his real interest was in Armorel herself. Elizabeth had realized that on their visit to his club. She knew (how well!) what effect a body like Armorel's had on men of the monastic kind, she had noticed how austerely he kept his eyes away. And he should not have her now; for Armorel was Gordon's, and what could Elizabeth do for Gordon, for Gordon's unfathomed power of loving, the bitter loneliness in which all his talents were starting to rot, if she could not restore her to him in the end?

"Listen," she said. "You want my own opinion about Armorel?"

"Yes."

And she had the answer ready phrased, beginning, 'I'm perfectly certain that she's not the right woman for dealing with a young delinquent.' But she never said it.

It was inveterate honesty which warned her that the phrase itself was false before it escaped. How could she say whether Armorel was fitted to handle delinquents or not? She paused, and the day's tiredness, the gathered tiredness of all the months since her pregnancy with Michael, swept up on her like the first sweet fumes of chloroform. Why attempt to set the course of others' lives, when she had achieved such small success with her own! This shiftless, blustering man might expect her to make up his mind for him, but Armorel had no such indecision. To Armorel—as Elizabeth had found her—the allotted course was marked with ghostly flags to be accepted with a child's dreadful simplicity. What use to argue or protest, to explain the complexities of what she had left behind or to warn her that men of an intrinsic structure less stable than Gordon's might be found along the road she had chosen. She was faintly influenced, perhaps, this tired woman, by an impulse of her own; for the desperate hopes we have once clung to can make their magnetism felt long after we have thrust them away; but she was not conscious of this tenuous, insistent drag when she hesitated, changed the conformation of her mouth and said with the same sincerity:

"Well, I'm certain of one thing—you won't find another girl with more fundamental honesty, or one with more courage."

"Are you?" he said tersely. "That's interesting. Well, I may fix something, I may not."

And without even a gesture of leave-taking he marched away.

Nurse Wimple was at the door again.

"Now, Mrs Kinfowell, if you'd like to come along! Only it mustn't be more than five minutes this time—then it'll be time for His Lordship's little din-dins."

8

*T*OWARDS THE middle of June, Elizabeth was writing:

My dear Armorel, I had thought of writing before to remind you how much I hope that we shall meet again, but I fancy you have not much patience with letters which have nothing in them except what you know already!

Mr Grist—who came to see me some time ago—tells me in a letter that he has some suggestion to make to you about Gian Ardree. I don't know if you will be pleased or not—I remember that you didn't much care for Mr Grist when we saw him. Personally (though I suppose one shouldn't judge a man on such short acquaintance) I doubt whether he's a person I should care to have much to do with. He may be all right with other men, but he talks about women in such a contemptuous tone that one suspects he is hankering after them all the time, in a way one would rather not be hankered after! I think I myself should prefer to approach Ardree through any other route but the Grist highway—and I fancy you will see what I mean, whether you agree with me or not!

But probably the Ardree chapter is over, since I gather he has finished his sentence and therefore nothing more can be done about it. You won't be offended if I say how much I admired your courage in trying to get what seemed to be an injustice put right. I've never been the sort of person to attempt anything like that, and I wish I had. I suppose I belong to the nineteenth-century type of women, the sort who said 'I'm sure these things are much better left for our husbands to deal with'! Still, having resigned myself to mid-Victorianism I have the Victorian woman's consolation— the belief that we can sometimes do more by loving one man intensely and almost blindly—the one who loves us—than by passing the wisest laws or starting the noblest revolutions.

Duffy has just had another letter from G.A.—I don't see why I shouldn't tell you. Much the same as the last one, but more fervent still. How I wish there was some way of cancelling parts of history—I mean, making it not to have happened. If only that was possible there would be such happiness for you, I feel, within your grasp. Armorel dear, I should so love to know that you were happy . . .

Almost every sentence in this letter had the effect which Elizabeth had hoped to avoid. It fortified Armorel's decision.

Trevon's postcard, scrawled in pencil, had told her of Ardree's release a week before. '. . . I imagine your interest in the case was purely juridical, but if you are still interested in the man himself (who, I may say, does not seem responsive to influence of any kind) you may like to call here again.' The card bore no address or date, was signed illegibly and understamped.

It is nonsense to say—as relatives were saying a few weeks later, and were to repeat in years to come—that at this stage Edith Cepinnier could have prevented what occurred had she been a little more perceptive and more resolute. Let it be granted that Edith (though of sharper understanding than people realized) was limited in her powers of sympathy: can it be seriously argued that a woman of subtler perceptions would have succeeded where she failed! If the course of lovers is unpredictable, how much more so the way of those whom the furious current of love no longer carries. "I simply cannot understand it!" Edith repeated, that September day when the news came; and that was largely true, because in the fifties, with the bold light of late afternoon making all the landscape clear and steady, one remembers little of the sensations of immaturity. Yet surely, thinking with her blood, as the Germans say, she did obscurely realize that Armorel had faced some kind of challenge; and perhaps she had realized in the same way that the power of her own good sense would be mere feebleness against the fierce resolution which such challenge provoked in her brother's child.

And after all, what objection could she have made to what was broadly described as 'social work'? If Armorel was not to return to college it was time she had some definite occupation. Hollysian House seemed to be a thoroughly estimable institution, with the names of several clergy, including a bishop or two and a well-known headmaster, appearing on its stationery: the proposal that Armorel should work there as librarian in the afternoons and evenings, leaving at half-past eight and getting home before ten, was reasonable enough by post-war standards of *convenance*. Presumably one or other of the bishops would look in from time to time to see that everything was respectably managed. Gertrude had made no objection, beyond saying that it sounded 'rather prosaic'. And in any case it was only a trial arrangement, of which Armorel herself might soon grow tired.

9

SHE WAS at the job for more than four weeks before she saw Gian at all. Every now and then Trevon told her that he was doing his best to get the fellow along to the Club: he said it sometimes impatiently, sometimes with a grudging note of apology. One afternoon he informed her quite casually that Ardree had been round the night before, a few minutes after she had left. But patience was not a discipline to which she was unaccustomed.

The building was an exhaust-chamber which muted all the sounds except its own. The shouting and the noise of hoofs on the granite sets of the wharf, a compact uproar from the traffic of Kembury Street, the gobble of tugs in the tideway, these came as recorded sounds through an instrument faultily tuned. Within, the place was a romping ground for echoes, which the many partitions at both ends of the gymnasium only distorted, so that the ear was always confused about distance and direction. Flock's grunt as he polished the taps in the lavatory often sounded as if it were just outside her door. The scraping of Trevon's chair, his nervy cough, came to her as acutely as if the party-wall which Flock had laboriously constructed between her room and his did not exist. Like the city's voice, daylight came circuitously and enfeebled. In the library, with its small high window facing the wall of Thomson's repository, you were but faintly aware of the day's lightening or darkening; and in the second week of July, when the heavy clouds which had long protected the city from summer, were pushed apart for a few hours, she was astonished, going out for some cigarettes, to find the yard broken into a pattern of shadow and sun.

On most afternoons a negligible person known only as "Slimey" came, who was understood to be a tradesman. He would hunt out a chisel from his gladstone bag and perform some desultory operation on a wall bar which had got loose, or climb on a ladder and fiddle with a window catch, while Flock, for once neglecting his own work, stood with hands on hips at the other end of the gymnasium and monotonously abused him. "Call yourself a ruddy carpenter! Coming up for tradesman's pay, I s'pose—'performed his duties with efficiency and zeal'. Blokes like you, I s'pose, what built the perishin' Empire—take the whole of a ruddy fortnight to get a perishin' screw put in, and then he don't know what he done with the ruddy screwdriver." From Slimey himself there was never any reply, except a noise like that of a locomotive shunting. But occasionally Trevon would go off like a two-pounder gun: "Flock! You obfuscated acrobat, why the devil can't you get on with your own job! Leave Slimey alone, blast you! How do you expect the poor blithering nincompoop to use the twopence-halfpennyworth of mother-wit God gave him if you're chipping in all the time!" "Very sorry, Mr Grist, sir!" Flock would roar. "Didn't know as how you were having romantic thoughts, sir. Wonderful the way a bloke gets romantic thoughts, come this time of year, get me. Writing poetry, perhaps you was, sir!" "Flock! Hold your vulgar and revolting tongue!" But in this masculine ritual the voluntary librarian had no part. And when shop opened, and fifty voices were trying to shout each other down in an endless tourney of revilement, her sense of isolation only increased. They came into her room in ones and twos, as shyly as if she were naked. The way they spoke to her varied between shame-faced incoherence and flashes of nervous impudence; they jostled each other and went off into furtive giggles, there were often heavy whispers of

"Dare you! and "Get on—the tart won't eat you!" before the door was wrenched open and an under-sized boy, violently projected, landed like a carcase at her feet. "You, you perishin' Bakewell!" Flock would bawl from the other end of the gym, "don't you know better'n that the way to treat a lady!" and from his own room Grist would shout: "Flock! Get hold of that yahoo and teach him some manners!" "You must have tripped on the floorboard," Armorel would say politely to the new arrival. "Now what sort of book are you after?—I've got a new index in this box over here." She was never hustled, she treated them all with the courtesy which the Boots girls show to imbecile old ladies. But the plywood wall which fenced her from the gym remained a moral as well as a physical barrier. She belonged to the furniture of the library, and the library had ceased to be part of the Club.

"I've been wondering," she said to Trevon, on one of his rare visits to her table, "do you think my being here is a nuisance to the boys? I mean, do you think it spoils their freedom—do they feel they've got to use less bad language, and that sort of thing?"

"I shouldn't think so," he said gloomily. He stood with one foot on top of the other, biting his thumb-nail and staring at the home-made filing cabinet to which she had given so much labour. His shyness was constantly returning, he was like a novice actor in her presence, not knowing what to do with his eyes or hands. "No, I can't really see that it makes any difference. But of course, if you're finding it all a fearful bore—I mean, I realize I still haven't got hold of this Ardree fellow you want to look at—"

She said quickly: "No, it's not a bore. So long as I can feel that I'm being some use."

"Oh, of course!" he said. "Yes, it's useful having someone to do my bits of typing. And this library business. Only when you get fed up with it you've only got to say. I mean, I got along all right before."

"I shall stay for a year, anyway," she told him.

"A year? Good God, you can't stand a place like this for a year."

"Well, you have. Much longer than that."

"Yes, but that's not the same thing. I'm paid for it, it's my job. Besides, it's a habit I've got into." For a moment he actually looked into her face, as he said defiantly: "I like it, if it comes to that. I always imagine that one day I shall be able to do something with some of these God-awful boys."

"Unless you turn me out I shall stay for a year," she repeated.

She thought that in some peculiar way he liked to have her there. At least he paid some attention, in his brusque, nonchalant fashion, to her comfort. He said one day, almost as if blaming her: "You're not getting enough air in here. I'm having that window enlarged as soon as I can get hold of a builder. The Club'll have to pay up—it's all nonsense their supposing they can run this place without spending a sou on it." Then he complained about her chair: "You can't sit on a chair like that—I told Flock to find you something else. *Flock!* Flock—for God's sake take this chair away and burn it. Get Miss Cepinnier the chair from my room, the one from my table, I can use that other thing." He found her a table-cloth from the dramatics chest, and a piece of carpet. "It's no good pretending this place is fit for any civilized person to work in," he said morosely. "Shall I tell Flock to stick in some flowers or something? I don't know anything about flowers, I've never bought them . . . Of course, when the trustees bought this mausoleum they never thought of having a woman about. Nor did I, for that matter. Can't do anything about the draughts, I'm afraid. All this building does is to split 'em up. Oh well, you wanted to come!"

Most of their conversations took place in the gymnasium. As often as not, when their ways crossed, he would walk straight past her, frowning as if the congestion of traffic vexed him. But sometimes he turned back and called abruptly, "Oh—Miss Cepinnier!" then stood with his eyes fixed on the wall-bars, making her feel that she had committed some act of sabotage.

"Oh, Miss Cepinnier, that fellow—what's his name? Ardree—I saw the manager of the place where he works this morning. They say he's not being any particular trouble, not at present."

"But—has he been?"

"Well, he threatened a man who made some joke about him in the canteen. That was just after he got back. He's not misbehaved himself since."

"You don't think you can get him here fairly soon?"

"No, I doubt it." He climbed up on the parallel bars, sat on one and leant back with his hands on the other. "You can't hurry these things," he said, with a note of irritation. "Some of them, of course, they charge into the Club the moment they're released. Almost expect us to get the band out. The other sort don't want to see anyone they ever met before. It takes time to get them out of that. And after all, he's a free man, he can't be forced to go anywhere he doesn't want to."

She said: "I realize that. Do you think it would be quite wrong policy for me to go round to his home?"

"I do!" he said emphatically. "When a chap's got himself slightly mucked the last thing he wants is any sort of improving person barging in at his own front door." He lowered himself to the floor and made off towards his room. "Well, I mean, do as you like! I don't advise it, that's all."

Just a week afterwards she spoke to Gian for the first time. On an evening when business was slack and she was reading *La Révolte des Anges* in a corner of the room she looked up to see him standing by the table. She knew him at once.

"Yes?" she said.

"I want a book, miss, Mr Grist said I was to come here and get a book."

"Well, now, what sort of a book?" She had moved over to the fiction stack, where she stood half-turned, ready to follow the customer's wishes or to make suggestions: it all came very easily as she went through the practised routine.

"Well, I don't know," he said.

"Do you like stories, or real life? Look, this is rather good, most people like this one."

She gave him *The Broad Highway*. He opened it in the middle, looked at it dumbly, shook his head and handed it back. He did the same with *Barlasch of the Guard, The White Company, The Emperor's Candlesticks*. In every gesture he was the faithful copy of a dozen other boys.

"Book about gardens?" he asked unexpectedly.

In one movement she took a pace along the shelves and stooped to get at the bottom one, while he watched her as if he had paid for admission. There were four of them in: *Amateur Gardening for Profit, Be Your Own Greengrocer, Practical Gardening for Towndwellers, Bedsell's Horticultural Calendar*. He looked cursorily at them all.

"No, not that sort," he said.

"Well, it's all I've got in at the moment. Perhaps you'd like to take some other sort of book for now, and come back another time. There are some other gardening books which are out at present."

He shrugged his shoulders, "I don't care, miss, really," and turned to go. That tempted her to her first venture.

"Your name's Ardree, isn't it?"

"Yes—why?"

"I thought it must be. I hadn't seen you here before, and Mr Grist told me about you."

"Told you what?" he asked.

"Oh—it was just when we were going through an old register—I saw your name, and he said 'He hasn't been round for some time.' "

"Yes," he said, "they all keep checks on y'."

"It's a nice club, isn't it! Everyone's so friendly."

"I suppose so," he said, and went away.

10

A FEW DAYS LATER she was writing to Elizabeth:

I am so ashamed of not writing before to thank you for your sweet letter. I was interested—I need hardly tell you—to have news of poor Gordon. I'm very sorry that he is unhappy, I hope he will soon find something (or someone) to make him forget about what happened last autumn. I wonder, though, whether he can ever be really happy—isn't it true, as some of the philosophers say, that happiness depends on singleness of mind?—and I don't see how you can be single-minded once you've started covering your tracks. But as I say, I don't in the least want him to be miserable, especially as it's more than likely that that other girl, whoever she was, was chiefly to blame at the beginning. One knows how girls did get hold of men when they'd been through the strain of fighting. But I don't see how one can blame her for his being dishonest afterwards. Well, I'm glad I've got other things to think about, since brooding doesn't do anyone any good.

Elizabeth dear, we must meet sometime and have tea or something together. I've been meaning to come to the flat and see you both, only I've been so fearfully busy at Hollysian House. Oh, but I haven't told you—I did take on the job that Mr Grist was offering. I really wanted a job of some kind. I'm so sorry that he bothered you about it—why ever should he? But of course he is a queer man, as you say. Actually he's really very simple. (And at bottom, I should say, religious—the two things rather go together, don't you think!) He is rather pompous and spasmodically sentimental—I think he probably made a mess of some love-affair, in the dim days of yore—full of good intentions, morbidly frightened of girls and hopelessly bewildered by boys. I should think he must have been an only child, with a large, fierce, angular mother who made him brush his hair before every meal (so he hasn't brushed it since she died) and really the poor dear would be much happier if she were there to bully him still!

I have had some contact with Gian, but I haven't got to know him yet. It's better not to rush things, anyway. As I expected, the prejudice against him continues—not much is said, but it sticks out a mile. Certain people are very anxious to justify themselves—when the Contessa Street incident happened they immediately concluded that he was a dangerous savage and dealt with him accordingly, so now quite naturally what they really want is to prove he *was* a dangerous savage and still is (especially as they've probably heard about my raising the matter in rather high quarters)! Actually he is not quite normal at present, you can see at once that the experience of prison has left him nervy and with a deep sense of injustice. But in general he's very much like the other boys who come here, only extra large in body and in a way rather good-looking, and his accent's slightly different—better, I think. I fancy he's got quite a good brain if it could be developed. What he wants is to be interested in something positive, if possible something which will help him to improve his position. Of course it won't be easy, but if I wanted an easy life I'd spend the whole of it at Cromer's Ride! I know that I was a failure over Gian before—I was determined to get his case re-heard by a competent judge, and I was beaten. But that doesn't mean I'm going to be beaten always. I believe that in the end I can show the great Mr Cuddish and all the others that the man they light-heartedly threw into the dustbin was worth something—that they were wrong and I was right . . .

She had, in fact, seen him just once more. Early one evening Trevon, passing her in the gymnasium, had said over his shoulder, "Ardree's down in the yard. He doesn't want to come in, apparently." At once she had put the library in charge of 'Nibbley' Toms, a boy with the face of a facetious otter who was always ready to stand-in, and had gone outside to the telephone-box at the corner of Balt's Lane.

There, pretending to make a call, she watched him. He was only a few yards away, leaning against the side of a railway truck, hands in pockets, an unlit Woodbine in his mouth. His clothes were striking, the shirt of brilliant canary yellow with a rash of triangles, the green scarf zigzagged with mauve, a light-grey cap violently checked with blue: but his attitude was so like that of a dozen others who lounged about the yard, lacking decision to go up to the Club or over to the Frobisher, that without forewarning she might scarcely have noticed him. At that distance he did not look wretched or even bored: he was detached, faintly amused by his detachment, impregnable: when he spat on the rail it was a gesture without significance, like the flourishing of handkerchiefs in Regency plays. She left the box and approached him boldly:

"Good-evening! You were asking me about gardening books— I've got a new one in, only just published. Would you like to come up and see it?"

Not even moving the cigarette he stared past her at a lorry manoeuvring on the other side of the yard; he might have been an astronomer intent upon some rare conjunction, she a small boy pestering him for cigarette-cards. Then some current in his mind made him grin, but the grin had faded long before he spoke.

"No, thanks."

"Well, I'll keep it for you," she said, "and next time you're up there you can have it."

He nodded, as if she had repeated a lesson correctly, and went on staring over her shoulder. Already three or four children had left their game of Five Stones at the other side of the yard to form a compact audience a few feet away: they stood quite still, flimsy and tarnished copies of the human model in their elder brothers' and sisters' clothes, devouring the spectacle of a bloke and a tart noodling with the empty curiosity of cattle. But Armorel was not put out. In her daydreams there had been bright pictures of the coming encounters with Gian, artistically designed and informed with purpose: but she had known that reality was made from less tidy patterns. Something in his grin encouraged her; whatever thought had provoked it, the grin was not contemptuous; and though the still eyes, watched closely, had no light for her, she thought they were neither dull nor inhuman eyes.

She said: "I don't blame you for staying outside on a lovely evening like this. I get an awfully cooped-up feeling myself, sometimes."

He said: "Yeh, nice weather."

"An evening like this I'd like to go on the Thames, on one of those steamers."

He considered this remark, actually examining her face, as if she had spoken of walking barefoot to Halifax.

"What for?" he asked.

"Well, to see the scenery."

"There's nothing of that sort," he said, and again he suddenly grinned. "You won't see nothing but houses. You can see them where you are now."

She laughed. "Yes, but nicer houses!"

"You can have the whole lot," he said tersely. "There's too many houses, if you're asking me."

"Well, people have got to have somewhere to live!"

"Uh-huh?"

"You're obviously not a Londoner!"

"Who said I wasn't?"

"I only guessed—Londoners can't see anything much wrong with their own city. At least, they always long to get back to it. Would you like to live in the country—work on a farm or something like that?"

"Nobody I know, in the country."

The lorry, having dumped a load of deals, was coming towards them in reverse, intending to turn into Balt's Lane. The children, London-wise, stood like a terra-cotta group as the tailboard came towards their backs. All at once Gian let fly with his voice.

"You—come out o' that!"

The children, who had plenty of time, were away like lizards, but he wasn't satisfied. Brushing past Armorel as if she were a gate-post he strode to the front of the lorry and as it stopped opened the driver's door.

"You!" he said in a voice like a blow-flame, and for a dreadful moment she thought he would hit the man. "D'd' you see them fuming kids? Where's y'bloody eyes! . . . knock y'bloody face in next time!" Satisfied—to her relief—with that, he lit the cigarette at last, spat, and sauntered off with a schoolboy dignity in the direction of Kembury Road.

That had been a disappointment. Their next meeting was more unsatisfactory still.

It was several evenings later that she caught sight of him in the gymnasium, leaning against the wall-bars. He was in the same clothes, his cap and the cigarette at the same angles: he might have been moved up in one piece like a toy soldier from his former position in the yard. She had the new gardening book all ready and she took it out to him.

She said: "I'm so glad you've come! Wasn't it stupid of that lorry-driver the other night—I really believe he'd have knocked those children down if you hadn't shouted to them."

The time lag before he could lay his mind on her remark was one she expected now. Waiting, she was aware that the uproar in the gymnasium had slackened perceptibly, that the tall Ormison and the inseparable Fidgley brothers were staring; but she had grown impervious to such attention.

"I told him," he said.

With sudden audacity she said, "You know, I was half-afraid you were going to sock him!"

His eyes wandered away between the heads of the Fidgleys. He sniffed, as if a waiter had brought him something slightly rancid; and announced from the corner of his mouth:

"I don't hit a bloke for nothing."

"Of course," she said quickly, "the children would have been a good deal to blame themselves. Really, they seemed to be quite deaf and blind."

"Well," he answered surprisingly, "a kid's not to blame if it's blind, is it!"

"No, I didn't mean really blind. I meant they were just dreaming."

"Not much to dream about," he said.

This was an impasse, and she turned to the book she had for him. "Look, I think you may find this quite interesting. It's got awfully good diagrams—even I can follow them, and I'm a perfect fool at anything like that."

He glanced at the book and put it on a bar beside him. He said at large: "I've got to see Mr Grist."

"I expect he'll be free before long," she told him. "Would you like to come and wait in the library? It's a bit more comfortable."

"I got a message he wanted me to come."

"Yes, well, I'll tell him as soon as he's free. He's got some visitor at present—I think it's some sort of police inspector."

He turned to strike a match on the wall behind him and lit his cigarette. "I know," he said.

11

*S*HE HAD to wait till the next afternoon for a chance to discover what it was all about. As soon as Trevon came in she went to his room and tackled him.

"Mr Grist, was it something to do with Gian Ardree, the police coming here last night?"

"It was," he said, and began paring his nails. "I've been expecting it—I don't like his present behaviour, and I don't like what they say about him at the Hibbage Lane depot. He's being very sullen and sometimes offensive."

"But that's not a crime."

"No, but screwing up the door of a man's room is—when the man's inside and hasn't another way out. Especially if you've already smashed a window to get in and broken up a piano to use for the job. Or if it isn't a crime it's an unneighbourly act. I mean, you can do that sort of thing at the older universities, but they don't approve of it round Lambeth."

"But did Gian do that?"

"That's the question. Somebody did—and they did it to a deputy foreman from Hibbage Lane. Man called Empire—fellow Ardree's in contact with every day."

"Yes, but—"

"And moreover a fellow that used to work alongside Ardree, and got put up higher while he was in jug. A man that Ardree doesn't like—he's threatened him more than once, with half-a-dozen other men looking on."

"But is that all the connection they can find?"

"Well, yes and no. He wasn't at home the night it happened—his father's let that out, though the mother said he was—and the story he tells about his movements sounds to me like a flabby story. Also he had a cut hand when he got to the depot next day."

"And that's all?"

"Just about, I think. In fact, I rather doubt whether they'll prove anything—or whether they'll bother to go on trying, now they've given him a fright."

"So you're certain he did do it—you yourself?"

"No. I just think it's ninety-nine per cent likely."

She was angry then; but she kept her voice in control. "You know, I wouldn't have thought it," she said, "I thought that was a thing of the past, dogging a man who's made one mistake, suspecting him of everything the police can't account for. That's what it is, isn't it! The police don't like it because one of them got hurt, and now they're out to catch him with anything that comes along. And so are you, as far as I can see."

"No" he said. "I can't speak for the police, but I'm out to catch him before he's caught, which is different."

"But if you're taking it for granted the whole time that he's a hopeless criminal—"

He interrupted sharply, but actually lowering his voice. "No, not hopeless. That's the point. Not a criminal either, if it comes to that—I use that word for a man who commits crimes, not just for a man who has an inclination to commit them, which we all have, one way and another. I suppose you wouldn't believe it, but I'm actually rather fond of Ardree—"

"I don't even pretend to be fond of him," she said, "I don't believe in being sentimental about these boys. I merely believe in getting at the truth about them."

"But can you?" he asked. "Can you get at the truth about people you're not fond of?"

"I don't see what you mean."

"No, well, it doesn't matter."

He had evidently reached the evasive stage, and she would not waste more time with him. But as she was going he called her back.

"Look here—Miss Cepinnier—I want you to realize, it wasn't my idea your coming here, it was someone else's in the first place."

Whose? she wondered; but it was more dignified not to ask. "Yes—?" she said.

"So I'm not altogether responsible for the present state of things, though I am partly—I thought it was worth trying. If I'd imagined that Ardree was going to be quite like this I'd never have let you come—he's much worse than I thought he was going to be, he looks to me damned dangerous. And I know what I'm talking about, I know what men can get up to when they've got something on their minds."

"So do I."

"No, if you'll excuse me, you don't—you don't know the first damned thing about it. Anyway, the point is there's nothing you can do for him. I can't get really close to him myself, and you've got much less chance than I have—that's in the nature of things. If you did by any means get into his confidence at all—well, it might land you in one hell of a mess. You may understand what I mean and you may not—"

"So you want me to clear out?"

"Yes—I'm sorry—"

"But you can't make me."

He stood up and looked at her thoughtfully, as a tailor might. Then he said, with a sudden, tired anger, "Oh, for God's sake!" and sat down again, facing his table. Over his shoulder he said: "Miss Cepinnier, will you, please, at least do me the favour of taking an evening off. Yes, I can dish out the perishing books myself. No, I haven't any letters for typing, I've only got the hell of a headache and a lot of work to do."

She understood, now, that his whole attitude came from a niggling jealousy. This tiny realm belonged to him: his oddity and grossness, the smell of his belongings, his capricious ardours and frivolities, made him not only its ruler but a very part of its texture. The boys accepted him because he was only a summary of themselves; and taking that acceptance for the highest loyalty he had resolved that it should shine towards him alone. Realizing that he himself lacked the essential sympathy to do anything with Gian, he was terrified of seeing a mere woman overtake him. Perhaps he noticed that in the last few weeks the library had become more popular. That alone could have started his resentment; and because he had no means to halt the tide which flowed from him to her, because she herself had never flattered him as the boys did, he had to relieve his vanity with a growing insolence, hoping to send her packing before she won the whole of their allegiance.

Very well! This evening she would do as he wished.

She had arranged already, on the 'Bespoke' shelf, the lately returned books which boys had specially asked for, each with the applicant's name on a protruding ticket. She set out the new register with the date-stamp she had bought herself, a brief, typed instruction (. . . *Member's number* only *in Column 2* . . .), the Suggestion Book open and dated, the special index to the month's magazines. She put new nibs in both the penholders, saw that the inkpot was filled to the right level, straightened the corner of the table-cloth and went out into the maturing afternoon.

A discreet telephone-call to the Hibbage Lane depot got her the address of Empire, the deputy foreman. She decided impulsively to go there on foot.

This city was not made for summer. It is plaited with machinery which cannot repose. The trains pass at the height of bedroom windows, or a little below your garden fence; with the doors and the sideboard constantly trembling from their violence you cannot feel that the year has reached fulfilment. In high, overhead light the river itself loses nobility. The odour that follows people coming out of the tube is one that should belong to winter, like the smell of a bakery; it joins the odours of exhaust and benzine, which the heat makes fatiguing, and when there is little wind the close, high cliffs of dirty brick will keep these bilious airs as an inverted tank would. If the sky is hazed, which is natural with the London sky, and there are no hard shadows, you have the sensation not of summer but of November noon cooked with an oil-stove. You sweat all day long in clothes unsuitable for sweating, and the sweat is soiled.

The passage to which a man had guided her was a series of elbow bends; she had lost all sense of direction by the time she came to a slightly broader street. A tobacconist at the corner had some idea how you got to Bidault's Place, through another passage under the railway; "If that's the place you're after!" he added, biting his small moustache, absolving himself from all responsibility; and the little, elderly woman with Irish eyes whom she consulted next was sure that Bidault's Place was where Mr Jenkins had lived before he moved to another part, the name of which she could not remember; they could only look, the woman said, and continued at Armorel's side, dragging beside her the forlorn terrier which she had on a piece of cord.

The regular approach to these was from the north side. At the side where Armorel arrived you reached them by a passage which cut through the centre of Coronation Building. The sign, 'To Bidault's Place,' had been covered by a cocoa plate. The other sign, 'Commit no Nuisance' spoke of people who could not read.

"That's right," the boy leaning against the wall told them. "Through that hole, hold your nose and keep straight on."

The drab street she was leaving, remote and self-occupied, its pulse enfeebled by the dead weight of the sultry day, was still connected with the known world: a sweeper's barrow with the borough arms stood there, at the far end you could just see the red flash of a bus passing. To enter the passage was to cross a last border. Sounds changed, as when a tuning knob is turned; the air, cooler here, fetid and still, closed in upon her like an anaesthetist's mask. For one moment she hesitated, turning to look back at the street; and her eye caught its title, Mickett Lane.

The door of the first house was open, showing a workshop of some kind, the entrance cluttered with empty bottles and a mangy cat. She put her head inside. "Can you tell me which is Number 3?" From a litter of leaking mattresses and chairs stripped of upholstery a sallow foreigner emerged in his undervest, blinking towards the daylight. "Number 3?" He shrugged his shoulders, his furtive eyes behind steel spectacles looked past her, calculating escape. "Who is you seek?" he demanded. "I'm looking for a Mr Empire," and he directed her at once; the third house from this one. She left him and the old woman together, discussing with acerbity where Mr Jenkins had once lived if he had lived at all.

Number 3 stood back a yard from its neighbours. It was larger, with four windows to the front, and two of these were flimsily curtained. When she rapped on the door a crinkled voice upstairs called: "Daise! See what that is!" Presently the door was opened a few inches, and a new, timorous voice said, "Yes?"

This was a woman or a child; in the shadow where the figure stood Armorel could not immediately tell. She asked, smiling, "I wonder if Mr Empire's at home? He lives here, doesn't he?" and the girl, after a pause, said, "I can see," shutting the door again. From somewhere at the back of the house her voice called: "Dad! You there?"

The girl came back and let her in, to the linoed passage and then to the living-room. The hot room, gorged with furniture, was clean; the window, tightly fastened, resisted the smells of the street, and the room itself gave a decent smell.

While Armorel sat on the one free chair the girl stood dumbly by the door, where her profile was lighted from the window. Yes, she was perhaps a young woman of twenty: twenty-five? The head, with hair done up in pre-war style, was abnormally big, her skin sallow, the coarse features almost elderly, except for her timid eyes, which were a child's eyes, wide and softly coloured. The most striking part was her mouth, which was very large but scarcely large enough for the great discoloured teeth which filled it; the upper lip, which appeared to be rolled back, almost joined her broad, flat nose, as if she wore a moustache of wrinkled flesh, and this deformity she had tried to turn to her advantage with a coating of vermilion rouge. These peculiarities would have caught attention even had the head been mounted on a body of proportionate size. It was not. The childish frock she wore contained a grown woman's body, perfectly matured, but on a miniature scale. She was less than four and a half feet tall.

Tired, now that she was sitting down, a little faint from the room's closeness and the ordeal to come, Armorel made conversation. "I hope it's not a nuisance, my coming like this . . . I had quite a job to find the place, it was silly of me, I came round quite the wrong way . . . It has been hot all day, hasn't it! I think we're in for a thunderstorm presently." The girl occasionally turned her eyes to Armorel's face and back at once to the window. "Aio," she said, her voice matched with the size of her body. "M-m . . . oh dear! . . ." she said. It was better when she looked away: receiving those darted glances from the young, gentle eyes, you felt that someone unseen was peering at you from behind a grotesque mask. There were sounds from upstairs of agitated talk and movement: Armorel guessed that Empire was putting himself in social trim.

He was, indeed, in ceremonial order when he arrived, with a double collar showing a gold stud, his big, cushiony hands washed up to the wrists, his fair hair damped down. He took the hand that Armorel offered, as if she had given him a baby chicken to hold, quickly let it go and dropped back to stand in line with his daughter, while Armorel sat down again. Inevitably she was hostess, they two were visitors.

"I hope you won't mind my coming like this," she said. "It's about a friend of mine called Gian Ardree—I think he works with you?"

He nodded. He was a small man, except in feet and hands, anxious to please, like a country parson in cheap cartoons.

"He's been in trouble lately," she said, "and I'm very anxious to do what I can to get him firmly on his feet again."

"In trouble?" His brow was rather like a Dalmatian's, his eyes had a dog's puzzled fidelity. "Oh, yes, yes, he went to prison." He laughed slackly. "Bit of a do with the police—knocked one right out of business, they tell me. You heard about that, Daise?"

"M-m," his daughter said.

Armorel said quickly: "Yes, I believe that's about what happened.

But he's not really a vicious young man—I know something about him from his mother—and in other ways."

With the grin hustled away, Empire nodded earnestly: the lady, of course, must know. Armorel was relieved: she had pictured herself dealing with a very different kind of man.

"On the other hand," she continued, "I think it's quite likely he may give some trouble if he isn't handled carefully—I mean, I think this is a time when his friends can do a lot for him. It's always a dangerous time for a man, the period after he's come out of prison."

Daise, with one of her glances, said "M-m." Her father, desperate to answer as the lady wished, said nothing at all. He looked at Daise for inspiration, he looked at Armorel's feet. Was it some society she had come from, was she just a plain ordinary nosey parker, or did she want to sell him a flag?

"Who's that?" he suddenly asked.

The old woman had appeared at the window.

"Oh," Armorel said, "that's someone who was helping me to find the way here . . . What I specially wanted to ask you was this: if you do find Ardree being troublesome in any way—"

But now he was giving her only a polite fraction of his attention. The old woman's nose was pressed against the window, her dog stood up with its paws on the sill. "I can't get any sense from him, dear," the old woman shouted.

"Put up the window, Daise," Empire said, and his daughter obeyed.

"Telling me," said the old woman, "that he's never heard of Davie Jenkins!"

Armorel smiled to her. "I've found the house I want—thank-you *so* much for helping me!" She turned to Empire again. "Do tell me frankly—has he been a nuisance to you at all?"

"Ardree?" he said, looking at the floor. "I've known him for a long time—haven't I, Daise?" He spoke as if his tongue were too large, damp and furred. His smile came like the crack in a blancmange, with no reflection in his eyes. "Used to come here—didn't he, Daise?"

"M-m."

"If he didn't live here, where did he live?" the old woman demanded. "You can't tell me I can't believe my own two eyes!"

"I'm afraid he must have gone somewhere else now," Armorel told her. ". . . And of course," turning again to Empire, "you still see him at work every day?"

"Mr Jenkins?"

"No, no; Gian Ardree."

She had lost his attention again. "Perhaps your mum would like to come inside?" he said. The dog was in already, smelling his trousers. "I don't think I ever heard of a Mr Jenkins. Have you heard of a Mr Jenkins, Daise?"

"I don't know all their names," his daughter said.

Armorel said rapidly, "That isn't my mother, I don't know her at all. Listen, please, Mr Empire, this is rather important—"

"It *is* important!" the old woman echoed. "Mrs Inch, my name is."

"—I've heard something about a practical joke being played on you. I want to know if you think that Ardree had anything to do with that. Because if you do, I want to take the whole business into my own hands, for your sake and for his. It was a very stupid affair, and it must have been a great annoyance to you—"

His mind seemed to be working in some fashion now, though its gear was painfully low. "I remember him coming here as a young lad, Sunday afternoons. I had five or six of them in a Bible class. These lads, you know, miss, they get nothing of that kind, if someone don't learn them. You can't live without Holy Scripture, can you miss?"

"Well, I—I don't know. But I'm sure you must have had a good influence on him."

Surprisingly, and rather dreadfully, his daughter laughed. Her great mouth, when she laughed, became a crater from which the thin notes of her mirth trickled grotesquely.

"That'll do!" Empire snapped, and the laugh fell dead.

Mrs Inch sniffed. "I never did hear of Mr Jenkins going to no Bible class."

"Yes, I did a lot for them lads," Empire went on. "It's like as you might say I got a way with young chaps. You can always send 'em along to me, if you're having trouble with any young chap."

The voice from the window broke in again: "But he's not a young chap."

"Of course," he persisted, "there's some lads you can't do nothing with. There's what you might call a spirit of evil inside them. I'm not saying aught against the young chap you was speaking of . . ."

He was set to a fair wind now. His eyes might wander, coming to Armorel's face in sliding glances like his daughter's; his soft, friendly mouth might bunch and droop alternately reminding her of a marionette's; but the liquid voice ran smoothly, earnest and humble, charged ever more warmly with the eloquence of the simple-hearted, tireless, because it had no nervous force to be exhausted. Fallen into stupor, his daughter watched him as children stare at the traffic through misted windows; Mrs Inch herself had come at last to silence.

Would it always be like this? Armorel wondered. As the curded voice went rambling on she grew desperate to get away: to escape from the smell of Bidault's Place and the stuffed flowers on the broken piano, from the need to sit as a lady should and to wear an understanding smile. The girl Daise was frankly watching her now, as primitive people watch the first explorer who comes their way, while Mrs Inch, leaning on the window-sill, was quietly crying. Together with Empire himself, still standing politely in his place and intermittently smiling, helping his endless digressions with the lame gestures of his soft, ungainly hands, they made a picture like the careful tableaux of a village pageant, living creatures eerily reduced to waxwork; and she felt, with increasing malaise, that she was part of this peculiar tableau herself.

"I can't waste my time standing here all night!" Mrs Inch said suddenly. "Who's to get Alfred Inch's supper for him, that's what I want to know."

"Of course, yes, you must get back!" Armorel said quickly. "I must be going too. It's so kind of you . . ."

She put out her hand and this time Empire held it firmly, smiling. He leaned towards her, so that she caught the smell of his breath. "You understand," he said, "I only want to help folk all I can, no matter who it is. The police or anyone else—after all, the police have got their job to do, the same as other folk."

She could not get her hand away. "But you know," she said urgently, "I'm nothing to do with the police. I'm only interested in Gian Ardree."

He smiled gravely, continuing to hold her hand. Mrs Inch still watched them curiously from the window, Daise from the stairs. "He'll be all right, young Ardree," he said, "I'll keep an eye on him, I always do what I can for the young lads—short of anything as come against the law, you understand. He knows that right enough, Ardree does—so long as he's not up against the law he's not got a better friend than me."

She did not try to answer, her mind was fixed on getting away before laughter overwhelmed her. Not that she saw anything amusing in Empire's earnestness: the room's sepulchral respectability, the damp hand cherishing hers, the great head of the creature timidly looking down from the stairs, these were a waking, liverish dream that started in her head and throat the laughter which visits mourners at a funeral. Without another word she pulled her hand away and went out into the street.

Her obvious course was to turn right and go out into what she afterwards knew as Sea Coal Street; and by this route she would gratefully have avoided the passage under Coronation Building. She started to go that way; but a group of men idling in the roadway, men with hungry faces and nothing in the world to look at, made her lose her nerve. She turned abruptly and went the way she had come, walking with dignity but more rapidly than she was used. She had not reached the passage when she heard the old woman shouting after her. She took no notice at all.

At that point something happened which frightened her. Someone close by said, "Excuse me!" and she saw a man standing in the darkness of a doorway. She stopped dead and said in a wholly unnatural voice "What do you want?"

The man's accent, when he spoke again, slightly reasssured her and though he did not come right out into the roadway, she could see, now, that he was at least respectably dressed: the kind of young man—her impression was—who sells motor cars in Long Acre. "I'm so sorry," he said, "but I saw you come out of Number 3; can you tell me if Empire's at home?"

She answered that he was, and started to move on, but he spoke again: "Do you mind telling me if there's anyone with him? Any visitor, I mean?" He was very polite, like a well-drilled schoolboy.

She answered: "Not as far as I know."

"You—didn't see anyone hanging about?"

"No."

"Who was hanging about?" Mrs Inch demanded, steaming up like Pheidippides. "There's no sense talking that way to me. If people don't tell you nothing you've *got* to hang about."

The chance was too obvious to be ignored.

"Listen," Armorel said, "if you talk nicely to this gentleman he'll tell you all about Mr Jenkins." She left them and hurried on into Mickett Lane.

A few drops of rain had fallen, but the storm held off. Absurd, to have been so scared by a polite young man—probably, she realized now, a plain-clothes man on the look-out for any further mischief at Empire's house. But the pulse of her heart still felt like an engine left to race, her feet still hurried. This street was narrow, and its houses, loopholed walls thrust hard against the narrow pavements, had the groping look of a blind beggar's face. She would not recover all her calm till she reached the main road.

The sweeper and his barrow was still there, a few women gossiped on the pavement, some boys were kicking a tin along the gutter. Her eye was caught by a man some distance down the street because of the way he walked, with the springy slouch of a young Londoner, but with something furtive in the movements of his head. Coming in her direction he kept close to the houses, stopping every few yards to look about him, and when some thirty yards away he turned sharply into the one narrow passage which broke the block. By then she had seen that it was Gian himself.

Instinctively she looked back along the street. Mrs Inch and the plain-clothes man were advancing together in the middle of the roadway, the dog dragging ahead. She went quickly to where Gian had stopped with his back against the wall.

"You—what do you want?" he demanded.

Just beside them the back door of a house was ajar, she pushed it boldly and saw that the house was an empty one.

"You'd better come in here," she said prosaically, "the police are just up the street."

He hesitated for a moment and then followed her inside. Followed her upstairs, having bolted the door behind him, and stood with his white face a few inches from hers, his hands and his teeth clenched.

"See here!" he said, scarcely parting his lips, "are you going to keep out of my tracks or not?"

"Not," she answered.

Relaxing, after a few moments, he sat down on a painter's trestle, biting his lip and staring at his ragged shoes.

12

She was to think of that house, No. 83, with something akin to sentiment; to grope in the falling and distorting light of memory for elusive details of that hour. For their friendship started there.

"I can see that room now, the trestle Gian was sitting on, the look on his face—as if he thought I was a kind of wicked fairy and Scarlet Pimpernel rolled into one." She said that—to Christine—many weeks later. It was not, in truth, the memory of that hour at all. Gian's face, as he sat on the trestle, was first livid with anger and then merely sullen; the face she afterwards 'remembered' was built out of several occasions—his bewilderment when she told him (casually, in the Strand) that she had scarcely any money of her own, the incredulity in his eyes when she gave him a leather cigarette-case for his birthday, his dumb astonishment at her remark, among the Florentines in the National Gallery, that "hardly any educated people think those miracles really happened." No, in reality she could not recapture that first proper meeting at all. The broken window and the peeling wallpaper, painters' tins and brushes, shavings and cigarette-ends all over the floor: these remained in outline. The curious light which a window opposite threw back from a sun fallen below the storm's rim, that was too subtle to be etched on memory, and the smell, sawn wood and plumber's paste borne in the evening odours of the hot street, could only by chance come to her again. She could have repeated months later some of the things she said—"Well, honestly, it is my business. We both belong to Hollysian House. ... I know it must be maddening, but then you couldn't expect Empire to refuse promotion, and in any case it's no good going for people when they've got the police looking after them"—but never again in exactly the same voice, its quiet good-temper warmed and lit by the evening's excitement, its studied cheerfulness softened by caution and by a hint of tears. Such an hour does not stand by itself, it emerges from those before it already nurtured, as live beings are by their parentage. The day it was born from had been fretted with small terrors, heavy with frustration. At the sight of Gian it changed, ceasing to be purposeless. Fear remained: of the outcome of so outlandish a situation, of Gian himself; for at the moment when they arrived upstairs and he faced her, standing in the doorway, his eyes looked murderous. But this new fear was blended with triumph (she thought already how in a casual sentence she would recount the affair to Trevon) and the wasted day had seemed to be restored.

So little speech passed between them. "My business, isn't it! . . . No harm in a bit of sport . . . Deputy foreman don't make no difference —make him boss, for all I mind. Won't make him nothink different, a jag's a jag, no matter what he is. . . . It's not the same as butting in, honestly it isn't. . . . Yep, I seen you meant all right. Gettin' books and that. I reckon on what Mr Grist said, what he said you don't come from the Court nor yet you're not in with Sally's Army nor any other noseys. Yep, I reckon that by what Mr Grist said." But excitement had quickened him, as the scuttle of a mouse changes a drowsy cat into a shaft of sensitivity. Even in the first few minutes, when he sat on the trestle with his mouth glum as a schoolboy's in detention, his brow was intent. They heard foosteps halting below the window, the short bark of a dog followed by voices, "This way, you're certain?" "Not up to nothing —that's what you think! The word I use is 'bitch', and I don't mind who hears me—B-I-S-K-H. . . . " and when those sounds had died away he grinned, sniffling at the same time. The grin came and went as he walked up and down the small room, putting a cigarette in his mouth and back in his hip-pocket: a private grin, not to be shared with her; but sometimes his wandering glance came nearly to her face, and once it rested on her dress, dispassionately, the gaze of a town child upon open moors. He was showing off now, shifting his scarf, playing with the cigarette, shrugging his shoulders: she was surprised to see so much mobility in a face which had looked so lifeless before, to catch the signs of cogitation. He admitted, presently, that she existed as a separate being, "You'll get your dress mucky, sitting there," and when she replied that it didn't matter he brought a piece of sacking from the next room and put it for her to sit on. "You got no call to stay about," he said more than once, "the cops a'n't after you!" but she answered evenly that she was not in a hurry. She asked for a cigarette and he gave it to her, much surprised. That seemed to lessen his irritation, his face showed interest now, as the molten faces of very dour people will sometimes light up at the antics of a kitten. "Spoil your inside," he remarked, and then, as one knowing his world, "Cop goes off at eight. Change the shift then."

"Pay you, at that club?" he asked.

"No, I don't get any money for it. Of course it's not a whole-time job."

"What d'you do it for?"

"Well, I like it. I like books—and people."

"What, those blokes round the Club?"

"Some of them are very nice. There's Eddie Peters, I think he's absolutely delightful."

"Eddie? Gor! Bloke that can't hardly talk."

"Well, that's what makes it interesting, that sort of thing. He may not be able to talk much. But he knows things. He reads an awful lot. Then there's Terence Hubbitt."

"The cop's son?"

"Yes. I like him very much too."

He nodded, "Yes, he's all right," and went off into a day-dream. He would have talked freely, she was certain, if he were practised in conversation; she could see him getting sentences ready and then throwing them away because they were too clumsy to carry his thoughts. All her apprehension had gone, and since he looked so seldom directly at her face she could study his as she had studied only one face before, wondering that features cut in so hard a substance could yet suggest mercurial alternations of inward cloud and light. In the Court, watched from her awkward place, these hunting eyes had seemed animal and childish; they were strange eyes still, but their light no longer came from a flickering source, and the mouth which had shown like leather became a pliant instrument, responsive to a range of impulses. Her instincts had been just, then: this man whom the upright Mr Cuddish had so casually put in prison, whom the knowing Mr Grist had been content to classify as difficult and dangerous, was a creature no smaller in sensibility than themselves, perhaps no poorer in natural intelligence. In knowledge he might be behind his fellows, slower in understanding, less balanced in temper, less able to distinguish between good lines of conduct and bad. What else would you expect from his shoddy parentage, a childhood walled by the Contessa houses, the crammed, uproarious, chancy schooling of Sand Street? And if he was far behind, was not the task of coaxing him forward so much the more rewarding? To make him what he was meant to be, to show the scribes how hopelessly they had misjudged him, might be a labour not of months but of years. So long as it was hers, she did not mind.

Here was the genius of this curious hour, her sense of final dedication and of boundless strength. In the moment of his frenzy one word of hers had calmed him; and surely if she could penetrate his mind with eyes of understanding, if she set herself no limits in labour or patience, she was destined for an achievement which few would have dared to attempt. She watched him moving about the room like a beast newly caged. From where she sat on the floor he seemed gigantic, in height as well as breadth: a creature devoid of graces, his thick hair unkempt, a dirty scrub on his angular cheeks and jaw, his jacket torn and his greasy trousers shapeless: not a boy but a man, coarsely mature, with dried and dirty sweat on his forehead, dirt in every crack of his workman's hands. Somehow the picture which had grown in her mind was of a boy with some physical weakness, a shrinking and sensitive being, crushed by the weight of misunderstanding. In this reality there was nothing that cowered. His sniff was contemptuous, the movements of his chin and wrists were a fighter's. Here was someone to be broken, rather than mended, before the best in him could grow; not by the old and fruitless cruelties, but with the supple penetration of intelligence. Simply by coolness, by taking his manner of life for granted, she had made the first step. Even as minutes passed his perplexed hostility was waning; without her asking he clumsily dealt her another cigarette, and actually a rasher of his thoughts.

"In with the cops—Empire. Got 'em all round, whenever he wants."

"Well, that's a sound enough reason for keeping clear of him, isn't it?"

"Maybe."

He examined his knuckles, hideously broken, and smiled again. The look of fury returned, he spat on his sleeve, shook out his massive shoulders and loped back to the window, where he stood and looked defiantly into the street.

"Better not stand there," she said, "they might see you."

"What of it?"

"You know well enough—you don't want to be seen within a mile of Empire's place."

"They can't do nothing."

"Except get you back into prison—that's what they're trying to, isn't it?"

"Prison's all right," he said.

"Not for people like you. It's all right for brainless people—they might as well be in prison as anywhere else. You've got brains—you know that. Anyway, I don't want to see you going to prison again—no, don't tell me it's not my business, I'm sick of hearing you say that." She was smiling, but her voice had taken a man's intonation, the phrases falling like the dull, even blows of a lumberer. "Listen, it would be a silly sort of life, a man spending half his time in gaol just because he's too bone lazy to use the brains that nature's given him. If you haven't the gumption to see that—if your own people are too feeble to make you see it—then it's going to be my business, whether you like it or not."

With some solemnity he considered this manifesto, coming slowly towards her, his lips tight and twisting in a way she hadn't seen before.

"If it weren't for you being along with Mr Grist," he said, giving his thoughtful decision, "I might crack your face for you."

She stood up, taking her time.

"I suppose it's all right if I hit you back?"

Feet astride, hands withdrawn from his pockets, his mouth still oddly wriggling, he scanned her face and neck with precise eyes, as a chess player examines the board before his move. She realized in those moments how quiet it was in this small room, with the children's voices from the roadway stilled. The footsteps that she heard were a long way up the street, the noise of a goods train shunting came from another world. Strangely, she was cold, though the day's heat seemed to have stayed in the stagnant air against her face, resisting the fresher smells of evening. After a time he seemed to grow tired of his preoccupation, and turned about nonchalantly to stand beside her, leaning against the wall, whistling with his teeth, occasionally smiling. Something in his tired face forbade her to speak again: with the light weakening he grew almost as distant as he had been in court, and having captured ground that day she would not trespass any further. The darkness of the threatened storm was slowly intensified by nightfall. He did not move about any more, and until the darkness made them almost invisible to each other they stood side by side, like strangers early in a theatre queue, dumbly sharing (she believed) a kind of contentment.

As they walked together to the end of Contessa Street (with a yard between them, like a preparatory schoolboy and a mother wrongly dressed) he made one remark: "You certain it was a tec you saw? . . . Maybe lucky you come." The air had freshened a little from the dark street she saw one spray of stars.

In the tram, when she had left him, she was unconsciously smiling: there was a lingering pleasure in the feel of the people jammed beside her, in their overworn clothes and stale odours, because she had travelled a little in their country: the pattern of light which the Old Richmond threw across the pavement, the torn fly sheets and the little crowd round the barrows at Haig's Corner, these, slung past the windows, had caught the virtue of a new possession, like the names of places you have passed through in the early marches of a long campaign.

13

*P*ART OF the magic remained, making her immune to the set-backs and the disappointments. It changed the feel of life, it altered her behaviour, her looks. On the day after her visit to Bidault's Place Gian strolled into the library and took out a book as one takes a ticket for Charing Cross; but paused at the door, looked her in the face, grinned, took off the grin, said curtly—addressing the highest shelf of books—"Nice game of hide and seek!" and left the Club. The fact that a week passed before he came again scarcely diminished the silent exaltation in which she lived. The advance had begun.

The sense of triumph gave her new confidence, she ceased to be merely a conscientious underling, Hollysian House became partly her own. The boys were immediately aware of the change. She was far less shy, she started to call some by their Christian names as Trevon did and even tried to joke with them, though joking was never her forte: but books had to be returned by the proper date now, either that or no more borrowing, and she listened to no argument. "And, Gus, will you please not shut the door with your foot, it's got a handle." On the whole they liked it. And on the whole, though he grumbled, Flock liked it. "Sergeant Flock!" she would shout right down the gymnasium, "I asked you quite distinctly to get all the books off the top shelf and dust it thoroughly . . . No, I'm not asking you again, I'm telling you it's got to be done. Get me?" she added fiercely. The shelf was dusted. She emerged of an evening and marched confidently between the groups, calling "Where's that scalawag Fisher? Oh, there you are—you owe me one and fivepence cigarette money, come on, I'm not going to climb up after you!" 'Susie Bitch-rod', they called her among themselves, loud enough for her to overhear; 'Miss Susie' to her face, sometimes just 'Susie'. She liked that. She put up notices signed 'Susie' and sometimes 'S.B-R'.

The change would have been obvious enough to Trevon, but she gave him particular chances to observe it. She started by returning a draft he had scrawled for typing. "I'm not going to waste my time unravelling that, you'll have to make a fair copy and then I'll do it." She argued with him, quietly, inexorably. She had decided to retard the library hours by half an hour, and nothing he said would alter her decision. No, she would not have books of faintly disguised theology, even if they were a gift from one of the Club's most generous patrons; Trevon could keep them in his own room if he wished and give them out himself, that was his affair, but they were just not going to clutter up hers.

"Did you know that Ardree was in last night?" he asked on the Thursday afternoon.

"Last night? Oh, yes, yes, I saw him."

"He came into my room fairly late, I had quite a long talk with him."

"Oh, yes?"

"He said something about his having seen you a few nights ago. In Mickett Lane, I think he said."

"Mickett Lane? Oh, yes, I know it, I walk that way sometimes. Yes, of course, that was where I spoke to him."

"He seemed a bit puzzled about you."

"Puzzled? I shouldn't have thought there was anything puzzling about me. Look here—I wanted to tell you—I've decided to spend fifteen pounds on new books. We really do need them."

"And where's the fifteen pounds coming from?"

"Well, that's what I want you to tell me . . ."

And now that her last fear of this blustering creature had gone she could find some kindness for him. More and more he was making excuses to come into her room and talk, sometimes in a nervous fashion about Gian (to be adroitly side-stepped), sometimes about herself. "You don't feel you're wasting your brains in this God-forsaken outfit? . . . It must be nice to get down to Streatham, after stewing in this place all evening. I suppose you've got a pretty room, all chintzes and hand-painted lamp shades and things? I suppose, really, it's very pleasant to live respectably—I can hardly remember, but I think it must be. Look here, if you feel you need flowers and that sort of thing you must tell Flock to get them and I'll settle with him. And if he tries to be funny, tell him I'll kick his backside for him." She was too sensible, too mature (with Gordon behind her), to be highly flattered by such attention; yet too quick in observation and instinct to overlook the little signs which had broken out, his more careful shaving, the occasional brushing of his hair. In most ways, he was the same as when she had first known him. He stayed for hours in a tightening fog of smoke and flatulence, he sulked, he dogmatized and ranted. He delivered vast lectures on the rottenness of civilization, bemoaned the crass indiscipline of his boys in one breath and sentimentalized about them in the next; lit one cigarette from another, belched, hiccoughed, roared his self-pity across the gymnasium. *"Flock!"* he would yell, "Flock, you lousy meddling, muddle-headed mercenary, what the hell do you mean by emptying my waste-paper basket, damn your bleeding eyes—don't you know there's always something in it I'm going to want later on, curse your drip-nosed interference!" "Mr Grist, sir, if you was to inquire," came back a distant voice embalmed in cosy innocence, "you might hear as how it were an angel come and took your basket, sir. Small-sized angel about six-stone-ten, sir. I seen her come and cart it off with love's dainty fingers, get me, Mr Grist, sir!" Another bellow: *"Miss Cepinnier!* I will not have you reorganizing this hell-begotten club without my express permission, do you understand!" yet in a minute or two he was beside her, staring censoriously at her skirt. "Look here, Susie, I've got to have a new coat, this thing's falling off me. I wish you'd get me one, I never go near any shops. . . . That must have been very expensive, that dress. You know, I like seeing you sitting there now I've got used to it. It's a change after seeing nothing but old Flock—I do so hate the sight of Flock's muscles—utilitarianism gone crazy. Yes, I feel there's something to be said for having a librarian—a small, blue one. It seems to go with the books. Well, I suppose it's like everything else in aesthetics, you like what you get used to . . ." And there he was right, she thought, and aesthetics was not the only field to which it applied: inevitably, you grew fond of chairs that had been in your nursery, of old baskets which had lost their handles and aged, rusty bicycles; you had some liking for a desk you sat at every day, for the smell of a place where you had enjoyed some happiness, the noise of familiar traffic; for the cough and the heavy breathing, the foolish ebullience, the sprawling, nervy, graceless presence of a man whose job happened to lie close to your own.

This too, this quickened and full-flowing response to the tones that radiate from shadow, she may have owed to the fresh urgency of her mission; as, when a windjammer puts out to sea, her every timber seems to come alive.

Her need was for patience but also for speed. In a week or so she might lose as much of Gian's confidence as she had gained, and if she failed to find some interest for him now, when his fractured spirit was still bent towards mischief, there might not be another chance.

They taught her, these creatures of many shapes and sizes jostling and ragging round her chair, that almost any boy would respond to flattery, even such minor flattery as your knowing his name and something about him: and she learnt that some of the most uncouth among them, the most laconic or surly, were pleased with the chance to do her a personal favour. On that principle her earliest traps for Gian were set. Getting word that he was hanging about in the yard she went downstairs with a pair of suitcases which she had kept handy, weighted with old books; with these she laboured towards Balt Lane, calling "Goodevening, Gian!" as she passed him. It worked. She found him slouching beside her, mumbling "You can't do that, that's not a kid's job," and he carried the cases the whole way to the cloakroom at Waterloo. It 'chanced' next time he wandered into the library that a heavy box of books had to be got down from the top of the cupboard. "Wait," she said, "here's Gian Ardree, let him do it, he's as strong as a lion," and she stood gasping with admiration as he performed the simple task. Another evening there was a new page of the register to be ruled. "Gian, be a dear, you're good with your fingers." This was trying him high, and the first lines he made were far from parallel, but he rubbed them all out, laboriously marked the intervals in the way she showed him and did it again. Perhaps he had not cared for such kindergarten work: he was absent for three nights afterwards: but when he came again she praised him lavishly, and at once set him to putting returned books back on the proper shelves. (The job was foolproof, now that shelves and books were carefully numbered, but she made him understand that no one else in the Club could be trusted with work of such complexity.) She saw him slamming at the punch-ball, in the somnolent fashion of one peeling a twig and went to try her own hand, collecting a circle which shouted "Gor—look at Susie! . . . Bleeding cruelty to the ruddy ball! . . . Here, miss, let me show y' "—but only Gian was allowed to demonstrate, and she joined in the 'Gor!' at the vicious power of his blows. By expert contrivance, by cautious stage-management, she began to give him a new status in the Club.

She persuaded him to come on a Sunday excursion to Regent's Park, with Terence Hubbitt as companion (since he had manifested a kind of bovine attachment to this undersized, bespectacled, spotty and uninteresting child) and this was a partial success and the inclusion of Terence put him in an entirely different mood. He looked at the trees with something like appreciation, he smelt the air and said, "All right, out this way!" as if the park were his own handiwork. Of Armorel he took scarcely any notice, except to buy her, in an offhand way, a cup of tea; but to Terence he was almost garrulous. "Could do worse, of a Sunday . . . Better get something to take back to your mum—go on, course you can pick 'em, I won't let no one hurt you!" She was much heartened; and two evenings later, leaving the library in charge of Nibbley Toms, she persuaded him to come to St James's Park with her, alone, and listen to the Green Howards' band. For this adventure he wore a new jacket, with a clean collar and sober tie.

She prepared conversational openings as diligently as an actor studies his part, hunting not only for subjects which might interest him but for language which she could use naturally and which he would understand. To begin with it mattered little, she thought, what they talked about, if she could only get him talking at all. Here again the earliest attempts left her almost without hope. Her mention of Empire and his daughter made him evasive and sullen. She spoke of his mother —how strange London must seem to one brought up in the sun-drenched loveliness of Italy—and all he said was "Mum? She's all right." Contessa Street was 'all right', his job was 'all right'—no, there was nothing in it, anyone could do it. Had he ever thought of trying for another sort of job? No, he hadn't, he expected all jobs were much the same. No, he didn't expect to get promoted—well, he just didn't think it was likely, that was all. No, he didn't play football; that sort of thing was all right for kids. He had once been to see the Arsenal, his dad had taken him. That must have been fun? Well, no. Had he ever done any carpentry, tried to make things? He hadn't. Allowing for the high, thick walls with which his life had been surrounded, she began to doubt if they were his only limitations.

But at least he was getting used to her, accepting her eccentricities as he accepted the rest of experience; and on an evening when she said, "I simply must stretch my legs, do come for a walk before the library opens!" he came as unconcernedly as a carriage dog. His face, indeed, was that of a martyr who has frequently been taken to the stake on the wrong day; his gait aggressively detached; but he had the slightly possessive air of one leading rather than being led, and when a friend in Flanders Street called "Where y' taking Susie, Toughie? Maiden's End?" he did not look abashed at all. It was in that short walk that he first spoke to her spontaneously. As they were passing the Sand Street Schools he stopped to stare, holding on to the railings which go all round the playground. She waited patiently, and all at once he said, pointing to the Girls' Entrance, "All wrong! Bleeding death-trap, them steps."

"Oh?"

"Seen a kid cut her head open. Tripped, see? They come out all together, the ones in front get pushed by the ones behind. This kid come down head first, give her head a crack on the stone there. Cut it right open. Blood?—you never seen nothin' like it. Covered with it, I was, just pickin' her up."

"Yes," she said, "it does look dangerous. But I don't see quite what they're to do about it. I suppose they could make a rule that the children have got to come out in an orderly way."

"Rule?" he said. "Rules is no good."

"Well, what would you do?"

"Take away them steps," he answered, without hesitation. "Sort of platform thing, you want there, with a wall this side, about this high, see? Path goin' down close up against the building—not steps, a slopin' path, see? With a rail both sides, a wood rail, not iron, see?"

The incident was sufficient guide to one alert for guidance. She persuaded him a day or two later to visit the Civic Design exhibition at the Institute of Civil Engineers. Cap in both hands, unlit cigarette at the usual angle, he dutifully examined one model after another with the eyes of a tone-deaf man in the Wigmore Hall.

"They're beautifully made, aren't they?" she suggested.

"Yes, they're all right."

A failure, she thought. By tomorrow she would think of a new line to pursue. She looked about to see if there was anything important that they had missed and when she turned again he had disappeared.

There was a screen near the entrance with a group of photographs to illustrate the Lowes-Beddling scheme at Liverpool. One showed Gold Purse Street as it had been, with a child swinging on a piece of rope fixed to a lamp-post: there were views of the same street half-demolished, and pastel drawings to show the court which would take its place. She found him studying this screen, not with any look of intelligence but with a kind of rustic gravity. He put his eyes close to the child swinging on the lamp-post, as if she were someone he knew. The drawings he passed over cursorily, but the photograph of a Wicken demolisher at work held him fascinated. She said, after a time:

"It must be fun to use a thing like that—to press a lever and see a wall toppling."

"That don't do nothing, that lever," he said without turning. "That's the brake, that is. You got an extra clutch pedal down at the bottom what puts in the working gear."

"You're interested in machinery?" she asked.

"Not specially."

The photograph of two bricklayers at work, with a small girl looking up at them, stopped him again. He scrutinized it with contemptuous concentration.

"What are they doing that for?" he asked at length.

"Well, I suppose they may be building a house for the little girl to live in."

"What—that kid? A house like that?"

"I don't see why not."

"Do better get her something to eat!" he said laconically.

"Well, for all we know they may be doing that as well. One of them may be the girl's father, earning money to get her food."

"What, that?" he said. "That's not her dad. That's a silky."

"Why, how do you know?"

"You never seen a bloke lay bricks like that, not a bloke that knows how."

"What, isn't he doing it the right way?"

"Right way? What—laying on bricks without nothing to hold 'em fixed!"

She said quickly: "Oh, you've done some bricklaying, have you?"

"Only in the locker," he said, with a note of defiance.

"It would be rather a nice job, wouldn't it, to build houses?"

"Depend what sort of houses," he answered; and although she

led him back to the subject with all the skill she had, as they drank coffee together in the Bridge Street A.B.C., she could penetrate no further.

Yet her patience had narrowed the field of possibility. Plainly his dormant interest was in things, in the making of things, probably in the making of houses. She had been foolish to put him at so high a fence as architectural design: that was a level he might reach in time, but at present it was as far above him as the rush-tops above a tadpole. Meanwhile, he had powerful hands and observant eyes; if he could be taught the lesser crafts in building he might progress to the higher; the things he saw and felt, above all the things he did, would nourish his mind for the more adventurous journey she intended. Within a few hours she had letters on their way to everyone she knew, or knew at second hand, who was concerned with the building trade. Within two days she had seen the principals of three technical schools and received particulars of two more.

Some hold that a jockey in the first flight will exercise more than the skills of judgement and of touch; that by some esoteric means his will-power flows into the horse he rides. If by such means one human being can command another, Armorel must have used them. But it can scarcely be argued that Gian had, at that time, no will of his own. Impossible, of course, that he would have travelled on the course she set—or even dreamed of it—without a powerful impulse outside himself. Yet surely he possessed some kind of ambition, or at least some kind of hunger, which she in fact wakened and directed. So much the facts seemed to imply. For in less than a week after their visit to the exhibition they were walking side by side up the steps of the Grover Technical Institute in Stamford Street; and a fortnight later, alone, slouching, with fugitive and hostile eyes, he was mounting those steps again for the fifth time.

What young man, after all, could have held out against such insidious flattery, so gentle-voiced as well as so tremendous a persuasion. She had learnt some gestures of his own, the off-hand manner which a man of the streets wears to separate him from the sucker class: with them she had found a smile like his, a shrewd and corner-mouthed grimace which dawned from an obstinate frown and sank into the frown again before anything was given away. She kept that smile for him. She made him seem to take his own decisions, brought him problems which he could solve from his own field of knowledge—"Gian, look, that man at the corner has charged me 3/6 for doing these shoes. Have I been a mug again?"—and treated his grumbles as if they belonged to her as well. She was casual: that was the secret. Her invitations and appointments were made as if she didn't care a damn: 'Might as well.' 'You coming?' 'Feel like the baths?' these were phrases that belonged to comradeship and she learnt almost to dispense with any others. What wonder that at last he was giving her some particles of his confidence in return. He told her in a casual fashion that he had been stood off for three days for some jugglery over clocking-in which the deputy foreman had spotted; that his father was 'gone all out on himself', being out of a job; that a sister who'd married a Birmingham chap was in the family way again and 'trying like mad to get it ditchered.' These came spontaneously, a recognition of her interest. Of the evening classes he said that most of the teaching meant nothing at all to him: it was really for silkies, for blokes with a lot of schooling, 'same as you'd be yourself.' But because she made his attendance a favour to her, exactly as if he were earning money from which she somehow benefited, he went on attending.

By seven o'clock the mob which comes each morning to earn some remote kind of living has mostly been taken away, leaving the city to its own people. The congestion loosens and the tired streets can breathe a little. This was the city they chiefly shared, on evenings when the classes were not sitting. There was a tea-shop called the Liverpool in Southwark Street (it is a shop for electrical appliances now) which stayed open till eight; once or twice, between his working and her library hours, they had glasses of lemonade there, with rather noisome pies, watched curiously by the marble-eyed old woman who kept the place. They got on a bus one evening which went at a joyful speed down Kingsland Road while she tried to explain a passage in a text-book which had bothered him, and afterwards they stood in the middle of St George's Circus to settle conscientiously about the fare. Often you might have followed them, in a small excursion like these, without realizing that they were meant to be in company: he was usually ambling ahead or lagging behind like a puppy on a generous lead, sometimes he would stop dead to look at children playing on the kerb or an old man pushing a barrow and she would go some distance before she realized he had strayed and stopped to wait for him. But he in his turn waited patiently if she turned to look at a shop window, and sometimes he smiled then, and even made a remark: "Won't do you, Miss Susie, you don't get class shops in this part." On an evening when the sun sank from a clear sky into the haze over Notting Hill they both stood still to look southwards from Lambeth Bridge. They were the length of a tram apart, and he could not be seeing what she saw, the promiscuity of sooted stone and brick turned by a diffusion of light into one incomparable masterpiece. But he had stopped of his own accord, and when he caught up again, face resolutely bored, his teeth were whistling.

For her in this summer of contentment, each day rewarded by the inches climbed, the town wore that aspect of a new possession. It was a harmony too fragile to be kept, but such that once and again in later years her ears might prick to it. In the grey light of a London evening she might see a boy pushing his small brother in an orange-box along the cooled pavement by the shuttered shops in Pegg Street. Perhaps with twenty minutes to kill she would drop in at the Liverpool and leaning on the stained American cloth would imagine she saw Gian coming over with the glasses, callow, embarrassed, his eyes lit faintly by a fugitive pride. But it was flecks of experience slenderer than these, more transient, which would hold the genius to take her back. A glance up at the clock as she stood on the Embankment waiting for a tram; the fresh, sunset air which sometimes catches your face as you turn from Stamford Street to go over the bridge; a moment when the traffic in Waterloo Road seems to have petered out, and you catch, with the smell of trains and a chop frying, the gurgle of a tap-room pianola: if these should touch like hairs her nerves of memory the sober enchantment of that August might all return, its ardour and tranquillity, the expectancy coursing beneath its flat fatigue. This season contained perhaps the afterglow of another summer's tenderness; but the complex music was its own, the tone austere, the basal rhythm hard and urgent like the beat of hoofs.

14

She knew when that season was over. So often the feel of life alters imperceptibly, you cannot tell when a period of contentment began or ended. But she felt this change, reflectively, when it occurred.

The day to be recorded for anniversaries was the second Tuesday in September. That was the date of finality. But the end really came five days before, and she recognized it by what they call a feeling in the bones. Nothing physical altered. The weather, which had been steady and warm by English standards, remained so; there was no hint of autumn. On this Thursday afternoon she went to the Club by her usual route, through the familiar odours of Balt Lane. There were stripes of sunlight across the yard, a brown smoke beyond the buildings on the river side. She thought suddenly, as she went up the creaking stairs, I suppose I shall go on doing this, day after day; but it has become a weariness now, it has lost its meaning.

Gian had let her down the night before. She had arranged to meet him at the usual place and go with him to the Grover; he had not turned up, and she had heard later from one Ernie Heald who attended the bookkeeping classes that 'Toughie' had not been seen at the Institute. As Gian was the last person of whom you expected regularity, that one default would not have put a curse upon this day. Something in his manner when she had last seen him, a furtive look, a hint of new development, may have started her train of uneasiness; or she may have felt superstitiously that the fair breeze which had followed her for several weeks was overdue to fail.

Trevon arrived in a dry and poisonous humour: not one of his usual tempers, in which he would bounce and bellow at everyone who came near him, nor one of the sulks in which he wrapped himself when some boy was being a nuisance. Today he was cold and competent, he said a frigid 'Good-afternoon' and told her to bring in the petty cash book as if she were a junior clerk of doubtful honesty. Presently he called for her again (instead of making the room-to-room journey himself, as he usually did) and in a prosy, let-you-off-first-time fashion pointed out an error in casting. "Oh, and by the way—" he said, and stopped. "No—nothing." She went back to her own room.

So that was how the wind was blowing!

When four days had passed, and Gian had not shown up at the Club or at the Grover, she decided to question Trevon explicitly.

"I'm sorry to barge in, but can you spare me a few moments?"

"Well, I'm really rather busy."

"I only want to ask you one thing: have you stood Gian off for any reason?"

"No, I haven't." Then, as she was going, he called after her: "Miss Cepinnier! I'll be quite honest—I've advised Ardree not to come here for two or three weeks. Advised—not ordered."

"May I ask why?"

"No, you mayn't. Well, yes, I suppose you ought to know. The boy's unhappy, and I think he'll be happier if he keeps away for a time. That's what it amounts to. Whatever's right or wrong with that chap, he's very honest. At least, he is with me."

"And does the Club make him so frightfully unhappy?"

"No—but you do."

"How?"

"Look here," he said, with his lips like stretched rubber, "you're forcing me to speak a lot more plainly than I want to—well, I was brought up in a vicarage, so perhaps my ideas about plain speaking are rather out-of-date. Listen: you probably imagine that Ardree thinks of you as just a nice kind friend, a sort of vest-pocket Sunday-school treat served up by the management every evening. Well, he might if you'd got a body like an old sack. Only you haven't—you know that. You may have been told by some blithering maiden aunt that only nasty-minded men ever think about a girl's body. Well, you might as well know from now on that that's plain pop-eyed balderdash. Every time you smile at Ardree you put just one idea in his head. And because you're what's called a lady, which means that he can't do anything about it, it's driving him pretty nearly cracked. You think you're being kind to him, and what you're really doing is giving him a special kind of hell."

"I'm not trying to be kind," she said quickly, "I don't believe in all that sloppiness—I'm only giving him the chance that he ought to have." She paused, and a few moments passed before she said, with perfect steadiness: "But I think it was you who suggested my trying to do something for him?"

"It wasn't, originally," he answered. "However, I made a crashing blunder, if you like it that way. There were things I—underestimated."

"I suppose, then, my being here is a torture to all the boys?"

"No," he said. "You've paid no special attention to any of the others, so they're comparatively not affected. At least, not the same way."

"Because if so," she continued evenly, "I suppose I'd better leave, as you wanted me to. It's a pity, because I'm interested in the job. And of course I can't help having a body."

"No," he said seriously, "you can't—of course you can't."

"Well, I'm to leave, then?"

She waited for him to speak, and in those few moments, with her mind sparked into incandescence, she seemed to see the issues wholly and clearly. By a final twist of stupid cruelty in the nature of things the campaign for Gian Ardree was evidently lost. Must everything else go overboard: the sense of vocation, the daily escape from Cromer's Ride, the boys' friendly cheerfulness, old Flock's good-humour, Trevon himself? She realized how much she had missed Trevon these last few days, in which he had been as much a stranger as if some other had taken his place. He was like an old mongrel that you keep from sentimentality, ill-tempered, lousy and diseased, but loved for its residue of loyalty. He had called Ardree honest, and she was ready to apply that term to Trevon himself. She had come to see him as a simple man perpetually confused by good intentions, raised high on crests of self-esteem and plunged into deep troughs of self-abasement; a creature with neither rudder nor ballast; yet one free from polite and hollow poses, incapable of malice, whose devotion once bestowed would not easily be displaced. There was something else which had a certain importance: she was not a woman for nothing, she had not read books without enlarging the field of her observation or been betrothed to Gordon Aquillard without learning anything about the symptoms of secret tenderness: she was all but certain that Trevon was in love with her.

"You see, Trevon," she said, when the silence was no longer endurable, "it's all rather difficult for me to understand. It's only a few weeks ago you wanted me to go away because you said I hadn't the smallest chance of influencing Gian—and if I did he'd probably cut my throat. And now apparently I am influencing him and he hasn't cut my throat but I'm torturing him by having a body." All that came as if she were reciting from Euclid. "So I suppose the answer is that I've got to go anyway."

He said slowly: "I've told you already—some time ago—I like having you here. I—well, I do. Only that's not the only thing we've got—"

But she would not let him meander again.

"Please, Trevon, do you want me to go or don't you?"

He hesitated once more, gnawing his lips, looking out of the window. One could almost pity his abject irresolution.

"No," he said. "No, I don't."

"And about Gian—" she pursued— "that of course is nothing to do with the Club at all. No, I'm not disputing your right to keep him away—of course you must do as you think best. But if I want to go on seeing him anywhere else I think you'll agree that that's my own affair."

"In a sense it is. Only—"

"It was very kind of you to tell me just what you think about it. I understand perfectly—everything you said. But of course I'm—well, I'm not a child, and I've got to do what I think best."

The sting of a vicious blow may produce something akin to exaltation, pain comes a little way behind. In her own room at Cromer's Ride, her mind quieted by the dullness of things she knew, the little doll Christine once dressed for her, the stylized poppies of the wall-paper, she could start to measure the catastrophe: to wonder, presently, if something could be reclaimed. A year before she had seen the future as a tracing for her embroidery; and when a dozen words in a man's hesitant voice had rubbed the tracing out she had been left entirely purposeless. Since then she had drawn a pattern of her own and given all her powers to filling it. Could another man, with a sentence or two, destroy that one as well? The dragging, solitary hours in a graceless room, the embarrassments and terrors of Bidault's Place, the long struggle against successive disappointments; were these all to pass into limbo with nothing achieved?

She began a letter to her cousin Raymond, whom she often used as a tank for the overflow of her thoughts: he was a well-intentioned man of impenetrable stupidity who would always give her a kindly answer without understanding a word she said.

> It looks [she wrote] as if the Gian business will have to be abandoned. They're accusing me now of trying to vamp him—it's

extraordinary the number of ways people can find to prevent you doing what is obviously your duty. This is a disappointment, but I've been through so many of those that I feel thick-skinned enough to bear it. I think I've got older this last year or two. Anyway, I see everything quite clearly, I know there's no one to help me—I've given up expecting any news of Father—and having to decide everything for oneself does give one a certain power, as well as a kind of excitement. I don't think anyone could dispute the fact that I've had some influence on Gian, and that surely means that I can influence other people as well. And I honestly believe that one can find value in all kinds of unexpected places. This man Trevon Grist, for example, he's so obstinate and wilful and childishly jealous, and yet I believe there's something lovable in him if it could only be brought out . . .

The door squeaked and she found Aunt Georgie standing behind her with a letter in her hand.

"I did knock," Aunt Georgie said, "I don't think you heard. This came by the afternoon post. Rellie, darling, are you feeling all right?"

"Yes, Georgie—why?"

"I thought you were looking—oh well, I'm glad you're all right." The letter was from Elizabeth Kinfowell.

. . . Surely it's time we saw each other, or we'll think we've quarrelled! I'm in my own flat all this week—Henry's in Shropshire with some friends of his and I'm getting things straight for him. Won't you come and have lunch—any day, only perhaps you'd ring beforehand just to make certain.

No, definitely not! She had long since determined that her next meeting with Elizabeth would be on a day of triumph, and this, however stoically she might face it, was one of defeat. But the need for sympathy is more compulsive than dog-eared resolutions. Next morning she telephoned immediately after breakfast. "Elizabeth dear, I'd love to come. Today?"

15

SHE LEFT early and went to the Club to get some work done so that she need not hurry back after lunch. Trevon was not there, no one was about except Slimey. "Slimey, do you happen to know where Mr Grist is?" Well, Mr Flock had said that Mr Grist had gone to see the doctor. "The doctor? Why, is there something wrong with him?" "Not that I know of. Mr Flock tell me Mr Grist go to see the doctor regular every week." At twelve she tidied up, put a note in Trevon's room to say that she would be in rather late and set out for Elephant Station. But here her programme was interrupted.

As she went downstairs she saw that someone was standing in the entrance, in the posture of molten apathy which the poor acquire from interminable waiting. Anxious to get away, she hardly looked to see who it was, but this was a figure one would recognize in a race crowd: Daise Empire's. She stopped and put on her smile.

"Can I help you?—I think we've met before."

Daise answered the smile faintly with her eyes. She said in her twitter of a voice, "It was Gian I was looking for. I thought he might be here."

He had not been to the Club for several days, Armorel told her. "But in any case he wouldn't be here at this time of day—he'll be at the Hibbage Lane depot."

"No, miss, he's finished there. Got his pay-off."

"What—dismissed?" But she did not at once take in the full significance of this. The girl was staring at her with those childlike eyes which she had found so disquieting in Bidault's Place, while the fearful mouth lolled like a half-deflated airship: Armorel's chief thought was of leaving that stare behind.

"Well, then," she said, "you're most likely to find him at his home. You know where he lives?"

"Yes—but he isn't there."

"Is it something very urgent?"

"Well—yes."

Armorel said sensibly: "Well, look here, the only thing you can do is to leave a message with me. You'd better come up to my room and I'll give you some paper. Then if by any chance he does come in I'll see that he gets it."

They went up to the library together. The message, which as far as Armorel could see had only a dozen words, took a fabulous time to write.

"Do you want to put it in an envelope?"

"Yes, please, miss."

When she had stuck up the envelope, and painfully written 'G. Ardre' on the front, Daise stood still. Her mouth began to gather, evidently there was something she wanted to say.

Armorel said: "Now I'm afraid I shall have to leave you and rush—I've got to keep an appointment. You'll find your way down all right, won't you?"

"Yes, miss, only—"

"Yes?"

"I was wondering if I could stay here till he come. I haven't got nowhere else to go. I'd do something—I'd scrub the place out—"

Armorel said patiently: "But it isn't at all certain that he'll come in at all. I promise I'll give him your note if he does come."

"But I can't go back without I seen him."

"Well, then, I think your best plan is to go and wait at his home—I'm sure Mrs Ardree would give you a cup of tea or something. I'm so sorry I've got to rush away."

In the tube she thought, Exactly! They whip me off and the first thing he does is to lose his job. For a moment she felt that she must go and try to find him before library opened; but no, people must learn.

Relaxed on Elizabeth's sofa, she felt that she had been right to accept the invitation. The last few days had been like climax in arrest, as when the purpose of a party is exhausted but no one comes to announce the carriages, and the sense of overhanging storm had followed her into sleep, drawing Trevon's face into her dreams, rousing her in the early hours to lie half-awake with her head grinding in indecision. This room with its tall windows looking on to Treasurer's Court gave her what sleep had failed to give. Listening to the soft gaiety of Elizabeth's voice, describing the changes which were to be made in the flat, she felt detached and secure. She knew that Elizabeth herself was the main source of her tranquillity, and a shadow of resentment lingered that this creature had so much to give while she herself seemed always to be cast as receiver. But for this one hour she would let pride rest and give herself up to a passive contentment.

"But why should you want to change it at all?" she asked, her eyes touring the masterly panelled ceiling, the Pergoles medallions, the Amboyna and mahogany chairs. "It looks perfect to me."

"I don't really want to," Elizabeth said easily, "only Henry's bringing the Nicholedds here—you know the people? rubber and that sort of thing—and he wants the place re-done for them."

"What, just for one visit?"

"Oh, they may be here some time. Hilda Nicholedd's delicate. She doesn't like to have children about—she lost her own boy, poor thing—so I've had to send Michael into the country. And she doesn't like anything 'old-fashioned', it depresses her."

Armorel said decisively: "People ought not to be like that."

"But they are. You see, she's been rich all her life, which means that she hasn't had any real life—that's sometimes the disadvantage of starting off rich—so she has to find her interests in other ways. Some specialist in Geneva has told her that she will only be really well so long as she has blue and orange all round her."

"And does she believe that?"

"Yes, for the time being. Later on she'll feel off-colour and she'll pay the man another ten thousand francs and he'll prescribe a dash of purple. No, I mustn't laugh at poor Hilda, she really does have a lot of trouble with her health. And her husband's a very busy man, and sometimes perhaps—?—rather difficult."

"Aren't all men difficult?"

"Well, perhaps they are. But in different ways. They're more complex than we are."

"Do you really believe that? I mean, really complex, not just full of whims and postures?"

Elizabeth said: "Well, yes, I do. But perhaps I oughtn't to generalize. Nearly all the men I've known really well have been soldiers, and I've known them best when they were homesick and frightened. Perhaps you get a wrong idea then—you see them too large. Still, I like to go on thinking that men are nearly all like those. You see, when they're miserable they're so terribly unselfish, so unbelievably kind."

The curried eggs were on the table. She went to close the hatch and stopped at the wheeling tray beside it to pour out sherry.

"I suppose Duffy's told you the news?" she said. "About Gordon coming back early next year. He's decided not to do another year in America."

Armorel said: "Oh, that's rather a pity, I should think."

Elizabeth brought the sherry over.

"Of course, he'll want you to meet him."

Armorel shook her head. "I'm afraid I shan't." She took her place at the table. "How awfully good this looks! You know, this is quite marvellous after having lunch in a tea-shop almost every day for weeks."

But Elizabeth was abstracted. She asked presently, as if their talk had not been broken:

"You definitely don't—you haven't any feeling for him any more?"

"No, I don't think so. I really haven't thought about it for quite a long time."

A silence came like a ground mist rising. Then Elizabeth said: "I only thought—now that that other interest of yours doesn't seem to be coming to much, that boy you wanted to help—"

"But, Elizabeth dear, who said it wasn't?"

"No one. Only, as you hadn't said anything, I thought—"

Armorel said slowly: "No, I haven't done with Gian. I've got him on to a building course at the Grover Institute—that's the sort of thing he's likely to be good at—but whether he'll stick to it I can't say. Anyhow, I'm not going to interfere for a bit—it's no use spoon-feeding a man all the time. I'm going to leave him quite alone for a week or two—perhaps a couple of months—and see how he gets on."

That was truthful by the time she had finished saying it. For here, with the Venetian tumblers and the repoussé silver, with this woman who dispassionately accepted all experience, she felt a coolness and assurance of her own coming first to her voice and then to her mind. When the babas au rhum arrived she was describing the life of Hollysian House, lightly and with touches of exaggeration, as she felt that Elizabeth herself would have described it. ". . . Yes, Slimey's a darling, quite terrified of women, the poor dear blushes whenever he sees me, and he sort-of puts a collar and tie on his voice before he speaks. . . ." Coffee came through the hatch and Elizabeth called: "Lucy dear, you ought to go now or you'll be late for your show. I'll clear these things away." They took the coffee into Elizabeth's own room. "It's cosier here," Elizabeth said. "This is the one that's going to be Hilda's room. I shall miss it, rather." Armorel said absently: "Yes, that does seem a shame."

She had meant to say nothing at all about Trevon; for with Trevon she was at that stage where thoughts are too delicate to withstand the gentlest daylight. But the little chair she sat in enclosed her with comfort, and Elizabeth, curled on a cushion and restfully stirring the coffee beside her, smiling with closed lips at Armorel's lovely arms and hands, was like a pool where only gentleness and grace would be reflected. She found herself saying:

"Yes, to begin with he had quite a wrong impression of me, I suppose he'd suffered so much from meddling females and naturally he thought I was just another of them. You see, he's really a very simple creature, all that bluster is just put on for self-protection. He *could* be awfully kind, but he's frightened to be. What he really wants is someone to look after him. But he's obviously had nothing to do with girls—I shouldn't wonder if he's still brooding over some frightful warning his housemaster gave him in a solemn end-of-term talk. So on the face of it he's rather a hopeless case. Only one can't help being interested in hopeless cases."

Elizabeth did not immediately answer. An answer did come to her tongue but she put that one back into hiding. She said, "You'll have another cup? Well, I'll just put these things out of the way," and took the tray back to the dining-room. Returning, she sat on the side of her bed. There she seemed taller, and for the first time today she looked as if she were in pain. She said abruptly, with that serious smile which must belong to some memory:

"Armorel dear, they're not! They're not simple. It's one of those catchwords which women pass on from one generation to another, it makes men suffer and then we suffer in our turn."

Surprised, Armorel protested: "But that wasn't exactly what I said. I only said—"

"It's nothing that you said," Elizabeth interrupted, "it's what you've been thinking all this time." She paused, she looked wretched now. "You see, I just happen to have known a lot of people, and I've been in love, really in love. You don't know people until you love them intensely, you've got to give everything before you get everything. I've known what men are like when all the barriers are down, I've known them when they're loving and when they're dying. That's why I'm frightened when I hear girls talking as if men were just children. It's become a complex with me, if you like Duffy's word, I hear that sort of talk going on all round me, and I think, 'That means more misery—for him and for her.'"

"You mean—?" Armorel asked very quietly.

It looked for a moment as if Elizabeth could not speak again, as if her lips had frozen and she had to thaw them with her tongue. "I mean," she said, "you've made one man most desperately unhappy because you thought he was simple and were shocked when you found that he wasn't—"

"—No, it wasn't that! No, I never thought he was simple! I only thought—"

"—and now because you're disappointed and restless you're trying to persuade another one to love you. You imagine you could be happy with him because you think he's fundamentally naïve. Well, yes, his feeling for you is probably simple enough, it's what any man's feeling is for a girl who's young and beautiful—supremely beautiful. But that isn't the same as love. You can't make happiness grow from anything as superficial as that."

"You mean," Armorel told her, looking away, "that you yourself haven't."

"Yes—if you like—that's what I mean."

"So you think I ought to go to Gordon and tell him I made a mistake—that I wasn't really angry with him for deceiving me, or that I shouldn't have been!"

"No, not that," Elizabeth said. "Only go to him. Or just let him come to you."

Armorel answered: "It would mean that."

Presently Elizabeth slipped down from the bed and sat on the arm of Armorel's chair.

"You know," she said soberly, "you are a very sweet and tolerant person, I don't think anyone else would be sweet-tempered enough to put up with me in the way you've done."

It seemed as if Armorel did not hear those words. She sat as still as if some fever held her, looking at the pattern of the carpet and faintly smiling. It came as a surprise when she spoke again, in a voice that seemed to come from a distance but was neither tremulous nor husky:

"I don't think that Trevon would marry anyone he didn't love. You see, I know him rather well. No, he wouldn't marry anyone unless he loved her."

Elizabeth said: "So he's asked you?"

"No. But I know he's going to. And even I can't always be wrong."

Elizabeth touched her shoulder. It was hardly a gesture, it could have been only an accidental movement. "And now," she said with sadness, "I've spoilt everything—everything between us. And I did so want not to spoil it."

"Why should you have spoilt it?" Armorel answered distantly. She had not moved her shoulder. "I think it's better when people know about each other. You see now—don't you?—that I'm quite grown-up in the way I understand things. I know where I'm going, and I never give in. I've always wanted you to understand that."

There was another silence, until Elizabeth said: "One moment—I think I heard someone at the door."

The entrance halls in those flats are small; the front doors are only a few feet away from the doors of the principal rooms. When Armorel heard a man saying "Can you give me five minutes?—I'm fearfully sorry—rather at my wits' end," she could not fail to recognize Trevon's voice. She just heard Elizabeth saying, "Armorel's here." After an interval they came into the room where she was sitting.

There was hardly any awkwardness: they were civilized, and civilization gives a drill for behaviour on which people can fall back. "I don't think I need introduce you!" Elizabeth said. Trevon said: "Hullo, Susie, we seem to have picked the same day." His smile, Armorel thought, was peculiar, as he stood enormously just inside the door, holding his appalling hat; had she not known that he never drank anything she would have thought he was slightly drunk.

"I got your note, thanks awfully," he said rather absently. "I was out visiting all morning."

"Slimey said you'd gone to the doctor."

That seemed to startle him. "Slimey's a know-all," he said curtly, and turned to Elizabeth. "You know, it's very agreeable to look at Susie in an appropriate setting. I'm so used to seeing her in that filthy Club, it makes me feel like an ogre holding the fair maiden in captivity." He threw his hat on the bed and sat down, knees wide apart, as if the chair had been reserved for him.

Armorel said: "Perhaps I ought to be getting back."

"But why?" Trevon objected. "There's nothing you can do in the Club at this time of day unless I'm there. You know, Mrs Kinfowell, Susie's got to think she runs that outfit."

"She was telling me only a moment ago," Elizabeth said, "how you've got the whole thing at your fingers' ends."

"I have," he said gravely. "After—what is it, four, five, six years?—I really have got these yahoos under control. I've stopped them smoking by pinching their cigarettes, I've abolished bullying by calling it 'leadership', I've stamped out bad language by telling them it's bloody undignified." He was standing up again, he began to move about as far as the small room and his large body allowed, flapping the sides of his jacket like a wet hen, relishing fiercely his own garrulity. "So Susie thinks I'm good! So do I! I think I'm magnificent. A very prince among club wardens, a virtuoso in club-wardenship."

"Tell me," Elizabeth said rather shortly, "did you really want to see me about something? Because if not it's a pity you've come and spoilt our nice party."

"It can wait," he said, lugubriously collecting his hat. "I didn't mean to interfere with a nice little women's chat. I return to my treadmill. Ladies, your most obedient!"

Armorel stopped him. "Trevon, listen! If you want to talk to Mrs Kinfowell I'll go away. I can clear the table and wash up, can't I, Elizabeth?"

"No, I'm going to do that. You stay where you are and keep Mr Grist amused till I get back."

"She can't," he said. "I see her every day. She no longer amuses me. Lead me to the scullery and show me your clouts."

With determined quietness, Armorel asked him: "Was it about me and Gian?"

That was a question which had to be answered more promptly than a man's wit allows. Smiling, Elizabeth said: "It was more probably about his health. Just because I was a nurse during the war he thinks—"

"When," asked Trevon stonily, "have I talked to you about my health?"

"I thought you told me, some time ago—"

"I didn't!" he said obstinately and with a note of childish temper. "I talk to my doctor about my health, and to no one else."

"Oh, I'm sorry, Trevon. I really didn't—"

Armorel said to Trevon: "So you come here quite a lot?"

"Two or three times so far," he said. "Is that a scandal?"

"No, only it's just—curious that you never told me."

She was looking at Elizabeth; who, where another woman might have turned away, looked back at her rather as a mother will look at her son when by some sentence or gesture he shows that his dependence on her is coming to its end; and who said slowly:

"You see, he was worried about you—you and Gian. He knew I was fond of you, and so he came to me. Armorel dear, I know it all sounds horribly furtive, when I put it just like that. But you see, we were both so terribly anxious not to hurt you, not to hurt any of your feelings."

Armorel said with control: "I don't quite see why neither of you could have come to me and explained."

Trevon said: "But I have, haven't I! I've explained it as far as you can explain about a creature like Ardree. Only it's perfectly hopeless, because you insist on thinking that I'm prejudiced against him, whereas I'm exactly the opposite. At least, I am now. I think he's a very unhappy man, and I'm fond of him. But I also think he's damned dangerous, and anyone who doesn't understand him had better keep miles away from him. I've tried and tried to persuade you of that."

"Yes," she said, "I know you've told me over and over again that I don't understand him. Only since I'm perfectly certain I do—"

"You can't! You can't understand a man like that unless you're a man yourself—and fundamentally a rotten one."

She said wearily: "Must you be cheap and theatrical!"

"Yes," he answered, "I must. I must do something to try and get some sense into you."

It was Elizabeth then who said, without raising her voice: "Trevon, in my house you're not to talk like that. Certainly not to Armorel."

"Oh, I'm to clear out then?"

"But surely you won't, without apologizing? No, not to me—you've only been ill-mannered to me. Bad manners don't hurt me any more."

"Elizabeth," he said, "I'm frightfully sorry. I'm always like this after I've seen that doctor. He gets on my nerves."

"Listen!" Her voice came like a line drawn against a ruler. "You've got to try and be sensible, both of you. Armorel, you know what I've been thinking. And so do you, Trevon. I think you're dangerous to each other and I think you'd better keep apart. If I were you, Armorel, I'd get some job and if possible go abroad. So long as this disappointment over Gian is on your mind you'd do much better to keep as far away from London as you can. I'm sorry if I sound like a schoolmistress, but I see no point in talking gently to people who are fogged with disorderly emotions. I've seen too much of that. Well, I'm going to get the washing-up done. You can both do just what you like—there are cigarettes in that box over there. Please go exactly when you want to—and I personally don't mind if you don't bother to come back."

But having left the room she returned immediately and stood regarding them both with the look men have in the earliest hours of bereavement. In a voice emptied of virtue, like elastic that has perished, she said: "I didn't quite mean that—the last thing I said." She went to Armorel, bent swiftly and kissed her hair; waited for just an instant, with her still, shocked eyes on Trevon's face, and then left them. Presently they heard the jingle of a tray being carried, and the kitchen door opening and shutting.

Clumsily (for he fitted an elegant room as poorly as he fitted his clothes, he was the wrong size and shape for life above stairs) Trevon moved towards Armorel's chair and sat on its arm. She, guided by intuition as precisely as an actress is directed, got up to replace the book she had taken and stayed on that side of the room, leaning against the bed. She said:

"I'm going to stay here and rest for a bit. I'll be back at the Club by about half-past four—that'll give me time to finish your letters before shop opens."

He seemed not to hear that. Assuming, as men do, that her thoughts should run the way of his own, he said rather quietly: "It does seem to me that Elizabeth—dearly as I love her—is sometimes more dogmatic than she should be. When I said the doctor had put me on edge she seemed to think I was spinning a yarn. As it happens, it was perfectly true."

She did not answer. There was a night-gown of Elizabeth's on the bed, she picked it up and studied the exquisite Venetian rose point at the collar.

"I go to him once a week," he continued. "This was a special visit, actually. I wanted him to tell me if I could leave off the weekly visits now. But I suppose all this doesn't interest you."

"You look very well."

"Yes, but unfortunately his answer was 'No'. Not for the time being, anyway. Later, perhaps—he couldn't be sure."

"Oh."

"Well, anyway, that was one of the things I wanted to talk to Elizabeth about. The other of course was the Ardree business. I wanted advice from someone who wasn't involved, and it had to be a woman, because I don't follow how women look at things. I thought I did once—but it was only the way they look at some things. Well, there you are. I was to apologize, wasn't I? Well, I'm not very good at that."

She said quickly: "I don't want you to. Of course, it hurt me, your coming here without letting me know. I thought—I thought you knew me well enough, I didn't think you'd need to hide things."

"Yes," he said, "looking at it that way, I can see it was treating you fairly badly." He moved to sit beside her on the bed, he hung the hat on the toe of his boot and there rotated it with a juggler's concentration. "I suppose I've always treated you badly. That's because I'm always frightened of myself. Not that that's an excuse."

"No," she said, "you've really been awfully kind to me. Letting me come in the first place, letting me make changes in a show that was going perfectly well already and didn't want any interference. And I know I've given you a lot of anxiety."

"Kind to you?" he repeated.

"Yes," she said, "tremendously kind."

She had not meant her voice to go flaccid and moist. The effort to keep it steady seemed to have defeated itself. Wearily, she leaned right back to let her head rest on the counterpane where the pillows were and put her arm across her eyes.

"How?" he asked.

"By being just what you are, by not treating me as a young lady." She went on presently: "That's why I've loved it so, being accepted, being just part of something. I know there were things we didn't agree about. But that hasn't really made any difference. Whatever you said, I knew you were never really hostile. I shouldn't have felt I belonged if you'd always been polite, I'd have felt I was in the way all the time. I couldn't be fond of a place where people treated me as a sort of Sacred Institution."

"Isn't that just how Flock does treat you?"

"Flock's a darling, but . . . you've all been very sweet to me. I've loved it all, I've been so terribly happy."

Waiting for him to answer, she lay perfectly still. With her eyes closed she could feel that he was watching her intently, that his face had come nearer to hers. But the weight of his body beside her knees did not move.

When a few empty moments had passed, he said: "I think it's about time I was getting back. Are you coming along?"

In the automatic lift, standing feet apart with his face to the wall, he said: "I think on the whole that Elizabeth was right . . . I suppose a taxi is indicated—have you by any chance got any money on you? I'm afraid I never seem to have any." While they were waiting on the pavement, he said: "What I mean is, I suppose we'd better get right away from each other. You see, I'm the sort of person that you—don't want to have too much to do with. At present, anyway. Well, give it a few months, a year perhaps—I may be a bit different then . . . There never is one of these bloody cabs when you want one." When he could no longer fail to see that she was weeping, he said: "Susie, I hate having upset you like this. I only wish to God I was the sort of person it was worth you or anyone else getting upset about."

When a taxi came he put her in with as much gentleness as he had at his command, and they travelled together as far as the turn into Knightsbridge. There, as they waited for the traffic to open, he said as naturally as was possible even for him: "Oh, damn, I've forgotten something. Look here, you go on, I'll come along in the tube." Without looking at her again he jumped out, just as the car was gathering speed, slammed the door behind him, recovered his balance, apologized angrily to a man he'd nearly knocked over, and walked off quickly the way they had come.

16

Back at the Club it took her less than ten minutes to get her own things together: a propelling pencil and a wooden paper-cutter rather crudely inscribed 'For A. Ceppinier, a Popular Dorm Monitor, Michaelmas 1918'; the small hanging mirror with the snapshot of her father stuck in the corner, her brush and comb and slippers. The whole lot could be squeezed into her slim attaché-case. She allowed herself to open the index box and glance over the neatly headed cards: it was some sort of memorial to leave. But she knew they would go back to the old sloppy methods before she had been gone a week.

An envelope lay upside down on her table: she remembered only when she had turned it over that this was the note Daise Empire had left for Gian. It was poorly stuck-up, and naturally, now that she was alone, she opened it. It said: 'Dear Jan He is bringing them in again you said to tell you Your loving Daise.' She stuck the flap down again and took the note to Flock, who was in the billiard room: "Sergeant Flock, if Ardree happens to come in this evening you might give him this. It was left by some friend of his. Don't forget." "You're not coming in again this evening?" he asked. She said: "No, not this evening. Not at all, in fact." She hurried down the stairs, anxious to be right away before Trevon came.

From the call-box at the end of Flanders Street she rang Duffy's flat but got no reply.

Her course now was erratic. She walked rapidly to the place where she most often got her bus and waited there for perhaps a minute. When no bus came she went on in the same direction and turned into Alderman's Field, where she rested for some time on one of the seats. Then, with the energy which increases in some when there is no load for it to take, she walked north again towards the Elephant, and in twenty minutes she arrived at Mrs Ardree's shop.

When she had waited for some time in the empty shop it was Simon Ardree who came; unshaven, very dirty, and looking as if he had just been wakened. Seeing a customer of this rather unusual kind he automatically wiped his sleeve across his face. "Yes?" he asked.

"I haven't come to buy anything," she said; her voice was deliberate, gentle, dignified. "I'm a friend of your son Gian's—we know each other at Hollysian House. He hasn't been there for some time and I just came to see if he was all right."

"All right?" Slowly digesting her words, he twisted his head on the long, peculiar neck which appeared to work like an adjustable reading-lamp, peering at one side of her face and then the other with bunched eyes as a milliner does. "You're from Damien Street?" he asked.

"No, no, I'm nothing to do with the police. I'm from Hollysian House—the boys' club, you know."

Before long he arrived at her meaning, and he asked: "Would you be Miss Spinnier? Ah, then I've heard tell about you."

"Yes, Gian and I are very good friends. He isn't in at present, I suppose?"

"Been in," he said closely. "Gone out again."

"You don't know—where?"

"I'd like it if I did."

As anyone could have seen, the main flow of his thoughts had been through another channel. The streams came together now. Without warning he raised the flap in the counter and came to the front of the shop.

"See now," he said, "what are you to do? A lad like that, all but a grown man, you can't thrash him, you can't lock him up, can you now? If he don't want to say what he's about, well, what's to make him? 'I'm not doing nothing what's wrong,' he says. 'Nothing what seems to me wrong,' he says. Same now as with this dwarf young woman who come round, he can't mean no harm with her, it wouldn't be natural, with a creature like that, not the way I look at it. We're none of us saints in heaven, as you might say—"

Armorel interrupted: "You're talking about Daise Empire? Has she been here today? Did she leave any message?"

"Nothing but what she wanted to see him. I had to tell him that —that's only keeping a promise, see. He come in not long after dinner, bit of a mess he looked to be in, looked as if he could do with a bite. 'There ain't no jobs, Dad,' he says, 'there ain't no jobs in the whole of London,' he says. (He got no contax, you see, the same as what I have. There's people that know me, no matter where you go.) 'Been a young woman in after you,' I says. 'Who?' he says, 'young lady from the Club?' he says. 'Well, she didn't say nothing about no club,' I says, 'young woman with a dial the size of Big Ben, kind of a freak,' I says. 'Well, I'm off,' he says, without never taking his cap off or a bite of some't to eat. 'Back sometime,' he says. Only then he come back— well, ten minutes, as it might be. 'That knife,' he says, 'the one you got from America, I know a bloke what'll give it a clean-up for you. You just let me have it,' he says. 'Now listen,' I says, 'you want to be careful with a thing like that,' I says, 'You get in a bit of scrapping with a lot of other lads,' I says, 'someone gets himself hurt, and then what?' I says. Well, what's the good? You can't talk to a lad like that, not far off a full-grown man, see. I ask him where he's going, 'Oh, nowhere,' he says, 'Back sometime,' he says. Well, what can I do?—I got the shop to mind, the missis being out and all, you see the way it is." He jerked his head into a fresh position and searched Armorel's face forlornly, as if he would see the answer to all his problems written there as soon as he could get it into focus. "I mean to say, with an English lad you know where you are. Not that I'd say a word again his mum, she been a good mum to him, you won't find a better nor truer woman than what she is no matter where you go, an I seen some places in my time. Spent most of my time sailoring, though the theatre business is my profession as you might say, just to put a word on it. I mind the time I first see Gian—in Genoa that was—well, you wouldn't have known but what he was pure Grindie."

There were two more customers waiting now, but it made no difference: he was obviously ready to go on all night. Armorel said briskly:

"One minute! These people are waiting to be served."

He dealt with them quickly enough. Sock suspenders? Well, he had some, but he wouldn't recommend them. The customer would do better to go to one of the drapery places in the main road . . . Threepennorth of peppermint diamonds? There she was—twopence, that would be, they weren't worth more, the stuff they sent you nowadays. But before the business was finished Armorel had smiled, murmured something about a call in Mickett Lane, and slipped away.

No faltering now, no self-questioning, no searching back through the feverish, haunted pathways she had traversed today.

The catch of the overloaded attaché-case had broken; once already the contents had fallen into the street, and since then she held it clinched between her arm and her party frock, where it fidgeted and rubbed. A shoulder-strap tore loose, letting her slip fall below the skirt; and as she walked at top speed, occasionally breaking into a run, one of the new shoes was sawing deeply into the back of her heel. They stared, the children sitting along the kerb, the women at their doors, as she hobbled and ran; a boy on the back of a lorry yelled "Late for Ascot!" but for the most part they watched her in tolerant, unsmiling silence. The breeze, up-ending her wide-brimmed hat, had dragged a shock of hair out of its place, and however often she crammed it back with her free hand it tumbled loose again across her damp forehead and her eye.

She stopped just once; that was at the entrance to Bidault's Place; stopped and fiddled with a safety-pin, trying to get the slip fixed up, recovering her breath. In five minutes or less her body would have cooled and then, perhaps, she would have considered this last throw coolly. That did not happen. She went on into the place, which absorbed her as an old, recurring dream does. It was six o'clock.

The men that she had seen there before, or others out of the same press, stood listlessly against the wall almost opposite Empire's house; men with grey, slack faces and dead stumps of cigarettes stuck to their lips. From them she had the impetus she needed. She knocked fiercely at Empire's door, and when Daise answered it went straight inside.

She asked rather breathlessly, rather peremptorily, "Is Gian here?"

Daise had withdrawn a pace along the passage, which was dark with the front door shut, and heavy with her scent. There she stood planted, looking about her like a trapped field-mouse, and her great vermilion mouth started to giggle.

"Is he, please?" Armorel demanded.

"No . . . No, he was here, he's gone away now."

And at this moment Armorel heard, from the back of the house, Gian's cough.

"I think you've made a mistake," she said. "Perhaps he's in the back yard?" and she tried to push past down the passage.

Daise immediately moved her small body to block the way. "He's ill," she snapped. "You can't see him. This is my dad's house, you've got no warrant nor nothing."

Armorel called loudly: "Gian! I want to see you!"

"Who's that?" a woman shouted from upstairs.

Daise suddenly moved aside. "All right!" she said, "you can see him if you want."

The shallow back room, lit from its lean-to roof, was hot and stale with the smells of cigarette-ash and rancid butter. The remains of a lawn-mower were spread all over a basket chair, there was a gas-cooker which prevented the door from fully opening and beside it a tin bath on a folding table, a plate rack festooned with socks and underclothes. Gian lay on a sofa smoking.

Armorel, standing just inside the door (there was barely room to go further), said: "Gian, your father's sent to ask you to come home.

He wants you as quickly as possible. He'd have come himself, but he had to look after the shop."

"I couldn't stop her coming in," Daise told him.

Gian did not move. "You tell him I'll be coming," he said.

Yes, he was ill. Ill or drunk, but she thought it was illness. He lay in the stillness of exhaustion, pallid and sweating. His eyes, wide open, were fastened on her face, but she could not be certain that he saw her: she had seen eyes rather like these in people trying to concentrate after standing all night in a train, and she had the feeling, which comes occasionally in the presence of the very sick, that she stood upon the far circumference of a circle in which he was the centre. With his body lying so still, as the effigies lie in the twilight of a cathedral transept, his individuality had grown.

Abruptly, but without roughness, Daise pushed Armorel aside and went to stand by his head. "You better do like she says, Jan. You make me scared, you being here."

He smiled then, looking up at her; took a mouthful of smoke and blew it out contentedly through his nose. "You won't be scared long," he said.

Daise said urgently: "I get on all right, I do really. You go on home, you leave me, I'll get on all right."

"Course you're all right!" he said with obstinacy. "Only I want to see your dad, that's all. Old pals, that's all. Should be here by now. What's the time?"

"It's gone six."

"Gone six?" He seemed to come awake, he turned and let his feet fall to the floor. "I want another fag," he said petulantly. "These your dad's, these here? Well, he can stand it. It's hot in here. No, don't you open that, I want it shut, see! Too many folk in here, that's what's wrong with it. That one over there, that one from Mr Grist's, you tell her to go, Daise, I don't want her round here."

"I'm not going," Armorel said quietly, "unless you come."

Daise, sitting beside him now, stroking his shoulder as one idly strokes a kitten's fur, said: "You better leave him, miss, he's all right with me."

The thump which sounded on the front door brought the three of them, the house itself, to silence. Gian was on his feet and they stood like actors in the wings. Perhaps five seconds had passed when Gian said in a small voice, "Well, aren't you going to let him in?"

Daise went out into the passage, shutting the door behind her. Gian pushed past Armorel to stand with his face close to the door. They heard Empire's voice saying: ". . . nine o'clock, see?" and immediately afterwards Daise's: ". . . wants to see you, she's been bad all day." Presently the room shook slightly from the fall of Empire's feet on the stairs.

Armorel found that she was sitting on the sofa. The pain in her heel where the shoe rubbed had become acute, but in the translucent lethargy which had absorbed her she could suffer it almost with the interest of a detached observer. From this tired stillness of the body her senses were drawing a peculiar sharpness. Her ears searched for noises within the house, but as men fighting will notice and remember the song of a blackbird she heard with great distinctness the contingent sounds of the world outside, a factory hooter which might be out towards Herne Hill, a tram going over the points at Mickett Cross. Her gaze came round to Gian's back, and having reached it, rested there. His body was trembling a little, as if he were a child put to stand in a corner and weeping with shame; she was nearer to pure pity for him now than she had ever been. Even when his hand, shaking, came round to the back of his trousers, felt its way into the pocket stretched by a shape she could not mistake, she experienced no fear of him except the fear that her body started of itself, slowing the response of her muscles, tightening painfully the mechanism of her throat.

He turned round very slowly, controlling his body as an acrobat does at the climax of his performance. He had on his face that smile which men will sometimes wear when their stomachs have been torn by shrapnel. With his fingers on the handle of the door he said softly, almost voicelessly, "You're going now, see! You do best keep clear away from this place. You better be sharp—I'm telling you."

She went towards him. Matching her voice to his she said: "Gian, look—you've got to be sensible. Listen! Everybody loses a job at one time or another. What I'm going to do is to help you find—"

He caught her by the arm. "Shup! You're going, see!" Using only his left hand, with its fingers gripping like a dog's teeth, he got her facing the door, while with his right hand he carefully opened it. He said in her ear: "Out through the yard, see. I don't want you nosing round any more, see!" His pinched voice was one quite new to her, less the voice of a man raging than of one choked with bitter, childish tears;

he was still holding her arm. "There'll be things happening if you don't keep off. You understand!"

He pushed her out into the passage and let her go. He would have shut the door immediately behind her, but she put back a foot to stop it. She turned and said very quietly: "I'm going to get the police. I'm sorry, Gian, but it's all I can do."

She went out into the yard as he had told her, and through a broken gate into the patch of waste ground beyond. There, in a moment's faintness, she stopped and leaned against a derelict wash-stand which was propped against the fence. Her ears went on straining for some sound from Empire, but all they caught was the sick, peevish voice of the woman she had heard before: "I won't have it, Charlie, I've told you, I won't have it . . . There are things I can do . . ." She hurried on to a gap between the houses which led her back to the road.

She went as fast as she could without actually running towards Mickett Lane, still clasping the attaché-case under her arm, oblivious now of the pain in her heel, of the broken shoulder-strap, the men staring. But when she had covered only a few yards she heard rapid steps behind and then the voice of Daise, panting, "Miss Spinyer! Miss Spinyer, will you come back, please, and speak to Gian!" Without turning she answered, "I'm going to get the police," and increased her pace, but Daise caught up and seized her by the arm, crying, "No, not the police! Please, miss, not the police!" and they went on side by side, with Daise repeating, "There's no call for any police, truly there ain't, he's just wrought up, he's out of work, that's all it is," until they were nearly opposite the upholsterer's shop. There a third figure came up behind them: it was that of Gian himself.

Some of the people looking idly from their windows in Mickett Lane had watched her on her way to Bidault's Place. They were now to witness a still more interesting spectacle. From the passage under Coronation Building the Bond Street-looking girl emerged again, walking with a combination of dignity and speed which appeared more curious because at every second pace one foot seemed to be giving way. She had the attaché-case in both arms now, rather as the inexpert carry a baby; her hat was down over one ear, the slip hung far below her dress; and her face, which some recounting the affair were to describe as terrified, others as merely angry, was glistening with the pin-heads of sweat which trickled from her temples down her cheeks and nose.

Close behind her and a little to one side, keeping position as an outsider would, a young workman whom some recognized by his yellow shirt was slouching along with his hands in his pockets, chin down on his furred chest, his dead eyes set forward as if on an aiming mark; while at his left side the misshapen girl who belonged to Empire, her vast mouth in ceaseless gesticulation, kept up to within a pace or two by working her tiny legs like a hedger's shears. This small procession, with its own escort of ribald children, moved steadily down the street and looked as if it would go straight through to the main road; but as it drew level with Begbie's Store an elderly woman, coming out of the shop with a dog on a piece of cord, ran up to the Bond Street girl calling, "There! You're the one who knows about Mr Jenkins!" and the girl, faltering, wheeled off into Amersham Row.

Heald, the owner of Begbie's Store, with a villager's nose for local interest, came out on the pavement in time to see the girl stop by the back door of old Mrs Pewell's house, which had been empty and under repair. Even at a distance of thirty to forty yards he could tell that she was rattled. He stood gazing with mild curiosity while she tried the handle, shoving against the door with her shoulder, and when it would not give he saw her turn to face her pursuers. At this point, after calling to his wife to mind the shop, he wiped his hands on his apron and crossed the street for a better view.

The scene, when he approached, rewarded him rather tamely. There was no movement at all. The girl, standing with her back against the door, was faintly smiling in the way that sick people smile when they want to spare their friends. With Mrs Inch and a trio of inquisitive children the young workman and his companion made a small crescent before her, the man a little closer than the others with his eyes intent upon her body in a way Heald didn't care for, his right hand working as if the fingers were frozen and he was trying to thaw them. Only Mrs Inch was talking, as an old trouper goes on with her patter when the rest of the company have forgotten their parts: holding precariously to her place on the kerb, while her dog strained towards the livelier smells of Mickett Lane, she delivered a crackling fire of petulance, calling Heaven and Daise Empire to witness that this woman of the streets had stolen her lover in the early months of 1912.

In this situation Heald, a Lambeth man by birth and unbroken residence, presently took a hand. A taxi-cab was coming empty down the lane; with a single 'Oy!' he stopped it, opened the nearside door, and signalled to Armorel with his left eyebrow and his thumb. She accepted that invitation as if a servant had summoned her own carriage; walked to the taxi with dignity, got inside, and gave one startled, grateful smile to Heald, who, with a casual nod, slammed the door. But her difficulties were not yet over. Mrs Inch, grey and vociferous with rage, was standing close to the cab, attached to it by three feet of cord; the cord was jammed in the door and at the other end of it the dog was standing with its paws on Armorel's lap. While this embroilment was being disentangled Armorel sat back with her eyes shut. The driver, sliding the partition window, asked "Where to, miss?" and she told him "Damien Street—the police station." She did not open her eyes till the cab was under way; and then she saw that Gian, having swiftly entered by the other door, was sitting beside her.

She leant forward to close the partition window and then she said, "Gian, you'd better give me that knife." "What knife?" he asked automatically, and she answered, "You know." Presently he took out the cheap 'Mexican' knife, of a kind which is sold in any American port to tourists, and fiddled with it dreamily. "Can I have that, please?" Armorel asked. He answered "No" and stuck it into the waist of his trousers. "Very well," she said, "the police will find it."

Gian hunted about the inside of the taxi with his eyes, as cats will explore a strange room: now that his body was still again he had fallen back into remoteness, he looked like one who has taken a beating in the ring. He did release a smile, in that new, strange way of his, as he repeated the word "Police!" but Armorel, closely watching him, could not tell what kind of thought had prompted it.

He said a little while later, quite quietly as if to himself: "You do know when to stick yourself in, don't you!"

She answered with simplicity: "I heard about you losing your job. I knew you'd be after Empire again."

That seemed to set his thoughts on a new course. "Empire?" He sat screwing his fingers in turn, as men do who must struggle to keep awake, his knees were drumming together in loose rhythm. "You don't know nothing about a bloke like that."

"Perhaps I don't. Only I know that a bloke like you has got to keep away from him."

"You don't know nothing," he repeated. Then, "You got to do something. You can't let a bloke like that do just what he wants." His eyes fell shut for a moment, his mouth was working like a stammerer's. "No good talkin'!" he said rather wearily. "They all go talkin' and a bloke like that do what he wants. They get a bloke what do no manner of harm and in he go into choke. An that Charlie Empire, they don't do nought on him, he just go on the way he likes, no way to stop him. I reckon *I* know a way. Don't make no difference to me, choke or nothin' else. They feed you in choke, no matter what. You don't get nothin' right but what you pay for it, see."

"I don't understand," she said.

The taxi-driver, turning round, asked sourly, "'Ere, was you keeping this cab for somewhere to live? Damien Street police station, I thought you said. Maybe this is the Crystal Palace—my mistake if it is."

Armorel said: "Will you drive on, please!"

"Where to? Folkstone Pier?"

"No . . . Contessa Street. Number 14, Contessa Street."

Gian, squeezed into his corner to leave a foot of empty seat between him and her, stared rustically at the upper windows of Beak Street, the tailors' dummies, the Brasso plates, the letters of *Shaving and Chiropody* in levitation upon dingy windows, passing him as strangely as the common sights of a foreign town. Armorel was saying:

"You see, I can't help you if you won't tell me anything, if you only run away. If you found the course too difficult you could have brought the books to me, I could have explained a lot of it. Why didn't you tell me about losing your job? I'd have gone and seen your employers, or I'd have helped you look for something else. Don't you see that's what I want to do!"

He did not answer at all, he seemed to have retreated into some valley of his own. The cab slowed up and she saw they were in Contessa Street already. The dirty shop front with its jumble of transparencies slid up and stopped beside the window; a notice hung askew in the door said 'Closed'. With his gear in neutral the driver sat still, an essay on human perversity written on the back of his head and shoulders. Neither of his passengers moved.

"Gian," she said rather rapidly. "I know you loathe the sight of me. Only you know I have tried to do something for you—I did try to get you out of prison, I tried to get you a decent chance. There's only one thing I want you to do for me." Something was wrong with her breathing, so that her words came rather like people crowding out of a cinema. "I want you to promise me you won't go anywhere near Empire again. I've got to ask you that—otherwise it means I've got to tell the police what you were doing this evening—the knife and everything. You see, I'm not going to let you make yourself a criminal. I can't do that. I've told everyone you weren't like that. I can't let it happen, it would mean I'd lost everything. Gian, you will promise me that? You will, please?"

"What?" he said as one just waking; and then, surprisingly: "No, I won't promise nothing. Not to you or no one else."

"Go on to Maples?" the driver inquired. "Fit you out with beds and things there—make the old bus a real comfy home for you."

Gian stood up and tried to work the unfamiliar door-handle. She stretched and held his arm. "I'm not going to leave you alone till you promise. I'm coming in to see your father—"

"You're not," he answered. "You leave me alone!"

"Driver!" she said briskly, "will you go on, please. Back to Damien Street. No—to Belsize Park—Paisley Gardens."

The driver took his foot off the clutch as if it had stung him. "Crike or blee dinmitey!" he said.

He looked in his mirror once or twice, when he had turned into the Waterloo Road. By Belsize Park the clock would have put up fifteen bob, or something near, but the girl could stand that, with the silk affair she was wearing and a brooch the size of a duck's egg. He was hungry. The day was aging, the lights came on as he drove over the bridge. Winter coming, he thought, smelling for an instant the river air. Was that a knife the chap had been showing the skirt? He didn't want that sort of thing, not hanging about all day at the Bailey and nothing to show for it. He jerked the car out of a sluggish stream and pulled it across a lorry's bows from Aldwych into Drury Lane.

She said: "I'm going to get you something to eat. I've got a friend at Belsize Park, we can be comfortable there."

"I'm not taking it," he answered. "I'm not taking nothing only what I buy myself."

"Well, you can pay for it if you like."

"I can't," he said.

"When did you last have something to eat?"

"That don't matter."

The driver's odyssey ended in Seymour Street. He was moving behind a bus, the girl called to him to stop and simultaneously he realized that the man was getting out. A fool, he thought, to try it at that speed; and sure enough the chap had landed on his bottom in the middle of the road, where another taxi only just avoided him. The man got up and went to the farther pavement limping; it looked as if he had pulled a muscle in his leg; the girl, having shoved a ten-shilling note through the partition, jumped out and went after him. 'Put it the other way round,' the driver thought, turning off into Barnby Street, 'and it might make sense to me.'

Aldenham Street, almost empty, was a darkening groove of quietness through the muted uproar from the railways; it magnified the noise of their feet as they went like yawls racing in a headwind towards the gas-holders and the smoke of the Great Northern yards. Without the strained ankle Gian would have got away: he had six yards' start, and he knew that Susie could not move fast in her stupid, fashionable shoes. He was, in fact, still a yard or two ahead when he crossed the tramlines in Pancras Road. There she drew level and they limped on side by side as in the old days; when he turned into Jubilee Yard she followed, and they continued slowly, erratically, towards the canal.

He stopped in the shadow of the trucks by Newland's Wharf and turned to face her. He had his hands stuck under the tabs of his braces, in the draining daylight she saw his eyes like bits of glass in his grey face.

"Now!" he said. "Are you going to let me alone?"

She said inconsequently, "I've got to rest, you must let me rest!" There was a heap of stuff beside the truck, deals with sacks laid over them, she went and sat there. Gian started to limp away.

So long as she was moving her nerves had been under control. Now she knew that she was more tired than she had ever been before, that the pain in her heel was intense, that she had been without food for seven or eight hours; and this knowledge, coming suddenly through body rather than mind, carried her defences by surprise. She put her forehead down on her hands and cried without restraint.

It felt as if the rush of tears flowed warmly over her misery as music does; as music turns defeat into a kind of majesty, weeping turned hers. When she looked up again her tiredness and her tears brought all the scene into a gentle harmony. Far over, Highgate was smudged on a sky which sunset had left still faintly green; here, beyond the canal, arc lamps dropped yellow pools on the grey confusion of the Midland yards, the trellised gantries showed like blackened lace against the red-shot plumes which locomotives bore into the wilderness of Camden Town. In this beauty of shadow and smoke all her sensations were absorbed. The near sounds sharpened by evening, harsh voices of men at work on the farther bank, a ceaseless rattle of couplings, were overcast by the soft, conglomerate tide of distant sound flowing in from Euston and York Road: the stink of locked water, of tannage and yeast, a throbbing pain in her heel, the feel of drying sweat and the rough boards cutting into her thighs, by these realities of wretchedness she was woven in the scene's reality, enfranchised to its mysterious splendour. Her thoughts falling into an easy stride, she supposed that Gian had gone: by now he would have limped as far as Pancras Road and perhaps be getting on a tram. A movement behind startled her, and she heard his voice again.

He was asking, "What's up, Miss Susie? What are you crying for?"

There was no simple answer to give; the one she used came without premeditation:

"My arm, it's hurting."

He came close to her and studied her bare arm: the sparse light from a high lamp above the loading sheds just showed the marks where his fingers had gripped it in Bidault's Place. This had an extraordinary effect: he started to tremble violently, so that Armorel felt the vibration through the boards on which his foot was resting. He said shakily: "I didn't mean to do that, honest I didn't. I never meant to hurt y'. I just wanted you out of it, I didn't want you mixed up with me an Charlie. I didn't meant to hurt y'—Bible oath!"

Instinctively she took hold of his wrists and gently pulled him so that he had to sit down beside her. She said, holding his hand with both of hers, stroking his bony fingers with her thumbs, "You didn't hurt me. I know you couldn't ever mean to hurt me, we've been friends too much for that."

In daylight their attitude would have been ludicrous: she in the damp and creased organdie dress, he sitting forward as shy young men are supposed to have sat in Victorian drawing-rooms, pulling at a dead cigarette, letting her keep his hand as if he had disowned it. Clumsily stacked, the boards they sat on were ready to topple over: a frivolous breeze, loaded with all the foul smells of the wharf, had chased up a dirty sheet of newspaper and wrapped it round their legs.

With his free hand he had started to fiddle about his waist, the knife came out and he held it on his knee as if he were fascinated by the way its blade caught the light. "There you are!" he said suddenly, and he put the knife on her lap. She gave it back. "I don't want it. I know it's all right with you."

Presently he said: "I'll get you back. Back to where you live. There'll be one of them taxis, I'll get you on one of them."

"Not yet," she whispered. "I must rest for a bit. My shoe hurts when I walk."

"Carry y' if y' like."

"No, I can walk if you'll give me an arm."

So they walked for a few yards, she still holding his hand and with her other arm supported by his. It was he who stopped.

"Can't go like this!" he said.

"Oh, your leg—I forgot. Gian, I'm so sorry!"

"Leg's all right!" he said; and then, his governed voice smoking with excitement: "Listen here! I'm not one of them that mucks about with women, that's not my kind of biz, see! I'll get a girl sometime—or maybe I won't—a girl what know my kind of life, and then I'll have it fixed, church and everything, and then it won't do her no harm." He stopped, and she could not help him; she could only murmur, "I hope you will." "You don't know how it is," he said with something near to anger. "You're pretty, see, you're fumin' pretty. A bloke see a face like yourn an he want to do somethink to it, he can't help it no way."

She turned quickly and moved one hand across to hold his other arm. "Gian, you needn't be frightened!" Her voice was steady but very small, the words only reached him because her face was so close to his. "There's nothing that makes us really different. You won't find anyone to care for you better than I can. I don't want any life except looking after you."

Then he carried her back to the pile of deals, kissing her cheeks and forehead with a surprising gentleness; and there, holding her carefully so that her head should not touch the dirty sacks as she lay back in his arms, he put his tearful eyes against the tears on her cheek, his trembling mouth on hers, drinking its warmth and softness as with a desert thirst.

It was towards midnight, and Duffy was reading Havelock Ellis in bed, when the door-bell rang in her flat. Supposing vaguely that it was Irene, Margaret Wellard, Pamela or Audrey she called, "Come in, darling—the door's on the latch." There were voices in the sitting-room and then Armorel came into the bedroom, still blinking from the force of the electric light, and shut the door behind her: an Armorel whom even Duffy had never seen, dishevelled and dirty in such a frock and hat as one kept for garden parties in deaneries, exhausted, frightened, triumphant; making the too slow, too careful gestures of beginners in the dramatic schools; wearing the remote, fey smile of those rescued from the sea.

"Duffy," Armorel said, standing with her back to the door and holding the handle, "Duffy darling, I just wondered if you could give us something to eat, we've had nothing for ever so long—"

"—But, darling, of course—"

"—I know it's fearfully late—"

"—Darling, it isn't! It isn't twelve yet, it's never been so early—"

Armorel laughed a little, still holding the door; it was the laugh of the desperately tired.

"Listen, Duffy, I've brought a man as well. I know it's awful of me—"

"—Awful? Rellie, how silly you are, I *love* men—"

"—No, but, Duffy, listen! It's Gian. I'm going to marry him."

Duffy went to the corner where a curtain made a hanging-cupboard and rummaged for her dressing-gown. With her back to Armorel she put it on. She turned, smiling, and said simply, "That's lovely, darling, I hope you'll be terribly happy!" and kissed her. Armorel opened the door and Duffy went ahead of her into the sitting-room, saying over her shoulder, "Will you be a sweet and get the milk—in the bathroom—you know where I keep the things that go bad—in the basin under the telephone."

Gian stood near the wall in the darkest part of the room, with Armorel's attaché-case under one arm and a cheap American knife in the other hand: distress and terror sculptured in salt. Duffy went straight to him, and in an uprush of her kindness kissed his cheek. She said: "It's so sweet of you! Coming here—and marrying Rellie and everything. You'll love her terribly, she's so awfully sweet." He did not try to answer, or even to smile; but when she had coaxed him into a chair he mumbled something in which she caught the words 'best I can'. He sat bolt upright, while they were rattling about him with cups and kettles, and fiddled with the knife, pressing the blade into his palm, staring at his dilapidated boots. He smiled just once and the smile, instantly passing, left his mouth in the shape of stoic resolution: it was such a face as you would commonly see, in the earlier war, on the leave platforms at Victoria. When they gave him his coffee he sipped it cautiously, and ate very slowly the bread and cheese which he had cut into tiny pieces. His eyes, beginning to move furtively about the room, rested on the golliwog perched astride the volumes of Taussig, on Lemminard's brash cartoons. He seemed to listen alertly to the distinctive sounds which came through the open window with the breath of exhausted summer: footsteps on the pavement, a rustle from the plane trees, the last tram grinding towards Haverstock Hill.

PART TWO

17

'Somewhere among all these documents one must discover truth and reality.' So Raymond thought, some twenty years afterwards, as he was industriously sorting them.

A suitcase, three feet long, two feet wide and nine inches deep, stuffed tight with papers and photographs: to say nothing of three or four exercise-books filled with shorthand records of conversations: here, surely, would be material enough to represent with fidelity some eighteen years in the lives of a few people. But in this bundle of letters there is one you wrote yourself; the colour of the ink already gives it a certain historic air, although it is dated 1933—only six years ago; and does it recall to actuality the smallest impression of the events about which you were writing? The snapshots, records made by a faultless mechanical process with no intrusion of an artist's eyes, seem to correspond less closely with what memory has retained than the boldest caricature. A child's painting-book, with the inscription 'Tonie from her Dad' has got into the collection, among the lawyers' letters and the rent receipts. That will bring to anyone but the mentally moribund a panorama of his own live memories; but only to Tonie herself, and to her very faintly, a portrait of her father's face as he stands by the sink and whistles awkwardly, hardly daring to look, while her fat, small fingers tear at the envelope's flap.

Raymond possessed to the verge of lunacy a middle-class reluctance to destroy anything which could be remotely described as having 'family interest'. He was one much given to puerile hobbies. Having failed as a doctor he had taken to writing books (as Gertrude rather unkindly said,

"Raymond is a man who needs variety; at the age of thirty-five he felt he wanted a change of failure") and some residue of nervous impulse in the man's make-up had to be absorbed in collecting things—second-rate paintings, tram-tickets, anything that came along—and tying them into packages with labels. He applied this mania to his own correspondence; and if anyone asked him for the date of Cousin Edith's baptism (such a request as would reach him once, perhaps, in a dozen years) he would say immediately: "Well, yes, now I come to think of it, I believe I have got the baptismal certificate—I picked it up with a lot of other stuff when I was going through Lawrence Cepinnier's papers," and he would tear away to some dreadful glory-hole and be back in ten minutes, shrouded with cobwebs, triumphantly waving the certificate itself. Or he would murmur, anxiously combing his moustache with a middle finger: "Now, there must be some reference in one of Gertrude's letters to her mother. Or, wait!—Lawrence would have given some sort of donation at the time, or at least a tip to the verger. I know I've got some old account books of Lawrence's . . ." It was a pleasure, then, for this harmless creature when Michael Kinfowell, during his second Long Vacation from Oriel, went out to Finchley to visit him. He had liked Michael as a child, when, for reasons beyond casual benevolence, he had visited him at his preparatory school and taken him to lunch at Cartacre's; he had watched the boy's development with something like a botanist's interest; and now that the thinness of Michael's face had assumed a patrician shape, the perplexity of the brows changed to a hesitant intelligence, the extreme shyness to a sensitivity of manners, he was more than flattered that the youth should find him of any interest or value. "Of course, my dear fellow, rout about as much as you like! Or take the stuff away, anything that interests you—only I should be grateful if you'd keep things in the proper bundles. Now look, most of Tonie's mother's letters are in this one with the blue tape . . ."

It was Michael who had come across the painting-book, on a lonely visit to Weald Street. The tenants of 16a, full of kindness, had let him walk about the house; in the tiny attic room which had once been Tonie's bedroom he had found the book sticking out from behind an old packing-case, and they had gladly allowed him to take it away. He was a young man with the sentimental kind of curiosity which is sometimes found in students of history: he liked browsing among old letters, and he liked to see the places where things had happened, his father's school at Bedford, Balkan villages which his parents had known, the hospital courtyard which his mother had so often described in telling him of his early illness. Perhaps he suffered a little from a malady of his time; for the years of his growing had been those when a boy with eyes in his mind could look forward only into darkness and would often seek refuge, as the old do, in retrospection. With a certain melancholy (which you saw in features increasingly like his mother's) he went bicycling in a part of Sussex where with his mother and stepfather he had once spent a holiday full of small delights and of lingering contentment. On a winter morning he idled in Paddington Station, hoping to recover in the tangle of movement and odour, in the raw and thunderous air, the ecstasy of his first return from school. That hope was ill-founded: the chords were all there but the tune did not sound the same. And he was no more successful when he tried, visiting the scenes of remoter memories, to find in them the cause of shapeless fears and anxieties which had troubled him in earliest childhood. The tessellated hall where a man in uniform had said, "Mr Kinfowell is waiting in the car outside, Master Michael"; the long avenue with the wellingtonias at Easterhatch: he recognized these places, when chance and fancy combined to lead him there, as if they had first come into his mind through reading rather than through sight and touch. He said in a letter: "No, my dear, I am not so stupid as to think that we can retrace our steps. I do not really expect to feel again the hideous terrors of my first term at school by smelling chalk and ink and hearing the clanging of 'Old Joe's Gong'. Neither do I suppose that if I saw my mother coming to me across a newly-mown lawn, wearing the curious hat and the low-waisted dress of the earlier 'twenties, I should be overcome by a tide of mysterious sorrow and fall sobbing into her arms. Just as I know that these sensations were real I know that they are lost, like the bouquet of those wines which will not travel. But with the world as it is at present we have to face the fact that our time may be a short one. Things of which there is little are precious. I am greedy, I want to take everything that has come to me and wrap it securely in a watertight parcel, I don't want to lose one jot of past experience which can any way be got at, mine or yours..."

So in that characteristically impulsive visit which he paid to Raymond it was the past they talked of. They understood it differently: to Raymond, as far as anyone could tell, the past was a list of dates, of births, deaths and marriages; to Michael, a fabric of sensations, here broken, here worn, here so thickly covered with grease and dust that the pattern could not be seen. Yet for Raymond there was pleasure enough in showing off the well-trimmed garden of his recollections, with its paths turning and intersecting, even to a visitor who kept stopping to smell the flowers. A generation apart, the two men found that their kinds of reserve were complementary. They liked each other very well.

"Of course all this district has changed completely in the last few years," Raymond said sadly. "Down that way we used to get into open country almost at once, then over the playing-fields towards Mill Hill. We used to picnic over there—you felt you were miles out in the country. However, I mustn't bore you." That was a phrase he put in automatically after every sentence or two, as nervous tennis players say 'Sorry' at the end of every rally. He pushed up his horn-rimmed spectacles and looked curiously at Michael's forehead, as if he hoped to see a name-tab there. "I sometimes think of moving, but I hate the idea of watching my desk being taken to bits and flung about by the removal men. They'd be bound to lose something. And it would feel like running away—after all, I was here before all these damned arterial roads and things, I don't see why *I've* got to clear out . . . Now, look here, you said you'd like to see the church where Tonie's mother was married. You'd like to walk?—it's no distance—one wastes petrol horribly on short runs. You may find it a trifle depressing—one feels that the builders wanted the Deity to have a place for spending the week-end more or less incognito."

"I suppose it feels to you as if the wedding happened yesterday?" Michael said as they went up the hill.

"No, I wouldn't say that. I'm not old enough to think of eighteen years as nothing at all. No, I really remember very little about it, except that it was hell. I mean, all weddings are hell, don't you think? You find women powdering themselves in your study and looking at your books. Oh, yes," Raymond said (they were opposite the unlovely church now), "I do remember one thing, I remember a photographer falling over, just where we're standing now. Forgot he was just in front of the kerb. Smashed his camera and hurt himself—fellow from the Press. I did enjoy that just a bit."

With that small stimulus the rusty wheels of his mind began to turn.

"Yes, she went through it very well. Of course you'd expect that —if anyone faints in the vestry these days it's the man who's giving the girl away. Hideous dress. She wanted to wear powder-blue, but then she was afraid the bridegroom would think that wasn't absolutely correct. I never knew a girl who bothered so much about what the bridegroom might think."

Michael said: "I suppose at that age she looked very much as Tonie does now, except for being fair?"

"Well, I never know what people look like. She was always supposed to be the image of her great-grandmother. Of course, so is Tonie supposed to be. And of course you can see it—even I can see it."

He leant back with his buttocks on the handle of his umbrella, winded by such a burst of cerebration. He was in the middle of the road and a laundry-van, hooting petulantly, had to graze the kerb to get past him; he stared after it, stroking the rather long grey hair above his ear, with the distant, disapproving glance which sometimes caused old maids to mistake him for a man of intellect. Michael waited politely. The sun had come out again, up here the quick North London air stirring the captive trees gave a certain pleasantness to the gauche suburban street.

"You know, I've often pictured it," Michael said, "from my mother's description. It's interesting to see how far one's picture matches the reality." He smiled, and this was exactly his father's smile, which charmed without intention, the phosphorescence of rippling thoughts. "It's a curious period to contemplate, don't you think, the time when you were alive and knew nothing about it."

"Yes, I should think so."

Only Raymond's ears were listening: his mind would not slide over to a new subject as quickly as that, it was working now like a terrier at a hole where a rabbit has disappeared. "The eyes were wrong," he said abruptly. "I looked at her in the vestry—they weren't Dorothea Truggett's eyes at all, people said they were, but they weren't. The mouth was Dorothea's. Well, at least, that's how I saw it then." He got out a cigarette and put it fussily into a holder. "She didn't want to be married in a church at all, the one thing she had from her mother was a perfect abhorrence of all that sort of thing. Well, I mustn't bore you. But there again, the important thing was to make her husband feel he was getting a proper show, that's how it looked to her. She wasn't going to have any hole-and-corner business. She kept on saying that—pages and pages of instructions she sent me. And, oh my God, that man from the caterer's, he treated me like a sort of deckhand. Well, I suppose it went off all right—people said it did, only of course people always say that. Absolute hell, I thought it was."

Michael would have liked to go inside the church, but Raymond evidently did not want to: swinging his umbrella with the air of a Loamshire squire on a stroll through his estate, the senile pussy-cat had started walking back towards Regents Park Road.

"Trying to remember the name," he said, "Uncle Percy or Uncle Albert, some name like that—some relation of the bridegroom he must have been. Of course really it's quite a long time ago, all sorts of things have happened since then, the General Strike—that was 'twenty-six, of course, quite put the wind up me—and then this German nonsense starting all over again. Yes, Percy, I think it was. Wanted me to turn my garden into a sort of tea place, he said I could make a pile of money that way. He kept showing me how I could knock out a new passage through the drawing-room. I do wish people would recognize a snob when they see one, it makes it all so embarrassing. I must look up the name—I expect I had to send him some money at one time or another. Percy or Albert, I'm not quite sure which."

Of course, Raymond was thinking, there were trams then, not these damned trolley-buses. The unwieldy trams had possessed some kind of absurd, archaic dignity, he thought, forgetting how bitterly he had abused them when they came. The weather, he fancied, had been much as it was now, perhaps a little colder, he couldn't remember, he would have to turn up his weather diary for 1920. Somehow umbrellas had come into it; somewhere—at the church? at the house?—he had sheltered Armorel with his own umbrella, and she had said with her touching smile, "Cousin Raymond, you are so terribly sweet!" But why umbrellas at all? Surely the reception had been mostly in the garden. What was it that fellow had said about the weather, that fellow who had married Christine Cepinnier—Liske, Everard Liske—what was it he'd said? He was odd, that fellow, you could never quite understand what he said, or rather why he had said it: taken at its face value it never seemed to have been worth saying. Well, there had certainly been umbrellas up, so there must have been some rain. Yes, now he came to think of it, rooting about the corners of his dim and dusty little mind, he remembered there being some rain.

Yes, there had been rain, and it did not surprise James Ardree at all. "I said to my old lady," he told the porter at Finchley Station, "—she couldn't come, seeing there's the kids and the business and everything—I said to her before I left home, 'You mark what I say,' I said, 'there'll be rain. Always rains at weddings,' I said. Now, see here, how far to this St Luke's Church? If it's got to be a cab, I'll *take* a cab. It comes just the same to me—I can *pay* for a cab. Only there's no sense in laying out brass if the church is half a mile up street, is there now! Brass is brass, whether you've got it or whether you've not."

The lady and gentleman over there, the porter said, were going to St Luke's as well: it was a mile or so, and they were waiting for a cab.

If Everard was already miserable, if he loathed the sad, suburban station and the rain dripping on him from the edge of its roof, if he thought it was madness to take his wife in her present state on such an expedition as this, no word or glance betrayed it. "Rellie is going to marry a policeman-basher," Christine had informed him over the toast-rack. "So original. So possibilitous." "Dear me!" Everard had said, making a note to get Mappin and Webb's catalogue. And when she showed him a few days later the dress she had bought "for Arthur Augustus and me to wear at the wedding" he had only remarked, with the faintly vibrating voice of one who hears that he is now to be drawn and quartered as well as hanged: "You really think, dear, that Dr Heugh will approve of this?"

"But, sweetie, what does poor Heughie know about girls' frocks!"

So here he stood in his brown week-end suit, dignified, patient, gravely affable, holding his faultless umbrella over Christine and carrying in his other hand the bag with all the trifles Christine had supposed an expectant mother might need in Finchley, a brush and comb and various medicines, a novel and a thermos, a Bradshaw and a pair of goloshes. He wore his kid gloves, not the wash-leather ones, which might have been too showy, and to make sure of hurting no one's feelings he had substituted a simple brown for his Old Carthusian tie. Everard Liske differed from other men by being perfect. He never raised his voice, he had never said anything to wound, nothing in his manner or dress was even faintly ostentatious, nothing stuck out. He was said to have married Christine because she had the same unobtrusiveness as his socks and his Bayswater flat: at the time, no element in Christine's composition had stuck out either, and her voice, if a little high in pitch, was never loud.

"Not a taxi on the horizon," Christine said good-naturedly. "So soothing. So rural."

But a horse-cab presently arrived, and with gentle efficiency Everard put her in and took his place beside her. A porter appeared at the other window.

"Can you take another gentleman—going the same way? Save you half the fare."

The long, brick-and-tile face of James Ardree, mounted between a bowler hat and a vast chrysanthemum, and now rising like an operatic sun above the porter's shoulder, took the question outside the field of debate. "A little one like me," James said, opening the door and folding and then unfolding his long, unwieldy, funereal body, "you won't hardly notice. Now was that the lady's toe, or yours, mister?" He lowered himself carefully into the narrow space which the couple had left between them and offered Everard a cigar.

"Perhaps we'd be more comfortable," Everard suggested, "if one of us sat the other side."

"Aa, I'm right enough where I am now. As snug as a bug in a rug." He looked from one to the other with a wealth of friendship. "Aa, she's ploomp, I will say. But I like a lass to be ploomp. The name's Mr Ardree. Right pleased to know you."

"Liske. My wife. Atrocious weather," Everard said.

Christine said, "So kind!"

The cab with its pleasantly bouncing gait, its smell of forgotten comforts, went creaking down the main road.

"They tell me," James said, sitting forward with one large, comradely hand on Everard's knee, the other on Christine's, "that my brother Simon's boy has got himself a juicy piece—a real slice of undercut. Though whether there's any brass in contract Simon don't seem to know. Well, Simon, you see, he's got no head for business, never did have nor never will. Going sailoring like he did—you tell me, where's the brass in sailoring? Now see here, there's brass all round, waiting for someone to come and pick it up with a shovel, anyone that's got any eyes. Take this road. Wants widening—there isn't a road that doesn't. You start people talking about 'the Finchley bottleneck'— no matter whether it is or it isn't—then you go to that shop at the corner, buy a packet of fags, talk about the weather, give the old girl the tale. 'They tell me they're going to widen along here—spoil your front a bit, I dare say.' That goes all along those houses. Next thing you find a chap on the peep-see for a block of houses he can make into maisonettes—you know, a few feet of breeze-blocks and a length of bell-wire. I'm not saying you'd be in it yourself, mind! You don't want to be *laying out* brass, that's what the Good Lord made the mugs for. Where you come in is on the rake-off."

"Ah, yes."

"It's like this, see, you go to some builder chap, what you know has got a dud lot of breeze-blocks, been sold him by another chap you know. 'Now see here, Dick,' you say, 'I wouldn't wonder but what I know a chap what'd take those blocks off your hands. Mind you, the brass won't be a masterpiece,' you say. See?"

The cab turned into Mountfield Road, Mr Ardree steadied himself with his right hand against the window and with his left re-lit his cigar. "Now what would your line of business be?" he asked. "Something high-class, I dare say. Wines and spirits?"

"Well, as a matter of fact, I'm a member of the Stock Exchange," Everard confessed.

"Right!" said Mr Ardree, pouncing. "And what's the answer to that? The answer is 'Get out! Cut clean away!' Let those lads go their own way, any way they like, but as far as you're concerned they've got the push-off, see?" He turned to wave his cigar under Christine's nose. "Now I ask you, Mrs Licks, what do those lads do for your hubby? Strangle him! Strangle him into a corpse with their rules and fads and fancies: no publicity, no competition—what I call competition—no enterprise! 'Cut it out!' That's what you want to say to your hubby, 'Hubby,' you want to say, 'cut 'em adrift!' Now I know a chap in Stockport, cousin of a friend, runs an office all on his own—I'll give you the address, I've got it on me somewhere—nothing very big, no swank about it, you could look in there yourself and you might say, 'Aa, strike me, not much brass finding its way in here, not that I can see!'—and, Mrs Licks, do you know, old Dave Elleridge—that's the chap I'm telling you about, the chap that runs that little business—well, I say 'little' business—"

"I think this must be the church," Everard said.

The Kinfowells had arrived early in their Daimler and Flock had put them well forward on the left-hand side. Much as she disliked this prominence, Elizabeth realized that he was right: to place Henry farther back would be to have the vessel down by the stern. Physically Henry was not a large man, but one thought of him as large, just as a bare, solitary hill standing against a town appears to be a mountain: at fifty-one he was, indeed, mountainous in everything but size, his handsome, Ayrshire face had the look of erosion, his thick, grey-shot hair lay as if fastened in its shape by the steady drive of coastal gales. In the dark suit which he wore for his less important boards he sat very straight with his hands folded on his knees, apparently unaware of the barrage of curious glances from the other side of the church. His head never moved, only his quiet eyes turned slowly, appraisingly, from the pulpit to the choir-stalls, to the lectern, and back to where, in the foremost pew, the bridegroom sat with his wrists on his spread knees, exactly as a boxer sits in his corner of the ring. Yes, a prize-fighter, Elizabeth thought; a small-time bruiser stuffed into his Sunday serge to be shown for threepence at a charity fête; but when he turned a little, so that she saw his profile, pale with fright and resolution, her feeling turned to pity and immediately to a colour against which pity faded. In Serbia she had ceased to pity soldiers, whose acceptance of their day made that emotion seem anaemic and shrill: was it a trick of light in this baldly daylit building, a twist of circumstance, a mere aftertaste of old associations which showed her in Gian's face something she had watched so long in theirs? She turned her eyes away, as one does from prisoners, to glance covertly at the dozen of his friends who were packed protectively in the two pews behind him. These, while the people behind her leant over each other to whisper and even to laugh, were as dumb as children awaiting punishment, they only fiddled nervously with service sheets, coughed into their handkerchiefs, shot furtive glances across the aisle. The stout, foreign-looking woman must be Gian's mother, and his father presumably was the man on her right, the one who looked as if he expected a keeper to get up in the pulpit and throw him bird-seed, while the two men on Mrs Ardree's other side were not to be identified. The dark girl behind, with her luxuriant display of charms, would be a sister of Gian's; you could tell from her facial likeness to the mother; and the slack-mouthed, hungry-eyed youth whom one instinctively connected with the motorcycle trade was probably this girl's husband. But who could the strange creature at the end be, the deformed woman or child who seemed to be quite alone and whose repellent mouth Elizabeth was forced to look at again and again?

In a whisper that cut through the tide of whispering like rifle fire Flock was giving his last instructions to the bridegroom:

"Now mind, there's not a bit of need to get the sweatin' horrors. You don't do nothing, nothink at all, except stand up alongside Miss Spinyer and say what the parson tells y'. You don't want to worry about the ring, neither. Young Hubbitt get it off me when the time comes, an' you get it off young Hubbitt, get me. Cautionary word is said by Miss Spinyer, 'and thereto I give thee my tooth.' On the word 'tooth' you catch her by the left hand—*left* hand, mind—cant the left arm to an angle of forty-five degrees, insert ring on fourth finger of the left hand and ram home with easy downward movement of forefinger and thumb, in this manner." The whisper rose to gale force. "Oy!—you perishin' Toms, don't stand there gapin' an' gauspin' up round this end —what'd you think Miss Spinyer pay your fare for? Whole lot o' new customers down the other end, backers of Miss Susie's by the looks on 'em, off you go, m'lad, an' chivvy 'em in alongside the rest of the gentry!"

A fresh stir behind, where the frantic Ormison was trying to separate James Ardree from the Liskes, made Elizabeth turn round. The Cepinnier wing was filling up, with the kind of people who belong to County Cricket Weeks and who seem slightly out of drawing in church. Some few were local. A heavy nucleus, in solid clothes which appeared to have been too casually shared out among them, could be recognized as members of what Gertrude always termed the Kilburn and Cricklewood Branch Line: with all their oddities of feature they retained in common a faintly insolent shyness, and you could not mistake the Truggett brows and chin. Joined with this group, but clearly alien, a vigorously tailored man of horse-dealing aspect was querulously talking to a ripened blonde in the height of pre-war fashion with a very small, hard mouth and a chicken's darting eyes: in her, for one instant and never again, Elizabeth caught some indefinable resemblance to Armorel. Her glance went on at once to the end of that pew, where a hat like a chocolate box, devoutly inclined upon an ivory prayer-book, proved to be the outworks of Duffy Elwin in her ceremonial trim. Of half a hundred people now in the church only one seemed to regard it as a place of sanctity: far back on the Ardree side she had a glimpse of Trevon Grist in his seedy overcoat, kneeling with the top of his tousled head against the book-rest, his body locked in a deathlike stillness except when his hands, with the slight, feverish movement of worshippers at Latin shrines, made the sign of the cross.

Seeing Elizabeth, Duffy raised the prayer-book to screen one side of her mouth and discreetly sent a message with her lips and eyes; by what is known as intuition Elizabeth could read it almost word by word: "My dear, you won't believe what happened—a hellish ladder, just as I was starting, and the ones I've got on now aren't even a pair." Elizabeth sent back a smile of sympathy and Duffy's face relaxed into the serenity of devotion. Soon the organ started and the choir wheeled in.

How many weddings, Elizabeth wondered, in the last twelve months: Olivia Bairdley, the Pinthorpe girl, Hilda Nicholedd's niece . . . the recurring carnival of bobbing and whispering pews, *The Voice that*

Breathed o'er Eden, Henry sitting beside her as he sat now, collected, amiable, competent, ready to show his Maker and the bridegroom's mother exactly the politeness that each seemed to require. Fashion, she thought, had buried this drama beneath the silt of its vulgarities, the very words of the rite were so worn with use that they had lost for her their intrinsic nobility. She could escape by setting her mind adrift in the familiar streams, Michael's whimsied charm, Gordon's set face as she had told him the news, the old, threadbare days at Dinstead Fen; but this actuality which she had helped to make forbade so easy a refuge. She shut her eyes, but the florid perfumes of the women behind were still wrapped round her, the banal words of the hymn which Henry was gravely singing in a key of his own were like the jolting of a train when you are trying to thread a needle. In a curious fashion she was frightened; and she was on the point of doing what she had never done before, of saying, "Henry, I don't feel well, please take me out!" when a flutter behind told her that the curtain was up.

Looking past Henry's nose she saw Raymond's pseudo-distinguished head, with the mildly apologetic face which made her think, What, hath this thing appeared again tonight? But one's eyes remained on him no longer than on the horses drawing a royal coach: she looked at Armorel and Raymond ceased to exist.

Armorel was more than the centre-piece of this motley gathering, more than its occasion. As she advanced, very slowly, very erect, the climate changed: as if, in a shop cluttered with bric-à-brac, you moved some piece away from the window and the daylight washing in to a far corner revealed a Rembrandt head. She did not smile; a smile would have weakened her sublimity; she only let her eyes and mouth repose, so that her beauty could lie still in them. Just then it was not a woman's face we saw, though the flow of her walk in the long dress was an empyrean of womanhood: no, this face was not man's or woman's, and pallor had bleached its loveliness; it was one shared by both parts of the human breed, getting its dignity from age and endurance, its power from quietness, its genius from being alone. I know that when I looked at it that afternoon I had to restrain tears; tears such as transmute and glorify the day. Gian, waiting for her, had his feet apart, his big hands hanging like captive balloons in the void, his eyes on the floor. But when she came near and he looked at her his face showed nothing which the understanding could regard with contempt. Armorel took his stiff arm like one long used to that support, the organ stopped and a little, aging man said with peculiar gentleness, "Dearly beloved, we are gathered together here in the sight of God . . ."

"Of course she was my closest chum at Hilda Abbess's," Daphne Steaben said to Everard, standing in the French window of Raymond's drawing-room.

"Oh, really?" Everard said. He had felt that his business experience was not varied enough to make him a congenial partner for James Ardree, and seeing this girl standing all alone he had excused himself and fetched her a sausage-roll. "That must be a delightful school," he said.

"It's a quite perfect school," Miss Steaben told him, "but it has no soul. It was useless for Armorel and me. I don't know if you're an esoteric?"

"Well, no, I'm a stockbroker, actually."

Miss Steaben, looking distantly at a cabinet full of Raymond's dreadful china, took hold of Everard's sleeve. "You know," she said, "it's a very curious thing, but I feel that I've been through all this before. A long, long time ago. Do you ever get such a feeling as that?"

"Well, actually, I don't think I do."

"When I was quite small Daddy took us all to Egypt for a holiday. It was utterly shattering—you know, modern Egypt has no soul. But a most extraordinary thing happened to me as we went round the Amen Temple at Karnak. The dragoman was being most awfully rude and repulsive, so I wandered away from the others, and I suddenly came to a little sort of bas-relief of an ancient Egyptian queen. I mean, a very young queen, but in ancient Egyptian times. Of course I'd never been anywhere *near* this place before. And do you know, I suddenly had an awfully strange feeling in my head, like very wonderful music, and I suddenly realized perfectly well that I knew who that queen was. Who do you think?"

"Well, I haven't done a fearful lot in the way of travelling, actually—"

"Me!"

Everard scanned the sea of heads all round them. Christine was nowhere in sight.

"Would you care for another sausage-roll?" he asked.

"Are you all all right?" Raymond inquired vaguely, squeezing his way into the garden. He realized now that he should have taken the

King Edward hall; as usual he had miscalculated the number who would accept the invitation, and Mr Gigg from the caterers had just told him that it was going to be a damn close thing with the pastries. Well, it wasn't his fault that the rain had started when everything had been set up in the garden, so that all the tables and things had had to be carried inside; or that the sky had cleared just as the guests were arriving and that Gigg in scrupulous observance of the contract had made his almost mutinous squad take everything outside again, bumping into people and getting the women's dresses caught in the hinges of folding chairs. Another hour or so, he thought, switching his bedraggled smile to right and left, and this auto-da-fé would all be over. It was going all right, he supposed, everyone seemed to be jabbering or eating or blowing the filthy smoke of Turkish cigarettes about, and that seemed to be, God save us all, what people liked doing. He caught sight of Christine talking to Captain Desterin. (What classic impudence of Arthur Cepinnier's wife cadging an invitation for that mountebank!)

"Are you all right, my dear? What have you done with what's-his-name, that man you married last year?"

"Oh, I left Everard having a glorious run with a harpy in green. I do think husbands ought to be let off the lead sometimes, don't you? I mean, when one is expecting, I think one's husband needs ever so many girls. So re-invigorating."

Raymond hurried on towards the Dutch garden, where Gigg and Flock had fallen out of sympathy about the placing of deck chairs. ("What I want to know is, who's got the contract on this wedding, you or me?" "Well, you, by the looks on it. Setting all them chairs where the ladies and gents get the sun come smack in their perishin' eyes—why, a lance-corporal'd have more bloody sense than that!") Irene Cepinnier was calling after him, "Cousin Raymond, I do want a little talk with you!" and he steered over to the right, hoping that the laburnums would hide him; but here was Charybdis, the twin Martello towers of the stern belonging to that unbelievable person in the bowler hat who had already buttonholed him for several minutes to talk some gibberish about tea-gardens and who was now nudging the tiresomely successful-looking Scottish creature right back on to a bed of prize-winning dahlias. He sheered off to the left, but James had spotted him. "This gentleman here," James said to Henry Kinfowell, "will bear out what I say." "Back in one moment!" Raymond called, with a smile like a bicycle lamp short of oil, and almost ran into the arms of Mr

Gigg, who wished to know whether this particular pestilential wedding was being done by Portwood Brothers of Squire's Lane or had it by any chance been turned over to the War Office.

"Now you can take my advice or you can leave it," James continued, "but the pay-as-you-ride class of business has come to stay. You take typewriters. I get to hear of a young lass that wants a typewriter—earning ten half-cracks a week, we'll say, wants to make a bit of brass in her spare time, fair enough. Well now, I don't try to *sell* her a typewriter. And why? Because I know she can't afford to *buy* a typewriter. So what do I do? I *give* her a typewriter. I get it off Leary's the wholesale people, down by central station—decent stuff, mind: no use taking on a charge for what the lass is going to make into tinker's trash before you get it back off her: Court Kensington, that sort of job, stand up to a bit of wear—I get this job on quarterly account and put it on one of George Hinchliffe's vans (he won't charge nothing, seeing how I put a bit of business in his way, come one week, come the next). I go the front door—the *front* door, mind—and I say 'Miss Pratt?' I say, 'I hear that you been wanting a typewriter. My name's Mr James Ardree, here you are, it's yours, sign on the bottom and nothing to pay—*nothing—whatever—to pay* till Friday three weeks.' So what happens next?"

"So you think the Court Kensington a good machine?" Henry interrupted.

"Good? Listen: you take a word of advice from me—Mr Ardree, the name is—and don't you touch that job with the mucky end of a sewage pole. It'll last, mind—it'll last for ever. But what's the good of it lasting if it won't type! Listen: it's the *works* is just a misery. Speaking mechanically, it's muck, plain honest muck like father makes it."

"I'm interested," Henry said agreeably, "because one of my companies manufactures that machine."

"Ah, then listen, and I'll tell you right now what you've got to do to make a mucky machine of that grading fetch you in a decent bit of brass."

A tow-haired boy bobbed up between them. " 'Ere, gimme that glass—get y' a refill—gimme yours too, may as well, all goes on the boss's bill."

There were really too many helpers. From a sound position between the serving tables and the rockery Flock had got his team organized, and with all the advantages of youth and amateur keenness on their side they were cutting out the opposition. "William—over there!" Gigg would bark. "Whole dozen of 'em—standin' there starvin'!" but before the puffy old waiter was half the distance across the lawn a brace of boys slipped by Flock had reached the group with three assortments of sandwiches. "You—Jordan—" shouted Gigg, apoplectic with frustration, "get hold of this tray, sharp now!" "On it, boy!" spat Flock, seizing Toms by the collar, flicking him round and launching him like a catapult. "You, Slimey—catch!—that way—ole basket by the hollyhocks, top her up!" House and garden seemed to be awash with haggard, wrathful waiters and tearing, twisting boys, you were battered and stunned with service. Before you had drained your glass a grubby fist snatched it away and in half a minute it was back refilled. A plate was plunged between your stomach and the woman you were talking to; you hesitated, a remorseless voice said, "Goo on—last two!" and one èclair was thrust into your hand, one into hers. You left your chair to walk across to the lily-pond and the chair followed you, as you knew when its sharp edge was bumped against your thighs. "There y'are, mister—nothing to pay—might as well rest y'r arse!" The Fidgley brothers, competing in the issue of cakes, had got out of hand and were running like madmen from group to group, bellowing their scores. When Everard put a cigarette in his mouth the elder Fidgley tore at him with a lighted match, the younger leapt and blew it out, transferred the cigarette from Everard's mouth to his own and lit it, cried "Got y' skinned, cock!" to his rival and put it back. "Yes, friends of my sister-in-law's, I imagine," Everard said to Miss Steaben with a trace of awkwardness. Beyond the shrubbery Maria Ardree, nervously smiling, damp with sweat, shedding occasionally a few insistent tears, rinsed glass after glass in a bath of soapy water while Duffy dried them.

Irene succeeded in separating old Frederick Hutchinson from a group of the Kilburn-and-Cricklewoods and got him pinned against the wall of the summer-house, with Roger Desterin supporting her.

"I've not had one word with Raymond," she said. "Nonsense!—he's not a bit too busy, he's not doing anything except wander about and beam at people who don't know from Adam who he is. Of course he's avoiding me—I'm not a fool! And I can't say I wonder at it either, after the hand he's had in this. Still, it's not him I'm blaming, it's Edith."

"Ah, poor Edith!"

"Poor Edith? Poor smug!" Her voice settled to the squeezed monotony of a phonograph recording. "I've written to that woman time and time again, I'm in a nice house here, I told her, there's a room Armorel can have to herself any time she likes to come. But, oh no! Not a bit of it! Armorel can't stay with her own mother because Armorel's having a proper Christian upbringing and her mother's a wicked woman! Armorel must stay with her good, kind, Christian, charitable aunt Edie, and learn to be a nice, respectable, high-class Christian girl! If Armorel started seeing her own mother it would make her all nasty and low-class—oh, yes, of course it would! And what happens? The first thing that Armorel does is to go and marry a van-boy off the corner of the street!"

Frederick brought a yawn to still birth. "But you know, Mrs Cepinnier, your husband's side of the family do make rather unexpected alliances now and again."

"That's not the point!" Desterin said sharply. "The point is, Irene had got every right to be consulted. The girl's own mother—it's a damned insult, if you ask me. I'm not a snob, mind you—a snob's just what I can't stick, saw too many of 'em in the war. (No, blast you, I've told you nine times already *I do not want* any coffee!) But when it comes to a thing like marriage, there are limits."

"In what way?" Frederick inquired.

"And what would her father have said?" Irene pursued. "That's a thing I'd like to know!"

Frederick's gravestone face fell into a new posture of courteous distress: each moment seemed to intensify the happiness of his day. "One has never been certain about Arthur's prejudices," he said thoughtfully. "I don't feel that I know the bridegroom, I've only had about three words with him. Is he at all interested in motor-racing, do you know?"

Christine, twirling her long gloves, came swaying over the strawberry-beds. "Isn't Cousin Frederick a sweet!" she piped to Roger. "So oldy-worldy. Cousin Freddie, don't you think it's awful for Mums, seeing the last little chick fluttering away from the nest! Only of course the nest rather fluttered away first. I've been seeing all Rellie's new relations. So intriguing. The sister's awfully pretty, we've been talking baby for hours. She knows all about weaning, and keeping hubby interested, and abortion and everything. Oh, and Roger would simply love the sister's husband, he makes money on motorcycle tracks, as well as all sorts of things. Rellie looked awfully sweet, didn't she!"

"From where that man put me in the church I could hardly see her," Irene said. "I was thinking she might come and talk to me."

"The least she could do!" Desterin agreed.

Christine spread across the three of them her ready-made and harmless smile. "I expect Aunt Edie's told her all the essentials," she said consolingly. She turned to Frederick. "Don't you think Mums looks angelic in that little frock! So chic," she said, "so chaste," and wandered amiably away.

"Such lovely flowers!" everyone was saying, avoiding—except in whispers—the most obvious and least comfortable topic. "How nice that the rain stopped just when it did! All these pretty frocks, and the waiters and everything—it gives you a pre-war feeling, you can almost believe that the old times are back." "Such a lovely afternoon, after all! Really we might be back in August," people said. But the breeze blowing across the lawn, a little salty to the nostrils, made older women glad they had kept their coats; and the fall of afternoon light across the shrubs and pergolas, limpid and subtle, did not belong to summer.

"Do you think everything's going all right?" Raymond asked Elizabeth; he had to ask her something, he must always have a word or two with any beautiful woman, as the chronic tourist maddened by railway posters must have one sight of Clovelly and Florence and the Midnight Sun. "They all seem to be shouting in each other's faces, I suppose that means they're all quite happy. I suppose really I ought to introduce people, only I never can remember anyone's name. I haven't the faintest notion what yours is."

"I'm Elizabeth Kinfowell—I'm just a stray friend of Armorel's, so you don't have to work out relationships or anything. You have met my husband?"

"What? No. This one? Ohowdudu, yes, I think we have." (They always had these husbands, stuffed and senseless and smiling, like guardian eunuchs.) "I feel I can forgive anybody anything," he said, with the confused intention of being friendly, "so long as he's not a relation and not going to be."

"A very enjoyable occasion!" Henry said, as if declaring the bazaar open.

"Good God! Do you think so?"

"Ah, it may be that I have an element of romance in my nature." Henry's voice, which charged each syllable with separate importance, was unexpectedly soft in timbre: he was one who could show in every radiant gesture the gladness with which he suffered fools. "You know, when I go to a wedding I feel that the joy of the happy pair overflows into the hearts of those all round them, like the burns that flow down from Bendeoch to bring all the glen into leaf and flower."

"Yes, I suppose so."

"And can be turned into electricity, too," Elizabeth added.

"Ah," said Henry, "there you have a very interesting proposition."

Having steered the men towards suitable pastures, Elizabeth slipped away, intending to find Duffy. So: the hearts of all these twittering people were soak-aways for the bridal happiness? She was sure that Henry believed so, that the sunshine had found a response in his sensibility, that he was alight with friendliness towards everyone in this Frithian paradise and saw his feelings reflected in the faces about him. For in such a mind as his, where the working-parts were as snugly fitted as a launch's engines, there was room for all the emotions to alight and dance without risk of fouling the cogs. Perhaps he was right. Perhaps it was merely her own solitude which made her see this gathering as a carnival of loneliness, where the flags on the little houses waved to each other and the people crouched singly behind drawn blinds. She had talked for a while to Simon Ardree, who had failed to find a place in Flock's team of blacklegs and was fecklessly trying to mend a broken chair with a piece of bootlace: he had stood up, rubbing his hands on his serge trousers, had reluctantly told her that his son was "a good lad, as far as he go, but rough, as you might say, which is only natural," twisting his long neck, peering over and round her as if he thought she was holding a summons behind her back; and had smiled, with manifest relief, only as she left him. She had caught the same expression, the look of a man hiding, in the eyes of Gian himself, when Armorel, moving with sober grace from group to group, had brought him to her. Gian had said carefully, with a dignity of its own kind, "Pleased to meet you, m'm, very glad you could come!" and she fancied that his eyes, in one momentary liaison with hers, had added, "That's all I'm allowed to say in this performance." It caught hold of her, this notion, so that the shreds of conversation glancing her ears, the amiabilities, even the whispered troubles, had become a trellis of deception. And nothing I say myself, she reflected, is born in my mind; my tongue is like a piece of glass sending darts of borrowed light into people's eyes, preventing them from seeing inside. She caught sight now of the misshapen girl she had noticed in church, standing by herself on the far side of the lily-pond, and instinctively she went to join her.

"I'm a friend of Armorel's," she said, "my name's Elizabeth."

Daise Empire said, "Oh," and half-turned away.

"I suppose it's rather rude of me, but I felt I must tell you how much I admire your frock." It was a crude assembly of green satin. "I saw it in church."

"Oh, it's just a cut-up of an old one my mum used to have."

"Did you make it yourself? I do think that's clever, I can never get the collar to fit like that. It's a jolly party, isn't it!—only I hardly know anyone here, I have to be content with watching the others. You're a friend of Gian's, I expect? What a fine, strong face he's got."

"Yes, 'm."

"You've known him for a long time?"

"Yes, 'm."

The creature was all but hopeless. To her repulsive deformities was added, in the canary voice, the coy turning of her head, a callow affectation hardly easier to surmount than the dreadful fixity of the insane. But there are those who must travel in a strange country merely because they know there is nothing but discomfort to be found there. Elizabeth signalled to Ormison, who was passing and who brought two chairs; she sat down so that it was natural to look a little forward of Daise's face, turning only now and again to meet her eyes.

"You're a Londoner, I expect? I wish I was! I lived in the country right up till the time I was married. Of course that was nice in a way, but now I've got to live in London I always feel such a stranger— I'm ashamed of myself all the time for being so slow about things, never knowing which bus goes where and all the things which are so easy for people like you . . ."

In a little while Daise was talking: not fluently or with any show of pleasure, but giving out short lengths of speech like the strips of ticket which the box-office girl releases. Yes, she had always lived at Bidault's Place. Her brother had gone away, to Canada, she fancied, and her elder sister had died. Mum had always kept the house really nice, like houses where she had been in service, but she was ill in bed now, had been for quite a time. Gian Ardree had always been kind. Well, in all sorts of ways, "only he don't get on with Dad." Of her father she spoke negatively: he never did touch the drink or put his money on horses; he had been a preacher of some kind once, but he didn't do that now . . . But that was not all, Elizabeth thought. This picture of an existence framed by four close walls, so commonplace that a score of words were enough to draw it, was not the whole picture. Some accident? A midwife's shameful incompetence? or something further back? She tried, looking across the lawn at the frocks and the smiling faces, to imagine the possession of a body which made people stare and then turn quickly away. That should be enough, God knew, to account for everything she saw in this girl's eyes: enough, except for one who had felt the first terrifying signs of Michael's coming, who had sat beside him when the doctors thought he was certain to die. She asked, merely as an idler throws pebbles into a pond, easing a silence, "Do you have any visitors at all?" and the result of that innocent question was frightening. It was as if a gentle, friendly person had turned without warning upon a child, barking, "Caught you! Thief!" In a voice suddenly roughened Daise said:

"Why? *I* don't ask them!"

Elizabeth said quickly: "I was only wondering if I might come sometime. I thought your mother might like someone new to talk to occasionally. And perhaps you could show me how you get the collar of a dress to fit so beautifully."

Trevon was coming across the lawn; with his hands in his pockets, hulking and contemptuous, parading his shabbiness and his detachment.

"Oh, Trevon, there you are—I was trying to find you." And how fatally, she thought, this man chooses his moments to appear. "This is a friend of mine, Daise Empire. Daise has known Gian for a long time. This is Trevon Grist—he's another friend of Gian's."

Rather to her surprise, Trevon behaved well: his manner changed as when an actor comes back into the wings, the contempt fell off, leaving a gracious simplicity. He said, stooping to hold Daise's hand, smiling as if she were a woman of charm and distinction: "I want to know all Gian's friends! Are they looking after you properly? This party's a terrible muddle, you must come to our Christmas party at Hollysian House, we'll run that properly—perhaps you'd come as one of the hostesses? Susie's going to be one of them, I hope."

But Daise would not respond to his warmth. She mumbled something about "better be getting on" and walked away, looking for a new place where she could be unnoticed and alone.

Trevon stared after her, and then turned round to look at Elizabeth's dress.

"Who got her here?" he said with closed teeth. "That poor fool Ardree, I suppose. She's not fit to be in a show like this."

"What do you mean?"

"I mean, among all these titivated baboons. I don't know her, but she looks an honest creature to me, she comes from an honest part of this filthy capital. These people here—my God, have you looked at them? The pullulating aftermath of the Disraelian age! That chittering opossum who's supposed to be running this circus—some cousin or something of Susie's—have you seen him? Just hanging on in the hope of being bought up for the South Kensington museum. Well, they're having a run for their money, aren't they! Nothing these sort of people like more than a mating, and when you give 'em a really first-class piece of miscegenation, from the way they look at it, it's worth a couple of hangings and a whipping thrown in. Still more fun if she'd married me—God, how the Cepinnier clan would have rushed to buy up old copies of the Sunday mucksheets and get all the details! Really I think I should quite have enjoyed that wedding—I'd have gone round with a camera and photographed every one of Susie's relations in the act of inspecting me. I—"

"Listen," Elizabeth said peaceably, between the fall of the waves, "I want to take you and introduce you to my husband."

"That man over there?" he asked. "Ben Lomond back from the dry-cleaners? Yes, I thought it was—that type always has a woman like you. It's not that they have any real taste—they just have the rich man's instinct for value. What on earth's the point of my meeting him?"

"Well, I want you to stay with us tonight—"

"Stay with you? Good God! Why in the world—?"

"Because tonight I think you're quite likely to do something stupid if you're not looked after."

"Stupid? What do you mean?" He looked into her face and then he said: "Oh, I see, you've been turning up old newspapers! Juicy reading!"

"Surely," she said patiently, "it's only very childish people who go to the newspapers for excitement. People titillate themselves with second-hand scandals when they've never been within a hundred miles of getting mixed up in one. I shouldn't think that anybody who's once been in a sordid situation finds sordidness amusing."

He did not answer that directly. He said: "Anyway, I can't stay with you, not tonight. Very kind of you, but I've got to have some sort of amusement tonight. I can't go on living like a monk—what's the good of it?" And then: "In a way I'm glad this has happened. At least it's got Susie clear of me—that would have been the worst thing that could have happened. Look here, I've been very rude, I'm sorry. It upset me a bit, being in a church—even a church like that. I hadn't been inside a church for weeks. You know, they oughtn't to have that sort of thing in a church. It's just about the same as having the money-changers in the Temple."

"But you were there of your own accord."

"I know. I was hunting for magic. I always imagine that something will happen and I shall find myself where I was in the old days. It doesn't and it can't, it's just an illusion."

He started to walk away but she followed him; through the kitchen garden, past the rubbish heap and through a gimcrack gate into the meadow beyond. He turned to her there and said: "Elizabeth, my dear, you'd better keep away from me—as far away as you can. London's large enough, thank God, for two people never to meet each other."

"But why?" she asked. "Just because you're miserable today, and don't really want to see any of your friends—"

"It's not only today," he said. He spoke painfully, like a man with severe pleurisy. "Really, I don't want to have any friends, I can do with having the boys at the Club, people like that. You know, you're most frightfully kind, I wish to God I could repay it in some way, I wish I could even accept your kindness. But you see, I'm the sort of person—well, I'm beyond the reach of goodness. Well, goodness from anyone like you. I've gone much further than people like you can picture—I'm glad you can't. There's one sort of virtue left for people like me—if you can call it virtue—it's to keep their leprosy to themselves, not even to let people know what it's like. I mean that, I'm not just making a speech."

This affected her in a curious way. She was not a woman whom anyone could imagine crying: you would have said that she, if no other, had done with that. Yet when she spoke it was clear that she was crying inwardly, and that only the spartan hold she had upon her body prevented tears. She said in a whisper: "But don't you see that you're denying me the only kind of purpose that can make me worth anything at all—a creature who's muddled her life as much as I have?"

For just a moment he put his forehead against her shoulder. He said uncertainly: "Perhaps I do see, or almost." He manufactured a kind of smile. "I'm sorry. *A chacun son enfer.* I can't let you into mine —not you."

They went back together towards the house, smiling and bowing to people they knew. He said as they walked: "I suppose I'm more responsible for this calamity than anyone." She asked, "Do you really think it's that?" and he answered, "What else can it be? How could she possibly understand him!" "Isn't it a fact," she said, "that love is the same thing as understanding?" "That's what I mean." The guests were all beginning to work their way towards the front of the house.

Duffy had arranged to drive the Ardree parents home. "Now you just stay exactly where you are," she said, having collected them at the foot of the front steps, "and I'll bring my idiotic little car and you can use it as a grandstand." Close to the steps, the luxurious car which Raymond had ordered to take the married pair away was sleekly waiting in the half-moon drive. A few yards behind it, having entered the drive by right of costliness, a similar car also waited. Oblivious of Raymond's elaborate parking plans, dead to the niceties of caste in the motor world, case-hardened against every kind of embarrassment, Duffy fetched her small saloon from the queue of cars in the road and succeeded, by a series of volcanic manoeuvres, in placing it between the two landaulets.

This was at least a welcome diversion for the guests, who were waiting for the climax of the party with a slightly bilious impatience. The conversation of relations who meet rarely—"Tell me, do you hear anything of Louisa nowadays?—" was petering out, and the special strains which this occasion had put on their social resources were reaching the limit of tolerance. They had the pleasure now of watching this round and red-faced girl tugging her wheel first this way then the other in impartial and affable response to the conflicting directions of Sergeant Flock, of Reg Ormison, Captain Desterin, Ed Hugg, Mr Olleroyd and a rubicund coachman-turned-chauffeur in a frenzy of anxiety for the rear wings of the hired car. They saw Simon reluctantly climbing up to sit on the roof of the saloon, and the peculiar Mr Olleroyd, who looked and moved as if he had lately been unpacked after long storage, being shoved and hoisted after him. Then it was Maria Ardree's turn; and Maria, who for some time had been quietly but openly sobbing, was astonishingly changed into a giggling, squealing schoolgirl as Flock and Desterin, locked shoulder-to-shoulder and crying "Steady—hup!", slowly raised her formidable bulk into the air, while Simon hauled valiantly on her gigantic arms, her daughter and son-in-law steadied the load with their hands on her stupendous ankles and Ormison with his innate gentility hung on to her skirt and kept it in place. A moment of doubt and alarm, a short, heroic struggle, and she was up, the roof of the car was bending ominously in the middle, and Duffy returning to the driver's seat was joyfully calling that the roof didn't matter a hoot in hell. "Room for all!" Mr Olleroyd suddenly cried, and Ed and Rosie got up too. "Really!" the Cepinnier faction murmured, doubtful like Malvern Festival audiences whether one smiled on such an occasion as this. "Stand-by!" Flock ordered sharply. "Wait till you see the whites of their eyes!" and the Club contingent, wickedly grasping their bags of rice, edged back into the firing line.

And still the principal actors did not appear.

It was Raymond's avowed and sincere belief that he was an unlucky fellow. In truth, he was one whose rare gift for mismanagement invites from fortune a co-operative provision of disaster; just as a man too incompetent to board the right train will generally find himself on the one which takes him furthest from his destination in circumstances of the highest discomfort. His intentions at this stage were faultless. He realized that his guests were nearly demented with embarrassment and boredom, that the Lambeth boys might get beyond control at any moment, that he himself was in danger of seizing James Ardree, who went on and on about the tea-garden scheme, and wringing his neck. He therefore said explosively, "Wait! I'll go and hustle up those two!" rammed his way through the crowd and charged upstairs.

Gian was waiting, as if for execution, on the landing. Raymond, almost felling him with a friendly pat on the shoulder, said, "These blasted women!" strode across to the room where Armorel was changing and hammered on the door. "Armorel, my dear, will you be a sweet girl and for God's sake stop trying on fresh suspenders and come and take your husband to Jericho or wherever you're going!" In half a minute Armorel emerged, but the interval was long enough for Raymond to be visited by one of his Good Ideas. "Look here!" he said brilliantly, taking one arm of hers and one of Gian's, "the hall's absolutely crawling with relations and things, I'll take you down the back way and we'll cut out most of that nonsense with the confetti." Life had taught this man nothing at all.

The manoeuvre seemed to work well enough. From the side door of the house a clump of lilacs reached out to the drive. Advancing behind this screen, Raymond made a dart for the door of the Daimler he saw there and pulled it open. The pair were inside the car before anyone had seen them.

The Kinfowell chauffeur was wakened from his habitual doze by the sound of the door being slammed and a voice saying authoritatively: "Right away, driver!" Mr Kinfowell was a man usually in a hurry, the chauffeur a master of his craft. The chauffeur's hand had started the engine almost before he woke, his eyes told him in less than a second that the way forward was finally blocked by Duffy's saloon; in seven seconds he had reversed with perfect artistry into the road and was moving forward on the other lock.

Pleased with the success of his strategy, Raymond strolled towards the steps, gently rubbing his hands and smiling. He considered every show of enthusiasm un-English, he detested the custom of bombarding married couples, and above all else he loathed the thought of any vulgarity in the quiet avenue where he and his neighbours had spent most of their lives. All this he seemed to have avoided by one stroke of shrewdness, and the sight of a white-rosetted car in front of him, with its driver holding the door open, failed to disturb his complacency. The fact that something might be wrong was first conveyed to his intelligence by Henry Kinfowell. Arriving at the front door, Henry had observed some £2,000 worth of his property moving smartly towards the main road, and like others who can well afford to lose £2,000 he regarded such a prospect with a slightly pathological distaste. He let out a pistol-shot of "Hech! They've stolen my motor!" and simultaneously came a bellow from Flock, "Oy! The bleeders have got away!"

The boys were out in the road like a pack of hounds and went in full cry after the retreating car with Flock at their heels. With a sharp "I'll catch them, sir!" Desterin had jumped to the wheel of the hired car and propelled it towards the gate, while Raymond and Henry together pushed the bewildered driver aside and jumped in the back. But Duffy was quicker still. Designed by nature to embellish the folly of others, ignited by a passion to serve, she called "You leave it to me!" and while Desterin was threading the Daimler through a tangle of guests she shot her car in one faultless backward curve out onto the road. The Huggs jumped down as it started to move, Mr Olleroyd came shoulders first into the lilacs, Simon hung on as far as the gate and there dropped off into the arms of Everard Liske. Too scared to scream or weep, Maria remained aloft. As the car stopped in the road she slid to the side. As it moved forward she glided back. When it gathered speed she slowly rolled over on to one elbow and remained like Madame Récamier, semi-reclined and statuesque but still slipping aft an inch at a time, her face identical in shade and expression with the face of Lot's wife. "Stop her!" yelled Simon, tearing in pursuit. "You let Mum off!" screamed Ed, as a hand waved cheerfully from the driver's window. "I'll stop them!" Duffy called back. The spray of charging boys across the road forced her to slow down, Desterin raced the Daimler up beside her, and Raymond's agonized face appeared. "You've got a woman on top!" he yelled. "I'll make them stop!" Duffy echoed, smiling and waving, steering with her left hand and cramming Desterin on to the kerb. "Keep over, you silly bitch!" Desterin roared, as the two cars went on side by side, yawing in harmony. "Faster, man!" Henry grunted, while Raymond writhed in the corner muttering "O my God! Hell take and damn these lunatics, God knows what everyone will think!" The sharper-witted guests had joined the pursuit in their cars, the rest followed on foot and the toughest caught up Simon and Ed, who with arms spread wide were running hard upon Duffy's tail, ready for the moment when Maria would finally slide off. "Disgraceful!" moaned Irene, hobbling in the rear as fast as her high, tight shoes would let her. "I know he'll kill himself this time!" "So dramatic!" Christine panted, lurching along beside her. "So bad for Arthur Augustus!" With Flock now in the lead and lengthening his stride the boys increased their pace, hysterically shouting and scattering rice as they ran. Through the rear window of the leading Daimler, now sixty yards ahead, Armorel smiled and waved, while at fifteen miles an hour the whole Gadarene concourse poured up the genteel avenue, bawling, "Stop him! Stop her! Stop that car! Come back!"

A coal-cart coming up Hendon Lane set limits to this parade of indignity. Henry's car was obliged to stop and the pursuers drew up on both sides. All the doors opened at once.

"That happens to be my motor!"

"Armorel, you nanny-goat!" (This was Raymond.) "What do you mean by going off in this old fool's car!"

"Rellie dear," called Duffy, "there's something wrong. They say you've got the wrong husband or—*oh, my aunt!*"

The saloon had slackened speed just when Maria had travelled as far to the rear as she could without coming off. The laws of motion operating with perfection, she had started to move the other way, slowly and quite passively, ignoring equally her husband's, "Hold on where you are, Maria!" and Ed Hugg's "Jump for it, quick!" As the car came to rest her pace slightly increased. Fascinated, Simon stopped dead, while Ed crashed into the door of the other car: it was Flock who reached the spot in time, the sportsman Liske came up beside him and the Fidgley brothers closed in behind. "Get set!" squealed Flock, and Everard murmured, "Mine, I think!" as Maria's person reached the forward edge of the roof and hovered there for a moment, like a tree at the last stroke of the axe, before descending with a curious majesty, upside down, by the sloped windshield to the bonnet and thence to the arms of the Field.

"At my age tsat is not right!" Maria said.

As if Raymond's humiliation needed some outside help to arrive at his standards of unpleasantness, the rain had started again.

"Somebody get an ambulance!" Raymond barked; in his daydreams he was a leader of men. "I don't care if she *is* all right, I said 'Get an ambulance'! You, young woman, you must be mad. I don't know where the proper driver is, somebody find him—no, no use wasting time, somebody get a taxi! And someone for God's sake drive away these infernal boys!"

But while Raymond fumed and blustered Henry had seen what had to be done. "You will honour me," he said to Armorel, "by stepping back into my car. No, no, the pleasure is mine. You, sir," to Gian, "please tell my chauffeur to take you exactly where you wish." He bowed, he gave them both his enchanting smile and ceremoniously reclosed the door.

As the car started to move again a dowdy, breathless and wet-eyed woman whom no one had seen before ran up to the window calling weakly "God bless you!" and thrust in an envelope with a cheque for a hundred pounds; she was lost at once in the surge of boys who saw their prey escaping once more and were rocketing after it like a horde of banshees, hurling the last of their ammunition at its tail. The Daimler beat them; it was off like an arrow and away down Gravel Hill, leaving the spent affray behind: the Ardrees and Duffy bunched together in a babel of laughter and explanations, Irene sobbing and upbraiding her protector, Maria embracing Flock and Everard in turn;

while Raymond like an anguished ghost shambled from one group to the next, still issuing vague commands, still telling everyone that he was not to blame, and Georgina, whom hardly anyone had noticed, was hobbling back towards the station, and a little way down Hendon Lane with her dreadful face to the wall Daise Empire was strangely and bitterly crying.

18

Saturday. Wet nearly all morning. Read Edsell's *Case Records of Industrial Neurosis*, stiff but brilliantly logical. Got *Daily Mirror* and *Wide World Magazine* for G, but he spent most of time amusing adenoidal Cupwin children. Mrs C free to concentrate on *Film Pictorial* and v. grateful. Walk on promenade before lunch. G agrees to resume tech course to please me. P.M. Got blue tie for G, 6/6, very bright but good. G v. pleased, I think. He wanted to get me night-gown we saw in window of Bon Marché, but I said he must not pay so much. I think he thought I didn't like it because it was so very revealing at bust, poor darling is full of inhibitions. Tea Miranda's Parlour. Evening Pavilion to hear Julia Barelli. G stood this well and said, "I reckon she know her job," which makes me see possibilities. I thought her treatment of Chopin grotesquely over-romantic. The woman *has* technical power, but prostitutes it to sentimentalism—the right commercial policy, I suppose, in a popular resort like this.

Sunday. Morning wet. I read. G played with C children. P.M. Mrs C who never deviates from respectability thought children must go to local Sunday school, and G said he would take them as Mrs C busy placing stars in order of popularity for F.P. competition. G thinks he is nominally Catholic but "don't mind a bit of a service." Shall not interfere with this, G not yet far enough on to understand insoluble contradictions in Messianic hypothesis. He evidently thought I might join S.S. party. Said I had letters to do, G perfectly complaisant. Wrote Eliz re Henry and details of job for G. Tea Miranda then walk to far end of promenade. G quiet but I think quite contented, he evidently enjoyed singing rowdy hymns with C children. Tried to lead on to subject of Empire family but G not disposed. Saw gay socks in Bon Marché which I will get for G.

Monday. G had letter which he told me came from Trevon. Rain all morning, I read *The Approach to Adult Education* (Cheames), early chapters sound but then Cheames gets fogged with Messianic hocus-pocus. G took C children to pier in mackintoshes. P.M. Meant to walk to Hawkes Cliff, but rain came on when we reached end of promenade. Tea Miranda. Saw Trevon's letter in bedroom, nothing except male heartiness. Before supper some trouble when G alone with Cupwins, apparently Mrs C slaps little Désirée for persistent disobedience (little D continually interrupting when Mrs C trying to read). G incensed, goes for Mrs C, and offers to knock block off negligible Mr C who feebly supports her. Took reasonable line as one always can and affair more or less blew over. Explained afterwards to G that one cannot interfere between parents and children, certainly not in boarding-houses. G penitent though I don't think he altogether understood.

Tuesday. G slipped out and bought the expensive night-gown with some of the last of money his uncle James gave him. Shall wait till later to explain that we mustn't go in for extravagances—do not want to hurt G's feelings in smallest way. Rain cleared and we set out for Hawkes Cliff, but rain started again when we reached end of promenade. P.M. Heavy rain.

Intermittently the record trickled on for nearly two years, filling four 'Law-Students' notebooks. She came upon them twelve years after the first was begun, and wasted half-an-hour (she called it waste) dipping and reading; seated on the floor of the attic in Weald Street with her back against a tea-chest, covered with dust, her tongue just showing between her lips.

They have value of a kind, these invertebrate and toneless diaries. Occasionally, at least, they mean something later on to their authors, especially if these are women: something of the 'historic site' order, an object to regard with respect and tenderness, a stimulus to memory. (Mrs Cupwin? But of course—the blue and white dress designed for a woman ten years younger, the idiotic fuss about using the bathroom!) The handwriting, the naïveté, will provoke a faintly agreeable wistfulness: how young I was, how callow then! And almost certainly she will say, in the formula that belongs to necromancy, 'How it brings it all back!': seeing no contradiction there.

No, in 1932 those days on the Suffolk coast could not return. It is true that most of the elements might have been recalled, for the small resort, already fallen from social esteem in 1920, had altered little in twelve years. The North View Hotel was still open, with its shallow verandah, the zigzag steps which led through a waste of blown sand and tamarisk to the promenade: Miss Exel remained proprietress, one or two of the same end-of-season guests still came each year. Had Armorel returned to the second-floor room she would have found the furniture almost unchanged, the door of the wardrobe held shut with a piece of paper and groaning eerily when it was opened; the view identical, with the bay windows of the Alderney, the sparse hedge of a bowling green, the pierhead just showing over the signboard which said *Mrs Harper's Family Bathing*. On any October morning when the sun suddenly burst upon the dripping promenade, while the spray of high tide whipped against the beach huts, the sound and smell of the place would have been the same. But between the ages of twenty-one and thirty-three the senses are slightly changed, eyes fastened to much mending will focus a little differently, the palate is matured and dulled by many hurried meals of left-overs in the acid London air. Experience continually shifts the point of view: when you have been out to work, borne children and moved house, the breath of changing seasons will have lost its quintessence and the stir of a crowded street will not excite you in exactly the same way.

What no diary would return to her, as she sat in the dusty attic and pretended not to hear Tonie calling, was her own response to all the incidents of those few wet days. Nowhere had she written, "I was happy." And indeed, so bald a phrase could have carried no meaning through such a space of time. Yet it was happiness, of a sort, which pervaded the opening of her married life; a kind of contentment which belongs more often to men than to women, and is proof against many discomforts, outlasting the long terms when no progress is made, the sharp set-backs: it was the embracing happiness of purpose.

There was one hour when the realization of her sacrifice overwhelmed her, when fear and misery convulsed her in tears. This was on the third morning, when the sun coming through thin curtains woke her early and she lay listening to the sounds which penetrated the thin walls, to the sneeze of small waves and the scrape of shingle. There was light enough to show her trousseau clothes on the chair, the dressing-case which the Kinfowells had given her and Gian's rexine valise, the florid set of bedroom china on the jerry-built washstand: a smell of bacon already rose from the kitchen, mingled with the house's permanent smells, linoleum polish and bathing dresses drying. Something, perhaps the shift of the curtains and the breeze touching her face, made her think of the room she had shared with Christine at Hayward's Heath, and with that flick of memory she felt the loneliness and terror of exile. The tears came like a jet of steam across her eyes, she thrust her face into the pillow and could feel the bed moving on its castors with her sobs.

Gian lay fast asleep with his face toward the door. She had almost recovered when he turned and half opened his eyes to regard her cloudily. "Something wrong?" he asked. He moved a sleepy hand to touch her arm, but feeling no response drew it away. He turned over again and she got up to wash and dress.

But that was only a passing feebleness which sprang—she decided later in the day—from some physical cause. When, with some dim recollection, Gian asked if she had slept well she told him that a silly dream had made her wake in a fright.

For the present her single concern was to make him content: to give him everything he needed for comfort and recreation, above all to nourish his self-esteem. How carefully she had planned this holiday. She would avoid the big and crowded resorts, where Gian chancing to meet his friends would feel awkward in the new holiday clothes, but the place she chose must have at least some of the pleasures he was used to, the shooting galleries and the winkle bars. She would not launch him into a showy hotel, to be alarmed by tail-coated servants, but she rejected equally the poky lodgings which might make him feel she was ashamed and hiding him. Everything must be done cheaply, and yet there should be a flavour of extravagance, it must appear that she herself was having not only the best but the first treat of this kind. In all these meticulous calculations she had little to guide her: there were no terms in which she could consult Gian himself, she could only estimate his feelings by a species of arithmetic based on her own. Continually on guard against anything which might injure his pride, she phrased her plans as suggestions, leaving decisions, as it appeared, to him. She was careful to see that Raymond's cheque, which was to keep them going for a month or two, was made out to Gian. When there were letters he could not write she asked some favour which would keep him occupied and told him afterwards, "Oh, Gian, as you were busy I just wrote to Carter Paterson myself." At every chance she pretended some kind of ignorance—did he think they ought to ring the bell or wait till someone came? would someone come in to take her shoes for cleaning or should she put them outside the door?—and if he only frowned and scratched his head she laughed, squeezing his arm, and said what a lot they had to learn. There was pleasure in the mere contrivance, and he increased it by the gravity with which he played his part. The anxiety which his eyes and forehead showed had already dwindled. He even smiled when he made mistakes she could not conceal—that curious, fleeting smile which she had first observed in the house in Mickett Lane—and he learnt rapidly, repeating any point she tactfully gave him with a quick, assenting nod. It was wrong to call Miss Exel 'Mum' and to shout loudly at the waitress? "I got it!" A man could wear his cap in the vestibule but not in the lounge? "Got that!" And she saw with delight how, when he came a second time to some piece of routine he had mastered, his head went up with confidence. There were other factors which might partly account for this increase in stature: the rich air, the sensible meals which he was getting for the first time in his life: but as she covertly observed his face, when he sat at ease in the verandah gazing at the life of the promenade, she could feel like one who cuts away an overgrowth of trees and sees the stunted plant below just starting to push up towards its natural height.

Miss Exel quietly explained to Mrs Cupwin, taking her into her own room, that this Mr Ardree was not the kind of guest they usually had at the North View.

"You do see how it is, Mrs Cupwin, the letter came from *her*, really nice paper, and the writing and everything, and when you've had the experience I've had, well, you do know how to judge that sort of thing. So naturally I thought he'd be the same. Though of course with the war and everything you don't quite know where you are, the same as you used to in the old days."

The deception (as she secretly called it) was indeed hard on Miss Exel, whose grandfather had been mayor of Lowestoft and who brought a sense of duty to her calling. No hotel can be run without a policy, and the pains she took in placing her advertisements were equalled by her care with all the minutiae of management. She was a woman of practical charity. She wanted her guests to be happy, class distinction was the enemy of happiness and she stoically repulsed it from North View by telling the unsuitable that her accommodation was already booked for the entire season. Small gradations she recognized—you would find them, surely, even in such an establishment as the Alderney—and these she sought to mitigate by her skilful allotment of tables, so that people of the same kind would find themselves neighbours. Long ago she had moved her own things into a smaller room so as to make the front room of the entresol into a second lounge: the label *Private* stayed on the door, and she would only mention the room, choosing a tactful opportunity, to one or two guests whose letters had come on die-stamped paper. "If you do find the lounge a tiny bit crowded, Mrs Duntisbourne, I hope you'll make use of my little drawing-room. You will have it quite to yourself, except for Captain and Mrs Bede and the two Miss Leppings." And in every approach to what she sometimes called 'my North View family', in wishing them good-morning, suggesting appropriate excursions, calling attention to the little rules she had made for the general harmony, she showed the same sensibility towards their individual feelings. "What I want," she said, directing Gracie to put the napkin with the darns on Miss Green's table, the newer one on Mr Filleul's, "is to make everyone—no matter who they are—feel they are getting just as much atttention here as they are used to everywhere else." Her benevolence shone all day in her puckered, rather mournful eyes, it was reflected in a score of little notices: *'Guests retiring after 10 P.M., are kindly asked to remember, that Others may be Asleep. Thank-You!'* *' "T-O-W-E-L-S." To avoid Loss and Possible Inconvenience of Guests, who will follow, You are asked to kindly not use them, on the Beach. Thank-You!'* She was a small, stout, friendless woman of forty-six, all day long you heard the whimper of her glacé slippers as she sped from room to room upon her duties and her little kindnesses, opening a window in the lounge, adding a dash of pepper to the soup in the kitchen, straightening Mrs Duntisbourne's quilt and popping a vase of flowers on the Miss Leppings' chest of drawers; wondering with threadbare optimism if the Bedes would remember to send her a card at Christmas-time.

"And you see, Mrs Cupwin, now they *are* here I can't very well ask them to go, can I! I mean, I couldn't send a lady like Mrs Ardree to one of those places in St Michael's Road—that isn't at all the sort of thing *she* would be used to, would it now?"

Mrs Cupwin lit a new cigarette from the old. "Well, I wouldn't worry if I was you, Miss Exel. I'm sure *I* don't mind. What I say is—I was saying to Mr Cupwin only last night—you can't expect to pick and choose in these days, it's no use minding who you rub shoulders with, you've got to take the rough with the smooth, I said. I said the same to Miss St Estwyn and she agreed with what I said. She's nice, isn't she, Miss St Estwyn! Old-fashioned, of course. Lovely place she used to have in Berks, I'm told."

In truth, Mrs Cupwin did not at all mind Gian being in the hotel, especially as the Ardrees were up on the second floor and had the table near the service hatch, while hers was next but one to Miss St Estwyn's. She liked a mystery. At night, when she drowsed over a magazine in bed and Harold lay on his back already snoring, she conjured a semblance of Gian's face, the brutality of his brows and jaw, and the current of her thoughts would run warm and pleasantly. By day the young man had practical uses: in the unaccountable fashion of children Eileen and Désirée liked him, and as long as they didn't pick up his accent that attachment was much to her convenience. But he yielded values beyond these. Watching the incongruous pair at their almost silent meals, following them along the promenade, the man jacked up in his brand-new collar and sports coat with the slimly tailored girl holding his docile arm, she could re-assess her own spare fortunes. How well-mannered, after all, her Harold was, how quick to open doors for ladies, even if he smirked a little and followed through with a quick, washing movement of his hands. If the clothes he got for holidays were never exactly what she would have wished, how unself-consciously he wore them; and if he was not a tall man, a height of sixty-seven inches was nothing to be ashamed of. Those thoughts were scarcely formulated, they refreshed her mind as the sea air brought refreshment to her lungs and skin. She said to Miss St Estwyn:

"Well, I suppose the girl's made her own choice, and it's not for anyone to interfere now. It's up to her to make what she can of him." (How fully she understood that.) "And you know, I do think I've seen some improvement in the young man already. I can't help noticing the way he watches Mr Cupwin, little things he sees my hubby doing. It makes a difference, don't you think, to really *see* how things ought to be done—you know, *little* things, I mean."

"Yes, I'm sure Miss Exel does the best she can for all of us," the deaf old lady said agreeably, playing with her locket, graciously smiling, bowing herself away to the safety of the little drawing-room on the entresol.

In different degrees they were all grateful for so rich a source of speculation, not less stimulating because it had to be handled rather as the slipper which is hunted at children's parties and to be tucked away adroitly whenever the couple appeared. There was mystery here (as Mrs Cupwin had confided to each in turn) and it brought closer together a group of people who were themselves rather sadly unmysterious. Mrs Askell knew there was a baby behind it somewhere, and Mr Askell, whose views in the last nine years had turned out to be the same as hers, knew that as well, while Mr Bishop from Southampton said firmly with one side of his close, sagacious mouth, "Money—if you ask me!" But the elderly Miss Geswick met all such theories with her dim, elusive smile. "That isn't what *I* think!" she delicately said. What Miss Geswick thought no one was informed, and in Mr Bishop's opinion Miss Geswick did not know. But if she lacked a theory she had visions which made her lock the door of her room and keep the light on all night.

"Well, he's a quiet enough sort of chap, anyway," Mr Bishop said, passing the scones to Miss St Estwyn.

"That's exactly what I *don't* like!" Mr Cupwin shrewdly commented.

Mrs Askell agreed with Mr Cupwin. She said with meaning, "It's the quiet sort that cause the trouble, more often than not," and her husband said, "That's right!"

"I mean to say," Mr Cupwin explained, "you see these photographs of these fellows in the papers, fellows run in for housebreaking and worse things than that, and you'd say from the look of them they were quite ordinary sort of fellows."

Unexpectedly Miss Geswick broke in, playing her ace. She said triumphantly: "It's the *eyes* that tell you! Aren't I right, Miss St Estwyn?"

Miss St Estwyn graciously shook her head. "No, thank-you, no more for me."

Mrs Cupwin said: "Well, all the same, *I* think he's got quite nice-looking eyes."

"Now then! Now then!" Mr Bishop mechanically interposed.

"Yes, but have *you* looked at the shape of his chin?" Mr Askell demanded.

"Or at the top of his head?" asked Mrs Askell.

"Chap who's done a bit of boxing, I should say."

"Or butchering."

"Exactly!" said Miss Geswick with finality.

Mr Cupwin said hesitantly, "Well, you do get decent enough fellows in the butchering business, same as any other sort of business," and his wife added at once, "If it wasn't for the butchering trade I don't see how we'd get any meat. Harold, pass the biscuits to Mrs Askell."

"Is Mr Ardree a person who kills cows," Eileen inquired, "or does he only chop them up, like—"

"Now, Eileen," her mother said promptly, "If you've finished your tea you can wipe your hands and run along and play in the verandah."

Mr Cupwin, collecting his own and his wife's tea things and carrying them back to the tray, felt suddenly the need to establish himself. He was, after all, a man who had come a long way under his own steam—he had his kids at a private school along with the doctor's little girl—while most of these folks here were pretty much where their parents had put them, neither further back nor further on. He moved deliberately to the fireplace, stood with his heels on the fender and put his thumbs in the arm-holes of his waistcoat, so that the silver mounting of his wallet and the top of the Eversharp pencil showed like insignia of rank. With a small, distant smile he scanned the confusion of china and occasional tables, the giant cameo on the mauve landslide of Mrs Askell's chest, the haunted, pin-head eyes of Miss Geswick, Mr Bishop's glistening dome; and his gaze travelled on into the outer world, the Salisbury Hotel, the Belvedere, the pollard chestnuts along St Asaph's Terrace and the scarlet call-box.

"Well, I'm just a plain Englishman," he said slowly, "and I've got plain English views. Fair play for all, that's what I say, and I'm not speaking ill of any man, no matter where he comes from, till I've got something proved against him." He gave a look to his wife, needing her overt sympathy in this emotive hour, but she had taken up her knitting and her eyes were on the needles. "All the same," he concluded, "I've got a right to my own opinion, the same as everyone else, and you can tell me what you please, but there's something about that fellow I don't like the look of, and that's the end of it with me."

He released through his nose the breath that he found left over.

"Oh, look," said Mrs Askell, feeling for her jumper in the corner of the sofa, "the sun's come out!"

But the mystery was in some ways a disappointing one, it had the untidiness that spoils most of reality. The girl never played the part which her situation demanded: she seemed to accept the abnormal as a standard pattern, she was neither shamefaced nor defiant, neither scared nor innocent, neither furtive nor loquacious. In a comradely fashion each of the women made some opportunity for a quiet talk with her, not without hope of some confidence which would have a high retail value; but in the broad daylight shed by her even voice what should have been dark hints and reluctant half-admissions were as boldly outlined as the signboard of a sixpenny bazaar. The puzzle somehow remained. She gave at once too much and too little, and they were left like spectators at a conjuring show, confident that everything is done with mirrors but not quite knowing where the mirrors can be.

Mrs Askell got her in a corner of the lounge while Gian was out with the Cupwin children and told her how bad things were in the leather business. "I hope your husband's not connected with that trade at all, Mrs Ardree?"

Armorel looked up from her darning and smiled. "No, he's not. He was a jet washing hand in a traction depot, but he was dismissed a few weeks before we were married." Her voice was the quietest in the room, but no one had the smallest difficulty in hearing every word. "So at present he's not in any trade at all."

Sincerely grieved, Mrs Askell made kissing noises with her tongue. "It's terrible, putting men out of work. I suppose they were making room for some demobilized man?"

"Oh, no, it was just an ordinary sacking. I mean, a straightforward case of indiscipline."

Mrs Askell would not have pursued the matter. She was in the slightly embarrassing position of one who, discreetly asking for the loan of twopence, finds a wad of bank-notes thrust into his hand with the words 'I really can't think what to do with these.' But sympathy drove her one step further.

"Oh, I do hope that won't stand in the way of his getting something else?"

"Probably it would, if one meant to be quite honest about it. I'm getting him a job in the building trade, I hope."

"Oh, I think architecture is so interesting."

Armorel quietly corrected the implication. "Oh, nothing like that —I mean bricklaying. That's all he could do at present. He had some experience of that in prison. Do tell me where you got those lovely beads!"

That evening she informed Mr Bishop, who had ventured to beat about the financial bush, that her private income came at present to roughly forty pounds a year, and that she meant to look for some kind of domestic work. She casually told Miss Exel that the aunt with whom she had lived till lately had virtually refused to see her again, but that she was going to live with her parents-in-law for a time, "because they're delightful people and I want to know them better still." To Mr Askell's carefully introduced remark, that he had known extraordinary cases of men being reformed by good influence, she replied without ill-nature that she thought reformers were generally humbugs. At breakfast she was heard to say, "No, dear, nothing matters in the very least as long as I know you're happy." And a few minutes later, when Miss Geswick trapped her in a corner of the hall to exclaim with misted eyes, "Surely love is the most wonderful thing in the world!" she answered with her friendly smile and with the gentlest candour, "Well, you know, I never quite understand what that saying means."

No, when every fret-sawn piece they asked for was instantly produced they were still unable to make a recognizable picture. And obviously they would get nothing out of the young man himself, whose conversational resources were mainly limited to the phrases 'Morning!' 'Nice day!' 'All the same to me!' and 'I reckon that's about right.'

Not that he was exactly shy—his initial shyness had worn off quickly. He looked at them unflinchingly, but without a great deal of interest, standing against the wall with his hands in his trouser pockets and softly whistling. No manners at all but no ill-will. When Gracie stood holding the heavy tea-tray while the gentlemen scuttled about to clear a table and put it in the centre he would seize the tray himself with a brusque "Here, gimme!" and nod her out of the room, working the door with his heel. If Mrs Cupwin needed a light for her cigarette he threw her a box of matches across the room, or when Cupwin was handy he would rap him on the arm and say tersely, "Light for your missis!" With obviously kind intention he told Miss Geswick, in the manner of a provost corporal, that her dress was undone at the back. And when Mrs Askell circuitously described her husband's importance as manager of a wholesale firm in Nottingham he gave her a patient hearing before he remarked with untainted cordiality, "Well, good luck to him! Good enough, a sit-on-your-bum job, for a bloke with no body to him." He could not be quite ignored or ever patronized. They regarded him with discomfort and with a subtle, lingering trace of fear.

His behaviour to his wife was in some respects the same. Generally, at meals, he seemed to be looking past her, and though the ladies observed him with the tireless concentration of Boer snipers they never caught him in a gesture of tenderness. Yet it could not be said that he was neglectful. Indeed, he was remarkably quick in detecting her practical needs. She had only to feel about her for something that wasn't there and he would murmur "Want y'book?" and nod peremptorily and crash upstairs. If she needed pepper and the pot was empty he promptly marched across the room and with a casual "Lend us, half a jiff!" snatched one from another table. The chairs had been moved one morning, so that Armorel found a hard one in her place, while the chair with an upholstered seat which she had used at previous meals was now waiting for Mr Askell. Calmly, under Mrs Askell's eyes, Gian changed them back. When Armorel went to get her sewing after dinner and he arrived before her in the lounge he would stand like a bulldog in front of the small arm-chair she favoured there, and once, when Mr Cupwin tried to move it for the use of his own wife, he turned and said curtly "Leave that alone!"—which was enough. He seemed, in fact, to regard his wife as having peculiar and absolute rights. Directly the morning papers were brought in he strode up and seized the *Telegraph* for her before anyone else had a chance to pick. At tea he saw that she got her cup first, and would have no argument about it, when Mr Askell and certainly Mr Cupwin would have made the first delivery to Miss St Estwyn. Whenever Armorel wanted to leave a room he posted himself like a sentry to give her clear passage, and if one of the men through inadvertence was about to go in front of her he would put an unmistakable hand on the trespasser's arm. These manners, which the men regarded not without resentment, were extremely disturbing to Miss Exel. The other women, while they joined their menfolk in condemnation, reserved in their hearts sentiments not of unqualified disapproval.

He was nobody's idea of a husband. A watchdog, if you liked, or a personal servant, though he lacked a servant's obsequious airs. Her treatment of him was wifely, and the other women could only admire its skill: she never neglected to thank him for each small service, her orders were all the politest requests, she was stone-blind to all his gaucheries. To all that delicacy he seemed unable to find the smallest response. She smiled and he just nodded in reply. She gave him choice of plans and he only shrugged his shoulders. The little gestures of eye or hand that a lover watches, the special movements of a woman's neck and shoulders when one she cares for is helping her put on a jersey-coat, these enchantments appeared to impress him no more than a breeze ruffling his hair. But in his own fashion he repaid her with an almost ferocious loyalty. If he never studied her face he scarcely glanced at anyone else's. Waiting for her in the hall he seemed hardly to realize that others were passing by, and if they spoke to him he answered with a sullen brevity. He carried her things along the promenade—everything, it was a strict point with him that she should be empty-handed—with an air not of sufferance but of privilege, and the looks he shot at passers-by made many feel like footpads on the verge of arrest. In any small request on his own behalf he spoke to Miss Exel with a humble shyness, but when Armorel's comfort was concerned his applications had the shape of authority. The hotel, his expression and his stance asserted, was an object earmarked for his wife's convenience, like her handbag and her shoes. And the other visitors? Evidently he saw them as at best part of the hotel's furniture, supplying that background of movement and chatter to which his wife would be accustomed, a modest setting for her graces; but principally as a corporate incubus to be elbowed out of her way.

To this there were exceptions. With the Cupwins' peaky and fretful children he was on terms of intimate understanding which the others found hard to understand. Mrs Cupwin had hoped for boys; and as if to atone for their sex as best they could the little girls were so calamitously like their father that, as someone said, you could almost see the pince-nez sprouting from their little dribbly beaks. Their parents were bringing them up with care: they were dressed all day in frocks which would not have looked odd at a Christmas party, they were almost incessantly clean, and every attempt they made to disturb the North View peace, to shout, to whine, to create untidiness or demand their mother's attention, was met from an armoury of measured threats and ambiguous promises, of practiced demurrers and nimble evasions. The policy left a certain overflow of restlessness for someone to mop up, and among all the visitors (who were generous enough with casual affability) this husband of Mrs Ardree's alone took on the task, with an enthusiasm which seemed to argue some feebleness of mind. For long periods he lay on the floor to let the children roll about on top of him, take off his shoes and rake his hair. He made peculiar faces and what Mrs Cupwin considered dreadfully common sounds, and when Désirée cried "Again! again!" he repeated the performance tirelessly.

To Eileen he brought paper and scissors for cutting-out, which she liked to do lying on the sofa, with her legs over the pommel, or wandering with a slow dance-step about the room. He would go round after her, collecting the clippings in the waste-paper basket, which Désirée would presently get hold of to sling the contents half-way across the floor; then he would grin and go down on his knees and pick them up all over again. Once or twice Armorel ventured a hint that this treatment of children was open to certain objections:

"You see, dear, if they get their own way every single time when you're amusing them they'll get to think that other people ought to treat them in the same way. And you see, if Désirée keeps on throwing waste-paper all over the place at home, when her mother's got all the housework to do, there's bound to be trouble and tears."

But he seemed unable to follow that reasoning. It was remarked by those who were interested that the matter of the Cupwin children was the single one in which young Mr Ardree betrayed an inclination to take a line of his own.

Miss St Estwyn was the other exception to his neutrality.

All the others put an extra polish on their manners for the benefit of the dim old woman whose face and body had collapsed like the walls of a cheap candle, leaving only the heavily-browed eyes to suggest her former presence. They bowed to her in a way they had learnt from period films, they ran to pick up the needles and the spectacle-case which constantly slid down the taffeta slopes of her lap. For it was understood that she had been an early friend of Mrs Pankhurst and herself a person of some significance in her time. Perhaps Mr Ardree would have approached her with equal decorum had it been within his power; he so far lacked the means that he appeared to overlook the necessity; but he plainly recognized her existence as of one belonging to a higher order of creation than sofas and hearthrugs, his eyes occasionally strayed towards her, and on only his second morning in the hotel he said sharply to Mr Bishop, who was idly picking up a book from the lounge window-seat, "You can't have that, it belongs to the old girl!" By tea-time Mr Bishop had hammered the incident into one of his jokes: he told Askell that "Miss St Estwyn maketh the dumb to speak."

She had a rubber-ferruled stick for her little walks outside, and kept it for safety in a dark corner of the hall behind the grandfather clock, where it was rather difficult to find. It became a habit of Gian's whenever she appeared in outdoor clothes, to fetch the stick and bring it to her at the foot of the stairs; where he would push it into her hand, say "There y'are!" and slouch away. In the town one morning he saw a conductor trying to hurry her as she was hobbling to catch a bus; he left Armorel and crossed the road, lifted Miss St Estwyn bodily on to the platform, slung a dozen words of undiluted Kennington in the conductor's face and then took his stand in front of the bonnet till he saw that she was safely in her seat. When she came to thank him for this service, he did not seem to hear. And on other occasions, when he pulled away her table to let her out after meals, or spontaneously got something she wanted from upstairs, his manner was so off-hand that it almost looked as if he meant to insult her.

And yet she accepted that treatment without any sign of offence, sometimes with a smile which it was difficult to interpret. It was wonderful, everyone said, how good-natured the old thing was. Perhaps a little too good-natured, when Mrs Askell offered to hold her wool for winding and she answered, "No, if you please, I'll have Mr Ardree if his wife can spare him—it requires such a lot of patience." But at her age such eccentricity was pardonable; for she was, they felt, superlatively English and the sister, they had been told, of a major-general's wife.

One late afternoon she beckoned the young man as she sat in the verandah, and made him bring his chair beside hers.

"They tell me you have been in prison recently," she said in her deep and friendly voice. She was not as deaf as she seemed, she had merely learnt in seventy-six years that very little of what people said was worth the trouble of listening. "I suppose the prisons are just as silly and shocking as they always were? No, I've never used one myself, but two of my nieces have been put away from time to time and they both speak very critically of the *organization*. Of course they're by way of being 'ladies', and 'ladies' have lots of silly fads. I make allowance for that . . . you know, you're a very fortunate man. You have an extremely beautiful wife, beautiful and clever. She reads silly books, but the sort of silly books people *should* read at her age. I hope you're going to look after her very carefully?"

He replied, more fluently than anyone but she would have expected, that his wife was far too good for him.

"You see how it is," he said, "I got no means of knowin' what sort of things she wants. No cash neither, if it comes to that. She's gettin' me fixed up on a job of some kind, she says. Well, a bloke do what he can. I mean to say, she wanted the hitch-up all right, that's the way it looked to me. Of course she ought to have had a silky, you don't have to tell me that, I can see that just as plain as the next bloke."

"No," Miss St Estwyn said almost fiercely, "that's quite wrong! You must try to be sensible—you're a very sensible man indeed, only men never are quite sensible about their womenfolk. No, a silky wouldn't have suited her at all! A woman with Mrs Ardree's brains gets the *sort* of husband she ought to have—if she really needed a silky she'd have found one and made him marry her. Don't ever forget that! I've lived long enough to know what I'm talking about. Now I want you to move my chair, round this way, and yours this way . . . That's right."

"Get the sun right in your face that way!" he warned her. "Give y' a bad head."

"I know. But it's better than being where I can see all the ridiculous people in this hotel. I want to look at your hands. Of course I'm an old maid, I suppose that's why I like looking at men's hands. You've got really splendid hands, so strong." She smiled and actually caught him smiling. "That's a thing you hardly ever find in a silky, the beauty of strong and useful hands. You must always make your wife realize how good they are, how useful and how firm and beautiful, these hands of yours." She chuckled, so that when he had passed through his surprise he was forced to smile again as he watched the many folds of her dilapidated face in the bright, sloped sunshine, the young, defiant eyes. "How lucky—what a wickedly lucky girl! Having such a lovely body and a man with glorious hands!"

It was only on the last afternoon of their stay that the old woman had any but the most casual conversation with Armorel herself. She found her alone in the lounge, writing, when Gian had taken the children to see MacAndrew's Curiosities, and she took a seat close beside her.

"Too aggravating!" she said presently. "You thought you had found an hour's peace to get on with your letters, and now this old person comes in and starts chattering."

Armorel smiled and closed her writing pad.

"I'd always much rather chatter. These are only business letters."

Miss St Estwyn nodded approvingly. "In every family the woman ought to do all the business. Men think they *understand* business: they have phrases they like the sound of—you know, 'glad if you will proceed in accordance with the terms of your quotation,' that sort of thing —and that makes them a prey to all the rogues in the world. It takes a woman to grasp the great philosophic truth that if you take a pound out of a stocking the stocking holds one pound less than it did before."

"Well, perhaps so. But I mean my husband to do all the business as soon as he knows how."

"You're teaching him?"

"I shall. But of course I can only take things slowly. He's got everything to learn."

"Everything? I should have thought he knew more about some things than you and I ever shall know."

"You mean—?"

"Well, what life is like before it has been soaked in sauce and sprinkled with bread crumbs."

"Oh, of course. No, I only meant that he's had practically no schooling, never been anywhere, no technical education of any kind."

"And you're going to get him all that?"

Armorel nodded. "By degrees." She spread her left hand on her knee and examined her rings, the gold one and the one with the huge synthetic ruby. "Of course we've practically no money, but we shall both be in work—a friend of mine is getting him a job in a constructional firm. I've already paid the fee for the course he's taking in elementary building technology. That may put him into a slightly better position, and then I think I'll be able to get him a rather more advanced course—"

"You mean, really, that you want to get him into something better than a labourer's job? Something you do in a collar and tie?"

"Do you think that's absurdly ambitious?"

It appeared unlikely that Miss St Estwyn would reply. As a kitten quivering with the ardour of a protracted stalk will suddenly relax and start to wash itself, so, when her expressive mouth was already shaping for an answer, her interest seemed all at once to fade. Her eyes had turned from Armorel's face towards the window, to hunt some ghost along the windy, makeshift street. She had known so many women and their belongings, their hard-wrought attitudes, their men, their anxious clothes; she was too tired now to remember how the pieces were supposed to fall. But at length she did speak again.

"No," she said negligently, "I only wonder whether it's worth the cost. The cost to him, I mean."

Armorel said slowly: "Yes, I expect anyone would ask that. Anyone who doesn't know him as I do. Well, that means everyone, really. You see, when a man's never learnt any form of self-expression at all—when he's merely been chucked into the first roughneck job that comes along, just treated like a mill-horse by the people who employ him and like a cross between a lunatic and a criminal by everyone else—well, he doesn't realize himself that he's got anything inside him, and it stands to reason that no one else can either. Not unless they happen to notice odd little things. You'd never imagine that Gian had any ideas about architectural design. Well, of course, he hasn't, in the formal sense. In the practical sense, he has—ideas and instincts that no one else's ever bothered to look for. It's all there, but it hasn't grown because the ground's never been tilled. You know, people give their whole lives to a few acres of soil, cleaning it up and making it yield its richness. Well, surely a human being's worth as much trouble as that."

Her English voice, not meant for urgency, had gradually slipped a little. She brought it back into its groove.

"Of course he needs everything, and I haven't got such an awful lot to give him. I've got a certain amount of intelligence, that's about all. Still, when I start a thing I don't give it up. That's what's going to count in the end."

Miss St Estwyn had begun the process of gathering her things together; she could never sit very long in the same place. She stood up, trying her balance like a sea-lion, smiling obscurely at her own reflection in the mirror on the wall.

"Yes," she said, "there are things he needs," and she started her progress towards the door. "He needs love—really a very great amount of love."

Armorel slipped ahead to open the door for her; and having gently closed it again returned to her letter: ". . . may be living at Contessa Street at any rate for a few weeks, if I feel that Gian's mother really has room for us—there are three storeys and Gian says there are quite a lot of rooms. I feel so strongly that he will be far more comfortable with me when he sees that I am quite at home in his own surroundings. I do think your Henry has been good about the job. I promise that Gian will work his hardest and make it a success . . ."

The fracas with the Cupwins occurred towards the end of their stay. Since a storm in the tea-cup you live in is bound to be disturbing, the affair was a little more disagreeable than Armorel's reference in her diary reveals.

Mrs Cupwin had been indoors all day, partly because of the rain and partly to finish an *Ideal Marriages* competition from which she hoped to win £250. She sat smoking, knees wide apart, with photographs of the Stars and an entry form spread out on her lap. On the other side of the lounge her husband was noisily asleep with his head on last Sunday's *People*, the windows were all shut and her head was aching.

Eileen was being good. She had stopped begging to be taken to the beach and lay on her front near the door, drawing many-petalled flowers on the title page of a *Playbox Annual* and rather monotonously humming the air of *Daisy had a Dandy*. Désirée, left without employment, was making a leisurely tour of the room, jigging the ornaments on the cabinet, teasing the blind-tassels, spinning a castor on an upturned chair. In less than an hour she had asked her mother three times whether there would be Grape Nuts for supper; to which Mrs Cupwin had answered on the first occasion that she did not know, on the second that Désirée was to keep quiet and not be a worry, on the third that if she asked the question once more she would get a good slap. The warning was unambiguous: it is hard to believe that the child did not understand it.

This background was unknown to Gian. Returning from an abortive walk towards Hawkes Cliff, he came into the lounge just as Désirée, on the completion of her circuit, was quietly running her fingers round the panel moulding of the door which led to the dining-room. He was smiling at Eileen, and rolling her over with his foot, when Désirée said in a tiny voice, without turning round:

"Mummy, do you *think* there's going to be Grape Nuts for supper?"

Mrs Cupwin in one swift movement gathered up all the papers from her lap and put them on to the arm of her chair. She said:

"Désirée! Come here!"

Accustomed to obey that tone (for she had once tried the experiment of ignoring it) Désirée went to her; slowly, thoughtfully, but to outward appearance trustingly. Mrs Cupwin's mouth made a little smile of a curious kind. She glanced obliquely at Gian, and it may have passed through a corner of her mind that she was giving him a demonstration some time overdue. She waited till the child was close to her, then pounced on her wrist and slapped her hand with a good deal of force.

Perhaps three seconds passed before Désirée let out her first wail. (In that interval the worst of the physical pain was probably over.) There was time, before the noise began, for Mrs Cupwin to add her footnote, "You know what I said!" and for Gian, white, stiff and trembling, to reach her chair. Gian said:

"You got no fumin' right to hit a kid like that!"

Mrs Cupwin did not reply. The phosphorescent rage in Gian's voice gave her the same kind of shock that the blow had given the child, and his eyes, as he stood over her, made her more frightened than she had ever been in her life. Her husband did answer. The sound of the slap had roused him, he had caught Gian's obscene adjective and realized that it was addressed to his wife. From his position he could not see Gian's face and he was not frightened at all. He stood up, and raising his thin voice to overcome the uproar which Désirée was making, he said with all the force that indignation could gather from his narrow-chested body:

"Here, that's enough of that!"

The second shock, from hearing her father speak in such a tone, brought Désirée to a heaving silence; while Eileen, still on the floor, gazed at the grown-ups' singular behaviour with a petrified curiosity in which there was a faint tingle of delight.

"What do you mean by it," Cupwin fumed, "talking to my wife that way! Language like that!" His voice, as Gian turned towards him, lost a little of its ring, but he had enough impetus left to carry him on. "Time you were back where you come from—I don't know what they're thinking of, having the sweepings off the slums in a house like this, meant for decent respectable folk!"

Mrs Cupwin, recovering her nerve, said: "I suppose I'm not fit to bring up my own child!"

Gian answered: "No, you ain't!"

Cupwin said: "I'd like you just to repeat that!"

"She ain't fit to have nothin' to do with any kid," Gian said.

To that point the situation had developed when Armorel came in. She grasped it instantly. It was not difficult to know all about the Cupwins, and the spectacle gave her clues enough: the two men facing each other, Gian smiling as he waited with a dangerous patience for Cupwin to hit him, Cupwin feeling about for a mask of dignity and muttering that he'd a good mind to put the matter in Miss Exel's hands. But if a résumé was needed, Mrs Cupwin in her own fashion supplied it. She spoke rather fast on one high, slightly unnatural note:

"Perhaps you'd like this room to yourselves, Mrs Ardree, you and your husband? I think your husband thinks I and my husband aren't quite fit to be in the same room with him—we're people who aren't fit to bring up our own children, so it seems. I suppose the children never do get slapped in Bethnal Green, or whatever part your husband comes from. Little tiny touch that wouldn't hurt a kitten! I suppose they can make themselves a plague all day long and no one says a word to them. What some may call upbringing, I don't doubt, only there are some who don't much care for the results, only judging by what they see."

"Gian," said Armorel, "would you be a dear and run along to the post office before it shuts. I meant to get some three-halfpenny stamps—you'll find half a crown on the dressing-table." She waited till he was out of the room and then said, "I'm sorry, I interrupted you. You were saying—?"

"What *I'm* saying," Cupwin interjected, "is that I'm not going to have Mrs Cupwin insulted in this hotel, and that's flat!"

"Yes, and if you find Mr Cupwin smashing your husband's face in for him," his wife added, "you needn't come laying the blame on me! He's got plenty of patience, my husband has, but when it comes to having guttersnipes putting their tongue out at him, that's trying him a bit *too* high!"

Désirée, standing scared and forlorn by the cabinet, had started to whimper again. Armorel, turning her back on the Cupwins, knelt on one knee beside her. "Désirée, is your hand still hurting?" She took Désirée's hand in hers, but the child, crying "No! No!" snatched it away.

"You'll kindly leave that child alone!" Mrs Cupwin snapped, and her husband echoed, "You leave her alone!"

This broadside appeared to finish the battle. The young wife stiffened as with a sudden and violent pain, she turned to glance at the avenging pair with eyes that seemed to be blinded by their fire, and then without a word went to the door. There, however, she turned again, and stood smiling with her fingers on the handle.

"Listen!" she said, and the calm of her voice surprised them. "If Mr Cupwin wants to give my husband a thrashing I don't see any objection at all. Only I hope you'll let me watch, because it ought to be interesting. Or if he thinks it would be simpler to make a fuss with the proprietress—well, I can't object to that. All *I* shall do in that case is to make an equal amount of fuss with the N.S.P.C.C. And in the meantime I don't really want to hear anything more from either of you till you've got yourselves under control."

The door had very gently closed behind her before they thought of any reply.

Superficially, the results of the skirmish were negligible. The Cupwins ceased to say 'Good-morning' to the Ardrees, they discovered ostentatiously that they and the children needed a walk whenever Mr Ardree or his wife entered the lounge. There were consequences reaching further in time, a small but perceptible change in the attitude of the Cupwin children towards their parents and of the parents towards each other. But those mutations had to adjust themselves in one of the new estates on the outskirts of Bristol, many miles away from the North View Hotel.

To Armorel it gave a heightened sense of her powers: she had met with trouble slightly different from any she had envisaged and handled it with success: but it gave her also a new conception of the magnitude of her task. In the talk she and Gian had that evening, gentle and good-humoured on her part, laconic on his, he had shown himself not only blind to Mrs Cupwin's point of view but unable to conceive as possible a world of sensibilities differing from his own: and in one moment of cold despair, when he sat on the edge of the bed staring woodenly at an evening paper and repeating the very words he had used ten minutes before, she felt as Annie Sullivan may have done when Helen Keller first came into her care. But if the mountain looked higher from the foothills than from the plain there was still no limit, she thought, to her muscle and wind.

> The great thing, [she wrote to Daphne Steaben next morning] is never to lose your nerve. One's intelligence will do everything that's wanted—in time—so long as one doesn't let it collapse in a fit of the shakes. We go to Contessa Street tomorrow, and then I shall be in it up to my neck. It's so frightening that I feel joyously excited . . .

After all, people pay money for the experience of danger. They cling to each other screaming with fright as the scenic railway cars make the first vertiginous plunge and five minutes later they are queueing up to pay their shillings for another ride. But the perils belonging to reality are not so nicely measured out; in reality the tensions go on, ugliness takes new forms to turn the stomach by catching you unawares, danger like the rub of an ill-fitting shoe is a dire familiarity which attenuates endurance, to snap it perhaps at the moment of maximum strain.

Danger? Fear? When she looked back across the twelve years to the first days of her marriage such words as those would seem grandiloquent and false. Yet her physical sensations, as the train settled to its homeward stride, as the sprawl of villas and workshops thickened to obliterate the Essex fields, were precisely those of fear: a draught through the loins, bubbles in her throat on which a word or two would slip and tumble. From there North View, with its incessant calls on her tact and contrivance, looked like a harbour which no storm had ever reached, the last nine days a season of untrammelled contentment. For a time, at least, her memory would keep securely a few scraps of that sharply-lit experience: a strip of sunlight across the blue quilt, sand on the linoleum, the routine of absurd, grave courtesies: and she realized already, with the grimed houses of Forest Gate crowding past the window, that the feeling those shreds recalled would be one of safety, of safety starting to leak.

She was pinioned in her corner of the carriage, which was full and nauseous with smoke. Gian, pressed up against her, sat staring balefully at a sailor who had given her a casual grin, and she was surprised when he suddenly turned to look at her face.

"Something on your mind?" he asked.

She smiled. "I was only thinking, it's a bit hard on your mother, having a daughter-in-law thrust into her house like this."

He considered that remark with lowered brows, as if he were really trying to imagine thoughts and happenings outside his present experience. He said at length, off-handedly:

"You don't need to worry your head, Miss Susie. Mum, you see, she take things the way they come."

His eyes had returned to the sailor's face, but his hand slid cautiously between the back of the seat and her waist; reminding her, in a moment of distress, of a journey to the other Stratford she had made with Gordon Aquillard. "It's stuffy, isn't it!" she said, and the hand slid back to its place. The train ran screaming through Bethnal Green, the funereal faces swung in unison as it lurched across the Shoreditch points and the dark chaos of Liverpool Street gathered to hold it fast.

19

BEFORE the door to the back room was opened the smell of tomato ketchup came out into the shop. The noise of forks and of laughter drowned the squeak of the door, and no one looked up when they went inside. The weak bulb which hung near the dresser was already turned on, for the closed windows resisted the dwindling daylight and the room was clouded with smoke.

Ed Hugg sitting sideways to the table was reading the outside sheet of the *Star*. Rosie's baby was on Simon's knee, where Rosie fiddled with its wrappings, and at the other end a man with strange growths on his face and neck tried to tempt it with sugar melted in his teaspoon. The laughter came chiefly from Maria, who with her face to the company was stirring a saucepan on the range with one hand and wiping the sweat from her forehead with the other; but a tiny desiccated woman at the farther side was laughing too, shaking so much that she could not get her cup back on the saucer and from time to time relieving her mirth with a piercing squeal, which the florid man beside her accompanied with resounding slaps on his thighs and a chain of snorts like a locomotive going uphill. The grey, stained table-cloth was loaded with pickle and ketchup jars, jars of chutney and mayonnaise, bottles of vinegar and Daddy's Sauce.

Gian, still holding two suitcases and with Armorel beside him, stood patiently just inside the door. It was Ed who first saw him and called out, "Coo, it's Gyan—Gyan, how are you, boy!" Then stillness came, the utter stillness which comes upon a room when the whistle is heard of a bomb falling.

Maria recovered first. Still with the spoon in her hand she rushed upon her son, put her arms round his body as far as they would go and held him to her breast, laughing tearfully and plunging one wet kiss after another upon his mouth. The rest came round, they shook his hands, they struck him on the shoulders and behind, crying,

"Cheerio, Gyan boy, how does it feel!" while Rosie held Evangeline's face against his neck. But the weight of his agonized shyness crushed their welcome and the scattered silence flooding back rose up to hold them where they stood.

They knew that they had to do something about Gian's wife, but they could only look at her sidelong, each hoping that someone else would act or speak. She stood wearing a smile that had begun to pinch, she said in a voice she hardly recognized: "I'm afraid we've come back at a dreadfully awkward time!" But no one answered her, no one could think of a word to say.

20

No, the honeymon had given her no cause for self-reproach. That was how she had felt as they humped their baggage from the Elephant to Contessa Street; and years later, when she was turning out boxes for the move from their Weald Street home and an old tie of Gian's sent her thoughts back to the North View Hotel, her judgement was the same. In those first days she had aimed at limited objectives: to acclimatize herself to things that would offend her delicacy (his grossness in digestion, his habit of lighting a cigarette before he got out of bed) by making her wish in these physical matters wholly subservient to his; to give him confidence in her and in himself; to perfect her own knowledge of him. Perhaps she had not entirely achieved the last of these. Seeing him asleep and waking, learning all his gestures as he shaved and dressed and ate his meals, discovering what things would interest, amuse or anger him, she was always conscious of some room to which she had no key. But perhaps, after all, that room was empty. Circumstances had furnished her own house richly; it might be wrong to suppose that every corner of another's was filled. She said to him, on the night when Antonia was conceived:

"You enjoyed the holiday, didn't you, Gian?"

He answered drowsily: "Yes, I reckon that was all right."

A little afterwards, when she thought he had fallen asleep, he said with his head turned away: "You know, Susie, I'll get things the best way I can for you. A place of your own, some sort of a place, soon as I earn any chink. Do the best I can."

She told him, letting his forehead rest against her side, that he was never to be anxious about her comfort; that he should work only to make the best of his own gifts, that he must be patient, remembering that the early stages were always laborious and dull. "You know, Gian, I'll never lose my faith in you." (And surely—as she stood at the window looking at the familiar Weald Street houses and waiting for the remover's van—she had never lost faith in his power to advance.) "And you know, even the early stages won't be so desperately hard, with me there to help you. We can do such a lot together, I can explain all sorts of things . . ."

But his thoughts did not seem to be marching with hers. In this house where all the sounds and smells which penetrated the gimcrack walls were those he had lived with from childhood it was he who appeared, just then, to be lonely and afraid. Her voice had not been quite free from tears; for in their strange country the whole of her existence was narrowed to her hopes of Gian, and at a moment of such fatigue her calm was overstrained by his dreadful importance. Those tears must have frightened him, in the way that young children are frightened by some look in the mother's face which they do not understand. He murmured something, and she caught the words ". . . know it weren't right." Then she could only say, "Aren't you happy, Gian? Nothing's wrong if only you're happy," wondering with the swift mind of weariness what the shape of happiness could be in one of his simplicity. She put her hand in his (remembering what Gordon would have wanted) but he held it only as a sensitive child will hold the body of a bird he has killed in thoughtless mischief.

In the smaller room to which Gian's parents had moved (the room previously used by Mr Olleroyd) Simon was telling his wife that he thought Gian had changed already. "More grown-up, see what I mean. More hold on himself, see what I mean." Maria, with most of her face in the pillow, gave out that laugh of hers which had nothing to do with comedy. "Ssuss! Why would you tsink! Gian?—a married man, tsassis what Gian is now! Aa—but he still issis mother's own lil-ragazzo!" And in the room next to theirs the Huggs were talking at the bottom of their voices so as not to wake Evangeline. ". . . All right then, have it your own way, she *is* pretty. Only what she'll be like after Gian's had her a year or two . . ." ". . . Oh, yes, quite the little bloody gent he is now. *Delahtful holidah, mah dear fellah! Pass the potatahs to mah wahf, there's a good fellah! Mah wahf's secuahed me quaht a decent appointment as a bricklayer, doncherknowah . . ."*

Yes, it was clear in distant retrospect that the plan of starting in Contessa Street was the one which had been miscalculated. But her reasons still seemed to have been sound enough. She had wanted his evolution to be as natural as it could. When work and study were making unprecedented demands on his patience it would not be fair to burden him with the embarrassment of new surroundings and an altogether new way of living.

"Besides," she had said, "I think your mother would be disappointed if we didn't accept her invitation. Of course we'll start straight away and keep on looking for a home that's within our means. But we've got to make sure of our income first, don't you think? You know I'm perfectly certain that the man with real intelligence who's ready to put everything he's got into the job will do better work in bricklaying than the man next him. So much better that it'll show, I mean . . ."

The trouble was that Contessa Street proved a poorer vehicle for companionship than she had supposed.

The narrow house, built originally for the manager of Dibdin's Cooperage, was a storey higher than its neighbours. In the 'nineties, when a certain Albert Moldenhauer had bought it and converted the front room into a harness shop, there had been an L-shaped yard at the back which belonged to the Roundel of Ely in Eton Street. Moldenhauer had taken over the yard and filled a great part of it with sheds of varying construction which had since been used as store-rooms, chicken-houses, and even as impromptu bedrooms for the lodgers whose plight and whose shillings Maria could never refuse. In time he had acquired the Roundel itself, when it had lost its licence and was going for a song, and had connected the two properties by an ingenious closed bridge of his own design and partly of his own workmanship. He had also joined one of the sheds to the Contessa Street house as an extra back room and built another room above it, to be reached from the bridge, but he had not thought of enlarging the original stairway or making a new one. In 1912 the freehold had passed to his son, Ernest Molinar, and at about that time the Roundel portion had been sentenced to destruction. While it lasted, however, Maria as lessee saw no objection to using those rooms in which the floors were tolerably safe for any purpose that from time to time occurred to her active intelligence. She liked to go through that way to Eton Street, where she did some of her shopping, and it was a route often taken by friends who came to see her.

She was not lacking in friends, for she was a good listener and her singular combination of lethargy and vivacity had a tonic property for those who suffered from melancholy or boredom. Indeed, her regular customers were all her intimates. During shop hours, which were never precisely limited, the chair by the glass-panelled biscuit chest was seldom without an occupant, generally a woman some way past the years of personal vanity, who would wait contentedly while chance customers were served and then pick up the conversation at the point where it had been broken. Often, when Maria decided to close the shop in order to rake a meal together or to feed her hens, she would transfer the visitor to the kitchen-living-room in the way that a later generation carries the wireless set from one room to another: she liked to have voices about her when she was cooking or washing, even when she was killing a chicken, which in itself was one of her keenest pleasures; she was always pleased to find that someone had come in through the Roundel and was waiting for her in the second back room. Simon also had his friends, former shipmates, fellow tradesmen from the halls, who never minded waiting. Occasionally, dejected and slightly furtive people came to ask for Mr Olleroyd and were directed across the bridge to his present room. And while the Huggs were staying in the house (which seemed likely to be for a long time, since Ed was making useful 'contacts') there were girlhood friends of Rosie's coming in to admire her child and talk about their boys. The place, then, had the feeling less of a house than a railway station. Maria was not English and had learnt no prejudice about homes and castles. She required no boundaries, she even disliked them. As her shop was a continuation of Contessa Street itself, her kitchen was a continuation of the shop. For the resultant congestion of the kitchen the remedies supplied by Moldenhauer were always to hand: people could overflow into the second back room or if necessary to a shed which had been empty since she had given up breeding Belgian hares; pans waiting to be scoured and clothes to be ironed could be put on the stairs, and if the stairs were choked the corridor above could take the superfluity. In the fact that most of the rooms were passages to others Maria saw no disadvantage. It accorded with her intuitive notions of freedom. She eluded the tyrannies of time as successfully as those of space, letting instinct and necessity divide her day as they would. Of a dozen clocks in the house the only one with its machinery in working order was without a minute hand.

In this field of liberty the newly married pair were not left much to themselves. Even the bedroom which Maria and Simon had generously surrendered gave them only a limited privacy. The little room to which it led was uninhabited, but Maria still kept some of her clothes there, together with shop stores, cleaning tools and a certain amount of food for the hens. Whenever she had to go through at night or in the earliest morning she did so with prodigious tact, handling the stiff latch of the door like a burglar, creeping as softly as her fifteen stone allowed and keeping her eyes towards the wall; but the exercise so worked upon her nerves that she seldom completed it without a burst of laughter, to be followed by torrents of confused apology, a plunge towards her son and a noisy kiss on both his cheeks. Under the threat of these incursions every conversation was inclined to be anxious and hurried, like the plotting of conspirators in a house infested with police. Museums, parks and cafés were still the only places where their companionship was in any way secured.

To all appearances Armorel was at home. She showed no surprise at food appearing on half-washed plates, at Simon's table customs or the things which were done to Evangeline between the dining-table and the range. She seemed to accept the whole of Maria's economy, only mitigating its worst effects by deft adjustments, surreptitiously opening windows, clearing a top layer of rubbish into the yard, creeping down late at night to scrub out the room. It was Gian who appeared at sea. The look of strain which had showed on the night of their arrival hardly lifted. Trivial features of daily life—the way that Simon cleared his tubes after eating, oblique witticisms about the underclothes drying on a line across the kitchen—set him glancing nervously at Armorel's face. He spoke very little, and less to his family than to his wife, though he found soft, shy grins for Maria whenever he caught her alone. To Ed's incessant jocularity about his new status, to Rosie's tiny, silken sarcasms ("Very kind, your missis is, giving me hints about my baby, very good of her to spare the time!") his answer was a sullen stare (though once, when Ed went so far as to couple Armorel's name with a sly obscenity, there was such a tightening in his body that Ed found it convenient to stroll out of doors). People who had known the household for some time remarked to Simon that his son did not seem himself. "That lad of yours," old Vincent the cobbler said, "he's got such a dainty dish it give him the whole-time bellyache." And even Maria, who regarded English weather and English moods with a tolerance hardly short of amaurosis, noticed the change.

On a Sunday morning when Simon stood in the yard, staring despondently at the little plot of clay and cinders which he always hoped would become a flower-bed, she came and stood beside him, holding under her arm a cockerel she had chosen for execution.

"Magnifico—allse lovly bloom!"

She pointed to the few tired leaves lying amid the groundsel, uttered a squeal of laughter and pinched his cheek.

"I reckon they done me down over the seed," he answered. "Ted Eeley got it, he reckoned it was all right."

She nodded: "You are *good* garden-man, Simon, ifse give you *good* seed, *good* ert'—'njussa tiny-tiny-tiny piece of brain, sisi?" She laughed again and put the cockerel's feathers against her cheek. The job in hand was one she liked to do at leisure and with loving attention to a ritual of her own; having caught her bird she would fondle and talk to it, she would hold it at arm's length, laughing, and show it off to its fellows, telling them of the beauty and agony of death. "You tell me, Simon," she said suddenly, "Gian—why isse not happy? Tsegirl—Miss Susie—you tsink she will not go to bed, hn?"

He stooped to pull out a weed. Though he refused to believe that any trait in Maria was an absolute imperfection he disliked her direct approach to matters of importance. In his last years at sea he had never uttered the word 'torpedo', believing that this was the way to keep you clear of them, and his faith in that policy had scarcely lessened when he had been torpedoed twice in seventeen months. He said cautiously:

"The lad's all right, nothing wrong with him, not that I can see. He got to get used to it, that's all. Been a good boy, see, never had nothing to do with skirts, he tell me that quite straightforward, nobody but that freak from Biddle's Place, and he can't have meant no harm by her. You got to get used to it, same as everything else."

With a firm hand on the cockerel's neck she stroked its breast with her forehead. She was not listening. She seldom listened to Simon, whose English—she complained to her friends—was very bad; but she picked up the sense of what he said whenever she felt inclined.

"You tsink she lov Gian?" she demanded. "I tsink he lov her vereverevere moch."

But he in his turn evaded the issue. "You see, Maria, it's not like what she's been accustomed. You see how it is. I'm not saying the place isn't all right. I'm not saying it isn't run very nice, having the shop on your hands and everything, you can't expect a house to be run the way a ship is. Well, you see how it is, I might see Ted Eeley sometime, see what he might get them serviette things, make her feel like what she's been accustomed. I'm not denying it's a lot of fish-an'-fancy, but that's the way it is. First-class saloon, passengers all get them serviettes, clean every meal. Second-class, clean every two days—all the big lines."

His tone told her again that he was saying nothing worth her attention.

"You tsink I speak?" she demanded. "I tell Miss Susie she mus' go vereverevere kine wis my ragazzo? I tell her, you go to bed, you makse *good* wife, hn?"

"Well, no," he said, "you leave it to me, I'll talk to her. I know how they talk, see—I done first-class serving, times they was short on staff in the old *Semiramis*, I done it on the Singapore run, too—I know the kind of talk they use, folk in that way of life." He started to move towards the house, he couldn't bear to see anything killed. He said over his shoulder, "You do better and leave it to me."

That undertaking gave him two anxious days in which his friends at the Warwick Palace found him curiously silent and abstracted. Not altogether unhappy days, for he was conscious of dormant powers which he believed would rally to the cause of his son's well-being. At night, as he walked from the theatre to the tube, stirred by the cold air, the moving lights and the equalizing darkness, his mind lit up as if a match were applied to shavings and dry wood. Words came to him like manna; the jewels of Miss Braddon's art, once tumbled from seamen's libraries into the dark recesses of his memory, rose to the surface like new creations of his own brave spirit. Yes, he would speak to Gian's wife. He would approach her not as a suppliant but as a person of equal rights and equal dignity demanding justice. She might very well suppose that in giving herself to a man of humbler status she had done him a favour; ah, but humility was often a disguise for nobility of spirit, and the day might come when the name Ardree would be one which the highest in the land would sigh for. Let her ask herself, then, what was her duty. What was the duty of any woman who had pledged herself in the sight of God and man? Could she be content to enjoy the fruits of the married state, the honour, the security, while the man who had given her these benefits was languishing sick at heart? He bought a threepenny ticket and went on into the lift, unconscious of the crowd shoving him into the corner, the vast, steely eyes of the girl on the other wall proclaiming, 'I've found Romance since I learnt the *Ida Rossignon* Way.' "I address you," he said, all but aloud, "with the passion of a man deeply wronged, with the authority of a father. I speak kindly now. But let me once be satisfied that my son has been treated with contempt, his happiness sacrificed to a woman's vanity and whim, and neither womanhood nor pity shall restrain my arm." Yet pity was not outside his thoughts as the train carried him northward. In the window, where the grey pipes rose and fell above his own reflection, he saw scenes of noble forgiveness and reconciliation; of Miss Susie embracing his knees, the tender gratitude of Gian, Maria's eyes shining upon him with wonder and admiration. But first, he thought, his mind chilling a little as he turned into Newington Causeway, I must get her alone.

Half-way through a five-week season he had not to be at the theatre before ten, and on a morning when he came down for his breakfast at nine o'clock he found Armorel washing Evangeline's napkins. Maria was serving shop and the Huggs were in their own room, Olleroyd had already gone out "to try for a bit of luck" as his formula was. Armorel said without looking round, "I'll do your bacon in one minute —I just want to rinse these through." He walked deliberately to the sink and stood beside her. It was the wrong moment, he realized that now; the fire was not alight in him; but having got so far he would not retreat.

"Now listen, Miss Susie, I'd like to have a few words with you if you don't mind." He was perfectly calm, he thought, and yet his heart had begun to hammer, sending up a wind on which his words shook and bounced. "Now I know right well that this is not the sort of house which you been accustomed," he said skilfully, looking round at the litter of unwashed china, clothes and shop stores which covered the tables and most of the floor. "You see the way it is, things is very uncertain in the theatre business, chap may be earning a bit one month, show crack up, no sort of work the next. Well, it isn't as if people got all that money to spend, no munitions or anything, it's not like a running a shop before the war. Of course I reckon I could clean the place up a bit, only Maria, you see, she like to have things the way she put them, seeing they do things different in the part she was brought up in as you might say."

His voice was settling, and he was moving steadily towards the kernel of his argument. But she interrupted:

"You know, Papa Simon, I think it's so terribly sweet of you and Madre to have us here. Especially when you've got Ed and Rosie on your hands as well. And giving us your own bedroom. It's making all the difference, having time to look round for a home of our own."

"Well, as I was saying," he continued, "I reckon that lad of mine would want to look after you proper, the best way he know how. Mind you, he's not what you'd call highly educate. Me being away sailoring, away two years together maybe, Maria, she had to do the best she know how, not knowing nothing about English ways of schooling and such. All the same—"

"That's what I want to do for him," she said seriously. "Of course I've hardly any money, but I do know my way about—I mean, I know something about education, I've got friends who are teachers and so on. It's just a matter of patience. He's really getting down to this technical course now. Of course he does find it frightfully hard—he's never been taught how to use his full powers of concentration. But that's where I can do a good deal to help him—"

"Well, you got to understand," he said with what he thought was some firmness, "a boy get to eighteen or thereabouts, something like a grown man, as you might say, and he feels it's past the time for schooling. Come to working, that's a different thing. Gian, he ain't afraid of hard work."

"Or of hard study!" she said, smiling. "I'm sure he hasn't got any silly notion about it being undignified to learn anything after you've grown up."

She put the last napkin on the pile, ready for wringing, cut the rind from two rashers of bacon and started to fry them. It was the way that women had: possessing no power to argue they could always cover their weakness with manual fuss, clattering things about. Still standing, he tried once again.

"I mean to say, all I want is to see the boy happy. What I mean to say—"

"I think we agree about everything!" she answered.

Maria called from the shop, "Si-*mone!* Somebody 'ave movese Wright soapsetis underse Quaker!" and simultaneously a wail broke out overhead from which Ed's infuriated voice emerged, "I tell you, I didn't even touch the bloody kid!" Simon took the plate which his daughter-in-law handed him and sat down. When Maria asked him that evening if he had tackled Miss Susie he replied that he had got the whole situation summed up and would talk to the girl again later on. He must manage things his own way, he said.

His own way would be to consult Gian himself; and that again was not easy, for the boy had to leave early to get to his job over at Hammersmith, he was at evening classes three times a week and on other evenings rarely out of Miss Susie's sight. If only there were one room where he could get the boy to himself! Simon was not dissastisfied with his home, even if it was not the one he had dreamed of through many voyages: it was a plain marvel, he thought, the way Maria kept things going, the way there was always something to eat and his shirts eventually got washed and darned. He could not dislike old Olleroyd, he was glad to have darling Rosie under his roof again, even if that sharp-faced, clever young fellow of hers made him continuously uneasy. Yet there were times when he did allow himself to think a little wistfully of the Everton house he had been brought up in: where people knocked before they came in, where, however crowded the other three rooms, the Best Room was kept for special occasions, and where the intractable old Methodist who had brought him up with her four other children could hold the lot of them in silence and submission whenever and as long as she required.

Beyond that, he was a little frightened. He had been away through most of Gian's and Rosie's infancy, seeing them only for short periods and very much as a visitor would. With Rosie, who responded quickly to his petting, he had maintained an easy relationship. With a boy it was different; Gian had belonged to his mother, she seemed to understand him, and Simon, the last to disturb a peaceful situation, had seen neither cause nor means for interference. Yet affection of a kind had grown, a sympathy like that which underlies many contented marriages, seldom risked in the dangerous vessel of language. "You managing all right, son?" "Can't grumble!"—such speeches had generally been all that their friendship required, though there were moments still clear in Simon's memory when they would have valued a greater fluency: times when the boy's quick temper had got him into trouble, when another of Simon's jobs had proved a failure. In the Damien Street Court they had been given five minutes together, just before Gian's removal to Spenwick; on that occasion neither had uttered more than a few words, but in a curious fashion they had understood each other more closely than ever before. Simon cherished that fugitive intimacy. It was weakened now: this son of his who had a woman to share his life could not be entirely the same, he had grown a little older and stiffer in his behaviour, already his speech had noticeably changed: but the essence of it must still be there, Simon obscurely thought, and a man whose appetite for friendship was never satisfied would not lightly let it go.

"Take a bit of getting used to," he said, "being married and all that." They were on the top of a bus, Simon had worked it out that he could go half-way to Hammersmith with Gian and then get back to Ladywell in time to clock in. "Still, I reckon she'll treat you all right, same as you treat her, once she get the feel of it, see what I mean."

Gian suddenly grinned: it was something Simon had not seen for months. "She got the feel of pretty near everything!"

"She's not treating you unkind?" Simon asked anxiously.

Gian said, folding his ticket into a concertina: "There ain't a better girl than Sue, I don't care where you look. Someone tell me there's another girl as good as Sue and I'll smash his face in for him, an' that's flat."

Simon could only say: "You're gone on her, I reckon?"

"Bet y'life!"

Well, that was the great thing, that was all that really mattered, the important thing was not to say or do anything which could interfere with that. But as the bus broke loose from Parliament Square and charged towards Victoria he was not entirely satisfied. He had got up early for this talk and it was putting an extra fivepence on the day's outgoings; he wanted to be certain he had achieved his purpose.

"She help you with the studying?" he asked.

"She do that."

"Come easier now?"

Gian, working his mouth rather as a cow does, straightened his ticket and began re-folding it. He did not answer till they were past the Army and Navy.

"She think I ought to have a silky's job. Well, you got to try, see, come you like it or come you don't."

Simon nodded, his eyes fixed on the neck of the man in front.

"This job she got you—that go all right?"

Almost imperceptibly Gian shrugged his shoulders.

"Do all right! They pay y'." Then he said: "Fumin' great block on offices—'surance or some such. Half a million fumin' bricks, I wouldn't wonder. Lot of fumin' use!"

"Still, they pay you!"

"Yes, they pay y'!"

"An' it don't really matter, so long as the job's good."

"The way I see it, it's no sort of fumin' good. Kids all over the place—they want somewhere to live in, somewhere to muck about. Lot of fumin' good a bunch of offices is to them."

Simon was out of his depth. "Well, you never know," he said. "May find yourself in a breakin'-up gang, next thing that comes along! S'long, son!"

He started moving towards the stairs. Then he stopped, came back and stood with his hand on the back of the seat he had just occupied.

"Course, I don't know nothin'," he said. "I'm nothink, only an old sailoring man—don't get much luck to speak of along in the theatre business. Well, there it is, I'm supposed to be your dad, just the same. See what I mean? You find things the way like they give you the belly-ache, up in crow's nest, I mean. Well, you can always come along to me. I'm there to listen to what you got to say, you know what I mean."

Gian, only just turning his head, rapped his father's fingers with his knuckle. "I get y'," he said.

"Would you be gettin' on the bus," the conductor inquired, "or gettin' off the bus, or jus' walkin' up an' down for a bit o' exercise?"

Still unhappy, Simon felt nevertheless that something had been achieved. "Boos?" he said absently. "Call this ole boombat a boos!" and got down into Sloane Square.

He was distrait all that day. "Ole Simon Ardree," they said at the Palace, just within his hearing, "he's fallen in love, that's what's the matter with him." "What, ole Simon what got a wife and kidth of his own, about seventy-five ton of wife an' kidth all told? Ga-ah! He'th dreamin' of hith ole seafarin' days, time he had a great battle with a nundred man-eatin' sharkth, along off the coath of Bulawayo!" "Sweet dreams, Simon boy? Back on the quarter-deck, was you?—heave-ho, m'lads, treasure ahead, all change here for the desert island, step off with the right foot first, this way to the enchanted castle, turn left for the be-eautiful princess, all hung round with pearls an' diamon's an' lost her bloomin' drawers." "Quiet over there!" Mr Epsom bawled. But Simon was not disturbed. Izzy Brooks and Lofty, they must have their fun. Very slowly he planed the board which was to replace a worm-eaten one on the port side of the stage; a job was all the better for being done slow, someone had once told him. No, with a lad like Gian there was no getting to the bottom of him. You never would have fancied his picking up with a girl like that, regular lady, right off the saloon deck. Queer little cuss, he'd looked, Maria holding him the way all the Eye-tie women did, alongside the Molo Vecchio at Genoa. ("Si, Simono, sissisa figlio, you figlio, Simono carissimo!") Come to that, he never was the sort you'd fancy in the clink, neither. Temper, yes. Hit about a bit with his fists, same as any lad what got that size of a mitt on him. But prison! A quiet sort of a lad like that Gian—keep hisself to hisself—no vice in him what you could see. "Sure, Mr Epsom, gettin' on with it just as quick as ever I can! You, young Izzy, if you'd keep your perishin' head out of my light—!" And suddenly he was angry. The girl wasn't going to make a fool of the lad, that much he knew—she wasn't going to make a fool of his son! The lad wasn't nothing out of the ordinary, didn't pretend he was, but he was Simon's son, there was a way Simon felt about him and he wasn't going to have the lad suffering in his mind, come all the cabin-class bits of fluff that ever minced and mauked in Burkley Square. That look of Gian's in the dingy room at Damien Street; that little tap of his on Simon's fingers this morning . . . The grain in the board he was planing became indistinct, "You got a cold on you, Simon boy?" Lofty was asking. Yes, a sort of joke he was, not having a face like a picture-postcard, nobody understanding what he was made of. But there might come a day when the joke would end.

"Yes, Mr Epsom, I *am* getting on with it! . . . Here, Izzzy, you're supposed to know about buyin' and sellin', with a sniffer the shape yours is. You tell me, where's the cheapest place I put my hands on them serviette things?"

Yes, he might be nothing but a monkey-faced old sailor-man, but there wasn't any man or woman going to do just what they liked with a decent-hearted lad like his son.

21

*T*HE YOUNG FELLOW was working, there was no question about that. A sight of him now would have shaken the men at the Hibbage Lane depot (all except Charlie Empire, who was surprised by nothing, least of all by what a man would do when a pair of legs and a tidy bosom were in the contract). At Hibbage Lane, to all appearances, the boy had done his stint merely to save himself the bother of not doing it. Especially in the days after his bit of police trouble they were used to seeing him come through the clock with only seconds to spare and then lounge in a corner of his pit all day long without a civil word to anyone, biting his lips, working his jet as the laziest of Satan's servitors might play the flames upon the damned. A version of that dour expression was familiar now to the men of Timble Vale Construction, but the slouch and the contemptuous sniff had given place to a nervous concentration. He cadded for one 'Stumper' Bead (from which he derived the name 'Stumper's Tosser', reduced in time to 'Stosser') but when Stumper was having one of his stand-easies Stosser would fetch and carry for anyone who needed it. For this assiduity he was mocked but not disliked. "The boy can't hold himself!" they said. "You keep at it, Stosser boy!" they said, "they'll be making you foreman come this time next week." "Foreman? Ain't you heard—director of the company, that's what they got Stosser chalked up for. Mr Peglett tell me he got the chitty this morning, with 'Secret and Continental' written all over . . . Oy, Stosser, them two ladders, jus' before the Rolls-Royce come for y', get 'em over 'ere, will y' . . ." He bore it patiently, he acquired one of those grins which nature's butts put on like a face cream and continued to work twice as hard as anyone on the job.

It suited Stumper well enough.

"Ardree, boy," Stumper would say, "you'll never make a bricklayer. Not if you live for a 'undred years. It's an art, bricklaying is. You go rushin' at it, mus' get the next course finished by dinner—well, that's not bricklayin', that's jus' navvy work. I done a church job down over at Blackheath—that's real brickwork, that is, the sort you get on a church job—and d'you know how long it took me to do the first course of the arch over the vestery? One whole month, that took me, jus' before the war that was, an' me been in the trade thirty-seven year. Now that was what I *call* bricklayin'. . . . All right, yes, you can go on as far as where the angle starts. It won't take me no time to knock that bit away and do it again . . . Drive me well-nigh loony," he would say, "standin' here watchin' you muckin' an' messin', treat the stuff like you was diggin' up a field of turnips—ploughboy's mate, that's what you oughter've been!"

But in truth, the risk to his mental stability was small, for his mind was in English bond and as safely founded as the work he had done in his prime. Nor had he ever been blessed with a better pupil to do his job for him. This Ardree, for all that his fists were like a mistake of the butcher's, had already learnt to handle a trowel as if it were a thing with nerves in it; his work was neither slap-dash nor sluggish, he could listen while he trowelled and sometimes ask sensible questions. At sixty-three, with a body shaped and weathered by use, you may feel that you're as good a man as ever, but your hands, working at chest level, are stiffened by the cold more quickly than in the old days. Stumper had no dislike of work, taking his own time, on a job where his matured skill got him better results than the next man's, a bit of arch or chimney work, a job of corbelling; but with stuff like this, all worked out in the drawing-office so as a casual could barely slip up on it, it was pleasanter to stand back on his good leg with his hands in his pockets, an old sack tucked cosily round his shoulders, to watch and criticize, to talk of the beauty of work on intersecting angles, of a job he'd done copying an old fire-place out Barnet way.

"That Ardree," Mr Peglett asked, "he do you all right?"

"Ardree? Ay, he's willing enough. Give him of a bit of trowellin' to try his hand at, now and then—not that you'd make a bricklayer on him, not in a 'undred years."

But Peglett, dry Northumbrian, knew better than that: old Stumper was not the kind to let a bit of brickwork stand with his name against it unless it was as near perfect as eye and trowel could make it, loving craftsman that the old basket was; and yet he was doing precious little of this piece himself. Shy as a girl, Peglett never seemed to look at anyone, he merely glanced up as a miller does when he emerged from his wooden cabin. But he saw things. Up on the staging at the north end, bending over the ventilation plan that Mr Roberts had brought down from the office, he kept one eye to sweep across the job as far as the Cricket Street turning, over the web of ladder and scaffold, the iron roof of the masons' shop, the tortoise movement of the casuals steering their barrows along the bridge of deals from the brick stacks to the hoists; there, on a stage a few feet lower than where he stood, he had glimpses of Stumper, a grey Napoleon in corduroys, leaning back, leaning forward (like a bleeding artist, Peglett thought) without ever taking his hands from his pockets, while the young bullock beside him never once put down his trowel. Hm! So the chap was handy enough to please old Bead, Bead who said there was never a man you could call a bricklayer unless he came from Dorset and none at all apprenticed since '77. Peglett spoke to the youth, seeing him waiting for a bus. "Getting hold of it, son?" A ghost of a grin, and then the sullen look again. "Uh-huh!" Perhaps a little wrong in the head, Peglett thought. Or merely one of those who looked no further than the next meal and the next young woman. But the face had something of its own, you knew it when you saw it again. And the lad could work, take him any way you pleased.

This was a winter of some severity, cold for men enjoying in the streets the world they had fought for. Soon, when the long spell of rain was done, there was snow on the staging which froze your feet all day; and now that the boisterous gusts from the river side had ceased a steadier wind was born which came down Fulneck Street like a wire broom. Up here, level with the dismal roofs of Auberry Terrace, so that you saw right over to the Middlesex Water Works, you were consigned to a region fashioned uniquely for your wretchedness; where, with the mind so numbed that it would not reach beyond the pain in ears and hands, you came to regard the ordinary people walking in the street below, the tops of buses passing through King Street, as a crudely realistic modelling shown under glass. From that life to which you had once belonged you were still divided by four, five hours of endurance, and the clock-hands just visible above the roof of Straker's Stores moved as if they too were stiff with the cold. Deliverance came at last with the sky's darkening. You hardly felt the rungs as you climbed down, dimly trusting that hands or feet would do their work from habitude. And in the street, with lights coming on in the windows, you looked at people sitting to their evening meal as one from the jungle would, still doubting their reality.

He thawed a little sitting in the bus, rather faint, confused by the sweep of crowding lights. But his feet stayed dead, and the slow walk along Borough Road chilled him again.

It amused Ed, looking up from the *Star,* to see his brother-in-law blinking in the doorway, ears red, eyes bloodshot and wet, the white lips just parted in what might be a grin or just a canine imbecility.

"Well, Gyan boy, got your foreman's job?" And Olleroyd, nodding affably, would push some plates aside to make a place at the table while Maria, squealing with laughter, ran to and fro between the dresser and the range. Perhaps he was happy in that half-hour, with the warmth and familiarity surrounding him, though he spoke very little and gave his smiles as if they were small change he could ill-afford. At seven, most nights, he was off to the evening class.

In 'G' lecture-room at the Grover Institute you had your choice: you could sit close to the stove and be scorched or sit away from it and freeze. But here the agony was to keep awake. "Now listen, gentle-men—I don't surely have to go through *that* again!" and the nine survivors in the course would stir uneasily, feeling for some new position where neither buttocks nor shoulder-blades were tortured by the adamantine seats. Mr Cood took off his spectacles and seemed for some moments to be in prayer. "Surely *one* of you can tell me the difference between 'plan' and 'elevation'?" They rubbed their eyes and looked despairingly at the board, they woke up little Davies and whispered the question to him, little Davies coughed and bit his nails. "Parker?" "Well, I mean to say, it's like what you was telling us last time." "Kind of you to say so!" Mr Cood remarked with a trace of bitterness and sniffed despondently. "Ardree, now?" A spark of mirth ran across the dismal room, and a kick on the bovine Hobb's ankle was passed along till it got to Gian's.

"What? I didn't hear you."

"Perhaps I might suggest, Mr Ardree, that you try listenink with your eyes open. You might find it easier, if you don't mind my mentionink it." The titter went round again: really Mr Cood was a comic in his own fashion, whatever you might say. "I was askink," Mr Cood continued, "if you could help these gentlemen here" (Sarcastic old bastard! they thought) "with a definition of the difference between 'plan' and 'elevation'."

"Well, I don't rightly know how you say it."

"Ah!"

"Only I know the way they look. Them plans, if you see what I mean, if you look at 'em from on top—well, I mean to say, what you call a levation, it's the same as if you look at it—well, the other way, see what I mean."

"He mean, same as if you was to crawl underneath and look at it," Davies suggested.

"Or sneak up on it round the corner," murmured Hobbs.

"Now listen," Mr Cood said, "I'm put here to help you perish—to help you gentlemen improve your minds (as you call 'em) and get you up on to better jobs. Now it's all the same to me, whether you do or whether you don't . . ."

They all shifted again. This speech came at least once a week, it was the sole item in Mr Cood's tutorial repertoire which every one of them could recite verbatim. They liked it, since it filled up nearly five minutes, and for that space they were released from the obligation to look like eager students momentarily baffled by a problem of unique complexity. Ten-past eight—they were already half-way through. Most of them had a day's work behind, on a new estate at Charlton, in the permanent twilight of a warehouse on Softer's Wharf, the narrow ledger-room of a toothpaste factory where another clock like the one above Cood's head fought stubbornly against the advance of time. The flame of ambition which had first brought them to the feet of Mr Cood had long since died to embers. One or two, struggling to keep their heads above the waves of sleep, still tried to absorb a little of what he was saying; a few went on attending the classes as some agnostics go to church, vaguely expecting a mystic conversion into scholarship; the rest because they had paid the fee or because this musty room was warmer than the street outside. They leant against each other or crouched over their note-books, staring at Mr Cood's high forehead till it became an undulating mirage, turning for relief to the row of Useful Charts, so long under dust and gaslight that they blended with the brown distemper of the walls; always, from the tail of one eye, they watched the crawl of the minute hand from eight to quarter-past, to the half, to quarter-to, to nine o'clock. "Well, I s'pose you gentlemen'll be gettink brain fever if you learn any more in one evenink." When the magic sentence fell they loosened out like unpacked silk and herded towards the door, shivering and yawning as if they were soldiers roused for early parade, to join the crowd from other class-rooms which clattered through the windy twilight of the corridor and down the concrete stairs to the cold, quick-scented freedom of the street.

Home again at twenty-past he saw Susie, these evenings, for the first time since early morning; at Boughton's, where she had found a job, they had changed her to the later shift, so she had to do suppers and didn't get back till nine. He found her as a rule finishing her own supper, and with the shyness that returned in those fourteen hours of separation he sat down gingerly at her side. "What sort of a day?" she would ask, concealing her own weariness, and pushing the treacle towards her plate he would look nervously at his dirty finger-nails.

"Not so bad!"

"And this evening's class went off all right?"

"Much the same."

Earlier, they had sometimes found comparative privacy in the second back room, but this was too cold to sit in now. In the kitchen the general noise—Ed and Rosie sparring, Maria's clatter, the wail of Evangeline when she was being held out—would serve for a time to protect their quietness; but as they laboured tiredly to dovetail their thoughts some separate voice would constantly break in. Maria, scrubbing her pans and chaffing old Mrs Bentlock about her corns, would suddenly whip round to utter her stinging laugh, crying, "Ayee! Serris my Gian—my *marrit* son Gian—allo, mi' picciolo!" Then the courteous Olleroyd would put down the *Furrier,* brush a few crumbs from the folds in his waistcoat and address himself to Gian's wife with some solemnity. "It's my belief, Mrs Ardree, speaking from sixty-three years I've been in this world of ours, that we live in strange times—strange and *remarkable* times." Or Ed, snapping the book in which he jotted his day's profits and losses, came round and pushed his thin, pointed fingers into Gian's hair. "I reckon it's a marvel, Mrs Susie, the change you've made in our Gyan. You'd say he might be a bank-manager now, just to look at him! Keeps his trap shut so as he won't give anything away, don't you, Gyan boy!" As soon as they had washed the rest of the supper things they retreated as a rule to the cold bedroom.

"You don't think this lecturer is any good?"

"Well, you see how it is—all book stuff, don't mean nothink. I get on all right Tuesdays, down in the shops with Mr Benfellow. Something a bloke can get his hand to, that kind of teachin'."

"Yes, but you see, dear, so many other blokes can too!" She smiled, looking at his wrists. "Of course it's a marvellous thing to be able to do things. It's all I should want for anyone—except my Gian. But then, *you've* got more in you than that! You're going to count for more than other men—after you've learnt a few things that they haven't."

She saw he was hardly listening. Staring numbly at the gravure of *Marigold and Her Friends* he buttoned his pyjamas, lit a final cigarette and got into bed. She could have fallen asleep at once, but the value of this one hour was worth the struggle to keep awake.

"Gian," she said, "I think I may possibly be on the track of a house that would suit us."

That roused him. "Cor, honest truth?"

"Well, it's all rather indefinite, but Mr Olleroyd advised me to see the barman at the Old Richmond, who's rather a friend of his—a man called Herb Evans. Apparently Herb Evans knows all about everybody and everything."

"I know him."

"So I managed to slip along there this morning. Well, he doesn't know about any houses himself, not at present, but he told me of someone who he thinks does. Only—listen, Gian, it's someone you don't much like, but, you see, we do really want to find somewhere before young Arthur arrives—"

"Who is it?" he asked shortly. He was not devoid of intuitions.

"Well, it's that tiresome creature Empire—"

"Charlie Empire?"

"Yes, Gian, I know he's been anything but a good friend to you—"

"That's neither here nor there. I'm having no dealings with Charlie, and that's the end on it."

"But, Gian dear, what is it you've got against him? It was only a rotten job you had at Hibbage Lane."

"It's not the sort of thing as concerns you, or anyone of your sort," he answered stubbornly.

"But anyway, we could probably do everything through a third person—possibly through Herb Evans himself. I mean, if this is our one chance of getting a home—"

He said fiercely: "I'll have no muckin' about with Charlie Empire, neither you nor me!"

He had not used that tone with her before. She lay on her back, wide awake now, with her eyes closed and her lips together, confident that she could resist the impulse to weep. She heard him stab out the cigarette and presently she could feel that he had turned to bring his face close to hers watching her intently.

This was a moment when she might well have given way to crying; not in order to break down his immediate opposition but for a larger purpose: to gain him finally and wholly. She knew that. But still she did not cry. She had a kind of honesty, guarded as people guard old flags or stones, not for their loveliness but for their intrinsic virtue; and that virtue would be polluted by the sentimentality of tears. She opened her eyes and looked quietly at his face.

It was a beaten face, transfixed by grief and fear. He did not speak or even move his lips. His eyes, not often lit to reveal the half-tones of emotion, spoke by themselves of what he wanted now: to see her weep, so that he might smother her tears in his comfort; to feel her arm come round his neck, to be given only a small sign or gesture to which his narrow means could respond. It was a strength surely outside the commonplace which kept this very tired woman from yielding then to the assault of tears, from giving him the semblance he wanted of an emotion she did not feel: strength, or a peculiar lucidity: helped, perhaps, by the clouded memory of a woman standing by the nursery window whose voice, as the door opened, changed from a ripple of sarcasm into heaving, histrionic sobs. Turning away from him, she said:

"I'm sorry you feel as you do, Gian. I think it's foolish. Still, I must try looking somewhere else."

For some time they lay awake, he with his forehead thrust deeply into the bolster, the sleeve of his pyjamas between his teeth; still hearing through the flimsy walls Eliza Bentlock's wheeze and Maria's cackle, the tireless flippancies of Ed Hugg's adenoidal voice.

22

CHANCE, helped by the mechanics of the household, presented her with three letters on the same day. The post brought them over a period of two weeks, but Maria, who presumed that every letter contained a wholesaler's bill, was used to stuffing everything that arrived into the shoe box where she kept her marriage lines with other old papers and darning wool and bottles of Aspro. Rosie found them there by chance just when Armorel was starting for work and threw them over.

"Must be yours, Sue, envelopes like that—must cost a bit!"

The first she opened was from Elizabeth in Shropshire: Elizabeth had heard that Trevon Grist was in the Kennington Royal Hospital, possibly Armorel had been to see him and could give her some news? Sitting in the bus, she merely glanced at this one and put it away in the bottom of her attaché-case: that life was done. To the second, which came from the principal of the Grover Institute and was headed 'Confidential', she gave more attention.

In reply to your letter of the 29th ultimo, I have called for interim reports on Mr G. Ardree's progress.

Mr Ardree is doing well in the manual classes, and it is our opinion that he has the ability to become a first-class tradesman in any of the branches in which he may decide to specialize. He shows particular aptitudes for Bricklaying and for Joinery, and we think that he might with advantage attend more advanced classes in either of these Trades.

His theoretical work is not of the same standard, and we have reluctantly concluded that it would be a waste of his time to go on to further studies of this kind. If, however, he is determined to do so, we think that he should first attend a more general course, since his general education is not, in our view, at present up to the school leaving standard, which is the minimum standard we assume all students in our theoretical classes to have attained. The Education Department of the London County Council would doubtless be ready to give advice in this matter.

That letter seemed to be of first importance. But the one with the Streatham postmark, which a kind of nervousness made her keep till the last, pushed it into a lower place.

My dear Armorel:

It falls to me to send you news which has brought me great grief, and will not be less grievous to you. Like me, you must have continued to hope, however faintly, that your father had survived. That hope we can no longer retain. Today I have received from the War Office a letter informing me that Arthur's death in the second Battle of the Aisne has been definitely ascertained from the report of a warrant officer who was with him and was afterwards taken prisoner. There is no detailed account, but the report says that early on the day of his death Arthur received severe shrapnel wounds in the neck and shoulder, and was ordered by his commanding officer to go back to the casualty station. He avoided doing so. For me that is enough.

I shall not attempt to offer you consolations—these I think would be as useless to you as they are to me. Neither shall I say anything about what kind of man your father was, because you were old enough to know him well. We shall remember him, I suppose, in different ways. But we both know that he served his fellows selflessly and his God without fear.

It is impossible for me to finish this letter without including the message of goodwill which I have long intended to send you but which has been delayed by an old woman's weakness for procrastination. Your aunt Edith, as you know, has for some time past been mistress of this house, which I no longer have the strength—or perhaps the interest—to manage myself. That position—and the fact that Dr Eustace now forbids me to travel prevents me at present from saying that I should like to see you again. But I see no reason why the estrangement between Edith and yourself should continue indefinitely, or even continue at all. You will not, I feel sure, allow the smaller kind of pride to interfere should the opportunity occur for what one may call, perhaps too grandiloquently, a reconciliation. Meanwhile let me say, without raising again the question of your choice of a partner (which would be tedious for us both), that I, at any rate, have never doubted your possession of the fibre needed to make a success of the life you have resolved upon. Perhaps I myself should have made something less negligible of my life if the choices before women of the middle classes had been less narrowly restricted than they were in my time. But that is a question of academic interest, and for you of no interest at all. One thing I can say: that in following the notion of absolute duty to our husbands—a notion long since indignantly discarded—many of us Victorian females did discover a passion of the heart which burnt steadily enough to light us right through our days. Possibly it was the passion and not the duty which really counted.

This is as much as I can write—I no longer have the nervous force to stay at one task for any length of time. Please—I do not ask you to try to cultivate any sentimental feelings for or about a disintegrating and rather boring old woman. But on this occasion when we are at least partners in sadness I hope that the daughter of my dear son will accept the blessing—and the true affection—of her loving grandmother,

         Gertrude M. Cepinnier.

It was fortunate that when this letter came she had worn her new life long enough to have it fitting in the way that shoes, even if roughly made, will fit with use. With the advance of her pregnancy the days' discomfort had increased: in Maria's house she felt more keenly the lack of any place where she could be at ease and undisturbed, at Boughton's the fatigue of standing by a table while customers debated whether to take the cod or the plaice almost defeated her endurance. But she hardly noticed the smells now, noises like that of Ed's voice had grown so familiar that they scarcely grated, there was no longer any strangeness in the sight of Olleroyd making do without a handkerchief or of hens exploring the kitchen floor. Her surroundings yielded few positive pleasures in which she could share; these people's bouts of cheerfulness were pitched still further from her compass than the hearty ribaldries of Hollysian House. But the law of familiarity had again begun to operate, by which dead matter assumes a kind of friendliness and routine, and having at first curbed the pace of time, begins to quicken it. Acquiring new tricks of hand and mind, she could total a bill faster than her fellow waitresses. At home she had discovered shelf and cupboard space outside Maria's orbit, so that when Maria was calling on St Anthony and the Blessed Virgin for a packet of soap-flakes it was she who produced them and she, when the drain of the sink was clogged, who magically cleared it with a piece of wire. From such bits and pieces of activity, methodically sewn into the fabric of her surroundings, she had achieved a pattern which the others recognized and which she could feel to be a private possession: a pattern of no elegance, but one to give that negative contentment which serves as understudy when happiness is not at hand.

Thinking of the child inside she was hungry for a place of her own. But Contessa Street with the noise of steam saws and the smell of railway belonged to her a little now. Lizzie Bentlock would wave from the window as she passed, she knew the policeman who was generally on duty at the corner and the newsboy gave her a good-morning. These were stakes more authentic than those of her student days in a concern of some repute. The tawdry patchwork of shops along the Causeway and the thresh of traffic about the Elephant's grotesque façade, pigeons waddling slowly out of the way of buses and the Lion Brewery growing from a river fog: this drab conglomerate of kickshaws and commotion held you in bonds not wholly different from a lover's embrace.

The crowd unloaded by the bus was ravelled with a stream debouching from the tube, shoppers and clerks swarmed up the street in a cloud of chatter and smoke. As unconcerned as they in the loss of all identity she let herself be swept along to the door marked *Oswald Boughton Ltd. Staff*.

"I'm putting you with Doris today, Mrs Ardree. That's the window side down as far as the orchestra. D'you think you can manage this lot on one tray?"

In some way Gertrude's letter had cleared the issue. The final tie had gone. And another lingering question was solved as well. From her earliest years of understanding, her mother, child of Rhondda Calvinists, shrewd about the tricks life played, had taught her to rely on herself: "It's people with no will of their own who talk about their trust in God—it's just an excuse for weakness . . ." Hitherto she had not wholly accepted that. She had never tried to understand her father; for few had understood that man of infinite lights and shades, who would throw out a clue and follow it immediately with one that pointed the other way; but her love for him, that deep, warm stream which was the source of all her gentleness and whose channel no other stream would find, demanded her loyalty to those of his beliefs which she could comprehend. She knew that the centre of them all was his faith in a God of compassion; and in a tacit bargain of the sort men make within themselves she had given that God the chance to prove his goodness before she finally discarded him. On the platform at Hayward's Heath, wriggling in his uniform and staring sardonically at a cocoa poster, Arthur had said in his off-hand way: "You know, Rellie—whatever happens, one doesn't get out of the range of God's love. I never have any doubt about that." And now Irene was living as she wished, and her father was some sort of crumpled mess beneath the Picardy slime.

"Are you feeling quite all right, Mrs Ardree? Terrible colour you do look today, if you don't mind my saying!"

"Yes, thank-you, Doris, I'm perfectly all right. I expect I've put on too much powder—I always do when I'm in a hurry!"

So now it was Gian or nothing, and the doubts which had returned these last few weeks must be finally put away. The letter from the Institute crept back into her thoughts: she would read it again going home and work out a plan of attack. But no, not today, her mind would not be clear enough today.

"Oh, I am so sorry—I thought you said mashed potato. No, I'll take it back and get you fried—no, it's no trouble at all!"

Yes, she thought (leaning against the counter, repeating "Two mashed three fried, please, Miss Harvey"), I must find somewhere for us to live, quickly, quickly, I must get him away from Contessa Street where all the old life still encircles him.

He was altering. She could watch the changes as a mother watches the growth of her child, glorying in her percipience and power: the quietening of his voice and behaviour, the rare, faint flashes of sensitivity. His devotion was unfaltering: he was never too tired to run her errands, he could not rest if she was on her feet, grew nervous and forlorn, and sometimes rude to the others, whenever she betrayed her weariness. But there was more in his development than that: a hint of increasing shrewdness, of something akin to savoir-faire. Perhaps he had listened more than she supposed to the chatter at the North View, to Mr Bishop's obiter dicta and the bits that Cupwin read aloud from the *Sunday Express*. A laconic remark or two showed that he knew a little about the surreptitious activities at the building site, the wangles on overtime, the small rake-offs earned in the allocation of tasks. And he would say of a lecturer at the Grover, "Always has it pat on a Tuesday—that's the night the principal look in most often." Yes, his mind had moved into a higher gear since the day when he had sighed and sweated over a simple job on the library register. And that, surely was what she had looked and laboured for. But was the advance in just the direction she had wished?

"No, it's fourpence extra. Perhaps you were looking at the 2/6 Special—coffee's included in that."

She caught from tags of conversation between him and his mother a scattered glimpse or two of a life still far outside her reach. And often, while she talked to him, she could see from the shift of shadow in his eyes that he was wandering in a country which no map of hers even faintly resembled. Then there were times, rare till now, when he showed a flicker of his old independence. "Wensday? Can't do it—I got myself fixed up on a bit of overtime . . . Well, the way I look at it, we've got to get the chink, see." And once he had said: "That Cood, I give him just what I got on my mind tonight. Him getting on to that nipper of a Davies, all sarcastic, and that's a little bloke that tries all he can. I tell him, 'That's enough of that talk,' I said. I said, 'You get paid to do the teaching on us blokes. You just get on with it!' I said." That again was what she had wanted: to see him acquiring confidence, moving towards the time when he would have a position and authority of his own. But not outside her leadership. She had given him everything and she was ready to go on giving. He, on his side, must have no secrets, no hopes or anxieties in which he did not come to her for guidance. In a hundred small affairs of dress and behaviour he had followed where she gently led, at times he seemed to have submitted wholly to the design she had drawn for him. But the tree she had pruned so carefully might yet grow to a shape she had not intended, and now that she was utterly alone she could not tolerate the itch of that uncertainty. In such a mind as his, so crudely made in comparison with hers, there could be no corridors sealed permanently from her reason and patience. She must know without the last film of doubt that she possessed him.

He told her that night that he had heard of a half-house which might be going; he would see the man on Saturday afternoon and try to fix it.

"But, Gian dear, I've got to work on Saturday this week. I do think we ought to do the house-hunting together, it's the only way to be sure of getting something to suit us both."

"It'll be gone if I don't fix it quick," he told her. "You can't go pickin' and choosin', not nowadays."

"Well, I do intend to pick and choose," she answered quietly. And then, seeing that she had hurt him, she said: "I'm sorry, dear, I'm rather tired, I got some bad news this morning. My father you know, I've told you about him—well, they've found out definitely that he's dead."

He was changed at once. He came nervously to her side, dry with distress.

"But—you was gone on him, wasn't you, Sue!"

That was all he managed to say. He would have taken her hand, perhaps kissed her, but evidently he did not know if that was the right thing to do.

She saw something like a scene opening: people of his sort went in for scenes on these occasions, and she must teach him gently that sensible people did without them. She started to brush out her hair.

"Yes, he was a very dear man. But of course one's parents have to die sometime, don't they!" She gave him over her shoulder a smile full of kindness. "What I was thinking about Saturday was that we might have dinner together somewhere before I go on to Boughton's. We've got to work out some sort of a plan about what you're to do when the present course comes to an end."

AN INTERPLAY of accidents, not remarkable, merely fascinating to those who like to browse over the mechanics of chance, caused Weald Street to be the background of Antonia's childhood: a casual remark overheard in a dingy bar, a resolution made at a moment when any decision seemed better than none. That background was perhaps less important than some would suppose. For a young child the immediate is what matters, the smell of a dress, the warmth there may be in rooms or in voices; the country beyond is accepted, it is only required to stay put.

The freehold of the south side of the street was owned by something or somebody called Irving's Beneficiaries; the leasehold by the Curtison Trust. Twice a year two elderly sisters living in a village near Carlisle received from solicitors in Worcester a cheque for £64. 15s which made their lives a little easier; this came from the Curtison Trust and was "something to do with Great-aunt Maud," but that was all the old ladies knew; and half a dozen people living in Southampton, in Manitoba and elsewhere who received similar but smaller cheques probably knew still less. It is a point of interest, though of no importance whatever, that through the will of one Thomas Curtison Gribble, who died in Calcutta in 1889, a twenty-sixth share went to Lawrence Cepinnier, and thence 'in equal parts to the male children, legally begotten, of the said Lawrence Gribble Cepinnier,' which meant to Arthur; from whom it passed, on the establishment of his decease, in equal parts to his two children legally begotten. All that machinery worked from the impetus of periphrastic documents, brown with age, which lay in black tin boxes in the vaults of various banks; it was operated at several points by aged clerks who engrossed abstractions of titles in a spidery hand and by captive youths whose thoughts were on next Saturday's football; and few of the parties concerned knew anything about the others except, in some cases, their names. But below this upper crust of ownership came another stratum still more difficult to investigate. Shortly after each Quarter Day an elderly man called Mr Vision arrived at the offices of Folliage and Son, Solicitors, in Leadenhall Street, was admitted to the office of Mr Gerald Folliage, drank one glass of port and placed under the corner of the inkwell stand, folded, his firm's cheque for £53. 2s 1od. Once a month, when a certain Mrs

Driver was having her small rum and stout in the private saloon of the Old Richmond, Charles Empire would slide in, nod to her, put three or four bank-notes into her gloved hand, pat her shoulder, whisper, "Now you be careful of that, Kate," and disappear. Those two transactions were related. It has not been discovered precisely how.

For that matter, no one—not even Herb Evans, who had an inside knowledge of most things in the Weald Street district—knew just what rights Charlie Empire had over his 'little properties'. Empire himself disclaimed all ownership. He 'knew a man who might fix things up,' he 'could take the money and give it to the right man, so that no one need worry'—and in fact, when that had happened, no one did need to worry. But he himself, he let it be understood, had no interest in the matter: he was a very poor man supporting an ailing wife and a dependent daughter, with medical expenses and one thing and another he could barely afford to keep his own little house going. Yes, fortunately he had friends who occasionally did him some kindness; one of them, for example, had let him have some rooms at a very low rate to use as storage space. And he in his turn did what he could to help others who were as badly off as himself. He could sometimes put people on to something he'd got to hear of. If he had any money in his pocket —which at the moment of speaking he did happen to have—he could tide you over with a quid or two, cheaper than what old Prestwich in the tobacconist's would let you in for. To young people, especially, he would always lend a helping hand—he had even taken two or three children, motherless girls in their teens, under his own roof for a time. He was a shy and modest man.

At the Richmond his place was in a corner by the entrance to the saloon bar, where he would make a half-pint last all evening. He never talked much, he didn't want to spoil the conversation of his superiors, he was content to give them his shy, self-effacing smile.

Ed Hugg really fixed it. Ed could deal with a man like Charlie— there wasn't anyone that Ed couldn't deal with. He was twenty-nine, much older than he looked, with the lean, downy face of a schoolboy who has matured too early. Two years in the Army Service Corps had merely underlined the lesson which he had understood well enough from childhood: that everything was against you except your own wits, that the other man was like yourself, just as smart and wanting precisely what you wanted. Wearing those axioms as frontlets between the eyes he could afford to be agreeable. And indeed, he was always smiling. He was small in body and particularly in his hands; quick but easy in his movements, especially when he offered cigarettes to women, who enjoyed his humour and his flattery. There was something in him of the Regency buck, turned out by Brummagem at a quarter the price. His bold shirts and cheap, dark suits fitted him like a skin.

"This house of Empire's," he said to Herb Evans, in the privacy made by other people's chatter, "does he have it on a straight tie-in?"

Herb said, as usual, "I don't know aught about a house of Empire's."

"Oh. Old Olleroyd thought you might."

"Oh, him! Talk like a carpenter's mate, old Olleroyd. You better ask Charlie himself—he'll be in tonight."

"He keep the flies off—Charlie?"

"If he gets what he wants."

Ed said "Ta, Herb!" and went to play snooker.

So this Empire had a house, or part of one, and would want about fifty over the market rate, allowing for Herb's cut, and could be relied on to ward off any supplementary tenant that the man next above might try to squeeze into the circus. It might be a deal. Come to that, he might take the place for him and Rosie and the kid, only Contessa Street was good enough and as near as twopence buckshee. Or perhaps if he fixed it for Gian he could get his own cut off Charlie, though that seemed unlikely on a seller's pitch like there was these times. No, the cut, if any, would have to come off Gian himself. He'd push it along for a bit of sport, anyway.

At supper, with both Gian and Rosie out, he had asked Armorel in his friendliest fashion whether she yet had any hopes of a place to live in, and she had wearily shaken her head.

"No. I did hear of a place from the barman at the Old Richmond —he's a friend of Mr Olleroyd's. But the house seems to be owned by a man Gian specially dislikes, a man called Empire. He was Gian's foreman, you know, and he got him tricked out of the job somehow."

"Pity!" he had said.

And the situation was one he rather fancied. This girl was out of his line, he was clear enough on that: she might have tumbled right off her perch to get tied on to Gian—women did that sort of thing because they liked to be hurt a bit—but that didn't mean she was down to his weight or anywhere near it. Good enough: there was still nothing to rule out the chance of simple, Sunday evening fun. More and more he felt for Gian's wife a kind of chivalry, chivalry bent a little at the edges to fit the shape of his mind. She was, after all, a woman: cut away the trimmings, the Park Lane behaviour, the *feahfully-sorry-to-have-troubled-youah*, and she was just the same as the rest, with the same requirements—cuddle, flattery, fun, a sense of danger. And if Gian gave her the first of these—which within Ed's observation he did on something like a bank-holiday schedule—he neglected all the rest. So Ed pitied her, and being practical he set himself to supply what was needed. He gave her a private, sidelong glance when Olleroyd fell into one of his more bovine pomposities, he was careful to notice anything new she wore and to praise it in such a way as to hint his admiration for the shape below as well as the garment above. He was cautious: not in avoiding offence to Rosie or Gian—he could dodge those two like the ghost of a pickpocket—but in keeping just on his own side of Mrs Gian's line. That was easy enough. Man of the world, salesman, he infected every customer with his own confidence. "As you like," his face, his shoulders said. "All the same to me, whether we do business or whether we don't." This affair of getting a house was right up his street: beauty in distress; the fairy godfather, shrewd, kindly, self-effacing; just a suggestion of secret conspiracy. Gian, of course, would be cross when he found out who was in the deal. Too bad, too bad! However, he had a few bits owing to Gian for one thing and another, for his smugness, his threats, and most of all for being such an insufferable fool.

The game finished. "Lucky tonight!" he said with his friendly smile, put the half-crown in his pocket and went back to the bar.

Olleroyd was there, benignly drinking what to Ed's exact knowledge had been owing to Maria Ardree for eleven weeks: his great, bald, browless head incongruously decked with grey tufts beneath the pouches of the eyes, the fishlike mouth raggedly screened with a tawny thatch, two hundredweight of mournful dignity loosely parcelled in the ultimate marasmus of a respectable black suit. "Well now, I've broken my rule this evening," Olleroyd told him. "In the usual way I only just look in here to say how-d'y'-do to one or two old friends. A man gets lonely—an old man in the position I'm in—and what with things being so bad in the fur trade—"

"I get it!" Ed said shortly. "That over there, that's Charlie Empire, ain't it? Gyan's old boss! Right, I want him over here. Get him a wet, see, and one for yourself—that's on me, only nothing over a gin and Perkins, got it?"

So Empire came over and sat nervously on the stool they gave him, hating to be so conspicuous. The loaded air of the dark bar was vibrant with loud and confident voices, with the shrill laughter of steel-faced girls, and this little woman of a man seemed to have got here by mistake, seeking a cup of tea at the Salvation Army. Ed smiled at him, while Olleroyd went on explaining:

"Mr Hugg here, you see, he married the daughter of my old friend Mrs Ardree. Yes, I think I might call myself an old friend—very gracious, Mrs Ardree has been to me, and there have been times, I think I might truly say, when I have had the privilege of being of some slight assistance to Mrs Ardree. Mrs Ardree was saying to me only the other day—"

"She was saying to him," Ed continued, "it was time he looked for somewhere else to go and put himself. You see, Mr Empire, my wife's ma don't want to be selfish, her chairs've all been nicely warmed by Olleroyd's bum these last two years, time someone else had a go."

"He likes his little joke," Olleroyd said despondently.

"You wouldn't know of anyone that's got a couple of small rooms old Olleroyd here might have?"

Empire looked sad and ashamed. "Well, now, I was telling Mr Olleroyd, not more than three weeks back, about a house a friend of mine mentioned to me—empty house, it was, all but one room on the second floor and one on the ground. There might have been some kind of an arrangement—"

"Ah, but then I didn't say I was looking for a house," Olleroyd interposed.

"And now it's gone?" Ed asked.

"Well, practically, as you might say. At least, that's what they told me. There's just the deposit still owing, by what I understand."

Ed nodded. "I know, I heard about that one. Forget who—some bloke told me. Well, you won't forget old Olleroyd if you hear of another one?"

Empire said thoughtfully: "Of course, if this gentleman they tell me of is having a bit of difficulty over the deposit—"

"What sort of deposit?"

"Somewhere about ten pound, my friend said, the best I can remember."

"Ten quid! And two rooms out of four taken?"

"Well, it was a case, you see, the old woman down on the ground, she was all ready to take herself off—wanted to go really—only naturally she'd have expenses, seeing she's nothing only her Lloyd George money."

"So ten quid covers the buy-out—all but the one room on top?"

"Oh, I wouldn't say that. Not for the buy-out as well. I'd say he'd have asked for more like fifteen to include what the old lady wanted."

Ed offered him a cigarette, threw one at Olleroyd and lit his own. "House business—it's right out of my road," he said through the smoke. "I'd have said that ten quid might do the whole job. Now, Olleroyd here, he might give a leg up to the old girl."

"Mr Ed, he must have his little jokes!" Olleroyd repeated. "He knows as well as I do I got no money coming in at the present time, the fur trade being the way it is—"

"You know," Ed told him with serious eyes, "if Mother Ardree heard of you giving Mr Empire two quid ten to help out a poor old woman, I shouldn't wonder but what she'd keep you another month or two, instead of doing what she was saying to me this morning." He pulled his trilby forward into the out-of-doors position and turned to Empire again. "Well, if you did hear of that house going again—ten quid opener and the old girl clean out of the down room—well, you might do worse than let me know. Olleroyd here'll pass the word along, same time as he might want to see you about the two quid he was talking of. Pleased to have met you, Mr Empire!" He gave them both his amiable smile and shoved his way out to the street.

So on a wet Tuesday morning, when Gian was at Hammersmith and Rosie bargain hunting down at Lewisham, Armorel found herself going towards Weald Street with Ed holding over her an ancient umbrella of Maria's. She walked, now, a little stiffly, the rain had damped her stockings and got into her shoes. But her carriage had scarcely altered, her calm face had the dignity of purpose, she nodded to Ed's chatter as agreeably as if he were exactly the escort she would have chosen. For one who spent some hours each day with the trickling voices of the Boughton girls such company was not, indeed, detestable. The words this creature uttered were not blown like spume from the crests of his mind, they came with vigour and point, with a certain art of his own, modulated for a lady's hearing. He was candid. He confessed that he had always lived an inch or two outside the borders of strict honesty, had tricked his way into one job after another, gathered a few quid on the side as he went along—what else? You had to live! Why hide it? And now that she was used to it his voice itself, thin, nimble, slightly hoarse like the spare-time voices of street orators, did not positively displease her. Yes, you could make a bit on the cycling tracks, he said, if you kept your eyes and your ears open: you just had to know which of the items were fixed and which were not. 'Left-overs' of linoleum, art drawings done from photographs, wine corks bought off servants and sold to hotel waiters, write-ups for private schools in sheets that nobody would hear of, there was cash in all those lines of business if you didn't stay at them too long. Not always quite the strait and narrow, that he would grant. And of course she couldn't approve. Neither did he, come to that. Only you got so many mugs about, queueing up and well-nigh weeping for someone to come and take it off them—well, if you didn't have their money the next man would, and the next man might be nothing but a downright rogue. He looked at her sidelong, finishing with a twist of his mouth and a trifling lift of his shoulders. No, he said with that quarter of a glance, he didn't expect a lady in her position to approve a man in his: but you're grown up, his eyes said, you're a woman of the world, you can see the funny side of it. He was suave, detached, faintly ironic. "Yes, poor Mitch, the cops had him in the end. Funny thing, I had a sort of notion they'd be on to it, the day before it happened—that was the day I gave up my lodging and sent all my things down to old Jake to look after. Bad luck on young Mitch, him being the one that got pinched. I'd have stayed and helped him out, only I had business over at Newcastle and that was a job that couldn't wait." He shook his head mournfully. That kid Mitch was one he really had been fond of. Sad, the way life played you tricks like those. Tragic, when you came to think of it. But not quite so bad if you saw the funny side.

"Oh, I should've told you," he said as they turned into the street. "This bug-trap we're going to look at, it's one of Empire's places. Yes, I know Gyan don't get along with Empire, but then you see he hasn't *got* to get along. No reason Gyan should know that Empire's in the deal at all. If there's got to be a ticket, well, Herb Evans signs on the top side of it—or Olleroyd, if you like—it don't really matter who signs it. Herb takes the cash—once a month'll suit everybody, seeing the deal's all as tidy as mother makes it—and for all anyone knows it's just a straight bind-in between him and you."

It was not a point easy to argue with a man who had just told her, as if it were a part of normal education, how certain post offices could be induced to pre-date the postmarks on letters. And in any case there was no time for argument. They came to No. 16A and Empire was standing at the door to greet them.

He was sorry, Empire said, that his friend Mr Johnson who owned the house could not be there to show them over. Mr Johnson had asked him to do so on his behalf. Mrs Ardree must understand that the house was by no means in its best condition: the previous tenants had, unfortunately, proved to be very careless people. Mr Johnson would, of course, put the place in perfect order just as soon as the necessary labour and material was available . . . His humility, this morning, was lit with a special kindness. He did appear to be seeing the proposition from Armorel's point of view, to be honestly concerned to fit her up with a comfortable home; and it jarred upon her when Ed, standing half-way up the stairs with the face of a gourmet examining hounds' meat, kept knocking the damp, flaked wall beside him and muttering, "Struth! Call this chicken-coop a bleeding house!" Yes, Empire explained, there was an elderly gentleman already established in one of the upper rooms, but he had his own cooking stove and was the kind who gave no trouble whatever. Mrs Eustace, downstairs, would definitely move out as soon as Mrs Ardree arrived—she had been planning for some time to go and live with her sister-in-law in Plumstead Road. No, Mrs Eustace would not be the smallest trouble . . . And that at least seemed likely to be true, for Mrs Eustace, skinny and grey, found sitting listlessly beside the gas-cooker in the back room, revealed no sign of truculence. She looked with fleeting interest from one face to the other as animals look at the people who pass their cages and went on pulling an old cloth button to pieces. Her mouth was working loosely and jerkily, but she said nothing at all.

"If I did decide to take the house I should want a written assurance that Mrs Eustace's interests had been properly cared for," Armorel said.

Empire was absolutely certain that Mr Johnson would provide her with such an assurance.

She had already made up her mind to have the place at almost any cost; for she felt now that everything depended on getting away from Contessa Street, that any place she could call her own would give her a frame in which to build up Gian's life as she intended. There were distastes to be overcome: but she was not without practice in that exercise.

She loathed the street, which looked its dismalest on this grey morning: it had none of the crude variations which relieved the face of other streets close by, not one bay window, nowhere a railing or a row of struggling bushes between house and pavement. But that, to a realist, was of no account. The house itself was no more abject than its neighbours, and with a whole row to support it on either side it could not very well fall down. The smell, when she went inside, revolted her. She had got used to the odours of careless feeding and dirty clothes, but here was another, sweet and sickly, which for a moment reminded her of Empire's house in Bidault's Place. Well, that too was something a sensible person would disregard: a thorough cleaning, after all, would banish it for good. So they solemnly visited each of the small, square rooms in turn, she being bowed ahead, Ed with his hands in his pockets talking behind her, Empire and Olleroyd, who had unobtrusively joined the party, moving like pall-bearers in the rear.

"This now," Empire said, "this would make you quite a nice room. Of course it looks empty without the furniture."

"It looks lousy," Ed told him.

Half the worn linoleum was up—rolled in a corner—and the scraped walls showed several layers of paper. There were broken chairs about and a good deal of broken glass clinging to bits of picture frame, an old stained mattress with its stuffing falling into a pool of grease, the remains of a mangle.

"Would these go with the house?" Olleroyd asked politely.

"Well, Mr Johnson might come to some arrangement."

"I should like to see upstairs," Armorel said.

They had to go carefully, one or two of the stairs were practically non-existent. Empire said that Mr Johnson would see to that.

Mr Brodie was not at home, so they had a look in his room, Ed working the lock with a penknife. It was a crowded room, Mr Brodie appeared to need a vast amount of furniture, including a double and a single bed, two sewing machines and no fewer than nine budgereegahs in four cages. "He's the kind that wouldn't give you any trouble at all," Empire repeated. All over the larger bed there were skins of a raw appearance fastened to boards, which Olleroyd examined with interest. Armorel saw no reason to linger there and they moved on to the front room.

This was where the paramount smell came from, the barber-tobacconist smell. A bottle of scent must have been spilt here, perhaps several bottles. There were, in fact, empty bottles all over the room, lotions on the window ledge, jars of face cream on the broken bed-frame, bottles of Honey and Flowers, Modeste Amour, Moonlight of Araby, Charmantine, Baiser de Douces Vierges, scattered about the floor; and there were scraps of glazed chintz and most of a suspender-belt lying among the cigarette-ends and the torn pages of glamorous magazines. "Of course it wants a bit of a clean-up," Olleroyd ventured to say. "And then," said Empire, "it would really make a very nice room.

"And then there's the attic up above," he said. "There's rather a lot of stuff there now, but Mr Johnson'll clear all that away. That's going to make you quite a nice room."

They went downstairs again, and through to the asphalt yard, where there was a closet with coke in it, a dressmaker's dummy and parts of bicycles. Empire and Olleroyd stood nervously side by side. The high, brick walls hid all the view except a cumulus of underclothes, there was nothing much to be said about this yard.

As Armorel looked at Empire's embarrassed face she thought she could see what the issue really meant to this frail, impoverished creature: whatever rent he got for this house would nearly all go to the man above him, it would need a dozen deals of this kind, a dozen long-drawn arguments over almost worthless properties, before he scratched together the extra few shillings needed to keep up the pathetic respectability of the little house in Bidault's Place, to buy a few small comforts for the woman lying all by herself upstairs. He was looking miserably at the dummy, only now and then giving a quick, shy glance towards her face. He had no overcoat, and his clothes looked very thin. She said suddenly:

"How much a week do you want for this place?"

He was startled by her abruptness. "Well, now, it's like this," he said. "Mr Johnson's got several different parties after this house. There's a gentleman in the printing trade—"

"How much?" she repeated.

Olleroyd said nervously, "Of course you know, Mrs Gian, Mr Empire here would rather you had it than anybody else—"

"And then you see," Empire went on, "it's what you might call in a good position, no way to speak of from the buses—"

Armorel said: "Yes, but, Mr Empire, all I want to know is the price."

He nodded as if he understood. "Yes, I do really think it would make you a nice little home—"

"Oh, it would that!" Olleroyd said.

"—I know the way it is, with a young lady that's got married, might be looking forward to a family of her own one of these days—if you'll pardon me speaking of such—naturally a young lady wants a place of her own, somewhere she can do up a bit and make nice. Now you take a little house like this. It's not a mansion, I'm not saying it is—"

Ed said violently: "This young lady here's asking you what you want for this crike-orful shed. Will you for crisake tell her what you do want!"

Empire breathed deeply. "Well, I couldn't say to within a shilling or two just what Mr Johnson would be asking, not with rents the way they are now. I do know he wouldn't take *less* than fourteen and six—"

"Fourteen and what?"

"Not *less* than fourteen and six."

They were back in the passage, where the smell seemed to have increased. The wind came straight through the house, and the customary crowd had collected in the front doorway. Nervous, chilled and weary, Armorel framed the words "Very well . . ."

She was stopped by Ed's laughter. He did not laugh often, he preferred to greet the ludicrous with a tiny action of the muscles at the corners of his eyes and by taking up a stitch in his ductile underlip. But now he rocked and bellowed, he poked the unhappy Empire in the stomach and struck poor Olleroyd between the shoulder-blades. "Fourteen and bloody-six!" he squealed, with one incomparable gesture in which he seemed to sweep the house over, squeeze it into a pellet, chew it up and shoot it out through his left nostril, "*and* a ten-quid put-down! D'you think Mrs Ardree here's a crackpot or just a plain ordinary Christmas Club! Charlie, boy, it's this one, single, solitary pig-box of a cart-shed Mrs Ardree was talking of, not the whole fuming block." And with that he sharply patted the cheeks of both the men, caught hold of Armorel's arm and wheeled her through the onlookers into the street.

Empire followed, not seeming to hurry but managing to move fast, with Olleroyd still trotting behind, and in a few steps he caught up.

"Mrs Ardree," he whispered, "there's something I'd just like to say. There was a bit of trouble, you'll remember, between me and your husband. Well, it wasn't any fault of mine, nobody had more liking and respect for your husband than I did. Only seeing we had that little bit of misunderstanding, well, when Olleroyd here tell me you was looking for a nice little home, I thought I ought to give you the first chance on this house I hear of. You see, nowadays, with houses being so short—"

For a moment Ed stopped whistling. He said in Armorel's free ear: "Sheer bleeding wholesale robbery! You don't know where you are these days. Bloke comes along with a likely proposition, next thing you find he's nothing but a low-down crook."

"—You see, Mrs Ardree, if I was to take less than what Mr Johnson's asking it would just have to come out of my own pocket. I'm a poor man, Mrs Ardree, I got a wife sick in bed, not been up for months, and my girl's no use for any sort of real work—"

"Sheer downright swindle!" Ed muttered. "Get blokes nowadays that don't know what honesty means."

"—One thing I do know, Mr Johnson won't come down a penny under ten bob. Of course I'd try all I could with him, I'd tell him it was a young couple looking for a home—"

"—Not even pick out men to do their tricks on! Go hunting out a lot of helpless women and kids—"

"—Mr Johnson, of course, he's as nice-hearted a gentleman as you would find, only he can't afford to lose money on that little bit of property, which is all he's got to live by."

"And you know, Mrs Gian," Olleroyd panted, "that would make you a nice little house."

They had reached the end of the street. Ed stopped so abruptly that the children following the party nearly fell over. He said without looking at anyone:

"Seven and a tanner. Yes or no, it don't matter to me."

Empire stood still with his mouth working. There were tears in his eyes. He said with difficulty:

"It's hard, you know, Mr Hugg. With a wife ten months in bed. If you'd said nine and a half now—"

Ed looked at Armorel. "There's ten quid got to go down first," he told her. "That's usual. Any time before Sunday. Then eight and six a week, and it's not worth half that." He shrugged his shoulders and left the ball in her hands.

It was still raining. She looked at the gaping children and along the melancholy street. What she wanted now was to sit down; and she thought, In that house there would be a chair, and without asking

Maria if she was using the small kettle I should be able to make myself a cup of tea. She nodded to Empire.

"All right, eight and six." She added, "Thank you very much, Ed. You'll fix it up for me?"

She smiled to Empire, still sorry for the way that Ed had bullied him, and went on to get the bus that would take her to Boughton's.

"Your little home, too, one of these days," Ed said to Olleroyd when she had gone.

The three men, talking comfortably about the afternoon's racing, made their way to the Richmond, where Ed bought the drinks with the pound note which Empire handed over, one of the two which Empire had received from Olleroyd the day before.

How sensible she had been! It was not even necessary to go to the Richmond to pay Herb Evans; she gave the money to Olleroyd each week and he brought her a receipt (sometimes on the back of an envelope, sometimes on a piece torn from the margin of a newspaper) which Evans had signed 'p.p. H.Johnson'; Empire's name never came into it and Gian had asked no questions.

Since Mr Johnson's labour difficulties seemed to continue indefinitely they resolved to put the house in order themselves. She calculated that it would be ready for habitation two or three weeks before the Event.

And the work gave them an immediate return of contentment which neither had foreseen. They were there on every free evening and for most of the time at week-ends (the whole of one week-end was occupied in clearing the attic alone) and during those many hours of labour they were seldom out of harmony; for they understood and accepted their separate functions, hers to make decisions, his to carry them out. There were things that Gian would have had quite differently (in the lunch hour he gazed with yearning at robustly flowered wallpapers in the King's Road windows) but clearly he did not dream that any choice of hers could be wrong.

There was conflict only when Armorel tried to do her share of the harder work as well. When he had got a heavy box of rubbish down to the passage she wanted to drag it out into the yard, and protested that it would do her no harm. But he soon stopped her. On that issue alone he asserted a husband's authority with a vehemence that amused, pleased and occasionally frightened her. He was intensely nervous about her condition, supposing that the smallest physical exertion would be disastrous; and when she tried to pick up something which he himself could have tossed in the air with one hand he would seize it from her with a roughness bordering on brutality. "You lay off that, Sue—understand!" Then he would spread his coat on a box for her to sit on, and smile shyly and happily so long as she remained there. She learnt by degrees to respect his absurd anxieties: for his own sake she would call him when anything weighing more than a pound or two had to be moved, and only when he was thoroughly absorbed, scraping the encrusted dirt from the back-room floor, filling up holes in the walls by a method Stumper had taught him, did she venture to do some scrubbing herself. She fed him constantly with praise; and when she smiled with admiration at a section of wall he had rendered he would stop for a moment, look at her sidelong, draw his wrist across his face and permit himself a grin. But her encouragement was scarcely needed: she could see in his eyes, in the laconic gestures she had learnt exactly to decipher, how he rejoiced in the results of his handiwork; how he marvelled at the light brought in by polished windows and bright distemper, at the unimagined freshness. With such discovery the tiredness of long hours on the building site fell away. He attacked the jobs she set him as if his body had been idle all week, he whistled as he moved on hands and knees along the passage to scrub and then to stain the worm-eaten boards. When she made him a cup of tea with a kettle borrowed from Mr Brodie he stood and looked at the bit he had finished, and then at her face, with the pride of a child; he even lapsed into little jokes which she did her best to laugh at: "Reglar Bucknam Palace, it's turning out . . . That Johnson, he'll think he's hired the outfit to a gang of perishin' fairies, he'll be stickin' out for another two bob!" In those moments they shared the sun.

But they were not always alone. There was carpentering to be done, and Simon took it on with enthusiasm though not always with success. He was unlucky in the timber he used, mostly odd bits "that Mr Epsom give me," and the tools he brought always proved to be a little out of adjustment. "Of course," he said, "theatre carpentering, that's a different sort of trade, now," and he would speak regretfully of the faultless tools possessed by Jesse Guiseborough, the chips who had first taught him the craft. On fine Sundays Maria arrived in her remarkable hat and stood just behind him to titter and give advice. When he had put a new board in the stairs (the work of more than two hours) she used her weight to test it, and when it snapped with a report like pistol fire she fell into helpless mirth, rolling and squealing on the bottom step, gasping, "Si-mone—*mio carissimo*—you call himself a lovely carpentiere!" while huge, affectionate tears ran down her hot, fat cheeks and nose. At times like those the faithful presence of Olleroyd was invaluable. Too stiff and too obese to work himself, he served as Simon's mate and chief consoler; when wood split or the heads of screws came off he would take him aside and talk as one man of experience to another. "It's the wood you get these days, it's not like what it was before the war, it's all this foreign stuff, you see." And with delicacy he would nod towards the rolling and chuckling Maria as if she were a possession he had the honour to share. "A wonderful woman, your Mrs Ardree! Wonderful the way she can always see the interesting side." Ed was often about, keeping up a ribald commentary, and then there was Slimey, who had got to hear of the enterprise and came to lend a hand out of sheer good-nature. He and Simon got on well. For half an hour at a stretch they would stand nodding at each other, exchanging technicalities with gentle, inconclusive earnestness; while Maria, left to amuse herself, would go and stand over Gian, douching him with love and correction, or would proclaim her own ideas to the company at large.

"Hereser will be a *grant* armadio forser sospon, hn?"

"You mean you want shelves there, a sort of cupboard?" Olleroyd asked.

Slimey came over, eager for some new thing. "Well, that'll mean pluggin' the walls. I couldn't rightly say if the walls'd stand up to that. Got a bit o' chalk?"

Simon fumbled. "I got a bit o' pencil somewhere. A rare bit of wood that's going to take—half-inch it ought to be for the shelves—got to take the weight, see." He measured roughly, drew lines where he thought the ends of the shelves might come, and then altered them.

"What would the shelves be for?" Brodie demanded from the skirt of the group.

"For saucepans, Mrs. Ardree here was saying."

"*An* forse dustan broom."

"But this ain't going to be the kitchen, not by what the young lady was saying to me."

Slimey was testing the wall with his penknife. It was a wall that Gian had finished distempering the night before.

"Or you *could* have it this way," he said. "Lend me that pencil, half a jiff."

"*No!*" said Maria fiercely, "tsat is not what I mean!"

One of the women who hovered all day about the front door came forward sympathetically.

"I'll show you what she means. It's like the way Elsie Cupplegate had it, the time she had that room with Will Sandy. Gimme that pencil and I'll show y'."

And then Maria was pleased; for though she loved to have men about her, things to be mocked and bussed and bullied, she found the lot of them incomparable fools and looked to her own sex for understanding. The whiff of debate set light to her social powers, this stranger was immediately her oldest friend and they would fight together through thick and thin. Here was life, here was drama on the grand scale, and she herself, endowed with every gift of passion and command, was cast by Providence to be its epicentre.

"Siss ladee, she sesat I am all right. Give it to me sehammer!" She uttered one fierce bark of laughter, she kissed the top of Slimey's head, she ran, flourishing her arms, propelled a box to the wall and surged upon it. "Simon, you holdse nail, where I tell, *tsere!*"

"Eh, but listen now, Maria—I reckon I ought to ask Miss Susie—"

"*Hold it up senail!* Meestrolleroyd! Stand tsere—*tsere!*—so for if I tomble . . ."

So the arguments went on all morning, and the hubbub poured out into Weald Street, crowned with Maria's shrill commands and her high, explosive merriment. And this gave pleasure to a narrow street where the drunks lay in of a Sunday and the grey hush would be varied only by the sudden screams of children. The door of 16A was not yet fitted with a latch; such boundaries as obtained were not in force when rooms were still unfurnished, and where Maria was at large no boundaries could exist. The life of the street first lapped against the threshold and then crept inside. The women stood along the passage, chatting in undertones and smoking; children ventured into the back room and even up the stairs, where people of bizarre appearance were constantly moving up and down upon business with Mr Brodie. Through these groups and eddies Armorel picked her way with grimly guarded patience, ignoring the old women's speculative asides about her figure, murmuring, "Excuse me please . . . If you wouldn't mind! . . . . No, Madre, I'm very, very sorry, but I'm not going to have shelves in this room at all."

It was not in Gian to be vexed; he had known no home that

strangers didn't walk about in; he openly encouraged the ragged children, who, finding he kept a grin for them, and sweets in his pocket, were thickest wherever he was working. That, too, Armorel would tolerate, since their presence seemed to give him pleasure. There was only one occasion when the nerviness of pregnancy undermined her self-command.

The trouble derived from a wood-and-wicker cabinet, an affair of wings and brackets and many artful embellishments, which Armorel had found in the front room and thrown into the yard. Maria, poking about for things of value, had brought it back; upon which Armorel had told her with great politeness that she did not want it in the house, and Maria, secretly, had given it to Simon to repair. On the next Sunday a debate of more than usual vigour and prolixity was going on in the back room, and Armorel, coming downstairs to look for a pair of pincers, found the men, under Maria's excited directions, screwing the cabinet against the wall. She said quite calmly:

"Papa Simon, will you please take that thing right away. And please fill up the holes you've made. I've said that I don't want it anywhere in the house."

Maria said: "But sissis so pree-tee! You put allse pitcher, seflower, s'ornamento—"

"I'm sorry, but I just happen not to like it."

The men stood back, staring at their hands. Simon looked ready to weep. Maria took three short paces towards Simon, snatched a screw and the screwdriver from his hands and continued the work herself.

Armorel returned to Gian upstairs. She was just able to get out her words: "Gian, are we getting this house ready for ourselves or for your mother? Do I have any say at all? Because if not she can have it and I'll go—somewhere else." Then, standing against the window, without noise, she wept.

Gian went slowly downstairs. His mother was working on the screw with the kind of energy she used for tackling vermin when that was her whim. The others had not changed their positions. Simon tried to speak, "Been a bit of a misunderstanding—" and then gave up. With his eyes he said, "You see how it is—your mother—my son's wife—"

For several seconds Gian himself was dumb. Then, turning upon the Slimey group, he let fly.

"You get out, all you! Clutterin' up the place! This is my house, see! Too many of you, comin' clutterin' round!"

The men shrugged their shoulders and wandered in an untidy file to the street, leaving Simon and Maria behind. Maria, grimly relishing the situation, went on with her work, while father and son looked hopelessly at each other. In the silence which had come upon the house they could hear Armorel sobbing.

Olleroyd, last in the withdrawal, had lingered by the street door. He turned now. He had seen Simon's face when Maria snatched the screwdriver, and Simon, after all, was one who had treated him well. With that curious motion of his, a stage caricature of a nobleman's dignity, he travelled slowly back, sucking the ends of his moustache, to where Gian stood near the foot of the stairs. There he arranged his loose dentures in a smile.

"Now it wouldn't do," Olleroyd said, "for any little misunderstanding to come between a young fellow and his ma. It's natural," he said, "you don't get the ladies all seeing things the same way. Mrs Gian, you see, she been brought up rather fancy, as you might say—"

But by then he had given Gian what Gian required.

With his body tightening like a cat's, Gian said: "You, that's enough out of you!" His skin had lost all colour and his eyes were like frosted glass. *"Get outa here!"* he yelled. "You—*you get out.*"

For once quick off the mark, Simon jumped forward and held him; tightly, by the arms and the cross-over of his braces; till the murderous fit had passed and he fell into violent shivering and then tears.

24

*T*HE INCIDENT left him subdued and more than usually shy. For several days he hardly said a word at Contessa Street except in answer to questions. He gave Olleroyd a packet of cigarettes, with so gauche a gesture that a stranger would have thought he meant to insult him.

It did not make much difference. The household at Contessa Street was not one to be depressed by the silence of one of its members, and at St John's Hill, where he was working now, they did not depend on young Ardree for social liveliness. In both these compartments of his life he was left, sensibly enough, to get over his sulks or whatever his wan taciturnity might imply. As for his wife, she treated the malady as if it were physical and simply increased her gentleness. She had told him, after the storm, that she was sorry to have made a fuss. Having said that, she did not discuss the incident further or ask him any questions. What would be the use of saying 'Gian, why are you unhappy, is there still something wrong?' She did not even know for certain that he was unhappy, and he would hardly realize what she meant by such a question. What more could she do than surround him with her kindness?

No one outside his own circles would have noticed anything peculiar in his expression. Passing him in the street you might have thought the face was striking, with a mouth suggesting truculence and the eyes a shamefaced timidity; but he was palpably of foreign extraction, and in foreigners a sullen look might signify nothing at all. In a maritime city of that size a man must go to extremes of oddity before he is remarkable: with little Korean women chaffering in the New Kent Road, with puggarees and Franciscan habit in the tubes, you do not pay much attention to a tic or an outlandish beard. This variegation affords a kind of privacy. People may declare their love in Ludgate Circus, a homesick girl can blubber in her sleeve as the tram jolts through Camberwell, and no one will turn his head to look. The young, slightly foreign-looking workman had the London gait; without appearing to look either way he would cross over Newington Causeway with a narrow margin of safety and swing himself on a bus already in second gear, mechanically scoop out his twopence and stick the ticket inside his cap. Balanced with one knee against the end of a seat he would gaze through the outworks of a girl's hat at the cheerless fabric of Wandsworth Road and see, as Londoners do, nothing at all. Once in a week somebody—a woman most likely—might glance with curiosity at such a man; by chance someone of the speculative mind would stare at him long enough to wonder what sort of life he belonged to, a young fellow so aggressively detached. Following him along the pavement you might have wondered at his sudden hesitations, his habit of stopping and looking about him like one who fears pursuit or has forgotten where he is. But that, again, was an eccentricity barely remarkable in a place where the squeeze of living must engender some curiosities in behaviour. In working dress he blended well enough with the dun brickwork which prevails in that jungle, he was a background figure, an item of that breathing litter which is swept about the city's channels, heaped and re-dispersed, to serve as corpuscles from which the dead, mechanic mountain derives the semblance of life.

Yet when Nibbley Toms saw him waiting for his bus at the Elephant he said: "How go, Toughie boy—what's up with you? Look like an ole doughnut somebody stepped on, that's what you look like to me!"

It happened that in the week after this encounter he found himself with an evening unexpectedly free. He was attending night school in Bewley Street now, where a Mr Duckett taught him multiplication of money by practice and what was wrong with the sentence 'The doctor done him no good'; and when he arrived for the Friday class there was a notice on the board to say that Mr Duckett was ill. "Well, on Monday," a fellow student said complacently, "we'll know if the doctor done him good or not," and they went their several ways. Gian sauntered in the direction of Weald Street, where Susie would be working on curtains.

This was one of the occasions when he seemed a prey to impulse. He had not gone far before he halted and changed his direction, and from that point he walked faster, looking straight ahead, like a man late for an appointment. But having reached Mickett Lane he stopped again a few yards short of Coronation Building. There he stood for perhaps three minutes, leaning against a wall as in the old days. His face betrayed no sign of thought; he might have been a marionette waiting for a fresh jerk on one of the strings to set him in motion. The jerk presently came, a mild one: he turned and went off in his former, lackadaisical fashion towards Hollysian House.

There was another interval of irresolution when he came out of Balt Lane. He stood beside a railway truck, just as Armorel had once seen him standing, sucking a cigarette which had gone out, looking at nothing in particular and patiently waiting, one had said, for the end of the world. But at last he stirred again, crossed over the yard and went slowly, negligently, up to the Club.

He asked the first boy he saw—one he didn't know—if Mr Grist was in. "In his room," the boy said. "Came back yesterday, look like a fumin' corpse." Gian went on across the gym.

They all saw him then. "Oy, it's Toughie!" they said. "What, ole Toughie come back!" "Miss Susie turn you out, Toughie boy?" "Not the coppers after y' again!" They formed a little crowd round him, hitting him on the backside and offering cigarettes. "Well, what do it feel like, Toughie?" "Brought the wife and kids?" "How many little Toughies you got now, Tough?" For their approach to the topic of marriage was like that of the Book of Common Prayer. Then Flock saw him and came over.

"Well," he said, "if that ain't that perishin' Ardree! Hans in his pockets as per usual. Well, here's another of 'em all run to seed, I reckon. *Caam* on, Ardree lad, hold your head up, life ain't as bad as all that! Miss Spinyer been knockin' yer about? What you want to do, lad, is get them shoulders back, an' knock off some of them perishin' fags, get me. Might last out another year or more if you treat y'self careful!"

Gian grinned sheepishly and went on into Trevon's room, where the Interview Hour was in progress.

There was one boy playing draughts with Trevon, one sitting in the sink and reading the evening paper, while the Fidgley brothers, muttering "Cor, that was a foul!" "Well, you hit me below the bloody nivel!" were happily wrestling underneath the table. Trevon looked up and said, "Why, it's Gian! God, it's nice to get a sight of you again!"

The boy who had said that Trevon was like a corpse had not erred very far: Gian himself, not one to be much affected by men's appearance, was startled when he saw the change. Trevon's body had shrunk like a punctured tyre, so that his suit, never a good fit, now looked like a father's clothes passed on to a schoolboy son. The fat of his face had gone, leaving its structure cadaverously sharpened; the eyes seemed to have sunk further into their cavities, the lips to have been unpicked and more tightly sewn; and where his skin had formerly been blotched and unhealthy it was all of one colour now, the colour of paper in old books. This was a curious experience, to find a familiar personality so disguised: like hearing from behind the false whiskers of fancy dress the voice of a friend. The twitch was still there, and all the nervous mechanism of the body; but it was slowed and softened, the voice quietened, the movement of head and hands fatigued. His laughter came more gently. Only the half-cocked, rather painful smile was the same.

"Huff you, James!" Trevon said, and removed a king. "You don't know Gian Ardree, do you—before your time. He's gone and married into the bloated artistocracy, the old snob. Still, you wouldn't blame him if you'd seen the girl. I'd have married her myself only I hadn't the looks. Dark horse, you know, this old Ardree!"

The tone was scarcely altered; and in a style of his own he could convey affection with his raillery, affection that would make boys shy if it came in any other dress. With only the tail of an eye on the draughts-board he was scrutinizing Gian as minutely as a doctor would, noting the improved barbering of his hair, the tidiness of collar and tie. And Gian knew that he was being inspected, and was not put out. The smell of the place and its hollow uproar came gratefully to his senses: this was home-coming of a kind. Only a few months had passed since he last sat in this chair, but within that segment of time lay the dread ordeal at Finchley, the long nightmare of the North View Hotel; and here was wonder, to return from such a voyage to a country where scarcely anything had changed. Flock, upon some excuse, had come in now and was standing as he always did in this room during shop hours, strictly at attention.

"Sorry I didn't dust the chairs, Mr Grist, sir. Would've done if I'd known Mr Ardree was paying you a call. Trouble about this West End tailorin', you know Mr Grist, sir, the dust get into it something horrible. (You, young perishin' Fidgley, you come out from squeakin' and squawkin' under there!) Put 'em out, shall I, this lot here, sir? Doctor said you was to be kept quiet and laxative in soul an' body, get me, sir."

The door crashed open and two more boys shot in.

"Been an accident, Sergeant! Young 'Ooper, he's fallen off the 'orizontal, we think he's broke his leg."

"That Hooper!" said Flock, not stirring: the joke was six years old. "*I'll* break his perishin' leg."

"He really is bad, Sergeant. Cryin' like a pig at the butcher, God's truth he is."

"I'll make *you* cry like a pig in the butcher. An' I won't have no swearin' in this club, what is paid for by a squad o' bishops and other God-fearin' personnel. Not in Mr Grist's presence I certainly won't. Nor in Mr Ardree's presence neither, now he's been and signed on with the perishin' gentry."

"Oh, it's Tough Ardree, is it!" said Ormison, grinning over their heads like a lighthouse. "Beg pardon, Sergeant—mistook him for the Prince of Wales. The light ain't too good in here."

"Smash y' face in for another one like that," Gian said automatically, without ill-humour.

"Cor, listen to Toughie! That ain't the way they teach you to talk in the Burkley Hotel, surely it ain't!"

"What you done with Susie?" the elder Fidgley asked, mopping the blood from his nose.

"Yes, why ain't you brought her? We miss Miss Susie round here. You get blokes like Fidgley here puttin' their names in the wrong register, makin' the Club a byword an' a mockery."

"Yep," said Gian, "I reckon you could do with my wife back here. Keep yer in order!"

"They can do with that!" Flock said.

"Reckon she kep you in order, besides," Gian told him calmly. And amidst the "Cor!" and the "Listen to 'im!" he put himself to the expense of a smile.

He leant back and rested one foot on his knee, he frowned at the well-polished shoe, savouring his wit. The absurdity of coming here in a sports jacket, clean and carefully ironed, no longer troubled him; now that the first embarrassment was over it actually increased his confidence, like having won a quid on the St Leger. The familiar voices played upon him warmly. Yes, there were changes: Mr Grist so worn and still, quietly laughing all the time but never bursting out and shouting the whole lot down; and it made a difference, as they were saying, Susie not being in her place. He would never have acknowledged it, but just now he was glad to have her gone. It increased his freedom. Here you could talk as you liked, sniff, clear your guts, and never feel that you were adding one more pebble to the load of anyone's patient endurance.

"Naoh!" he said in answer to Terence Hubbitt. "Nothing in it, them stuff-shirt hotels. You knock over a cup o' char—who cares? Jus' tiddle the bell, an' a bloke come an' mop it up. Easy!" He changed his legs, put one foot on the table and tilted back his chair. Even Flock was listening with attention. "Bung up with perishin' ole tarts, natrally. Well, you don't mind them. Do a bit of how-de-do, pick up their snitchers when they drop 'em, open the doors for 'em, shut the doors after 'em, 'Pleasure is all mine, who's the next customer?' Coupla fumin' kids one of 'em had—knocked 'em about somethin' horrible. I tell her one day, I say 'That's no way to treat them kids, an' you know it!' 'Crike!' she say. 'That's a piece of fumin' sauce,' she say, 'can't I do as I like with my own bleedin' kids!' she say."

He commanded his audience now, the audience he had never had in his life. He was standing up, he kicked the chair away and in an instant he had passed from the being of Gian Ardree into that of Mrs Cupwin; not the floss, frustrated Mrs Cupwin of reality but a creature that rose from his kindling fancy, a twisting giantess, a princess of Edwardian grandeur, a flaming hell-cat guarding with tooth and claws the right to torture her young.

"'Listen!' she say, 'I'll put my husband on to you! Knock the liver 'n' lights out of you, my husband will!' Well, then, in come her ole man, just as she say the word. Little bloke about so high, couldn't see over that table. 'This bloke been insultin' me,' she says. 'Well,' I says to her, 'the poor bloke can't hit me from where he is now. You better put the little b— on the pianer,' I tell her. So we stick him up on the pianer, and she hang on to the bum of his trouses to keep him fixed, and I stand up close in case the little bastard fall down an' get hisself broke. Nex' thing I know, the little perisher up an' give me all he got, right here on the trap. ' 'Ere, wait a *bit!*' I says. '*Crike!*' he says, dancin' about an' suckin' hisself an' carryin' on like a load o' barmies, an' nex' thing, the ole tart she come on at me a masterpiece. 'You c—!' she says. 'You look what you done!' she says. 'You been an' broke his fumin' hand!'"

It went all over the Club, it reached the Quiet Room and the billiard room and the carpenters' shop downstairs. "You seen ole Toughie?" they said. "He's goin' on like a circus." "Cor, what that Susie done to him! Dress him up like a fumin' peacock, done him all over with sandpaper, college accent an' all the rest, an' he come on here and give out the 'istry of his life like a fumin' conjuror. Cor, you oughter come an' listen to him—Happy Days I Spent in the Riz Hotel, How I Knock Out Joe Beckett with One Biff from my Top Hat— coo, you'd think it was the Daily Fumin' Mail!" They liked him in this new rôle, they brought him such drinks as the Club afforded, "Goo on!" they said, with admiration mixed in the chaff, "tell Higgins here about the tart what thought you was Lloyd George!" till his newfound powers had all run out, and he sank a little way into his former shyness, but happily, smiling with wonder at his celebrity, nodding in a comfortable fashion to these people who, once trivial features in a familiar scene, had come back to him in the soft warm hues of ancient comradeship. When eleven o'clock had passed, and Flock with his accustomed sarcasms had chivvied the last loiterers out into the yard, he stayed to smoke a final cigarette while Trevon polished off the day's correspondence. And his face, as he watched the smoke twisting, was that of a man home from a long campaign.

Trevon got up and fastened the window-catch and took his hat off the handle of the cupboard.

"Now I go home too."

"You don't sleep here now?"

"No, my friends think I ought to live as if I were a civilized being. I've got a room—two rooms in fact. (I've been in hospital, you know.) Come and see them."

"Well, Susie might be wondering where I've got to."

"Yes, she'll think you've been run over, and she'll get a hell of a shock when she finds you haven't. It's not much out of your way, anyhow. You know Mickett Lane?"

In the warm, clear night they set off at Trevon's old pace, but before they got as far as Flanders Street he had to ease up.

"It's odd," he said, "I don't feel ill now, I feel just the same, only other things have changed. The stairs up to the Club have got steeper and there seem to be more of them. It puts me in a shocking temper. Yes, I've had quite a time—I got ill shortly after your wedding. They had me booked to peg out, as a matter of fact, only I somehow didn't. I suppose that would have been too easy a solution—in life you don't get any easy solutions. Tell me, how is Susie? Why don't you bring her to see us?"

Gian said shortly: "She's all right." They had covered another fifty yards before he added, "No, she ain't all right," and then in one long stream: "I didn't ought to have done it, and there you are. Don't make any difference, anythink I say now. I'd go to clink for it, I would 'n' all. Clink ain't nothink. Only that wouldn't do *her* no good."

"But what is the bother, old thing?"

"I put her in the family way."

They were at the corner of Donnier Street, and the bright light from Macqueen's Supper Room was on their faces. Trevon had to turn his head away sharply. But he saw, in an instant, that there was nothing comic in this. He said gently, holding Gian by the collar and rocking his head:

"But, my dear old thing, that's what a husband's for. That's what they expect, it's what they want."

"She ain't fit for it," Gian persisted, in a voice that sounded angry, "not a chip of a kid like that. I do' know why I done it. She never been used to anythink like that."

Trevon stopped dead. The crowd released from the New Victoria was all about them, but he never took any notice of crowds.

"Balls!" he said. "My dear Gian, little tiny twits of women produce one great thumping child after another and feel all the better for it."

That was like calling 'Cheer up, chum!' to a man dying from cancer. Gian said huskily, as they went on: "It ain't that, you see. You see, she got gravel enough for anythink. It ain't that. See how it is—she c'd get it off her own kind of bloke, an' that would be all right. Mean t'say, a kid like that, she want a sort of a silky, know what I mean, got to be a bloke with schoolin' 'n' that, not a sort of a hairy bloke out of Contessa Street."

"Listen," Trevon said, when they had turned the next corner. "You're a very nice bloke, and I don't mean you're any stupider than I am, but there are some things you've simply not begun to get hold of. Now look here, if you weren't the right sort of bloke for Susie she wouldn't have had you. For God's sake get that into your head. Susie isn't a fool, she's a very clever girl indeed. She knows all about the silkies, she's seen dozens of 'em, she's had 'em chasing her and wanting to marry her. One of them was a college professor, and I'm told he was as good-looking a bloke as you'd ever see, with a D.S.O. and all the rest of it. He asked her, and she sent him off with a flea in his ear. *You* asked her and she said 'Snap!'"

That was useless too.

"Y'see," Gian said, his speech rushing and stumbling, "she got me wrong. She thought I only had to have a bit of schooling an' that, an' I'd be just the same as what she was used. Put me in the building trade, see—well, that's all right, I got the hang on that, they put me on a skill job now when I ain't hardly started, use m' hands as well as the nex' bloke, shouldn't wonder—only she got the notion I'm to do a sort of clurk's job, see, all fixed up in a drawin'-office, bloke what see the customer and make out the plan the way he likes. Well, you got to have y' words right for that, 'n' a lot of figurin' an' such. Well, I go along under that perishin' Duckett, an' what's the use of that! You've only got one life, a bloke can't learn all that, not if you've got to make a livin' 'n' that. She been all right to me, I didn't mean to do her no wrong. I reckon it all come out of havin' muck 'n' all in y' thoughts. Well, I reckon no one ever tell me the way out of that."

Trevon said: "No—God knows how you get out of that!"

He was cursing himself for being a sick man. Through the skelter of jostling words he could see a good way down into the thoughts of the youth wandering and all but blubbering beside him, and at his normal power he would have known what to say next. He didn't, now. It had been a habit of his, passing through the gymnasium, to seize the rings and pull his chest up to their level: on returning from hospital he had found it an effort even to hang from them. That feebleness seemed to have touched his brain as well. He could run the Club all right: do the letters and accounts, make the everyday decisions. This needed a brighter, steadier flame, and the fuel was no longer there. He said, stopping and opening a door which was on the latch:

"I'll make some tea or something, then we'll talk. My head's not frightfully good."

Gian followed him into the house, where the door beside the foot of the stairs opened and a grey woman popping out her head said, "Oh, is that you, Mr Grist, that's all right!" He noticed, remotely, how very slowly Trevon went up the stairs; and he noticed also that something about the house was familiar: it was the one that Armorel had hustled him into to keep him clear of the police.

A light showed under the door at the top of the stairs. Trevon was saying, "Now how in hell did I come to leave that on!" when it opened, startling them both. Looking past Trevon's arm Gian saw a woman standing there in outdoor clothes and heard her say: "I was round this way so I thought I'd just get you some supper—it's by the fire. I've got to hurry back now."

Exhausted by the dozen stairs, Trevon leant against the lintel, blinking at the light. He said feebly: "You shouldn't have done that. It's terribly kind."

Gian had turned and was trying to slip away. Trevon called him. "Gian, come on! This is a very nice person called Mrs Kinfowell."

Elizabeth turned her smile to him. "You wouldn't know my name," she said quickly, "but I'm a friend of Armorel's—I'm Elizabeth. We did meet for a moment or two at your wedding."

Gian nodded and said, "Pleased to meet you, m'm!" but this was more than he could deal with. The evening had taxed him heavily enough, with its sense of truancy, the ordeal of facing old acquaintances, the struggle to pay out in sentences the barbed tangle that lay inside; and now, without warning, he was faced by a creature of infinite delicacy and grandeur who behaved as if he were one of her own kind. He could not even find the words to get himself away.

"See how it is," he mumbled, looking half-way between them, "very kind, only Miss Susie she'd be wondering, I reckon. Thank-y', Mr Grist."

He had one glimpse, as he turned, of the simple room: the fire, the shaded light on roughly carpentered bookshelves; a room of which the walls had possessed some meaning for him once. With another nod he stumbled off down the stairs.

But the solitude he wanted now was denied him. He had only gone a few yards down the street when he heard the door open and shut again, and light steps running. The woman was coming after him. She called "Mr Ardree!" and he stopped.

"Yeh?" he said.

She said, "I'm going your way as far as the main road—can I come with you? This isn't a terribly nice street to be in at night."

"Nothing wrong with it," he said as they walked on together, "not this street. Biddle's Place now, back there, you want to keep clear of that."

"I've been there this evening," she told him.

"What! Biddle's Place?"

"Yes, I've been to see a friend of mine. Oh, of course, you know her—I met her at your wedding first of all. Daise Empire."

He was slow at getting hold of this. "Daise?" he said; and a few moments afterwards, "I knew her dad, I worked under him."

"Oh, I've only seen him once. I've usually been in the afternoon—I read to Daise's mother sometimes. She hasn't got much to entertain her, poor thing. Of course Daise is awfully good with her."

"She all right—Daise?" he asked.

"Yes, I think she's quite well."

"Huh-huh!"

She asked him: "What do you think about Trevon? Of course *I* think it was sheer madness to let him go back to work. He should have had at least a month's convalescence. I suppose they found him a difficult patient at the hospital—that sort of man always is."

"I ain't heard what he got wrong with him," he said. "I ain't seen him before tonight."

It was her turn to fall silent; and they did not speak again until they reached the main road, where she took her leave.

"I'm going to wait here and hope for a taxi," she said. "I've had rather a tiring day. Listen, you'll give my love to Armorel, won't you! And I wish you'd bring her to see me—she knows where I live."

"She don't do much visitin'," he said.

"Well, I suppose we must say 'Good-night'!"

"Goo'-night!"

She watched him sauntering off in the direction of the Elephant; leaving me, she thought, as if I were a bus he has just got down from! Then, as he reached the next lamp, she was surprised to see him stop and turn round.

He came slowly back and stood in front of her, quite silent, and looking at her feet, so that for one moment she was faintly scared. Then he murmured something which she had to ask him to repeat.

"Weald Street," he said. "Sort of a house we're going to—have it to ourselves, most of it. You could come round there, see. See Susie 'n' all. 16A, it is."

"Of course!" she answered. "I'd love to come."

But he seemed unsatisfied.

"See how it is," he said, after another silence, "she'd want someone to talk to her, nor I wouldn't know how. A sort of lady like yourself, see how it is."

She understood perfectly. "I shall enjoy it so much," she said. "She and I haven't had a talk for ever so long."

And still he stood looking at her feet, working his mouth, fishing for something else that lay in his thoughts. He said at last:

"Then, y'see, you could likely tell me the way I ought to go on. See what I mean? I mean, I got to do right by her, best I can. Only I reckoned you oughter know—you being a friend of Mr Grist's—Mr Grist don't know just anyone as his friends, see what I mean."

Why to me? she thought: he has hardly seen me, I've only been a shape walking at his side: why to me, always to me? But her impulses worked as if no confidence like this had ever been given to her before, and she only managed to say, putting her hands on his shoulders, "I understand, Gian, I do understand!"

With that he did seem to be satisfied, and after one slow, frightened look at her face, a sculpture of compassion in the faint light of the street, he went off again without trying to say anything more.

25

*N*o, they had only been peeling him, them Fidgleys and that lofty Ormison with a tart's grin always stuck on his mug. Same as before. Come down to it, he was a short-arsed bloke with a mug like a gorilla and his thatch more like what you'd see on a nigger than any ordinary bloke's. Like a Grindie's, come to that, though they didn't try that on him any more. So of course it was better than a circus, the way they look at it, him toggled in with Susie; flash dosses and all the rest. They weren't seeing the blind side of nothing, they knew how it was, him standing on that carpet outside the bedroom door, wishing to crike a flash of lightning come and strike him dead. See it himself, come to that, supposing another bloke go getting toggled outside his class. And a Grindie at that. Good as a Punch and Judy. 'How are y', Toughie! Nice to see you, Toughie!' Not so green as he couldn't see the back side of that.

And yet there was a vein of happiness, a sensuous warmth of the emotions, as he went on slowly towards the Elephant: with the street almost empty now, only a cop flashing the doors of the shops and a single drunk crooning to himself against the post office wall. A shower earlier in the evening had left the roadway moist, the tramlines were threads of silver under the high lamps. At this hour sounds were separate and clear, as you hear them when lying in harbour; the air, loosed from the smells of oil and ferment, belonged again to the sky. In stillness this city of his possession calmed him, and he caught from its stertorous sleep a faint tingle of bravery.

He was tired, and when he turned off at Wilson's auction rooms the stages of the evening had lost their boundaries, leaving it an almost formless memory of excitement, of mingled contentment and fear. How shameless to talk to Mr Grist like that, to give himself away, like being sick on the pavement. But like being sick it had relieved him. With another bloke like yourself you couldn't talk that fashion, he'd look at you the way as if there was something wanted tightening and he'd pass it on to the boys. Nor yet you couldn't give it off on an educated bloke, like Mr Duckett, say (or Susie, come to that), because a gent like Mr Duckett never put his mind on that class of fancying at all. Mr Grist, he might answer or he might say nothing: he didn't look at you, leastways he didn't look at you like any other bloke—'Crike,

259

you must be balmy! Call that a headpiece you got, what ain't nothing but a nine-inch sewage pipe! Time you got a hold on yourself and read y' fumin' Bible!'—he only looked as if you tell him a bit of bad news what was interesting just the same, like what you get in the Sundays. 'Might happen to you or might happen to me': that was the kind of notion you got off Mr Grist. Pity, in a way, about the skirt showing up. Might have got a bit more in the way of an answer with Mr Grist all to himself, sitting there comfortable. A nice room it look, so much as he'd seen. Not a silky sort of room, like what Susie was after fixin' up. But a room a bloke would feel all right in—better than what Mr Grist had at the Club.

"Well what if I am late!" he replied to Ed, who was still sprawling in the kitchen doing calculations in the margin of the *Star*. "Don't have to report myself to you, do I! Or punch a clock in this place! Susie gone up?" He found her in bed and nearly asleep. "I knocked into Mr Grist," he told her. "Got talkin'."

"Oh, I see. Yes, Trevon's a fearful talker," she said.

Born out of the street's darkness, it remained the clearest picture of that evening, the room he had seen for just a few moments: the shaded light warming the colours of books, old crimson carpet slippers on a bedside rug. And Trevon's exhausted face, as he dropped into a basket chair, that was so sharp an image it would stay for a time in Gian's memory, the look of a man beaten and bewildered, the faint, surrendering smile. The woman's face, turned away from the light, he had hardly seen at all: it came into that picture, obscurely, as a form shaped in snow, darkly framed in the close cornice of hair and the silk foliage of her neck. Her voice he recalled as something separate, a thread of warmth which had seemed to come without the mechanism of tongue and lips: . . . *I'm Elizabeth* . . .

"We met at your wedding," she had told him. At the wedding? Vaguely, he felt he had known that shadowed face before, and even heard that voice. But not, surely, in all that confusion, not in a trim suburban garden. The scene that gathered round her, faint like old painting, had a brown wall and a line of gnarled trees.

His mind cleared a little, as with clouds rising, while he was at work. He was on a fancy job now, a window shaped like a shell, where he could use some cunning that Stumper had taught him; high up again, thirty feet or more above street level, so that he saw the funnels of steamers passing and over his shoulder the trees on Clapham Common; and with the weather becoming more gentle your thoughts ran pleasantly here. At half-past ten on any fine morning a mob of children tumbled out like gooseberries from the little school he could see in Pillage Road, where an aged teacher formed them up like soldiers and marshalled them across the street to the park. Sometimes he took his lunch bag over there, so he could watch them at their games; and by degrees he collected nerve enough to address their governess, who sat and knitted on the seat beside him. Yes, they were nice children, she told him, her loosely-articulated eyes swivelling to right and left as if there were spies in all the bushes; but often so very difficult, downright naughty at times. That little Mellarby, for instance, in the green knickers, a regular terror he could be. Of course, it was all on account of his father . . . At four o'clock, when the children were formed up again and marched back to school, he waved to them with his trowel; occasionally one of them saw him—as a rule, the villainous Mellarby—and a grubby handkerchief was waved in reply.

A brown wall and the grey-green, twisted trees. The sky like blue glass lit with electricity. And now, sharply in the heavy and still air, the intermittent, cracked note of a bell.

"Beautiful thoughts, Ardery?" "Don't you talk to him, Bert, else he can't concentrate. Can't you hear, the angels is calling him. Get him, too, if he step back another half a yard!"

He grinned, he liked this gang. And almost at once, with the grin floating away, he was back among the twisted trees.

Not that it mattered, and he wasn't puzzling about it: the scene developed by itself, like an autumn landscape, as he shaped a brick to fit the corner where a curve and a straight line met, as he paused to look across the factory smoke at the refreshing green of the common. Waiting for his bus at the end of Eccles Road, watching the lorries which splashed through the mud on Lavender Hill, he heard Elizabeth's voice again as voices are heard in the first moments of sleep, and through the dun façade of the Public Library he saw, though he did not recognize, a turn in the dusty Pontedecimo road. "What is your name, little boy? Have you lost your mummy? Why are you crying?" The woman stooping so that her serene face was level with his and her dismal draperies no longer frightened him: there, with the road hot under his bare feet, with the drivers cracking their whips on the steep slope, he had seen her first of all.

He could not have found his way, now, from the house in the

Vicolo Sant' Agata to the slope of green, ruled with olive trees, where she had played with him and the other children. She had come to fetch him, perhaps, or Mama had taken him there. It had happened so often, he thought, it was part of everyday life, the warm grass and the trees, the sound of the cracked bell. Monaca Pieta, that was her name, and she lived in a large house on the other side of the hot, brown wall.

He had supposed, when he was younger, that he would be taken back to those places before long, and go without shoes again. He had once talked to little Rosie about 'Where we live'; 'You don't remember where we live!' But since his first year at school he had realized that the past is all shut up and you do not go back. He could remember a little of how it had ended: Mama complaining and scolding in the dim, swarming belly of the ship, the way the ship's sides curved over the narrow bed he shared with Rosie, the waves thumping and trying to get in. The nearest passengers still kept their place in his memory, a shrunken Englishwoman who was always coughing, the oniony man who shouted at her to be quiet and then prayed aloud with his arm round her shoulders, holding his cigarette in the other hand; and he knew exactly what the smell had been, for in Flanders Street on certain days he had caught a whiff of it again, the smell of sickness and dirty clothes and tar. Yes, that was the boundary where the old life ended: with Rosie whimpering beside him, baggage and people sliding about as the floor tilted over; and then the man in a steward's uniform had grown to something more than a shape, as he picked his way with a flash lamp between the sleeping bundles and came to stare at them with dumb anxiety, the peculiar, long-necked man he had been told to call 'Papa'. That had seemed to go on for a long time, the swinging motion, the queer shadows formed by the garish bulkhead lights and the moving bundles, 'Papa' returning again and again; a lifetime in itself; and he could not remember how it had changed to the chilly, grey-brown life which had followed. He had simply found himself, as if he had been there always, on the kerb in a straight-sided street which was sealed by a factory wall.

No Pieta there. No Francesco Gioielliere in blue velvet trousers or scarlet birds in a cage, never a sky alight with sun. He had stood shivering by the broken door which led to some passage-way, holding Rosie close to his side, watching the pale children who sprawled in the garbage and yelled at each other with words he could not understand. From a window far above a woman had bawled down at him but he had pretended to be deaf, determined not to move till they brought

Mama back. "Ospedale!" the woman had said, laughing horridly and sounding the word in her own strange way, when she came to grab them both by the arms. When Rosie cried he had seized the woman's leg and bitten it, and afterwards, lying almost naked in the dark cupboard and twisting from the cut of the strap, he had screamed Pieta's name until his voice gave out.

He had pictured Pieta exactly, he thought, in those hungry and despairing days (though his picture had corresponded little enough, perhaps, with the peasant features, scarred from smallpox, which Scorzini's portrait shows in the Palazzo Cadorna). Now her face was no longer a shape that his mind could re-fashion, it was only an area of paleness within the shadowing headdress, a distillation of light and of tenderness: a face that was sad but always smiling, so that it lit immediately a child's answering smile. Her voice, even now, he seemed to recall distinctly, a voice far softer than Mama's, crying "Catch me, lovelings, catch me!" as she ran up the green slope, laughing and stumbling in her morass of skirts. Yes, and once, when she fell over, he had sprung upon her shouting "Prigionere!" and she had seized and covered him with kisses murmuring, "No, Gianito, you are *my* prisoner, mine!"

Always that hillside and the olive trees. No. Once, he remembered (walking slowly towards Bewley Street, hating to shut himself away from the sunlit evening), once he had seen her on the balcony of their own house. That day, among these clouded recollections, was like a group re-outlined in a faded drawing, the day when the polizia had come for Carlo Ferrara who lived in the room above. He had watched the struggle through the half-open door, the polizia blaspheming and Carlo's scarlet vest being torn to shreds as he was dragged downstairs; he had seen Matilda Ferrara in her night-dress clutching the sbirro's belt, heard the curious, animal whimper she gave when the other one struck her on the mouth. (He had stood perfectly still, smiling, thinking that this was a performance like one he had seen in the Piazza Cavour last All Souls' Day, and knew no reason why he was sick on the floor a few minutes afterwards.) But how should Pieta have been there? Perhaps it had not happened all at once, as memory seemed to tell him; but he thought the alley had still been full of people, shouting and gesticulating, with Matilda lying on the stone steps between their feet, when he had looked up and seen Pieta with one of the Ferrara children in her arms and the rest clustering about her knees.

A long time, years and years, he imagined, since he had consciously thought of that: and yet the names came back, with a sharp, small portrait of Matilda's young face and her spread-eagled hair, the blood trickling from her mouth onto the dirty steps. ("And now," Mr Duckett was saying in his gentle, coaxing voice, "I want to see if we can clear up these Subordinate Clauses once and for all—play hard and really get them licked.") Perhaps he had fleetingly recalled the scene during those hungry nights in the park after his sacking from Hibbage Lane. For at that time, certainly he had needed Pieta; and Pieta, faint, elusive presence, a woman stooping over him, a girl romping between the olive trees, Pieta was first of all the figure which stood so calmly, so protectingly, upon the Sant' Agata balcony above a cauldron of noise and rage. Of all which belonged to that buried time, that dream which could only recur in dreams, she alone, less visible than the Ferraras, dim in colour beside old Francesco, had kept her strange reality, so that loneliness in him was a longing for Pieta, and the small flame of hopefulness which had burnt in the Digg's Yard days, and through the futile weeks in the Spenwick, was the expectation of Pieta, the sense that she could not finally desert him. The dream, the echo of a dream, was framed in no language; if words had ever fastened to it they were in a tongue which his ear scarcely recalled and his mind had forgotten. The vignetted shapes and tones remained, breathing their odour as old and valuable things do, sometimes faintly, powerfully in certain still airs; and like the spray of thin white scars across his shoulders the impress would not be erased by growth or by the current of time.

So much in his life had changed, so many new demands had been made upon him, that this subterrene nostalgia increased its hold. Often overtired, he suffered the new experience of sleeplessness. He would wake as early as two or three o'clock, vexing himself about some small affair of the previous day, the foreman's little sarcasms, some spitefulness of Rosie's; and labouring in the twilight between sleep and consciousness he would struggle to explain himself as Mr Duckett might approve. Susie's presence at his side disturbed him then; her breathing seemed to be uneven, often she was murmuring to herself and occasionally she would speak as loudly and clearly as if she were conscious; "Georgie, don't go away! I didn't mean to hurt *you!* . . . Quiet, please, quiet! I simply want to show you that I can manage all right. The point is that you didn't tell me. That just killed it, *killed* it. I know I'm right." Again and again he thought she must be ill, and he asked, "What's wrong, Sue, what's the matter?" nervously touching her arm. But she would answer coldly: "You mustn't bother me now. There were six extra coffees, that's what makes the two shillings difference," and would turn over to face the other way. Then he was in misery, certain that she was suffering from some unkindness of his own; fearing to waken her, longing for daylight and yet dreading the moment when, as he tried to explain his anxiety and his remorse, the words he required would scatter and crumble. In those enfeebled hours, with senses working too slackly to embank the flood of thoughts, it was easy to imagine that Pieta, somewhere at hand, would stretch her arms to him. She had been there, mysteriously, when he was alone and lost at the turn of the Pontedecimo road. Some magic had brought her to Fr'esca and 'Vanni when their mother was like rubbish thrown out in the vicolo. In this long, half-lit corridor she could not be far away.

He wanted to see Mr Grist again, and he thought of going to Mickett Lane; he would have liked to refresh his memory of the warm colours in that room, and if the lady who called herself Elizabeth were there he would enjoy hearing her voice. (Like Susie's voice, and yet so different; deeper, older, the edges of the words more gently curved.) But the cost in shyness would be heavy, and he was busy in those days.

They were working overtime at St John's Hill. On Sundays he was helping Susie and on most weekday evenings he was either at Bewley Street or in the Grover workshops. The joinery class was a part of his routine that he could easily have sacrificed; his thick squat body was fitted with a joiner's hands, and he had mastered most of what Benfellow the instructor had to impart; but somehow he enjoyed those evenings more than the rest. He had his uses here, giving a hand to the novices and duds: he could tell them nothing in words—somehow Mr Duckett's lessons never enabled you to explain the method of sharpening a chisel—but he could show them. Hearing somewhere behind him the exasperated grunt of a boy bungling an interior curve he would wander over rather sheepishly, take the spokeshave himself and silently demonstrate; then, giving back the tool, he would delicately hold the boy's wrists and make them the channel through which his own sense of the curve was transmitted to the blade. They sniggered over this interference, but took no offence; you could not be offended by such stolid amiability; and in time they were all demanding his services. "Lumpy, here 'alf a jiff! Somethink all gone to bowery with this fumin' wood, maybe those mutton chops o' yourn'd shift the beggar . . .

Cor, ain't nature a masterpiece! What you can learn them gorillas!" Benfellow, elderly, one-legged, wearied to the verge of lunacy by pudding-fisted students, was ready to tolerate the practice with only a rare sarcasm to protect his patent. ("What I say is as this is the way a workin' joiner do it, though of course I wouldn't argue with an advance man like Mr Ardery!") Benfellow knew, obscurely, that the providence which had given him a strong and subtle pair of hands had denied him the art of teaching; and he saw that this clod from the back streets could somehow do with other men's bodies what he himself did so effortlessly with tools. "That chap," he told his wife, "he got some sort of a hold on 'em. Make 'em act like as if they was tradesmen instead of lumps of dough. Bleeding miracle, if you ask me." So Gian stayed on the course, an old-stager, relishing the smells of resin and glue, unconsciously enjoying a sense of possession which Weald Street would never give him. When Armorel proposed that he should drop the joinery and continue only with the plumbing he answered that Mr Benfellow still had plenty to learn him. Those evenings, she suggested, could be spent more usefully at an interesting course of lectures on 'The Citizen's Responsibility' organized by the L.C.C. But on this matter he was quietly determined. He wanted to make himself a joiner, he said. It might come in handy with his job. He would see about being a citizen later on.

Then, when he wanted to unlock one evening every week, it was the English course that he dropped.

Trevon had sent him a letter: he was opening a new show over at Three Tuns Road, something similar to Hollysian House but for younger boys; he had rented half a house and some waste ground, and he was getting senior members of H.H.B.C. to do most of the running, taking it in turns.

> All I want you to do is to go regularly one evening each week and put the fear of Satan into these brats, who require it. Knock all their heads together and kick their backsides until they begin to grab what civilization means . . .

It excited Gian, for he had received only two or three letters in his life (apart from those alarming notes of Susie's with endless 'suggestions' about the wedding and assurances that she would do her best to be a good wife to him, to which he had answered, 'Dear madam, this is wrote to thank you for what you have figured out, which is all O.K. and thanks . . .') Digg's Yard, where Simon had planted his family for their first wretched years in London, was in the Three Tuns district, and a certain curiosity inclined him to revisit the scene. Without saying anything to Susie he laboriously wrote a reply.

> Mr Grist. Dear sir, I beg to acknowledge your esteemed letter of the 29th ult. I take this opportunity to advise that I will go to your new 'Club' on Monday 5th at 7 o'clock P.M. This is the best I can do Sir since you have done fine on me, and I have never met my Wife except on account of 'H.H.B.C.' I will not hurt any of the young boys as you know Sir, that is just your joke. I shall not say that I would go each week. I will do my best sir. With kind Regards, in which Mrs Ardree joins, Yrs respectful, G. Ardree.

With that, in the event, another evening every week was earmarked. Earmarked and apparently wasted. For Trevon's creation at Apostles' Court, born from a capricious impulse, swaddled in every conceivable discomfort and reared on a bountiful diet of misorganization, looked like a failure cut closely to the pattern of all enthusiastic failures. In the back first-floor room with a broken window giving on to the Pan, Gian found a trestle table and two benches, a coloured print of Landseer's *Dignity and Impudence* and three paper Union Jacks. Here a lean and shamefaced youth known to him as Snitch was in charge; he was standing by the wreck of a piano playing *There's a Long, Long Trail a-Winding* with one finger, grinning feebly and at intervals saying dejectedly, "Look 'ere now, it's no fumin' good me playin' to you blokes if you don't sing." His audience was five small, ragged boys. One, who had been sick, was crying bitterly, while an elder brother was viciously and tirelessly beating the table with a curtain-rod. The two smallest, pinched, verminously dirty and with savage, adult mouths, were squatting close to the door, evidently longing to bolt, and the last, a ten-year-old grotesquely tall for his age, stood all by himself and stared towards the window with less than an animal's understanding. None of them looked likely to burst into song. When he caught sight of Gian, Snitch stopped playing.

"I got to amuse these little baskets," he said dourly, "that's what Bulky Grist tell me. I got to bring sweetness and joy into their fumin' lives, an' give 'em a noggin of esperrit de corpse."

"I get y'," Gian said.

If he did, he was no help. He sat on the table, merely increasing

Snitch's discomfort, until one of the door-watchers said desperately, "Gone eight o'clock, mister. I 'eard it strike, Crike's truth I did. Gent said we could fume off at eight!" upon which all five made a rush for the door and Snitch without a word went after them.

There is no obvious reason why Gian should have gone near the place again. That he did go may be attributed mainly to his odd sense of gratitude to Trevon, which demanded some practical expression; and a little, perhaps, to the influence of Armorel. Not that she encouraged it. When he told her in a foolishly casual fashion that he had given up the English course "to muck in on Mr Grist's new club," she could barely hide her annoyance, and let out the comment that anything started by a man like Trevon Grist was doomed to be a waste of everyone's time. Yet it was she, surely, who had taught him that time out of work was something to be used and boredom something to be overcome. He had learnt to submit with regularity and without reward to the misery of Mr Cood's lectures; now, having embarked on a new form of discomfort, he easily accepted it as routine.

Nor was it wholly disagreeable. The drab dilapidation of Apostles' Court could not positively oppress a denizen of Contessa Street; and a man who had once been pursued up Blackfriars Road by a dozen boys of his own age singing *'On goes the Grindie, the Macaroni Ape'* was not too much embarrassed by children ten years younger than himself. The harmlessness of these infants, behind their shrewd and often hostile faces, was calculated to put him quickly at his ease; while in Alb, the imbecile, he found a curious kind of fascination. He spent the whole of one evening knocking nails into a piece of wood in the hope that Alb would try to imitate him, and most of the next two sessions showing him over and over again (without result) the way to put new laces in his boots. It was reward enough to see just once, in the wandering, goat-like eyes, something that might be taken for a smile.

This was a country different from the region of Contessa Street, where you could trace some threads of purpose in the motley of shops and houses marshalled against roads which took you somewhere in the end. When you crossed over Three Tuns Road you were in a prospectors' encampment where even the tallest building with its broken windows looked makeshift and incomplete; a village of women and their broods, a caravanserai for sailors, so that children kicking treacle tins along the gutters had the bright fair hair of Oslo or the smoked eyes of Nagapatam, sometimes dark heads with thick and wiry hair. A year before, Gian might hardly have noticed that he had crossed a boundary; for the grey-yellow brick was the same, and there was nothing strange to him in foreign voices; but the North View had waked new sensibilities, and at Weald Street under Susie's close direction he was creating something which differed from his parents' home as musquash differs from coney. He was becoming alive to new gradations. Visiting Alb's home he saw that by some standards his own was respectable and clean; and if his mother was slatternly in her ways she was a paragon of neatness compared with the mother of Alb. (He could put Alb in the river and she wouldn't complain, the mother said, standing at the entrance to her room with a soldier's greatcoat over her nightgown: Alb was one of her slips, she told him, adding all the unvarnished details, and after that she shook with laughter until a slightly drunken man arrived to take her inside and slam the door.) Compared with Digg's Yard, which he found only a furlong away on the other side of the Pan, the decency of Contessa Street was almost smug. Standing at Digg's Yard Turn he could see smoke-stacks that he recognized, and a faintly remembered rubbish-tip on the other side of the barge wharf. For the rest it was all strange land, except that a smell from the houses stirred some memory, and the odd notion passed through his mind that the children squealing and tumbling in the roadway were children he had known.

Not a place to be loved or to be proud of. But his having lived here hastened the sense of possession which grew in his recurrent visits to Apostles' Court. This was a region of no privacies and no restrictions: street doors were rarely closed, amorphous families disengaged from each other only, and not invariably, for sleep, children took food in their pockets to eat on the Pan while their mothers fed on the steps or at the Carpenter or lying in bed. They recognized him now as he came from the bus-stop, and he would smile when the women in a friendly way threw bawdy comments from the windows, when banana skins whizzed past him in the road or a grinning child deliberately messed a step he was about to walk on: here as elsewhere he was a joke perhaps, but remembering the solemn courtesies of the North View he felt that this was a masonry he could understand. To forget, on this one evening in the week, the artificial speech he was trying to learn was like changing from uniform into old civilian clothes. He could swagger and shout here; when an infant who could not control his wind went into peals of laughter he laughed as loudly as the rest. He liked to feel himself so strong, to let the whole of Tim Paipi's 'Shanghai Gang' pin him to the floor and shake them off with one ferocious heave; and when he heard them saying "Cops? Ardy Rhino'll deal with them!" he felt that he had found a kingdom. A boy who had mischievously thrown slime in his face brought him the chewed remains of an apple as peace offering, and he was oddly moved: he understood that gesture. In some sense he had come back home.

But often he was miserably angry. For there was ugliness here, which no one bothered to hide, of a kind that played directly on his sensibilities. There were children with impetigo and with sores on their spindly arms, some had hare-lips or goitre, pot-bellies or crooked spines. Walking across the Pan he would see a tub-like creature struggling to keep up with the older ones on bandy legs and feet that turned over sideways, and later, when it was chilly and dark, he would find her fallen asleep in the mud. Then there was a house by Leakly's shed where a pair of mulattoes about five years old were pushed outside whenever a customer went in; they were skinny children with watery eyes who seemed to have no ideas for play, they merely stood and shivered by a wall which gave them some protection from the rain. Those were sights which hung like a drag upon his thoughts, and there were strands in the skein of sound which chafed his nerves more painfully still. From certain houses you could hear a child's continuous keen beneath the raucous voices of a man and woman arguing; and more than once he caught the sound of broken, frightened screams alternating with the clap of blows. That noise, running like icy water through his veins, made him huddle and bite his thumbs, and when nausea turned to rage he beat on the bolted door till his hands were running with blood. Afterwards the weakness returned, while the anger stayed like an abscess gnawing his mind; at night the faces of children followed him into sleep, they called to him and he answered them bravely (so that Armorel was sometimes woken by his cry and his frantic movements) but when he tried to approach them he found that the Spenwick officers had got him chained to the ground.

"You don't mind coming here?" Trevon asked him, darting in one evening, hasty, confused, pitifully tired and out of breath. "It seems to me worth going on with. Or do you find it a ghastly bore?"

"It's all right," Gian said.

Such hasty visits were all he saw of Trevon in those days, all he expected to see; for it was plain to the least observant that the man was spending far too lavishly what little health he had regained. And that was unfortunate for Gian, with no one else to listen to him in just the way that Trevon could. In the forest he had come to none of the tracks was marked, and the travellers he had started with had gone off some other way. He could have done with a guide who at least understood the language he spoke.

Perhaps the schooling of a human creature is bound to include a stretch of solitude, where daylight fails and the country no longer corresponds with the explorers' charts. He was simply unlucky in having wandered to a route for which he had received no maps at all. At Sand Street they had taught him about arithmetic and Henry VIII's six wives, he had heard that there was Good, such as giving to beggars, and Evil, like stealing food. For other boys this seemed enough to get on with; they learnt the rest from the streets they lived in, from sardonic foremen, hook-nosed dealers and accessible girls; but to Gian it now appeared, vaguely, that existence was more complicated than he had been told. He did not go over his feelings with a glass, since that was a trick which no one had taught him; when he was wretched he did not study his misery as the highly-schooled do. But he knew, as animals can rarely know, that other beings could suffer hurt; he faintly understood that those more delicate in body and complex in mind might experience distresses unknown to him; and it seemed to his unformulated thoughts that in taking possession of a creature so much more finely wrought than himself he had made a signal contribution to the sum of existing pain. That belief lay like the shadow of a cloud across his mind's chequered countryside, and in the face of a paralytic creeping along Borough Road, in Alb's drifting eyes, the whimper of a very thin child who stood on the pavement entirely by himself, he seemed to see a reflection, an echo of what he had done. Dimly he awaited some kind of retribution, and he was frightened; not of fatigue or pain, for he knew no limit to his own endurance, and his body was so fortified by use that memory only whispered how it felt to flinch from a blow; he was afraid, rather, of his own feebleness in understanding, his clumsiness, his power to hurt more fragile things with so little effort of body or voice. Some power he did not comprehend had slyly made him the instrument of an unfinished cruelty. That power might still be unsatisfied.

He had his work, his classes, the pressure and traffic of the back room at Contessa Street. These, from hour to hour, were sufficient freight for a mind unused to navigating far from the shore. But in moments when he was tired and his thoughts fell slack a loneliness he had not imagined before possessed him like a sickness in the blood, and against that infection neither anger nor the stoicism of one unused to coddling sympathy was of any avail. Then he was desperate for another creature at least to recognize his distress. He would have taken it to Susie herself, but he could build no bridge between his awkwardness and her sensible, sweet calm. And Mr Grist with the troubles of a hundred boys pursuing him was tired and ill, and Pieta, though he thought he had heard her voice not long ago, stood somewhere out of sight.

It became his habit to return from Apostles' Court by Mickett Lane, which meant going a little out of his way; always hoping he would run into Trevon there and be invited to his room again. Once he took the cut through Bidault's Place, out of curiosity to have another look at Empire's house. There was some risk of meeting Charlie Empire himself, but he felt equal to that situation: in his off-duty clothes, and walking with his head up the way Susie liked, he was as good as any deputy foreman; he would nod to Charlie in a casual fashion and walk away.

It didn't happen—the planned situation never happens. But on one of those evenings he did see Daise. It was nearly dark; he was walking rather slowly past the house where Trevon lived when a girl with a heavy basket hurried through the patch of light thrown from Begbie's window onto the wet pavement. He, at any rate, could not fail to recognize that figure, the great head on the small, delicate body. He called out, " 'Lo, Daise!" and it was she who merely nodded and went on.

He ran after her, calling: "What's the hurry? The war's over now —ain't you heard!"

"I got to get back," she said.

He seized the handle of her basket, "I'll take it for y'!" but she would not let it go. She said: "Leave off, Jan, do—my dad might see you."

"Your dad—what about it! He's not my boss any more. I can carry anyone's basket, can't I?"

He walked on beside her through the Coronation passage and into the place. There was a sheltered corner near Zadolski's shop, much used by lovers and sometimes by plain-clothes men. He led her there as he had done more than once before.

"Goin' on all right?" he asked.

"Yes, I'm all right." She was nervous, she kept looking towards the passage, where an overhead lamp would show up anyone who came. "You all right?"

"Huh-huh!"

"Like being married?"

"It's all right."

"Got a job?"

"Huh-huh. Bricklayin'."

"Does she—does the lady think that's all right?"

"Huh-huh. Yes 'n' no. She want to get me on a drawin' job. Own the whole outfit—see the mugs. 'What can I do for you today, mister? Church you're wantin', workhouse? Run you up a nice factory, any size you like.' That's me, the way Susie wants it."

"Fancy!"

"Yep, fancy's right! You got to do more book-learnin' than a college professor for a job like that." He re-lit his cigarette and spat sidewise with the old swagger. "What you up to, these days?"

"Oh, nothing."

"Mum all right now?"

"No, she's still bad. Lady come round and see her. Sundays it is mostly. Weekdays as well sometimes."

"Uh-huh!"

"Mrs Kinfole, she said she was. Knew you, she tell me."

"Uh-huh. She all right?"

"Yes, she's nice. Help me do out Mum's room sometimes." Her eyes were on the ground except when she glanced guiltily towards the passage, it looked as if her one idea was to get this interview done with. "Well, I got to be getting on," she said abruptly, and moved away. Then she came back, and for the first time looked up at his face.

"Been nice, seeing you again, Jan," she said.

"What's all the hurry?" he asked once more.

"Dad don't like me dawdling about. He says it ain't respectable."

"Oh, your dad said that!"

"He wants everything respectable."

Again she would have gone, but he caught hold of her arm; not roughly—that wasn't necessary.

"Listen," he said, "did he ever find out I come round that night? That night Susie come after me."

"Yes. He come into the back room and smelt the cigarettes."

"What did you tell him?"

"I said you just wanted to see him, only you couldn't wait."

"Uh-huh."

She said fearfully: "You wasn't going to do anything to him that time? Not really?"

"Scare him." He reflected for a moment, shifting his cigarette across his mouth. "Pity she choose that night to come after me."

"It wasn't, Jan. It was a good thing she do come, you know that!"

"Uh-huh?" And then, bending down to her, he asked: "He don't still bring them in?"

She hesitated and then laughed in the way he hated; a nervy, twittering laugh. She whispered: "Not much."

"What do you mean, 'not much'?"

"I don't mind, anyway," she said. "It don't make no difference now, reely it don't." Then, sobering, becoming almost matter of fact, she said: "He got a new place going over Three Tuns way. Doris Pinchley tell me—Doris walk out 'cause she had a row with Dad. A proper set-up, the new place is. Swank, I mean, so Doris tell me."

"Uh-huh—respectable!" he said.

But she did not understand jokes of that kind, which he had never made in the old days. She said in a voice of wood: "He don't bring back nothing but the left-overs. Them as kick up about the tally. He got to do something to keep them quiet, dockers 'n' all. It's no good makin' trouble, you get used to it, reely you do."

She was all sincerity. She didn't want any trouble. No, she never wanted any trouble—"You go and get Dad upset, an' then he upset Mum," that was what she had told him again and again. It was right, he supposed, you got used to it. And the men got used to it, some of them. Some didn't, and a few found it funny. He was back for an instant at the Hibbage Lane depot, with young Bickie Schneider going on and on in his earnest, nasal, outrage-loving voice. 'But her *fice*— well, you know, honest God, I never did see a fice like that, it ain't human, honest God it ain't,' while Stommeridge, with his camel's mouth, wallowed in laughter. 'Goew on—you don't want to look at her *face!* Cover it up, boy, that's all you got to do with the ——'s *face!*' And then the ham-fisted sketches, brazenly labelled on the cloakroom wall. He said, letting his thoughts tear out:

"See here, Daise, I reckon I can't do nothink, see. Married man, see how it is—you got to go on like a shiny once you get toggled the way I got—"

"I don't want nothing," she said.

"—It's not what you want!" he pursued, between anger and misery, "it's what he want done to him—"

"No, Jan, you can't, reely—"

"No, I can't. Only you can tell him, just the same. About that knife I show y'—I got it still—"

"—But, Jan, you never would! Not on Dad!"

"*Dad!*" he said, and a spurt of obscenity escaped like sputum through his fastened teeth. "You can tell him, just the same. He knows what I said, back at Hibbage Lane. Tell him I only got to hear once more—tell him that, see!"

"You're talking foolish, Jan. There's Mum an' all. I got to get on now—"

"Listen, you got to tell me, see—next time he bring one in. You got to, see! God 'n' oath!"

"All right," she answered mildly, "God 'n' oath," and he let her go. "It's been nice seeing you. Jan."

"Yep!"

He knew perfectly well, starting to walk home, that she wouldn't tell him. She had never told him, he had always been obliged to find out by talking to blokes at the depot, watching from the end of Sea Coal Street. Well, come to that, it never had been no business of his, and it certainly wasn't now, with him toggled and Daise a grown woman, eighteen she must be by this time. But he was slow to think in general terms. He could not argue, as the well-informed do, that things which happen everywhere and every day are unimportant, because he had no means of casting his reflections as widely as that. As he went slowly past the fish bars and billiard saloons in Kirk's Squadron Street he could only think of the time when he had found himself alone with Daise in that top back room, the shock of realizing that the submissive, tearful eyes were human, her voice the voice of a child. That scene returned with so much force that he stopped and swung about as if he meant to go back; and as he saw in the lamplight the tobacconist's at the corner, the Lifebuoy plate, the porch of St Andrew's Mission Church, his memory shifted to that other terrifying evening when he had come this way, famished and slightly giddy, with the summer wind blowing the dust in his face, to have things out with Charlie once and for all. Then he had been free, and what happened to him was no one's affair but his own. He was suddenly enraged that Susie had taken that freedom away.

It was raining again, but he did not notice that: in this country it was always raining. Someone said, "Oy, look where you're goin', cock!" colliding with his arm, and "What are y' bloody eyes for!" a driver yelled as he stepped off into the road.

Everyone else was free. At the Old Richmond, as he passed, young men and women laughed together while the restful agony of an accordion spilt out from the saloon; across the tide of lugubrious basses chanting *The end O-O-OF a PER fick-die* a cheap and cheerful voice broke from the pavement. 'Well, Joe, I said, your loss, not mine!' and the girl clinging to the speaker's arm laughed shrilly as they danced along in step towards their tram. The entrance to Vedander's buzzed with the stubborn tones of Jews and kerb-touts arguing about the day's receipts, a Pullman streaming over the viaduct showed for an instant the stolid profiles of homebound city men, outside the tube a bunch of shop-girls moved in a swarm of giggle and chatter through the portière of lighted rain. No one but me goes out by himself, he thought as he turned into the darkness of Cord Street, not noticing the undersized clerk who passed him, the old woman picking her way to the pillar-box across the traffic slime. He sniffed, he could almost have found his way from here by smell as a dog would. And yet, he vaguely thought, tired now from the day and the labour of feeling, You are up above this crowd, and able to fight back, so long as you stay alone.

The door of the shop was wide open and a light came through from the back room. It was Lizzie Bentlock, standing like the Rock of Ages at the inner doorway, who greeted him:

"And here's the cause of all the trouble! About time you *did* come home!"

26

THEY STARED at him, as on the night when he had brought Susie home. The usual people were here. A part of the table had been cleared for ironing, the rest was strewn with pages of the *Star* and the remains of supper. The change was intangible, as in a house where news has come of some disgrace.

"Your mum's with her," Simon said.

There were people on the stairs, Rosie and one or two others. He pushed past them to the bedroom and opened the door.

Maria was standing against the bed. Beside her bulk he could just see Armorel's hair. Swinging round, Maria said violently: "Gian, you is not to comesin sair!" He went downstairs again.

Simon leant against the sink, ostensibly drying a cup which had been in his hands for five minutes or more. He was trembling, and his breath, for the first time in months, smelt slightly of gin. He came shamefacedly to Gian's side.

"It'll be all right, son. Your mum, she seen a lot of that, see what I mean, she'll do all right."

"That's right," Olleroyd echoed from his chair, "Mrs Ardree'll do her all right."

It was a point of pride with Lizzie Bentlock that she never came right into the room unless Maria asked her. But this was an occasion for breaking rules: Mrs Oestermann and Mary Toble, her juniors in Maria's friendship, were already inside. She sat comfortably in the basket chair, smoking a damp cigarette as if she were paid so much an hour to do it.

"Maria had a bad time with her second, so she tell me."

Miss Toble nodded. "It run in families," she said.

"She don't look a strong young lady, young Mrs Ardree don't."

"And they do say you want a strong girl for a strong fellow's baby."

"She'll come out of it all right," Simon said again.

Needing to sit down, Gian took the chair that happened to be empty next to Ed's. The paper lying in front of him said *Mayfair Shooting, Ex-Public Schoolboy at Bow St, £780 on Scent and Lingerie.* Ed, sitting back, smoking with *jeune premier* ostentation and doing accounts on his knee, surveyed him with guarded amusement.

"How go, Gyan boy? First time's the worst for fathers, they do say. Still, I reckon you'll get through all right, all the fresh air and exercise you get, pickin' up a brick and handin' it to the other bloke, wipin' the kid gloves with a nice, easy motion."

Gian took his chair round the table and sat by Olleroyd, who said hoarsely: "I know all about it, I know just how you're feeling. I lost my first wife that way."

The window was tightly shut. All the cooking utensils which Maria had used for supper were still in the sink and a bundle of Evangeline's napkins lay unwashed on the sewing machine. Someone had upset a jug of gravy, it was all down the back of a chair and formed a lake on the floor in which Ed's cigarette-ends had opened out and were now congealing. Useless bitches, all these here! Gian reflected. Susie would always deal with such untidiness, and it seemed to him a deliberate affront that the rest had taken advantage of her absence in this way. But he was too tired to do anything about it. Something was out of order with his breathing, and he felt as he had done in the police court. He was more lonely than he had been in the street.

The door from the stairs opened and the gnome-like Mrs Diddus, who appeared at meals sometimes and was believed to be one of Maria's Roundel lodgers, brought one more odour into the room. In her dressing gown and Wellington boots, with her hair peculiarly parcelled, she stood waiting for attention, heavy with evil news.

"Lizzie," she said huskily, "Steve's not riding tomorrow. I heard them calling it in the street." She turned despondently to Gian. "Your ma says you can go up now if you want."

Rosie stopped him as he went upstairs again. Her make-up was channelled with tears. She said almost fiercely, squeezing his arm against her small, full breast: "I never meant her no harm, Gi, truth I never did! I'd do it for her m'self, truth I would, it's nothing to a girl like me." He was grateful for that, and kissed her cheek as he had not done for a long time. After listening for a few moments at the bedroom door he opened it cautiously. He didn't really want to go into the room now.

Maria was creating as much fuss as if there were four of her, laughing, crying and careering about the room. She seemed to have the place half-full of towels and kettles, she was tearing things and spilling things and calling on her saints first plaintively and then with fury, like a customer grossly insulted. "Two minute!" she said ferociously. "Two minute and then *out!* No more else!" Then, laughing again: "Ah, so pehle, s'poor lil-ragazzo!" Gian removed himself from her embrace and went cautiously towards the bed.

There seemed to be nothing wrong with Susie at all. She lay quite restfully, she smiled at him. "What sort of a day?" she asked in her ordinary, pleasant way. "Have you been to Mr Duckett?"

He kept a yard away, as if his breath might harm her.

"Well, you see how it is, Susie, I been with the kids tonight. That business of Mr Grist's. Wensdays, you see . . . I don't like seeing you bad, Sue."

She said: "Oh, all this is perfectly natural . . . You're only going to this affair of Trevon's once a week, aren't you? You see, it's very nice and all that, only it won't *help* you in any way, and you can't afford to let any chances go past, not at present, anyhow."

"No, I reckon it's like what you say." One of her arms was outside the bed-clothes; he would have liked to caress it. "Nothin' I can do? Get you anythink?"

"No, thank you, Gian. I shall be perfectly all right. Only it takes some time, you know."

"Where is—I put him now?" Maria was demanding of her protectors. "I say I put him onse chair, segrade bowla—satisa liddle *bicker!*"

"Oh, there's one thing I'd be glad if you'd do," Armorel said, "if you're not too tired. I'd like you—" She stopped as if her source of breath had been cut off, he saw her face tautened with pain before she turned her head away. In a second or two she went on speaking with her voice unaltered, and he could only tell from a movement of the bed-clothes what it cost her to keep it so. "I'd be so grateful if you'd—get on to Aunt Georgie. It's Streatham 7701. If you'd ask for Miss Georgina Cepinnier, and just tell her—tell her my baby's coming and I think it's going to be all right."

"I got it," he answered automatically.

If she had uttered one cry he could have bent down and held her; but the Truggetts had never behaved like that. With the spasm still upon her she said distinctly: "Perhaps you'd do that straight away."

He lingered at the door; long enough to hear her catch her breath, to see her turn and open her eyes and compose that smile again, patient, friendly, encouraging. After that there was nothing for it but to go away.

At least he had something definite to do; and without cap or coat he went straight off towards the call-box at the corner of Eton Road, nursing the Streatham number on his tongue. But before he got there he remembered that he had never used a telephone in his life and had no idea how it was managed. With that, the task assumed a fantastic importance: why this Miss Georgianna must be told he could not imagine, but it was Susie's one request and he must not fail her. Mr Grist, he thought; Mr Grist would know. And he ran without stopping the whole way to Hollysian House.

The Club, as he should have realized, was closing down and Trevon had gone. Only Flock was still there.

"God love a chicken-coop!" Flock said bitterly. "Pass on out of my hands a matter of two month, and what happen to your trainin'! Come on here puffin' an' blowin' like a trackshin engine! Spec Mr Grist to wait about all night to see y'! Call yerself a full-grown man, put the King and Parliament to the cost of givin' you a slap-up edgercation, and then you say you don't know how to use the fumin' phone! Come on then, for crikesake!"

They went together to the box at the end of Balt Lane.

"What's that—Miss Spinyer got started on her time? An' whose perishin' fault is that, I'd like to know! You got a sawbones on her?"

Gian had not thought of that. Within his experience you had Miss Beavle or old Mrs Lodge, and his mother—she had told him—could beat them both. He had supposed that only women of fabulous wealth had doctors.

"Now all you got to do," Flock continued, standing in the dark box, "is to strike one perishin' match on top of the other while I organize the civvy signals. Miss!" he suddenly bellowed, "I want Strettim double-seven-oh-one, an' I *don't* want Strettim double-six-one-oh, an' I don't want any fiddle an' faddle and larkin' about in any manner whatsoever. Number of *this* box? How should *I* know? Here, Ardree, give *me* that match, for crikesake. What, *another* copper you want! Look here, miss, you're not talkin' to the bloke what organize the bleedin' Mint, nor yet the Bank of Bleedin' England . . ." He went off raging and found a drunk in Flanders Street, got a penny off him 'for the Earl of Haig's Memoriam' and came back cursing the man for having stepped on his toe. . . . "Jus' the same as I tell you before, Strettim double-seven-oh-one was what I said—oh, yes, you did, an' I don't want no more of your sauce, young miss—Well I *am* holdin' the perishin' line, aren't I, what d'you think I'm doin', cuttin' it off and takin' it home for the wife an' kids?"

A doctor, of course! Gian thought, standing miserably in the rain. Fool that he was! A lady like Miss Susie ought to have a doctor to her, that was as plain as horse-drop.

"What?" yelled Flock. "What's the good on sayin' hullo-hullo-

hullo-hullo! I can 'hullo' you jus' the same, go on all night, come to that. Miss Spinyer, I want. You *is* Miss Spinyer? Well, then it's *your* turn to hold the perishin' line . . . Ardree, come on, lad, quick about it, keep those heels together and breathe right up from the navel!"

Shivering with alarm, Gian held the receiver tight against his ear and steered his lips into the mouthpiece. He said sepulchrally: "I been asked to speak to Miss Spinyer. Miss Georgianna, that would be. Much oblige . . ."

The voice that miraculously came back had been strangely squashed in the wire, but it still sounded like the voice of a queen: "I'm afraid my sister has gone to bed. It's fairly late, you know. Who is that speaking?"

"Well, m'm, it's like this here. I'm only speakin' for Miss Susie, well, I mean Miss Spinyer as you might say—Mrs Ardree, that is."

"*Pull yourself together, for crikesake!*" Flock groaned in his free ear. "No use diggin' round the dung-heap—give the ole perisher your number, name an' rank!"

"I'm afraid I don't quite understand," the queenly voice said.

"Well, it's like this here, m'm, my wife, you see, she's got a sort of a baby coming, she's down with it now. She said I was to tell Miss Georgianna Spinyer."

The far voice changed a little, but the note which made his face hot and damp stayed uppermost: "You're speaking of my niece Armorel? You say her confinement has begun? She's not in any danger?"

"Well, yes, m'm. It look to me like it's took her proper bad."

The voice, utterly controlled again, said: "Do you mean that there's some risk of her dying?"

"If the ole girl's tellin' you the story of her life," hissed Flock, "you just cut her off! Replace the implement on the hook provided, apply safety-catch and stand at ease."

Gian said, with his breath pumping awkwardly: "I don't know, m'm. It do look as if it might be that way to me."

There was a pause, and then Miss Cepinnier said bleakly: "I see. Thank you for sending the message. Good-evening."

Gian let the receiver hang on its flex and went outside: "I'll get the penny back to y' temorrer," he said.

Now that his programme of action was exhausted he was lost again and he stood quite still in the rain. Instinct told him to run all the way back to Contessa Street, but a wall of dread rose up against it: the fear of seeing Susie in agony, of finding her dead; a terror of all the interested faces. He said miserably to Flock: "I don't know any doctors. I don't know as how you can get a doctor on a job of work this time of night. I reckon she want one of them shiny doctors out of Regent's Park. I don't know but what you got to pay 'em off before they come out."

Flock's gorilla hand came round his neck, which it shook gently forward and back. "I'll tell you what you are," Flock said, "you're nothin' but a chump, you're the mutton-headedest young b I ever come across in seven years workin' for a clubful of perishin' loonies. Listen to me now! Point One: Miss Spinyer ain't goin' to die, that sort never do think of dyin', they don't do anythink so common, not before they've got to ninety-nine an' been a bleedin' nuisance all over the fumin' lanskip. Point Two: Reference medical, I will indant for same, what will report for duty at your home. Point Three: What you want to do is to take this five-bob I'm now givin' yer, go to the Rosy Crown what keep the back door open half the night, get yourself so pickle-me-Thomas you can't hardly find your way home, *find* your way home, find yourself a bed-roll, doss down an' go slap off to land of fumin' nod and stay there till it's over." With a final shove he sent him off towards Flanders Street. "And don't you let me find you pantin' and squawkin' an' raisin' hell round my perishin' club any more tonight, get me!"

Back at Contessa Street, sober as when he had left, it was hard for Gian to believe that he had been away for more than a few moments. The company had scarcely moved, it was almost like seeing a film for the second time. He had supposed that something important would have happened, that the baby might be born already, and it added to the strangeness that no one told him anything; this time, indeed, they were so much engrossed in their own talk that they hardly noticed him at all. He heard the heavy sounds of Maria moving above, and once, he thought, a sharp cry. Too much frightened to go upstairs again, too shy to ask anyone here for news, he sat on the floor close to the range, trying to recall the comfort of Flock's words, which had flickered and gone out.

He would have valued Rosie, but she was busy; she came down now and then to hunt for something in the cupboard and ran distractedly upstairs again; while Ed, ignoring him altogether, was telling interminable jokes about expectant fathers to Olleroyd, who gravely blinked and nodded like one who listens to a lecture he has paid for. In the women's group Mrs Oestermann had taken the floor, and her low, heavily accented voice filled up the interstices as if cumbersome furniture were being dragged about in the next room. ". . . a *boxing* fellow, do you see. Come from *Litauen,* do you see. Well, you see, he get her with a chile who is *six*-teen poun'—*six*teen poun, do you see—and do you know what *her* time is? —*for*-ty-seven hour and a half, *for*-ty-seven hour and a half, do you see . . ." Occasionally Mrs Diddus came in, wiping her face, and stood by the door for a few moments with the expression of one whose need for calamity is being slowly satisfied. An hour passed, an hour and a half, and still nothing seemed to have happened. No one except Gian appeared to remember that anything was expected to happen.

Then Simon's nerves let him down. He was not accustomed to so long a stretch in the evening without Maria to bully and comfort him, her absence made him fancy that the framework of his life was falling to bits. So, obscurely, he felt the need to get things straight, and started to steer himself about the room, picking up bits of paper and wondering where to put them, looking for a cloth to wipe up the floor and then for somewhere to wring it out, since the women formed a barrier between the sink and the rest of the room. It was never an easy room to move about in; and now Olleroyd, hypnotized by the tide of Ed's wit, had his chair planted right against the pram in which Evangeline was sleeping, so that the passage on one side of the table was blocked. This meant that Simon had to go a long way round to get to the cupboard where everything useful was kept, and the sense of frustration rubbed through the last strands of his control. "You all go on talkin' and talkin'," he suddenly burst out, "with one of God's own creatures twisting and dying in mortal agony right over your heads!" and thereupon began to cry.

But they did not take much notice, because Simon was subject to these fits of depression and was never a noticeable person. "Now don't you be takin' on so, Mr Ardree!" the women said, with the offhand professional kindness they used for children. Fortunately two of his workmates had arrived on one of their regular visits and having seen him in such a mood before they set about his re-establishment with promptness and goodwill. Kind Izzy Brooks brought him a cup of water and made soothing noises close to his face; it was the weather, Izzy said with conviction, which sneaked up inside a bloke's bowels and got a hold of his conscious; while Lofty Chiffop, bent over him like an adjustable reading-lamp and gulping with benevolent laughter, pulled his hair, patted his cheeks and blew on his forehead, causing him to be slightly sick on the corner of the dresser. "You don't want to tease yourself, Simon boy," they said, putting him in a chair they had dragged away from Lizzie and fanning him with a dish-cloth. "Allth well that endth well!" Izzy told him. "That's right, Simon boy!" and Lofty gave him the story of the undertaker's wife and the queer taste in the Irish stew. "If you get a grandson it'll *compensate* y'!" they earnestly reminded him, and he did at last stop crying aloud and sat with his head in his hands, very white and heaving and asking again and again to be left alone.

"I knew another old fellow what was took that way," Lizzie said. "The time his cousin was taken, poor soul, having her baby."

"Really!" they all said, squeezing past Gian to look at Simon more closely. "They do say it's the fellows what suffer the most!"

"I reckon it's touch and go," Mrs Diddus announced from behind them, suddenly entering and immediately departing again.

No one had so far noticed the shabby and furtive Eurasian who had come in through the shop. He stood casting his quick, yellow eyes this way and that as if he were looking for the gas meter.

"Please, where is this trouble?" he suddenly asked.

Olleroyd, who saw him first, said intelligently: "Ah, you'd be the doctor! Mr Ardree over there, he's been took queer, very queer indeed."

"Queer? What is the matter with him, please?" said the doctor, forcing a passage to Simon's side.

Gian would have interfered then, but his attention was drawn back towards the door by the sharp whistle on two notes which Flock always used as a kind of hunting-cry.

"Well, Ardree lad, this is the quickest I could do. Dr Wainsel this is, all the proper tickets, slap-up practice t'other side of Wandsworth Road and itching to strip for the job."

The man at Flock's side was, in appearance, less like a doctor than the Eurasian: he might have been a hire purchase agent, a race-track scientist or the manager of a suburban dance-hall. The heavily ringed hands suspended from his fraying cuffs were like a quarryman's, and as he stood with his heels planted apart, his dark chin rammed on his chest and his eyes full of sleep, he looked as if he only wanted something to punch.

"Well, come on!" he said shortly. "Where's the patient? Someone show me, for God's sake!"

The Eurasian looked up sharply and detached himself.

"Excuse me, please! I am the doctor here—the name is Dr Hahmied."

Dr Wainsel, dragged from his bed after a stretch of sixteen hours' work, was not inclined to waste his time with casual buffoonery. "Where is the patient?" he repeated. "Upstairs?" And knowing how this sort of house was put together he went straight for the stairs door. Dr Hahmied, however, was there first.

Dr Hahmied had dignity. "You will please excuse, Doctor," he said in his high, rather sing-song voice. "I am very well understood there is much prejudice with a licence practitioner of my own kind. You will allow me to show you my certificate of the London Hospital—please! I am of British nationality. My father was of Aylsham in Norfolk and his marriage was in St Jude's Church, Church of England. I have the certificate—please! My grandmother also was of Greenwich, London."

"All I know," said Dr Wainsel, looking at Dr Hahmied as if a smut had got into his own eye, "is that this gentleman has brought me here without the smallest regard for my convenience to attend a confinement—"

"Correct!" said Flock.

"—and since you, sir, do not appear to be doing anything about the case, not as far as any plain, ordinary man can see—"

"Toss for it!" Ed suggested.

"Perhaps I may clarify," Dr Hahmied said without losing his composure. "I arrive here, I find a gentleman in a state of grave nervous exhaustion—please! I have reason to expect the encephalitis case. I would be most happy for a second opinion—please."

"What, that fellow over there?"

The tone of that question roused Simon from his tearful lethargy.

"Ay," he said with emotion, standing up, "I know folk think it's comical when a chap suffers from his feelings. I know right well this isn't a *grand* house, Doctor. It's a poor man's house, I'm not denying it. And I'm a poor man, I'm not denying that either. Ship's steward, that's what I've been most of my life, and now I'm nothing but a tradesman in the theatre—"

"Beth trademan that ever wath!" Izzy put in.

"And a better man you won't find this side the river," said Chiffop, "or t'other side neither, come to that."

"—But a poor man has his rights, you know, Doctor. He has his rights and he has his feelings—"

"That's right!" said Miss Toble viciously.

"And what is more, he has his pride."

"*And* his pride!" Mrs Bentlock said.

"You might call me just a simple, seafarin' man, Doctor. I come of good stock, all the same. Irish stock, I come from. You trace back among the folk I come from—"

"The Sinhalese also are an ancient people, of great honour," Dr Hahmied explained in a voice now tinged with excitement. "Five century before Church of England they have found a great nation in that most beautiful of lands, with extremely equable climate, please."

Dr Wainsel's reply to this argument was broken short. The door behind him was opened with violence, striking him on the shoulder. Maria was there.

"*Why issa dottore not come?* You tsink I makese baby live 'n' semozer not die, all in one pair of hand, hn? Diddus! Whassiser use of tsat Diddus!"

Dr Hahmied stepped forward again. "I am ready please!"

"Right, then—you don't want me!" Dr Wainsel said furiously.

Flock, with a sidelong wink at Gian said, "Well, that there's the bloke who's down on the bill for father. Up to him to say."

Gian had not moved an inch. As if trapped beneath the room's load of stale air and voices he sat with his stupefied eyes wandering slowly from the doctors' sullen faces to the abject figure of his father whimpering in the corner, to his mother's damp face and scattered hair. What he saw, against this room's crapulous disorder, was the seedy room upstairs: the faded pattern of the yellow wall, the skewed pillow, Susie's grey face with the taut lips just vibrating and the dreadful resolution of her eyes.

"I'll lend you a copper to toss with," Ed said.

But it was Lizzie who gave a decision. "Well, look at it what way you please, it don't seem to me right to have a nigger doctor on a young lady of her class. You don't know what it might do to the baby, for one thing."

"Make up your mine!" shouted Maria.

Dr Wainsel had made up his mind already. He was half-way to the shop door. But Dr Hahmied did not quietly accept his victory.

Quiet he was, for perhaps two whole seconds; quiet and trembling like a stalking cat, while his eyes, first pitched at Lizzie Bentlock and then seeming to look in every direction at once, changed colour disquietingly; but while his body appeared to be locked in paralysis his mind was working. It was a mind which, under unusual strains, worked fast but without precision, like a river in spate which, challenged by cliff-locked narrows, will break the easier banks and flood across the countryside. He could see, though everything was shaking in his eyes, that Lizzie was a woman; and he knew that in this country a woman must never be attacked. It seemed to him then, by the confluence of many darting thoughts, that the real author of the outrage was the British doctor who had chosen—he supposed deliberately—to come here a few moments after himself and who was now, with every appearance of withering contempt, making his escape. He took two paces, therefore, and seized Dr Wainsel by the belt of his overcoat; and he said at large, in the strained, windy voice of one who has run a long distance:

"So everyone think that all British doctors are good baby-doctors! Sh! *Good* baby-doctors! And that is a lie and a falsehood and an untruth, because I have work in the baby-hospitals so I can see for myself the way it come the mother die, the baby die, always someone who die with the British doctors, because where there want to be some big healthy baby and mother also they say 'Where is that Dr Hahmied?' —oh, yes, please, the mothers cry for Dr Hahmied all the time, every day. You ask this British man here, you say to him, 'How many babies you have dead this month, last month, month before that?'—"

Simon's eyes had moved from Gian's face to Maria's.

"Now listen!" he said, addressing Wainsel unsteadily but with simplicity and a certain stature. "You're a doctor, and I reckon you belong to a great an' noble calling. In the name of my son here, what has the woman he loves dyin' on her baby up there, in the best bedroom, that is, an' in the name of my good wife Maria as done all she can, I ask an' I beg an' beseech you to save that human life as good as you can."

The dignity within that appeal meant something to Dr Wainsel, who turned towards the stairs again. But it had cost Simon a little too much. For an instant Simon stood perfectly still, as a sawn tree seems to hover for a moment before its fall; but it was plain that there was no force holding him together. Ed, quicker than the rest, cried "Look out!"

Dr Hahmied realized that his prize was escaping. With a boxer's agility he twisted and sprang to get between his rival and the stairs, and would have done so cleanly had not Wainsel, turning back at Ed's cry and instinctively moving towards a collapsing man, caught Hahmied on the side of the neck with his elbow. The blow was probably quite accidental, but Hahmied could scarcely be expected to realize that. Quicker than a snake he spun round, dived on to Wainsel's thigh and bit.

"Mindse plate!" Maria squealed, bursting unreasonably into fresh laughter.

That was addressed to Simon, whose head, as he fell, came hard against the table. Flock started forward, barking, "Someone for crikesake get hold of that Chink!" but Lizzie was on to that already. Within a foot of where Simon now lay groaning on the floor she had the Eurasian prostrate with her giant knee wedged on his neck, while Mrs Oestermann sat on his legs and in a dull, workaday fashion was bastinadoing his loins with her very sharp, small fists. There were cries of "Goo on, Liz, dot him one!" with counter-cries of "Easy now, don't kill the por booker!" "T'other bloke hit him first!" " 'Old 'ard, Liz—play to the fumin' whistle!" and Izzy, squirming in, did his best to drag Bet Oestermann away, but in a moment Miss Toble had him by the hair and was banging his head against the table-leg. In sudden alarm Maria stopped laughing and thrust herself towards Wainsel, who was kneeling at Simon's side. "Blood!" she squealed, "he drop all his blood!" "Oy! Steady there!" commanded Flock. "Steady!" a man or two repeated, coming in from the shop. "Come now," panted Olleroyd, struggling to get to Maria round the table, "easy now, Mrs Ardree!" "Damn that Hottentot!" Dr Wainsel roared as Dr Hahmied, with Lizzie holding on to his ear, kicked out at him with his one free leg, gasping, "I kill you—all of you—just the same!" From the stairway Rosie was calling, "Mum! Do come up!" but Evangeline had woken and Rosies' voice was lost in the wails from the pram. Mrs Diddus brutally pushed her aside. "It don't matter to no one, I s'pose," Mrs Diddus bawled into the smoke and din, "only it do so happen the baby is come."

In the puff of silence which saluted Antonia's birth a new voice said: "Will someone show me, please, to my niece's room."

Gian recognized the voice, and recognition shocked him into reason. He got to his feet.

It was curious that Edith's presence made so much difference. She was, of course, a tall woman, but the contractions of rheumatism took something from her height, her shapeless hat and raincoat were such as an elderly, impoverished servant might wear and the Cepinnier shyness hung upon her like a veil. She did, however, command that room, simply standing and looking at the scene, the men on the floor, the overturned chairs and dirty crockery, with the staled, incurious gaze of a licensed valuer. And except for Evangeline's cries, now fallen to a whimper, the silence into which Mrs Diddus had plunged them continued like an afterwave of Edith's voice. Even Hahmied got up quietly and stared at the wall like a boy who is going to be caned.

An echo from the North View came to help Gian then.

"I reckon you're Miss Spinyer—how-j-do—I'll show y'."

With those words, spoken with modesty and composure, he quietly pushed the women aside to make way for Edith and the old man who stood with her, motioned them up the stairs and fell in at their heels. Maria, prompted by Ed, came panting up behind, for once speechless and shaking with alarm.

Edith painfully mounted one stair at a time. Gian heard her say, in the flat voice of a broker, "Dr Jacquelin, if any blood should be wanted I am in Group II." She went on, as of right, into the bedroom, and the doctor and Maria followed. Gian did not know if he ought to go in with them. The door shut again, leaving him outside.

He stood by himself on the top stair. The noise below was starting again, as in a class-room where the master is seen slowly retreating across the quadrangle. From the bedroom he heard nothing except feet moving and low, indistinguishable voices.

He waited patiently, schooled to loneliness and patience. Freed from the pressure of the room downstairs his senses were lively now; his ears hunted after little sounds, he saw as if under a glass the shape like a monstrous bust where the distemper had been rubbed from the wall, the shawl of cobwebs between the light-flex and the lintel; but his mind was curiously stilled by fatigue and pain. He was bitterly ashamed. For the wrong he had done in stealing something not made for a man of his sort the requital seemed to have been screwed to the furthest point. To be supine with helplessness while she suffered; to encounter that old Miss Spinyer's eyes and suddenly to see through them the place where he had brought his wife for her miracle of agony and creation: these last humiliations had reduced him to the stupefied calm which physical pain sometimes gives in the end. He no longer wondered what was happening on the other side of the door. The cry he heard, at once small and piercingly strong, meant nothing to him since it was only Susie's cry he listened for. His thoughts hardly moved at all.

Mrs Diddus had come a little way up the stairs. She said crossly, "Well, you can't say I didn't tell you what would happen. I said to Mrs Ardree, clear as clear. That's another apron to be washed out, and a lot of thanks *I* get!" He took no notice and she went away.

His eyes did not shut, but he must have slept as he leant against the wall there, for when the door did open he started exactly as one roused from sleep. It was Edith who appeared. She closed the door behind her and stood still, looking down at him. Except for the eyes, there was no alteration in her tired, impassive face, no trembling of the lips, no trace of tears; but in the ruthless electric light he saw, at first with astonishment, that the eyes themselves were unutterably sad.

There was no sadness in her voice when she spoke to him. She said in a tone that he associated with police courts:

"I expect you're needing money. It's—it's going to be expensive, all this."

Money? On most days many of his thoughts were about money, what margin the rent at Weald Street would leave them, how he could get things more in Susie's style; but—money, now?

"I'll do all right," he said shortly, without meaning to sound offended. And then, as his thoughts caught him like a gust of wind, he said: "I can raise it off Mr Grist. The buryin' job an' that."

She was lost. "Burying job?"

"Well, I d'know—no one tell me. I s'pose Miss Susie's gone."

"Gone?" And then so slowly, so wearily, she said: "You mean—died? Did you think she was dead?" She shut her eyes for a moment. "There's been a lot of difficulty. It would have been all right if Dr Jacquelin had been there earlier. Dr Jacquelin is very good. You know, one must have a good doctor. I think she's all right now—I mean, she will be all right, with Dr Jacquelin there."

"All right?" he echoed stupidly.

"The doctor seems to think so."

She could scarcely believe that this ox-like man was weeping. She could not turn away, because his eyes were still fixed on hers, and she watched him, dumbfounded, while he struggled to speak against his sobs: "I reckon she might have been as bad with a proper fellow, I know I done her wrong, I never wanted that. I never want to see her have nothink like that . . ." She could only answer, in that voice of hers which refused to wear anything but working dress:

"It has all been very foolish, I suppose—I suppose all kinds of people were to blame." And as one who suddenly remembers a trifling loan that has to be repaid she added, without any change of tone: "I suppose you'd like to see this."

Intent upon her face, he had not realized that she was carrying anything particular: some sort of a muff, he might have said, perhaps a bundle of soiled things such as Rosie had brought down earlier in the evening. Now, as awkwardly as she had held it, she planted the turban of blanket in his arms.

He first glanced up at Edith's face again, and was puzzled by what he saw there; for instead of matching the dryness of her voice her mouth had slightly relaxed, and her eyes were actually less aloof than they had been till now. That gave him a new shyness and he looked down.

In the clumsy hand-over the wrappings had slipped a little, and something had escaped. It was the model of a human foot, shorter than Gian's forefinger, too roundly fashioned to be thought of as a thing for standing and walking, but complete. Yes, each of the five curled toes, fantastically small, had even its nail. Automatically he slipped his hand round to this small object and held it for a moment, feeling the flesh warm and endowed with a perceptible movement of its own; then he tucked it carefully away. He had not thought of this at all: that the creature Susie had been forming would be so perfect or so real. Forgetting that the grim Miss Spinyer watched him he moved a fold of blanket from the part that lay on the crook of his arm, and saw there the head; not so minutely scaled as the foot had made him expect, and yet tiny for all that it contained, the doll-like ears, lips, nostrils, even wisps of brow over the screwed-up eyes. Those nostrils moved a little, and a piece of thread which a towel had left there was agitated by the life that came from them. This was a person: a new person that Susie had made. Instinctively he tried the experiment of speaking, he said, in the Italian voice that occasionally came back to him, "Antonia!" and it chanced that the baby's eyes, no longer shielded from the light, opened just then: dark eyes like Rosie's, very still, but seeing; he was certain that they saw. Probably it was the light over Gian's head to which the eyes were directed, but he thought that they looked straight at him, calmly; human eyes, the eyes of a new individual, belonging to Susie and in some remote way to him. He had sense enough, born from the sunlight which fell like fire into the Vicolo Sant' Agata, to turn the child so that her eyes were protected from the electricity. Acutely excited, he held her delicately but closely, enjoying the little weight she put on his arm, and bent his cheek right down to feel the warmth she gave and if possible the faint stir of her breath. For a few moments he was almost happy.

"Antonia?" Edith said. "That's what you're calling her?"

"Susie said that would do, supposin' it was a girl. She's a girl, I reckon."

"Yes. Shall I take her?"

Reluctantly, he gave Antonia back to her awkward arms. She could not really have wanted her, he thought, she looked at the bundle so distantly, almost with disdain. She said with a nervous glance towards the bedroom door:

"I suppose I may as well go. I don't suppose there's anything I can do. You could tell Dr Jacquelin that I'm waiting for him in the car."

Her irresolution made him say: "Get y' a cup o' tea?"

"Tea? Oh—thank-you—no."

But Rosie had thought of this earlier: she came up the stairs now with a cup and saucer, put them into Gian's hand without a word and went down again. They could just hear the babble of inquiry, 'Did you see it?' 'How's it goin'?' as the door at the foot of the stairs closed after her. That was a reminder to Edith that she had to go through the crowd in the kitchen again in order to escape. She glanced at Gian despairingly. With some difficulty and embarrassment they exchanged their burdens, he taking Antonia and she the tea.

"This is very kind," she managed to say, trying to swallow the scalding tea, continually watching him as if she expected him to throw the baby away. "You must realize," she said abruptly, "I'm not a rich woman. My mother is more or less an invalid, that adds to the expense of our household. But of course—I should do what I could. I mean—there are things you'll need for the child. If you will write to me—I mean, I shall do what I can."

"Yes, m'm," he said. "Only we'll be all right."

"I mean," she persisted, trying to keep her eyes right away from him, "I could always come here if I were wanted for anything. I—I understand a little about simple nursing. I've done work of that kind—not professionally, I'm afraid. Of course I don't want to interfere with any of my niece's plans. That would upset my mother, for one thing. Oh, yes, I was going to say—I expect my mother would like to see the baby sometime. Perhaps someone could bring her to Streatham—I don't know."

"Susie'll do that," he said.

"Yes—well—I don't know. Perhaps she would let that—that very pretty girl who brought the tea, perhaps Armorel would let her bring the baby. Of course we should like her to come herself. You can tell her, perhaps—if she would rather I were not there I could arrange things, she could come some day when I am out, I'm out all day sometimes." She put the cup and saucer on the floor. "I think I ought to go now."

Without meeting his eyes again she set off down the stairs. But half-way to the bottom she stopped, hesitated for a few moments and then dragged herself up again.

"Perhaps you will tell Armorel—well, perhaps you will say goodnight to her from me."

"Yes, m'm."

"And you will look after them—after them both?"

"Best I can."

It appeared from the way she looked about her that she had forgotten something, her gloves or umbrella. Suddenly she put out her arm, and he realized that she meant him to shake hands. As he took her hand she stooped—the action could not have been more clumsy—and kissed the blanket where Antonia's head was, whispering something from which only the word 'bless' came to his ears. It took an absurd length of time, that gesture, as if someone were shouting 'Hold it!'; and when she straightened she was still grasping his hand. Glaring at the wall again, she mumbled, "I expect—I'm sure you're a kind man." Then she dropped his hand as one throws away a bus ticket and began the descent once more, very slowly, almost concealing her lameness, erect and self-contained. He could feel, up here, the path of silence which she cut through the kitchen on her way to the street.

The sense of being on parade which Edith had brought to the house remained behind her like the dust which hangs in the desert after the passage of a caravan. Only when Dr Jacquelin had left, and the genteel purr of the car bearing them both away came faintly to the back room, did freedom return.

They swarmed upstairs then; the women seized Antonia as if she were the common spoil of battle, they passed her from hand to hand, they held her this way and that, untucked her hands and feet as if to price them, kissed her on the cheeks and on the mouth, while Olleroyd took Gian's hand in both of his and Ed, laughing raucously, belaboured his shoulders and posterior with festive blows. Maria emerged from the bedroom harassed and subdued by Jacquelin's directions, but the sight of ordinary, comprehensible folk was like the sun bursting upon her soluble spirit. She had worked—ah, name of St Anthony, had she not worked! Her experience and skill, her powers of organization, her resolute heart, these and these alone had won the triumph which her friends were clustering to applaud. Generously she caught hold of Mrs Diddus, kissed her cheeks and displayed her to the crowd as a singer displays his accompanist, crying "She aid! Sis poor Diddus aid me also!" She caught the cigarette which Ed threw her and stuck it in her mouth like a cigar, she seized Olleroyd's handkerchief to wipe the sweat from her face and arms, and with tears continually misting her crimped and weary eyes she laughed as in the day she had first brought Gian out into the street, glorifying with her salvos of mirth the marvels of creation which Nature could work in partnership with Maria Prudenza the municipal scavenger's child. Bewildered and enraged by their presumption, Gian looked round for his father, but Simon's friends had carried him off to get a heartener from a place they knew of. All the life of the house had shifted to the stairs, and in the back room, dense with smoke, he found no one except Evangeline whimpering in her pram and Rosie bowed upon the table, fast asleep with her pretty head among the unwashed cups and ketchup bottles, the head-shawls which the women had left, the crumpled paper and cartons and butts of cigarettes.

Holding Antonia like that, treating her like a kitten or a doll, sticking their dirty faces against hers—some of them people he hardly knew! Mum, of course, encouraged them, but with a heart so great and good as hers Mum would pet the wolves devouring her feet . . . The anger they had lit in him turned against the room: he must get away from here, he would go and walk in the streets. But while he dared not visit Susie until she summoned him he was equally fearful of moving far away. There was nowhere, in fact, for him to go or to be, no one to tell him anything. Damn Rosie for going asleep—he hadn't the heart to wake her, she looked so childlike and so used-up—and damn Izzy and Lofty for taking Dad away. He wanted just a word with Mum—'Susie doin' all right? Didn't say she wanted to see me?'

—but Maria, careering now upon her own obstetric memories, was embedded like the heart of a lettuce among all the gap-toothed bitches of Contessa Street. He was a man, that night, without a home.

Well, Sue was his wife, wasn't she! And the room—he was pulling out three bob a week for it. Couldn't be nothing he mustn't see, nothing he couldn't stand up to if he keep a hold on himself. With his mouth tight, hands in pockets, he barged his way upstairs again, ignoring a squeal of "Fancy him a papa now!"; went boldly into the room and shut the door quietly behind him.

Yes, it was all in a mess as he had expected, and full of alien, hospital smells. Someone had hitched a towel round the bulb and the light seemed to fall with special force, like stage lighting, upon the litter of rags and basins which covered the chest of drawers. The bed was in shadow. He advanced towards it almost like one playing Grandmother's Steps.

He could see that the bed at least was tidy: clean sheets—who had got those, and where? Susie was murmuring faintly but she seemed to be asleep.

Like a child bemused by the lights of a shop window he stood still, biting his dead cigarette, intently watching. He knew—it was the talk of every day, like weather and wages—what childbirth meant: he had prepared himself half-consciously to see her blanched and crumpled after the long struggle. Not for this tranquillity. It gathered in one image of a substance more ethereal than flesh, this young, reposing face, pale in the shadow, framed by the white pillow-slip and the sheaved foliage of hair, the firefly glimpses he had caught in boyhood from marching songs, street-corner preachers, the covers of sentimental magazines: a vision, till now inchoate, of innocence and splendour, of infinitely tender things fused by valour and hardship to a loveliness outside men's power to comprehend. He knew these features as he knew the old, patched counterpane: the curve of the forehead, the little creases below the eyes: to the slender, faintly stirring mouth he had often pressed his own. But this face, sublimed by the agonized yielding of new life, was something that he saw for the first time. Not a possession: he could never possess a distillation of beauty such as this: it was a treasure to be guarded as soldiers guard a city whose gates they have never passed, an image to be worshipped as pilgrims kneel before Our Lady of the Covered Eyes.

He had forgotten his anger now, the evening's long fatigue. His senses had all shut down, so that the dwindling hubbub on the stairs beat like the noise of a street's traffic only against the outer wall of his mind.

Her eyes slipped open and she looked at him perplexedly, as if trying to identify a once-familiar scene. But in a moment or two she knew him. She said rather faintly:

"Gian, what's all that noise?"

He answered in a whisper, as if there were still the risk of waking her: "It's just friends of Mum's. Lizzie and that lot . . . Do anythink for y', Sue?"

"No," she said vaguely. "No, I'm all right. Where is my baby, Gian?"

"Well, Mum's got her."

"Oh. Is she all right?"

"Yes, I reckon she's all right."

"Oh."

He was not sure how far, in this exhaustion, she could understand anything he said. Should he speak as he wanted to now? It was all ready, like a crowd of people waiting for doors to open: he wanted to tell her that Antonia was perfection, he wanted to praise her bravery, to pour out his gratitude for the miracle she had performed, to say that he loved and worshipped her beauty, her heroism, her womanhood, her calm and gentleness with a passion he had hardly conceived before. Without moving, he said "Susie!" and with her tired eyes falling shut again she responded:

"Yes?"

"You had a bad time, I reckon?"

"Oh, just the usual, I suppose it was." She was very sleepy. She asked, with her eyes still closed: "Did you see Edith?"

"Miss Spinyer? Yes, I seen her."

"You know, you made a mistake. It was Georgina I wanted you to send the message to."

How could he explain? His nervousness, the telephone, all that. He said, dreadfully ashamed:

"Yes, I reckon it went wrong."

"Edith didn't bother you, did she?"

"Her? No. She was all right." It came to his ears curiously, that phrase: 'bother' him? A lady like that bother him, Ardree? He said: "She'd like her mum to see the baby, she tell me."

"Oh, I see—she's been making plans."

"Well, that was what she said."

Armorel said, after a pause: "Yes, Edith thinks she can still run my life for me. That's what she always thought. She'll never forgive me for trying to run it myself."

He did not in the least understand, but he knew that people who were sick often wandered a little in their talk. He said:

"I'll get the baby fixed, best I can. Get her her schoolin' an' that. I reckon I can get cleanin' jobs at nights, hotels an' places."

"Oh, no!" she said quickly, perfectly collected now. "No, Gian, you've got to keep your evenings, I want you to use them for increasing your own knowledge, so that you can get higher positions later on. No, you mustn't worry over the baby. I've got it all worked out."

"Well, I thought we could figure it out together, see what I mean." She did not answer.

"You and me," he explained.

But you could not suppose that a woman in her state would follow the direction of his thoughts: he did not expect it. A strong impulse made him move close to the bed, he put his hand within an inch of hers; but he could not actually touch her, now, when he had witnessed her transfiguration, before she invited him; and since her eyes were shut she could not see that the invitation was awaited. She said very wearily, but with her voice quite steady (for she never lost her sweet good-sense):

"I think you ought to find somewhere to tuck down and get to sleep, Gian dear. In Olleroyd's room, perhaps. It must have been upsetting for you, all this."

The door had opened, letting the simmer of the house flow in as through a breach in a sea wall: the hoarse, persistent voice of Eliza Bentlock, Olleroyd's sympathetic rumble. Yawning noisily, Mrs Diddus brought in Antonia and put her in the basket on the washstand, while Maria, thrusting past Gian as if he were a piece of furniture, started to fuss with the bed-clothes. From downstairs, with all the smells of sauce and grease, came the noises, now forlorn and now exultant, of men singing: Simon's friends had brought him home.

Gian couldn't be here all night, Maria told him. The girl must get some sleep. He said, "Goo'-night, Sue," and she answered sleepily:

"Oh, good-night Gian."

Perhaps she had opened her eyes again, perhaps stretched a hand towards him; but Maria was between them, so he could not see. At any rate, she must be terribly tired. He seemed to be in Mrs Diddus's way as well, she said angrily, "Oh, you!" when he peeped over her shoulder, trying to get another glimpse of Susie's child. He went downstairs and looked about for a cigarette; not thinking, as common sense alone might have bidden him, about where he should sleep.

## PART THREE

27

*A*LL THE LETTERS which Raymond wrote to Elizabeth Kinfowell, from the time of their first meeting at Armorel's wedding, were in the same voice; and their matter was often very much the same.

> On Tuesday, [he said in one of them] I make my customary New Year pilgrimage to Weald Street. The usual dressing problem rises—and I have always prided myself on being a man without sartorial perplexities—how to clothe myself so as to flatter Armorel without infuriating her neighbours. To the finer points of Weald Street sensibility I am without a guide. If only you, my dear Elizabeth, were here to instruct me . . .

In December 1928, when their friendship was seven years old, he was writing:

> Elizabeth, my dear, I am in really urgent need of your wisdom and experience. Do you not feel that chicken livers *à la Madère*, with perhaps a Mittel Mosel wine of some kind, would be an admirable thing for your general health on Tuesday or Thursday of next week at 12.30 at the same place as last time? The question of Michael's Christmas present is giving me grave anxiety. When I took him out at half-term he said 'a book,' but books are sold in so many different sizes, and are said to be bad for the morals as well as the eyesight. Then I require advice and encouragement for my New Year visit to Weald Street. How I wish that Armorel had not chosen that particular passage to live in! —To the olfactory

mise-en-scène I am now hardened; but not to the manifest hostility of those strangely shaped ladies (I make a guess as to their gender) who stand all day long in the doorways of No. 5 and No. 12, or to the ribaldries of their children, or the peculiar abigail and other supernumerary members of my cousin's establishment. I ask again, why Weald Street? The genius of martyrdom I understand (though I could never approve it); but surely when the martyr insists on being fastened to the stake with barbed wire he crosses from holiness into mere pedantry. Well, that is Armorel's affair, and I do not pretend to understand her better than I understand the rest of her sex. You, my dear, I do not understand at all. But you understand me, and you can be my Beatrice when all others fail. Since it is modish in these times to have what is called a temperament I can say without disloyalty that Armorel appears to be acquiring that adjunct—a small one, nothing ostentatious, I assure you; and I really doubt if I can be of any use to her except under your minute directions. I think I have already told you that you are a woman not only of physical perfection but of singular gifts and unique perceptions. Elizabeth! I insist that you pay attention, and stop grinning—yes, I said grinning—in that aloof and cynical fashion. My dear, I implore you to take me seriously . . .

'Unique perceptions'! Elizabeth echoed when she read that passage again in the tube; seeing reflected in the window what appeared to her the most commonplace of middle-aged faces, feeling the pinch of a corselette she had not troubled to put on carefully, thinking of people she had entirely mis-read, situations woefully mishandled. 'Singular gifts'! She remembered the hours it had once taken her to write a letter telling Gordon Aquillard that Armorel was finally lost to him; she thought of Henry's lectures on household account-keeping ("But, my good woman, when you draw a cheque you're not *adding* to your income, surely even you can see that!"), his familiar "Ah, well, we'll see what Hilda thinks—Hilda's generally right about matters of style." Poor Raymond! she thought: too slovenly in mind to come to terms with people as they really are, he uses them as lay figures to be clothed with preposterous garments, faintly redolent of naphthalene, from the presses of his baroque, Edwardian mind.

And yet there was significance, had she perceived it, in the very fact that Raymond pursued her friendship for year after year. He was, of course, an amateur of women, but not of women advancing into middle age. A few old ladies he liked, mostly relatives of his own; among the necessities of his life was that for people (like Gertrude Cepinnier, with whom he had maintained unflagging correspondence until the week of her death) who could respond like dancers in a minuet to his archness, his courtly preambles, his gravely constructed flippancies. For the rest, he liked his women friends to be young, and fresh from stock; not because he was pained to see them lose their bloom, but since, with a limited equipment for gallantry, he realized instinctively that when once his tricks had all been performed—the little dinner at Fothergill's hotel, the slightly risqué story about Fanny Beaconsfield and the Princess of Wales—he must discover a new audience. Obscurely, he knew that he was a bore, and had just sense enough to avoid the humiliation of being shown so. And yet, having once added Elizabeth to his collection (and not doubting that she saw through all his pretensions), he was ready to cultivate her society with almost painful strategy for the rest of his life. He conferred that distinction on no other young or middle-aged woman of his acquaintance.

The wretched blunder about Kinfowell's car at Armorel's wedding had given him an excuse to call at Munster Place, ostensibly to make his apologies. He had been lucky, as he was so often; Elizabeth had been alone, and in twenty minutes, working on stereotyped lines, he had learnt approximately at what times and seasons her husband was likely to be out of town. In the spring, motoring in Shropshire, he had visited Easterhatch and exhibited himself to Henry as a harmless, rather old-fashioned person who shared Elizabeth's interest in ceramics; for he liked his tactics to be without fear and without reproach; and thereafter his access to Elizabeth's society had been limited only by the bounds of her tolerance. He was careful not to lose so precious an amenity by extravagant or clumsy demands. He never sent her an invitation when his conversational funds were low, seldom when he had nothing to offer besides his own companionship. In March, if she cared to see Pavlova, he had two stalls, and afterwards she might possibly be amused by an Italian place he had lately discovered, particularly good for supper? Then he would let three or four months elapse, punctuated only by an urbane letter or two, before he asked whether she had any interest in polo: for himself, he regarded the game fundamentally as a misuse of fine horsemanship, but the skill of the American visitors was said to be fascinating to watch, and Archie Stanhoe had asked him to bring a lady to Ranelagh on the 10th. Once he made no attempt to see her for as long as seven months. But in that space he twice travelled to Dorset, upon the flimsiest excuses, and took Michael out for a half-term holiday; and those were occasions for particularly long letters. ("He was looking extremely well; I stayed overnight to watch him run in his heat of the 220, and experienced an avuncular pride in his performance—he is not a strong runner, but all his movements have an Athenian grace, as I should expect. Really I take the warmest pleasure in his society, and I am so grateful to him—and of course to you—for again giving me this indulgence. How wise that young man has been in his choice of a mother . . .") After that she could scarcely refuse his invitation for the Ladies' Night of the Odd Volumes; and in April next year he invited her and Henry to lunch with him at Finchley (only Henry proved to be away on business at Amsterdam) and drove her up to the Spaniards, and they walked together on the Heath, where their faces were licked by the London wind and splashed with sunshine falling through fresh leaves.

There was always Weald Street to talk about; for if any sincerity was to be found in this man of wayward sentiments it lay in some kind of devotion to Armorel. Her beauty and gentleness in girlhood had charmed him, as her steadiness of mind had pleased him later on; he had been fond of her father; and since Arthur's death and Irene's dereliction he had felt a certain responsibility towards their child. He realized, moreover, that he was much blamed by the relations for having helped her to make a ridiculous marriage; and having no small respect for the man she had chosen ("a thoroughly honest tradesman" . . . "devoted to Armorel" . . . "chap who doesn't pretend to be anything but what he is—I can get on with people like that!") he was constantly determined, with a touch of the Truggett obstinacy, to prove them wrong. "You see," he would say, leaning on the arm of Elizabeth's chair, "it's not merely that Armorel knew her own mind—every girl says she does that—the point is that she had a mind to know. Of course, I think she has made tactical mistakes. She has asked for too much, and she hasn't asked for enough—do you see what I mean?" while Elizabeth nodded gravely, sympathetically, never disputing anything the old windbag said . . . But surely he needed Elizabeth as something more than an audience for his meanderings about Armorel, this painstaking hedonist who clung so tenaciously through the years to what friendship she had for him. He never made love to her: he could not have dreamed that she would respond. She had not been young, as he thought of youth, when he first met her. There was hardly anything similar in their characters, and he must have known that she gently laughed at him.

Perhaps it was chiefly that, living without close relationships, he hungered for emblems of permanence; and Elizabeth changed so little. the years passing the grey increased a little in her hair, the small creases about her eyes and mouth were deepened, the fit of flesh to bone in her face slightly altered. But these modulations did not matter, because she had never been a belle of the sort that soap-makers publicly delight in. Indeed, he had never seen her a woman in full health, her skin and the stitching of her mouth had always been those of a convalescent. Her beauty, he thought, was of a kind that a sculptor will achieve just once, perhaps when he himself is sick, too tired to regard the conventions which have become a part of his equipment, so that his elemental genius goes to the stone unmodified and he can say when it is done: "There, there is my first intention!" Yes, she was a work so finished that age could make no difference; for she was already aged, he thought, in wisdom and in suffering. In her eyes, her walk, the movements of her hands, there was repose; not lassitude, but the quietness of one who has discarded the needless gestures of impatience, surprise, alarm. Upon that stillness of regard chance and the seasons would work without organic effect, as waves, beating on a strong sea wall, subduing its colour, wearing the stone-face, will leave the foundation unimpaired. Her voice, soft like the wines of the Médoc, did not alter at all.

And then, romantic that he was, he liked a woman to be mysterious. He knew so many of the facts: her father's early death somewhere abroad, the struggling, impoverished life at Dinstead Fen, her work as an elementary school-teacher: yet often she seemed to him as darkly framed as the allegorical figures in cloudy paintings, and he was fascinated by the huge extent of the country he did not know. She spoke so little of herself, except in direct answer to his questions; so little of how her days were filled, what friends she had and which she cared for. She did not belong, as others did, to any world that he knew. From the way she behaved in restaurants, the people she bowed to, the cast of her occasional sarcasms, one would have classified her as adhering to the straitest sect of rich men's wives. But when she said, casually, "Of course Matilda has a theory that all our bad weather comes from America," he found that she was referring not to Matilda Llandovery but to a certain Mrs Empire living somewhere in the Southwark hinterland; and she would say "No, I shan't be in the West End again this week," exactly as one of his own neighbours might say it. Of her husband she spoke in terms of positively Victorian deference: "Henry and I didn't really like living in Turkey" . . . "Henry thinks that small hats don't suit me" . . . "Yes, I did mean to go to Michael for his half-term myself, only I don't like to leave Henry at this time of year, when he nearly always has a cold": deference, almost affection, with never a hint that her marriage was not all she wished: while Raymond was certain—for it made no demands on anyone's perspicuity—that a mere sum of objectless capacities like Kinfowell could give her nothing that she needed. Why this façade, with a man so discreet as himself? —for surely by now she could trust in his discretion. Did she never lose her detachment, was she really content to go through the social motions as brainless beauties did and to live entirely within herself; or else, in whom did she confide? But the mystery was deeper than that.

He could understand neither her sorrow nor her happiness. He did not doubt that she endured much physical pain, but the suffering he saw when he caught her unawares was not from a physical source; not, he thought, from any one source at all. From the tiredness of her eyes, the slow, tugged framing of her lips when she smiled, you had said she was a creature ordained to suffering; but no one could have called her melancholy. She could be gay, she responded easily to what pleasure you had to share with her and lingered in that delight, slipping back only by degrees to the still shadow from which you had brought her. Even when she was pensive, when old sicknesses betrayed themselves in the movement of little veins beside her temples, the ebb and flow of stiffness in her lips, you would not have used the word 'unhappy'; because unhappiness brings dullness to the eyes, and in hers there burnt, however far away, an untroubled light.

No, Raymond did not understand her, and perhaps he was content not to understand; for with all his small, childish conceits he had some notion of his limitations. There was music which meant nothing to him because his tympanic nerves lacked sensitivity to perceive its elements; and so, he supposed, her mind and heart were illumined by lights too exquisite, too transcendental, to penetrate his own. It was enough that she was kind to him, to feel that perhaps the little treats he devised for her, the few small jokes they kept to unwrap and play with at their occasional meetings, were a fraction of her life which she would miss if they ceased to occur; enough to get her answers to his letters, beginning *"Mon vieux"*, to see two or three times a year the light breaking in her mysterious mouth and eyes when she caught sight of him across the foyer of a theatre (a faintly different smile, he told himself, from that which she kept for other friends), to watch the infinite delicacy of her body as she sat down in the Russell chair he had bought specially for her, murmuring, "Oh, Raymond, it's nice to be so quiet, not to have to think!"

How delicious her silences are! he thought, that afternoon in November 1933 when they had lunched at the House and he took her home, as she desired, on foot. In the park's quiescence, with the mist drawn as a net curtain across the Whitehall buildings, the thresh of taxis in Birdcage Walk already remote like the sounds outside a dream, another woman would have needed to chatter, 'How sad the trees look! ... How slowly a year dies!' while she was content to reflect the tones of the falling day in the quality of her silence. And then, of course, it was he who broke it.

"You must be horribly cold, with those thin stockings. You know, I think you ought to go in for politics yourself. If we must have women in politics then we might as well have a few sensible ones."

She loosed and re-hooked her smoke-fox tie so that it lay still more becomingly, he thought, on her narrow shoulders.

"Oh, Raymond, I'm sorry I look so dowdy. And it was such a nice lunch, and so many friends of yours saw me!"

"My dear, I didn't say you looked dowdy."

"You said I was a sensible woman."

"Well, I didn't mean it. Honestly I didn't."

"That's very sweet of you, Raymond! I've felt so lonely all these weeks, with Henry in America and no one to tell me that I'm mentally deficient."

He said dejectedly: "Elizabeth, surely you needn't talk to me in that débutante fashion. You know perfectly well that you've got ten times the brains I have."

"Ten times?" She stopped on the foot-bridge to break up a piece of bread she had slipped into her bag and throw it to the waterfowl. (It charmed him to watch her doing that.) "Oh, dear," she said, "what a terrible load to carry!"

"What load?"

"Ten times your brains."

"No," he said firmly, "no, you really cannot make this fish rise with *that* old piece of orange peel. One thing I do realize, which is that I am not a clever man—"

"—But I thought you told me—"

"—My cousin Frederick made the whole position clear to me some time ago, when I first talked about a political career. He said, 'Raymond, my dear fellow, I love you very dearly, but intellectually I rate you as a minus quantity.'"

"But how sad for me!"

"Why?"

"To know that you put down my intelligence quotient as minus ten."

"I must ask you to excuse me," he said rather pettishly, "while I go back and drown myself in that pond."

"But, Raymond, it's so unlike you to start breaking by-laws, especially in a Royal Park."

"I hope you'll feel sorry when you see the headlines: *'Girl's cruelty brings death to well-known season-ticket holder. Complete misunderstanding, says wife of Financial Tycoon.'*"

"*'Thought he could swim.'*"

"As a matter of fact, I am quite a good swimmer."

"*'Thought he would interest moor-hens.'* Tell me, do you really think that politics would be my métier?"

"No, I don't. You're neither the one thing nor the other. You're not earnest and dull, you're not fundamentally cynical, and you're not a wool-gathering idealist."

"Are those what they want?"

"It's what they get."

"Do you think that Armorel would make a politician?"

They were exactly in the middle of the Mall. He stopped dead, looked at her sharply and then at the ground, standing like a golfer with his feet apart and menacing a tram ticket with the point of his umbrella. His capacities were not unlimited, he could not walk and pursue fresh notions at the same time. He said:

"Armorel?"

"Your cousin."

Yes, but they had not been discussing Armorel, Armorel had scarcely been mentioned today, they had been talking (he vaguely thought) about moor-hens. A pity that even Elizabeth had this feminine trick of leaping from one topic to another.

"But I mean to say—Armorel, she's got two children, Antonia must be ten or eleven by now, she hasn't got time for that sort of nonsense. Of course she did think of it once, or so she told me, before she met that fellow—what was his name? Achilles Appleyard or something, some damned silly name—"

"Gordon Aquillard."

"Well, it doesn't matter. Of course you go through that stage, even girls nowadays, she was reading economics and all that sort of eyewash."

"Do you think we ought to get on to the footpath?"

"Well, I've got as much right to this road as all these dyspeptic brewers in their damned motors, haven't I!" But he suffered her to take his arm and lead him on towards the Green Park. "Of course the point is that she was too good-looking. You can't expect a really pretty girl to settle down to anything like political life."

"Yes, you were saying that before we got to the moor-hens."

"Was I? Well, it's a pity, all the same. I feel that if she had some outside interest these days things might be better. I'm not saying there's anything wrong. All I mean is, she'd have less time to worry over her husband not becoming president of the Guild of Master Bricklayers or whatever it is she wants him to be."

"You think she worries over that?"

"Me? I don't think anything. I mean, not about Armorel. I don't understand married life and all that."

"But you think she's changed a bit?"

"Well, everyone changes, don't they?"

He wished there were not so many people about, clerkly young men and their girls, a seedy governess with a whole cohort of children, even ragged people such as he had never seen in this part, as far as he remembered, in the old days. They distracted him. In this Atlantis, with the grey, Whistlerian light drawing rails and litter bins into harmony with the gentle distances, the portentous mass of the Palace imparting to the background a secure theatricality, he could have thought of Armorel in peaceful and heroic terms: against this sombre cloth, and with Elizabeth beside him, he could have contemplated her situation as one watches drama, objectively, with the oblique satisfaction of fastidiously ordered griefs. These loiterers with their effluvium of scent and poverty brought whiffs of the reality he had been steering away from all these years. The man coming towards them now had a keloid from ear to lip—interesting, in a way—and Raymond had seen the exact copy of that disfigurement on his last visit to Weald Street. Really, when so little of dignity was left, it would surely not be unreasonable to make such people cover up their scars, at least at this end of the town. And now Elizabeth, with that weakness which even the best of women had for pursuing topics far better dropped, was saying:

". . . you think she's happy?"

"Happy? Armorel?"

He went on for another twenty paces, a part of his timid mind wondering whether anything could be done to tidy up that dreadful fellow—should he run back now and tell him he ought to try Butterthorpe the dermatologist in Aybrook Street? He said:

"I don't see how you can talk of people being happy or unhappy in that general way—ordinary people, I mean. People jog along, they have their good days. And then, I mean, a girl of Armorel's intelligence must know what she's in for when she marries a very poor man. She knew she'd got nothing but a hole-and-corner sort of life to look forward to—she told me so herself. I've offered her more money but she doesn't seem to want it. I don't really see what else one can do."

He had stopped again and was gazing over to the blurred skyline of Grosvenor Place as if something there might help him.

"I mean to say, she must be used to that sort of life by now—nearly twelve years, isn't it! And you know, last time I was there she really seemed quite cheerful. She made some joke about what's-his-name, that dreadful little man who lives in the back room upstairs. And she's not a girl who makes jokes as a rule."

Elizabeth said slowly: "I doubt if poverty or wealth has anything to do with it. I know a bit about these things. People from the opposite ends of the economic pole can join up and live in perfect contentment—on less money than Gian earns now. Armorel doesn't want luxuries, anyway, she's not that kind. The question always is whether people accept the same fundamentals."

Heavens, what words the girl used! Like Armorel herself in one of her *studentisch* moods. He protested:

"You're really going a bit too deep for me to follow!"

"It frightens me," she said.

Those words affected Raymond almost as if a gun had been fired behind his head: Elizabeth, a creature who took life so serenely, 'frightened': and in that terribly quiet voice!

"Frightens you?" he repeated foolishly.

"Her living so completely alone. All the doors locked and bolted."

"Locked and—? Oh, I see what you mean. At least, I suppose I do. But then some people enjoy living like that, in a kind of moral hermitage. I can imagine it being exhilarating, in a curious way."

"Not for a woman. And not in a place like Weald Street."

And now the pleasure had gone out of Raymond's day. Disturbing as the world had grown—the newspapers black with unreasonable discontents, everybody wanting more wages or more colonies—one hoped at least to find a little peace in familiar places, in civilized manners, among friends of one's own kind. He had looked forward so much to this meeting, when if they talked of Armorel it should be with friendly warmth, perhaps with some very gentle, allusive laughter at her trifling weaknesses. That fragrance was lost for today. There were lights in the Piccadilly windows, the cars flowing towards the Circus were like fishes with incandescent eyes: here the stink and chatter of the town came to them like an offshore wind across the sodden turf, and slowly as they were walking they must presently be embedded in the barn-dance. He said with nervy abruptness:

"That man—what did you say his name was? Aquillard—is she still in touch with him, do you know?"

"No. He writes to her sometimes. She doesn't answer."

"Well, that's a relief, anyway."

"Is it? Contented people aren't afraid of writing letters."

"That welfare-worker fellow—Grist," he said doggedly pursuing his own line, "there never was anything between her and him, was there?"

"There was, in a way."

"But that's all over, I suppose."

"Yes. Except that these things are never quite all over. Not for us, at least."

He stopped once more and gazed at the diorama of mist and light like a child at his first pantomime.

"Well, there can't be anything much to worry about," he said

Of course women would always talk in that fashion; it was the way their minds worked, even in such a woman as Elizabeth. Having gorged themselves on the entremets of fiction they scoured the lives of their acquaintance for equivocal situations, and where nothing was to be found there was everything to be invented. He had asked her in sufficiently plain terms whether she thought Armorel was at all involved with other men and she had practically confessed that there was not the smallest evidence of it. What then? In this business there was an element of jealousy, perhaps, since that feeling was seldom entirely absent from the relationship of two handsome women. Elizabeth had everything that money could buy, yes. But did she not faintly envy her friend the almost canine devotion of a husband so curiously chosen? Envy her, perhaps, the pluck with which she had built a life on such crazy foundations? For that was what he himself saw first in Armorel, a courage amounting almost to heroism. Possibly he over-admired it, having no courage himself: with the caprice of heredity, that part of the common strain which she possessed in such abundance had been denied to him. But surely no one who saw how spotless she kept that dismal dwelling, how calmly but how firmly she managed all the affairs of her overloaded and heterogeneous household, could fail to marvel at such unwearying fortitude; and must not a woman in Elizabeth's position, with the brambles swiftly cut away from any path she chose, be at least a little envious of one who had heart and muscle to carve a road for herself? That would account for everything, Elizabeth's change of voice, her curious innuendoes: and perhaps the damp tristesse of the Park had worked on her a little—she must be cold, with those fanciful stockings.

"A marvel to me how she manages," he said, his thoughts slopping over.

But why had he received such a shock when she said 'It frightens me'? Had there been, these last few months, some subterranean stream in his own mind to which those words had given escape? He had suffered, of course, from the common anxiety which hung in the air like the breath of coming snow, a malaise reflected alike in the faces of the prosperous and the hungry as he saw them in his morning train. Ten years ago, with the German nonsense settled, one had presumed that things would return to normal: and so little had this happened that even he had begun to doubt whether there was such a thing as normality. Now, from over in Europe, and even in this city of his own where omnibuses ran to schedule and all the traffic stopped in obedience to one man's arm, there were voices questioning the very axioms of order and civilization with such persistence that he had changed his newspaper and begun in a superstitious way to go to church again. All that, he supposed, was at the bottom of his disquietude—no need to call it his fear. And yet, as he tried to trace the source of this faint reverberation of danger, and would have searched far out in the wilderness of general anxieties, he was led inexorably to the spot where Elizabeth had placed it: to Armorel herself. It was at Weald Street that he had begun to be frightened.

"Of course," he said, "you go there more often than I do." And trusting her good manners, which should prevent her giving undue value to vague suggestions, he added: "You must tell me if ever you think there's anything I can do."

Yes, coming away after that last visit to Weald Street he had been uneasy. Of course he was always low-spirited in that part of London, which in some incomprehensible way made him feel inferior and even slightly unreal. But his mind had fidgeted all the way back in the train and even later, when he sat at home surrounded by his own things and writing one of his graceful, faintly ironic letters to Edith Cepinnier, it had not been entirely stilled. Rellie had been so bright, but he thought there had been a note of falsity (no, one could not use the word 'hysteria') in her cheerfulness. "Yes," she had said, "Gian spends most of his Sunday at that sub-Utopia of Trevon Grist's—he's getting to be called the Uncrowned King of Apostles' Court!" Well, a fellow of Ardree's callow perceptions could not have been affected by the whisper of sarcasm in that remark, since her smile had been fully lit by the time she turned her face to him. And after all, husbands and wives did give each other these little pricks, and suffered no harm. Gian had been very silent all the time that Rellie was talking about little Gordon's difficult-ness, the way she had dealt with the trouble over Mrs Lewis's broken milk bottles, the psychiatrist's recommendations: that, presumably, was because such talk was far above his head. No, it was a little later that Raymond had been slightly disturbed, when Gian said something about taking Tonie to hear the carols at Southwark and Rellie had casually interposed: "Oh, Gian dear, I meant to tell you, that's off. I said she couldn't go if she disobeyed me and went into Mrs Shermy's house again, and I found her going in this morning." Tonie, sitting in her little chair in the corner with a book, had merely thrown a questioning glance at her father. Gian had not looked angry, only disappointed; or rather, something more than that—stunned with disappointment, Raymond would have said: and presently, without having spoken, he had gone very quietly upstairs and Raymond had not seen him again.

He caught just the end of Elizabeth's answer: ". . . You see, there are certain things which you could say and which I can't."

"What?" he said. "Well, I don't know."

The words 'frightened . . . danger' were repeated in his mind like a silly tune that one picks up from the whistling of errand boys; they had started the small current of physical fear which he had felt in August '14, phlegm in the nasal sinuses, a continuing tachycardia. That look of Ardree's . . . Well, naturally the fellow had been disappointed, having arranged a treat for the child and finding his arrangment spoilt; but life was full of such small disappointments. Better, he thought, if the man had been firm, even given vent to a burst of temper; for when the simple conserved their emotions there was a risk of fermentation.

"I've got a good deal of faith in Gian Ardree," he heard himself saying. "Very quiet, very patient; a thoroughly honest sort of chap." (And that, surely, was true enough.) "No polish, of course; but really, you know, his manners astonish me—he's got the true *sense* of good manners. Much more so than half the men in my club."

Rellie would come to me, he thought, if there were any danger. (Danger?) For he imagined that every married woman kept in her mind's recesses the name of someone she would turn to if things went wrong. He was straining to make his own faint memories of marriage project a picture of what it might feel like from the other side: the utter dependence, the terror that must descend if the safety of that dependence wore thin. Fantastic, to let such notions wreathe about the figure of Armorel, with the tranquil command she held over herself and those about her! How she would mock him if she knew! And then, 'Like being locked in a high room,' he thought, 'and catching the smell of fire.'

"You talk about my thin stockings," Elizabeth said, "—it's you who are cold! You're shivering."

Shivering? Surely not physically, so that anyone could see!

"No one can take care of herself better than Armorel," he said didactically. "The one thing she simply would not tolerate is any interference—even from me." And then, nervous of contradiction, aware that he had used a rougher-grained voice than the one he kept for her, he stumbled on: "And you know, my dear, I really feel—I mean, women can lay their hearts open to each other in a way they can't with men. I mean, supposing you had some sort of emotional trouble, you know what I mean (I'm not suggesting that it's likely)—well, I'm the very last person you'd tell about it. But, on the other hand, you might very easily go and talk it over with Armorel."

She smiled then, rather strangely. "Not Armorel," she said. And then: "About her troubles, yes—if she wanted. Not about mine."

"But listen," he persisted, "supposing Michael was being fearfully difficult, as all boys are at one time or another. Well, then, surely you would want to compare notes with another mother. Of course it's unthinkable that Michael would ever be difficult—"

"He is sometimes," she said. "Not naughty, I don't mean—he's a wonderfully good boy. But nervy at times."

"Nervy?" Raymond felt himself relaxing, like a traveller who chances on a familiar route after days in unmapped country. Michael —what safer and more sympathetic subject had they in common? I am rather a clever man really, he thought. "Oh, no," he said, "I should never use that word for Michael. Or 'highly strung', or any of those other tiresome phrases. He's merely a child of very delicate perceptions."

"Like his father."

"His father?" They had come out into the street at last, and though he regretted leaving the Park—its loneliness, the tones of smell and colour with which it responded to the year's mood—he felt safer with these more robust familiarities, the tissue of busy voices and the odour of wealth which hotels spilt out across the damp pavement. He crooked his arm for her to take. "Curious, I've never thought of your husband just in that way." (All this was deliciously trodden ground.) "Of course, I see him as the man in the street does, and his major qualities dim the minor ones. I think of his immense capacity for detail, the extraordinary nerve he must have to carry so many responsibilities at the same time. You know, when a man doth bestride the narrow world like a Colossus one finds it difficult to think of him in ordinary human terms. What I mean is—"

"Henry isn't Michael's father," she interrupted.

He said, although he had heard her perfectly: "I'm sorry—what did you say?"

"I'd rather you kept that to yourself," she continued in the same voice. ('Quite casually,' he thought afterwards, when he tried to recall it.) "It's possible that everyone will have heard before long. But at present no one has. I know you won't talk about it." (Then she did trust him! So much, at least, was retrieved from this spoilt, disturbing, oddly humiliating day.) "I think perhaps I'll ride the rest of the way— I did rather a lot of walking this morning."

315

And that, at any rate, was characteristic of the Elizabeth he knew: to say the right thing at the awkward moment, never to leave embarrassing gaps. She had given him the chance to cover his confusion with masculine fuss and he took it with both hands, he sprang at a commissionaire, "You—get me a cab!" and stabbed the man's palm with half-a-crown, he stood far out in the road himself and held his umbrella like the forbidding angel's sword, shouting at the nonchalant taxis with the voice of a demented sergeant-major.

"Oh, Raymond," she said, when a driver had been scared into submission and he had seized the door of the taxi and jerked it open, "have I made you late for something?"

"Me?"

"You seem in such a hurry. I shouldn't have talked so much."

"But it's you," he said almost indignantly, still holding the door for her. "You said you wanted to get home—of course you want to get home. I've kept you wandering about for hours in that draughty park, I've never behaved so badly in my life. Get in, my dear—I'll have you home in ten minutes."

"But I'd rather go by myself—may I, please?"

"Oh, but—"

"It was a lovely lunch! *Mille remerciments!*"

Well, better that way than to sit beside her for ten minutes fumbling for something to say. He must have breathing-space, it was all too upsetting, that badgering over Armorel and then this quite incredible statement about Michael. Surely it makes her a different person, he thought, standing a yard outside the kerb and watching the taxi's rear light as it was sucked into the swirl of Hyde Park Corner. It may even damage our relationship.

"Another cab, sir?" the commissionaire asked.

"What? Yes. I mean—certainly not!"

Haunted as the well-to-do are by capricious notions of economy, he joined the crowd waiting for buses. He was pitiably depressed. At lunch he had been in superlative form, the P.M. had spoken to Elizabeth charmingly, Raymond had felt that everyone was admiring his taste. Then, in the Park, where their talk should have been as intimate and agreeable as a game of bezique, it had passed right out of his control and all the proficiency on which he so prided himself had failed to restore it to their private key. Something to do with those damned moor-hens, he thought; and he had actually found himself wondering if Elizabeth had changed.

"King's Cross," he said to the conductor. He invariably came to town by the steam line instead of getting the tube at Golders Green as his neighbours did nowadays: if the electric railways were going to push right out into the countryside they would get no encouragement from him.

And on top of that she had calmly told him, herself, that she was something different from what he had always imagined. At the first instant he had supposed she referred to an earlier marriage, one of which, astoundingly, she had never before spoken a word: but, no—if she had meant that, she would not have required his secrecy. Well, he was not the man (he told himself) to be perturbed over the peccadilloes of the distant past: he had his views on these matters, but they were now, as he recognized, unfashionable views. The real trouble was that the disclosure removed her, if only a little way, from the special class to which, in his mind, she had always belonged. A delicate friendship with himself, where all the proprieties were scrupulously regarded on both sides, was one thing: a clandestine liaison was something different, and however you looked at it, whatever allowances you made for the stresses of youth and an incongruous marriage, there was in such an affair a taint of vulgarity. Ordinary women did these things in moments of frailty. Hitherto, he had not regarded Elizabeth as an ordinary woman.

"Not running!" he said to the man at the barrier. "The 5.17!"

Something, apparently, to do with the coal situation. There was nothing you could rely on these days. For a few moments, standing near the bookstall and reading the headlines of the evening paper, he was soothed by the movement of the stream pouring past him, dark coats and flesh-coloured stockings, blue overalls, a couple already in evening-dress. (*Wife Strangled with Pyjama Cord—Alleged Confession* —how oddly people behaved in the unimaginable country west of Maida Vale!) The faces emerging from shadow and passing on towards the platforms were resolute with trivial intentions, strangely uniform of mien despite their variety of feature, composed and commonplace faces. Democracy, he thought, and that was something he liked to watch, so long as no one asked him to get mixed up with it. This current would flow while the world lasted, and the schooled, impervious faces would not change. But the curious winds that dart and flutter in that station were creeping up under his coat, the sense of disquiet came back like flood water through a flimsy dam. It no longer satisfied him to murmur that the times were out of joint, and the pronouncement that people get on best when left to manage their own affairs came only in the hoarse voice of a peddling quack. He was faintly conscious of some inadequacy within himself.

A foreigner passed him, cutting across the stream; a Sicilian, he thought it might be, a swarthy, short-backed fellow who looked confused and frightened. What were such people doing and thinking, did the police keep track of them? He must try once again to persuade Rellie to come out to Finchley, with Tonie and Gordon if need be, and there, in his own room, he could talk to her more easily: in a general way, of course: about the prejudices that simple people had, with perhaps a passing reference to the way in which the Latin temperament differed from one's own. Or perhaps he would write, getting Elizabeth or someone to deliver the letter by hand. He could express himself so much better in writing, taking his time, enjoying the feel of his padded chair and the exact, harmonious movement of the gold pen over the faultless surface of his notepaper. Really the effect of writing might be better. He was most anxious not to be alarmist, to avoid giving her the smallest hint that he suspected any maladjustment. After all, if one steadfastly believed a situation to be entirely healthy there was always a reasonable chance it might become so.

He turned up his collar, instinctively glancing round to make sure that his tailor was nowhere about, and started moving towards the platform for the 5.46. In the train he might feel better; there would be faces and opinions he knew, and the pressure of his own realities would make the sitting-room at Weald Street a little more unreal. The noise wrapping thickly about his ears, shreds of talk woven in the screech and snore of locomotives, was a lenitive for his senses: it subdued, though it could not silence, the recurring whisper from that inexplicable Elizabeth, 'It frightens me!' *Frightens me!* Frightens me? In a child's questioning glance, a workman's look of disappointment, there was no cause to be frightened. Unhappy, he went on towards the front of the train, where the first-class carriages would be; walking a little faster, as if with that physical show of resolution he could leave the whisper behind.

28

*R*EACHING THE flat, Elizabeth changed quickly into older clothes. Then, with half an hour to spare before starting for her regular visit to Bidault's Place, she took out the letter which she had begun to write this morning:

> My own precious Michael,
> All the proper news is in a letter inside the parcel I am sending you. This is one which you can keep to read carefully when you have a little time to yourself. It's rather a difficult one to write, because it's about a lot of grown-up business. But you are a most understanding son, and we do know each other so very well, don't we, and we do absolutely trust each other.

She read that over twice, wondering if it carried her own voice, if Michael would hear her speaking and feel her hand in his armpit. Then she tore it up. She would go down at the week-end and take him out in a car: it should be within the will power of any human being to keep emotion under control for an hour or more, to speak without letting tears come into the voice.

Lying down, she turned up the shade of the bedside lamp a little so that she should not fall asleep: in the early morning, when she desperately needed sleep, she would have to pay for any she pilfered now. She said to Lucy, who came with a cup of tea, "No, thank-you, dear, there's nothing else I want," and the elderly maid went back to her own room.

A wasted day: in trying to make Raymond a little less supine she had merely thrown him off his balance and spoilt things for them both. Earlier, she had rather wildly thought of asking him to break the ground with Michael, who had some fondness for such an amenable 'uncle' and would have listened at least without alarm to anything that reached him in that sedate and pompous voice. But the idea was palpably hopeless: if Raymond ever agreed to so positive an undertaking he would probably forget the object of the journey before he arrived at the school. Wasted: yes, but all these years had been wasted. She had been no use.

By remaining very still she fastened the evening pain, which was bad today, in one place behind her eyes; there she could hold it as one holds a hot cup in accustomed hands, and the dim, continuous noise of the Knightsbridge traffic, filtering into the quiet room, dulled it a little. It would stay keen enough to keep her awake.

Use? "Nothing is worth giving unless you give yourself." The voice, Northumbrian in shape, smoked by the passage of almost thirty years, still sounded like the voice of God. She could remember the feel of the carpet giving place to naked floor where she stood barefoot and shivering by a communicating door in the Glasgow hotel; hearing Mother's tearful voice and then that single sentence in her father's, the quiet, the ultimately certain voice of one who has hacked away all but the core of his beliefs. Her impression of his face, as he stood looking up to her window at Dinstead, as he sat impassively in the Greenock tender, had lost all outline; the photographs awoke no recollection. He remained as one whose rare gestures of tenderness had been immeasurably precious and whose wisdom had been absolute for her. Give yourself: but to what, and with what intrinsic object? They had kept the letter from the British Association which came just after the news of his death: ". . . with his unique analytical gifts and his selfless devotion to archaeological science there is no doubt that, but for this tragedy, he would greatly have enlarged our knowledge of Aymara and Quichua cultures . . ." Give yourself to a notion, then, to a bloodless belief, the filling of gaps in codices on dusty shelves? Or if, as she thought, to people, then to what interest of theirs?

On the little chest-of-drawers, half-full of Hilda Nicholedd's things, the photographs stood like the epochal, unrelated illustrations which punctuate illustrious Lives: the Cottage taken from Jowett's farm, Mother with Caesar and Jemima, Henry in court dress. Only two had retained the power to move her, and one of those was of Armorel in her wedding gown. She stretched and brought it to the bed to study more closely the delicate shaping of the face, the sweet immaturity which surrounded a faintly smiling mouth and still, decisive eyes. 'For Elizabeth, with my love.'

"I implore you to give her all the love you can find," Gordon had written in one of his half-hysterical letters, "since she will no longer take any from me"; and to Gordon, with the cavernous loneliness beneath his towering assurance, she could refuse nothing. The passion she had summoned to answer his desperate need in the tumbled village on a Greek hillside, once in a drab hotel in Cromwell Road, had sought an afterglow when its ephemeral life was spent; and it was natural that the strong current of her pity should flow to another whom her precipitancy had helped to injure. Was this all that had happened? Could remorseful pity pretending to be love have endured so long that even now she was stirred when the rare letters came in Armorel's hand, still beginning 'Dearest Elizabeth'? And was not the unreason in her continuing emotion the very hall-mark of love? For bare pity, she thought, does not demand a return, it scarcely asks for gratitude. Perhaps what she had hoped from Armorel was to see fulfilled in her the kind of future she had once imagined for herself. In Armorel she had found a creature endowed with the grace and gentleness which are power translated into other terms, together with a resolution which would accept no compromise, no facile satisfactions: the heroic brought to dear reality in a knitted jersey and small, skilful hands, in easy gestures of affection and responsive smiles. With her own life drained of nearly all its meaning she could not have been impassive to one so rich in promise: all the discerning tenderness with which experience had uselessly endowed her had been ready to serve so steadfast a traveller on so dangerous a journey, and it was ready still. But there was between lover and loved that thin, tensile surface which reflects without absorbing; they had drawn no closer and the years were gathering speed; she wondered now if in their long, shy friendship she had been of the smallest use, if loneliness would at last narrow the gap, if she could ever truly serve her at all.

From the Rouvray photograph Henry's clear eyes looked out at her with the kindness of contentment. She had been of use to him. Not only, she believed, as a decoration of his progress. He had never asked her for advice, for it was not in his nature to request advice from his subordinates: but in their early years he had left a hundred decisions to her judgement with casual phrases, 'You have it the way you like, my dear!' . . . 'You must make up your own mind, lass, I haven't the time'; he would deftly lead their talk to get her opinion on people's social value; and he had never ceased to cock his note-taking ear (his eyes still fixed on whatever he was reading) if she spoke of things which were being done, worn or seen by people who had no need to worry over what they did, wore or looked at. Yes, she seemed to have done what he required, and now that her service was drawing to its end she doubted if a personal secretary, trained and paid, would have given him better value. It was foolish and no doubt unjust to complain that he had required so little. In five years' time, she thought, as her eyes were drawn magnetically to the small boy gravely fondling a toy

Dalmatian, Michael will be starting to make his own engagements and to feel gayer when I am not there; then my use as a person, as myself, will be finished.

The telephone chirred and the voice of Norah Chilcott arrived like a carriage and pair rolling into a sleepy homestead.

"Elizabeth, my dear, I've only just heard the news about Austin Nicholedd. I *am* so sorry—so is Matthew. It's a terrible thing—I suppose he was only in the early forties. Of course there's so much reckless driving over there. I suppose Henry's dreadfully upset—he's always been devoted to Austin, hasn't he!"

Elizabeth said patiently: "Yes, it was a shock to Henry—I've heard from him, of course. They'd worked together for a long time."

"What do you think poor Hilda will do? I suppose she'll come home at once?"

"No, I think she's staying over there for the time being. She has a lot of American friends."

"Oh, I know she has! Tell me, dear, do you know which hotel she's staying in? I feel I ought to write."

"She's at the Wethouder."

"Oh, and could you give me Henry's address? I know Matthew wants to write to him."

"He's at the Wethouder too."

"Oh. Is there any chance of your going over to join him?"

"No."

"But you know, you ought to have a change."

"Do you think so?"

There was a pause in which Elizabeth, hearing Norah's breathing, could picture the lacquer crinkling at the corners of the old woman's mouth. Then she heard:

"I mean, I should have thought it would be a good thing from every point of view. Of course, dear, it's no business of mine, but you know what stupid things do make people talk."

"My own friends don't," Elizabeth said: she was, after all, in pain. "And I don't so terribly mind about Henry's."

Norah said: "My dear, how peculiar your voice sounds! I suppose it's the telephone. Listen, Matthew and I want to have a little party, specially for you. A sort of consoling party, you might say. At Sagrestano's, we thought. Just to get you out of yourself a bit."

"Out of what?"

"Out of yourself, dear. You do like Sagrestano's, don't you?"

"Yes, except for the people who run the place and the people who go there."

"But, Elizabeth, you told me once that you loved it!"

"Perhaps I was out of myself then."

"This line's simply dreadful."

"Yes," Elizabeth said, letting the receiver alight on the cut-out as gently as a butterfly, "it gets worse and worse."

'Out of yourself': so much of her life had been spent out of herself that she began to doubt whether she had ever lived within, whether there was any self to return to. In the end it did not matter: you lived in other people, in Henry, in Michael, in Armorel, and your flame survived only in the heat of their fires. Hers would flicker, perhaps, so long as Michael cared for her, spared her a few of his secrets. But after that? Could any fire be livened by a faggot which had stood so long in the rain, would there be anything left to burn? In these last months she had felt herself beginning to grow old. It frightened her, but not exactly as others are frightened. She was not much troubled by the prospect of ageing in appearance, for hers, she thought, had been chilled by early illnesses; or of being friendless, since she had many friends; or of the slackening that must come in her powers and sensibilities. Rather she dreaded that as the few who seemed to need her dwindled she would gradually lose belief in human need and at last in human values. Lying here alone in a room she had come to hate for its infections, troubled by the light but fearing to turn down the shade, she foresaw herself an old woman living upon a thread of transient impulses; selfish, and bored with her own selfishness; hungry for pity and despising those who gave it; spiteful, not from malice but because the faiths which would have moved her gentleness were all dried up.

She stirred, shifting the pain into a fresh position, and held it there grimly as she slid her feet to the floor. "Michael!" she whispered, seeing him in hospital again, watching him run and stumble on the lawn at Easterhatch, hearing his grave voice ('I expect I shall be decently treated, Mother') at the railway-carriage window, "You won't leave me altogether, Michael, whatever happens? You'll make use of me sometimes?" But the telephone was buzzing again.

"No, he's still abroad . . . Yes, this is Lady Kinfowell."

"I'm *so* sorry to trouble you—I wonder if you could possibly help me." The male voice was young, emollient, only a trifle over-varnished.

"This is the Collimator News Service, we rather want if we can to check up on an item about Sir Henry in one of the Pittsburgh papers. It's not really important, only—"

This, obviously enough, was where she should have broken off the conversation. Being human, she asked:

"What item? Which paper?"

"Well, it's a very unimportant paper really, mostly local gossip, you know the sort of thing, only naturally it would print anything interesting about your husband because of his steel interests there."

"Yes, but—"

"It's in a column by a man who calls himself Peeping Tom. It's all the most fearful rubbish, but some of his stuff gets syndicated—"

"You've got it there? Then you'd better read it to me."

"Well, it's about the death of a man called Austin Nicholedd—I expect you know of him. A lot of sob-stuff, you know—so young, brilliant tennis-player, that sort of thing. Then it says, 'Heart of all Pittsburgh goes out to lovely Mrs Hilda Nicholedd, noted star of London Social Firmament, well-known here and generous donator to Duquesne University—'"

"How moving!"

"Yes. Then we get this: 'Very small bird or maybe long-eared dormouse whispers your Peeper that interesting announcement on this Top Rank Beauty may break soon. And with coloured stars, making worthy Pittsburghers guess again where they come in with Britishers on speed record issue.'"

"Is that all?"

"Not quite. It goes on: 'Tom spoke London Finance King Sir Henry Kinfowell, business buddy of Nicholedd, handing condolences to Hilda in fashionable Kickapoo Bar on Allegheny Boulevard. Strong, silent Financier Kinfowell gave best imitation of strong, silent British financier Tom ever seen. But grinned plenty.'"

"Nothing else?"

"Well, there is. There's a picture stuck into the column—it's a very bad picture, quite unrecognizable—it shows a girl in nurse's uniform and an English officer. Sitting outside what looks like a sort of estaminet."

"Yes?"

"And the caption says, 'Back Home: Lady Elizabeth Kinfowell with soldier friend.' Nothing else. And that's the only picture in the column."

"I see."

"You see what I mean—there are half a dozen different inferences that people might draw—"

"As many as that?"

"And the reason I'm troubling you is this: If that column gets into some of the offices over here it's more than likely that the London papers will be on to us about it—we're very strong on the States side and they rely on us a good deal to tell them whether stuff that comes over in the Yank blatts is phony or otherwise. So I just thought you might be able to give me something which would kill this story stone dead. I mean, that would help us, because it's almost as much our business to kill phony stories as to dig out the real McCoy, and from your own point of view—"

"I'm afraid I've no point of view," she said. "If any of the London papers want to make use of that paragraph it's up to them to judge how near libel they can afford to get. I imagine they keep their own lawyers for just that purpose."

"Oh, but I hope you understand—"

"Perfectly!"

Having rung off, she hesitated for a few moments and then called Trunks. "Northampton 8655." In a restless, idle fashion her mind made varying sketches of Peeping Tom: a brassy blonde from some western university in a Stoltmann pinafore frock, a tired old gin-soak anxiously peregrinating between the speak-easies, grateful for any fag-end of scurrility which would help to pay the next instalment on his Chevrolet. Clever, to have got that photograph, exactly at the right time. She vaguely remembered the one, a pop-eyed little R.A.M.C. sergeant had taken it and sent her prints when she was back in London. Yes, this would be the "additional item" which Henry had spoken of in his letter, and someone in the Peeping Tom connection must have got to business with a room-waiter or a lawyer's stenographer. Did the sense of achievement glow brightly enough to reward such industry?

"Your call to Northampton—speak up, please!"

The voice that said "Hullo!" was faintly northern, a little strident with emancipation; from behind it there was audible the clamorous voice of a child.

"Mrs Aquillard speaking."

"Oh, Rhoda, this is Elizabeth Kinfowell—how are you, dear?"

"Me? Oh, going great guns—apart from this accursed prolapsus, you know. (Stephen, *will* you stop that filthy noise!) I'm afraid Gordon's out—did you want to speak to him?—he's lecturing some damned society. Sorry, can't hear, these kids are all out of hand."

From seventy miles away Elizabeth could hear how precariously the metallic assurance was kept in that voice. She remembered how Rhoda's telephone was placed in the sitting-room, where with the doors open you saw the pram, the gas-cooker and the dustbins almost in one line.

"How is he?" she asked.

"Oh, well enough, you know. Bit nervy. Still, that's what I'm here to look after. (No, Martin, you must wait!) He did get your letter. Was that what—?"

"He's told you, of course?"

"Yes, he's told me what's likely to happen. It's all going to be rather cheap and tiresome. Still, these things happen, I suppose. I merely hope the university shamans won't take up an old-fashioned attitude."

"Rhoda dear, I can't tell you how grieved I am—I wish we could have a talk—"

"I'm afraid life's terribly full just at present. I'll tell Gordon you rang."

"And you'll give him my love? And to you, dear."

"I expect he'll ring you back."

The voice, the cramped and anxious life surrounding it, were submerged in the effervescence of mechanical sounds. For a few moments she went on holding the receiver as if some message might come from that pandemonium, but the voice she heard now was faint from the years that had washed over it, "Yes, I know it's madness, but it's the only thing to save me from going mad." She sat by the electric fire to put on her shoes, shivering a little, and the picture which would never fade out lit in her mind for a moment with peculiar vividness, carrying its special aroma as the memory of a dream does: the shadow of the canvas bowl thrown by a hurricane lamp onto the stone wall, the restless stamp of mules in the yard outside; Gordon's dark shape on the camp-bed, his voice fluttering like a scared child's, "No, I had no idea that being frightened could be quite so bloody as this . . . Yes, my dear, I'm off in exactly four hours' time—Üsküb. So you probably won't be bothered with me again." I am being alone too much, she thought, putting on her coat.

She went to the Elephant by tube: it was all Henry's money, she wouldn't use a penny more than she need. How long had he known? she wondered again, floating like driftwood in the tangling currents of Piccadilly Station; no one saw far into the mind of such a man, the people he trusted most had keys only to one or two of its rooms. Perhaps his suspicion had begun in Michael's earliest weeks, when (to her at least) the structure of Gordon's temples and cheekbones had already begun to appear; for he had always shown even less interest in the boy than a general insensibility towards children would explain. As long ago as that he had probably commissioned someone to make inquiries about the Captain Aquillard whom he had once met at Victoria, to follow the lines of intelligent speculation and build up—in case he wanted it some day—another of the neat, grey folders she had often seen on his desk in London Wall. Well, she was in no position to complain. "You see how it is with women," a workman in the lift was saying, "they only go by what their feelings tell them, they don't have the power to reason." "Nobody knows," a boy sang cheerfully as the grille slammed open and the damp air, dragging at torn fly-sheets, bore coldly into her face the smell and clatter of the New Kent Road, "nobody knows —the trouble I've seen!" And if your spirit, she thought, could be possessed by the daedal anxieties and griefs of all these others, of a shivering lorry-driver who waited for the cross traffic to break, the tuberculous woman pushing a sack of coal in a pram, you might see your own as inflated, captious and trite.

" '*I am cold,*' *she faltered.*

'*You must fasten your cloak,*' *was his careless response, and then, with an almost contemptuous gesture, he turned and pulled it roughly about her.* '*If you think,*' *said he disdainfully,* '*there is any warmth to be had from the horses' breath and my own, I shall lodge no objection to your tenancy of the seat beside mine.*' *Fearfully, as if that were a command, she placed herself in the seat he proffered. And they drove on through the thickening dusk, and the winding road rose steeply, and the dark and ancient forest closed in upon them, till she saw only the horses' tossing manes, the snow flakes whirling in the pool of light which the carriage lamps cast forward, and above, where the pine tops joined like hands upraised in prayer, a solitary star.* '*Tonight!*' *the Marquess muttered.* '*Be it life or death, it must be settled tonight!*' *She slept; and when her eyes re-opened the lights of Chavencières showed like a circlet of diamonds in the valley far below. A weight lay upon her shoulder, close and warm. It was Dieulouard's hand. She sighed, and instantly the hand was withdrawn. 'October has passed,' breathed the Marquess, with pity and scorn burning like twin fires in his sombre eyes, 'and the necklace has not been found, and there where you see those lights your mistress waits for your reply.'* That's the end of the chapter—shall I go on?"

"I'd rather wait till next time you come," Empire's wife said. "I like to wonder what's going to happen next."

A stranger would have sworn that she had not heard a word of it. She lay as usual with her face towards the window, where the curtains were never fully drawn, so that she would have a glimpse of anything that happened in Bidault's Place; and while the reading went on her lips were tightly fastened, as if she were having a wound dressed and must struggle not to cry out. Sometimes it was hard to believe that she was alive; even her eyes remained so still, and her skin had the colour and feel of death: certainly you would have said, from the scantiness of her grey hair, from her greying moustache and the way the structure of her mouth had collapsed, that she was a very old woman. In fact she was probably still under sixty—she did not know.

She said, "Turn up the gas, dearie!" and Elizabeth obeyed. With the extra pressure the gas-fire poppled noisily, but Matilda did not mind that and Elizabeth had got used to it: like the smell of damp cupboards, the holes which castors had worn in the linoleum, it belonged to the cherished reality of this place where you could be at ease, where so little was expected.

"I'll make your tea," she said. "You like this book?"

Matilda was silent, still intent upon the gap between the curtains. Then she said: "Yes, I do remember that road."

A year or two back (as she often recounted) she had been outside the room, feeling so unusually strong that she thought she could go for a walk; but had only got as far as the head of the stairs, where the sight of the broken banister had given her a giddy turn and she had collapsed on the floor, staying there till Charlie had come and carried her back. Since then she had made two or three excursions each day to the far side of the room, occasionally unsupported, sometimes moving from one piece of furniture to the next as children do when playing touch-wood. From her bed she could see perhaps thirty yards of the street, and that view included the heads and shoulders of people walking on the farther side. She had not left the house for over eleven years.

She turned her head slowly and suddenly smiled.

"Silly," she said, "for her to go on like that! I'd have asked the foreign gentleman what he meant."

"She was shy, I suppose."

"Yes, yes!"

The old woman fell into another silence, but the smile remained in her eyes like a pilot light and she was preparing herself to speak again. Elizabeth, watching sidelong how her hands moved below the bedclothes, hearing the shift of phlegm in her throat, could tell almost exactly when the next words would come. But not what they would be; for though she had learnt the general movement of Matilda's mind she was still surprised again and again by the suddenness with which its gear was changed, the lightning alternations between lethargy and animation, the range of expression which the old woman commanded with her near-sighted eyes and with the gestures of her cramped, emaciated hands.

"They've got it wrong," Matilda said. "There wasn't a place called what you said. Aberdeyrn, they might be thinking of."

"Yes, they do make mistakes."

"Those lights, they must have been the school-house. Miss Lewis used to be there very late, making the lessons for next day. You wouldn't see Plas-Mawr, not from there. Dainty, the road is that way, the trees and all."

"Plas-Mawr—what's Plas-Mawr?" Elizabeth asked, knowing very well.

"Plas-Mawr? That's where I had my first situation. Yes, yes, very good Mrs Owen was. And Mr Owen, a very big gentleman he was. Fond of the horses, Mr Owen was, only they frightened me. 'You don't want to go to London Matilda Williams,' Mr Owen used to say to me. 'Nor anywhere near London,' he used to say."

"But you went!"

Matilda smiled at her hands with a certain cunning. She said abruptly: "I think she is in love with the foreign gentleman, what do you think? I think her soul goes out to him like the little flowers stretch up towards the beautiful sun, you think so, bach?"

"Well, yes, she seems to have very warm feelings for him."

"And what would be the use of it, if he is a *married* gentleman, heh?"

"Yes, that makes it all very difficult. Perhaps we shall find later on that his wife dies. I'm only guessing."

"Or perhaps the young girl can kill her?"

"Oh, I hope not! A gentle girl like Hortense wouldn't do that, surely!"

Matilda considered. "She is a wicked woman, the foreign gentleman's wife, a sinner before the Lord and evil in all her ways, indeed yes, bach. I think Tonce will find her having her lay-down one afternoon and cut her neck with a knife, heh?"

"But a girl like Hortense wouldn't know how to do that!"

Matilda shrugged her shoulders. "She is a young girl from London, maybe. In London the young girls can cut the neck of a person, oh, yes! Over Union Road, where Charlie come courting, do you see, I see it with these two eyes, out in the road, yes! I see a great man put his hand on a young girl, and then she cut his neck with a knife—like that—"

"But, Mattie, how dreadful! The idea of taking someone's life! Is your tea all right?"

Lost in the memory, Matilda stared with a face of boredom at the cup which Elizabeth had given her. "Maybe he was a *bad* man," she said, and a moment afterwards a new smile took hold of her face. "Yes, yes, it is *good* tea! But you have not washed the saucer as I would, bach. Look, one spot here, another there."

"I'm terribly sorry."

Matilda stretched her claw-like hand and caught hold of Elizabeth's wrist.

"You will learn, bach!" she said. "It is all patience—I tell you that and I tell my other girl too—you cannot learn it all in a day, to do things how they are in a *good* place. Ah, that Daise, she is so *slow*, do you see, she is so *blind*, poor childelie!"

"No," said Elizabeth firmly, "I can't have you saying that about Daise! Daise is a splendid worker and you know it."

Matilda shut her eyes. "She is an angel, bach, she is a cherubim and seraphim. But she does not know how to work. Look at this room, indeed—all spider-web, dirty, dirty!"

"That's nonsense, dear! You know I gave it a thorough do-out myself on Saturday."

"I said to that Mrs Jan, I said, 'Daise is a *good* girl, she will do you as well as she can, three morning and two afternoon every week. But she does not know much,' I said. 'She has never been whipped,' I said to Mrs Jan."

"Were you whipped, Mattie?"

Matilda laughed. "How would I be any use if I was not whipped! On Saturday—Wednesdays sometimes, but only if I had been idle. My father was a *good* man, do you see, in all the Bible Christians he was the *press*-ident, do you see. And the best quarry man in all the country. And then I was whip by Charlie too, when we was married a little time. Yes, yes."

Elizabeth asked quietly: "And you thought he was good, too?"

The answer was matter-of-fact: "Yes, then he was a *good* man. Every day he read the Bible to me—you see, bach, when I was ten year old I went to work and forgot my schooling—and then we prayed to the good Lord, Charlie and me side by side, to find something for us to eat and somewhere to live where the rain would not come in. Then sometimes he beat me, because he said it was sinful to be pretty like me. Yes, yes, then he was a *good* man."

She shut her eyes, but the smile that came to her mouth stayed there. So much talking tired her, yet Elizabeth encouraged it, feeling that the pleasure it gave the old woman was worth the price. And to listen was no longer a strain. Elizabeth had heard the tangle of dead ends and inconsistencies so often that she could fit the fragments easily into their place. Sometimes she could almost live within Matilda's mind; seeing with her eyes the penurious houses by the quarry at Llan-y-Troed, the lascivious face of Mr Livingwold appearing in the icy attic at Woolwich, hearing with the ears of a young Matilda the screams and blasphemies of the dark street she had looked at from the hovel in Rotherhithe. What she could not make her own was the calm acceptance, the stoicism verging upon relish, with which Matilda recalled those times. Perhaps this eleventh child had been so schooled in infancy to hardship that the roughness of later experience had scarcely bruised her; or else the screen through which she saw the past was opaque to misery, letting only the softer colours come through. But that was the picture of a simpleton; and in the wasted creature who lay motionless for hour after hour, clutched in a turmoil of shabby quilts like a root in the soil, and who would suddenly laugh or sing, could utter shrewd sarcasms on something you read her from the papers and flash at times with radiant anger, there was something besides simplicity. In a life like this, futureless, there could scarcely be any purpose; but with her, purpose seemed to be no necessity: she lived, and sometimes it appeared that she lived splendidly, upon the riches of her submerged, untrellised mind.

"You are tired, bach!" she said suddenly, without opening her eyes.

"No, only tired of my thoughts."

"What thoughts, duckie?"

"Just stupid ones."

Was it possible, she wondered, suddenly weak with fear, that Henry would take Michael away from her? Since she was to be the guilty party the law, she supposed, would give him that right, especially as the law could not treat Michael as unfathered. However little Henry cared for Michael he might value the dignity of having a son; and though he was not a cruel man if you thought of cruelty as passion (for a mind of that cast was aseptic to passions), his notion of justice—yes, that would be the word—might insist on his possessing what should have been his own. Would he risk his friends' opinions when he found she was ready to fight? And then, would the older boys at Michael's school get to hear of the contest, would there be covert grins in the dining-hall and snatches of crude innuendo across the forlorn untidiness of the change-room? How would he answer that—her Michael with his grave eyes, his shyness, his passionate loyalty? . . .

"I think I hear your husband coming," she said.

But Matilda's answer came before the street door had shut again: "No, that's Daise."

She might well have gone away, for she had stayed longer than usual and when Daise was at home there was little for anyone else to do; but as soon as she left this house the gyration of her thoughts would be unhindered, and she dreaded that as people dread the place where street lamps end. Here, in the cane chair between the gas-stove and the washstand, she could stay as long as she pleased, warming her spirit in their workaday intimacy; for they had grown used to her presence and could talk as freely as if they were alone.

There had been a time when she was jealous of Daise, for a skill that so far exceeded hers. That had passed, and now she could watch her bunching the pillow to support her mother's neck at the most restful slope, here loosening the bed-clothes where they lay too heavily, here tucking them to close a hollow space, with a respect in which only affection intruded. The repulsion once inspired by the girl's deformity had gradually been thawed by her tender submission: warmed by the gentle eyes Elizabeth had learned to kiss her, not dutifully but with the kind of pleasure there is in kissing a lover's scars. And this was tranquillity: to be with those who accepted her simply, to share for an hour a life which had no decorations and no pretence. It was Matilda's habit to grumble at her daughter: this bit of fish was undercooked, the bed-socks chafed where Daise had darned them, Daise was for ever putting things where they couldn't be found: and there were tart replies, 'Oh you!' 'Why can't you look where I *do* put things!' But one came to realize that the bickering was a fender which bore the rubs of a meagre existence, of illness and fatigue; beneath, there was a constant affection which showed itself in flashes of tenderness on the mother's part, in unwearying ministry on the daughter's. Here was love as the earth secretes it before the cutters and polishers have been at work. The narrow room which circumscribed their communion looked more like a theatre set than one where people lived; the deal wardrobe with its varnish graining, the caving wicker-chair, china mugs with the arms of Hartlepool, might all have been collected by a sedulous stage-manager as symbols of hopeless respectability in hard-fought retreat. There was none of the small poetry of softer lives, coffee and quietness by shaded reading-lamps, the admiration of old graces and new clothes, to sweeten the fellowship of this frowsty prisoner and the slipshod dwarf in stockinet who nursed her. And yet, it seemed to Elizabeth, they answered each other's needs in the way that lovers do, and from the meagreness of their field, perhaps from the very monotony of little actions constantly repeated, there had grown an understanding more exquisite and more robust than mere acceptance, rare like the flowers that grow from crevices in the Alpine rock. It was, she believed, enough for them. To her they had given their friendship, but they did not need her answering devotion; they could absorb only a little of the love she had waiting for a deeper channel to fill.

She was drowsy; but when she let her eyes fall shut the face of Michael smiling wistfully would always show through the curtain. And these others, she thought, own nothing except peace.

The argument that had started went on lazily, like a game of tennis between two idle players.

"Then if you cannot keep it mended you must ask your dadda for some money for a new dress, surely!"

"I don't get money off Dad."

"But Dadda has a lot of money, surely."

"I don't want that sort. Finish that up, Mum, and then I'll wash your face."

"But, duckie, I told you last night, I said. 'There is a hole under your arm as big as a bald head.' What does Mrs Crockett say if she sees her working-maid with a hole under her arm as big as a bald head?"

"You know quite well I wear an overall with Mrs Crockett. And anyhow I wasn't there today. Now keep quite still or you'll have the basin over."

"Of course you were there today!"

"You know I only do Mrs Crockett Saturdays now."

"Well, this is Saturday, dearie."

"It's not, Mum, it's Tuesday."

"Tuesday? Oh, dearie, my poor head, my poor old head! Get me one of the pills, duckie—now where did you put those pills, the ones that Dr Hammid give me? So it was Mrs Jan you went to with the hole under your arm? And what did Mrs Jan say when she saw the hole there, as big as a bald head?"

Daise said: "It don't matter what Mrs Jan says. I give her what she pay me for." Then she glanced at Elizabeth and her twittering voice went into a giggle of embarrassment. "Mrs Jan's got something better to do than to look for holes in my frock. She's on the go morning, noon and night."

The embarrassment remained and was pitiful to see. At such a moment the girl became conscious of her deformity, her eyes went left and right instinctively looking for somewhere to hide. Elizabeth asked quickly:

"Is little Gordon still giving her a lot of trouble?"

"Gordon? No, Miss Liz. Gordon's been sent away."

"Sent away?"

"She send him to one of those places—I don't rightly know what you call them—a sort of school, it is, for kids what make theirselves a trouble. It's what the doctor said, Mrs Jan tell me, a special sort of doctor she have on him."

"But how long for, Daise?"

"A year to start with, she tell me. An' she don't see him all that time. Then if it don't act they keep him on longer."

"And that is wickedness, indeed, yes!" Matilda said. In a spurt of indignation she sat upright, catching hold of Daise's dress as if she were the culprit. "How would a little baby boy be all right without his mumma, say you!"

Elizabeth interposed: "But he's not exactly a baby."

"And who will make him good again unless it is his mumma to kiss him and his dadda to give him the strap?"

"Mr Jan never would do that," Daise said quickly.

Off her guard, Elizabeth asked: "What *does* Gian say about it?"

Daise said evasively: "It ain't nothink to do with him. Mrs Jan, she see about it all."

"I expect they talk things over in the evenings."

"Jan don't talk much," Daise said simply. "He don't go studying up things what make into talk."

Matilda had sunk onto one elbow, but her excitement was not exhausted. A pronouncement had been growing within her, vibrating the whole of her contracted body, and it issued in one piece:

"That is wrong, I say, and I do not mind what anyone says at all. What would she marry him for, a great ugly man like that—what is the use of a great ugly husband if he will not tell his wife what to do! Indeed, she will make him angry. You say, 'Mattie Williams is a foolish old woman that never had schooling, what will she know about anything that goes on, yes!' But I tell you I have a forehead over my eyes, I listen, I think, when all the others are just talking and talking. I say if that great ugly Jan is not allowed to beat his own children he will get to be a *passionate* man, and that will not be a good thing for Mrs Jan, heh?"

"But, Mattie, why in the world should he want to beat his children? I think Gian's a particularly kind person."

The old woman smiled like a chess player who has set a trap and watches his opponent tumble in. She performed that shrug of the shoulders which was Gallic in feeling but peculiarly hers, her cratered palms turning slowly up and outward, her lips twisting slyly.

"So then it was another Jan Ardree, say you, the one that threw down the policeman in the street so that his arm could never be used again, indeed, yes!"

"But that was ever so long ago—thirteen or fourteen years."

Matilda nodded; her smile remained. She said ironically: "And now he is a *kind* man!"

"Why do you call him ugly, Mum?" Daise asked shortly.

"Because the good Lord in his mercy give me two eyes."

"Well, a person can't help what they look like, can they!"

Matilda did not immediately answer that. She pulled her daughter onto the bed, kissed her own fingers and pushed them up into Daise's hair. "But the good Lord give me other blessings also," she said. "He give me a baby girl with a pure and gentle heart, so the fornicators and the proud and froward men can do her no evil, childelie bach."

It was partly curiosity, partly an itch for justice, which forbade Elizabeth to leave the old woman and her opinion of Gian alone. She said with the gentlest reproach:

"You know, Mattie, you don't see him often. I suppose it's years since he came here?"

The answer came from Daise, who, quietly suffering her mother's caress, said laconically: "He come here last week, wanting to see Dad. Only Dad was out."

"He is a foolish man altogether!" Matilda said, stiffening into aggression once more. "What will it matter who will get the money for the house if it have to be paid, heb-heh? I say it is all his foolishness!"

Elizabeth said: "I don't quite understand."

"It's about the rent he pay on the house," Daise told her. "Mrs Jan always give it in to old Mr Olleroyd, and he pass it on to Herb Evans at the Old Richmond. Only most of it go to Dad, because it's a property he got a tally on, some way no one rightly understand. Only Jan don't know till that Freddie tell him—Freddie what Herb Evans have to put the empties in the yard and such—he got to know and he tell Jan over at the Apostles."

"And what will it matter if the money go to Charlie or where it go!" Matilda demanded again. "Spsh, it is nothing but a foolishness!"

"Have you talked to Charlie about this?" Elizabeth asked her.

The old woman lay right back and turned her head to her favourite position, looking towards the street. That was her habit when her interest in any topic collapsed: she had spent her day's force, Elizabeth thought; and the two younger women began to collect the used crockery that lay about, quietly, with the skill of old partnership, and to put the room in order for the night. But without moving head or eyes Matilda started drowsily to talk again:

"Thy desire shall be thy husband! How would little Mattie speak to the man the Lord gave to rule over her? For this cause shall a man leave his father and mother and cleave to his wife. That is for ever and ever, Mr Llewellyn said, until the man is dead. I remember Mattie

Williams when she was all alone, and it was cold in the little room up in the roof, and then that Charlie Empire came and she found he was a lovely man." Her voice was getting thick with phlegm, and distant, as if she were all but asleep. She stirred convulsively, and her hand came out of the bed again and searched along the quilt. "Are you there, childelie? Don't be angry, Daisie bach, don't be angry with poor Mattie—what can poor Mattie do? Only the good Lord know how to punish the wicked and ungodly, Mattie can only do what the Lord command." Those words were scarcely audible, but a fit of coughing which possessed her seemed to stir up some residue of power, and when she spoke again, panting, her voice was whetted to a trenchancy they had not heard before. "He seeketh out the evil that is in the heart of a man, and he will smite and destroy that wicked man and plunge him down into the fires of hell! Come here, Daisie bach, listen!"

But Daise was not listening to her. She said sharply, "Mum!"

And Elizabeth, without turning round, knew that Charlie Empire was in the room.

For his presence was felt more quickly than that of many to whom the quality of 'presence' would be applied. There was a smell attached to him, distinct from the compound fetid odour which the room continually inhaled from Bidault's Place; the smell of those barber's shops where the barber works with a Woodbine in his mouth and wipes the razor on sheets torn from the *Winner;* and you felt, upon the first encounter, that this emanation spoke for the whole man, effeminate, readymade, with a touch of varnish to hide the shop-soil. But his chief impression upon Elizabeth, on the rare occasions when he came home before she had left, was that made by poor actors when they perform with those of a higher class: from his own being he cast on those who surrounded him an awkwardness amounting to waxwork unreality. Just as a wretched actor does he stood, now, twisting his hat with one hand and rubbing his trousers with the other; looked round the room in a bewildered fashion; hurried his glance past Elizabeth, brought it slowly back, smiled as if into tropic sunshine and looked away again, murmuring, "Take it very kind, coming here to cheer up the missis. Very kind of the lady, ain't it, Daise? You ought to say thank-you, you know, Daise. Not much of a place to come to, a place like this, not for a lady."

Neither could find an answer; they stood quite still and watched him as he went uncomfortably to the bed. He had begun to look and to move like an old man, and Elizabeth cursorily wondered why she felt no pity for his feebleness.

"You goin' on all right, Mat?" he asked.

"Yes, thank-you, Charlie."

He seemed anxious to do something for her, but he was all at sea in the business of a sick-room. He gave a clumsy pull to the quilt, only making it come untucked on the other side. With embarrassment he stooped and kissed Matilda's cheek, mumbling, "I reckon you look better tonight, Mat," to which she answered:

"Yes, Charlie, thank-you."

"There was someone come in with you," Daise said suddenly.

"He can wait," her father answered abruptly; "I put him in the front room," and he turned to Elizabeth again. "You'd like Daise here to get you cup of tea, m'm, she make a nice cup o' tea, don't you, Daise!" He came to Daise's side and put an arm round her shoulder. "A marvel she is, m'm, though it's me that says it. Keep this place as good as she can for her ma, what can't do anything herself. Don't she, Mat?"

"Yes, Charlie."

"Of course, it's not much of a place, m'm—not the kind of place I'd have the missis in if I had the ways and the means. But it's home, you know, m'm. We make it all the best we can, me and Daise. And home's a wonderful word, you know, m'm, even if it's only a poor man's house like we got here. That's right, ain't it, Mat?"

"Yes, Charlie."

"Yes, of course!" Elizabeth said.

She was painfully preparing her formula for getting away. There is only one other man, she thought, re-living one of Henry's talks on household economy, who makes it quite so difficult for you to leave him; who has always something more he must say or perish and then repeats in slightly different words what he has said ten minutes before.

"It's very kind of you," she said, "but I've had tea already. I must be getting—"

"You see," said Charlie, "it's not so much what you got in a house as the feelin' in your heart what makes it a home. I often used to say to Mrs Empire, there, back in the old days—"

Upon an impulse, Elizabeth broke into his eloquence:

"Oh—Mr Empire—I do hope there's not going to be any trouble

about Gian Ardree and the house he rents from you. The Ardrees are old friends of mine, you know, and I heard—"

The question upset his balance only for a moment. A smile he kept in reserve came into position like the name of a station on a railway indicator. "Ardree?" he said. "That place of his along in Weald Street, you mean?—nice little house, that is, been looked after nice—that's no place of mine, you know, m'm, that's no business for a poor man, house-ownin' an' house-rentin'. No, I just take the money, now and again, to give it on to the old lady what own the house—that's just to oblige Herb Evans as does the collectin'."

"Oh, I thought—"

"Ardree, now," he pursued, "he's an old friend of my own, as you might say. Come to my Sunday classes when he was a nipper, young Ardree did. Got a job for him later on—I like to help a young chap the best I can, particular if it's a young chap that has a way of gettin' into trouble. That's right, ain't it, Mat?"

"Yes, Charlie."

"An' he always were a good enough lad at heart, that Ardree, weren't he, Mat?"

"Yes, Charlie."

"I'm glad you feel like that," Elizabeth said shortly. She had got into her coat, she went swiftly to the bed and kissed Matilda on the forehead; uselessly, for the old woman made no more response than a corpse would. "I can find my own way out!" she said, embracing Daise, and in a moment she was out of the room.

The door which she had shut behind her was re-opened before she reached the top of the stairs, and through the squeak of its hinges she faintly heard Matilda's voice again; but the words which came distinctly were in a voice of Daise's, different in timbre from the one she knew: "I tell you it don't matter, Mum, it don't do me no harm." The door shut once more; she paused for an instant, feeling that something was wrong and she ought to return; and found that Charlie was at her heels.

She had, just then, that very feeling of helplessness which had possessed another woman in this house some thirteen years before. Hitherto Bidault's Place had never scared her; she had travelled too variously to be scared by the insubstantial part of things. She was frightened now. "I got to say thank-you—" Charlie was breathing in her ear, nervously, confidentially, a little short of wind—"it do the missis a power of good, having a lady come to see her—it's hard for a man like me, you know, m'm, havin' his old sweetheart lyin' there and seein' her suffer . . ." while she, as in a liverish dream trying to say "Stop! Get back!" longing to run, went on down the stairs in silent dignity; and would have passed thus into the street, but the door of the front room was open, and a fungous, scale-eyed man came forward with a drizzling nose and half-cocked smile to wish her good-evening. Charlie was between them in a moment, saying "Half a jiff, matey, and I'll get your parcel for y'!" And moving so as to keep the other visitor screened he opened the street door and stood there ceremoniously to show her out; ageing, pathetically small, begging her with his eyes to forgive his poverty, his lack of any means to please; while she, with her chilled and fluttered mind repeating that last queer cry from Daise, could find no smile to answer his courtesy.

"I tell you it don't matter," the voice inhumanly flat, a dead voice, the voice of one too long defeated to have even the will to resist, "it don't do me no harm": the man with eyes like newly broken blisters, sweating at the neck, a drenched cigarette dangling from the loop of his sheepish grin: in this suppuration of men's infamy the years' evil and the gathered wretchedness of a day sultry with defeat broke upon her with a violence too swift for her seasoned defence.

She was not a novice in experience. Reared where pennies counted, broken to harness in the shifts and turbulence of board-school teaching, she had been in villages which Bulgarian troops had left the day before, had seen men still alive with their bodies turned inside-out, moved with open eyes and quick ears among the pimps plying their trade in the souks of the Levant. Yet this experience had caught her out. From Matilda's evasions she had long guessed the nature of Empire's spare-time occupation, had even suspected that in the past those activities had not been kept entirely outside his home; but no word from mother or daughter had ever prepared her for what she had just heard and seen. You suppose, she thought, stumbling, wanting to be sick, that there is nothing left to learn; that when you have watched to repletion the extremes of agony and filth no new and smaller twist can make you wince: yet no glimpse of wretchedness has ever frozen me as this has.

No (as the stagnant airs of Bidault's Place received her, familiar without friendship, chilled with fog, the last of the honourable workshop smells drowned in the stench of soiled clothes drying and food gone bad), this horror at another's misery does nothing to depreciate my own, it only turns me back upon myself. I try to escape from the drag of sympathy by saying this evil belongs to a world different from mine, which I can leave behind as I have left the water-front of Scutari; that a cruelty so mean as this can spring only from starved and blighted soil, that those whom it stings are so different from me in sensibility that they can scarcely feel it or be sickened by its stench. But these are my friends, sharing at least some part of their lives with me, bound to me by at least some ties of affection and understanding; and when I look at this needless wretchedness, this barbed embroidery which men have fastened to Adam's curse, I find my vision sharpened by my own distress as if both were of one shape and origin. What I suffer on my own account may, then, be only an aspect of universal suffering; but this neither diminishes nor dignifies the pain, rather it shows it to be at once contemptible and ugly, like a spreading disease of the skin. I can try to detach myself (as a stercoral draught assaulted her through the archway, as the sleepless commotion of Coronation Building, the raucous arguments, the ribaldry and wails of children pursued her down Mickett Lane), to say that my part is only a passive one, that the greed and blindness belong elsewhere; but when I look back to that shabby room in Cromwell Road—mauve walls and yellow eider-down, drawers that stick and cupboards which fly open—I catch sight of appetites the same in kind as those of the creature I saw just now. I peer inside the place which is secret from all others, as far and steadily as I can; and then I see that the greed was mine as well as his, that I lost all thought about injuring others in my headlong rush to appease it, that I should sacrifice the interest of others as recklessly again. I suffer because I have preferred to suffer; not as the martyrs do, but because it was the easier course to follow, the way of my kind: to yield without love, dodge the farther issue, cover with nimble deceits, live for the occasional delight. Yes, I belong to the rest, for essentially my passions are the same as theirs: the small, unshaven men who sell things in dark corners, the blowsy astrologers and cheap-Jack mediums of Camden Town, promoters of grandiose and shady companies, old, rouged women with Living-Art and Joy-in-Punishment saloons in the shuttered basements of Ismir. Darkness, nowhere anything but darkness and niggling desires. In faces at Sagrestano's and among the loungers in Bidault's Place I see a selfishness so absorbing that it blinds the heart alike to others' good and to its own; and when I have peeled off the last pretensions hiding the real creature within me I find a selfishness as hard and tawdry as any which revolts me in them.

The physical warmth she had brought from Matilda's gas-fire was exhausted, the damp wind coursing the street seemed to run unhindered inside her veins. She was walking unsteadily and in a pool of deafness, so that nearer sounds were stilled, while the farther noise of traffic in the main road, the clangour of trains across the viaduct, came with a strange distinctness to overscore the voices whispering inside her head. Her intention had been to call a taxi at the end of the street and go straight home; but she realized now that she might collapse before getting so far—it had happened before—and that would mean being caught in a tangle of kindness and fuss. From Trevon's window a light showed through the blue curtain she had long ago put up for him. She went inside the house, rested for a while in the passage, then brought her powers under command and pulled herself upstairs.

And Michael, she thought, as she slipped unobtrusively into the little chair beside Trevon's fire, would Michael, fruit of such transient passion, be like that too? Could she pretend to him, when he knew her story and saw it as an outsider would, that men were born to splendour and that evil was only an occasional mischance? There must come a time—it might come soon—when her influence over him would be finished. It was still not easy to think of Michael as a distinct and self-sufficient being, the centre of a cosmos in which she was a satellite less individual and less real than himself. But that was the fact she must accept; and in this hour of utter self-distrust she told herself it was better he should make his voyage alone. If there is any Good, she thought, he may chance to find it without help; or if he is to be guided, the guide must be one whose map is not obscured by corrections, creases and stains. Hitherto I thought it was only by mischance that from the seed of my friendships nothing grew which could stand against the seasons. Now I see distinctly that the genesis of failure was the corruption within myself, and if all my devotion flows towards Michael it will only stunt and wither him . . . Yet in this high fever of loneliness she knew she was merely a human being who would follow her primary instincts as abjectly as the rest. Michael was hers, never more hers than now, to guard and to live for. Beside that furnace of the heart the coiled filament of reason, charged to its highest incandescence, gave too little light to show.

"If you don't mind my mentionin' it," the man in the check cap said, "that do happen to be a diamond, the one Bulky jus' put down."

His partner winked. "Now don't you go interferin' with Slimey. Spoil his concentrationt."

"Oh, he's concentratin'? I thought it was somethink in his stomach, that gurglin' noise."

"Now don't you be nasty-minded—that's just his diallin' tone. Never mind, Slimey boy, you'll be dead some day. Put *somethin'* down—diamond if you've got it. Them square things with the square gone a bit arsy-tarsy, them's diamonds."

"It might be nice to get just one game finished before breakfast," Trevon said. "Fill up Slimey's glass, somebody."

"You havin' a drink, Mrs Kin?"

"Tea when the kettle boils," she answered, and the game went on.

They had taken scarcely any notice of her before: only Gian, who was puzzling over some text-book, had greeted her in his own fashion, with warmth and embarrassment in duel, and had put the kettle on to make her tea. And where else, she wondered, did good manners assume so grateful a form? It was Trevon, of course—they took their cue instinctively from him. More and more he seemed to control these people, without intention, as the fall of light controls the slope of flowers grown indoors. They caught his attitudes because of the difference between themselves and him, which they always remembered and which he seemed to have forgotten.

Yes, he belongs to them, she thought; covertly watching how his smile flickered and changed, warm for Slimey, mischievous as he caught the eye of Nibbley Toms; and as he gets older he is moving further away from me. The dangerous illness of eleven years before had reduced him physically, making the nickname 'Bulky Grist' a little absurd, and since then the settling process had continued, his frame tightening, the sparer lines of his face becoming permanent, so that his body appeared smaller than when she had first known him. But in personality he had increased. The twitches, the fits of sharp temper, had not quite disappeared; a watchful eye could see still the signs of an uncertain, even a timorous man; but he seemed to have measured his nervous weakness and got it under control, stowed where he could normally forget it. Here, with men he had known from their boyhood, he was as sure and tranquil as those who are born to live untroubled lives in gracious country houses; he rode their chatter as a Brixham trawler rides in crumpled seas, fashioned to sway and slide into the troughs but to hold a steady course.

"You're too bloody conservative, Frank. You never want to see anything changed. Why can't Slimey call it a heart if he wants to!"

The man in the check cap, spitting tidily into sleeve, said "Conservative? I'll tell you what I'd do with Conservatives—friends of yourn or not, Bulky—I'd stand 'em in one long row over on Tower Bridge there an' jack up the bascles. I mean that."

"Foul the works," Toms said disapprovingly.

Slimey pinched out his cigarette and parked it. "I reckon they got as much right to their opinion as you have to yours, Mr 'Ughes."

"Yes—an' what have their opinions done for blokes like you an' me? Keep the standard of livin' down to bedrock, then you get easy labour—any mug can see that. (No, ta, Bulky, I'll have one of my own.) Well, then, all they got to do is to run the laws accordin'. Send their lads to Eton an' such, work 'em into Parliament an' they got the thing rigged, world without end amen. Course, the workin'-man get wise to it now an' again—then it's time for the rulin' class to turn round an' say 'See here, lads, we got a war comin' on, all got to pull on the same rope for home an' country!' That's what's goin' on now—see it in the papers if you've got eyes in your head."

Spruce in his Burton suit, alert, faintly *père-de-famille* and manifestly a soft-goods man, Nibbley Toms eyed him with admiration. "Only four words left out, Frankie. Come in Chapter Five."

"You don't think there's any hope of re-educating the ruling class?" Trevon asked.

"Re-educate 'em with a noose!"

"Slimey here'll get it fixed up for you," Toms suggested. "Might try it out on Bulky."

Trevon nodded. "Suits me, so long as it's Slimey's job. Remember that rope in the gym, Slimey?"

"You won't mind my mentionin', Mr Grist, but that what you're puttin' down now ain't a diamond neither—not judgin' by what young Toms here was tellin' me."

"Blast!"

"Seems perhaps some bloke ought to start re-educatin' the rulin' class . . ."

The noise of the sleepless streets was audible even here, the floor shook a little as the trains passed. But the room, tight with smoke and fug, felt like the cabin of a small ship, a world alone in space. Nothing here was ever changed round: the cross-country vase on the gimcrack mantelpiece, the Minty chair, Everymans and Florentine prints had grown into the room as clothes appear to grow on those who dress for comfort; and as she sat with eyes half-closed, feeling the fire's warmth on her legs, hearing the continuous pat-ball of easy, familiar voices and the undertow of laughter, it seemed that these same men had never moved from their places about the table, that they had only grown older, fading into a new gentleness as the pattern on the wall faded.

"You feelin' all right, Elizabeth m'm?"

"Yes, thank-you, Gian, it's lovely here. I was just a bit giddy—it's cold outside. You've been at Apostles' Court? I want to come along soon and see how the garden's getting on. I suppose there isn't much you can do to it at this time of the year?"

"Well, we can get on with diggin' the pond, you know. I got some of Mr Grist's boys come and help me with the diggin'—rubble an' muck we got to get out, you see—an' then the kids help carryin' the stuff away; over on the corner—you know where I mean. I got a notion to have a sort of a rock garden over that corner. Look all right, you know, same as you might have in a private place."

"And the pond, is it going to be just ornamental, or will they be able to bathe in it?"

"Well, a paddlin' pond, you might say, that's what I got in mind. You wouldn't get it deep enough for bathin'. You get them kids paddlin'—in the summer, see what I mean—they'll like that all right. Get the bottom concreted over, so they don't muck their feet too much. Get a bit of cement off the firm, you know—Mr Belson won't charge it up too high, seein' I tell him what it's for."

The shyness which returned each time they met was thawing as he spoke. When he talked of Apostles' Court he grew in age and stature, speaking of landlords and borough surveyors as if they were men of his own kind, laying down the law even to Trevon about the need for new furniture and alterations in the rules. His Italian side showed more strongly then, often he became voluble and declamatory, free with gesture, and the fire of enthusiasm seemed to alter even his appearance, giving you glimpses of those lupine Tuscan farmers who will flash into oratory at railway-carriage windows. He would stand feet astride, thumbs in armpits, seeing over your shoulder every detail of the garden-playground he meant to create on the Pan and describing it almost with passion; and if you spoke critically of some boy who came to the court he would instantly contradict you: no, Steve was not really deceitful, he just didn't trust strangers, that was the way his dad had learned him, and he never cheated for his own benefit: as if he alone had the right to speak of those children or the intelligence to understand them.

". . . tell me it'll get all mucky and start up the flies an' that. Cuh! 'Think I never done no plumbin'!' I says. 'What happen to the dirty water out of your bath at home?' I says."

Nibbley said over his shoulder: "There go ole Toughie at it again! You ain't heard, Frankie—Toughie there's settin' up a new Hyde Park over Three Tuns. Hyde Park an' Wembley done up in one. Got a bit o' waste off the borough an' fittin' it up a masterpiece, gravel path right down the middle, Try-Your-Weight machine an' half a dozen ruddy dafferdills. Make the little baskets think they got the whole of Eppin' Forest come clusterin' round them."

"H-h- make 'em forget they ain't got nothing to put in their bellies!" Hughes said.

Slimey sighed. "Now you gone an' set him off again!"

Gian, with his eyes resting on Elizabeth's face, seemed to hear nothing. She said:

"It must take up a terrible lot of your spare time. Do you go to the court every evening now?"

At first he did not seem to hear that either. But in a few moments, returning from a far journey, he answered, "Well, no, I don't get round the same as I did. Fidge do it mostly—him an' Snitch between 'em. I give 'em a notion the way it got to go an' they put in the time, see." His eyes were just avoiding hers. "Susie put me on this course, see. Town Plannin'. Twelve lectures, that is, over at the London College, an' they give you studyin' to fill in—this here, that's one of 'em—it all come in with the course."

"That must be interesting."

Again a moment or two of hesitation. He was a different man now, and in spite of the settled look which the last few years had given him, the responsibility upon his brow, the dark suit worn naturally, the silver watch-chain, she saw for an instant the callow youth who had shaken her hand so stiffly in Raymond's garden. (And that, she thought as the glimpse passed, is reality: the rest an accident, mere overlay.) He said:

"Well, you see how it is, a lot of buildin's on paper, recreation halls an' all the rest. What might be for a lot o' blokes you never seen—it don't seem to signify. Might be a lot of folk who's fixed up all right where they are—same as you might be yourself, see—only want to shift 'emselves to somewhere else because they don't fancy the way the milkman say good-mornin', see what I mean. It's not like thinkin' up a bit of a place for a bunch o' kids an' that what you know all their names an' what they like and what they're scared of—kids what got no way to keep 'emselves from freezin', leavin' out the Covered Shoppin' Centre and the play-actin' circle an' that, what you get off the ole shiny as give out the lectures. See what I mean?"

She did see. She knew that if he lived to be a hundred this man would never learn to think in the larger ambit of theory. She said cautiously:

"Still, you may pick up some useful ideas—"

And he, instantly interpreting her caution, added:

"Well, you see the way Susie look at it. There's a sort of certificate they give out on you when you done the course. You put that up into the firm, see. You say 'What you got now is a ruddy expert. Plan your town for y'. Run you up a recreation centre, London College fashion, jus' like mother makes it.' "

("Cor, listen to ole Toughie now!" said Toms.)

"Might make a difference, see—leastways, that's the way Susie look at it. I got on a dead end, see. Mind you, I done all right reckonin' by what some do. Got twenty-two blokes do their work under me now—blokes of fifty or sixty some of 'em would be."

("Captain of Industry!" Toms remarked. "Coppers hold up all the fumin' traffic to let his Rolls-Royce go down Constipation Hill.")

"Only that ain't the same as what you might call a confidential job. The clerk give me over my part of the tracin's, an' the specication an' all, and I see the blokes under me do it all accordin'. Time schedule an' pay rates jus' the same. Only none of it come to me straight off the management, as you might say—there's always some other bloke put his fist on it before me. That's the difference, see. An' what Susie say, she say 'You can't go on all your life doin' jus' what the nex' bloke up says, you got to be up at the top of somethin',' she say, 'doin' somethin' out of your own napper. Then you get to mean somethink,' she say."

His voice had fallen to avoid the others' ears, he was looking straight at her eyes, beseeching her to follow the argument however obscure it seemed in his words, perhaps in a shrewd sentence or two to give it back to him so cleaned and polished that it would send a shaft of light into his own understanding. But this evening she could not do that.

"Tell me," she said, "how *is* Susie? It's quite a time since I heard from her."

"She's goin' on very nicely, thank-you. Of course, she's busy, you know the way it is."

"Yes, it's wonderful what she gets through."

"She do keep the house a treat. Everyone say she do."

"She does—marvellously."

At the table Slimey was holding the others mesmerized, and the room seemed to quiver with their stoppered mirth as his diffident, sorrowful voice crept on: ". . . did seem to me queer, but I done jus' exactly what my daughter said. 'The shop at the corner, Dad,' she said, as plain as plain. So in I goes, an' put the tanner she give me on the counter, where I don't see ought but bills for house-lettin', an' I says, 'Give me a Woman an' Beauty,' I says. Well, the bloke look at me rather queer, an' he says, 'As to the former,' he says—got a voice like a professor, this bloke had—'as to the former,' he says, 'you do best go down the street there to where you see a green door, an' there you give four raps an' say you been sent by Mrs Maconochie. An' as to the latter,' he says, 'you bes' kneel down and pray God to give it y', he says, 'because if he can't manage I don't rightly know of anyone what can.' "

"And did you?" Trevon asked in agony, as Nibbley buried his face and shook like a boiling kettle. "I found the green door all right," Slimey said pathetically, "but they tell me they never *heard* of a Mrs Maconochie . . ."

"Only we been thinkin' of goin' on somewhere else."

Gian said that abruptly, and he added at once, as if he would have taken the words back, "Well, that's what I got in mind."

"I suppose the house is rather small for your needs," she said, a little distracted by the laughter which was foaming about the table behind her, the bewildered Slimey's sibilant chuckle and Hughes's cannonade, "when you've got those other people living with you."

"Don't like what happens to the money," he said curtly; he was every year of his age now. "I didn't know, you see—hole-an'-corner business, Ed Hugg mixed up in it an' all. Well, I know now, an' I won't have my money goin' to that kind, and that's all it is."

The finality of his voice forbade her absolutely to pursue that topic. She said, too quickly, "Do tell me about—" and stopped. It was the boy Gordon she wanted to hear of, and she remembered only just in time that the honourable course for her was to listen to Armorel's account first. "—about Tonie," she said clumsily. "It's going to be her birthday before long, isn't it! You must be feeling that you've nearly got a grown-up daughter."

If he did think that he didn't say so. The word 'Tonie' lit a smile in his face and the smile stayed on his mouth, cooling till its light was that of a paint-and-paper candle in a Christmas bazaar. For a moment, when he spoke, it re-kindled as a wood cinder will before it finally goes out. "Took her along to the Apostles'," he said reflectively. "She enjoy that. Made quite a fuss of her, the lads did."

"Of course they did! I expect later on she'll be helping you over there."

He screwed his eyes. The cinder was dead now. "Susie don't hold with it," he said, and took her cup away to wash it up.

It wanted turning out, this room: a little shawl of cobweb at the side of the Giorgione, ink splashes on the door which might be skilfully removed with turpentine: sometime, perhaps, if she were well and strong, and if there were any sense in trying to alter things. Like the silk lamp shade, bleached and frayed now, swinging a little in the haze, the tapestry of voices seemed to be permanent, part of an arrested movement, a background she would see for ever enclosing Gian's defeated voice and eyes. "You don't know ole Slimey—terrible one for the skirts—caw, you never would believe!" "Ah, it's his looks, you know—handsome chap, Slimey is—that's what they can't resist." "You're dead right, Bulky—Mrs Kin, there, she'd tell you. Better lookin' than ole Toughie even, some do say." "Tell me he spend two hour every Friday in one of them beauty-parlours havin' his hairs permed—both of 'em." "I daresay it would do *your* 'air a bit o' good, young 'Ughes!" "You heard, I s'pose, the Borough Council's puttin' him in for the beauty competition nex' week. All done up in bathin' drawers an' a brassery. 'Miss Elephant an' Castle' they're goin' to put on his tally." But reality was Henry's letter, impartial, carefully phrased and faultlessly typed, and not this mellow dream of pleasantness; reality was a clock ticking in a hospital waiting-room and Nurse Wimple's calculated voice, "The doctors can't really tell until he comes round"; reality was the smiling, hungry, disappointed man in Bidault's Place, it was her own feverish voice saying, "No, Gordon, no, I don't mind about the risk!" Trevon, solid and at ease, throwing her a sidelong smile or two as she shrewdly added fuel to their enjoyment, Trevon himself was scarcely real. And already there were signs of the borrowed dream dissolving, a yawn from Frankie, a piece of coal tumbling against the bottom of the grate. Nibbley, glancing at his watch, had already said, "Well, this don't earn a frock for the wife, nor yet a pair o' boots for the baby."

With her body held so tightly in the hot repose which follows migraine her mind seemed to move as swiftly as in the moment of waking. Curiously, with her senses absorbed in the simple pattern men contrive for themselves, it was Armorel's view which she saw in brilliant clarity. She knew Three Tuns: a proud and happy Gian had shown her the glories of Apostles' Court, the makeshift workshop where boys with the vagrant eyes of imbecility were dribbling over fretsaws, the dank games-room in the basement full of children oozing with impetigo who yelled and tumbled and belaboured each other with ping-pong bats. She thought of the fairy-like Tonie in party dresses which her mother made so skilfully with materials from sales and ideas from Peter Robinson's windows; of the scramble Armorel went through every morning in getting her to a dame-school at Dulwich Park, to be given a glimpse of broader and fairer worlds than Weald Street. Could anyone call it unnatural, or even selfish, that such a woman should want to keep her child away from a stewing-pan of sailors' leavings, another Weald Street without even Weald Street's flimsy attempts at reticence! Surely it was not beyond Gian's compass to understand that: yet who would make him understand if not Armorel herself? He was beside her again; her eyes had closed but she felt his presence; and This is the time, she thought, in this warmth and friendship, when the vociferous presence of others only ensures our privacy: a word or two now from me, and he might grasp for always how her viewpoint must differ from his own.

A sentence formed itself, "Gian dear, you know how fond I am of Susie—of both of you," but before it was uttered her lips and throat fell slack. She was tired, so tired, and heavy with the day's evil. The continuity of sound was breaking, a chair fell over, Nibbley was blasphemously searching for his muffler. There would be danger, she thought, in anything I said.

So often a tranquil relationship depended on leaving words unspoken. Even between Henry and herself there had been subtleties of understanding and forbearance, certain words which both avoided when speaking of Hilda Nicholedd, questions of social distinction on which neither would ever touch. In a dozen years of marriage a fabric of such tacit understandings must have been worked between Gian and his wife, and if any part of it were strained an outsider could no more repair it than a seamstress could mend a spider's web. The little hill she had meant to cross had become a mountain as she approached it. That look of Gian's, the distress in it had seemed so disproportionate to so small a disappointment: had he worn that look when Armorel, carelessly perhaps, had given her decision about Tonie and Apostles' Court? And had it been unobserved? She opened her eyes just far enough to take in his profile as he stood with his shoulders against the mantelshelf: he was smiling now over some taunt which Trevon had chucked at him, he was part of the circle again. The crease in his temple was always there, she thought, belonging to no special anxiety. He was surely a man of gentle spirit, despite the roughness in build and features which sometimes made her think of Barbary corsairs; and if that knuckly hand of his was twitching a little it was only because so powerful and skilled a hand detested to be out of use.

"Well, get me own back next time, Bulky!"

"You will if you keep sober."

"Been very nice, I'm sure, Mr Grist. Quite a treat."

"Off to Mount Everest, Nibbley? Jus' thought you might be, with that thing round your neck."

"Pinched your lid? Whadu think I could do with *your* perishin' lid? Grow tomaters in it?"

"S'long, Bulky!"

" 'Night, Mr Grist! Ta! 'Night, Toughie!"

" 'Night, Bulky! Goo'-night, Mrs Kin!"

"Good-night, Frankie!"

She stood up, gripping the back of the chair and waiting for the giddiness to pass. "I must be off too," she said to Trevon, "I only meant to sit down for five minutes—the fog had got into my legs."

He answered over his shoulder, kneeling to revive the fire: "You're not moving from this room till there's a cab ready for you. Gian, you can nobble a cab on your way home and send it along here?"

"Yep."

He was in his coat, but he always contrived to leave a little later than the others and he stayed perched on the arm of the Minty, smiling remotely, till the sounds of Slimey falling half-way down the stairs, of scuffle and cheerful oaths and ribaldry, were broken off by the crash of the street door. (Yes, in a way he was older, he belonged to a category quite different from theirs, this knurred stub of a man with his paradoxical respectability, aloof, parentally fingering his watch-chain.)

"You been over in Biddle's Place?" he asked her casually.

"Yes, I looked in on Matilda. She was much better—full of talk."

"Daise there?"

"Yes."

Trevon, feet astride on the kerb, swinging the poker and enclosing them both in his mellow sunshine, said: "Best thing Susie ever did —or second-best, I should say—getting hold of that young woman to help her out. You can't beat Daise on housework. Look at the way she keeps her own home. When you think that Matilda can't help and Empire's living habits are half a length more grossly untidy than mine even—!"

"I've improved you a bit," Elizabeth said: she did not want to talk about Charlie Empire.

"Charlie come in?" Gian asked.

"What? Charlie?—yes, he was back just before I left. He was earlier than usual, I don't often see him."

"Anyone with him?"

"I think there was some man—" She checked herself too late to recover those words: her intuition had sounded the alarm too sluggishly: "I think it was the man to read the meter or something," she said confusedly. "I don't think it was a friend or anything. The Empires haven't many friends, have they, it's not a neighbourly sort of street, it's quite different from this one."

Gian nodded. "Yes, it's different," he said.

Trevon glanced at his face sharply. "Every street's different from the next!" he said as if trying to cover someone's faux pas; and in an instant his hands were on Gian's shoulders. "Why don't you sit down properly, for God's sake! There's no hurry—Susie'll know you're here." He was pleading with a curious urgency; Elizabeth had seldom seen such gentleness so forcibly exerted. "Stay and help me amuse this awful Ritzy woman—you know, she only comes here in the hope of seeing you."

"I bes' be gettin' on," Gian answered dourly. "Susie don't like it, me comin' in late."

Trevon stood back. "Yes, well, Susie's word is law, I suppose. But wait!" With his bottom against the edge of the table he looked into the reviving fire as if some message he had forgotten could be read there. "Listen, Gian, old thing, I'm not sure if you realize, this room's yours just when you want it. You don't have to ask or knock on the door or anything—"

"—Well, that's very kind—"

"—I mean, you may want it at any time. You may feel like talking to someone—it's much better to talk to someone than go on thinking and thinking over things, if you see what I mean. Even if there's only me here to talk to. And Elizabeth here, she's worth talking to, and I could always get her along." He smiled, still gazing at the fire, but he was perfectly serious. He stretched out and held Elizabeth's wrist. "She's a hell of a wise woman, you know. She knows all about her own sex and all about ours. And she happens to be bloody nice and she happens to like you just as much as I do."

Obviously Gian could not answer that: indeed, he was still in the almost cataleptic state to which the news of Empire's visitor had reduced him. He only mumbled something without meeting Trevon's eyes at all. But as he went to the door he did glance up at Elizabeth, with that same look (she thought) which he had given her on their first meeting in this room more than ten years before, a look which recalled to her the faces of young prisoners on the Salonika quay; and then, as if the invitation had come from her own lips, that anxious glance changed to a fleeting and shamefaced smile in which she saw with emotion a tormented gratitude. "I'll send a taxi round," he said, and fell into the little swagger he had kept from boyhood, nodding to Trevon in the Borough Road style and shutting the door with a jerk behind him.

"Yes, it's the one reason why I don't like him coming here. It slightly increases the chances of his meeting Charlie Empire in the street."

"Would that matter?"

"Yes. I think it's very likely that he'd knock him down. Good and hard and no nonsense about Queensberry rules. It's an act I should like to witness but there would be consequences. No, seriously, I think it might happen. He's been waiting to do it for twelve years or more."

"But he never has."

"I know—the moral restraints have just operated. But when a fellow's in a mood of despair the moral restraints do not operate. As I happen to know."

"And me. But is he in a mood of despair? What about?"

"Young Gordon, chiefly."

"What actually has happened?"

"Well, you know the child was quite out of hand—you must have seen that for yourself. Susie applied all her intelligence to the problem, but it didn't work. Something lacking in her make-up, you see—call it intuition. Dealing with that sort of child it's intuition that counts most. At least, I think so. I think Gian might have handled him if he'd been left to it, but—well, he wasn't. Susie meant him to be the strong element, the classic paterfamilias with a Lord Chesterfield voice and a horsewhip handy just in case—of course she wouldn't have put it quite like that. Well, Gian just somehow didn't see himself in the part. He's too simple to have any ideas about children except loving them—that's why I let him run Apostles' Court. So there you are. I suppose they both realized the business wasn't turning out right, but I don't suppose either of them thought it was his fault. Only humans, like us."

"Yes."

"So without saying one word to Gian she got a hundred quid off a cousin of hers—you know, that sub-Edwardian dummy who put on the wedding—and took the kid to a fashionable psychiatrist called Liedke-Urban—you've probably heard of him. About as much a psychiatrist as I am: a good, old-fashioned nineteenth-century moralist with some sort of a medical degree from the University of Leadville, Colorado, or God-knows-where and a bucketful of polysyllables picked up in a hasty misreading of Freud. Very charming, very impressive, absolutely honest, and a bigger bloody menace to society than all the confidence men within a two-mile radius of Marble Arch. You know, I'm not being nasty about Susie. After all, I've been in love with her, and that counts for something, believe it or not. But she is just that type of woman who flies to impressive quacks as surely and certainly as the cuckoo flies to the Cape."

"And this man said that Gordon was to be sent away?"

"In about nine hundred words of portentous jargon that's what he did say. And perhaps quite correctly. Only of course quacks deal with quacks, and the place he chose for young Gordon is run by a lunatic. Fundamentally one of the *suaviter-in-modo-fortiter-in-re* boys, only the *fortiter* is what is most apparent. Keeps the children segregated like convicts—parental visits absolutely barred and they're not even allowed to write home. Lectures them about the Self, the Development of the Rational Psyche, the Corporate Ethic and all the rest of the hocus-pocus till they wonder whether they're human creatures or something nasty at the bottom of a test-tube. Tells them all about the criminal strains in the stocks they come from and explains to them very kindly that they can't help being embryo criminals only they've damned well got not to be or God help them. No, he wouldn't say that, he'd say 'Liedke-Urban help them!' A friend of mine who was a very conscientious atheist was on the staff there. Got such a chill on the intelligence that he had to leave after four months—he found the place was undermining his disbelief in God."

"But Gian can't possibly realize all that!"

"All Gian knows is that his child has been taken away and shut up. And that situation he does not like and twenty thousand sensible Susies never will persuade him to like it. Because, for one thing, he's had a taste of being taken away and shut up himself."

She said very slowly—her eyes were shut: "I suppose we ought never to have let her come anywhere near him. You remember—at the Old Brompton Hospital? You made the suggestion and I backed it."

"I sometimes wonder," he thought aloud, "if it really could have been prevented."

"No," she answered wearily, "I suppose it couldn't. She'd made up her mind. Or something had made it up. We merely consented to be her instrument."

Those words provoked him in a way she had not expected. He said almost fiercely: "I don't believe that! That only leads to a hopeless fatalism. It would mean that we are creatures without any independent moral resource."

"Exactly."

"Bunkum!" he snapped. "That's the most cowardly and blasphemous falsehood, Elizabeth, and you damn well know it!"

This was the Trevon she had known first of all, and at other times she had welcomed such roughness as her patent to the friendship he normally reserved for men. But tonight she had no resilience for meeting so sudden an attack. She had imagined that the hour of helpless weakness was over, that with her nerves under control again she had been talking as calmly as on any other evening. That one brusque sentence knocked away the makeshift shores. She did not openly cry, but her head fell down onto her arms. She whispered:

"Well, that's how it looks to me."

In all their long friendship they had hardly ever touched each other except by chance; and it was curious (she afterwards thought) that she felt no surprise at what he did then: no shock and no excitement, only a grateful acquiescence. It was done very quietly. She felt his hands in her armpits, felt herself lifted as if she weighed nothing. In one effortless movement he sat himself in the wicker chair and took her on his knees exactly as a father would take his child, making with his arm against the wall a hoop on which her neck could lean in perfect comfort. Like that he let her rest, himself as still as if he were part of the chair they sat in. She had not opened her eyes, and though she stayed conscious, aware of the room she was in and of shaped thoughts calmly flowing, her senses were almost asleep.

The day's pain and despair had not gone: but in this unimagined repose, in the brown and crimson darkness, they seemed to lie in separate formes secure and quiescent as her body was; and as the weight of her body was borne by another's so her heaviness of spirit was supported upon his silence. She thought even then, It has altered, the loneliness is over, beneath the confusion there is safety. His voice when it came, so close that it seemed to reach her ears from within like the mind's voice, made no ripple upon her tranquillity.

"I hate your being so ill."

She answered a little afterwards: "Only in my mind."

"Just today?"

"I don't know." The restfulness continued, it was effortless to whisper so that he could hear. "It was silly. It was seeing that man that Empire brought in. If there's got to be cruelty, why must it strike at a creature like Daise, with everything else she's got to put up with! I've always known about these things. Only they've never got inside me the way this has."

"No. They don't until you're opened up by suffering someone else's cruelty." And after a time he said: "Has he done something particular?"

"He?"

"Henry."

"No. Well, he's going to divorce me. He's written about it."

"Because of Gordon Aquillard—all that time ago?"

"You know about that?"

"Well, I always guessed, you know." His voice was so quiet it was hardly more than breathing shaped into words. "Of course I've seen Michael sometimes."

"I don't know what he'll do about Michael."

"Poor Elizabeth!" he said. "Poor Elizabeth!"

Presently he asked: "Is he going to marry that woman who's always at your flat—Hilda someone?"

"I suppose so."

"And you—what will you do?"

"Look after Michael—if I'm allowed to."

"But if not?"

"Live by myself. Take some sort of job."

"Not marry again?"

"No."

He stirred for the first time, bringing his free hand round to hers, which he held for a moment and then let lie in his open palm as an amateur of gems would with a ruby. He said slowly:

"If you change about that, if ever you do decide to marry someone, I'd like to know beforehand. Do you think you could tell me?"

"Of course. Only I won't change."

The silences were rhythmic, his voice returning and returning was like the expected sound of small waves tumbling upon shingle.

"You know about my disease? What it is, I mean."

"I think so."

"If it wasn't for that—" the voice was strained and painful now— "I just want you to know—if it wasn't for that I wouldn't let you be alone. I mean, I'd try to persuade you to be my wife."

The silence now belonged to her, the next small wave was hers.

"It wouldn't matter to me, your illness."

"It would kill you," he said undramatically. "It's killing me—slowly and rather painfully. You would be just the same."

"That wouldn't matter."

When he spoke again his voice seemed less real; not false, but an instrument played with difficulty by one who found it too clumsy for his need.

"That man you saw at Empire's. I don't know what he was like, but that was me. No, not really as contemptible as me. I'm not making anything up, I'm telling you this because I've got to. In my case it

357

wasn't just buying something that was there for sale anyway—not to begin with. I was—in a special position. I can't quite tell you everything, it won't come out. These young things, you see—they were children, really—they came to me in trust. They came for—well, call it 'advice'. I was very good, you see, very wise, very understanding, they could tell me everything. They did, in fact. Well, those were the ones I started with. I could show you what the Sunday papers said about it, only I don't want you to go through more ugliness than you can stand. Well, when I came out of prison that kind of thing wasn't available. I had to go into the ordinary market. And when you get to the stage I was in then you require more and more exciting forms of satisfaction, and the bill mounts up. I don't mean the money bill, I mean the bill in cruelty—the recklessness with which you degrade human beings and the depths you force them down to. That was still going on after you first knew me. Right up to the time when I was in hospital. I still want it—sometimes. Only I haven't let it happen for a few years . . . Does that give you any idea of what I was like and what I made people suffer?"

"Yes, it does."

She could feel in his breathing what his words had cost and the effort he must make to speak again; as if a horse had fallen near the crest of a steep hill and was struggling to get on its feet. But she could only wait; her own voice would not work at all.

"I—I'm sorry to have given you all that. You've got enough on you without it. Only you see, I've always felt that our friendship was depending on a falsehood, your not knowing in the least what kind of person I am. That's spoilt it for me, I couldn't let it go on, however much I wanted to."

His voice petered away and she thought he would not recover it; but in a moment or two it came a little more calmly, as if a wider passage had been bored through the dam of his emotion.

"It's got to finish now, I knew that somehow as soon as you came in tonight. That's why I've told you—it's because I don't want you to come here any more. You've got to break away before you get hurt—more than I've hurt you now."

It was slipping a little, the calm voice; the stresses were falling wrongly. Like the corporal's at Monastir, she thought, the one who made jokes about incontinence when most of his stomach had been shot away.

"Of course if I was the heroic sort of person I wouldn't have told you. I'd have quietly faded out somehow, as they do in books. Well, I'm not like that. The fact is—well, you know, I suppose—you're the dearest thing on earth to me, you're practically the only good and the only reality in my life, and I'm making you go away—well, for the sake of your body and soul. It's the one unselfish decision I've made and I've spoilt that too by letting you know. It's a pity I can't do anything in the right way, but there it is."

When the stream of physical sensations flowed in again she found she was alone in the chair, while he sat on the floor near her feet. The loss of his body's comfort did not matter; even his presence in the room was hardly necessary now. In these moments, this miniature eternity, she had to bear his misery as well as her own; but the sense of liberation on which she was lifted, comparable with that of a man long and austerely chaste when first a woman shows him the whole of her body, carried even that load as well. You are freed from the narrow cell you live in only when another breaks open to receive you. Once before she had seemed to achieve that escape, but the skin of the other's selfishness had grown immediately to cover the opening. The barrier which this racked and stumbling voice had torn away would not close up again.

It is like hearing a shout, she thought, when you have been lost all night in pathless moorland. It is like the finding of another being by one who thought he was alone in animate creation. It is the stillness and serenity in which creation began.

The exaltation had no voice of its own. Only, melting the tissue of safeguards which divided the voice from the heart, it let her lesser thoughts pass into speech as easily as they flow in the channel of silence. At rest, she listened to this murmuring voice from her own lips as she would see her face in a mirror.

"Yes, it's better to know everything. All this time I've thought of ugliness and cruelty as something accidental, a few things growing out of the proper shape, like trees you sometimes see. Like Daise's head. That's how I thought about you, I thought you were all kindness with only little ugly growths."

His face and hands were grey-white. He did not stir, he appeared not even to breathe. Her voice went on:

"And I thought I was like that as well. Kindness with only ugly growths. I'm glad I've realized at last that it's always been the other way round."

He said—she just caught his words: "Not in you, no. There couldn't be ugliness in you."

"I think I'm glad because there isn't any difference. You'll let me have just that, won't you—you must let me have just that."

He said: "My mind won't tell me that."

"Tonight it seemed so hopeless, when I found there wasn't anything in myself to make up for other people's cruelty. It's hopeless now. But it's better with someone else, someone who knows it all as I do."

"Hopeless?"

"So much pain, and one relieves so little of it, so little it can't make any difference. You think that at least you're making some difference within yourself, building up some kind of value. Then you find you've made no change, there's nothing inside except the ugliness you see everywhere else. You don't get anywhere, it's a blind alley."

He moved then, putting his forehead against her knee. He whispered:

"That's when hope begins. Not till then."

"Begins?"

"Only when you're finished, when you've exhausted yourself. Before that you're only kicking against the pricks."

"I don't understand," she said; and watching the physical signs of his struggle for self-expression, the tautened zygoma, the hand crumbling imaginary bread, she remembered a sentence which someone had spoken in her hearing years before, 'They're not, men are not simple; it's an idea we have which makes men suffer and we suffer in our turn.' She heard him say in the voice of one struggling to resist the effect of morphia, to be natural and clear:

"You remember that day we went to the Tate together, the day I behaved so badly? I'd meant it to be quite different—I thought it was our last meeting. You didn't know, of course—I was going to destroy myself that night. Under a train, the way young Sippin did, it seemed so fearfully easy. Only I hadn't that amount of guts, I spent half an hour on the platform and it didn't come off."

She said faintly: "Oh, Trevon—"

"And then I sort of broke down and started praying, if that's the word for it. It was not in the least like any praying I'd done before, it was merely hopelessness and rage. I said: 'There's nothing I can do with my filthy life, and you won't let me chuck it away, so it's up to you. You can do what you like.' No, I suppose you'd hardly call that praying."

"Did it make any difference?"

"You mean, did it make me any different? No, to all intents and purposes I was just the same, I went on as usual, the Club and all that, making crazy blunders and losing my temper and cursing everyone. I found I could do without girls, but perhaps that was coming anyhow. I didn't become what they call 'a better man', you can't make a healthy limb out of one that's gangrenous all through. No, there wasn't any difference, there isn't any now, except in what I feel."

"You mean?"

"I think it's what a soldier may experience when he's half smashed-up and past being frightened, when he knows there's no more chance of living for another meal: that's when he starts to fight exultantly, because his private battle's lost and he suddenly realizes that the whole of the larger battle belongs to him."

She said: "They've told me that."

But he did not seem to hear her now. He went on groping for words, as if speech were a new and painful exercise for him. Like the men he had recalled to her, the men lying arm-to-arm in the stinking twilight of the long tents at Prishtina, this one with his head against her knees was a shabby heap of cloth and skin, used up and insignificant; as with them, only a part of him was here, the rest straining towards some view that he saw through shifting cloud; and like their voices, his was stripped of emotion, trammelled and spent:

"I wish I could explain, what it feels like to stop fighting in loneliness. It gives one's life its meaning—you can't find any meaning in a civil war that's only a procession of defeats, you've got to look for it outside. Only it's more than that. It's like what a plant might feel when it breaks the surface after winter, with its roots still in the dark soil. Do you understand what I'm saying? It's as if you were burnt alive and when your power to suffer was exhausted you felt your body turning into part of the fire itself. It's safety and peace."

"Have I spoilt that?"

"For a time. In the end nothing can spoil it."

There were footsteps on the stairs, a voice called stridently: "There's a taxi, Mr Grist, he says a fellow sent him."

Elizabeth did not grasp this: she had forgotten that there were taxis, that there were streets and people and time passing; but Trevon called in his ordinary voice: "Thank-you, Mrs Elm. Would you tell him to wait about two minutes?" He was on his feet. He took her coat from where she had thrown it and held it near the fire to warm, so that she, performing her part in the routine they had been through a hundred times, got up and held her cuffs. Then the mechanism petered out, and she stood quite still, looking gravely at his numb and anguished eyes. She said, as if there had been no interruption:

"It couldn't happen with me. I wish it could. It doesn't happen with ordinary people."

"You think it's just a part of my illness?"

"No. It's a power you've got and I haven't. I couldn't ever admit my own defeat."

"You have, to me."

"To you, yes. Anything to you."

He had dropped the coat; her glance came down to his hand fiddling at the point of his waistcoat as if with a tired life of its own, and she began to chafe it as one chafes a child's hand which the cold has numbed.

"We're different," she said. "I'm ordinary, I don't see far. I couldn't have that experience unless it came from some creature like myself."

"But it can't."

Without having to search for words she said: "I know that it comes from love. Isn't that what you mean?"

"Only from perfect love, divine love."

"Isn't human love the same?"

"No. Human love is always partly selfish, and selfishness is always cruelty."

She said: "I don't need perfection, I only need to love. I couldn't love you if you were perfect. You've told me what you are, and that's what I want. I want to know quite certainly that you'll always be as near to me as you are now."

"My heart will be. That can't alter. I can't ever want it to alter."

She brought the passive hand up to her face. "That isn't enough. I want these hands, and your voice. I want the way your mouth moves when you're shy and worried, and the smell of your clothes. I must have the whole of you, your body as well."

He took his hand away. "That's what I've been afraid of, that's why we mustn't see each other any more. I've told you—my body's not fit for anyone to touch, you least of all. It's nothing but poison."

"I've looked after poisoned bodies."

"You don't realize!" he said, with the kind of anger a frightened child shows, "you don't know what it's like, this thing I've got. It may get me paralysed all over and it may go to the brain—any time—they don't know—"

He had backed into a chair, his face was down between his knees and he was trembling. She said quietly, as she knelt beside him:

"You'll need me if that happens."

And then his control gave way.

"Need you!" He was weeping without restraint. "What good do you think you'd be when I'd given you my disease! What could you do when you were just the same as me!"

"You will need me," she repeated.

Her tears were flowing as freely as his, but to her, tears made no difference: with all her normal powers exhausted she moved and spoke, in this unimagined hour, as certainly as a homer flies upon release. With both her hands she forced up his head until she could bring her mouth to his eyes and then his lips.

"What does it matter, another illness in a body as sick as mine! What else could I do but lose my reason if you lost yours! My dear, my darling, do you think I wouldn't give as much as that for the glory of caring for you! My own beloved, my precious own, do you think there's anything better I can do with myself than give it all to you!"

From the meaningless world outside the voice of Mrs Elm broke on her ears once more. "I'm very sorry, Mr Grist, but he says he's tired of waiting. He says he wants to be paid off. Dreadful things he's saying, I don't know what neighbourhood *he* comes from!" and the arms starting to close upon her in surrender and conquest immediately fell limp again. Trevon called, "All right, I'll see him!" gently moving her so that he could get to his feet. He picked her coat up from the floor, put it unceremoniously in her hands and turned away.

It was reality that seemed unreal, as after a rough sea voyage the solid earth appears to tilt and heave. While he stood against the window-sill with his eyes on nothing in particular, his closed mouth twisting oddly, she got ready to go as on any other evening: fastened her coat, went over to the little mirror to put a comb through her hair, picked up her gloves and bag; but she seemed to be performing that routine as an actress would, obeying a producer's intention rather than her own. Sight and hearing were curious, objects about the room altered in size and level as her glance strayed to them.

Pulling himself together, Trevon said abruptly, "I'd better see that man!" and went off down the stairs, leaving her to follow. That was where she needed—in the strictest sense—his support. But the body works faithfully for those who drop the reins; her hand found the rail and her feet, feeling their way to each step with caution, brought her safely to the passage below. On the pavement a pound note had finished the argument with the driver, who was starting his engine.

"You'll be all right?" Trevon asked stupidly, helping her into the cab as he would have done with anyone else: no bending to let his mouth touch her hair, no pressure of the hand. There was something, she thought, that he tried to say, but it did not come. The street-lamp showed his grey face wearing the smile that Englishmen put on when photographers entreat them to look pleasant; he stood as still as a dummy while the cab drew them apart, an unwieldy derelict, growing, by some freak of shadow or of her exhausted senses, not smaller but immense.

Enough, the peace of emptiness, the stillness of a mind drained out; the remembered faces all withdrawn into the skirt of shadow, the many voices hushed except for his.

. . . *What it feels like to stop fighting in loneliness* . . .

The fog had lifted, the air washing her face from a broken window was clear and cold, smelling of trains. So these were real, the lighted meter and the moist, deserted pavements, the blind shop-fronts drawing away. A red light changed to green and from the dark lake silver-webbed with tram lines the Elephant rose like an island fortress and disappeared among the shifting lights behind. Had that been a dream, then, his tears, the roughness of his skin against her hands? Enough that the glowing warmth of it remained: *safety and peace.*

Climbing to that high country, breathing easily an air too rarefied for her lungs, he had left her far behind. But the sureness of his ascent seemed to be nothing beside the certainty with which her own spirit was filled, knowledge transcending reason, contentment hidden beyond the reach of fear, her first and full awareness of love's furious power.

These faces emerging in the band of light where her car waited for a van to pass, the woman who leant on her man's arm as if it was a balustrade, a trio of young men vacuously laughing, did they know love? *The only good, the only reality:* from a spirit wrapped in the feverish warmth and stillness of that returning ecstasy her pity flowed to them like sunshine on to frozen fields, creatures whose hearts must be blessed by the mere passing of one so enriched as hers. *The dearest thing on earth to me,* his preciously familiar voice suddenly broken beneath an emotion she had not imagined in him: so full a tide of sweetness would not be contained within one being, it gathered in possession the dark, deserted city, weaving from the shadows upon a yellow blind, a scarlet café-sign, the tumid figures of a lighted hoarding, the mysterious tapestry of love. Some imperfection lingered: he should be here, surely, where she might feel his hands and rest her cheek against his coat: something had happened which would have to be recalled. But the doubt was too far off, too weak to penetrate the motionless depth of love's security. The grey wall ended, in the silken black arena hedged with fragmented light a red lamp ran toward her like a falling star and vanished below her feet. She all but slept. She heard faintly through the hiss of tyres on wet macadam the raucous voice of someone singing, the sad face of a girl in evening dress appeared for an instant close to her own. But loneliness itself, she whispered, smiling from the darkness of the cab, is only an illusion. When the houses stood back again she smelt faintly the trees in Vincent Square.

 She knew, with the signs of morning creeping in, a paleness showing below the curtains, the rattle of a lorry in Brompton Road, that the first redoubt had yet to be taken. With his own love bound by selflessness outside her comprehension he had refused to surrender to hers. But when I have made him know my heart, she said, he will be blinded by his pity to the pity I feel for him. The reading-lamp was on, she was lying on her bed fully dressed with the finished life surrounding her, the photographs, Henry's letter on the chest of drawers. She had given something to the driver, she supposed, and brought herself up in the lift. She did not remember having slept.

 It is settled, she thought, there is no more misery of doubt about the country ahead. Upon the dark screen of pain and fatigue the outline of her mission was drawn now with an architect's thin, clear lines: no picture of a home's mellow contentment, tenderness broadened and deepened by succeeding years of close companionship; no fancy even of his weakness supported by her strength; only a grinding partnership of pain, the dreadful watch upon a man sinking into decay by a woman who struggled more and more hopelessly, against her own enfeeblement, to stave off ultimate collapse. And for what reward? She did not even believe, unless it was possible to believe at second-hand, in the transcendency on which his life was centred. Knowing so much of herself she could not imagine that her power to understand him would increase or that he would grow more open to her understanding. Denied the enrichment which other lovers find in sharing freely the past or the future, she could love and serve him only for what he was today.

The chink of cup and saucer, the soft brush of the door against thick carpet. "Oh, Lucy, did I frighten you! . . . Yes, I was feeling rather poorly when I got back, I'm all right now . . ."

With that she was satisfied. His outward roughness and the gentleness that escaped in his hands and voice, his sudden, private smile, even the agonies of his self-distrust, these her memory would cherish when they were lost in his dissolution. These were the blooms which love could gather and keep; and she had seen beyond them a preciousness which the grossest of his imperfections could not pollute. That mysterious value, belonging covertly to human spirits, intensely to his, depended neither on the body's wholeness nor finally upon the mind's. For what was left of her power to give and suffer she needed no greater object than this: no smaller could be enough.

The room, suddenly opened to grey daylight, seemed strange and foreign; the locked air, the sterile memories which haunted costly furniture, bore heavily upon her forehead, where the taxi's motion still worked like a clinging tune. With the opening of a window the noises of the town's recovered energy were starting to infiltrate; the lift-gate rattled for the first time and letters splashed into the corridor outside. Presently the telephone would ring.

"No, Lucy dear, no breakfast. But I'll be up in a few minutes. Yes, really, I'm perfectly all right."

It would lift, this weight of lethargy, she would be able to see people, talk, make decisions. It did not matter being so weak, and in such pain, when the new fire burnt so brilliantly within.

29

WHEN tea was over, the children who had come to celebrate Antonia's eleventh birthday were coaxed and shooed into the front room, while the grown-ups were led upstairs to the bedroom. "Gian will do all the organizing that's needed," Armorel said to Duffy, "he's wonderful with children." She was in her blue-grey velvet dress, six years old but so skilfully altered that it did not look out of fashion: indeed, it seemed more distinguished than Christine's afternoon frock, which Heurtel had made for her a month before. It was, of course, exactly right for the room, where the dismantled bed and the washstand had been screened off, and where her skill and taste had worked so shrewdly that you scarcely realized how absurdly small it was for eight people to sit in.

But Guy Filliard, Duffy's eldest boy, was the one who began the organizing downstairs. At tea his shyness had worn off alarmingly, and now, when his host suggested hunt-the-slipper, postman's knock, dumb-crambo, he shouted, "Oh, bosh! Girls' game—sloppy!"

"I know one rather good game," Michael Kinfowell began. "You start by getting into pairs—"

"I know—sloppy!" said Guy. Without malice he picked up a cushion and hurled it at Michael's head. "How's that? Out—middle stump! Bowler's name, Filliard, G. Listen—keep quiet, all of you! (Ned, you take this and slosh anyone who speaks.) We'll have try-by-ordeal, we play that at Torrage House. It wants hundreds of chaps, really. These girls will have to do as chaps. You start by getting into two lines: all except you—fudge-face—you're going to be Criminal. Come on, you others—two lines!"

Arthur Augustus Liske started to cry. He did not know what a criminal was, but instinct told him there would be no fun in being one. He had a bit of a headache, Arthur said, and would rather like to go to Mummy.

"Eats too much!" Guy shouted, and certainly Arthur was a little over-fleshed. "Ned, just slosh him a bit!" Guy said to his willing brother, adding rationally, "Then he'll see it doesn't really hurt."

"I don't think it's a nice game," Alice Derby said.

"Nor do I," said her sister.

"Perhaps I'd better be Criminal," Michael suggested.

Gian intervened. "Might be a bit too rough, that sort of a game.

367

Not much room in here, see what I mean. There's a game I know on, now, where you got to make the noise of an animal."

Guy gave him a glance of fury. "We'll have just ordinary sloshing, then. Got a snitch-rag, anyone?—we've got to blindfold one of the girls and then she points and the one she points to gets sloshed."

"Now see here," Gian persisted, "I want you all to get in a ring, see."

"This one," yelled Guy, pouncing on Muriel Derby. "Gosh—pinko, she's a wriggler! Get the snitch on her, Ned."

" 'Ere now, easy, that's enough of that! Get into a ring was what I said. Come on, now!"

"Slosh him, Ned, get on his legs!"

With some bravery Alice intercepted the small but bellicose Ned, seizing one ankle and holding it with all the strength of her thin and crooked body. "Mum wouldn't like it," she whimpered, "Mum said particular we was to behave nice with the boys."

The golden prospect of the party had filled her thoughts for three weeks past, and now, with her satinette frock already torn, she longed to be with the friends she could see through the window. In this august and alien room there were Muriel, and Mrs Bodwin's Elsie, and Tommie Ede from the shop: the rest outlandish strangers, except for Tonie Ardree herself, and to be so close to Tonie, object of trembling adoration, centre of exquisite shy dreams, was in itself an experience too rich to be borne for long.

"Coo, havin' a fight they are now!" The minute but virile son of Hull the plumber had got his elbows up on the sill outside, his nose pressed against the window. "Coo, he got on to Muriel, the big shiny, he's goin' to strangle her with his bloodstained snooter. Cor, doin' her in a treat, got her eyes protrudin' out like balls o' lard—pop!—there go one on 'em, woosh, rollin' about the fumin' floor!"

But his friends could see the show well enough for themselves: the Lanchester which the unteachable Raymond had brought to save himself the indignity of a short tram-journey was standing exactly opposite the window, and not fewer than nine of the younger inhabitants of Weald Street were on its roof, yelling and gossiping. "Alice—don't she look a masterpiece in that get-up!" "That's only what her auntie gone an' cut down for her." "Look like a fumin' duchess, if you ask me." "He don't look right, Tommie Ede don't, with nothink on top of his braces. Oughter have a scarf or somethin'." "Them? Them all come outa Buckn'm Palace!" "*Oy! Tom-eee. Had y'r eats yet?*" While those who had failed to find a place or had got shoved off were holding each other up to the window-sill or creeping into the front passage to have a squint by turns through the front-room keyhole. "See y', El-sie! Owsit go, Tom-boy? Got any eats left over? *Goo on, Mure, you hit him back, you plaster him, he ain't nothin' but a fumin' shiny!*"

"Yes," said Christine upstairs, sensuously fingering her fox stole, "it did sound like Arthur Augustus—not the last howl, the one before that. He always blubbers at parties the moment I leave him, poor sweet. Mother-fixation or something. So psych-whatisit! So vulgar and endearing!"

"Of course you know really Guy is most terribly sensitive," said Duffy, warm and smiling under a hat like one of the earliest aeroplanes. "Entirely different from Ned—Ned's just his father all over again, he's practical, always doing something with his hands. You really ought to see the pipe-rack he made for Gruff, exactly how it said in *The Young Handyman* only with cardboard instead of wood. Only Gruff never can remember to use it, poor darling. And you know he's quite fast for his size—of course Gruff's *hoping* to make a sloshing wing three-quarter out of him. Rellie darling, I do think it's just marvellous of you to give all these kids such a wonderful tea. And this house and everything, I always tell Gruff, I say it's exactly like finding a superb oasis in the very middle of the ocean. What a shame Elizabeth couldn't come—I suppose it's all the worry that's knocked her out. Such a sweet boy, Michael is. I suppose she won't be out of hospital for weeks and weeks. Tell me, has Gordon settled down all right at his new school? It all sounds terribly original and fascinating from what you said in your letter. Does he write to you every week?—Guy's wonderful about that, I get some sort of a letter every Tuesday in term-time, only of course not always terribly legible, but there's always the crosses at the end, he never forgets those, he's awfully sweet and good about it."

"No," Armorel said, "they don't allow them to write home."

Without appearing to take her eyes away from Duffy, she was casting lightning glances to assure herself that Simon had somewhere to knock out his pipe and Maria someone to talk to, that Raymond was not too bored, that Georgie had not been squeezed into one of those chairs where you couldn't keep your skirts as far down as an old lady liked. She did not so much dominate as pervade the room; her small, graceful gestures, the sweetness of her voice and smile seemed to bring the whole of it into the gentle radiance that is imparted by skilful lighting.

"You see, they work on Liedke-Urban's principles, which means they do everything to avoid the *drangvoll fürchterliche Enge* of conflicting influences. It's when you have the parent-love impulse and the man-fellowship impulse working on the undeveloped mind *at the same time* that you get an overload, and that means that something's got to snap."

"Oh," Duffy said. "Oh, how interesting."

"Yes, I do feel that I'm rather lucky about Gustav Leidke-Urban —the great thing is that he does let me see the whole process on which he's working. Of course he has to deal with a great many parents of the slightly unbalanced kind, religious repressives and Dartington sentimentalists and all the rest of them, so I suppose when he does find he's got someone of—well—slightly higher intelligence to work with he rather enjoys not having to beat about the bush, if you see what I mean . . . Yes, Daisy, what is it?"

Wearing a muslin apron for the first time in her life, Daise stood half-inside the door, staring at the carpet. "It's Mr Olleroyd, Mrs Jan, says he wants to help dry up."

The smile that played upon all Armorel's guests was spread to warm Daise as well.

"That's very kind of him."

"Only it's perks he's after. There's the rock cakes not touched, he's got his eye on them."

"Of course, yes! I hope he'll share them with Brodie." As the door closed again Armorel turned to Raymond. "Daisy's not quite herself today, poor thing. I think she's worrying about her father—he's had some sort of accident and they've taken him off to St Thomas's . . . Georgie, dear, are you comfortable in that chair? I'm afraid it's all a terrible squash. You know we're looking out for somewhere to give us a little more elbow-room. Of course I personally shall be sorry to leave this house—"

"—So original!" said Christine with her ready kindness. "So bijou!"

"—You see, I feel we made it ourselves, and it's full of memories. Only Gian feels he wants something rather more substantial, and it doesn't do for wives to be a drag on their men's ambitions. Madre, *did* you get enough tea—there was such an uproar I couldn't look after you properly!"

"If you felt like living in Coventry you might buy Mummy's house," Christine suggested, "the one she had with Roger. I know she wants to sell as soon as her lawyers have hoofed Roger out of it."

"Coventry must be an interesting place to live in," said Duffy, who was trying to pick out Ned's voice from the uproar below.

Christine was visited by her *chapeau-de-poil* smile.

"That's what Mummy used to think."

"But at this time of year," Raymond said to Maria with the laboured courtesy which induced a nervous depression even in the strong-minded, "you must often long for the sunshine of your native country."

"Aeh? Yes. But no."

Swaddled in layer after layer of bombazine, fastened in the low wicker chair by the weight of her own rolling flesh and of the occasion, Maria kept absolutely still. Only her eyes darted towards Raymond's face like those of a trapped mouse, and swivelled guiltily back to Armorel's.

"The ole lady got used to London," Simon explained. "Ain't y', Maria?"

The tangled voices from below and from the street were suddenly overridden by a burst of sound directly outside the door, the ripe and volleying voice of Mr Brodie: "Come on, Olleroyd, you old two-faced double-crossing devil you! It was two teapots I did, and they were the damnedest, and that was two more of them tiddling wee bloody cakes you said, on the Book you did!" Then the puffed voice, the little angry squeaks of Olleroyd were beaten down by the blast of Brodie's triumphant laughter, a plate went crashing down the stairs to destruction and the agonized voice of Daise rose from the last tinkle: "There now —just look at what you've gone an' been an' done!"

"My cousin's always been so fond of Italy," Georgina said helpfully. "He used to travel a lot when he was younger. Only now he's so busy with his politics and things. I think it's so nice when foreigners come and live with us. Only of course we don't think of them as foreigners any more. When they live with us, I mean. And these passports and things, it must make it all so difficult."

"Maria here never had no passport, m'm," Simon said.

"Oh. But then there's so much to enjoy in travel. I always wanted to travel myself, but I never seemed to have time."

"Two and a half times round the world I've been, m'm."

"Oh!" Georgina was a little faint from the stresses of the afternoon: the dreadful silence of Edith before she started, taxi-drivers grumbling over their tips, a hot and noisy tea, steep stairs, and now the feeling that many gigantic strangers were pressing in on her with complicated speeches. "Then you must have finished in Australia or somewhere like that. So wonderful and interesting. And then of course people go in aeroplanes nowadays." Aeroplanes, she thought, and the men who steered them were called pilots. Like Miss Wilberforce's nephew, only he was a sea pilot. And it was Miss Wilberforce's other nephew who had married and gone to New York. "Rellie!" she called, "—no, don't let me interrupt you—only I've just remembered who it was who had the jumper that might do for Tonie—it's a Mrs Lancaster. I've got the address written down beside the telephone—it got burnt in one of the elbows and she had to mend it with green wool because she hadn't any blue." She turned to Maria again. "It is difficult, isn't it, with wool! Do you think that Tonie's like you? I think she's got the wonderful colour of your eyes. You must be just as proud of her as—as my sister and I are. And the last time I saw little Gordon I thought he had a look of you, Mr Ardree. His mouth, I thought it was."

"Gior-done?" said Maria unexpectedly. "Tsey lock him up!"

Simon said quickly; "Well, you see how it is, Gian take it a bit hard, it go against his feelin's, that's natral. The ole lady don't mean no more than that, do you, Maria?"

But Maria was already back in her shell, her frightened eyes on her daughter-in-law.

"It might be you could say a word, m'm," Simon pursued in a cautious undertone. "Some time when it's no trouble, see what I mean. Might be you could put it the way it might sound all right, the way I don't have the use of the words without no proper schoolin'. Course, she got a very fine headpiece, my son's missis. Only he bein' my son, see—an' Maria's here—it's natral I can't put up with seein' him all down an' mucky in his mind, see what I mean."

Armorel's clear, soft laugh rippled across the room. "Oh, Duffy darling, you mustn't be so sentimental! *Of course* she doted on Tonie, Sunday-school teachers are *like* that. That's why she was so dangerous."

"Yes," said Georgina with her affectionate smile, thinking that Simon's grave eyes had become rather beautiful with age, that Maria must have some inner loveliness to inspire so steadfast a devotion, "I'm sure he's going to develop into a splendid boy in the end. Isn't he, Raymond!"

Raymond, after a second or two, answered firmly: "I've never had any doubt about that!"

And whom or what was the old dear talking about? he wondered. But he gave her the smile which he kept for very few, for he saw at that moment, completely unchanged, the one woman who thirty years before had been simple enough to understand him and to bathe his wounds with her selfless kindness. It gave him pleasure just to watch her face, on which a lifetime of subservience, of petty anxiety and self-distrust had worked as greater sorrows work upon stronger spirits, imparting to the clear skin of her cheeks and forehead the beauty of use and wear, enriching the gentleness of the recessed, Cepinnier eyes. For the moment his embarrassment was submerged. The ordeal of reaching this abhorred street, of meeting people outside his routine, was over. In the next few minutes there was nothing for him to do but to sit and smoke, to feel the ease and distinction of the suit his tailor had lately built for him, exchange the smallest conversational coin with people whose minds were as sluggish as his own. It made so much difference, having Georgie with him; his own kin and almost, as he felt now, his own generation; a failure like himself, another offshoot of sinewed stock which had somehow deviated into feebleness. Her presence drew his thoughts and senses comfortably back into the past: to summer holidays at Standle Minster, the breeze which moved on the hottest afternoon under Villier's elms, the smell of hay; back to the only London he really cared for and still vaguely hoped to find again, the different smell of fog in augustly sleeping squares, a Chancery Lane of tall hats and men darting to scoop up the horse-droppings, everything that started from the schooled pomposity of Dimber's voice, 'The carriage has arrived for Master Raymond.' Yes, as likely as not those brats downstairs were using his Scott hat for charades, while the urchins bawling outside were adding some thirty per cent to the normal depreciation of his motor. Yet beyond this proscenium of noise, beyond the grimed and meanly uniform windows on the other side of the street, he thought he perceived some afterglow of an early possession, a gigantic and pervading presence which soothed his timorous spirit. The chintzy smell which generally hung in this room was hidden today by a strange entanglement of odours, something exotic which Christine wore, the must of Maria's clothes; but from the open window there came now and then the subtler breath of the street, air that never wholly escaped, flavoured with damp smoke and ancient dust, stained with the very colour as it seemed to him of this city's yellow-dun complexion. The little table on which Rellie had arranged the flowers so beautifully was always trembling a little. Some new distraction sent the mob outside scampering up the pavement, and as a lull fell upon their cries he could hear through the mesh of jerry-built walls the low reverberation of traffic flooding all the knotted veins of Camberwell, the distant, continuous hubbub of trains: a fabric of sound so thickly woven that it had the quality of silence, movements so multifarious and persistent that their total effect was like repose. It belonged to him, after all, this most indestructible of men's creations, this bewilderment of brick and smoke in which he could never find his place; it was dearer to him, surely, than to Simon here, who stank of its dust. Some of his forebears had built these very streets, some whose names still showed in the wharfs by Greenwich Reach had brought the wealth of India and the Indies here in their wooden ships; and in Georgie's quietness, the gracious light that flowed from her eyes over Simon and Maria, the unstudied dignity with which she sat on the cheap bedroom chair, he saw a calm defiance not only of their present surroundings but of the cheapening wrought by time. There are spirits, he thought, and not only the bravest, which reassure us when we are frightened; and then, wondering why his mind should throw up that word, he seemed to catch for an instant the smell of sodden turf, a fleeting view through November mist of the skyline of Grosvenor Place. What was it this Mrs Filliard had said about Elizabeth being ill? *His* Elizabeth, did she mean?

"Is Mrs Ardree here?" The small, red face of Mr Brodie was stuck in the narrowly opened door. "I wouldn't be bothering you, Mrs Ardree, but I'd like you to know it wasn't me at all that had the plate broken. It might be Olleroyd would say I took it off his hands, and in God's holy truth it was all the other way."

Unruffled, Armorel broke off her conversation with Christine to answer: "Yes, Mr Olleroyd's always the smarter of you two when it comes to a scrap, isn't he! Aunt Georgie, I don't think you've met my co-tenant, Mr Brodie—"

That was enough: as abruptly as it had appeared the face vanished and the door was shut again. And who, Raymond reflected, could handle every situation as deftly as this cousin of his whom he still thought of as scarcely more than a child! Here, surely, was evidence that however much the Truggett strain had weakened in himself its sap was still potent in later shoots. Nodding politely to Simon, who went on and on about some technicality in stage carpentering, murmuring, "Remarkable! . . . I never realized that . . . Yes, it must call for extraordinary skill . . ." he kept her just within his view. How unperturbed she was by the tumult from below, how little trouble this party seemed to give her! She had noticed the miserable shyness of her sister-in-law, caparisoned like an old-fashioned trollop and dumped rather than seated on a Cromer's Ride chair, and had steered her adroitly into conversation with the kind Mrs Filliard. She was paying a sisterly attention to Christine's prattle and yet contriving to give encouraging smiles to Simon, a glance of affection towards Georgie, as if the simultaneous exercise of several personalities put no special tax on her resource. Like a musician, he thought, watching the little fluid movements of her delicate throat and chin, seeing how unobtrusively she turned her chair a trifle to bring Maria within command, how while Mrs Filliard's hands were always fidgeting with hair or dress Rellie's lay still: like a pianist from whose body the chords appear to flow so directly that one scarcely credits the intervenient mechanism of hammers and strings. Her voice was almost the quietest in the room, yet its very gentleness so held his senses that he hardly missed a word she said. Had civilization achieved a more perfect flower than this, a creature whose rarities of form and understanding were used to respond with fragrance alike to the choicest and dullest of those who came within her field? And had this woman, still young, discovered what the saints seemed to achieve and what he himself was for ever fumbling after, a way of living richly without the need for any intense relationship? For there, he thought, was the only security: to be independent of particular affections, to accept the kindness people were ready to give but never to hazard one's contentment in a vessel so exposed to wind and tide as the heart of another being.

"Most interesting!" he said to Simon with unfaltering urbanity. "And I suppose you find theatrical life quite different in some ways from life aboard ship?"

". . . Syrup of Figs," Duffy was saying. "Yes, I know it's most frightfully old-fashioned, but Gruff just won't approve of psychiatrists, and one must do something."

"I think that children nowadays crave for excitement much more than we did," Georgina said wisely but with diffidence. "Of course there used to be those air-raids when they were born. I suppose they miss all that."

"So monotonous!" Christine said harmoniously. "So unsettling!"

Maria, bursting free from the toils of shyness, said abruptly: "Air-aits? Hn! Mist Mar-shall, gelman conducse tram, Mist Mar-shall buy itse grant fiasca fis air-ait!" Her head jerked uncontrollably, there came as of old one frightening crack of laughter. "Now he have not one hair lef!"

The scuffle and hubbub from the front passage was amplified as the door opened and the embarrassing form of Daise appeared again.

"It's Mrs Eustace, Mrs Jan. She want to take off the bits of that plate Mr Brodie threw at Mr Olleroyd. She say she know a fellow as can mend it up. I tell her she can't have 'em, not without you or Mr Jan say she can, an' Mr Jan said I was to ask you."

For one moment Raymond saw the lines of Armorel's mouth hardening. But before she spoke she was smiling again. "Really, you know, Mrs Eustace did promise she'd stay out till six! I'll see her presently." And her voice fell back into its former softness as she turned to Georgie: "You know, Gian's so terribly tender-hearted about Mrs Eustace! I suppose *one* day the poor old thing will find somewhere else to live."

In the front passage the invaders were chanting in chorus:

> *"When their guts an' their bellies*
> *Are full up with jellies*
> *They'll* CHUCK *'em all over the plice!"*

"I do hope the noise doesn't worry you, Aunt Georgie."
Duffy, thinking of ringworm, said: "They all sound very happy."
"So uninhibited! So *quatorze juillet!*" Christine said.

Perhaps it was merely the starched collars and muslin frocks, but these children all seemed to Gian so different from the ones at Apostles' Court. Still, he had got most of them into some kind of order at last, Arthur Augustus had carefully dried his tears with a silk handkerchief and even Muriel Derby had stopped crying. Except for one or two rebels they were all in two recognizable circles on the floor, and the lean, overgrown Evangeline Hugg, blindfolded, was reciting once again in her high, nasal sing-song:

>*"And you and you*
>*By two and two*
>*Upon the field of Waterloo.*
>*One—two—three—* change over!"

They did not very strictly observe the rules. Tommie Ede in mounting excitement did a change again and again when Evangeline's finger pointed nowhere near him, using each change as an opportunity to barge his opposite number or blow down someone's neck. Tonie's round and rosy school-friend Marigold had formed a compact with Elsie Bodwin and they did a private change each time, both turning somersaults and getting their legs entwined, till the Derbys were impelled to join them and the floor became a tangle of brightly coloured knickers, legs weaving like antennae and red, inverted faces spurting hysterical laughter; while tiny Audrey, Terence Hubbitt's child, who had been slightly sick, lay with her head against Evangeline's legs and refused to change at all.

"I hope this doesn't bore you," Tonie said as she changed according to Cocker with Arthur Augustus.

"Oh, no, it's very interesting."

"Now you, Tom Ede," Gian shouted into the din, "you're gettin' too many turns an' no mistake! Come on now, back to places for the next change! Somebody different do Boney now—what about you. Master Ned? All right, you, Alice Durby!" Longing for the masterful presence of Flock, he wiped his forehead with his sleeve and put on the resolute grin again, while Audrey Hubbitt in a startling access of personality jumped on a chair and blew a tickler into his ear. "Now can't we have it just a bit quieter, for the sake of one an' all!"

Above the new crescendo of laughter the voice of Tommie Ede rose like an engine's whistle: "Cor—see what she done to the ole basket?"

"Well, I say she didn't ought!" came the voice of Alice in protest. "He's Tonie's dad, he's payin' for it, after all!"

"There are some what ain't never learnt how to behave!" Evangeline agreed.

In one bound Tommie was on top of Alice and pushing her paper cap down her neck. "Who d'y' think you are!—Don't talk s' daft!"

"You leaver alone!"

"Tommie, please, *please!*"

"Now, see here, Tom Ede!" With a careful movement of his powerful leg Gian hooked the boy away; he stooped to pick up Muriel, who had broken again into sympathetic tears, and covered her head with kisses. "Somebody see what's in my pocket!" and as they leapt upon him in a pack to seize and scatter the bull's-eyes, and got him down and rolled him about and sat on his head, his anxiety turned at last into happy laughter. "Goo on, Audery, have a tug! There's one of them ears still stickin' to my pore ole face!"

"Cor!" the outside audience yelled delightedly. "They got the ole bloke now, they're going to do a murder on 'im, they're tearing' out 'is bleedin' lights!"

"Uncle Gian is really most kind," Arthur Augustus said to Tonie. "I think these children are enjoying themselves a great deal."

The Filliards cared for none of these things. They had found that a small space between the wall and the end of the piano gave just enough room for Catchpole's questions, and in Michael Kinfowell, fair and slender, high in forehead and with rather dreamy, long-lashed eyes, they had recognized an ideal third man. Michael, whose approach to parties was quietist, had politely fallen in with their suggestion, and they had him upside down, his head and shoulders on the floor and the rest of his back supported by Armorel's sewing-machine, one leg pulled over and hooked under the piano's keyboard, the other held by Ned. Ned put most of the questions.

"What are *all* your mother's Christian names? . . . How old are you in *hours*—answer in one minute! . . . Time up!"

"Sloshing Number One!" said Guy in his businesslike way. "Heads or tails, Ned? Tails it isn't—my slosh! Wait a mo' while I roll up my sleeves."

"How long does this go on?" Michael inquired.

"No questions!" the Filliards shouted in chorus, and Guy explained: "You don't *ask* questions, you only answer them. Do you think, Ned, one extra slosh for asking questions? . . . Well, I think it counts as part of my turn, really."

"O.K. Then I have the first double-slosh that comes."

"O.K., lieutenant! Put a half-Nelson on that leg, will you, we'll want his shoe for the double . . . Right away!"

"Question Number Eight—Dr Catchpole wants to know: What is the feminine of 'My fathers wash a man'?"

" 'My mothers wash a woman.' "

The Filliards fell into a paroxysm of mirth. "Did you hear that, you scarks? He says his mother's a washerwoman!"

"Now don't you lads be hurtin' each other!" Gian said over his shoulder.

"Actually I didn't say that," Michael put in mildly. "The sentence I said hadn't got an article before 'wash'."

"What's he saying, Ned?"

"He says he hasn't got an article."

"Well, that's rude. *Double*-sloshing for that!"

The rest were wholly occupied in competing for three extra bull's-eyes with backward somersaults, and there was no clear evidence that Michael was at all worried with Dr Catchpole. Alice Derby did wonder that any mortal should suffer no hurt in being so incessantly belaboured with all the force two sturdy youngsters had at their command, but she supposed that a boy enjoyed this sort of thing. Only Tonie, looking round from the border of the larger scrimmage, saw that his face was over-red and his mouth held shut in a way that did not look quite natural.

"Hang on to that leg, you chump!" Guy barked. "He's trying to escape."

Ned hung on.

"If you don't mind," Michael said modestly, "you are hurting my leg just a bit."

"One more sloshing!" yelled the brothers in triumphant chorus. "Super-slosh for sissy talk."

"No!" said a voice behind them. "You're to stop that."

Without looking round, Guy took his stance for the next slosh. His wrist was seized.

"I said 'Stop'!"

"Girl Guides on the warpath!" Guy remarked.

He jerked his hand free, completed the super-slosh and turned round to face the interrupter with a bright, glinting smile. Then he scarcely knew what happened, only that something crashed against his face with the force of gunpowder, that he was in momentary darkness and then howling on the floor.

"Here now! Here now! What's all this?" Gian demanded, disentangling himself from the mob of little girls.

"I should like to show you where I sleep," Tonie said to Michael; and he, brushing his jacket, followed her submissively out of the room.

It was rather a formidable journey. Daise and Olleroyd had driven some of the invading children back to the street, but in the passage there were still half a dozen of the most tenacious, Reg from the horsemeat shop and Pete Roberts in his surgical boots, Maxie Aaronsohn and the two Wischnewskis with their baby sister, ripe, dirty and down-at-heel, insolent without ill-humour, avid without optimism for any scrap of drama or of food: they were all round Tonie the moment she stepped outside the door, shouting, *"Tonie, Tonie, lean an' boney, had her milk off the parsin's pony,"* "Cor, ain't she the Captain's Cuddle, reel art silk, I reckon!" and "Git us a bit o' coike, To-*nie!*" The foot of the stairs was blocked by the huddled and tearful form of Mrs Eustace, who wanted to explain that she had never thought of stealing the broken plate, while Daise, nervous and overwrought, kept saying acidly: "I tell you it's what I get my money for, looking after Mrs Jan's things!" "And that she does, by Paul 'n' Barnaby," Mr Brodie was jeering from the landing, "an' puts the half of them in her own small tricksy tum!" But as nimbly as a hunter Tonie maintained her course, holding in her skirt, gently using one shoulder and then the other as bowsprit, saying, "Hullo, Pete! . . . Hullo, Maxie . . . Good-evening, Mr Brodie! . . ." with the hovering smile that was so like her mother's and yet completely her own. "Ollie, do go and comfort Mrs Eustace," she whispered to Olleroyd, who stood against the linen-cupboard in the top passage with the countenance of Lear, "and tell Mr Brodie if he goes on like that I won't bring him anything for his ferrets." Outside the front room she paused, smiling faintly, and beckoned Michael to listen to Raymond's mellifluous rumble: "I agree with you absolutely, my dear Mrs Ardree, I entirely agree!" Then with a certain air of conspiracy she opened what looked like the door of a cupboard and led him up a narrow companion ladder, bidding him close the door behind them.

"You'll have to sit here on the bed," she said. "That stool's wobbly —Grandfather made it. This room was quite tidy this morning, only I left it too late to change for the party and I had to just throw everything down. Gordon used to sleep in that hammock arrangement. He's been sent away to have his character put right or something, he was always getting bored and breaking windows and things. Do you feel too cold up here? It's as cold as an iceberg when there's snow—the snow comes in sometimes—and when it's hot you get baked alive. But it's very nice to have a room of your own, I think. Have you got a room of your own?"

"Well, I used to have. That was in my father's flat. Only I don't think we're going to live there any more. I'm living with a sort of aunt person at present. My mother's in hospital."

"She isn't dying, is she?"

"Oh, no. She has to go to hospital rather a lot."

"That's Aunt Elizabeth, isn't it? She comes to tea sometimes. We don't go to her because Mummie thinks our clothes aren't right for the West End."

"Women worry about clothes," he agreed.

"Mummy worries about lots of things. So does Daddy, only he does it in a different way."

"I like him very much. He's rather like the master who teaches us gym. To talk to, I mean."

"He's perfect," Tonie said. "I think your mother's frightfully pretty."

"Yes, she's rather perfect too."

"Do you know what you're going to be yet?"

"Not exactly. I had an idea I'd rather like to be an intellectual—or do you think that's atrociously feeble? Of course I haven't really got the brains anyway, I was right down to fourth in maths last term."

"I should think it might be quite a good thing to be. I suppose you've never been in a room like this before?"

"Well, I don't think I've been in any girl's room. I don't really know any girls. Of course you don't see any when you're at school."

"I don't know many boys, except poor ones. I mean, poorer than we are. You can't get to know them really because they're always rushing madly about. I suppose you think girls are rather atrocious?"

He reflected for a moment, examining the one before him, the dark hair and large eyes that were like her aunt Rosie's, the Romneyan delicacy of nose and cheeks which she had from her mother: this was veritably what 'girl' (as opposed to 'schoolgirl') meant to him, a mystery of softness and slenderness; and yet as she spoke to him, from so close-to, the settled strength in her face made her much less a girl than a person. He answered:

"Well, no—you see, my mother was a girl, of course. That's rather what I go by. I say, it was frightfully pleasant of you to interfere with those Filliard people. They weren't hurting me really, you know. It was only a bit tedious."

"Well, they were enjoying it. That's really why I biffed him."

"I was wondering if he'd expect to be apologized to. I could do it, myself—I could say you were scrapping on my side and came in a bit harder than you meant. I just thought, from the point of view of it being a party, and him being a person who's been invited—"

"Well, not now, anyway—I'd rather you stayed here for a time. Unless you're feeling bored? No, I don't think he ought to be apologized to at all, he's such a skunk. If boys were all like that I'd never marry anybody."

"Well, I really don't think they are. We've got some people at school who are very civilized indeed."

"Yes, I thought there must be some of those." She swung up her legs to lie full length with chin on hands, feet in the air, and studied his face with quiet interest. "They'll probably turn out like Daddy."

"Oh, yes, probably." If he was embarrassed by her scrutiny he did not show it at all. "I suppose you will have to marry sometime? I mean, judging from what happens in books. I read a certain amount of rather advanced books—I've got to take School Cert next year and they set Jane Austen and that sort of stuff. It looks in them as if girls always get over-persuaded in the end. Or do you think that's only in books?"

"I think girls do, but I don't quite know how. I don't know if you know what happens when people are married?"

"Well, more or less. Of course there are people at school who know, and they rather spread it about."

"Well, in London here everybody knows it from more or less the time when they know anything at all. That's what strikes me about being married. All that would be simply atrocious with anybody you didn't really know."

"Yes, I can see that."

"In London," she pursued, "they make jokes all the time about kissing and that sort of thing. You get so used to it you hardly notice, only I think it's rather niffy."

"Yes, it's bad taste."

"There's a boy down the street who works in a barber's in Grange Road with beastly sneering eyes, he tried to kiss me once. Only Gordon was coming along and he carved him up. He went at his legs and got him right down and hammered him. Gordon's rather formidable when he gets an idea like that."

"Yes, he must be marvellous. So you haven't been kissed by anybody—except your parents and people? Or perhaps I ought not to ask that."

"Well, I haven't, as a matter of fact. I suppose I will be when I feel like it. I'm not sure when that is, I suppose about sixteen. That's five more years. But then it would have to be somebody very—well, you know, intelligent and clean."

"Yes, of course."

"I suppose we ought to go down again, as I'm hostess."

"Yes, I suppose we ought."

Tonie wriggled round onto her back and let her feet slip down to the floor. She said:

"I've enjoyed this conversation awfully."

"It's been delightful," he answered. And then embarrassment came. "Oh, there was one thing I thought of asking you. I mean, it just occurred to me. You were saying about when you get to sixteen. Of course I shall be a bit more than nineteen then. I may be more civilized than I am now, or possibly not. I was only wondering if I could see you then, and then if you found you'd got to the time when a person does want to try what it's like—being embraced, I mean—you could see if I might possibly be the sort of person. Or do you think that's a feeble idea?"

She considered it. "No," she said, "I think it's a sensible idea."

The door below them clicked and Olleroyd's voice, burdened with the double weight of phlegm and secrecy, came up the ladder: "Tonie! Your dad's calling after you!"

"Thank you, Olly! All right!"

As they passed the bedroom door again they caught Duffy's voice ". . . trouble about being in the army is that they pay you practically nothing . . ."

"That's Guy's and Ned's mother," Tonie whispered, "but *she's* quite all right."

Michael answered: "Yes, I know her. She is really a frightfully valuable person. You know, she was the one who introduced your mother to mine."

". . . Only it doesn't really matter as much as you'd think," said Duffy, "because you've simply got to spend a certain amount of money, because of the prestige of the regiment and all that sort of hocus-pocus, and if you've *got* to spend it, it doesn't make a fearful lot of difference whether you've got any or not. I'm afraid I haven't expressed that frightfully well—Gruff always explains it much better than I do, he's been a P.R.I. and he's got a marvellous head for money matters. The way Gruff puts it is that every bob you spend on gin is one bob less for the bookies. I think it's really the same as what one used to learn about Ricardo's Principles. Or am I thinking of Mill on Liberty?"

"I think it's Mill on the Floss, actually," Christine said, "but I do see exactly what you mean. It's like us. Everard says we're on the very verge of bankruptcy the whole time. So agitating."

"The whole thing," said Armorel gently, "is to scale things down to what you've got. Even if it means not going about with people you've been used to going about with. What hurts is trying to keep up a façade that you can't really afford."

Duffy said: "Yes, that's exactly what I was trying to say. Rellie darling, I do wish I could put things as neatly as you do."

"Does that mean," Raymond asked his cousin, "that if I could find you a decent, small house in somewhere like Putney or Ealing you wouldn't take it?"

Armorel nodded. "Definitely not! S.E.1 is where we fit, and I shouldn't dream of going anywhere else."

"But you know," Georgina said timorously, "there are parts of Putney which are really quite nice."

"Yes, Georgie darling, that's just the point. We can't afford to be quite nice, and I'm not going to try."

"But how funny," said Duffy, "that's almost word for word what Elizabeth said about her and Michael the last time I saw her."

"Elizabeth?" There was the faintest trace of gall in Armorel's smile. "I shouldn't have thought money was exactly one of Elizabeth's troubles."

"Well, it is now. She doesn't know in the least how much Henry will—oh—oh, didn't you know?"

A quietness fell upon the room like that of the moment when gunfire is first heard by civilians in the path of an invasion. Duffy, reddening, threw a scared glance at Georgina. Jerked out of his normal somnolence, Raymond began talking at high pressure about his recent visit to Kew Gardens. Armorel caught hold of Duffy's arm.

"Oh, Duffy, I've just remembered. I wanted to show you that painting of wallflowers that Tonie did at school. I've got it over here." Her voice fell. "There isn't anything gone wrong, is there? Not with Elizabeth and Henry?"

Duffy said in a flurried undertone: "I thought you'd know, it's been in some of the papers. That man's an absolute devil incarnate, he's actually raked up that old business about Gordon Aquillard, and—"

"Gordon? I don't quite—"

"Well, it's not because of Michael exactly, because apparently they can't bring that into court for some reason, but they *can* bring in one time when it happened in London." She stopped short. "Rellie, you do —you did always know—?"

Georgina ceased pretending to listen to Raymond. She had heard no word of Duffy's, it was only instinct that made her lean sideways to look past Raymond's arm and, seeing Armorel silent and perfectly still, rise and go swiftly to her side.

"Rellie! Rellie darling, are you feeling all right?"

To Raymond, staring across the room with an old woman's curiosity, it appeared that Armorel did not want to answer that question. But in a moment she had thrown off that curious hesitance.

"What? Oh, yes, Georgie dear, perfectly all right." She turned to Duffy, "Yes, of course I always knew," and then to Georgina again. "I did think it was rather stuffy for a moment, these windows don't open the way they should, nothing really works in this awful house." (Just the usual thing, Raymond supposed. Stuffy?—he himself had been incommoded by a damnable draught. Had something gone slightly wrong with her voice, or was it merely a fluffiness in his ears?) "You know Elizabeth Kinfowell—I must have told you about her, such a sweet woman. Duffy's been telling me—it's terribly sad—Duffy says she's having a wretched time in hospital. She's been ill, you know. Elizabeth, I mean. I really should have done something. I must remember to send her some flowers."

Well, that was over, or all but over, Raymond thought with satisfaction when he had packed Georgina into the front seat of his car and the Ardree grandparents into the back. True, he was not going to make the clean escape he had planned, for some fool had stuck a large saloon in front of his and the children sprawling right under his rear bumper made it impossible to reverse. But the sense of an appalling duty faithfully performed made him care-free to the point of heartiness. "Now you young people will have to move just a bit—otherwise you'll all get squashed into sausages . . . My dear," he said to Armorel, "I have never enjoyed an afternoon so much!"

Internal and external parties had finally merged, a strange medley of satin frocks with the robuster dress of Weald Street moved in tempestuous eddies between house and pavement, swirling up and down the stairs and flooding all across the road. The mothers of Weald Street were massing upon the fringe, children were caught and hugged and immediately raced back into the throng, a few of the guests made positive efforts to get away. "Thank-you so very much, Aunt Rellie, it was most kind of you to have me." "A most lovely party, darling." But the larger part of these civilities was lost in the unabating tumult of shouts and screams. The lustiest of all the yells came from some distance up the street, where Guy Filliard lay on his back beneath a group of hostile residents whom Ned was furiously but vainly assaulting with feet and fists; and while old Janet Veal, still lively from her four-o'clock refresher, was bellowing unseemly comments from the upper window of 29 a barrel organ in front of 24 filled every gap in the uproar with the limping harmonies of *Tea for Two*. Appalling, Raymond thought, when this was only one of ten thousand streets, when all these squealing brats would turn into people demanding food and employment, every one with a separate pride and loneliness, all falling in love and expecting what no lover could give, betraying and cheating each other, using the oldest, tested means to raise a new crop of miseries. Yet it appeared to him, just then, a friendly scene: if he could but forget what he had learnt about decent behaviour and respect for other people's belongings, about bacilli and hygiene in general, he might almost enjoy it himself. He stood patiently in the roadway, every inch a cultured suburban, tapping one foot to the organ's tune, giving way to shy and sentimental smiles, repeating, "Now come on, my dears, you'll be quite as happy on the pavement, come on, little girl—hell damn and blast the little beasts—come on, sonnie, just onto the pavement, come on, be good lads and lassies—O my God, are they all deaf or merely cracked! . . ."

In the doorway, as fresh and soignée as when the party had begun, Armorel was serenely smiling. "It's been lovely to have you . . . It was sweet of you to come . . . Good-bye, Tommy! . . . No, of course you didn't upset me, dear—what nonsense!—I'm only so terribly sorry for Elizabeth. . . . Good-bye, Marigold! . . . Yes, Elsie, you can tell your mother you've behaved very nicely . . . Good-bye, Arthur dear! . . ." A young man whose grey overcoat was as foreign to the street as Raymond's came up to speak to her. "Yes," she told him, "this is where Mr Ardree lives . . . Good-bye, Evangeline!"

And who the devil was that? Raymond wondered, catching sight of the newcomer with half a distracted eye and getting fussed as he always was by the unexpected: the fellow looked like a dun. He went back to the door, calling "Can I help, my dear?" and heard Armorel saying:

"No, my husband was attending a lecture at University College last night, he came straight home from there."

"Can I do anything?" Raymond foolishly repeated, and the young man turned to him.

"Oh, good-afternoon, I think you may be able to help me. There was an accident last night at No. 3 Bidault's Place. A man named Empire—I think you know him—he fell from the top landing where the banister was broken."

This was a little much for Raymond. To the nightmare of din and scrofulous children he had become acclimatized, accepting it as one of those preposterous realities in which he was sometimes strangely involved. But this: this young man popping up from nowhere—respectable accent, clothes nearly as good as his own, the type they let into his club nowadays—this almost-gentleman appearing out of the pavement like something at Maskelyne and Cook's and talking undiluted gibberish—

"Bidault's Empire?" he said. "What's that, a music-hall? My dear sir, do I look like a man who goes to music-halls! Or a man who goes round breaking banisters!"

"This isn't my husband," Armorel said. "Here is my husband now."

It was not the kind of young man which is embarrassed by small mistakes. He said pleasantly: "Oh, I'm sorry . . . *You* are Mr Ardree—Mr Gian Ardree? I believe you were at Number 3 Bidault's Place a little after nine o'clock last night?"

Gian said: "Yes."

"Well, I should be so glad if you could spare a few minutes to come to Damien Street with me—I've got my car here. Inspector Audwin thinks you may be able to give him some helpful information about a man called Empire who died in St Thomas's Hospital this morning."

"Empire?" Gian said. "Charlie Empire? Died?"

Armorel said, "But, Gian, you told me—" and stopped. "Well, if it's the police and they want some information, you'd better go."

Gian said nothing more and did not look at anyone. Bareheaded, and rather like one walking in his sleep, he followed the young man to the waiting car.

Raymond said to Armorel, "I don't quite follow, it's rather curious, all this."

And she answered: "There's always something curious in this part of the world . . . Good-bye again, Chrissie darling!"

Tonie asked: "Mummie, where's Daddy going?"

"I don't know."

"Can I go too?"

"No . . . Good-bye, Michael. Give my—tell Mother I hope she'll be better soon."

To Raymond's dismay, Georgina had got out of his car again: astigmatic and lame with corns, she was picking her way through the excited children on the pavement. She came and caught hold of Armorel's hands.

"Rellie dear, there's some trouble, isn't there? Darling, you must go in and sit down, you're looking so tired!"

"No, Aunt Georgie, I'm perfectly all right . . . Oh, Duffy, you've got them at last. I'm so glad! Good-bye, my dear, it's been lovely having you. Good-bye, Guy! Good-bye, Ned."

Then, however, she did let Georgina and Raymond take her upstairs and settle her in an easy chair.

Michael, lingering, whispered to Tonie: "There isn't anything wrong, is there?"

"No, I don't suppose so."

"You know I'd do anything in the world if there was—always."

"That's frightfully dear of you, Michael."

But really there was nothing wrong that anyone could see; no change, at any rate, which Raymond could observe from the window upstairs. If Armorel's absence from the scene made little difference, Gian's made less: this city was too large and too well occupied to notice the coming and going of one or two people. The day, he thought, had weakened; there was gaslight showing at some of the windows; but the children tearing round his car in a crazy skirmish between Tommie Ede's gang and Leslie Hull's were still yelling at the tops of their voices, and as the organ jerked into an altered stride they started to bawl out the words. *Ai want—ter be happy, but Ai—can't be happy, till Ai've—mai dew happy too!* The saloon in which the young man had arrived was already out of sight.

"I can't think why he didn't tell me!" Armorel repeated. "Why do people hide things? Why couldn't he just say he'd been to Bidault's Place?"

It was strange that Georgina's voice, squeezed so very small, still carried all its mellowed colour and warmth. "But, Rellie, Rellie my precious, I do feel certain of one thing—whatever happens you must go on loving him."

The voice answering was numb with weariness. "Georgie, it only muddles things, everyone talking so much about love. How can you love people when they're trying to deceive you? You've got to start by understanding their minds."

Mai dew happy too! moaned the voice of Weald Street.

Raymond said miserably: "Their minds? But, Rellie, is there any hope of understanding that? Do we let ourselves be understood?"

Yes, I thought, watching the light appear on the other side of the street, listening to that terribly familiar voice of Raymond's and searching the knotted undergrowth of his thoughts, we prisoners for ever demand from each other, in both understanding and love, a little more than any has to give. Subsisting on each other's wealth we get back only what we have given away ourselves; the air our spirits have exhaled comes round to be breathed again, and they must perish by degrees from asphyxia unless we can cut a vent towards some new supply.

The hubbub was subsiding at last, letting the city's profounder voice roll back, its pulse be felt again. They heard distinctively a newsboy crying the Late Night Final in Bekkipore Lane, and intermittently, from over towards the river, the comforting drone of trams.

". . . I know there's something I haven't done. Tonie's school bill, I left it somewhere, I think it's somewhere in the kitchen, I think it must be under the clock . . . Yes, Georgie, really! I was only a bit tired, I'll manage perfectly now. I'm almost sure it's under the clock. You know, I can always manage things, I always get along all right by myself."

PART FOUR

30

ONLY TWICE have I witnessed a trial at the Central Criminal Court. Although those two occasions were more than six years apart they have, at this distance, become so much superimposed that my memory is confused and I cannot be certain whether particular features belonged to one or the other. I remember them, in fact, almost as one protracted and miserable experience. Both cases were heard in Court I. Or were they? The Court looked exactly the same each time. I know I turned to the right at the top of the stairs. Well, I am almost sure about that. What I recall most clearly about both is getting a splitting head and taking an unprecedented number of aspirin tablets.

No, I am not one of those who frequent law-courts for amusement; and I do not visit them often for professional purposes, as some of my fellow-tradesmen do: I prefer to get someone else to give me any details I want. Fascinating, of course, when you get a good man in action, which is not invariable—as a rule counsel look to me like nothing more than carefully laundered little men who have been paid so much an hour to perform a part from a rather amateurish script and would be howled off the stage in any second-rate provincial theatre. With a good advocate, of course, it's quite different: even if he does not convince you of his sincerity you watch a highly subtle intelligence being used at full stretch and, in a curious way, concealing the fact that it is intelligence, disguising brilliance as that common sense which is what the jury looks for. Yes, I can almost lose myself in watching such virtuosity, as advanced amateurs of pianoforte technique will sometimes be so absorbed by a pianist's hands that they hardly hear what he is playing. Yet I never wholly enjoy the sensation, and afterwards I feel a little unclean; because one is continuously—however faintly—aware that behind this ballet of dialectic, this bloodless decorum, reality is hiding. By 'reality' I mean men and women experiencing sensations and emotions—which is all that reality does mean.

It's like being shown round the operating theatre in an up-to-date hospital. Nothing in the world so clean as that, so far removed from the grime and turbulence of life as most people know it: the immaculate walls and burnished chromium, silent mechanisms, lights pitched to cancel every shadow, the glass shield fixed to the gallery so that bacilli in the students' breath may not infect the sterilized air: and while the gentle voice of the theatre sister goes on explaining the marvels another voice whispers, 'Presently there will be a living body on this table, a blade will cut deeply through the tissues, blood will flow out and the body may die.' I was pleased, on both those visits to the Old Bailey, by the decency of the Court's interior design. I enjoyed the judge's decorative robes and the archaic tra-la-la which opened the proceedings, I liked the equally significant dowdiness of the jurors and the way His Lordship established friendly relations with them, the practised courtesies, the little private smiles between court officials and police. But wherever you are sitting you cannot forget that someone is in the dock, and even when it's as clear as day that the man is an unmitigated rogue you cannot stop thinking that something in his face resembles your own. It must be an abnormal person who does not murmur, 'There, but for the grace of God . . .' whenever he turns his head that way.

I have tried to refresh my memory from newspaper cuttings—there are dozens of them which I have kept in two box-files—but it is strange how little they positively stir it. Well, perhaps not strange at all, since the writers had other objects. There are the sober reports, which aim at bringing all the untidiness of cross-examination into a familiar shape where the process of logic can be discerned; and there are 'stories' (the right word, I think) from papers with much larger circulations, in which the writers' object was to extract and inflate such morsels of dramatic nourishment as they could detect in a scene wholly lacking in dramatic bravura. Of the second class, the treatment of Mrs Empire's appearance in the Court is an adequate example. Here, obviously enough, were the makings of a throb for the public pulse, and the cross-title writers have not neglected so plain a duty. *Widow Faints in Court* is the most temperate version I can find, *Sickbed Cry for Justice* is among the more imaginative. In the corresponding texts it is stated that 'Deathly pale, and anxiously watched by Harley Street specialists, the bereaved woman was carried into court by three hospital attendants,' that she was 'haggard and white-faced' and 'gave her evidence in a broken and trembling voice . . . twice losing consciousness and having to be revived.' In fact, as I do clearly remember, she came into court in an invalid chair pushed by a St John ambulance orderly; the court surgeon was present, and the court matron. She was not paler than anyone else would be who had lived indoors for years and I am fairly certain that she never fainted, though she did shut her eyes now and again from fatigue and possibly boredom. For the rest, she was sufficiently composed, and I fancied that on the whole she was rather enjoying the experience. Her evidence was somewhat difficult to hear—you do not expect an old, invalid woman to speak with the voice of a town crier or of Demosthenes—but it was unemotional and in my judgement remarkably precise. She described the quarrel that had taken place at her bedside between the dead man and the accused with sufficient assurance to give me, at any rate, a vivid picture of the scene, though she seemed unable to say what the quarrel was about. Cross-examined by Etchard Davies with gentleness but with no real lenience, she never wavered from her assertion that she had heard the accused leave the house, banging the door behind him, 'at least a minute' before Empire had left her room; and she gave an equally simple and convincing account of how she had heard the sound of her husband stumbling "like as if he'd caught his foot in some't', Your Worship," then "a sort of a splitting noise," then a single cry and "a long time after, so it seem to me" the sound of his body crashing at the foot of the stairs. There was nothing of the scared and anguished widow in all this: it was like listening to any old cottage woman telling a parish visitor how her little boy has had a tumble.

At the other end of the scale, I remember the surgeon's evidence in that case as being far less cut-and-dried than the more dignified reporters have represented it. According to a highly reputable provincial paper, 'The Witness stated that in his judgement the injuries in the neck, which were recent injuries, could not have been caused by a fall alone.' Actually this witness, who was an elderly, nervous and admirably conscientious pathologist (the type that is a bugbear to all but the best counsel), refused to commit himself to any such dogmatism. His halting sentences, always slightly corrected before they were finished, were exceedingly difficult to follow; but the gist of his evidence was that the injuries taken with his own examination of the broken banister rail and experiments carried out with dummies, had enabled him to make a credible reconstruction of the way in which the body had fallen, and that *if that reconstruction were accepted* the injuries to the neck must have been caused by some other means than the fall. In this instance the reporter has done his best to represent the evidence within the space allowed him; obviously he could not describe the witness's personality, his lisp, his fumbling, his corrections and caveats; and without that complete picture one is bound to get a wrong impression of the force of the evidence given.

The same thing applies to the more sedate reports of Swift's summing up. The account in the Manchester *Guardian,* considered as a précis, could hardly have been bettered for skill or fairness. What it lacks—what any written account must lack—is Swift's tone of voice, the utter honesty which we saw in his face, in the very set of his shoulders, while he was talking to the jury as one very wise and experienced man would talk to a group of sensible ones:

". . . Now this is the question which I think each one of you ought to ask himself: 'Supposing I was in a *very good job,* a very responsible and *interesting* job, and supposing a certain man had got me sacked from a very dull and poorly paid job twelve years ago, *twelve—years—ago,* would I—for that reason—go to that man's house and take hold of him and throw him down from the top of the house to the bottom? If I were in my right mind, and perfectly sober, *would* I do that?' Because that is what the prosecution has suggested to you that this man did do, and the case for the Crown as far as I am able to understand it very largely depends on that suggestion. And then—listen—there's another question which I think you should ask yourselves . . ."

Read the admirable Manchester *Guardian* report, which renders those sentences in *oratio oblique* but hardly condenses them, and you may still wonder why the jury arrived so quickly at their verdict. But if you had actually witnessed the change in his voice when he arrived at that passage, the significant pauses, the little, serious, confiding nods, you would not wonder at all.

The reports I have kept of the more recent trial I attended, the one which took place early in 1939, seem still further removed from the reality, and I find it hard to believe that they are recounting an event

I saw and heard with my own senses. (It's rather like hearing the adulatory speech which someone makes when you give away prizes at a school; you find yourself wondering who it is that the man's describing.) For the sake of interest I made a shorthand note of the cross-examination of Olleroyd, putting down what was said as nearly as possible verbatim. Here is an extract:

Mr St Anscar (schoolboy face, exaggerated Balliol voice to cover his nervousness; already exasperated): Now can you tell us what sort of relations existed between the deceased and her husband in the week before her death?
Witness: Uh?
St Anscar repeats the question in exactly the same terms.
Witness: *His* relations?
St Anscar: No—er—what I mean is, how did they get on together, as far as you could observe?
Witness (*wearing the expression of one sitting on a time bomb; wiping his face and brushing down his ragged moustache as if he feels it immodest to reveal his mouth to the Court*): Well, I mean to say, I mean, I known him since he was nothink more than a nipper, see what I mean—
The Judge: Could you speak a little more clearly?
Witness (*terrified*): Uh?
Clerk: His Lordship wants you to speak more clearly.
Witness: Uh?
St Anscar: Could we have it a little louder!
Witness (*in a voice so loud that it alarms the Court and himself*): I never done no speechmakink. (*His voice falls instantly to its former pianissimo.*) Mean to say, he never treat her anything but all right, by what I see, Lordship. Been good to me, as you might say. Give me a home. Both of em, I mean. Terrible thing that was, I couldn't rightly credit—
St Anscar (*slowly, clinging for dear life to his patience*): Now listen, all I want you to tell us is whether the way they behaved to each other altered during the last few days of the deceased's life?
Witness: Deceased's wife?
St Anscar: Life! L—I—F—E, life.
Witness: Well, I mean to say—
St Anscar: Did it or didn't it?
Witness: Didn't what?
St Anscar: Did it alter?

Witness	(*after several false starts, and after being soothed and skilfully prompted by the judge*): Well, I mean, I reckon—seeing how he wasn't in the house, a lot of the time, well, I reckon they was much the same as they always been, didn't seem no difference, not to me, only y'see, he never been what you might call a talkative man, nor her neither, come to that. Course, I never did see much of *her* relations, not but what an auntie she had come to see her, I do remember—
The Judge:	So what you're telling us, Mr Olleroyd, is that you didn't notice any change in the way the dead woman and her husband treated each other, or spoke to each other, during the last days of her life?
Witness:	Ay, that's what I been saying to that gentleman there. Lordship. (*Everyone relaxes, and one of the periodic fusses occurs. A juror goes out. The judge assumes the expression of a taxi-driver waiting with his flag up. There are discreet whispers and the passing of papers. People hurry in and out. I have the fleeting notion that I have been attending a rehearsal and that the producer has gone out to take a telephone call.*)
St Anscar	(*a little later, exhibiting a 'Mexican' knife*): Tell me, have you ever seen this before?
Witness:	Seen what?
St Anscar:	This.
Witness:	Well, I—well, you see how it is, it come on you with getting old, see—done a lot of close work in my time, as you might say—young chap at the shop said I could have them back in a week or ten days, see, them spectacles I give him—
The Judge:	Mr Stubbs, will you please pass the exhibit over to the witness so that he can examine it carefully.
Witness	(*after examining the knife for a long time, as if he expects to find a secret drawer in it; disdainfully*): Why, that been hangin' round for long enough. Over the chimney, that's where I always see that. (*The public gallery stops coughing. The jury become a little more attentive.*)
St Anscar	(*palpably aware of drama; clearly, but with studied casualness*): You mean a chimney at Number 83, Mickett Lane? The sitting-room chimney, yes! Do you happen to

	remember when you last saw it in its usual place above the chimney?
Witness:	Can't say I do.
St Anscar:	Recently?
Witness:	Well, I mean to say, there's always plenty of things alongside where that always has been. She use it as a place to put things, see, a lot of the chitties what come in, bills an' that—
St Anscar	(*with precision; using, as it were, his second barrel*): Do you know who is the owner of that knife?
Witness:	Uh?
The Judge:	Who does the knife belong to?
Witness:	Well, y'see—Lordship—well, o' course my memory don't hold as well as it did, I seen this knife, you see—well, I seen it a long time back, back in Contessa Street that was, time I lodged with Mr and Mrs Ardree. Well, I do remember he tell me—Mr Ardree—as how he got it off a Dutchman, or maybe a Norwegian, I can't rightly recollect, being as it's so long back—
St Anscar:	Just one minute—which Mr Ardree are you talking about?
Witness:	Why, that would be Mr Simon Ardree—he having been a sailor-man, see, it's natural he get about rubbing shoulders with all sorts, as you might say—
St Anscar:	Yes, yes, but this Simon Ardree, what relation was he to *Gian* Ardree?
Witness:	Well, that would be his father.
St Anscar:	Simon was Gian's father?
Witness:	Well, sir, still is, as far as I know.
	(*A nervous titter somewhere, and "Quiet there!"*)
St Anscar	(*patiently*): And Simon Ardree was at one time the owner of the knife?
Witness:	That's right.
St Anscar:	And did he within your knowledge give it to anyone else?
Witness:	Uh?
St Anscar:	Do you remember him making a present of it to anyone else? Did he ever say to anyone, "Here's a present for you, you can keep this"?
	(*The witness mumbles something with his hand in front of his mouth.*)
The Judge:	Mr Olleroyd, will you please try to speak clearly. Some of us in this court are rather elderly and we don't hear very well. Will you just speak slowly and as clearly as

	you possibly can. Perhaps you'll repeat your question, Mr St Anscar.
St Anscar:	Do you remember Simon Ardree making a present of the knife to somebody else?
Witness	(*suddenly letting out a nervous laugh*): Well, now, did he or didn't he, that's just what no one couldn't rightly decide!
St Anscar:	I really must ask you to control yourself! I asked you a very simple question.
	(*The witness is petrified, and it looks to me as if he is going to weep. He drags out his enormous parti-coloured handkerchief and wipes his face and neck as if he had just finished shaving. Clutching fiercely at the edge of the box he fidgets and twists like a child caught stealing apples. The spectacle of so old a man—and one not without an elephantine dignity of his own—in so abject a condition infects the Court with a general nervousness. There are shuffling and coughing, and a woman is led out from the public gallery.*)
The Judge	(*with extreme gentleness—but with a quick, dirty look toward St Anscar*): Just take your time, Mr Olleroyd! No need to get flustered—you've done very well so far, very well indeed.
Witness	(*abruptly, after a further period of silence*): Lordship. It wasn't any business of mine, d'you see—I've been a friend of the family these twenty year or more, very kind they've been to me, taking it all the way round as you might say, it wouldn't be any business of mine to put in on what can't be agreed between themselves. Well, now, take what the trouble was about this knife. Mr Ardree, you see—Mr Simon Ardree—he look up and say "Why, that's my knife you got up there!" see, and Mr Gian Ardree, he says, "Go on, Dad!" he says, "you give me that a long time back!" he says.
St Anscar:	When did all this happen?
Witness:	Well, I couldn't rightly say. Round about Christmas, that would be. Yes, well now, Christmas Day it might be, seeing how Mr Simon Ardree come along for his Christmas dinner, and then him sitting in the chair there, with just a small glass of port wine they got for him, and him lookink up over the chimney—
St Anscar:	Well, then, you think it definitely was Christmas Day?
Witness:	That's what I was saying.

And so on. . . .

The more exuberant dailies found material suited to their needs in that small-time interchange. I find that 'Family friend weeps in Box' and that there is some dark significance in a 'Knife of Foreign Origin'. Olleroyd's fumblings and mumblings are described as 'Furrier's Dramatic Evidence', he is reported to have said in moments described as 'tense' and 'before a hushed Court' that 'I owe the Ardrees everything,' that the knife, 'Most Treasured Possession of Dead Woman,' was 'Father's Christmas Gift to Son.' Working on opposite principles, the *Morning Post* summarizes the passage thus:

'Herbert Olleroyd, a retired tailor, gave evidence that friendly relations had existed between the dead woman and her husband up to the time of her death. He recognized the knife as one which had been kept as an ornament in the house where the tragedy occurred.'

I do not see how anyone could quarrel, except pedantically, with this last summary. It gives as concisely as possible the relevant facts which emerged: what it omits is immaterial, or almost immaterial to the issue. I only suggest that this illustrates how small a part of human experience is contained in what are commonly accepted as 'facts'. (When one says 'the fact of the matter is . . .' one only means, as a rule, 'the operative element in the situation is . . .') My transcript of the evidence can be examined in exactly the same way, and if I judged the *Morning Post* account to be omissive so I should judge my own. I have given with almost photographic accuracy what Olleroyd said. I have left out almost the whole of what he meant, although any attentive observer might have read a great part of it in the aspect of the man himself, in the hundred nuances of expression and gesture which even a painter of genius could only hope to convey by a long series of portraits made in succeeding moments. Here was an antiquated specimen of humankind, long since run to seed in body and reason. Here also was an honest man. He had read the Oath not in the formal or the stumbling, scared fashion of most witnesses but with great deliberation. I am certain that he was determined to tell the whole of the truth, as he understood it, despite what must have appeared to him the deliberate barracking of a clever young gent in fancy headgear. It did not occur to him that the Court really required only a particular kind of truth, or a limited portion of it: 'truth' for him meant everything he knew about the subject under discussion, and all the small details floating into his sluggish memory, odd sentences he had overheard, thoughts which had passed through his mind at the moment when he heard them, seemed to him to be part of its essence. One read that in the movement of what are called 'the poker veins'; one saw it in the agitation of his flabby hands, in his sniffing and mouthing and moustache-wiping, the dullness drifting through his irises as clouds pass across the April sky. I experienced no small sympathy with St Anscar; he had the limits of the Court's patience to reckon with, and no case would ever be brought to a conclusion if witnesses who were asked if they had ever been to Brighton were allowed to give a full account of all the days when they hadn't. All but a hundredth, perhaps, of what Olleroyd wanted to tell the Court was of no use to the Court whatever. And yet I felt that what he was trying to say (and could not have expressed in a hundred years) was not without its intrinsic value. In a depressingly unreal milieu where all the rest were on Sabbath behaviour, wearing so to say the uniform of their functions, correct and disinterested and a trifle bored, he in his undisguised simplicity made us think of values outside the narrow cognizance of this tribunal. His self-contradictions seemed to be symbolic of the conflict of human purposes, his sprawling body and recalcitrant clothes a demonstration of men's non-conformity with the tidy processes of formal reasoning. Here, in place of 'the thoroughfare to which m'learned friend has referred' was Mickett Lane itself, rancid and seedy but exhaling a warm breath, betraying through chinks in its commonplace exterior a huge entanglement of vital privacies. Those others, I thought at the time, represent the mechanics of morality, working smoothly enough. This decrepit creature reminds us of what morality is about.

Yes, my picture of Olleroyd sprawling over the front of the box, damp and husky and curiously immense in relation to his surroundings, has remained sharp enough. And I remember very clearly what the elderly judge looked like—so different from Swift in appearance and behaviour. A man called Cuddish, this was, whose career they told me had been an unusual one and who was best known for his work in earlier years as a Metropolitan magistrate. Where Swift's manner had been direct, man-of-the-world, this judge's was oblique and philosophical. I recall how, during his summing-up, his eyes constantly strayed away from the jury and found a resting place somewhere above the prisoner's head. He seemed, then, to be thinking aloud; I even had the impression that he was still feeling his way with perceptive caution towards his own conclusions. (Absurdly, I can remember scarcely a word he said, and should have to go to the *Times* report for it.) Not, I imagine, a good performance considered forensically: it is a judge's business, I suppose, to simplify arguments for the unlearned, not to lead them through a maze of half-tones. But again, my own feeling was one of peculiar gratitude; not only for the spontaneous pleasure of watching so delicate a mind at work, but because he appeared to be aware of a duty outreaching his immediate functions, an obligation towards truth itself. As the case went on I had felt a kind of weariness and desperation because, however good the intentions of these people, the actualities of human behaviour as I knew it seemed to be perishing beneath their expert vivisection. As one witness followed another, laconic or voluble, embarrassed or over-confident, honest within the ambit of their understanding, it had seemed to me that the machine which cut away the dead wood of their evidence was also destroying the living tree. Cuddish, if my impression was right, realized this: however little it concerned him as a lawyer, he knew that men's motives are not composed of a single strand, that between willing and not willing the dividing line is broad enough itself to be many times divided. To detect that recognition in his slow and careful sentences eased a little my uncomfortable sense of taking part in a superfluous and sterile parade.

But mostly it is the insignificant and often ridiculous things which memory retains. The man beside me had a pencil sharpener which he put on the shelf in front of him—I suppose it was a life-long habit—and at least three times he knocked it on to the floor with his wrist: I remember the large, neat darn which showed in the seat of his trousers when he dived like the ducks in St James's Park to retrieve it, and the wounded look in his eyes each time he returned to the surface. I remember a witness in a spotted scarf, a George Belcher figure, who kept saying as if it were a lucky formula 'Do it m'self—any day!' and always followed this remark with a bustling sniff which made the judge glance anxiously over his spectacles. Then there was a woman juror with a head like a Toby jug who spent her time whispering to the sallow, city-faced man who sat beside her refusing to take the smallest notice; and another juror, a little man of the back-door salesman type who sat slightly apart from the rest with his hands in his trouser pockets, whistling softly between his teeth and proclaiming with his detached, contemptuous eyes that none of these people were going to influence *him*. Did he belong to the first or the second of those two trials? It does not matter, and yet I am vexed that my memory will not work more tidily. Why should I remember the frivolous circumstance that on the first occasion I was wearing a brown suit and was worried because the waistcoat was rather ostentatiously cut? What was there worth recalling in a female witness's ponderous remark, "Two o'clock it was, as sure as sure, I heard the door bang, only you know how it is with clocks!"? Many such snippets return as vividly as if I were playing over a phonographic recording, but I cannot find the faces to which they should be attached; and those which belong to the second trial do not help me in trying to recover precisely the main current of my sensations when I heard them, the curious feeling that some previous experience of my own was being symbolically enacted before me, that the playing was desperately amateurish and the emphasis all wrong. It was not a mere breeze fluttering the surface of the mind, that nightmare sense of frustration; several times it was almost powerful enough to bring me to my feet. I wanted to call out, "Can you wait a little, please, there's someone else who ought to be heard, she's not so far away, I'm certain she can be got at somehow!" But the witness I wanted to summon was not to be brought within that court's jurisdiction.

The foremen of both juries stand before me stereoscopically: the one a cosy figure with a face that shone like a wet pebble, owner of a small drapery perhaps, pathetically anxious to perform his office without discredit; the other a sad and scholarly man who had bought his dark suit off the peg a long time before and who looked as if all life's chances had passed him by while he was discussing their possible flaws. It did not seem possible that either of those men was going to utter a sentence of such supreme importance to the man in the dock; and when the moment came for it, on both occasions, the artificiality which all these proceedings wore for me reached its highest point. This, I felt, is a crude sketch with understudies put in to read the lines until the principals arrive. On each occasion some minutes had passed, and I had the hubbub of the street about me, before I said to myself, 'Yes, it has actually happened, that was the thing itself.'

No one, I think, was at all doubtful how the shiny little draper would answer when the question was put to him: with Swift's analysis of the case for the Crown almost literally echoing in their ears, only a jury of certified lunatics could have reached a decision different from the one he had to announce. In the second case, according to my friend Paulet Shield who was present, there was a measure of uncertainty among the cognoscenti: they felt that the very length of time which the judge had devoted to examining every apparent weakness in the prosecution's arguments might have given the jury a wrong impression of what those arguments were worth. The time which the jury took to reach their verdict goes some way to support that view. But during their long absence there was never, I believe, any doubt in the depth of my own mind what the man in the shabby black suit would say when they returned.

By that I do not mean that I felt no tension when the question was put: a man must have peculiar or practised nerves who avoids that. And the moment of waiting for the reply, which must always seem a long one, was almost intolerably protracted by a special circumstance. The foreman proved to have an impediment in his speech.

The judge, glancing towards him in a curiously shy fashion (as I thought), asked the familiar question in the quiet voice of one business man to another: "Do you find the prisoner Guilty, or Not Guilty?" The foreman opened his mouth and it stayed open as if a fish-bone were stuck in it. Nothing came out.

I saw somebody's fingers doing a slow, stiff dance on the desk in front of him, like the fingers I had once seen of a man whose head had been blown clean off. A woman in the jury buried her face and at the back of the Court someone tittered. The judge, of course, betrayed no embarrassment whatever: he wore the calm of certainty, his part was virtually finished. Only, out of intrinsic courtesy, his eyes turned away from the foreman's struggling face, and in doing so met the prisoner's.

My glance turned that way as well, though not very willingly; and then it appeared to me that there were two people, not only one, who were quite untouched by the small wave of hysteria passing through the Court. That face, the prisoner's, was motionless; not with the stillness of stupor but with Promethean patience. There are people who make a livelihood by standing on a platform twice or more every day and having a cigarette knocked from their lips by an artist with a stockwhip; they know that once in a way the artist will not be in perfect form, and the whip-end which is like a white-hot needle will touch their mouth or cheek. Those people have a peculiar, professional face; and that was the face I looked at now. One other thing I saw, a glance which passed between the prisoner and the judge, swift as the touch of a bird's wing upon the surface of a stream, a look of surprise and recognition, almost of understanding. Just then, the foreman managed to clear his tongue and give the word for which everyone was waiting.

In the bustle on the stairs, where people were hurrying to get to another court, giving laconic instructions to their clerks, exchanging telephone numbers and names of restaurants, I caught snatches of sub-voiced opinion.

". . . . wuffy. Really too old for the job, you know, and not the right sort of experience."

"No, I think that's entirely misplaced sentimentality. All my feelings are with the woman . . ."

". . . previous cases. It happens like that, you see. A fellow has it in the blood, they treat him leniently and he just comes back and back."

"You call it leniency—prison for a mere schoolboy?"

"It's the birch you want for a type like that."

A man with the beauty of scholarship in his eyes was talking in a soft, perfectly modulated voice: ". . . a fairly commonplace psychological pattern. In the first stage you get the ordinary social repressions, using that term in a popular rather than a strictly scientific sense. Then a system of escape is built up, but the escape is illusory. The subject is first given the impression that all his inward hungers have been satisfied, but there's always a residue of discontent to remind him that he is not a monarch, only a shabby little man in royal clothes. That discontent operates like a drill, boring slowly into the surface crust. There comes a moment when it gets right through, and then the dormant volcano goes off with a bang . . ."

But those voices were like the babel which people let spill out of wireless sets, an intrusion which scratched the surface of my mind no more deeply than the dreary pretentiousness of the building itself. Just then I was not much interested in the categories to which men and women are shrewdly assigned by apprentices in moral anthropology. It is entirely correct and necessary, I was thinking, this performance we have just been through: for by means of recognized assumptions it operates a mechanism ably designed to limit the hurt that people can do to one another. More than that, it picks up incidents from people's lives and represents them in a moral diagram, bold, ingeniously drawn, and simple enough for everyone to understand.

And after all, what reason was there to reanimate the past! Some of it pursues us; the rest, whatever theories men may hold on the nature of time, cannot be re-lived or changed, and if we had failed in wisdom there was nothing we could do about it now. But finding myself in Ludgate Hill, crossing over towards the river with the vague notion of seeking fresh air and a chemist's shop, I decided abruptly to make for home and go through the old letters once again.

For to me, I thought, the past has not died, it lives within the present and only the moment in which I stand has not yet come alive. However painfully, I must go on searching through the evidence, the real evidence, scratching about for crumbs of recollection which would fill the gaps, wondering if at any point the course of events could have been altered, trying and trying to settle finally how much of the responsibility belonged to me. A bus that pulled up beside me was going over the bridge and on towards the Elephant; on a fresh impulse I went aboard, meaning to visit Weald Street and then perhaps screw myself to have one more look at Mickett Lane. The house itself with the mean doorway and ugly windows, the street's particular smell, might help to realize what felt just then like the returning impression of a vivid dream. If only the picture could be fully lit I might perceive some meaning beneath the rags and tatters which the Court had scraped together and treated as entirety; and then, as if that history had ceased to be part of my own, I might faintly hope to wrap it up and let it rest.

31

On the 10th of October 1938 Raymond had received a parcel posted (unregistered) at North Walsham. It contained a bundle of letters and a covering note from someone who, signing herself 'Daphne Scobaird', explained that

> You may possibly remember me by my maiden name of Steaben, I had the pleasure of meeting you at Armorel's wedding, of course that was centuries ago, only I do remember you quite clearly, and being so terribly thrilled to meet you. Of course I was really only a girl then and meeting someone like you and you being a cousin of Rellie's gave me a terrific thrill.

The thrill had lasted in the muscles of her hand, Raymond supposed, for the writing at that point assumed the semblance of a barograph recording. Where it re-emerged into legibility, he read:

. . . husband thinks it very feminine and foolish to have kept them like that, only we did know each other so fearfully well at Hilda Abbess's—even there I realized that she was a most specially wonderful person, she had a mind that could see into things and ideas in a way no one else's I've ever known could, and she was so absolutely honest, in the real sense, not just the bourgeois one— and naturally when you've known somebody as long as that you do feel about her differently to what you do of my other friends, especially when I feel that even when we were both married there were things she would tell me which she couldn't quite tell anybody else. I suppose there are some people who have a sort of gift for understanding people and naturally people confide in them a good deal, and then of course our views on some of the most important things in Life were always very much the same. What has been worrying me is the idea that perhaps somebody official ought to see these letters because there may be something in them which would be helpful to the Investigations. And of course Jack thinks that old letters only clutter up the house and I ought to get rid of them, in fact he did actually say Oh, do chuck all that b—b-ph in the bin. Of course Jack hasn't read them at all, they've always been in the drawer where I keep a lot of my old things. Only there's such a lot of what you might call private things in them that naturally I can't bear the idea of sending them to some total stranger (I do think that things can have a sort of sacredness, don't you—not in any superstitious sense, I don't mean) and so I had a bright idea and I thought as you were Armorel's cousin and she always told me how fond she was of you and at the same time respecting you most tremendously and as you probably know all sorts of government and legal sort of people I thought possibly you might go through them all and see what you decide ought to be done and possibly do it. I do hope you won't think this is an intrusion or anything, it's so very hard to put on paper what one really feels and of course Jack doesn't like me to spend an awful lot of my time writing . . .

The paper smelt of chypre. Having composed a correct reply Raymond put the letter away in a cupboard with an airtight door.

He was oddly reluctant to untie the ribbon in which Armorel's letters were bound. He, of all men, did not lack the housemaid's kind of curiosity, but the 'sort of sacredness' to which Mrs Scobaird had referred had equal power over his own own finical sensibilities. Curiosity won; and when he had folded the ribbon and stored it in the drawer he kept for such things, he found that he had forty or fifty letters to examine, containing almost as many thousand words. Late that evening he set to work.

Where nature withholds the greater gifts of the mind she often fills their place with a minor talent and major passion for being methodical. Although he sighed and breathed heavily through his nose, Raymond was in truth pleased to discover that the letters were all muddled up and that he had first of all to put them in date order. Even the laborious task of finding where stray pages belonged gave him a gentle satisfaction, such as short-legged and pot-bellied men obtain from running round the Park and imagining themselves 'in training'. The task of reading was less agreeable; not, as he had feared, because the contents of the letters were too disturbing but because they were not disturbing enough. One after another was devoted to matters in which he was totally uninterested or which he could not hope to comprehend. But since he was incapable of skipping (he was said to be the only man alive who read Hansard from cover to cover every day) he plodded conscientiously through the reminiscences of Hilda Abbess friendships, through accounts of Tonie bringing up her feeds, of shops in Camberwell which had failed to produce Size Fours for Gordon, of a man who had come to clear the drain outside the kitchen and made a competent job of it but was 'not the sort of man I like to have doing things—you will know exactly what I mean.' There were pages about the minutiae of domestic economy, long and repetitive accounts of a conflict with the headmistress of Tonie's school, all the paraphernalia, small in weight but vast in bulk, which covers the human mind's ground floor; and there were letters almost entirely devoted to what Mrs Scobaird must have meant by 'views on the most important things in Life', a tumbling sea of abstract nouns in which Raymond rightly thought himself too little a philosopher to swim. He read every line. When anything seemed to him of interest he marked it; not, as another might have done, by a pencil stroke in the margin but with a ruler and coloured inks. Where the name of Gordon Aquillard, Trevon Grist or Ed Hugg happened to occur he put a green asterisk above it, names of women were similarly marked with violet, and a number of passages which in some vague fashion he judged to be of possible importance were given a red underline. The contentment yielded by that occupation was enough to redress the boredom in most of what he was reading; for the exercise of neatness delighted him, and he was fond of colour. He might—as he often said—have been a painter, had he possessed some talent for design and the ability to handle a brush.

Especially, with plenty of blotting-paper and new nibs handy, he liked ruling lines in red.

'. . . Daise like all her kind enjoys making the worst of a bad job, and she can't understand how I can stay cheerful. It's no use explaining to *her*. The fact is that I am cheerful because I have no doubt whatever about the outcome of this ridiculous case. I know that magistrates make mistakes, but proper judges don't make them often, and if you knew Gian as I do you would realize that he could not possibly have had anything to do with Empire's death—which was caused by a simple accident. I don't say that just because I am his wife, nothing is sillier than the "my man can't possibly be wrong" attitude. Of course when he was younger he *was* quick-tempered, and didn't realize how much damage he could do with his fists, but he's an entirely different person to what he was in those days. (Or do people really think that a wife's influence counts for nothing at all!) He *did* have a quarrel with Empire—he had never really forgiven him for getting him sacked—men have a special amour propre which works like that—and the quarrel *did* take place very shortly before the accident, but to argue from that that the quarrel led up to the poor fellow's death is what they call in logic *post hoc ergo propter hoc:* and no judge worth anything would let a jury be convinced by such an obvious fallacy as that. What I mean to say is that the police are bringing up nothing against Gian except circumstantial 'evidence', and that 'evidence' just won't hold water. So I am keeping perfectly calm. My one fear is that Gian will cut a poor figure in the Court, because his upbringing has made him scared of every sort of official. Still, that can't be helped.

'Of course all this goes to show that when people are secretive it only leads to trouble. You realize, of course, that I'm telling you this in the strictest confidence. I have never quite made Gian realize that he would do best to bring *all* his worries to me. It's the masculine pride again which prevents him, obviously he felt that if he told me his feelings about Empire I might misunderstand and possibly laugh at him—though in reality I would never dream of laughing at him about anything, even when he utters the most absurdly old-fashioned sentiments. All this led to my telling one of these wretched C.I.D. people that Gian hadn't been anywhere near Bidault's Place on the night when

Empire got killed, and that may be said to have started the whole trouble—but since Gian had made out to me that he had been somewhere quite different I can hardly be blamed for that, can I? I just hope that when this business is over the dear man will have realized that it's in his true interest to confide in me over everything . . .'

'. . . She has been very kind indeed—and especially good to Tonie. I wish you knew her. She is the sweetest of women, and her boy Michael is charming, with those quiet, beautiful manners that they *do* instil—if perhaps at the cost of destroying some individuality—at very expensive schools. It gives me great joy that she should have him as some consolation for all that she has been through. There is just one unfortunate thing—I wouldn't breathe this to anyone but you—I don't feel that I can *absolutely* trust him. You will understand what I mean when I say that this is largely a matter of instinct—a particular instinct one has which isn't often wrong. I don't mean that I like the boy any the less for it. It's stupid and reactionary to blame people, especially children, for shortcomings which are no fault of their own, and a child is by nature straightforward or he is not. But it does make it more difficult to deal with a boy when you know that his personal charm is used, if ever so slightly, as a cover for things below the surface. He is not the sort who would tell a deliberate lie, I'm sure of that. But he *is* the kind who just keeps back things that he finds it inconvenient to talk about. For instance, I fancy he has friends that his mother knows nothing about. I feel a certain responsibility over this, because Elizabeth's very virtues, her sweetness and lovability, make her not perhaps in every way the ideal mother for a boy whose good looks and winning ways expose him to special dangers. She is rather one of those who would say (naturally, when you think how much he means to her) "Well, as long as he's happy—!" because such people, who give the world so much happiness by their own beauty and kindliness, sometimes forget that there are times when life demands something more of us than to be happy . . .'

'. . . Last night I made Cornish patties, which Gian loves, and afterwards I had a long talk with him about Gordon—such a cosy talk, all the odd people who officially or unofficially more-or-less live in this house as they did at Weald Street were out for once, and Tonie was so tired after the school excursion to Kew that she was fast asleep. I couldn't explain this, but then I don't need to explain it to you—you have your Jack, and so you know what it's like—the wonderful feeling when a man is rather tired and comfortable and very quiet, with his strength and masculinity all in repose, and you know that this being who is powerful enough almost to break you in two with one hand belongs absolutely and entirely to you. And oh his patience is so touching at times! Last night it was wonderful. I knew he could not really follow what I was saying, although I expressed it in the most simple language I could find, and put in some funny bits I'd thought of to make it easier (he loves jokes, though usually only the Lambeth kind of joke) —and yet he listened so attentively, with hardly a single interruption, and I could see he really was trying to make his own mind clear instead of just repeating the few stock sentences which he has for his own 'views', as he does sometimes when he's tired and worried. You know, I do think—although it may *sound* heartless to say so—that the ordeal he went through over that trial has been in some sort of way a good thing for him. It has made him less obstinate—no, that's not the word —I mean less inclined to think that because he's a man and I'm a woman his way of looking at things *must* be superior to mine. But oh how I do wish at times that he had a *little* more in the way of *background*. It's not just lack of education in the ordinary sense—I have done a good deal myself to overcome that—it's a complete blindness to proportion, a total inability to step over from one field of thought into another. Of course I shouldn't dream of trying to explain Gustav Liedke-Urban's theories to him *in detail*, he just hasn't the head for anything like that. All I am trying to do is to make him understand that *emotion* is the great misleading force, that every time reason starts to operate in the planning of someone's life, emotion—particularly what may be roughly called religious emotion—tries to interfere and get things back into the old muddle; just as, when someone plans a beautiful avenue with shady walks beside it, there will always be someone to make a fuss because it means the removal of one dear little old cottage. The main question is whether Gordon should come back here for a short period before he goes on to the agricultural school, which is Stage Beta in what Gustav calls his Theorem of Reclamation. Naturally Gian wants him to, and naturally so do I, in a sentimental sense—no mother could long to see her boy more than I do. But Gustav has pointed out—with that marvellous clearness of his—that it would be like washing clothes and then throwing them on the ground before hanging them out to dry.

Gordon would meet all his old Weald Street friends, or other friends of the same kind, Gian would spoil him, and by the time he got to Quarries Waste all the good he had gained from Peter Synvenor's influence would have been undone. That's what I just can't make Gian understand, and of course he can't at all appreciate the brilliance of Gustav's mind on these matters, but I think he does realize in his rather slow-moving mind that what I decide will work out best in the end—although that's always a hard thing for a man to admit. Sometimes I wish I *hadn't* the sympathy I have with Gian, I mean, the power to understand exactly how he is thinking.

'I don't know if it has ever struck you that motherhood is essentially a *lonely* business. Because of her special and supremely important function, evolution has given the mother a mind with special powers of interpretation, so that she can guide and educate her children's mental life as well as their bodily growth. But only she herself fully realizes that she *has* this power, and others with the best intentions are constantly trying to neutralize its effects by exerting influences of their own. One is sometimes almost frightened by the magnitude of one's responsibility. Gustav is a great comfort to me. He, with his extraordinary genius, does perceive both what is latent in me and to what interferences it is subject. In all our consultations over Gordon he has taken infinite pains to find the direction of my own ideas (as he puts it, there must be a 'master-source' in all such planning, and where the mother is of sufficient intelligence that master-source can best be found in her) and his own contribution is merely to systematize my conceptions and suggest scientifically the channels through which they can be executed. He has one saying which I find so very helpful—" 'Love' means the concentration upon a particular personality of a schooled intelligence." How marvellously that clarifies a wife's and a mother's duties. And how much less would the world suffer from the effects of religious and other cloudy emotions if only that truth could be brought home to everyone!'

It was on the day after he had marked those passages that Raymond heard from L. C. Sture. (According to his custom, he made a note on the top of the letter, 'Received 11/Oct/38'.) Sture wrote:

> I write D/O, that is to say, partly as an old friend and partly as a glorified policeman; in both personalities reluctantly; but however much you dislike receiving such a letter as this you know me well enough, I think, not to resent it.

The newspaper reports, fantastic as most of them appear, are at least correct in their implication that there are difficulties in regard to the Mickett Lane case. It is my business, in the interests of justice, to make sure that all the facts are known, whether or not some of those facts immediately appear to be relevant.

It is not impossible that you may possess letters written by Mrs Gian Ardree—you are, I believe, quite closely related—which would throw some light upon the general circumstances of her life during, say, the last two or three years; by 'general circumstances' I mean particularly the relations existing between herself and her husband or other persons with whom she was in frequent contact. It needs but little imagination for me to understand that it would give you pain to show such letters to anyone else, and most of all to deliver them to someone intending, if their contents made it seem expedient, to expose them to the always distasteful and sometimes hideous publicity of the law-courts. That, however, is what I am bluntly asking you to do, if there are any such letters in your possession. I ask it, of course, not as a favour to myself; but because I think you know that, however mechanical and even cynical we lawyers appear to most laymen, some of us at least are inspired and governed in our work by the belief that all truth matters and truth is all that does matter. To you I need not enlarge on that. I feel certain that you will understand why I make, to you, what might seem to others a preposterous request with hardly any diffidence at all.

If you have no such letters you may yet know of other relatives or friends who are likely to have them . . .

That worried Raymond at least as much as Sture had supposed. Private sensibilities—well, those of course must be sacrificed: the man was right in saying that only truth mattered. But truth on how accurate a scale? Timorous and mentally rheumatic, Raymond could never have disentangled his own ideas, but he realized in a dull, intuitive fashion that they differed from Sture's. He knew a little about lawyers—he had eaten his Dinners before turning over to medicine—and he did not question the high integrity of such a one as old Sture himself. But was it not ultimately an error to assume, as lawyers were bound to do, that it is possible to dissect any situation into propositions which can all be labelled 'true' or 'false'. "A struck B": that might be a demonstrable truth; but "A intended to kill B"—was such a statement, which a lawyer would use as a girder in his framework, so simple in nature that its absolute truth could ever be accepted? In the field of motive the fragments of which truth was made were never all to hand. Was it better to have a few of them discovered out of their proper place and disguised from lying in an unfamiliar soil, than to have none at all?

Nice fellow, Sture: and a first-rate mind, as Raymond had often told his friends (liking to boast of some connection with such a man). And at bottom Raymond was frightened of first-rate minds.

He put the letter aside, took the budget which Mrs Scobaird had sent him and went on reading where he had left off the night before. But he read now as if Sture were looking over his shoulder. He could see the man's face, beautifully kept, chin like a split plum, thin but kindly mouth, sparse brows, very light-blue eyes which never wandered but went to one point and rested there as the hand of a big clock does; and he heard Sture's quiet, agreeable voice delivering compact sentences like one who ties up parcels with bits of string cut automatically to exactly the right length. ("Only a madman would lead Germany into war with the British Empire. No madman could have united Germany as this man Hitler has done. In my view there will be no war." "She said it was impossible for her to meet her father again. I explained that her view of the nature of possibility was unrealistic.") How would such a man, hearing no live voice, seeing no familiar eyes, interpret letters like these? And now, as he continued reading, he found himself searching for that face of Armorel's, those many faces: the grave, intent face of a child sitting with chin on knees at the end of a sofa in the Hayward's Heath drawing-room, the mischievous mouth of a schoolgirl who teased him about his bourgeois manners, the pallor and the numbed eyes of a young woman creeping into this room late on a September evening, "Well, it's all over with Gordon. I suppose I should have known." Was it a fact, as he now imagined, that her voice had suddenly altered on that evening, or had it been changing a little ever since her mother's defection? Now and then he could hear the later voice in these sentences, but only in some of its moods; the note of weariness, seldom the warmth and sweetness which had made people turn their heads in a crowded room. But these words, he thought, are not for me; we have a separate dress to wear for each of our friends, dresses belonging partly to ourselves and partly to them: a complexity of disguises: and if all of them were put away, would one find a complete and integral being within? He went on doggedly, irked by his own dullness, fascinated by the notion that someone or something was eluding him. And at a late hour he was at work again, drowsily, often reading only with his eyes while his thoughts, warmed and perplexed, turned towards old familiarities, like people wandering through a village they lived in many years before: to the bashful smirk of Gian coming to meet him at the tram stop with a minute Tonie holding his hand; a strange, impassioned kiss that Rellie had once pressed into his cheek while they stood by the trumpery coat-stand in the spotless front passage at Mickett Lane. It was quiet now, the servants had gone to bed, the telephone would not ring again. There was pleasure of a kind, besides the pain, in rummaging through all the refuse of his mind, glistening trifles he had once treasured, scraps of forgotten clothes, while hand and eyes moved like a goods train along the uniform script, page after page, reading and hunting, constantly ruling the neat, red lines.

'. . . that Tonie did not after all go to Apostles' Court that afternoon, she and Michael were with the Bensons who are quite nice people. But why didn't she tell me beforehand?! I have explained to her now, and I think she understands, that what I dislike is *secretiveness*—I have seen something of the harm secretiveness can do. I think she does understand, when she thinks about it, that she can confide in me about everything. And really—though of course I shouldn't dream of saying so—she would be wiser to make me her everyday confidant rather than Gian, because Gian, with all his goodwill and affection, cannot possibly understand the problems and dangers that a young girl has to face. For example, he can never see *why* I don't want Tonie to go to Apostles' Court, and I think he fancies that I have some prejudice against that institution which makes me resent the amount of time he gives to it. I haven't! Although it *does* take up a very great deal of time that he might otherwise devote to study or to his home, I think it's a good thing that he should have a hobby which interests him. Only I feel—and it's so hard to explain this to him—that he ought not to accept *all* the burdens that well-intentioned people like Trevon Grist are always ready to put on the willing horse's back. Now that he is an older man I think that Trevon is wonderfully improved in character—not at all in health, poor man—he is a far more responsible person than in the days when we were developing Hollysian House together. But he still has—at times—a certain furtiveness about him which makes one just a bit wary in accepting anything he says. I do like people to be open in all their dealings—half the trouble in the world, I sometimes think, comes from people being secretive . . .'

'. . . a remarkable address from Joseph Vandeaar on "Obscurantism Today." A brilliant analysis of the logical stages by which theism leads to strife and injury (based on the Biblical aphorism, "Not to send peace, but a sword"). The theme he developed most strikingly was that the human mind has a normal tendency to deceive and that theism provides a convenient cover for any and every deception—the 'Believer' can always maintain that he has been transcendentally truthful (meaning that he has, to put it rather crudely, squared his *Theos*) and that a plain statement to beings of his own kind is therefore superfluous. We sang an anthem by Moff, the young rationalist poet—I didn't think it so very good but I suppose some people who have not been trained in mental exertion find relief in that sort of thing after a fairly stiff period of concentration.

'It was rather ironical that shortly after I got home Tonie came and asked me if I had any objection to her undergoing the rites of Baptism and Confirmation. (I wonder if you remember you and me being done at Hilda Abbess's? I felt fearfully uplifted and pious for at least four hours afterwards, especially as the whole party had chocolate cake in Pidgie's drawing-room!) Well, of course I told Tonie that she could do exactly what she liked—it would be dead against all my principles to interfere with a child's opinions, she must settle things for herself, make her own mistakes, and find her own way towards maturity of outlook. I did, however, venture to ask who had put the idea into her head, to which she replied that it was her own idea, and only by degrees did she let it out that a clergyman called (appropriately!) Squirelle had been on to her. A friend of Trevon Grist's, as I might have guessed—poor Trevon cultivates slightly furtive clergymen as others go in for guinea-pigs or ferrets! I asked Gian if he had known anything about it and he was fearfully abashed, and went into a most complicated, rambling explanation (for which I had not asked!). I am not sure that his influence hasn't been stronger than this Squirelle's even—it's no use my trying to explain to Gian the view every sensible person holds nowadays that children must be left to develop their own philosophies. I've tried, but it's a kind of reasoning that's quite beyond him, poor man—his notions of parental duty are all hall-marked 1887!

'So be it! But, oh dear, I do wish all these people would be open with me! Why, why all this concealment, all this subterfuge and back-stairs manoeuvring and deception! I try to make this a good home for them, it is *their* friends, not mine, who come here (and whom I work for)—is it really quite fair that I should be left in a corner while they are amusing themselves with little plots and schemes? *I* don't hide anything—what have I to hide? If there is one thing I loathe it's secretiveness.

'It's been very hot. I'd rather like to get away, but of course we can't afford that kind of thing if Tonie is to complete her education as I wish. And I couldn't really leave the house, it would be filthy by the time we got back, in London everything's covered with dirt five minutes after you've cleaned it. Whatever happens I am not going to have this house a pigsty. I had enough of pigsty-living in Contessa Street. I really ought to get the dresser moved so that I can wash the kitchen walls all over . . .'

'. . . absolutely determined not to let it alter my behaviour towards any of them in any way.

'The day will come when Tonie will turn to me for guidance. I'm prepared to wait for that—patience is not a virtue I've had no practice in! In the meantime she will have to go the way she wishes—I'm dead against interference with young people's lives—and if it proves to be a painful progress that will at least deepen our understanding of each other when the time comes when she ceases to accept without question the views of those who want her to think that her mother is an enemy. For the time being she will have these others to guide her, and the fact that I do not agree with the guidance they give will not alter my behaviour towards any of them in any way.

'I feel certain that her father, at least, would not deliberately exert any bad influence upon her so long as he is satisfied that he has got her away from mine. He was no ill-will at all towards Tonie herself. In fact, we go on behaving as if he had none towards me. I have got used to things, and though I have never learnt to admire secretiveness, and I still rather hate all the scheming and plotting that goes on, I find it quite easy to accept everything calmly. That's the great thing about cultivating one's pure reason—you learn to rely on it when everything else deserts you. Of course I have to be watchful, because he is being driven on by one man's influence all the time, and when a man gets to a certain state the sight of someone who keeps her mind absolutely clear and unprejudiced is like a red rag to a bull. But I am absolutely determined not to let it alter my behaviour in any way.

"We had a party for my birthday, not really a party, just ourselves with Papa Simon and Trevon etc: and of course old Olleroyd. Tonie had made a cake and actually got 38 tiny candles on to it, she made me sit in the chair that Georgie always used to sit in at Cromer's Ride and they all gave three cheers for me. Do you know, it's terribly silly, but I got rather a crying fit, I suppose it was because it all made me think of the old days, Weald Street and before that even—I never really wanted to leave Weald Street, it was Gian's idea entirely. It really was just as if nothing had ever altered, Gian and all of them were being so sweet to me. They wouldn't let me do any of the washing-up, Tonie and Elizabeth did it, I just sat there cosily and the men were smoking like chimneys and they were rather shy in a queer, nice way, they kept on asking if I was perfectly comfortable, and then they started making the sort of jokes they always enjoyed in the Hollysian House days. Of course I wasn't in that much, but I loved hearing them all guffawing and being happy. They had some sort of argument over that old knife we keep over the mantelpiece, Trevon said he wanted to borrow it for some reason, and Gian said it was still sharp and he would only hurt himself, and then Simon started up about the knife belonging to him, which is a favourite old idea of his. I said that in any case no one was to move it, because I specially value it. (I don't believe in being sentimental about things, certainly not about bits of bric-à-brac, but this old knife has particular associations which give it what I call *historical* value, and I think it has a special use in reminding Gian—who in spite of everything has a strong streak of sentimentality—of certain things that he owes to me.) Anyway the dispute ended in a great deal of laughing and cheeriohing and everything was so happy, and I didn't feel in the least bit lonely. I think I shall remember it all my life, it was so like the old days and I felt so perfectly happy.

'The weather has been very thundery. I am sensitive to thunder and I know when there's any about even if it's a long distance away, possibly in another continent. I think Tonie ought to have a new mackintosh, I could give her the money only she might not spend it all and then they would want her not to tell me. She has learnt to be very secretive.

'I have had to write this in rather a hurry because someone may come in at any moment, you're never alone here. I've got a bit of a head because the weather has been very thundery, but it doesn't alter my behaviour in any way. Gian keeps pretending that he isn't hostile to me, as a rule he has himself under perfect control and he isn't at all dangerous so long as I watch him carefully and keep him from coming under the influence of particular people who would like to use him against me for their own ends.

'I am sorry to have written all this in such a hurry, but I have got to move the furniture and get up the linoleum in the front room, I am perfectly certain there's thick dirt underneath it. Of course nobody else minds, so I'm going to do it all by myself, and then I've got to take down all the pictures in the bedroom and give them a proper cleaning, and wash the lamp shade as well . . .'

Before he went to bed (at three o'clock in the morning) Raymond had written an answer to Sture.

My dear Lionel:

Many thanks for your note. I understand perfectly that one's appetite for privacies must not prevent one from surrendering anything that might be useful in such a case as this. And I should most gladly help you if I could. Unfortunately I have kept none of Armorel's letters, which have never contained anything but trivialities of the kind reserved for the amusement of elderly relatives; and I know of no one else at all likely to provide what you are looking for. I do not think she ever went in for a regular or intimate correspondence. I am so sorry.

There was a small error in your letter to the *Times* which appeared on the 4th of last month. It was Goss whom Tom King beat on the 10th (not 12th) December 1863. He had, of course, already beaten Mace in the previous year (thus winning his belt). A very small slip and entirely pardonable (except when made by a lawyer).

Yours ever,
Raymond C.H.

32

"THANK-YOU," said Tonie to the helpful stranger, "it's extremely kind of you, but if you don't mind I'd really rather cross the road by myself. I find it interesting, when you take it calmly—my mother has taught me. You see, I always come home from school by myself now. Mother said I could when I was eleven—she's got all sorts of sensible views—and that was at least a month ago."

In the weeks which followed Empire's death and her father's arrest, Tonie was doing things by herself a great deal, as a matter of principle. In play hours at school she often forgot her resolution, and behaved for a time as she had done in earlier days; then she remembered and broke away from any party she was engaged in. "I think it would be best," she had told Marigold Oliver, "if you didn't speak to me too much. Till Daddy's been acquitted, I mean. Of course they haven't put me in Coventry or anything—Anne Harvey says Miss Ella's told everyone they're not to—only I'm under a cloud just the same as if I *was* in Coventry, and you might get under it too. Of course there's no harm in your saying 'Good-morning' to me and things like that—you can say that sort of thing to an absolute criminal and no one thinks it makes you into one yourself." And she had not been persuaded by kind Miss Ella, in an earnest little talk, to alter this view.

With head and shoulders very straight she crossed the road in her careful, scientific way and went towards home, wishing she could get there without going through Weald Street itself. At Miss Jamieson's, people's manners were extremely reliable and if you decided to behave in a special way people more-or-less realized at once what you were doing. Some of the Weald Street children were slower to understand, and it was of great importance—Mummie had always said—not to look as if you thought yourself better than them. So she couldn't walk along Weald Street in a stand-offy way, but if she looked as cheerful and friendly as usual they would think she didn't mind about Daddy being in prison waiting to be tried, and if she wore a shamefaced look they'd think he really had done what the Sunday papers said. Last week Tommie Ede, simply from his sense of fun, had been swinging one of his sister's dolls with a piece of string tied round its neck, shouting, "Oy! Look what they're goin' to do wiv Tonie's dad!" and she had been hard put to pretend that she didn't understand what he meant.

Today, however, most of the children were occupied with a rag-

and-bone cart pulled by a moulting donkey and hardly anyone noticed her. Only Alice Derby came across the road and mumbled, hardly daring to lift her eyes, "Ever s'sorry, Tonie—it's a cryin' shame an' that's what all of us say!" With a smile which fitted like a new dental plate Tonie answered, "Oh, thank-you awfully! It's gorgeous weather, isn't it!" and hurried on (hoping it didn't look rude) to get inside the house.

Standing quite still in the passage she could hear the voice of Mrs Eustace in the kitchen going on and on like a fretful baby's, occasionally punctuated by Daise's "Well, I d'know, Mrs Eustace, reely I don't." From upstairs the murmur of Brodie lecturing Mr Olleroyd flowed with the sweet monotony of plainsong, breaking now and again into a fountain of laughter. She went into the front room, which was empty, closing the door very softly behind her; pitched her satchel onto a chair, herself face-down on the sofa and deliberately cried.

She had not finished crying when Daise came in, so quietly that Tonie first knew of her presence by the scorched smell which always went with her. She said, with her face still in the cushion:

"I'm busy—go away!"

"Well, now, what ever are you cryin' for, Tonie?"

Since pretence was useless, Tonie cleaned her face as well as it could be done with a cushion and turned round.

"I don't see why I can't have any peace!"

"It don't look like peace to me, what you been havin'!"

"Oh, stow your guts, bitch-face!"

"Now you know your mum won't have you talk that way! What'll she say when she see that cushion all like that!"

"It ain't all like that!"

"An' you ain't allowed to say 'ain't' neither, you know that."

"I'll say what I fuming well like."

She was seriously angry with Daise: Daise standing and sniffing there with her eyes all watery and swollen, with paths down her cheeks, and making all this fuss because she, Tonie, had chosen of her own accord to cry for a minute or two in the same way as you sneezed or rubbed the sleep out of your eyes. It was people like Daise, snivelling for no reason at all, who made the whole business of crying soppy and stupid.

"What's Mrs Eustace going on about?" she demanded.

"She says she's going to lose her home and won't have anywhere to go."

"She's crackers! She's been saying that ever since I was born. Where's Mum?"

"She's busy."

Tonie pushed past Daise into the passage and called "Mum-mie" but got no answer.

"You do better leave her alone," Daise said. "She's goin' through boxes 'n' things."

"My mother isn't your property!"

"No, but I do her the best I can."

Everything Tonie knew about Daise was in that answer; and she suddenly remembered that Daise's own father was not in prison but dead. She turned and faced her again. Something had to be said, and because she had not enough experience to weigh the possible effect of words they came to her easily.

"Do you think it would make you feel better," she asked soberly, "if the judge said it *was* Daddy who did it and then he was—you know?" It was a little difficult to finish, but she managed it. "I can't *hope* that—you do see?—only I'm sure I'd mind a bit less if it was nice for you. So would Daddy, I'm absolutely positive."

But Daise had no such readiness in speech. She did not start to weep again as Tonie for a moment feared (that happened much later), she stood like a waxen image which has begun to melt in the heat, her repulsive mouth half-open, horror-struck and helpless. Tonie took her by the shoulders—she and Daise were of almost equal height—held her tightly and kissed her on the eyes and forehead. Then she left her and went upstairs.

As she reached the landing Olleroyd came out of his and Brodie's room, followed by Brodie's derisive laughter. He stood miserably with his back to the door.

"What's the matter, Ollie?"

"Saying I don't *try* to find work!" he answered, jerking his head.

"And he wouldn't recognize it if he did!" came Brodie's voice.

"Saying I only got m'self to blame if I find m'self put out in the street."

"But, Ollie, nobody's going to put you out in the street! You must know by now, Brodie just goes on talking to keep his mouth warm while he's thinking of something to say."

She gave him her smile, but today it would not penetrate the haze of gloom which encircled him and she went on rather sadly up to the attic.

Mum had pulled out the old packing-case from under Gordon's bed. She was sitting on the floor in her dustcap and overall, with papers and what looked like account books spread all round her. She said:

"Oh, is that you, Tonie? Do you want something?"

"No, not really. I've just got back."

"Oh. Have you washed your face and hands? No, you haven't. Ask Daise to give you some hot water out of the kettle—I don't suppose she's gone yet."

Tonie went downstairs again, washed in the kitchen and returned to the front room. With Wilson's *Empire History for Junior Forms* open on her knee she began to think of an animal—rather like a small monkey but with wings—which could be taught to do all Mum's work. She would keep it hidden (with Brodie perhaps?) till it was fully trained, and then one day when Mum was just starting to do this room she would walk in and say casually, "You just sit down, Mummie, Joe's going to do it"—no—"Tonietto's going to do it. Tonietto—on it, boy!" Tonietto would have cloths and dusters and a small broom with a telescopic handle in a little satchel on his back. With one bound he would leap to the window and rush up and down, polishing with five million strokes a second. For a time Mum would be quite speechless. Then, with her eyes shining like those of the lady in the Kleeno-kwik advertisement, she would say in a sort-of hushed voice, "Tonie, my darling, was it really you who trained him to do all this?"

"You'll have to wait a few minutes for your tea," Mum said, taking off her dustcap as she came in, "I've had to send Mrs Eustace to get some more milk." She stood kissing the tip of a middle finger, with the smile which Tonie knew had nothing to do with pleasure, looking quickly about for things that were slightly wrong, a chair cover or a doormat pushed out of position.

"Have you got much prep?" she asked distractedly.

Tonie slid Tonietto into the wings of her mind; he would perform for her another time.

"Only three sections of this. We would have had geog, only Miss Leecey's gone to look after her sick mother or something, and Miss Wyre forgot to set us any, thank goodness."

Armoral shifted one of the pictures and stood back to see if it was straight.

"But, darling, is that awfully sensible? I mean, you can't learn a thing you never work at by yourself."

"But, Mummie, the prep you get for geog is nearly always doing maps, and I just can't do them."

Looking out the window, Armorel caught a glimpse of the army hut where Lower Middle had done their prep at Hilda Abbess's; the ugly stove, the smell of geraniums coming in at the open window.

"I never could either," she said, and turned and sat down. "Only you don't really look at maps until you've got to draw them yourself, and you can't learn where places are until you do study them. Some day you'll go abroad and you'll want to know where you're going."

"But then all you've got to do is to get on the right ship. Grandfather's been to all sorts of places, and I'm certain if you showed him a map he wouldn't even know what it was."

"Oh, darling, don't be silly!"

"I'm absolutely positive he wouldn't! If you showed him a map of Africa he'd say 'Eh, look how they got the likeness of my ole girl!'"

She was thinking, 'Mummie couldn't draw maps either! Mummie couldn't draw maps either—she's *said* she couldn't!' and the whole, dull day had brightened. She came to the back of her mother's chair, leant over and planted a moist kiss on her neck.

"Darling, you mustn't talk—what's that for?"

"For being bad at maps. Oh, Mummie, I didn't think you'd ever been bad at anything!"

A little awkwardly, Armorel leant back, took the hand that was on her shoulder and brought it to her mouth. She tried to laugh, but that was not quite possible for a woman with the weight of so tiring a day on her forehead. "Precious!" she managed to say, wishing for an instant that she had the natural use of such a word, wishing almost to be a professional gusher like Edie's friend Mrs Forcres. And then: "You do see, don't you, why you've got to work at these things! I want you to be ever so much better than I was, I want you to go much further. And you see, you won't have any money to start you off, you've got to do it all on your brains."

Tonie said: "H-h! Where do you think I'll go abroad to?"

"Oh, darling, I've no idea. You may not go at all."

"Then all the geog would be just wasted." She was sitting on the floor now with her head against her mother's knees. "Somewhere like Australia, do you think?"

"Well, you never know."

"Where do *you* want to go?"

"I don't know—I'm too busy to think of going to places."

"But you must have wanted to sometimes."

"Well, Greece. I've always wanted to go to Greece."

"You mean, where the Greeks used to be?"

"Yes."

"Then we'll all go. When I leave school I'll go and work in Stevenson's until I've got about thirty pounds. Then I'll get the tickets, and then I'll come to you one morning and I'll just say, 'Mummie, stop doing whatever you are doing and start to pack. The taxi will be here at ten o'clock.'"

"Oh, Tonie, that will be lovely! Where shall we sail from?"

"From Blackfriars Bridge. And then when we get to Greece we'll stay somewhere and in the morning I'll say, 'Now, Mummie, you've got the whole day to rout about and find the fossils or mummies or whatever it is of the Greeks. Here are some sandwiches and I'll have tea ready at 4.30 and by then everything will be dusted.'"

"Lovely, darling."

This chair was not too comfortable, but it was curiously resting to feel Tonie's head against her knees, to have Tonie's eager voice playing about her like a cool wind. Swiftly, like the moods of April, the day's grimy and neuralgic weariness had changed to tiredness of another kind, bringing a faint aroma from other days' endings, the comfortable ache of back and legs beside Miss Ewing's fire late in the winter term, fields heavy and aromatic with summer moving drowsily past the Balcombe brake on the return journey up Cuckfield hill; easy voices, people who understood without your explaining, the sense of an unbroken circle.

". . . and as soon as I've done the dusting and all that I'll hire a pony, like Audrey Stewart's only grey and with a very long mane—do they have ponies in Greece? I suppose so—and I'll ride all round the country hunting for little native boys, all the ones that never wash and never get their clothes mended and the ones who've gone slightly crackers, and I'll round them all up and Daddy can make them into a club."

Armorel said, "Oh, then Daddy's coming too?"

"Well, of course!"

"You don't—you think he could leave his work as long as that?"

"Well, I suppose so."

A puff of wind had blown away the radiant, vaporous picture.

Another came for no reason, a Second Feature seen one Saturday in the Kennington Rialto where the bilious charms of a lacy nine-year-old had at last rescued a hairy man from those of the gaming-saloon, and then in some curious way the hairy man had turned out to be the soppy girl's father, although the wedding came at the very end of the film. Something could be done with the theme, but it wanted drastic alteration; to start with, the soppy girl must be removed and someone more sensible put in her place . . . Mum had just said something in the voice that never brought anything of interest.

"What?" Tonie asked.

"I said, You do know that we're going to move?"

"Move? You don't mean—out of this house?"

"Well, of course."

"Move to another house?"

"Yes."

"Mummie, how marvellous! Where to?"

"It's not absolutely fixed. Why, don't you like this house?"

"Yes, but it's always marvellous to move!"

And already she was telling Marigold ("I've got some absolutely terrific news! I'll give you three guesses—no, I'll give you five, you won't get it, I'm absolutely certain you won't!"), she was going up and down the street calling to everyone she saw, "We're moving—have you heard?—we're going away for always!" She was on her feet and half-way to the door.

"I must tell Daise and Mrs Eustace. Oh, and Ollie and Brodie."

"I've told them," Armorel said.

Like an excited dog when its owner says "Heel!" Tonie went back to the chair she had sat in before. She had realized instantly that the mum who had been with her a few moments earlier was no longer at hand: that accessible being had belonged to the important tickets and the white, luxurious ship, the sunlit island with broken columns standing between the palms. She opened the history book again.

"Listen, Tonie, you mustn't imagine it's a better house we're going to." The voice like that of an actress rehearsing who has already spoken the line a hundred times. "It won't be. It's just that Daddy doesn't like this one, and we've got to do exactly what he wants while he's away."

"Oh, yes, of course."

Moving! Tonie thought. Great vans and men with aprons, a strange kitchen, a new room to sleep in, everything entirely changed. *The founder of Britain's power in India started his career as a humble clerk,* her eyes read. Moving! Actually going away!

". . . old enough to understand. It's got to be a house where the rent is very low, and somewhere where we don't have to keep up grand appearances. I mean, it's much better to save on living expenses than to take you away from your present school and send you to the Sand Street Schools. Of course I may have to do that anyway."

Moving, actually moving! This house was almost as much a part of her as her hands and feet. The earliest memory she had was set in the kitchen here, a blue shirt of Daddy's and the row of blue-and-yellow porridge plates behind, a saucer twisting loose from her fingers and rushing down to crash on the floor. This frame contained her understanding of the order of things: that while Daddy liked to stand outside the street door of an evening, smoking a cigarette and greeting passers-by, it was not proper for Mummie to do that sort of thing; that the Derbys could be asked to tea in the kitchen sometimes, Marigold in the front room, because it was kind to give your guests the sort of surroundings they were used to. Here everything had some meaning. The patch neatly let into a panel of the door was where Gordon had made a hole with a table-knife, one hilarious evening ever so long ago when he was being Two-Gun Towzer the wild man of Mexico; Daddy, trying to repair it before Mummie saw, had suddenly remembered that he was standing in the front room in his braces, which wasn't a proper thing to do, and in his roundabout, self-conscious way had implored her to sneak his jacket for him out of the kitchen. Of course she had found Mrs Eustace sitting on it, and—

"Mummie, is Mrs Eustace coming with us to the new house?"

"Tonie darling, haven't you been listening at all?"

"Yes, only—"

"I was just telling you, we can't go on giving charity to all sorts of people. Don't you see it's a question of money! We just can't live on charity ourselves—Cousin Raymond's charity."

"But won't Daddy go on earning what he does now?"

"Well, at present he's not earning anything."

"But won't he? Won't he have the same work again?"

This seemed to be a difficult question. It was a way of Mum's, more than of any other grown-up's, to get hold of some apparently simple question you asked her and turn it this way and that in her mind, making little tiny movements with her lips as if the words she was preparing were like children trying to slip out of school before the clock strikes half-past four. Such a response made you feel babyish and awkward, and Tonie would have rubbed out the words she had just spoken. She ought to have known that when Mum had that special, stretched-back look in her eyes—

"It's always unwise to count on things," Armorel said. "I mean—things don't always go the way you want."

This did not immediately convey anything to Tonie's mind. What spoke to her was the voice alone, measured out to bear exactly that number of words, and the eyes that came to rest at a point on the wall as an animal seeks safety in a spot where it imagines it won't be seen. She kept quite still for a moment; she was a child inclined to deliberation; and then, stretching out, she put the back of her rather small hand against her mother's cheek. It was a slighter gesture than the one her feelings urged; for in those few moments, when all the voices in the house chanced to be silent and the street itself had fallen into a twilight stillness, she had the sense that her mother's place and her own had changed: the sense a novice mountaineer might have if the ice above him gave and he found himself supporting the guide's weight on his own harness. But she knew that her mother did not care for extravagant gestures. Later she might weep, but not now, for the sudden accretion of such vast responsibility was too violent a matter for tears.

When she managed to speak her voice was exactly the opposite to what she intended; boneless and childish; it had even the faint sound of a giggle in it.

"There is me. To do things, I mean. And I don't mind having things told me. I'll do everything—Mummie I can, honestly truly!"

Armorel sat quite still for a few moments more; she did not seem to be disturbed by having Tonie's hand against her cheek, or to notice when it was taken away. Then she got up as if her name had been called and shook out the cushion on which she had been sitting. She said, going to the door:

"You mustn't bother about things, darling, you must really put your whole mind on that prep. I must go and get your tea."

33

*T*HE REASON for her decision to move was not clear-cut. She had written to Christine: 'I want to get out of this house as quickly as possible—Gian has always had some curious prejudice against it. I hope to find something a bit cheaper before he comes back, naturally all this business has cut into one's savings.' At about the date of that letter she saw Herb Evans at the Old Richmond about payment of the Weald Street rent, and in a conversation which he remembers she said: "I've always detested that house. Everyone looks in at the windows and they feel insulted somehow because I keep it clean"—or words to that effect. At any rate the decision was made swiftly and with admirable boldness.

Flock was in one morning.

". . . been doin' a bit of investigation on me own account, been all round over at Biddle Place, seen the old perisher lyin' abed there. You can take my word 'n' oath, Mrs Susie, mum, or you may not, same as you please, but there ain't one mortal scrap of evidence what the coppers or no one else can muck up against young Ardree, your husband I mean to say, what'd hold as much water as'd drown a bed-bug. Bloke on tother side of the street, he's got it as plain as puddle, he heard the door slam—that was young Ardree goin' out—and he see a whole bleedin' five minutes or more go by on his clock before he hear a smack an' a squeak, an' that was the last squeak that ever come out of that pore bloke of an Empire—an' if you ask me, not sayin' anythink against a pore bloke what got the holy angels holdin' C.O.'s orders on him at this very moment for all you or I may know, what it do strike me is the pore bloke was just about screwed bung up to the eyeballs, takin' a dive-over like that when he must've known all along about that rail bein' broke, been like that for months the ole perisher tell me. Well, that's what that bloke I see mean to tell the judge 'n' jury, an' that's what I tell him he b-well *will* tell the judge 'n' jury, an' never him mind any fancy notions what them perishin' lawyers put in his nap—blokes what don't take one mortal scrap of exercise from one end of the year to the next and draw their pay for riggin' all the odds, get me."

"It's awfully sweet of you," she said, "to take all that trouble."

The old man frowned (even from Mrs Susie he couldn't stand a sloppy line of talk), loosening his muscles and returning to the stand-at-ease position. In the kitchen he sometimes sat down, but never in this front room.

"An' in the meantime," he continued, glaring at her as if she had come on parade wrongly dressed, "there ain't nothink put down on your ticket but to keep the home fires burnin', get me. You get on to frettin' an' moanin' an' sniffin', an' what happen? Slap it go right down into the bile, an' from the bile it upset over into the lights an' liver, an' up it come again as keen as clockwork an' knock you over cock-eyed. That drawn an' haggard look, see—same as you get in the adverts, 'I was losin' all my handsome looks through sickness and worry, doctor', quotation, see—constipation, flatulence an' nervous irritability, you get the whole perishin' issue come on at you like a load o' muck, an' what good do it do to you or no one else? I'm old enough to be your granddad—close on sixty-three, I am, an' feelin' as good as ever I did— an' what I tell you is you ain't got nothink on your detail only to keep the home fires burnin' while your hearts are yearnin' inside-out till the perishin' boy come home. Take it or leave it," he said.

"Only it's not going to be this home," she answered. "At least, I don't think so."

"Meanin'?"

"I'm looking for another house," she said swiftly. "I want to move as soon as I can."

"Uh-uh?"

He focussed his eyes on her face more carefully. The truth about women—he had got it shaped up these last few years—was that they were just the same as these perishin' boys: always hiding something, and you'd got to get round the back and jump out at them to find out what it was.

"Get y'down, this street? I know, bung up with nothin' but perishin' proletariat, lot o' nosey-parkin' ole girls want to know which way up you put on your undies an' all, nothink to do all day but stick out their tongues at what's better than themselves—'*My* hubby ain't never been in the clink, lor me no, wouldn't so much as know where to find the place!'—*I* know the ole baskets. Now of you'll jus' pay attention an' hearken to me—"

"It's not that," she told him. "I decided to move some time ago."

"Young Ardree know about that?"

"I'm going to tell him as soon as I've got to hear of a suitable house."

He shrugged his shoulders. Women, they couldn't live without a bit of hole-and-corner business.

"I got you," he said. "Move to a new house—what sort of a house? Sort of West End job you want this time—sort of Earl's Court set-up?"

She shook her head. "It's got to be cheaper than this one."

"An' what's the cough-up on this?"

"Eight and six."

"Struth! Bleedin' swindle!" He paused to put the muscles of his chin and jaw through a table of exercises. "Howsoever, you won't get an Earl's Court class of place on that money. Reckon you might not get a place this *size* on that money, no matter where it is, not with a roof on it an' all, seein' how the house racket come under a bunch of nothin' but screw-face double-crossin' civvies."

His normal look of severity darkened, as if someone had offered him so gross an insult that he could think of no sufficiently savage reply. His manual and dorsal muscles were working now, like the controls of an aircraft being tested for a long flight.

"Leave it!" he said abruptly.

A small parcel labelled 'Miss Tonie, with Regards' came out of his trouser pocket onto the piano, he nodded to Armorel as if allowing her to dismiss and marched away.

A note came that evening, borne by Slimey.

Hollysian House.
Wed.

Madam.

Inquiry re Married Quarter

Ref conversation this AM, I have the honour to say I was inform some days ago that occupiers of 83 Mickett Lane where Mr Grist have accommodation are moving to house in SURBITON (SURREY). Mr Grist being absent on leave, I proceeded there this afternoon and made inquiries re same. It is a bigger house than other houses in that street having been 2 houses joined into 1, only Mr Grist have 1 room (sitting) and 1 room (bed) on 1st floor and use of W.C. etc, and place to do a bit of cooking and there are 2 (unfurnish) rooms and 1 what you might call cubby-hole on attic floor, for which he pay Mrs Elm 5 shilling (which is a swindle) out of 11^s/6^d Mrs Elm pay to owner of same. Mrs Elm have 2 rooms (bed) and 1 room (small bed) on 1st floor and all ground floor where they are small rooms but 2 or 3 or more (with 2 rooms that must have belong to house they join into 1). So there is plenty of room only you got Mr Grist occupying some and Mr Grist go with the house, as is right. There is a man works on the lift on Elephant and Castle station put in an offer for this outfit only the owner has not told him yes or no, so Mrs Elm tell me. Well, there it is, and you won't get much better on the price these days with a lot of folk crying out loud for houses, so I have taken the liberty to tell Mrs Elm to tell the owner the man that works the lift is a rough lot and like as not to smash up the place as soon as look at it. Only if you do not want it I will report to Mrs Elm lift-man now satisfactory. Only I take liberty to suggest you carry out personal inspection of same at earliest convenience, and if it suit I will advise owner of best price offered and no funny business in accordance with esteemed instructions at all times.

        And oblige,
         Your obedient servant,
           S. Flock Sgt.

  She was at Mickett Lane within an hour, standing in the respectable front passage of No. 83 and listening with stoic patience to a discursive and minute account of why Mrs Elm was obliged to move. Perhaps she would like to see the house, Mrs Elm at last suggested; well, this now was the front room, it didn't really get much light and the fire was always smoking.

  It became a tour of the house's deficiencies. Nothing would cure the squeak of this door and that one let in such a draught it went right through to your bones—that was since Fred had raised the hinges, it had always rubbed against the carpet before. Three separate times Mrs Elm had spoken to Mr Horstead about the plaster coming down off the kitchen ceiling, and still nothing done. Dark in this passage, wasn't it, and very awkward the way this cupboard was placed, Mrs Elm said. She was small, grey and overworn, nine years a widow and one who still seemed to wait, glancing over her shoulder, for her husband to answer any difficult question. "And I'll show you another place that's always damp," she said, as one who sadly tolerates the caprice of an all-wise Providence, "Mr Horstead says it come up through the wall, so there isn't anything anyone can do." She was a connoisseur of damp places.

  "And you're paying eleven and six?" Armorel asked.

  "That's right. Now I'd like you to see where the window got blown in upstairs. Just after Christmas that was. Time and time again I've spoken to Mr Horstead."

Yes, Armorel said, with the diligent politeness of racing men dragged by artistic friends through Wildenstein's, yes, it was most negligent of Mr Horstead: how difficult, how tiresome, how awkward for Mrs Elm! Wearily following her guide's erratic course, she noted how many rooms there were and nothing else. What else was there to note? In such a street you did not look for elegance or even a dull utility, you expected the houses to be planned without a grain of intelligence and built with the shoddiest materials the builder could find; this was what your money was worth and you could take it or go without: it was probably the best house in the street.

"I beg your pardon?" she said.

Mrs Elm was looking at her with a certain wistfulness.

"I say I always have done my best to keep it nice."

Standing by the door which Mrs Elm had just opened, Armorel looked at the polished finials of the bed which filled two-thirds of the room, a vastly enlarged photograph of a man with whiskers, the pink china on the washstand. The windows were tightly shut, retaining the air of the previous night. The whole house smelt of drawers where extra blankets are kept and of bubble-and-squeak fried in bacon fat. She said:

"Oh, yes, of course!"

"And that over there is Mr Grist's room—his sitting-room, I mean. You couldn't have a nicer gentleman than Mr Grist—no hi-te-ti about him but a perfect gentleman just the same. Very kind he was when—"

"I used to know him," Armorel said.

"Well, now! Would you like to see his room?"

"Well, yes, if—"

"Well, of course I'm supposed to keep it locked up and not let anyone in when he's away."

"Oh, well—"

"But I suppose he wouldn't mind an old friend just looking in, would he now?"

"Well—"

Mrs Elm took the key from a nail on the wall and opened the door.

Armorel went inside and stood looking at the room. She asked suddenly:

"There is a back door to this house, isn't there? Out into a side street?"

"Yes, I was going to show you—"

"It's all right, I only wondered."

There were pictures, a table-cloth, a cup for cross-country running, which had been in his room at Hollysian House. Everything else conformed with those objects; the room's personality was distinct not only from the rest of the house but from that of other rooms of the same kind, in the way that a man's clothes, taken off and flung on a bed, may be distinct. A card stuck into the mirror over the fireplace was covered with memoranda in Trevon's handwriting. It was a seasoned, shabby and hospitable room.

"I was going to give it a dust and a sweep-out tomorrow morning," Mrs Elm said. "Thursdays, you see, I give a proper do-out to all the upstairs rooms."

Armorel said nothing.

"I did think really I'd give it a dust-over this morning," Mrs Elm insisted, "only you know how it is some mornings, the potatoes just wouldn't get done, and then the man come about the moving, asking me a whole lot of questions they could quite well have answered for themselves, as I told him. Of course when Mr Grist's at home he don't really expect me to go in his room at all."

"Oh, he does it himself?"

"Oh, yes, does everything for himself, Mr Grist does. Quite a handy sort of gentleman, he is—been used to living on his own before he came here, so he always tell me. Of course he has a lady come in and put him straight a bit, just every so often, you know. Of course you do get a handier sort of gentleman with an unmarried gentleman, don't you?"

"Yes, I suppose so."

"Although I do always say—though I don't say it to Mr Grist himself, of course, it being none of my business this way or the other—I do always say a gentleman as nice as Mr Grist ought to have someone looking after him properly, if you see what I mean."

"Yes, of course."

"Well, now, I'll show you that back door you were asking about. I don't know that I wouldn't rather be without it, really—it lets in such a draught. . . . Was there something else you wanted to see in this room?"

"I beg your pardon? Oh—no. No, there's nothing else."

At the front door, when the tour was finished, Armorel said:

"No, I'm afraid really it's not quite the house I'm looking for.

It's very kind of you to have shown me everything—I'm sorry to have given you so much trouble."

Mrs Elm's face betrayed distress.

"Of course if I'd known you were coming I'd have had everything as straight as I could. This morning, you see, I did mean to take up the mats and sweep down the stairs, only what with the man coming from the removals—"

"You've been very kind indeed—"

"Only, you see, it's a place I've always tried to keep nice—and you know, you've no idea the way the dust come in at the front—and I'd like to think of it going to someone who'd keep it nice."

"Well, I do hope it will . . . Most kind . . . Thank you very much indeed . . ."

Next morning, however, she went to Flock's tenement in Bowler's Tithe.

She had forgotten that Flock would be at the Club at that hour, and it was Flock's wife who greeted her. Mrs Flock knew nothing about any house, she was sure there must be some mistake or Flock would have told her: Flock knew—or ought to know—better than to start getting himself mixed up with house-renting business that she hadn't been into first to see it was all right. Yes, she would give a message—ten and six and up to twelve shillings if necessary—but her advice was to be careful of taking any notice of anything Flock might say: Flock would say anything that came into his head to oblige any young lady that came along: Flock was all right where he belonged, good enough at the drilling and all that, but he'd never had any head for business and never would: fair game, Sergeant Flock was, for every new swindler that showed his face over the wall, and if he hadn't had her to look after him hand and foot all these years he'd have been in the poorhouse long before this . . .

A little after five o'clock, however, when Tonie, curiously taut and silent, was having her tea, Flock appeared at Weald Street again; stood at attention just inside the street door, raised and lowered all ten fingers, raised one finger by itself, shut one eye.

"Fixed!"

And nine days later the two 15-hundredweight lorries were drawn up outside the house. Ted Orfit's lorries: yes, he had a covered van, and it was the covered van he had meant to bring, the same as he had said to Mr Flock, but only last night—well, just when he was locking up the yard, come to that—he'd had a message from Mr Drake, bit of very urgent business Mr Drake wanted the van for, he was a good customer, Mr Drake was, and not the sort that Ted Orfit could afford to cock a snoot on. The way it was, Ted Orfit had put in a special quote on this job as a matter of obliging Mr Flock, it wasn't a job he'd see any profit on, the way you got wages and all the overheads going up and up, more like a dead loss it would be on this job, which meant to say you couldn't disappoint a customer like Mr Drake and lose pounds and pounds of steady business, however much you'd like, with men got to be kept in work, just to oblige a friend the same as he was obliging Mr Flock.

"Well, I don't really mind," said Armorel, who was not such a fool as to think it any use minding, "only I do want you to tell your men to be careful how they handle the things."

And seeing it was such a short carry, Ted Orfit said, no distance at all really, and with the weather nice and settled like it was, it wasn't as if you'd get rain coming down on everything—or even snow as it might be—

"Yes, only do please tell your men to be careful how they handle the books and china."

"Men? Well, come right down to it, there ain't only Tiny. *He* won't do no harm—will you, Tiny boy!"

The man in a green jersey standing beside the second lorry gave the barely perceptible smile of one who is dared to jump off the roof of Selfridges for a fiver. He was sixty-four and just five feet in height. He weighed something over 250 pounds.

"They've come!" Tonie was calling, running upstairs. "Mr Brodie! Ollie! Have you seen—the moving men have come!"

She had wakened early and the idea had burst upon her like a trumpet-call—Moving! Today! At that curious hour the street still slept, though a misty sun shone on the roofs and flashed from the high fanlights of the toothpaste factory; and as she stood in her pyjamas at the sloped window the holiday smell of the day seemed to be quickened by an extra excitement which ran into her nose and loins. Seeing this panorama of tiles and chimneys almost for the last time was like seeing it for the first time; and with no one moving in the street, no voice but that of lorries far off in the main road, she had the feeling that this city, blackened and smoking as it was, was something freshly laid upon bare fields, a work no human eye but hers had so far seen. There should have been some grief in knowing that the new discovery was so soon to be lost; the room allotted her in Mickett Lane would give no such view as the one she commanded now; but to find this boundless intricacy of brick and fluttered smoke newborn in the magic early sunlight, to know it as your own, to think that by nightfall you would be almost a new person, one who had lived in two different houses, that was an intoxication which flooded over all regret. Just for a moment, when she was doing her hair by the tilting mirror Gian had fixed up for her, she was pricked by a sharp distress, as if the small, bitter stream of loneliness which had flowed underground in these last weeks had suddenly found escape to the surface: would Daddy feel, when that stupid business was over, that all his jobs in this house had been a waste of time? But of course he had thought of that when he agreed to their getting the new house, which Mum and he must have talked about when she went to see him. In the new house he would enjoy doing that kind of job all over again. And now, as she thought of welcoming him in a place he had never seen, of showing him where all the switches were, watching his dumb delight with the flowers she would buy and put by his bed, the splendour of the day swept over her once more. She prayed, doing up the back of her dress and treading into her shoes, Oh, let the van come quickly, I can't wait, I just can't wait!

"Ollie! Ollie, they've come! It isn't a van, it's lorries. Two of them. I don't think they'll hold everything. There's a man called Tiny."

"Well, now, that's exciting for you, isn't it! Lorries, bless me!"

"And if you'll take him away in one or tother of them," said Brodie, "you'll be doing an act of mortal goodness to the poor persecuted cre-ature you see standing before you. Blubbering like a board-school baby half the night, you'd say it was his darlint mammie being taken away off him."

"You know well enough you got no right to do any private fixing with that Evans!" Olleroyd exploded, continuing an argument which had evidently been going on for some time. "Mr Evans got a right to be told I'm ready to pay a half share just the moment I'm back in work again—it's no fault of mine, the fur trade being the way it has since the war."

"War! Are you still blathering about that war that finished fifteen years ago, and a new one starting up again by the looks of things! A whole week I'm giving you to find a kip for yourself which hasn't got a rent on it—a whole week of buckshee livin'—"

"But surely," Tonie said, "you're both going to stay here just the same, with the new people?"

"Tonie!" Daise's voice from the bottom of the stairs. "You best get your bed things done up the way your mum said! The men'll be wanting to take them. Then you can give me a hand here if you've nothing better to do."

"I'm sure everything will be all right," Tonie said to Olleroyd. "You know the way my mother always somehow makes everything all right."

"Antonia!" Armorel called from the street door. "I want you to help Daise finish the washing-up!"

No flurry in that voice, no trace of excitement or strain. She had been up at half-past five to make needful and needless preparations, rolling bed-clothes, packing and labelling china, writing little directions. (A note for Daise, 'Keep 4 mugs and the *tin* teapot where they can be got at easily—removal men will want tea frequently.') And now, though she was pale today and her eyes dark from lack of sleep, she wore a quick, quiet cheerfulness which Tonie recognized as belonging to occasions of stress.

"I don't mind what you did when you were moving the O'Donnells," she said to Orfit with the utmost gentleness, "the way you're going to move me is to take the bedroom things first as I've said."

But for the time being no one could get upstairs or down, for at the top Olleroyd was on his hands and knees gathering the bagful of biscuits which Brodie in a fit of boisterous waggery had thrown at him, while Tiny, clasping a pair of chairs, had got himself stuck at the bottom. Already there seemed to be an unusual number of people about the house. In the kitchen Mrs Bodwin and Mrs Aaronson, good-naturedly arriving to offer help, had settled down for tea; the man who had come to take the final reading of the meter, and whom Daise had furiously told to wait, was in the passage sharing cigarettes and chat with Slimey, sent by Flock to give a hand with the loading; and just inside the front room, where he had appeared like someone on the stage at Maskelyne's, a long, thin youth with a face like a death-mask and wearing a grey muffler tucked into the remnants of a dinner suit was whispering hoarsely to everyone who passed that he had a bit of a message from Mr Drake.

"So while we're about it," Orfit said, "I suppose at the other end we'd better put all the chairs and things in first and then nail down the carpets on top? You, Tiny, you may as well stop standing there grinning an' tell me what in piggery I done with a bit of chalk I have in my hand here not above two minutes ago."

A hawk-faced man whose name seemed to be Clip and who was apt to join in removals said, "I did see a bit of chalk," and squeezed past towards the street, carrying a box of tools, boot-brushes and coils of flex.

"Chalk, now where did I see a bit of chalk?" Tiny inquired of his guardian angel.

It was easy to lose such things, because at the very start of the house's dismantlement the smaller contents, loosed from old moorings, appeared to drift upon peculiar tides. It was Ted's idea to 'get all this truck on one side just for the time being', and in the execution of this policy fire-irons from the sitting-room found their way to the bedroom above, kitchen utensils appeared in the front room and books and pictures which Ted himself had put on the pavement were being carried back by Tiny into the house. The larger pieces of furniture seemed not to move or only to move a little way towards the doors of the rooms, but clocks and ornaments, cushions and stationery, were soon taking a confused and dilatory course towards the street; the front passage, thin for its present traffic and population, was further narrowed by a train of open boxes containing tins of Brasso, boot-trees, clothes-pegs and saucepans, a towel-horse stood askew on the stairs in company with the sewing-machine, a garden-rake, a basket heaped with picture hooks and teacloths and stair-rod eyelets, while rolls of linoleum, a frock of Tonie's, a carpet-sweeper and a set of Kipling in crimson calf were spread some way along the pavement outside. It was Slimey's view that everything would work out right when once they had got out the piano; and with the gas-man's help and that of the man who had brought a message from Mr Drake he already had it standing on one end. But the way was blocked by Tiny, holding a reading-lamp and waiting with the utmost patience for Ted Orfit's orders; and Ted, by now convinced that someone had hidden his chalk from deliberate malice was roaming the house in a frenzy of revilement and blasphemy and dust.

"Miss Tonie!" Little Mrs Roberts with the beady eyes and small, sweet mouth detached herself from the crowd of onlookers and ventured just inside the door with a pair of vases in her hand. "Do you think you could have a word with your ma, Miss Tonie, and just see if these is any good to her any more? There's a nasty chip in the bottom of this one, look. I just thought your ma might not be needing them any more."

Tonie said over her shoulder, smiling:

"I'm sorry, Mrs Roberts, my mother's specially fond of those. Will you please put them back exactly where you found them."

How lucky that the child was too young to understand about her father, Mrs Derby said to Doris Ede, as they watched the lithe body in the short, blue frock twisting as cleanly as a kingfisher's through the mesh of loiterers and lumber; and wasn't she getting more and more like her mum! Indeed, the child's countenance was becoming a clear reflection of her mother's, alert, composed, as the faces about her increased in boredom or exasperation. It did give you the willies, really it did, Mrs Bodwin said, mournfully surveying the shapes of pictures and furniture marked on the walls of the dismantled sitting-room: but if the desolation had the same effect on Tonie it was not apparent in her face. She was like a kitten today in the alternation of her moods, one moment swinging from the tail of a lorry, throwing back her head and laughing, a minute later gravely writing out an instruction of Armorel's to prevent the men from making mistakes at the other end. In exactly Armorel's voice, never loud but sufficiently incisive to be heeded, she had started to give orders of her own. "Tiny, help me with this box, please. . . . Clip, you've had enough tea, you ought to do some work. . . . I'm sorry, Mr Orfit, but Mum said that cabinet was not to go on till last of all": so that men who had been saying "Now then, twopenny, out of my way!" were beginning to keep out of hers. At intervals she was chivvying off the children who swarmed about the lorries after souvenirs; she was even taking the flustered Daise under her control.

"Yes, I know poor Mrs Eustace is in a state, but she's been sitting and crying like that all the time I've known her. You must simply go on telling her that Mum's got everything arranged—I don't know what the arrangement is but she's got something all worked out for Mrs Eustace as well. And will you thank Mrs Aaronson very much for helping and tell her she can go now."

The peculiar, confidential smile which people said she got from her mother was always hovering about her face, ready for each time her eyes met those of a friend. Her private world, with its own sun and cloud, seemed to go with her as she darted from room to room; yet there was evidence that she had a spy-hole, wide enough, on the other world as well.

"Slimey! What are they doing out there now?"

"Well, you see, Miss Tonie, there's a Mr Drake that says he's got to have one of the lorries."

"Well, please tell Mr Orfit that he can't."

"There's no good telling anything to Mr Orfit."

There wasn't. He was sorry, but Mr Drake was a customer worth steady money, and if Mr Drake wanted to have an extra lorry what was being held up on a cut-price job which was nothing more than to oblige Mr Flock, well, then, Mr Drake got to have it and there it was. So the chairs and bookshelves, the boxes and the odds-and-ends which Clip had laboriously arranged on the leading lorry were being cheerfully dumped on the pavement by Tiny, and Olleroyd was slowly picking them up and dumping them on the lorry behind, while Brodie leant against the wall and watched him, shouting ribald comments to the women on the other pavement and laughing like a man possessed. The rear lorry was already overfull. A chair that Olleroyd had just heaved up was lying with its front legs stuck through the glass of a book-case and another had fallen over into the road.

"Ollie, do be careful! Wait! Tiny, you've got to help him!"

"Young miss," Orfit shouted, "Tiny will take his orders from me and from no other fumin' suckin' quarter-size of a little bitch whatever. My orders is he's to get the clobber off this fumin' truck an' do it bloody quick!"

Brodie suddenly stopped laughing.

"You—will you keep your dirty blasphemin' tongue off that kid!"

"—It's all right, Mr Brodie!—"

" 'Ere, are you the kid's pa, or what?" Orfit demanded.

"I'll show you what I am, becrike—"

"Now, see here, I got a message from Mr Drake—"

"An' now you'll be gettin' a message from me, bejazy—"

"Cor—look at old Brodie!"

" 'Old y' braces for y', Ted?"

"Mr Brodie, stop! Thank you very much, only you'd much better—"

"Tonie! You got to talk to her, I can't do nothink with her!"

Turning round, Tonie saw Daise in tears. A few yards away Mrs Eustace was sitting on the kerb with a cardboard box which contained all her possessions on her knees. She was weeping; not as she usually wept, with an endless succession of triple sniffs and the moans of a child in troubled sleep, but convulsively, as a man will weep with a shrapnel wound in the lungs, and in silence, except when some animal inside her—as it seemed—sent out a sudden, tearing cry. It was a disturbing, a frightening spectacle; the black bombazine dress in shameful disorder, the dirty white hair straggled over her eyes, her grey face twisted almost out of the human shape; and the women who had started to cluster about her had fallen back. Only one, a stranger, was close and bending over her, a youngish woman tightly fastened in a sensible coat and skirt, whose kindness was painted on her face with a broad and overloaded brush. A car was standing a little further along the road with its driver reading *The Passing Show.*

"It's the lady come to take her," Daise explained.

"Take her where?"

"I do' know. Some place your mum's fixed up."

Tonie went to Mrs Eustace.

"Mrs Eustace, what's the matter?"

"Now you'd better run along, dear," the stranger said, "I'll look after her. I'm Miss Paulidge from the Queen's Road House of Eventide. They're always a bit upset until we get them settled." She turned to Mrs Eustace again, stooped and got her up off the kerb. "You just don't know how comfy you're going to be! Lots of nice old ladies there'll be for you to talk to. Let me take your things. Come along now!"

Upright, Mrs Eustace ceased to struggle or to cry out. The whole of her weight rested on Miss Paulidge's capable arms, her feet sprawled on the ground as if they belonged to a linen doll. To all appearance she was unconscious, almost lifeless; but as her head lolled over sideways her eyes opened just as a doll's might and came into focus on Tonie's face, her lips started to writhe and then, surprisingly, she spoke in a voice hardly different from the one Tonie had known from babyhood:

"Tonie! Tonie dearie! You won't let them, will you, Tonie! You won't let them take ole Maudie away—I ain't done nothin', I never been any trouble—"

It was plain that Miss Paulidge was used to old ladies.

"Now then, Grannie, don't you be fretting!" She was moving her burden very slowly, expertly, towards the car, flooding the scene with the searchlight of her kindness. "You'll be surprised how nice Miss Severil is, a lovely pink eidie you're going to have on your bed—"

"Wait!" said Tonie. "I'm going to see my mother—"

"That's right, dear, you run along and find your mummie—"

"But you're to wait until my mother comes!"

"That's right, dear!"

"Mrs Derby, you won't let her do anything till Mother comes?"

"It do seem a shame—"

"I never been any trouble—"

"Of course not, Grannie! Let's have a little walk together, shall we now!"

Tonie had broken away, dodging through the circle of women, running past Ted and Brodie, who faced each other like a pair of gamecocks, pushing Olleroyd aside from the door. "Slimey, where's Mum—upstairs?" She arrived breathless in the bedroom. "Mummie, there's a bitch—there's an awful person—she's dragging Mrs Eustace—"

"Wait a moment, dear!"

"But, Mummie, she's got a car, she's—"

"Tonie, you must not interrupt! I'm busy. I can't see to everything at once."

A youth of seedy respectability whom Tonie recognized as belonging to Mr Hoven the lawyer was talking to her mother in his small, lisping, pussy-cat voice:

". . . I was saying, Mrs Ardree, it's just possible it might come on this afternoon, but only if it's taken out of order. You see, Mrs Ardree, that does happen sometimes—if they haven't got someone they specially want for a case they sometimes take the next one instead. Only Mr Hoven says it's very unlikely, because Mr Swift never does like to start on an important case late in the day."

Armorel nodded. Her voice came as if on a bad telephone line.

"Yes. Yes, I see. Well, will you tell Mr Hoven that I—well, will you just tell Mr Hoven you've given me the message and thank him very much. . . . Oh, and will you ask Mr Hoven if he'd be kind enough to telephone my cousin at Finchley—yes, the one who came with me last time, Mr Hoven has his number—and give him the information you've just given me. . . . *Now*, Tonie, what is it?"

"Mummie, you must come! There's an awful person trying to put Mrs Eustace in a car, she's absolutely miserable, she's nearly dead, she's got no one to help her!"

Without answering Armorel slowly followed Tonie out to the landing. But she did not go downstairs, she turned the other way and opened the door leading to the attic ladder. Tonie said wildly:

"Mummie, aren't you going to come?"

Armorel stopped and looked over Tonie's head. She was still faintly smiling, but the smile looked as if it had no relation to her thoughts. All her movements had slowed down.

"What? Mrs Eustace? It's all right, I've arranged all that. She's going to be properly looked after."

"But, Mummie, she doesn't want to go!"

It was like talking to the very old, who must climb slowly and painfully out of the valley they live in to answer a simple question about the affairs of today. Armorel said:

"Doesn't want—? But she can't stay here. There won't be anybody here except those men—Brodie—"

"But she could come with us. She could be in the kitchen like she always has. I thought—"

Armorel caught her breath as if something in her chest made respiration slightly painful.

"Tonie, I—I've got an awful lot to think about."

Subdued, as when a theatre curtain goes up, Tonie said:

"That man—he was from Mr Hoven, wasn't he? Was it about Daddy?"

"Yes, but—"

"Did he say it was going to be today? Daddy being tried?"

"What?"

"Mummie, you ought to go! You ought to go at once, I'll find Slimey, he'll get you a taxi."

Armorel said: "What? No. I don't know, it isn't at all certain. There's a lot to do."

"But, Mummie, I can do everything. There's lots of men and people."

"Tonie dear, I'd rather you—just—keep out of the way for the time being."

That should have been enough for a sensible child. Tonie, instead of going away, took one step up the ladder and stood gripping the handrail tightly. Had Armorel been looking she would have seen that her face, losing colour and with the lips curiously tautening, had ceased to be the face of a child.

"You *are* going to be there if Daddy's being tried?" No tears in the voice: a voice of passion, but of passion controlled. "Mummie, you've got to tell me, I'm not a baby, I've got to know things. He is my father, it's my business as much as yours."

Pausing again, still looking over Tonie's head, Armorel said:

"What? Tonie dear, I'm awfully busy and I'm rather tired—we'll have a talk sometime."

Tonie went back to the street. The women, Daise among them, were still buzzing in a group, but Miss Paulidge and Mrs Eustace had disappeared and the car was gone. The leading lorry, the one Ted Orfit drove himself, had moved off as well. In the centre of a second group Brodie was leaning against the wall again, and now there was a stream of blood from his nose which Slimey and Olleroyd with an anxious babble of sympathy were gathering into grubby handkerchiefs. The second lorry, piled high for the first journey, had its engine going, and Tiny was at the wheel with Clip beside him. Without speaking to anyone Tonie climbed up at the back and found herself a seat on the bottom of a cupboard which was lashed upside-down to the driver's cab.

Clouds gathering in a thick, low screen had ended the promise of early morning; the street had recovered its everyday countenance, jejune and grey. As the lorry went noisily into motion the women were calling, 'Look at that child up there!—You be careful of yourself!—Here, Tonie, does your mum know you're goin'?' and a string of children tore after it with yells and cheers, 'Cor, look at her up on her ma's muckin's! Urcher, To-nie, give us a fumin' roide!' She didn't answer or wave, she never looked back at the house where she had spent the whole of her life. In Becket Street, where they stare at a tabby cat passing, people halted to gaze at the lorry with its elephantine driver and his cadaverous mate, the preposterous edifice of household gods which lurched and strained on the clumsy lashings; and there were shouts and laughter from the market barrows in Moravia Lane. But when it turned into the main road the interest of this unwieldy equipage was submerged in the confusion of carts and taxis fiercely shouldering their way towards the Thames. A man being shaved in Finchel's saloon did smile for a moment at the sight of an up-ended sofa swaying across a Gold Flake girl's enormous eyes; on the upper deck of a bus a typist said "Coo!" to her friend, seeing at her own height a doll's house jammed against Leighton's *Psyche* and the back of an umbrella stand; but in this simmering and ceaseless current, among the Pickford vans and market waggons crowding between the trams and the bustling pavements as if one city were threaded through another, few passers-by had leisure to notice the loosely-steering lorry with its jumbled freight of tea-chests wedged in the legs of chairs, old picture-books, a summer frock escaping from a trunk with a broken catch. As for the child perched up on top, she was perhaps of low intelligence; for she sat with her hands folded in her lap and looked straight in front of her with more than a Londoner's apathy, indifferent to the tangled life which passed, accepting the adventure with her delicate mouth severely shut, eyes never lighting in response.

The rain started late in the afternoon and as the light began to go it came on harder. The piano and some other furniture from the final carry were still on the pavement in Mickett Lane, and inside the house it looked as if nothing would ever get straight. Tonie was tired now; she could find nothing useful to do, and anything she sat on proved to be something that someone wanted to move. At present all the smells of the house were foreign and unfriendly, they were the smells of travelling rather than of living. The damp breeze which came in through the open front door whipped tiresomely about all the rooms: it was like being in camp, without the romantic excitement of camping.

None of the heavy stuff could be got upstairs because the electricians who should have come the day before had taken up several boards on the landing. No one could find the carpet which was to go in the front room. Sucking a dead cigarette, Tiny stood in the passage patiently waiting for orders as he had stood in the other passage for a great part of the morning. Most of the others were in the kitchen, where Slimey had got the gas to work and where Maria, arriving with Simon to see how things were getting on, was making a generous quantity of tea.

"Stand to reason, I can't put the stuff upstairs if there's no upstairs to put it," Ted Orfit said shortly and sourly, having negotiated the gap in the landing and reached the room where Armorel was putting up beds. "None of my orders, all these blokes fumin' round with the bloody electric. Can't keep my blokes here all night, neither—cut the bloody price an' do four times the fumin' work, that's what it come to."

"Slimey," said Armorel, "I wish you'd be very kind and see if you can buy two or three pounds of candles . . . I'm sorry, Mr Orfit, but you're not going to get one penny out of me until the job's finished and finished the way I want. If you hadn't taken off the second lorry you'd have had it done hours ago. . . . Yes, Daise, what is it?"

"It's an old lady in the kitchen, Mrs Jan. Seems she been sleepin' here these last three nights an' she says she's got a right to live here."

"To *live* here?"

"Well, there's a Mr Jenkins, she says, that bought the house for her and him to live in, some time back she says it was, an' she says she's got a right to the whole house only she won't ask for nothink only a place in the kitchen where she can have her food and sleep at nights. Mrs Inch, she says her name is."

"Oh . . . I'll see her presently. . . . Yes, what do you want?"

Clip stood before her like Death in a Morality. Sorry to trouble, he said; bit of a job he'd promised for a gentleman, it was gone the time he'd promised half-an-hour back, he'd just like to settle up if that would be quite all right.

Armorel called, "Mr Orfit!" but Ted was evidently busy now.

There was just himself, Clip explained, and young Charlie out there who had come in to oblige, he being a sort of a pal of Clip's, and Clip having the varickers the way they tell him over on the clinic he didn't ought to be raising heavy weights not by himself. Charlie wasn't going to charge nothing, Clip said—him being a pal of Clip's—only naturally Clip would give the lad a slice off his own quid what she was going to give him for himself.

"But you know perfectly well I haven't engaged you," she said. "Mr Orfit's doing this move, he's the one who's got to pay you if anyone has."

Clip said he perfectly understood: she was tired, naturally—knew himself the way she felt, sort of got on your mind, moving house and all—and he wouldn't want to trouble her at a time when she was as busy as she was. He was quite ready to wait, Clip said. He went off with a loosely fitted dignity to continue his conversation with Tiny and Charlie in the passage downstairs.

As far as anyone could see she was no more tired than she had been this morning: the day's fatigues and misadventures, the incessant bickering and confusion, had only increased her calm. Where she was at any moment things fell into shape, and when that shape was lost her team waited, like the duller children in a class-room, till she came round again. She had spared herself no physical labour: when anything heavy had to be lifted she was generally there to take her share of the load; and yet, working closely with the others, she had kept the detachment of a master-tradesman surrounded by novices. In the blue, belted overall she had worn all day she was still comparatively tidy, with her hair recently combed. Her movements were still precise, her voice as gentle as a mother superior's. Only another woman, and one of her own kind, would have noticed that the little things her hands did—picking up bits of paper from the vast untidiness, tightening the cap of a tube of toothpaste—were sometimes independent of her thoughts; and that when she was asked questions, now, a larger fraction of time elapsed before her mind had gathered warmth enough to answer.

"Yes, darling, is there something you want?"

"No, Mummie. I only thought—I only wondered if I could help."

"Help? Oh." She had got the large bedstead up and was looking about for something. "You ought to get to bed. I told that man—yes, your bed is here, I'll have it fixed up in a minute."

It was the bed key she was looking for, Tonie realized and found it. Tonie said:

"Mummie, have you heard anything more about Daddy? About the trial?"

"What?" Armorel gave a little shake to her head as one shakes a jar to loosen something stuck to the side. "I shall have to get curtains up, just in this room. Where are they?—Yes, over there. I think this rod will do if those sockets will work. Tonie, did you see someone coming upstairs? A woman, I thought I saw some woman going past the door."

"There's a Mrs Inch in the kitchen."

"No, not that sort of woman. Yes, the rings are in that box. Oh, just go and see if you can find Slimey, I sent him for some candles. And I'll want matches, you can probably find a box among the kitchen things."

"Yes, Mummie. . . . I suppose Mr Hoven would have sent another message if it had been today."

"What? Oh, yes, I suppose so. Darling, I'd be so grateful if you could find some matches."

There was no chair handy, so she had to move the bed over to the window and stand on that to get at the curtain rod sockets, which were rusty and difficult to work. A sash was broken (it was one of the items to which Mr Horstead had long promised his attention) and through the open window the rising wind drove a spray of rain onto her neck and shoulders; it caught the curtain and shook it with such violence that the end of the rod she had fixed already came out of the socket and a dozen rings immediately slipped off the end. Biting her lip, she got down, knelt on the wet floor-boards and started to replace them.

Someone came in and she heard the clink of china as a tray was put on the bed behind her. She said:

"Oh, thank you, Daise, that's very kind."

But when she turned she saw it was not the sort of tray that Daise would have prepared: there was matched china, bread-and-butter neatly cut. Looking up, she caught sight of a grey coat in the semi-darkness of the passage. She said:

"Oh—"

"I thought you might need a cup." A well-known voice: Elizabeth Kinfowell's: so unobtrusive it was hardly more than a whisper. "I'd like to help, dear, only I don't want to get in the way, there seem to be so many people swarming about like centipedes."

For a moment Armorel stared at Elizabeth's coat as if it reminded her of something she could not place: the bed was between them, it would not have been entirely easy for her to lean forward and kiss her friend. Then she said rather rapidly, returning to the curtain-rod:

"That's awfully sweet of you—it was sweet of you to come. You don't mind—I've got to get this room so that Tonie can go to bed, she's terribly tired. No—thank-you ever so much—I don't need any help, it's only just this room and I can sort out everything else afterwards."

"Won't you just have that tea?"

"I will when I've got this up." She was on the bed again, her voice was inevitably jerky as she stretched and struggled to refix one end of the rod in the socket. "It's all right, I can manage, I know how it goes. How clever of you—to find me here—I didn't think anyone knew." That end was steady and she moved precariously along the bed to put up the other one. "I just had to move. Flock found this place for me—Trevon Grist has some of the rooms. You remember Trevon, of course. He's on holiday."

"I know—a rather special holiday. Dear, I've got heaps to tell you, only—"

"Yes, I know!" The rod was in place. Armorel got down, went to the fire-place and picked up the frame of Tonie's bed. "I must just get this up for Tonie. Yes, it's a long time—I've been meaning to write, only I've been so busy, these lawyers and people—of course I heard about your trouble, I was so terribly sorry. (Oh, thank-you—if you could just hold it like that for half a tick while I get the other end.) Yes, I believe Trevon's coming back tonight, it's a nuisance not having the house to myself but I don't suppose he'll be any trouble—I could always manage Trevon. We must—you must come and have tea when

450

I've got settled. (Thank-you so much. I put the key down somewhere. I sent a man out for candles, I do wish he'd hurry.) Yes, it would be nice to have a long talk again."

Tonie came. "I've got the candles, Mummie. Shall I light some?"

"What? Yes, do, darling. No, I'll only want one in here, we mustn't waste things. Light one, will you—look, you can stick it in this—and then will you take the rest back to Slimey and get him to light some and put them where they're wanted, the men may do some work if they can see what they're doing. Thank-you, darling."

Elizabeth said: "Hullo, Tonie!"

"Oh, how do you do!" Tonie kissed her.

"Just take the others to Slimey, darling," Armorel repeated. "Oh, wait, take this bread-and-butter, I expect Daise will find you something to put on it for your supper. And then come up again and I shall have got your bed ready."

"Mummie, do you think Mrs Eustace—"

"We can talk tomorrow, darling."

The candle flame, stooping and fencing in the draught, threw on the open trunks and their scattered contents a darting light which was devoid of cheerfulness: the quivering shadows of naked bedsteads gave the room the look of a twisted cage. In a curious way, the small increase of light seemed to magnify the sounds that came, sounds foreign to the inside of a house, the chilly echoes of boots on bare floors, the whine and thump of the front door swinging on a short tether of string, continuous voices heard as if from the other side of a yard. Through those voices Tonie's came clearly from somewhere downstairs: "Does anyone know where Slimey's got to?"

"There's one thing I do want to tell you about," Elizabeth said.

Armorel, busy tightening the bolts on the bed frame, did not look up. She said, laughing unevenly:

"It's funny, we're always pushing things about. You remember—the first time we saw Trevon, Flock made us push the parallel bars." Then the laughter trickled away. "You mean about Gordon Aquillard?" she said quietly, with no flutter in her voice. "I don't think really we need talk about that. I—you know, it's all so long ago, I can hardly remember what he looked like. Of course he was most frightfully stupid, he ought to have told me about—about you, before—before anything developed. I do wish people would always tell me things."

Elizabeth said in a voice as quiet as hers: "Yes, people do go horribly wrong on that. They wait for the right time to say things, the time when they think it will hurt least, and then it's the wrong time. Darling—"

"If only Gian—"

"Oh, darling, how wretched of me not to say anything—as if I thought of nothing but myself—"

"But that's what I *don't* want! People keep expecting me to talk about Gian, but what is there to say! What can I do! I'm not allowed to give evidence, and even if I was—well, I wasn't there, there wouldn't be anything I could say."

The door had been left ajar. Elizabeth shut it. She asked timidly:

"When is it going to be—the trial?"

"I don't know. No one seems to know—they like to keep you in a state of uncertainty, the people who run these legal things. They tell me one thing one day and something else the next. I can't hang about the Court all day long just in case, I've got so much to do—this move, everything. It's no good working yourself into a state about a thing, even if that's what everyone expects you to do. People think you don't care about your husband unless you're moaning and moping all the time. *I* think one might just as well leave all that till—oh, well, what does it matter!"

She had started to make up Tonie's bed and Elizabeth was automatically tucking-in on the other side. Riding an impulse at its crest, Elizabeth came round the bed, put her arm about Armorel's waist and pulled her down beside her. Her voice came like sunlight flickering on broken water.

"It's going to be all right! You do know it's going to be all right!"

Neither resisting nor responding, keeping her face turned away from the candle, Armorel said:

"What do you mean?"

"They couldn't say he was guilty—I read it all in the papers when the case was heard by the magistrate. There just isn't any evidence they could possibly—"

Armorel broke in like a singing master when a pupil is doing his hopeless best.

"There's heaps of it!" she said.

"But not—"

"Elizabeth, there's no point in your talking to me as if I was a child. He won't get off—it's obvious, I've quite made up my mind about it." She spoke rapidly, but still with control. "You've got to face these things and I've done it. I've made all my plans. This house will cost a bit less than Weald Street, I shall take some more lodgers as well as Trevon, or else I'll get work again. I expect Trevon himself will be quite helpful, one way or another."

The pressure of Elizabeth's hand increased.

"Oh, but—oh, my dearest—but, yes, that's right, I suppose, I suppose it's brave and right, preparing for the very worst. Only—think if everything happens the other way, just think how wonderful—"

"You mean, having Gian back?"

Till then neither had moved. Sitting side by side, they might have been lovers in a park in the early, timorous stage; and in this carcase of a room furnished by stark shadows, the windows left bare as the curtain rose and thrashed behind them, there was nothing to generate the warmth of privacy from which tenderness is kindled. But the giant doors of safes are opened with small keys. For weeks past there was no one to whom Armorel had spoken that name; it had been 'my husband', 'Mr Gian', 'Mr Ardree'; and now, as if the word possessed some fairy-tale significance, the threads of will which kept her face and body in tension as a soldier's are kept on parade appeared to loosen and slip. Like nervous people suffering inoculation she caught her breath, the hand which had been playing with the top button of her overall fell down into her lap.

"Elizabeth," she said, half-turning her head, "Elizabeth—darling listen!"

And in that instant, recognizing in the muted light a profile she had once seen in the Lanesborough drawing-room, Elizabeth believed that the long estrangement of their spirits was over. She whispered into the expectant silence, "Yes, tell me, tell me—whatever I've done—" and the body leaning against her arm relaxed, the pale forehead came down towards her shoulder. "You know it's all right with me, whatever I've been or done . . ."

But there are words which must have tears to carry them, and the merciful gift of weeping like that of sleep is not at everyone's command. A moment was in bud: something lacked which should have brought it into blossom. When seconds had passed it was seen to have withered; and Armorel, cautiously moving her body free, standing up, gathering her tiredness and sending it away in a little, conventional yawn, said:

"Yes, it's been a trying time—everything's been fearfully different from what I planned. Still, one just has to make new plans, and not rely on anyone else. I'd love to talk about it—perhaps next week—it's terribly sweet of you being so sympathetic and kind. I must see what they're doing downstairs."

She was going to the door. In a windy, uncharacteristic voice Elizabeth said:

"I did want to tell you about Trevon, about Trevon and me. You know I've been fond of him for ever so long—"

"You? Trevon?—"

"And we were married a fortnight ago."

There was no chance, just then, for Armorel to answer as such news demanded. For Slimey was at the door in a sweat of agitation, Clip was just behind him and someone else stood in their shadow, while a volley of obscenities from Ted came crackling up the stairs, "—cross-eyed bitch suppose I'm payin' out on every bee she choose to hire on top of me own!" From the farther background Maria's elderly but still incisive voice was slashing into Ted's, ". . . a *bad* man, I say it, I say-itse Orfit have no honouren gentable at all!" A bloke had got to live, Clip was explaining, a bloke couldn't work for nothing, look at it whatever way you pleased; and at every break in this adenoidal litany the tearful Slimey was interjecting some sorrow of his own; there was nothing to be done with that swindling Orfit, he'd say as much to Sergeant Flock, it was near an hour since that Tiny had moved a foot from the spot he stood on now, and Mrs Ardree's lovely piano standing on the pavement there like a poor stray kitten in the rain. Within this vortex of dissatisfaction there was not much room for private pleas. But Olleroyd nudging forward like a barge in a narrow lock, soaking wet and with all the buttons of his overcoat in the wrong holes, clutching an eruptive suitcase and a wisp of draggled flowers, was evidently unaware of that. With the deprecating smile of one who has been applauded for some trivial feat he leant forward, tipping the rain from his bowler hat on to Armorel's neck, and whispered in her ear: a bit of trouble he and Brodie were having over the room they had at Weald Street; the way it was—with the fur trade so bad and all—there was nowhere for them to go just for tonight, and Brodie in a bad way with his eye closed up from a technical mistake. Would it be asking too much of Mrs Gian, for the true lady she always was, to give them a corner they could sleep in for a matter of two or three days?

Armorel stood listening to the several urgent voices with her lips together and with the impassive eyes of a cattle auctioneer. Then she spoke swiftly: "You and I, Slimey, can move the piano together—Clip says he's an invalid, he's not allowed to move things. If you want to earn ten shillings, Clip, you can put these boards down and then get everything tidy in the two front rooms downstairs. Otherwise nothing. All right, Mr Olleroyd—one night, and one night only: in the kitchen —and you'll both have to share it with a very tiresome old woman called Mrs Inch. You'll excuse me, Elizabeth?" She took the fish-paste jar in which Slimey had placed a lighted candle, pushed past the men and stepped nimbly over the gap in the boarding. She did stumble at the top of the unfamiliar stairs, her hand failing to find the rail, but she recovered her balance immediately. "Daise! Daise, will you be a dear and put on your mac and slip round to the police station. Ask for Sergeant Beard and tell him I'm having trouble here with Mr Orfit— spelt O—R—F—I—T. You've given Tonie her supper? . . ."

The sound of a car drawing up came naturally into Tonie's dream. She had not been asleep, she supposed, for all the time she had been aware of lying in an unfamiliar room; but her thoughts, slipping a little aside from the track of consciousness, had taken her to a curious station where she and Marigold and Gordon were waiting for a train to carry them to Greece, while Mrs Eustace, weeping bitterly, waved to them from the other side of the line. Gordon was being troublesome, he kept lying down between the rails, shouting that he could move in plenty of time; and when the train came, made up of a motor car with a string of boats behind it, it passed right over Gordon and stopped with him lying underneath. It was Daddy driving the car and she had tried to explain about Gordon, but Ted Orfit had kept on interrupting, saying that everything found on the line belonged to him, and all the time there were loud bangs coming from the engine. The bangs continued as the dream broke and dissolved.

Not knowing the time, she supposed it was towards morning, but there were sounds of movement somewhere in the house. Even now she could not quite believe that Gordon was out of danger; and with the idea that someone ought to be told, she got out of bed, felt her way across the room and out, barefoot, to the landing.

With the front door shut against the noises of the street the bare-floored house had assumed a chilly personality of its own. Its bustling activity had been reduced to the twitches of a body which sleeps. But there were voices everywhere, as if she stood in a dark cave surrounded by conspirators: from below, a woman's querulous murmur blended with Olleroyd's panting voice; from a nearer room, surprisingly, the silver voice of Aunt Elizabeth. A light showed from the half-open door of a room on the other side of the passage. She stole across, peeped in and saw her mother on hands and knees near the window, scrubbing the floor. "Mummie!" she called softly, but her voice was covered by the noise of the brush; and after a few moments, realizing that Mum was too busy to be bothered about a dream, she crept away.

The loneliness which had stalked her for so long took hold of her now, and she dreaded going back to her bed in a strange room. A child would have found comfort in the warmth she had left, a grown woman would not have needed it. For Tonie a part of childhood's safety had been taken away as the rooms were cleared at Weald Street; and if, as she believed, she was ready to cross the threshold of that other world where voices were lowered and sentences hastily altered in the presence of children, the one who should have guided and welcomed her there was the same who, with inveterate gentleness, with the smile of an inscrutable wisdom, was turning her away. Utterly alone, filled with a sadness she could only a little understand, she stood shivering in the middle of the landing and silently cried.

Then she grew frightened, for the knocking she had heard in the dream was repeated, and it sounded eerily in this carpetless house. Something must be wrong, someone was coming to tell them they had no right to be here at all. Downstairs the sound of arguing grew louder as the kitchen door was opened, she heard Olleroyd's stockinged footsteps in the passage below, the peevish voice of Mrs Inch, "I tell you I know it's Mr Jenkins!" and the sound of the back-door bolt being drawn. Overcoming her fear, of which she was ashamed even then, she went a little way downstairs.

All the light there was in the downstairs passage came from a candle in the kitchen. She did not hear what Olleroyd said when he opened the back door, she just saw him passing back into the kitchen with someone behind him. There was a moment's silence, as at the beginning of a children's party, then the men's voices started together with Brodie's uppermost in an incoherent jumble of exclamations, ". . . knock me all of a heap, begod an' all! . . . thought it was a ghost, I'll sware I did! . . ." and below them, faintly, another voice:

"... no one to tell me where they'd gone."

This moment was too much for her to manage, too sudden and too different from the one she had built and rehearsed in the class-room, in bed, in buses coming home from school. Instead of running she went down slowly to the bottom of the stairs, and slowly, as if she had been summoned to the principal's room, past the litter of unplaced furniture and boxes along the passage below. Only when she turned into the kitchen did the buried tempest of longing take her body into its power, throwing her into her father's arms, where she clung fiercely and speechlessly with her mouth pressed into his cheek, her throat and chest torn by the crying that would not escape.

Gian, quivering, almost brought down by her violence, mumbled: "Aw—Tonie! . . . There now! . . . Well!"

When the strength of the embrace gave out, when she had kissed his hands and he had knelt to kiss her hair and neck, a new impulse took charge of her. She ran now, colliding with boxes, stumbling on the stairs, flew across the landing as if demons were after her and came panting to her mother's side. Her voice was still locked, the words she tried to shout came out as gusts of breath, shaped but empty of sound.

"Mummie! He's come!"

Her mother wrung out the cloth she was using, hung it on the side of the pail, wiped her hands, stood up.

"Tonie, what are you doing out of bed? Have you had a dream or something?"

"He's come! Daddy—he's here!"

Her mother stood as if, from the darkness close by, a sentry had cried 'Halt!' She said:

"Tonie, shut the door!"

Then she said:

"What's today?—I can't remember what day it is—the clerk told me—can't you remember what the clerk said?"

Tonie had not moved to shut the door. As if she were a very stupid child she stood gazing at her mother's face, with such absorption that she did not hear—or did not look as if she heard—her father feeling his way up the stairs. They were both in the same positions, like children playing some game where you are out if you stir a muscle, when he came to the doorway.

Only professionals—actors, royalty—are a match for their own triumphs: the scorer of the winning goal, the record-breaking airman, can merely smirk and mumble when they are pushed in front of the exigent cameras. Gian, standing there with his tie askew, clinging to a parcel of his belongings, had not the air of a victor or even of master of this house; rather, he looked like one of the refugees who cluster like animals at the end of endless journeys, waiting for someone to tell them what to do. He did put on a smile, the smile of a schoolboy when an aunt congratulates him on some achievement she cannot in the least understand; and in that instant he appeared almost boyishly young. But he was too tired from today's journey to keep on smiling. He said only:

" 'Lo, Sue! Got off all right."

Armorel said to Tonie, without any unkindness: "I've told you, darling, you must get back to bed!"

And Tonie, hearing that exhausted tone of her mother's, seeing that smile of hers like a flame that the wind is blowing about, found her legs carrying her out of the room. She was a child not dull in intuition, she did not want to be present where grown-up people might be in tears, or to listen to what they said. A car was going noisily up the street, it was only by chance that she caught a few words spoken by her mother, "Gian dear . . . need to pretend to me," as she moved like a sleep-walker across the windy landing, and on (because she still lacked fortitude to be quite alone) towards the slit of light where she had heard Aunt Elizabeth's voice.

34

"SEE THAT CHAP going into that house over there?" Tim Heald would say with the corner of his mouth. "I could tell you something about that bloke. Got away with murder, that bloke did. Honest, same as I'm talking to you now. Judge let him off. Oh, yes, he done it all right. An' I could show you as easy as wink the ole girl that saw him do it—only she won't tell you. Dumb as Jumbo—got her head screwed on. Yes, he done it—to a bloke called Empire, chucked him down his own stairs, round in Biddle's Place there. An' a lot of weepin' an' moanin' there was about *that*—dirty twisting little fuming pimp, clock like a parson's, give his sluts a tanner out of every quid they pulled in . . . When? Oh, two or three years back."

He was never sure about years, now that his wife was gone: he could not have said, straight off, how long he had been the owner of Begbie's Store. At sixty-seven you see only a few division posts on the track behind, you just think of 'before the war' and 'since Mabie died'; and what was the use of worrying about the passage of time, or anything else that didn't concern you, like all this humble-bumble in the papers about the Germans and their perishing Jews, so long as you got your victuals and kept your own floor tidy.

"The way these chaps go on," he said to Herb Evans, "you'd think the world was nothing but a misery because they don't happen to own it. *I'm* all right, an' I don't even want to own the fuming street. All this gritting and grizzling about the times being bad—the times aren't any worse than what they always were. You ask me what was the best time I ever knew," he would say with a dry spit, "and I'll give you the answer, no matter when you ask me. 'Here and now,' that's my answer to that!"

For he lived precisely within his mental income: fifty to a hundred customers whom he knew by name and a dozen travellers who had been calling for years; a walk along to the Richmond after closing shop, the *Evening News* at five o'clock and *The People* on Sunday. His talk was mostly a drill, standard answers to standard greetings, terse and slightly cynical. ("Sights of London? What sights? In any case you can't see 'em, not in this fog. London? Nothing but ten million mugs that don't have the sense to go somewhere else.") Fifty years of taking down the shutters at nine, "Ta, Mrs James—*and* the next?" putting the shutters up again at eight: not much of a life for any bloke, they said at the Richmond. Yet it seemed to be all he needed. "Ruddy great Archangel come along the street" (Herb Evans put it) "blowin' the last toot—'Come on, Tim Heald, Big Boss wants you up aloft.' 'Well, if it's all the same to you,' says Tim, 'I'll just go on mindin' the shop.'"

Yet he was not entirely blind to change—how could he be, when a wing of the old Queen of Hungary had still been standing in his time, when he had watched the rise of Coronation Building and the long terrace of houses on the other side? To him Elephant and Castle Station was still newfangled, the electric street-lighting scarcely more than a whim; and beside these cruder scene-shifts there were transformations which came to him through nose and lungs, through the subtleties of sense and nerve which made him as good a weather-prophet, here in Mickett Lane, as a peasant is in his own valley. Yes, there were changes and he accepted them with contemptuous tolerance: they made no difference to him. The face of these streets might alter, but they still took him where he wanted to go, and the senile breath of the place would swiftly coat new brickwork to make it match the old. He had been born, a coster's son, in a tenement not half-a-mile away. He cherished Lambeth: not vocally or even consciously, often indeed with the petulance of consanguinity, but with a joiner's secret delight in the handle of an old tool. Knowledge is possession; not many knew as he did this cantonment of dingy brick, of dry rectangularity blighted with elaborate ironwork and florid archivolts, of mean, pretentious chapels frowning at the massive rococo of public-houses on the other side of the street; a country with the main road as its coast-line, on which the waves of restless living beat incessantly with small effect. He had often crossed that border north or westward into the jumbled tract where glue-voiced smarties swarmed about top-heavy office-blocks, anxiously making money or laws; he had once been down beyond Sevenoaks, to see how people grubbed about the naked fields for food; and those wanderings persuaded him, if he needed conviction, that civilization was fenced by Southwark Street and the Grand Surrey Canal. Here, while the crowded trains ran sweating towards Blackfriars, a man could go at a natural pace and live a life of his own, he could wear the clothes or rags he fancied, use the voice he chose for addressing anyone who passed, be it copper or borough clerk. In Lambeth you had friends. Here the thick-set noises of the town became a kind of quietness, its hundred smells were sieved; so that early on an autumn morning you would catch the river smells of Diesel oil and sludge, July brought with dust and lubricant a whiff from the stale breath of the tubes, on Sundays there were fatty smells, on some wet evenings, curiously, the odours of moss and brine. From this point of vantage, hedged with familiarities, Heald could watch the grey carnival with complacent, faintly sardonic eyes. Beneath the clock-tower only a mile away they might make decisions which would change the world: such decisions had rarely appeared to change his own. The frost returned in October, whatever they said; men went hungry and died, the young grew up to take their place. Living so close to the epicentre of half the world's traffic and fever, regarding it as one regards a fidgety neighbour across the garden fence, he seemed to look on change itself—covered tops on the buses, skirts in government—not as something organic but as a bubble floating in the changeless current of time.

Intuitively, he knew his limitations as an old cat knows to an inch how high a wall she can jump. What he thought about was people. Standing always in the same place, and that a narrow one, he saw them with steady and accurate eyes.

They wouldn't stay, not this lot, he had said when the unwieldy stack of furniture with a small girl perched on top had arrived at No. 83: there was more than one class took to Mickett Lane, but this crowd wasn't on the list. Within a few months, however, he had forgotten that prophecy: 83 was a house folk stuck to, he said—look at old Mrs Pewell, and even Mrs Elm had kept it ten years or more.

He continued to study them with an interest which grew into fascination. If Mickett Lane changed people's faces then they stayed.

Like old Frömel at 87, as solemn a little Hun as they made them six years before, and now with a wink which was good enough for any Lambeth man, to go with his English moustache. And the Webbels three doors further along, the casual, holiday-making faces they had arrived with had gradually taken on the apathy of the condemned. That pair would stay, and so would the old dressmaking woman who lodged with them. The houses in between had hardly a certain stayer among them: a trio of tarts at 93, dagoes of some sort, would move to a new pitch soon as all the tarts did, the girl next door who worked in a beauty place would be married within the year and the family of barrow-hawkers living above her were the kind who never paid their rent. Dapopoulos, the elderly waiter at 64, had looked like staying for ever, but the old gipsy expression had crept back into his eyes now that his sons had mysteriously grown into dapper Englishmen and gone into the railway. The Coronation people hardly counted: scavengers and lightermen, market porters and bookies' touts, maintenance gangers, half-time whores and warehouse cleaners, they lived in such inextricable confusion, sharing each other's noisy tenements and brats and beds, that Heald himself could identify only a few of them: stayers in the bulk, he supposed, like the mice he could never get rid of in his store-room, and in so far as they did stay he liked them; the honesty they generally showed with their own kind, their talk and their smell made up an element in his life that he would somehow be sorry to lose. It was the birds of passage he had no use for, the ones who had got themselves too well known in Battersea or Shoreditch, those who wore clean collars on

Thursdays, people who used the lane as if it were a railway station and showed themselves alien every day by their jaunty manners in his shop . . . These latest Eighty-threes, it took him a little time to see which side of the fence they came.

It was the girl who first made him realize that they had lived here long enough to be regarded as proper inhabitants. She had been so much a child when she arrived that he had found nothing odd in the sight of her tearing about the street with all the Coronation kids; and now, with a species of politeness which surprised himself, he was instinctively calling her 'Miss Tonie'. He was used to the speed at which children grew up: the little girls of Mickett Lane were toddling and blubbing one year, the next—it seemed to him—they had taken on the bosoms and calves of womanhood and were simpering after boys. But the change in Tonie Ardree was a different affair. No simpering with her. Side by side with her animation she had always possessed a gravity, plainly got from her mother, which she could draw about her like a veil; it was this gravity which came into the ascendant as she grew, and it seemed to govern her body's adolescence, carrying her past the loose luxuriance which came upon other girls of her age. Her laughter, instead of turning to coquettish giggles, became a recurrent illumination of the eyes which, matched with her live interest in whomever she met, was the other parent of her sympathy. She was not a solemn or a disdainful girl; she never deliberately drew away from the children she had tumbled in the road with, girls or boys; only, while they continued to need each other, as lovers or friends, she seemed to have resources which freed her from that necessity.

How like her mother in gentle dignity, in fugitive sadness, when they came into his shop together, often arm in arm; and yet how differently they affected him. He saw no trace of arrogance in Mrs. Ardree's behaviour; she would always stand back and take her turn, she spoke to him and to anyone she knew with a kindness entirely free of condescension; but she alone among his regular customers often found him without a word to say, and her entrance would change the shop from a social centre to a mere place of business. Folk were abashed, he thought, not exactly by a sense of her superiority to themselves, but by the kind of helplessness which everyone suffers in the presence of the deaf or maimed; with the quick eyes of those who live against the odds they saw some strain behind her friendliness, and there was nothing they could do to relieve it. Her daughter had no such effect. Often, when she came alone, she was wrapped so tightly in her thoughts that her presence in the shop was scarcely noticed; voices were never altered, women gave her just the quick nod they used for their other friends—they had long ceased to exchange among themselves that special look which meant "That man that done in Empire—his child!" But at other times someone would speak to her, and she would emerge slowly from her preoccupation, shy and surprised like a débutante whom royalty notices at a ball. And that was something of which Heald never tired: to watch the sobriety of this composed and graceful creature dissolving in the light which broke from her mature, peculiarly sculptured eyes, the pliant mouth tasting her smile before she set it free; to see how she surrendered the whole of herself to the delight of friendship, to hear the laughter in her feathered voice. ". . . Yes, Mrs Webbel, Timmie's always got a welcome for me. He'd starve if he didn't have mugs like me to buy the stuff you wouldn't touch with a bargepole . . ." Sometimes, if the shop happened to be empty, she would clear a space and perch herself on the counter with her legs on his side, twitting him for his untidy methods, his insularity; or she would listen silently to his deft comments on the affairs of Mickett Lane and the grocery world, while in the eyes resting on his face he caught sight of her thoughts like grave and merry children in the same dance. If only her mother, whom he admired almost fondly for her patrician quietness, would once do something like that! There was a day when she came across for a tin of Brasso and found Tonie standing at his side: she said, with the loveliest smile he had ever had from her, "I see you've got a new assistant, Mr Heald!" and then, the smile evaporating, "You mustn't let Tonie be a nuisance!" and with the scattered look of one caught peering through a keyhole she hurried away.

It was all wrong, he told Herb Evans: a woman like that being tied to a short-arsed hulking murderous brute of a bricklayer, whatever you might think of the bloke as a bloke in himself; and anyhow he didn't want people like that in his street, occupying houses that were meant for quite another sort, making decent people feel shabby and small. But secretly he was glad to have them there. He himself had come to feel slightly older since they arrived; a little oppressed now by the hot smells of the street in sultry Augusts, more impatient with the dank length of succeeding winters, less charmed by the Coronation waywardness, the changeless voices of Dapopoulos and Mrs James. At this age, and a widower, you required fresh interests, subtler flavours; and the people at No. 83, touched with mystery, foreign to everything the others had in common, brought him something like the sensation of an amateur who comes upon the Ecole des Batignolles for the first time. Their modesty, the apt simplicity of their clothes! This Mrs Ardree, how unwontedly shy she made him, and yet how he delighted in her walk, her easy gestures, the shadowed inflections of her voice. Years before, he had seen a girl of gentle breeding being threatened by roughs, just there on the other side of the street, and though the details of the incident had long grown dim her beauty had so impressed him that a semblance of it still remained: it was that half-lost impression of a young girl's loveliness which this older woman recalled.

The street would never throw its peculiar colour upon her; and yet, as the damp tormenting winds of another winter continued into May, as the fruit-pickers returned with their peeling faces and the year slid swiftly towards dark evenings and the garish Christmas windows, it changed her as it changed everyone who stayed. She had once appeared too young to be Tonie's mother; and though the child had moved half-way into womanhood she did not look so now. She kept herself in trim. He would never see her dashing over to the shop in an apron and old slippers as Mrs Elm had often done, even when she was rushed her hair was neatly combed. But the bloom had gone.

Her visits made a difference to his days, as in the lives of invalids the long morning may be gratefully broken by the sight of a certain train passing. On a hot afternoon when the shop buzzed and stank with women almost bursting from their clothes it was refreshing to see her slip in, bare-legged and nicely shod, in her plain summer dress. When it rained dismally all day he found himself glancing across the street, waiting to see the door of 83 open and the light-grey raincoat appear. Always the same precision and reserve, the air of one who worked to a table of energy and time in which there was nothing to spare. Ordering, she would bend over the counter ticking the items on her list and entering the prices—he respected that habit of not trusting anyone else's addition—and then he could watch her closely, admiring the clearness of her skin, observing small movements of the mouth which were so like Miss Tonie's, and how, sometimes, her eyes would become for a moment lightless, like the eyes of old women who have survived the people they knew.

"It's no place for your boss," he said to Daise, "she wants to be with her own sort."

"She's got her friends."

Her friends—of course! There was Daise herself, who seemed to be friend as well as half-day servant of the household. There was whatsisname, the brash-moustached old lodger who helped to carry her things from the bus, and that old perisher Mrs Inch who had found a corner for herself, the same as in Mrs Pewell's time—possibly she ranked as a friend. And a lot of use they were, to a hand-made copper-bottomed lady like Mrs A! There were others he saw once in a while, the green, willowy lady who wore smoked glasses even in winter, the doll-faced one (a sister, Daise informed him) with her fancy-ancy hats and her fat, pasty-cheeked boy, the stout, volcanic matron who always looked as if she had been chased out of a Turkish bath with scarcely time to fasten her tweedy clothes. Perhaps twice a year a hired car brought the little, nervous old lady whom Daise referred to as Miss Spinyer and Tonie as Great-aunt Georgie. Dowdy enough, she was, to belong to the lane herself, but the mob of children who ran and clustered about the car would always pay her the tribute of awed silence as the driver helped her out on to the pavement. And here was Heald's idea of breeding, which he recognized as he knew a trade-marked biscuit from the wholesalers' 'reduced assortments': the shy and grateful smile, the total absence of ostentation or self-esteem. Perhaps what really pleased him about her was that she was out-of-date like himself, and that her accoutrement—the unfashionable clothes, the shabby car with its elderly driver—was all in harmony, like the ingredients of his own street. He would arrange to be talking to the driver when she emerged with Mrs Ardree holding her arm, he would wish her "Good-day, m'm!" in the style of his predecessor and win from her a little bow. Her world was remote from his, but her single fluttered glance showed that she belonged to his own age, the age which had valued individual dignities. The luminescence which he saw in the older woman was reflected in the younger. On those occasions Mrs Ardree showed a peculiar gentleness, and he was glad she had such a friend to visit her. Yes, that was what he meant by 'friend'. A pity she had no one of the same kind who was also of her own years!

For in his eyes Mrs Grist, her sub-tenant and occasional companion, was a far older woman. Older? Well, the difference in years was a figure he never tried to guess; the impression which the two women made on him differed so greatly that although they often came to the shop together they were seldom side by side in his mind. With 'Matilda's friend', 'the joking lady', he did not need to put on the deference of man to woman or of servant to superior—civilities outside his professional manner; he scarcely thought of her as belonging to the bossing class. His feeling towards her might have been one of pity; pity for the marks of poverty in one who had experienced wealth, for the illness which her forehead and sometimes her breathing showed to the most casual eyes; but she treated these afflictions with so much levity that pity was blown aside. "Tim, I was sick in the tram just now, wasn't it frightful of me! No one will want to go in the trams any more." "Tell me, do you recognize this blouse I'm wearing? I've made a new collar and cuffs from the lining of my old coat, *I* think it looks very fashionable and spick!" Even the increasing weakness of her eyesight, which made her stumble over boxes in the shop, was something for her to joke about. "It makes me do such silly things—yesterday I poured the tea onto Trevon's porridge, and this morning I held up my hand in the Causeway to stop a pillar box. A policeman asked me in the sweetest way if I was drunk, and I said no I wasn't, thank-you, and walked straight into the nearest rubbish bin." Even when she was most obviously in pain she talked like that, and the griefs that she revealed were not the ones to make him sorry for her. A scared and ragged child stretching up to the counter, one of the Coronation women with her face bloody and bruised—sights too commonplace to hold his attention—those were the miseries which would utterly extinguish her radiance, reducing her to the frail and prematurely aging woman which at other times it disguised. Strangely, it was to this the remotest of all his customers from the men and women he had lived with, the most rarely compounded, that he gave his confidence. To her alone he sometimes spoke of his harsh childhood and the disappointments of his married life. And surely the burdened Mrs Ardree, so much closer in origin and experience, would confide in her no less! Yet as the seasons passed, Heald, who had stood in the same place for more than fifty years performing a task which left his faculties almost entirely at leisure, still wondered if that were so.

He would say to Mrs Grist, in his conventional style: "Mrs Ardree been across for her oatmeal just now. Don't look so good this morning, not to me."

And she would answer: "Oh—I haven't seen her this morning."

"Got something on her mind, I shouldn't wonder."

"Well, I—of course I don't know."

Just putting him off, perhaps: a lady, after all, knew better than to talk about her friends to any nosey-parking grocer. But when he saw them together they were often exchanging bits of news as if they lived in different streets, and the affection they showed was always trimmed with a narrow border of politeness. They were tender in the way they helped each other, one suggesting an item that the other might have forgotten, the younger swiftly reading aloud a label that the elder could not quite make out; they exchanged many swift smiles; but not much laughter. When he ventured, once, to speak to Mrs Ardree of his admiration for her friend she answered in her judicious way:

"Yes, she's a very unusual person. She—she's had a difficult life. And she's really very kind."

He had something like a stake in their lives since Daise, at Elizabeth's suggestion, had brought her mother to live in his front top room. To Daise he spoke of 'our Miss Tonie', 'our Mrs Grist'.

The arrangement suited him well. The old woman, dozing, gazing, sometimes talking to herself, was no more disturbance to him than a piece of furniture he might be storing; for a week at a time he could forget she was there at all; and Daise, besides keeping their own room in order, gave him unstinted help with the rest of the small house, which had not been so clean even in Mabie's time. He paid her to do his sewing, gave her her groceries, and put in the weekly bill for 3/6 rent marked 'Paid with thanks'. When she had settled her mother for the night she generally sat with him in the room behind the shop.

A catastrophe, it was, the dial that wench had on her, and no mistake or argument! And the twittering voice and mincing ways she'd picked up from the different folk she worked for—like a little fuming lady made to go on Woolworth's counter—they were enough to twist the lights of any honest tradesman. Yet he liked to have her by his fire. A chamber of fuming horrors like she had for her mug, you got accustomed to it, same as with other mugs that went up and down the street; at least it saved any sloppy talk from his nosey-parking friends. Shabby, she was, all darns and patches, but as clean as a parson's pipe. You could sit in your socks with that sort, and spill your thoughts as much or as little as you pleased. For she knew him well enough now to suffer his scrutiny without embarrassment—and when he looked in her eyes he forgot the distorted features below. What he saw then was the image of himself in childhood, when his father had been killed in a street affray at Greenland Dock and his mother had married again: a loneliness which was absolute and seemed to be final, an impotence in which bitterness had been drained away to leave only a cavernous despair. By that he recognized her as his kin. He knew the many faces of poverty, the fawning and the truculent, the vengeful, the resigned. But of all the eyes that passed his own—those of easy-come pedlars and their whining brats, casuals, ginsoaks, misfits, tiny, twisted beldams chaffering to get a farthing off the sago, a parade he saw stretching back to the dung-smelling, barefoot years—not many showed the stigmata he intuitively hoped to find. Externally he himself had changed, he was prosperous now and in danger of respectability. But when he had left the shop and got his collar off, when the crust of acquired behaviour was dissolved in tiredness, he could feel himself once more among those who laid claim to nothing but their own faculties and feelings. Undersized and blear-faced lads from the hovels of Bidault's Place, top-heavy sack-jowled creatures spawned in the alleys behind Three Tuns, cut loose and left to drift on the margin of the tide; men whose eyes never asked for fair treatment but wondered if they would chance to get it: these, for him, were still the innocent, the rest were tarnished by rivalries and accretions, these merely suffered. If he had a conceit of his own, beyond an unfaltering pride in the drab honesty of his surroundings, it lay in belonging to the secret fellowship of the hopeless and the lost.

"Time you got out a bit, Daise. You want to go to the pictures or something."

"Mum'd want me if she woke up."

"Don't you never want to go to no pictures or nothing?"

"You don't miss what you never been used to."

There, that was the authentic voice; not a note of self-pity or priggish self-esteem, simply the dry facts of the situation. He tried her on a new tack:

"You like it all right, the work you do for Mrs A?" and the same voice of dignity came again:

"There ain't no other kind of work I can do."

He persisted, then: "She treat you all right?"

"Yes, she do me all right."

"Ah!" And suddenly he crossed the line at which he had been hovering these months past. "Proper lady, you know, Mrs A. Kind that don't crawl out from under the lino, not in these parts. Same as the trouble-and-strife Mr Grist got—right up in the St Leger class, both the pair of 'em. Very kindly behaved she is, too."

He hardly expected an answer, but he got one quickly enough:

"Miss Liz? (Mrs Grist, I mean.) I reckon she's all right, Mrs Grist." She looked away from him, as if dared to some physical immodesty, and then let a sentence tumble headlong: "I reckon you won't find another lady like her, not anywhere, not in this world. She don't think about herself at all."

Of course! This creature might be simple to the point of imbecility, but there were truths she saw with the clearness of innocent eyes. He would not let her evade him now, however. He said:

"It was Mrs A I meant."

Her voice changed. "Mrs Jan? She's all right."

"She don't treat you hard any time?"

"No, she don't do that."

"Give you your money regular?"

"She's all right," Daise repeated firmly.

He sniffed in the non-committal fashion that travellers found so tiresome; and as if she had given quite a different verdict he said: "You got to remember, it don't come easy on a woman when she marries out of her class. And it don't come one bit easier when she get folk saying things about her bloke. Put a woman right off her track—"

"Saying what things?" she demanded.

He looked at her sharply. Was she really as simple as that?

"I don't need to go dragging up what's past and done with," he said. "Quite enough of all that, you must have had, the time it was on."

"You mean about Dad? You can say what you please about that, Mr Heald. It don't hurt me either way." She laughed a little unnaturally. "I reckon I got over that."

"It makes a difference, you see," he pursued. "To Mrs A, I mean—Mrs Jan, as you call her. *You* know he didn't do it, and *I* know he didn't do it, and the judge *said* he didn't do it, but no matter what the judge said you'll get blokes saying—"

She interrupted: "Difference to her? I don't see what difference. It wouldn't if he was my husband. If he was my husband I'd know what sort of man he was, I'd know I wouldn't find a better man than what Jan is, no matter if he was a toff or if he wasn't. I'd know you don't get better men than what Jan is."

She was full of surprises, he thought. He had never imagined that her twittering voice could be compressed into such vehemence, that her eyes could show such fire.

"You mean," he said adroitly, "if he was your husband you'd know he wasn't the kind of bloke that go pushing blokes off the top of their stairs?"

And another surprise followed at once: a single sentence delivered tersely, brutally, almost casually:

"I'd know he *was* the sort as'd finish off a man like Dad."

He bent towards the fire to knock out his pipe. "It don't matter what you say in here with only me," he remarked, "only you do better not talking like that anywhere else, see." He kept his eyes away from her. "You done enough of that stitching for tonight—time you got off upstairs."

Yes, such admissions were safe enough with him. He liked to collect titbits but he didn't need to show them off as others did, mostly he kept them tucked away as a miser does with sovereigns. Yet he was connoisseur as well as miser; he liked the bits to be in sets, fitting on to each other. His interest in Ardree increased.

When the days lengthened he had more frequent glimpses of the man, coming home from his work, going off again done up like an office clerk for some sort of evening job over at Three Tuns. In the matter of looks he made a better bricklayer than a stool man, but either way a decent-living family chap, a cut above the average for the street: half a dago, plain enough, and you could never quite tell with that breed, but in his experience a dago could be civilized well enough if you caught him young. What Heald specially looked for wasn't there, not that he could see.

He had no fancy notions about people who broke the law—he had known too many: skirts who pinched some gewgaw off a draper's counter, blokes who smashed up their old women now and again when they happened to be screwed, those, more often than not, looked as good and commonplace as a bunch of Baptists. But the long-stretchers were different. Men who worked the pre-postmarked letter game on the scale of business, professionals with syringes, fellows who got their weekly hushers off married tarts, he swore he could spot those cards a year before the cops closed in on them. Your killers might come in either class. Massen the Swede, strung for knifing a bookie's tout in a Saturday night mix-up, had been as honest an old matlo as any he knew; Jas Wiggs—strangled his kid—had looked like nothing but a belly-flopped old cop-house missionary; Eskisson—got off with ten years—was the sort they put up for the borough in the old days: but those were all men who had done the job in a moment of being worked-up. 'Biscuit' Baines whom he'd known well enough at the Richmond, Winson Harris who'd sometimes come in the shop, back in the 1910's, that Gadgels that he'd queued up to see at Marlborough Street—those were calculating performers, and he believed he would recognize another of their kind. He could not have defined in words their common quality, but he saw it as an overplaying of whatever personality they used: they were slightly too humble and helpless, or a little too eager to pay off a tick . . . If this Ardree had been laying for Empire for years, as men at the Richmond said, it was queer that he used no such overfinished disguise: for Ardree, as Heald saw him, was not a man trying to hide his real self, but one who struggled fruitlessly to reveal it.

He had known him vaguely quite a time back: one of a hundred young fellows he saw up and down the street, raw, tough, faintly insolent, bored and not averse to a bit of trouble to relieve the boredom. Their first encounter that he remembered had been quarrelsome. Coming in for a packet of Woodbines, the chap had slapped down half-a-crown and chanced to get a sixpence with a navel in it among his change. Heald, as he turned to go behind the shop, had heard a whip-like " 'Ere!" and the sound of the bad sixpence being banged on the counter. Swinging round, he had been confronted by a face stiff and shining with rage.

" 'Ere, you!"

"Hullo, give you a dud, did I! Sorry, lad—here's another instead."

"Ye'! Ye', I'll say you fumin' well did gimme a fumin' dud, you dirty twistin' little kite! What d'y' think! What in fumin' hell d'y' think I am! Think I'm some kinder bloody fumin' lapsuck, go unloadin' y' fumin' bastard chink on me! Think I do' know a bastard tanner from proper chink!"

"Yes, that's what I think! I see you comin' over the street, I said to myself, 'Here's what I been waitin' for, here's the bloke that'll take that dud tanner I been hanging on to all these years!' I gone and got it out of the special drawer where I been keepin' it ever since my old granmam give it me, and I slip it in careful so I reckon you won't get a sight on it. That's just exactly what I done."

Ardree, after aiming a vicious but undelivered blow at his face, had yielded a grin as a proper Lambeth man would; not a sullen grin, but one that broadened into richness. "Smash y' face in, next time!" he had said in a curt but not unfriendly fashion. And that grin was enough for Heald, who knew the difference between a bloke with a tearing devil in him and the real rat-bane, the sort with pretty smiles and a lifelong bellyache and a cupboardful of cheesy tricks.

He looked for it now, in this stolid bricklaying paterfamilias with a watch-chain to his Sunday suit, who came in occasionally on some errand for his wife. The wild bear in the man, the blustering bruiser, seemed to have gone; in maturity the ferocious power in the build of his face was oddly contradicted by the anxious patience in the dark, Italian eyes, the incisive voice had been blunted by a spurious refinement, intermittently he stammered a little. A man of unexpected nervousness, slightly overloaded by responsibility, rather slow in bringing his mind to bear; but never furtive, never ingratiating or obsequious; and when Heald flicked him with one of his amiable sarcasms, "I don't part with that stuff to the whole street, mind—that stuff's kept for the bloody nobs like yourself," the grin was lit again as if the boy he had known was always there, just hidden by the reputable citizen. He liked him then. He didn't care what a Lambeth man put on in the way of fancy clothes and fancy voices so long as the smell of the place still clung to him; so long as he kept, somewhere, his reality and his independence: the dour simplicity and shrewdness, the resilience, the short-grained laughter of the streets he came from.

It was just an impulse, he thought, him wiping off Empire the way he did. Heald could see this fellow doing a job of that sort, he couldn't see him working out the notion in cold blood, like Herb Evans and others said: you didn't get an honest grin, like Ardree could put up, off the sort of bastards who lay for a bloke for years. It was queer, all the same, the way he seemed to have it on his mind. The stutter and all. Done it when his blood was up; sort of job no one who knew Charlie would lay any blame on; got clean away with it, judge and jury playing like they'd been in the game themselves: so why should a rough-made bloke continue to chew on his guts about it the way he seemed to most of the time?

Once or twice when the shop was closed he came across with a message for Daise, and in the long summer evenings he began to look in occasionally with no particular excuse: to drink a cup of tea if one was going, to listen to Tim's talk, which improved in flavour with the age of the day. Seldom talkative himself, he sat on a hard chair, slightly self-conscious in his better clothes, nodding with judicious appreciation, now and then eyeing Daise as if he had to know her response before he risked his own. A little solemn, those meetings in the stuffy back room; but agreeable, as the meetings of tired friends are; with the back door open, a sense of coolness from the shadowed yard and the lowered voice of the town, of luxury from the band of mellowed sun falling on the factory's red wall and on a lilac bush which grew in between. By degrees, when he stayed long enough, Ardree would thaw a little. He would start chaffing Daise in a gentle, affectionate fashion for refusing ever to let her hands lie idle, or he would boast ingenuously of Tonie's successes at the North London Collegiate; occasionally he unlaced himself so far as to make caustic comments about the clerk of works on the dance-hall job he was doing at Ruskin Park.

". . . 'I don't care!' he says, 'it's down in the schedule plain black and white, all joinery work in the caif to be finish by the fourteenth when the decoratin' squad come on from the Brockley job. Can't have high-paid decorators hangin' about,' he says, 'they got to start on paintin' the moment they come.' Well, I tell the little bee, 'That's easy,' I says, 'you put the splashers straight on the job,' I says, 'knot, stop, prime and three coats paint, an' jus' the moment the timber come what you say you indented for, I set the joiners on puttin' in the doors an' window frames right close up against the primin' . . .'"

In that mood he lost the stammer altogether, he gave way to extravagant gestures, he was ten years younger. It was a delight to watch him then, to realize how much larger the real man was than the lugubrious householder he enacted, how much wider in range, more delicate in understanding: to see the mannerly smile dimmed by one that belonged to his private thoughts, and how quickly, when at ease, he could pick up some shrewd observation of Tim's to pass it on, twisted a little, in a glance at Daise. But those expansive intervals would always finish abruptly. Like Cinderella at the ball he seemed to realize that he had been too long at liberty from the country of his allegiance. Anxiety returned like homesickness to the eyes of children, he would stiffen and rise, take the feel of his clothes again, re-fit his Mohock's neck in the tight collar: "Reckon I best be gettin' along, the wife might be wonderin'. Very kind of you, Mr Heald, I'm sure!"

When Tim himself could find no way of warming him, a word or two from Daise ("Don't he look *tired!*" "All posh tonight, aren't you,

Jan?") would sometimes turn the valve. But when a fit of depression lay on him like a yellow fog they let him alone. Once he sat in abject silence for forty minutes, not even answering a question Daise put to him; and then, as he got up to go, he said laconically:

"You heard, I s'pose, Daise—got Gordon comin' home next week."

"Coo—not really!"

Tim said: "Gordon? Your nipper? I thought he weren't comin' home at all, not till he was through his fancy schoolin'. That was the way Mrs A had it planned out, by what Daise's ma tell me, and there ain't a lot *she* don't know."

"Well, then," Gian answered in the surliest of his voices, "you don't need to credit nothink what anyone says about my wife. Mrs Ardree got a headpiece on her, see, she ain't one of them weepin' and kissin' ma's what do their kids more harm than good. There ain't nothink but sense and goodness in my wife, see!"

"Well, now, I wasn't sayin'—" Tim began.

"All the same," Daise put in mildly, "she did have it Gordon weren't to come back home. She tell me so herself."

Gian said tersely: "Well, an' I had it he *was* to come back, see." For a moment he glared at them both, and then relaxed. "She changed her mind, see. Mr Grist and me, we chewed it over all ways up, an' Mr Grist put it up to Sue the way it look to me, an' she thought as how she'd change her mind. That hold to reason, don't it?"

"Oh, Mr Grist, was it!"

"What about Mr Grist?"

"Nothink!" Tim said. "Nothin' at all!"

He boldly raised the subject when Armorel came into the shop next day. "Someone tell me you got your boy coming home, Mrs Ardree. Nice for you, that ought to be, seeing your boy after all this time."

She did not appear surprised or offended by this display of inside knowledge. She answered in the sweetly rational voice he so much admired:

"Yes, it will be lovely to see him again. As a matter of fact I think it's all very unwise—well, for various reasons. Still, it's what his father wants. I never let my own views stand in the way of his."

Was she unhappy, a little frightened, behind her bright composure, or only tired by the spell of sunny days which turned the street into a bakery? The heat was tightening people's nerves, he thought, making them more sensitive to the discomforts and anxieties of every day. He watched her returning to the house and saw the door close behind her. That threshold he had never crossed since Mrs Pewell's time. He could hardly form any picture of what it was like in there. . . . They didn't sleep together, that much had reached him through Matilda, for women made a point of knowing these things. Why? Did she feel, in the way some women might, that there was something wrong in sharing a bed with a man who had killed another? And if so, how much had he told her about the sort of man that Empire had been? He could not imagine himself talking of such things to a woman of her refinement, but then he was not her husband. Which Ardree was. Only how much did that count for? He did not profess to understand the fellow himself; a part of him, perhaps—the part that belonged to his own bit of the town, rancid and uncouth, hungry, humane, spontaneous alike in charity and in self-defence—and that was all; but surely to God a book-read woman of Mrs A's intelligence could find her way to the bottom of a chap like him! Unless there was something—some quiff he didn't know about in the make-up of those dames—which made her disinclined to try.

None of his biz! If he wanted something to fret about, with the cold weather coming, there were out-of-works all round him and children who took turns for the family coat. But as the days shortened he found his eyes still drifting to the door of 83, fascinated by every appearance of people so different from any he had known who were yet becoming as much a part of the lane as himself; creatures who must in some sense be of his own kind, since he saw them altering with the day's mood and could feel their power to suffer as he did. He was aging, he supposed, finding the cold a little more troublesome than in past Octobers; the returning winter smells, Thames fog and the braziers lit by road-men, once dear reminders of a romanticized boyhood, touched him with melancholy now. No longer quite impervious to the alarms which thickened in the papers, he began to wonder, as the year sank, if the order and certainties he knew were doomed as well. Instinctively he turned towards those he would once have called his 'betters', as if minds more complex than his own could pierce beyond his range; and found, instead of a beacon light of understanding, a candle flame obscured by its own smoke, flickering in a tenuous draught of fear from a source he could not locate.

35

OF COURSE Gian liked it, listening to old Tim Heald give off his notions like a wireless, just as if the street—or all of London, come to that—had been run up to give him something to chew on. He liked the homely feel of the back room, and Daise, poor kip, sitting there so content. But the moment he got outside he was visible from any front window of Susie's house, and Susie would be wondering why he'd been with Heald so long. Only over at Apostles' could he lose altogether the feeling of being watched.

The time he spent at Apostles' Court was distinct from the rest in a way that his working time was not. As soon as he got off the bus in Three Tuns Road the air of the place enwrapped him as a familiar house does; the dingy façade of the Carpenter, rusted enamel plates, the draggled web of washing-lines across Lord Nelson Yard, these were a background of sensation which differed from Mickett Lane as, for a Sussex man, the profile of the Downs differs from any line of hills in the world; and as there is often one scene—the turn of an avenue, the pattern of photographs above a mantelpiece—which makes a man feel more himself than any other, the configuration of Three Tuns had become that scene for him. In the court itself, still a hulk of a place to any casual eye, there was evidence at every step of his own designs and often his own handiwork: walls had been rendered, treads of the stairs renewed, an awkward doorway from the games-room had been filled with breeze blocks and a new one made opposite the cloak-room entrance to take its place. The sense of ownership which these improvements gave him showed in his bearing as he came in from the street: he would put two fingers inside his collar and swing his jaw, he would kick the rubbish bucket standing in the passage and bellow, "Oy! Captain of the Squad! Who's turn to tip out the ruddy bin?" His name in this establishment had long been changed from 'Ardy Rhino' to 'The Fumin' Owner' or simply 'Boss'. They treated him, as of old, with every sign of scandalous disrespect. But they did what he said.

Crossing that threshold, he forgot that earlier in the day he had been a short-mouthed foreman, an anxious and blundering husband; forgot, because he no longer needed to think of himself at all. His mind was sometimes centred on Dozzy Field, sometimes on Ham Nissen; or else he was absorbed by the Rozinsky brothers, by Ted the Hun,

476

or Chet Imble or Rog or Stinkarse Steve. When he listened to a boy with a cleft palate trying to explain some quarrel with his step-father he seemed to lose his own existence altogether; in expression, in speech, he became almost identical with the child who talked. So occupied, he appeared to change in his moods as swiftly as an adolescent girl; he would be laughing like a drunkard at some fatuous practical joke, and then the face of a cripple watching his friend's performance on the horizontal bar would suddenly make him dry with misery. He would smile indulgently one moment, bark out an order the next. But beneath these surface fluctuations a close observer might have perceived a steady current of contentment. As he leant over a boy's shoulders to rectify a clumsily chiselled groove, or when he stood still for a moment to look out across the Pan, his tongue would show between his lips, the concentration of the eyes became clouded with vagueness, he very faintly hummed. Seeing his face just then you had said it belonged to an abnormally stupid creature, perhaps to an imbecile; certainly not to a workman of recognized competence and some authority in his trade. But in truth it was the face of a man who had escaped from the rubs and pinches of his normal experience as one steps from ill-fitting shoes into a pair of old slippers. There was much to try his intelligence here, much to bruise his emotions, but nothing alien to his understanding. And if happiness is found in the stillness of familiarity you might have guessed that he was happy.

A few years later Raymond, with his fiddling curiosity, was to pay a visit to what was left of the place. Mr Bertram Silkinson of the L.C.C. showed him the site and how the garden (where one circular bed of wallflowers still bloomed superbly) had been planned. Scrambling over the rubble which covered most of the Pan, Raymond asked what the official title of the Club had been, and the answer was:

"I don't think it had one. Everyone called it 'Mr Ardree's Club'."

"But Ardree didn't really run it himself?"

"No. Grist was the official head, and most of the organization—the paper work, I mean—was done by a fellow called Terence Hubbitt who was paid a small fee as part-time secretary. Ardree was sometimes in only two evenings a week, never more than four."

"Then why—?"

"I can't exactly say. The boys thought of him as boss, whatever anyone else did. If they wanted anything important settled they kept it till he came. There was a bit more to it than that, though. I used to look in myself fairly often, and the place always felt quite different if he wasn't there. Lacking in something—fulcrum, purpose, I don't know what you'd call it. It's odd, because he was an unimpressive man to talk to. To begin with, anyway.

"Certainly he wasn't an organizer," Silkinson continued, as they left the débris and walked back towards the main road. "That's to say, he could only organize things within his immediate reach, he couldn't plan ahead at all methodically. He was no use with pencil and paper, though he could do almost anything with bricks or wood. And boys. If he got them young enough. Just how, I don't know. If I'd been asked to choose someone to run a show like that, he's the very last I'd have thought of—I mean, if I'd only known him as one knows other men of that type. And yet, you know, Mackintosh—the man who runs the rehabilitation place at Bakewell—Mackintosh spent just one evening at Apostles' Court and then he said to me, 'I want that man. I'll pay six hundred a year for him.' "

"But he didn't make any offer of that sort to Ardree himself?"

"He did—by letter. He sent a copy to me."

"I suppose the Empire business stopped that?"

"No. It was just that Ardree wouldn't take it."

"He funked it?"

"No. His wife wouldn't play. The way he put it to me, he said: 'My missis don't cotton on to it. Bit of religion mixed up in it, she says, with this Mr Mackintosh, and she don't altogether hold with that. She reckon I'd likely make a muck on it, she reckon I do better stick to the buildin' trade.' "

A long goat-faced young man was cleaning the Carpenter's upper windows. Silkinson said:

"You see that chap? He was in an asylum for two years and directly he came out he tried to set fire to his mother's house—he said quite calmly, afterwards, that he wanted to burn her alive. The Tooley Street police put Ardree on to him, they said they wouldn't bring a charge if he'd go to Apostles' Court every night for six months."

He called: "Alb!"

The man came slowly down the ladder, stared at Silkinson for a moment without recognition and looked away.

"You remember Mr Ardree?" Silkinson asked.

Fumbling inside his jacket, the man dragged up a swaddle of oiled silk, unwrapped a greasy envelope and produced a photograph: Ardree at the age of perhaps twenty-five, spruced up like a chapel elder and grim with refinement. He examined it as a peasant examines his week's wage, nodded reflectively and stretched his mouth, just showing his black teeth; it was the nearest he could get—Raymond supposed—to a smile. With the dribble from his lips a few words leaked, "Don't get that sort, only once," while something like defiance flickered in his straggling eyes. He wrapped up the photograph again and went back to his work.

If only Grist had been a fit man (Raymond thought as his bus ploughed through the congestion of Tower Bridge Road) with time and strength to direct the affairs of Apostles' Court more closely, it might have grown into something large and important enough to survive the physical ruins he had just seen. As it was, perhaps some little had survived. If only Ardree had been there to see the way that fellow handled the photograph, almost as if it had been an ikon. . . .

But it is safe to say that Gian had never thought of Apostles' Court becoming bigger and more important than it was. He did not even think of it as having a larger purpose than the immediate one of giving fifty or sixty children some occupation for their idle time. Philanthropy is a habit of mind belonging to people with a different background—the background, for example, of Raymond's friends. He did not mean to do good to anyone, since doing good was the province of good people and he had too much sense to imagine himself one of those. He went to the place because he liked it. He listened to what the children told him because it was ordinary manners to listen and he understood them because there was nothing difficult to understand in being frightened or bewildered or hungry. He was kind to them in the way that anyone will help you up if you fall down in the street—an action almost as automatic as pushing aside something that gets in one's way; and if a measure of self-sacrifice was involved, it may be rejoined that the self to be sacrificed was not a luxurious one. Perhaps he possessed only what Leménager despairingly calls 'the indefinable genius of commonalty'. Perhaps: but if that phrase means anything at all, can it be applied to one who for years gave up his time to an occupation which others of his kind deserted after a few months at most, to one whom the abject, the incorrigible and the insane resorted spontaneously, expecting and receiving some peculiar need of their several spirits? His attachment to these scourings from the human floor, perhaps too stolid to be called affection, can hardly be considered a virtue, since he needed no effort to acquire it. But was it commonplace? Or was there in this rough-cast creature, whom a man so acute as Silkinson found unremarkable in appearance, some element which distinguished him immediately in other eyes? He had, in truth, a particular way of looking up at you, then turning his glance aside, and then—as if he had found some guidance in the void—letting it diffidently slide back to your face. The peculiar smile showed then, and when it had passed away it left in the set of his lips a softness which contrasted strangely with the pugnacious architecture of septum and chin. There were small, unusual movements of the folded skin above his eyelids, there was a humorous sniff he had, and an unexpected repose in his powerful hands when they were idle. On at least one acquaintance, who did not meet him very often, the individual man whom these traits combined to reflect made so sure an impression that Gian's personality, entire and full-flavoured, is with him now.

All those tricks of voice and expression, the sniff, the slow grin, the mock rages and genuine bursts of temper, were known and mimicked at Apostles' Court as nowhere else. They were part of the place, like the smells of glue and lysol, an incessant banging of lavatory doors, the slightly delirious air of a protracted party run by hosts who have no head for wine. Here no one thought of the Owner as having any other personality than the one they knew; scarcely anything was heard of his other pursuits, and with a new generation of members replacing the old, all but a few particles of the dust once stirred by the Empire trial had been allowed to settle. Once in a way some sharp-nosed youth who had received a dressing-down would mutter to a neighbour, "Him goin' on like a holy geezer! Done a bloke in once, the Boss did. Beat the cops on it, too." But the legend was generally regarded as facetious, seldom believed; and if the Club had lacked all other appeal for Gian it was still the place where the grey shadow of his reputation did not follow his steps.

Elsewhere, he could feel it following.

In daylight he never used the short cut through Bidault's Place, and he would even take a bus a long way round to avoid passing Coronation Building, where once or twice a woman had recognized him and shouted some ribald innuendo. When he turned into Mickett Lane his one idea was to reach the shelter of his own house, though even that was not a harbour safe against every wind.

He had helped to plan and make the home in Weald Street, although it was Susie who had found it: he himself had signed the tenancy agreement which Susie had got from the mysterious Mr Johnson. Here at Mickett Lane they had all the old furniture (still looking a trifle strange, he thought, in the slightly larger rooms), the same kitchen utensils, the rusty cabinet—a wedding-gift from Slimey—in which he had always kept his shaving things. Most of the Weald Street lino had been re-laid here. But the noise of his boots seemed to echo more loudly in this house, there were silences, and doors being closed softly.

At Weald Street, coming from work, he had liked to go straight to the kitchen and have a good clean-up. Then if Daise was there washing the tea things he had usually helped her, gossiping for a while. Nowadays Susie did not like him doing such chores ("Do leave that to Daisy and me, dear, that isn't man's work!") and in the kitchen passage he was always liable to be caught by Olleroyd.

"Don't want to be a trouble, Mr Gian, only I thought perhaps you might have a word with Mrs Ardree seeing how she don't like me upstairs in the daytime. It's that Mrs Inch, she seem to think she's got a right to be nearest the fire all day and every day . . ."

Or Mrs Inch herself would bar his way in a manner that old Mrs Eustace would never have dreamed of, standing with her little legs wide apart, holding a plate of food in one grey fist and furiously shaking the other.

"Look at it, look! Think I can eat that! That's what she give me for my dinner. Wouldn't give it to a dog, I wouldn't. I'm going to tell the constable, that's what I'm going to do. A fine pair you make—I know all about you, you and that Empire, poor Christian man that he was. And there's things I could tell *you* about that fine lady of yours, her and my Mr Jenkins she pinched off me, dirty little double-crossing tart she was . . ."

But these were tangible bugbears that he could deal with, a nuisance only because they prevented him from getting quietly to his own room. While he was removing his boots he shook off such encumbrances with a word of genial sense, a splash of unvarnished Kennington or obstinate silence. The next stage was the alarming one. Upstairs, he habitually paused on the landing, breathing deeply, listening: sometimes the chirp of a typewriter, the particular scrape of a chair, would tell him whether Tonie was home, or who was in Mr Grist's room.

Moving very softly along the passage, avoiding the places which creaked, he could often pass by Susie's door without being heard; but if it was a little way open, and she was sitting at the desk she kept there, she usually caught sight of his reflection in the glass of a picture and wanted to speak to him.

On such an occasion her musical voice called: "Hullo, dear, you're early!"

"Yes, I got straight on a bus, didn't have to wait." He stood still in the doorway, buttoning and unbuttoning his coat. "Well, I was going to give meself a bit of a clean-up—got all mucky on the site—"

"It doesn't matter—sit down and tell me everything that's happened today."

"Well, there ain't nothing to tell, really." He continued to stand, leaning against the little bed that Tonie slept in; he could never sit comfortably in this room. "You're tired, I reckon. I reckon there's too much on you, this house an' all. That Mrs Inch, she's nothink only a load of trash round here—'bout time she got her marching orders."

"But, dear, you and Tonie didn't like my getting rid of Mrs Eustace."

"She was a different sort!" He drew a long breath. "I don't want only to get it so you don't get so much on you, all this house cleanin' and that. Seem to me the house don't need to be all that clean—not as good you make it, not seein' it makes you tired the way it does."

She smiled, as when a child has spoken with a grace beyond his years. "Oh, Gian dear, that reminds me. I've something I wanted to show you. It's a letter from Duffy Filliard—you know her brother's in a building concern at Hatfield? Well, I asked her some time ago if there were any chances, and she's written to say her brother *is* looking for a new partner now, someone who has really been through the practical side. Of course it means putting in capital—about £2,000, Duffy thinks—but I know Raymond would lend us that. Dear, I know what you're going to say! You're going to tell me you're not up to writing work—"

"Hatfield? That's north, ain't it?"

"Only in Hertfordshire."

"I don't fancy movin' out of London," he said with decision.

"Oh." She closed her eyes for a moment. "I was only thinking that if we had a small house in the country—a cottage is all it need be—if we had a small house entirely to ourselves it would make things a good deal easier for me."

He hesitated, fumbling. With Sue you never could put it into words the way you wanted.

"We better look for another house somewhere round here. Might get on some sort of a small new house, labour-savin' an' all."

"But why don't you want to leave London?"

"Well, see how it is, I always been livin' here."

"Oh, but, Gian, is that a sensible reason?"

"Well, there's what I got on round Apostles' Court. They can't get fellows so easy, not fellows what'll muck in regular. There's the woodwork an' all, you got to have someone what can tell the kids what they got to do."

Armorel turned to look out the window, smiling with a quizzical patience. They had been through this so often. She said thoughtfully, without sarcasm:

"Of course I don't want to be selfish, I don't want to let my own interests stand in the way of Trevon's schemes."

"You put it the way it don't sound right," he protested.

At that she moved so that her smile, increasing in radiance, shone directly into his eyes. "Don't let's talk about it any more! . . . Oh, Gian, there's one thing I did want to say. About Tonie—she was telling me that she went to some church with you and Trevon and Michael last Sunday. Of course it's perfectly all right, only I do like just to be told where you're taking her any time—"

"—Well, you see, Sue, I didn't think as how—"

"—It's just that things go wrong if we don't let each other know what we're doing. You remember—well, of course, all that's past and done with."

Still smiling, she twisted her chair and reopened the account book on which she had been working. But now it was Gian who wanted to prolong the interview.

"See here, Sue, I was goin' to tell you. Ole Flock—I saw him at Hollies Club—he tell me about a bloke he knows, live in Biddle's Place, bloke what knew all about the Empire business. He seen me come out of the house that night, see. Old Flock'd get this bloke round so he can tell you just what he seen and heard—"

She sighed, swiftly copying figures into the cash-book. "Oh, but really, Gian, surely we've finished with all that, long, long ago!"

"Well, by what you was sayin' to Tonie—"

"Gian dear, I'm sorry, but this is my one chance to get the B.B.S. accounts done before tomorrow's committee."

Suddenly enraged, he said: "See here, Sue—"

"—And I have had a most awfully tiring day."

Her voice, thin with weariness, was only just free of tears. He saw all at once how small and ugly this street was in which she had to spend her days, how dreary her routine for one who had known the ample life you saw on the pictures. Seized by compassion, he took a step towards her, and would have put a hand on her shoulder, his forehead against her hair, had not the voice of experience warned him sharply that she would not tolerate such sentimental gestures. Dumb with distress, he crept away to his own room where, as he lay facedown on Gordon's bed, he thought he could hear her weeping. That may have been imagination: Mrs Inch had bouts of crying, in a quiet hour the flimsy house with its promiscuous cargo breathed uncannily with muted noises: but he could not stand it, he returned to the kitchen to put on his boots again, with Olleroyd staring in silence at his white face, and went out again to the lane.

When Susie was at home he kept away from the Grists' domain, for she insisted almost fanatically that the Grists should be as free from disturbance as if they had a house of their own. Even when she was out at one of her meetings he only ventured into their sitting-room if he saw the door open. Then, sometimes, he would go and sit in the small easy chair, talking spasmodically to Elizabeth or just looking at her while she went on with her machining. Her bare arms at work, and the way her lips moved in response to the voyage of her thoughts, were pleasant to watch; and she did not need to be talked to.

On the evening after that difference with Susie, Elizabeth came in and found him standing by the mantelpiece. "Is that you, Gian? Of course it is—how silly of me—only it gets dark so early in this room." She switched on the light and then felt along the mantelpiece for cigarettes, which she placed close to his usual chair. "Susie's out, isn't she? I've got to finish these buttonholes—it's a thing I've promised for tomorrow—and then I'll make some tea." She put her chair directly under the light and picked up the work she had left on the table, holding the material close to her spectacles; although she never appeared to be rushed she never wasted a moment. There were fresh flowers in the cross-country cup, mingling their scent with the old, bookish smell of the room; Gian could forget in a moment or two that his own room was in the same house and only a few yards away.

"Lot o' jobs?" he asked.

"Quite a lot. But still not as much as I'd like."

"Could you do one for me sometime?"

"I expect so. What is it?"

"Well, I give Susie one of them night-things once. Lace on it, up at the top."

"I know. You want me to make one of those?"

"Pay you, of course."

"If you like. I think I know the sort of thing, I've got one myself. Of course really good lace is frightfully expensive. But I might be able to find some, I've still got things of my mother's in one of the old trunks. I'd have a look now, only I don't want to disturb Trevon, I think he's asleep."

"Goin' on all right—Mr. Trevon?" he asked.

"Well—yes, I think so. He gets these headaches, you know, and they give him rather a bad time for a few days."

Gian nodded. He knew.

"He don't want to see anyone?"

"Well, no one except very close friends. He'd like to see you, of course. But I think we'd better wait a day or two."

The door to the bedroom had opened quietly, and they were both startled by Trevon's querulous voice.

"What's that? Who's that in there? Who wants to see me?"

"It's only Gian," Elizabeth answered. "Darling, I thought you were asleep."

She got up quickly, but before she had taken one step he was in the room, leaning against the bookshelf, and breathing laboriously through his nose; haggard and unshaved, with the coat of his pyjamas open and the trousers all askew. He said with violence:

"I'm not going to be made into a bloody invalid by you or anyone else." He was peering about the room as if his sight were no better than hers, and smiling narrowly like those who enjoy inflicting pain. "Where's Flock? I want to see him—I sent a message. Lazy bastard—why doesn't he come?"

"I'll get him as soon as I can," Elizabeth said, sitting down and picking up her work again. "Only I'd like you to go back to bed till he comes."

"I didn't ask what you'd like. I'm going to get dressed. *I'm going to get dressed, d'you see!* I'm going round to the Club, I can't leave it all to Flock, why should poor old Flock have to do everything when I'm still paid for it! You—that fellow—you'd better come and help me dress. Who are you? Elizabeth, who is it? Tell me—it's someone I know."

"It's Gian, darling."

"Gian? Gian Ardree?"

He stood by Gian's chair and looked down at him. He said hoarsely:

"Listen! Listen, Gian! You're Tonie's father, aren't you—I know you are. Listen, you've got to look after Tonie. She was crying, I heard her from my room. I can't do anything, not when I'm sick like this. I can't ever do anything, Susie won't let me. Poor old Susie! You'll have to look after her, you see—you must look after Tonie. You must get Elizabeth to help you. When Susie isn't there, you see. Elizabeth—where's she got to?"

Elizabeth put down her work.

"I'm here, beloved. I'm always here."

He stared at her across the table. "What are you doing? Sewing again? I don't want you to do that, it's bad for your eyes. You're not to, d'you hear me!"

He looked as if he was going to snatch the work off her lap, but a spasm of pain visible in his temples pulled him up like the crack of a showman's whip. He sat down with his chest against the table, his chin on his wrist.

Gian kept still; he had seen Trevon in a state not unlike this before. He said awkwardly:

"You don't want to worry about that club, Mr. Grist. Ole Flock got it all goin' on all right. I'll be round m'self tomorrow—see that everythink's all right."

There was no answer. Trevon's eyes had shut, he was breathing jerkily, his mouth working in the ugly convulsive way of a patient's in the early stage of anaesthesia. He said presently, feeling with his free hand about the table: "You mustn't—you see—you mustn't take any notice. When I've got this. Nothing I say. Are you there, Gian, are you still there? Listen, you mustn't let me do anything, d'you see! You mustn't let me, do you see! I might hurt her—Elizabeth—I might do something wrong."

When he spoke her name Elizabeth put her hand on the table, so that his should find it. Holding and nervously caressing it, he said,

"She's so good, you see," and a smile broke through the agony. "You've got to love her, she's so terribly good, so beautiful and good." He was speaking as if his mouth was full of blood, and for some time nothing more would come. Then he whispered: "I've got this head, you see, I can't do what I want, I can't even love her the way I should. And, Oh my God, my God, how I love her. My God, what she means to me."

Gian could not look at him any longer. His eyes turned towards Elizabeth, who sat holding Trevon's hand tightly against her cheek, her pallid face and body entirely still except for a small vibration which he could feel through the floor. "Gian, he doesn't know how good he is. I don't want anything else. I love him so that he couldn't hurt me": those were the words she framed, and though they were uttered too feebly for Gian to hear he understood far more than they expressed. In those few moments, when they spoke to each other with the voice of the eyes and with their equal knowledge of how the heart suffers, he understood her perfectly; so that he could remember that hour, where he had been embarrassed, grieved and horrified, as one enclosing a happiness he did not attempt to comprehend.

He was never to spend much time in that room, since for reasons he did not grasp his visits there were an annoyance to Sue. But the mere knowledge that he had these two so close to him, beings who seemed to find his roughness no hindrance to their affection, became an abiding solace. There were nights when the cold grip of loneliness kept him awake, and he would walk about for relief. Sometimes, when Susie had left her door open, he stood for a while beside her bed, painfully watching her still beauty in the suffused light which a street-lamp gave through the cretonne curtain. Once, imprisoned in the eerie borderland between consciousness and sleep, he lay and listened for a long time to the pitiful sound of Tonie sobbing. In times like those, when a shapeless despair caught hold of him, he turned towards the memory of Trevon's struggling devotion, of Elizabeth's endurance, as once he had recalled the compassion of Pieta's eyes looking down on the sun-shot turbulence of a narrow street.

36

*T*HE AGREED plan was that Gordon should go to the Quarries Waste agricultural school after three months at home. Liedke-Urban, having studied Synvenor's analytical reports, was confident that the boy came into his Category VII $\pm \theta$, and that the agricultural course was clearly indicated as 'the correct functional directionism for a partially reconstituted ethos within this category'. Later on he was able to point out with evident justice (besides some asperity) that his advice had been forsaken when the case was at its most important stage. For the plan did *n*ot mature.

Armorel had written to Daphne Scobaird:

> I have told Gordon that it is for his father to decide whether he shall go on to Quarries Waste or not. This seems to be the only logical way of settling the question, since my own opinions on the whole subject have already been jettisoned—it was totally contrary to my views, and of course Gustav's, that he was allowed to come home at all . . .

and in a later letter she simply notes:

> Gian has evidently decided that Gordon is not to go on to Quarries Waste.

This apparently casual acceptance of Gian's decision, does it signify that her interest and belief in Liedke-Urban had waned? Certainly her correspondence with him, once voluminous, had dwindled. Or was she just too tired or too busy to struggle?

There was enough, indeed, to absorb her energies. She was deputy chairman now as well as treasurer of the Belgrave Bradlaugh Society, committee meetings made a large demand upon her time. she was contributing not only to the journal of that organization but also to *Rational Woman* and occasionally to *Marching Mind*. She had thrice attended the annual congress of the Federation of Free Philosophic Associations as delegate of the South and Southwest London Group, had spoken twice, and had recently been nominated by her group as a councillor of the Federation. There were indications that she would go further. As a speaker she lacked both vocal power and the gift of dramatic gesture, but she was heard with respect. In committee she was exceptionally valuable, good tempered and clear-headed, tolerant of views which differed from her own but tenacious of essentials and ruthless with ambiguous motions. Her quiet but determined personality made an equal impression upon men of the stature of Edmund Gladstone Pea and Dr. Will Meshard (Chairman of the Executive from 1934 to 1938) and on such women as Millicent Towell and Henrietta Faun. "Councillor Ardree," Meshard wrote in the *F.F.P.A. Record,* "brings to our Cause a true philosophic temperament and mastery of logical reasoning which are by no means the less valuable for being contained in so gracious a personality. Her name is certain to become an important one in the annals of the Federation." "What I so greatly admire in her," Miss Towell says in a letter to Lady Stolebeach, "is that with all her personal attractions—which are, as you know, outstanding—she yet wins her case in any controversy with men by the use of her powers of reason alone. It is a delight to see men being so sturdily disciplined with weapons which they have always regarded as their own" (*A Correspondence,* edited by Rowena Stolebeach: Stillburn). And there is this tribute from Mrs. Hugh Goresworth: "Among the new generation of women Free Philosophers, Armorel Ardree seems to me the most likely to command a permanent influence. She is a crusader against shams and superstitions, not of the vivid and inflammable type once gloriously represented by Naomi Richel, but modest, shrewd, deeply convinced, indefatigable and utterly inflexible. Her whole heart is in our Cause, it is a brave heart, ever ready to strike a gallant blow for honest thought against the dark forces of emotionalism, a heart that may break but will never flinch or tire." When things like that were being said by the leaders, a woman of Armorel's intelligence could scarcely be unaware of her growing importance in the movement. To her personal friends, it is true, she spoke lightly of 'a certain amount of public work I do in odd moments'. Her home, she insisted, was her profession, and in a letter to Raymond written at about that time she said:

> As you know, I have had and always shall have just one object—Gian's career. When I was only a girl I dedicated myself to his vindication, and my life work is to provide the comfortable and secure background, the encouragement and inspiration, which will enable him to reap a full harvest from his ability. There have been setbacks, but my purpose is unaltered.

Yet secretly she cannot have been wholly unaffected by the homage paid to her in a world so much larger than that of Mickett Lane, wholly without personal ambition, blind to the chance of celebrity which these distinguished friends were offering with open hands. And for one who moved with confidence in circles of an advanced intellectualism, whose voice was already recognized there as a voice of authority, the field which Liedke-Urban so patiently cultivated may have begun to appear a small one, Liedke-Urban himself a prophet slightly out of date. In the fuller life of the intellect which she had entered, the need to win the smaller battles of reason against prejudice must have seemed a little less urgent than in the past.

Again, this rather lonely woman, with so few belongings to take a pride in, cannot have been quite impervious to the glory of exhibiting such a son as Gordon had grown. Just fourteen, he was already two inches taller than she, deep-voiced, manly in presence. "One realizes now," Christine told her husband after meeting the renovated Gordon for the first time, "that Rellie's poor darling Gian was never meant to be anything but a crude caricature of his son"; and most of Armorel's friends saw the boy as an idealized version of his father. Gian's strongest features, the thrusting chin, bossed cheeks, thick hair, were reproduced in Gordon's, but refined and more generously spaced; in him the cramped and faintly simian structure surmounting Gian's eyes had given place to a smooth, rather high forehead where the thick eyebrows, which also came from Gian, were a handsome ornament instead of a straggling stockade. His shoulders, again, were broad like his father's, but they did not appear to weigh down the rest of his figure, which was leaner and more flexibly built, a hurdler's body rather than a boxer's. He walked easily, with something of a horseman's swagger, and his gestures were if anything over-confident, like those of indifferent actors in social life. This confidence was undoubtedly a tribute to Synvenor's methods. As a young child Gordon had been gifted with an expression of insolence for use in street fights or with anyone he thought it safe to oppose, but the presence of anything like authority had reduced him to a snivelling bashfulness; at home, between outbreaks of savage temper, he had generally been silent, timorous and sly. Now, the furtive look had gone. "What he is afraid of," Synvenor had written at an early stage, "is himself. My intention, expressed in the simplest terms, is to exhume the buried origins of that fear, expose them to the subject himself, and thus destroy them." The treatment had evidently worked. The sullen child had become a youth of bold and easy manners; assured, quick in response, ready with laughter. Far from being secretive, he spoke of his earlier scrapes with frankness and humour, almost as if the quick-fingered brat who had taken Mrs Fulford's money had not been himself at all. Sometimes his talk even suggested that admission to 'Synvenor's Bin' was reserved for boys of sturdy character, while 'all the wets' were sent to more conventional schools. His accent was not precisely what Armorel would have wished, but he was quick to copy the inflections of those about him, especially hers.

Perhaps his conversation was a little thin in content, his range of behaviour rather small. But his laughter and his rank masculinity, even his untidiness, were refreshing in a household where the male element had always been submerged in a certain diffidence. At home all Gordon's attentions were for his mother; he would even take the trouble to escort her to her meetings, handing her in and out of buses with a gallantry which an upper-class schooling could scarcely have increased. Rellie was human. Could she really want to send such a son away?

Yes, theoretically the final decision was Gian's. But no one who knew both father and son had any doubt what actually happened. Gordon had lived in the country long enough to know that it contained damn-all but trees and cows. Since coming home he had never entertained the smallest intention of deserting London, where there were dance-halls, cinemas and amusement arcades, for the pastoral amenities of Quarries Waste. He made the decision himself.

For, although his life had for some years been minutely planned by Dr Synvenor, Gordon no longer seemed amenable to much planning. He turned up at meals when he chose, stayed out all night if he felt like it and made some laughing excuse next day. It was readily agreed that his education might as well be regarded as finished, since his prejudice against every kind of schooling was almost violent, and he was not the kind of boy one could picture at any school. He, for his part, admitted that he ought to have some work; but when Gian had been at pains to arrange for his apprenticeship to Bearstalls in Rotherhithe New Road he casually announced that he had found himself a job already. He was going to work with his uncle Ed.

He had instantly recognized Ed Hugg as the sort of man he could get on with, and Ed had not been slower to appreciate his nephew. The difference of thirty years in their ages counted little with men who discovered a common realism of intellect and a similar taste for the up-to-date—for magazines and records with a Manhattan flavour, shoes with half-white uppers and cars with hotted engines, sport of every kind which had a business angle to give it pep. They possessed, besides, a deeper community of spirit. Intuitively, they spoke of honest money with the same meiosis. A moulded brassière in a shop window would always join their eyes in agreeable sympathy. At their first meeting they had not been together five minutes before Ed, getting himself between the boy and the rest of the company, had murmured, "Heard about the Jew-bloke who took a tart on the Great Racer? The tart had got on blue cami-knicks . . ." and from that moment both realized that their understanding of life was the same.

A quid a week, Ed had offered, with seven-and-a-half cut on new business (on the net, mind!). It was up to him, he said, take it or leave it, only he wouldn't do himself better anywhere else. That was good enough to start with, Gordon had decided: it was a lousy cut, but he wouldn't need to put every bit of new biz through the firm, not if he knew anything at all.

"What *sort* of a job?" Gian demanded. "It don't sound like no sort of proper work to me, anythink Ed Hugg might be mixed up in. Muckin' round on dog tracks an' all."

"Well, he makes a bit, anyhow."

"Ye', but how does he make it?"

"Don't ask me! Well, he's got a radio business to start with—got the London end of a thing Aunt Rosie's uncle Jim got going up at Manchester. You know, Sales and Service. Does a bit with bikes as well, bit of burial club—commission biz. It all comes in—that's the way he put it to me—you go round after the tally and you keep getting new contacts. No good tying yourself down to one line of trade—where does it get you? Go on earning three quid a week for the rest of your life."

Gian sniffed.

"Better find out what your mum think about it."

"Okay, chief!"

Armorel, in her turn, asked, "What does your father say?"

"Well, you know how it is with Dad. Takes him so long to get his mouth open he forgets what he meant to do with it. Well, Dad, you see—he's not just what you'd call a racing model. 'You get settled down with Bearstalls, son, keep your snozzle screwed on the bench and it's two-to-one they'll make you foreman in thirty years' time'—that's the way Dad looks at things."

Armorel repressed a smile.

"Gordon, hush! Your father would be terribly hurt if he heard you talking like that. And you know, he got on very fast himself in the early stages. He was a most—he's a most conscientious worker."

Nodding solemnly, Gordon glanced sidelong at his mother's face and for an instant caught her eye.

"Must have been a great worry to Dad, getting taken into court and all that."

"That's all over now," she retorted swiftly. "You really think your uncle will give you a decent chance?"

He lit a new cigarette and put out the match with a flourish of his wrist. "Uncle Ed's okay! Course, he wouldn't take me on except for you, Mum. Always been a bit gone on you, told me so himself—when Auntie Rosie wasn't around."

"Oh, Gordon, what a lot of nonsense—that's a very foolish way of talking! Your uncle helped me to find a house once, and that's about all I ever had to do with him."

He grinned—Gian's grin without the smudge of self-distrust—and kissed her neck.

"Can't blame the bloke! Monday, I said I'd be around. Okay by you?"

"Well, if you're sure your father—well, at any rate it'll be something to keep you occupied while you look about for a more serious job. I do want to see you in a decent position—something better than being a mere salesman . . ."

In practice, the job did not keep him occupied so fully as his mother had expected. As before, he left the house when he felt inclined —he was sometimes breakfasting at half-past nine—and often came back before tea-time. Once or twice a week he took a whole day off and when questioned about it answered laconically that there was 'nothing much doing.' He would lie on his bed, reading and smoking, and at suppertime would have disappeared. (It was understood that he had taken up billiards and showed some promise.) Ed, however, reported that the boy was 'coming on all right', that he was 'a smart kid'; the fact that he rapidly acquired new clothes of decisive pattern and cut suggested that he was finding his way towards the money; and when his mealtimes coincided with the family's his bluff cheerfulness, a constant liberality with all the small change of his good-nature, made him as awkward to hold down as a floating ball.

". . . Makes you weep, the way some of these blokes go on! Chap moaning about an electric iron I got him on discount—same old thing —his old woman gets a smacker off the voltage every time she lays hands on it. Well, I couldn't have told him clearer: 'There's two models,' I said, 'Glideesi Champion and Glideesi De Luxe. You get a twelve-month guarantee with the De Luxe, only the sales conditions don't let me offer it as a discount line.' Couldn't put it plainer than that, could I?—either you get a guarantee job or you don't. These suckers, they just won't let you teach 'em. It's a tragedy."

Tonie asked: "But did his wife get a really bad shock?"

"Well, you know the way these blokes go on! According by what he said, the old girl jumps three foot up in the air and her false teeth shoot out and come smack up against the sink—ping!—cracked right across. 'Weh-el,' I said, 'you did ought to have the law on that dental bloke! Nothing but bareface robbery, a bloke selling your missis a flimsy outfit of teeth like that!'"

"Well, at least you ought to get the iron put right for him," Armorel said with severity. But she was almost smiling: his solemn impudence and droll precocity, his young, robust delight in playing his own shrewdness against the fumbling wits of the back streets, continually disarmed her. "You will do that, won't you, darling?"

"I've done better than that, Mum! Taken the whole job back off him—given him his money, every cent of it, all but five bob off to cover expenses, which you can't call unreasonable. And on top of that, I've put his old girl on the right joint for a new set of biters—straight off the peg, fit like an old sock, won't know herself—and five per cent off if she mention the name of Mr Gordon C. Ardrce."

"It don't sound like any sort of a straight deal to me—none of it!" Gian snapped. "That Ed Hugg—"

"Oh, Gian dear," Armorel said a little wearily, "we do know all your views about Ed!"

Tonie started to protest: "But, Mother, if—"

Gordon was smiling at his father with a good-humour which came close to affection. "You're just about right, Boss! Old Ed, he's got to thinking about nothing except the cash return. That's why he needs new blood in the firm. You've got to have ideals in business, same as everything else. Give a sucker a bad break the first time you sell him and what happens next time?"

"That's not what I mean," Gian muttered. "You know quite well what I mean!"

Gordon nodded thoughtfully. "You've got to pity Ed—he didn't have the advantage of a good father to bring him up." In his candid eyes and steady mouth, the respectful inclination of his head, there was not one hint of sarcasm. "Great loss to a man, never having had a good straight-living dad!"

No one could have argued then that such an open-natured boy, in love with the whole of life, disliked his father. He liked almost everybody, including what others would have called bad people, since he had been made to realize that 'badness' was merely a misfortune; and he could not be unimpressed by this man who had found the nerve to bump off a double-crossing pimp and the wits to get away with it. For the rest, he accepted his bricklaying father as he accepted his mother with her West-Endy voice and fancies, as he accepted Daise and Olleroyd. Synvenor had swept up all the dust and mildew of preconception about his own shortcomings and other people's: he was free, self-sufficient, ready to enjoy and to be enjoyed. His mother repaid his assiduity with a broad indulgence which he found entirely satisfactory; his father was censorious in the way laid down for fathers and Gordon bore him no grudge for that—he even took a quiet pleasure in the old runt's posturings as some grow to like the barking of a farmyard dog. Business taught him that fools were one of life's necessities; only pretentious fools were outside the scope of his goodwill.

The young man whom he met in the passage one December evening, a few weeks after his return home, was not of any kind he had much use for: a chap who looked as if he generally wore goggles and mooned around the Albert Hall. "You *live* here?" Gordon said. "Oh, I suppose you belong to the Grists—'No mystery ever baffled the lightning brain of Cat's-eye Kimberley!'" and raising his brown trilby, laughing gently in his nose, he turned and sauntered off to Bateman's Ring.

"He's very good-looking, your brother," Michael said to Tonie.

"Yes, I think he is, awfully."

"And I should think he's got brains. It's extraordinary what he seems to know all about—he's not fifteen yet, is he, over four years younger than me—and do you know, he was telling me yesterday that I ought to transfer my bank account to the Westminster because they'd let me go down to a lower balance without costs."

"Yes, he knows about money. So does Mother to some extent. I don't."

"I'm glad of that."

"Why?"

"Because money's muck. You can't even know about it without starting to be whiffy. I don't mean Gordon or anyone we know—"

"I know," she said.

He had come to meet her at school and they were walking along Camden Road, absent-mindedly letting the buses pass them. The dampness of roofs and pavements was turning into mist and the lighted windows began to take over from the lifeless January afternoon. She said:

"I like this road, it's so lovely and dull."

"It's a perfect road," he agreed. "Of course, you could say it's just cant, cocking a snoot at money like that. I mean, it's so easy when one's got some. And I've done nothing to earn it."

"I don't think it matters, having money," she said, "if you're the right sort of person to have it."

"Well, I suppose I have done something for it, in a way. It's meant spending more than half of every hols with Father, and—well, you know, playing up to the old thing."

"Is that rather frightful?"

"The playing up is. Having to admire him and like him."

"Oh. That's—difficult."

"You get used to it. Do it standing on my head most of the time. Only there are times when it's—yes, difficult. I oughtn't to say this—I'd never say it to anyone else. He's quite a pleasant person, you know, only he just never has seen anyone else's point of view. You see, if you give him any practical problem he gets to the answer about ten times quicker than anyone else, and it's always the right answer. So naturally he gets to think that if anyone disagrees about anything they must be just cuckoo. Well, that doesn't really matter either. What I loathe about the whole business is the feeling all the time that I'm being disloyal. A silly word, but you see what I mean."

"You mean, disloyal to her—to Aunt Elizabeth?"

"Yes, that's what makes it all fairly bloody."

Tonie glanced at his face, doubly pale in the dwindling light, and saw—though she did not know it—Gordon Aquillard's: the ascetic, enduring face of one whose mind must probe his griefs so skilfully as to get the greatest hurt from them. She asked timidly:

"But must you do it? Have you got to have the money?"

"Mother wants me to. You see, if I didn't, she and Trevon would think they ought to be giving me the same sort of education that he does now. And of course they couldn't—they've hardly got a bean—and they'd think they were letting me down and be miserable about it. You know," he said, echoing exactly one of Gordon Aquillard's voices, "when people are completely unselfish they're the very devil to deal with."

"I've found that myself."

The mist was turning into rain, Euston Road was like the Neva, black and scintillant below the phalanxes of taxis surging towards King's Cross. Where the soaked fly-sheets signalled 'Colonies: Hitler's New Demand' a flotilla of umbrellas tossed like capsized coracles on the swirl of breadwinners draining into the plug-hole of the tube.

"We're too late!" Michael said abruptly. "That's the hell of it."

"Too late for what?"

"Too late being born. We're decent and sensible people. If the world had started with us it would have been all right."

"I wonder."

"If we meant to improve things now we should have to start by rearranging our births—go back twenty years and get our parents organized on more sensible lines. (I don't mean Mother—you couldn't improve on her.) No, one would have to go further back still, one would have to remould one's grandparents." Four feet short of the kerb he suddenly halted. "Yes, when you come to think of it it's a retrogressive process. You've got to start at the beginning of creation."

A car hooted and its tyres squealed.

"It's a bit dangerous just here," Tonie said, leading him onto the pavement.

"You!" shouted the driver of the car, which had stopped, "are you cracked!" and from the rear window a woman like Madame de Montespan yelled: "Lucky for you you weren't killed, you silly bum!"

Michael slowly turned round. He said: "Madam, all the indications are that in quite a short time I shall be dying on some appropriate battlefield for your freedom to gallumph about in that rather repellent machine. So with all respect I think your views on chance and mortality are over-simplified. You should re-read your Plato."

"D'you realize you damn nearly caused an accident!" the driver thundered. "Might have got the whole lot of us killed."

"When I consider the very great number of people in this city,"

Michael said patiently, "and when I also consider your physiognomy—and that of Madame—in relation to all my own conceptions of the good, the true and the beautiful, I feel that that would have been a most desirable disaster."

"Oh, Perce, *do* drive on!" the woman wailed. "The man's bughouse, anyway."

"I wish you an exceedingly pleasant day," said Michael, taking Tonie's arm, breaking through the little crowd which had collected and moving on into Tottenham Court Road. "As I was saying when those gentlefolk interrupted, it's hopeless to imagine that we can take the world as it is and dose it with sanity. What we want is sensible ancestors, and there seems to be no way of getting 'em."

"Sensible?" Tonie echoed. "Aren't you fed up with sensible people? I am."

"What sort of sensible people?"

"Well, the people Mother hob-nobs with at her meetings—she tows me along there sometimes. You couldn't find anyone in the world more sensible than Mrs Paucrine."

"How?"

"Well, she's permanently happy, for one thing."

"Oh dear! Not good!"

"Yes, she's quite stiff with happiness, as if she'd got very tight stays, and she goes round making other people happy like a sort of microbe. She does it by explaining everything in a sensible way. If someone's little boy has fallen off the top of a tree and busts his ankle she says: 'Well, it's natural education, really. It's part of the evolutionary plan.' Then she finds somebody whose husband's gone off adulterizing with someone and she explains to her that you always get these neuroses occurring in periods of industrial depression. And she tells people who are poor that the great thing is to cultivate a healthy attitude towards poverty, and then stands there radiating healthy attitudes until her Lagonda sweeps her off to the Mirabelle."

"Broad-minded!" Michael said. The rain was increasing, Tonie's coat was thin and he seldom wore one. Absently, as they crossed over Oxford Street, he took off his jacket and put it round her shoulders. "Perhaps she could be sent on a European tour to cheer up the persecuted minorities."

"Well, she rather prefers London. (Oh, that's dear of you, Michael. You shouldn't, really.) She knows that everything will be all right as soon as our own politicians acquire the Modern Spirit. 'You see, my dear, they're all bogged down and encrusted with nineteenth-century superstitions—always one eye open for what the bishops are going to say about everything, always imagining that gentleness and kindness are a substitute for Good, Clean, Cold, Hard, Straight-from-the-shoulder Thinking.' Yes, those are the very words she did say. And she absolutely reeks of tuberose."

"And poetry? Can that be straightened out too?"

"Oh, it has been." Her voice rose again to the gale force and the Boars Hill inflection of Mrs Paucrine's, causing people they passed to turn and stare. " 'Got brains, that Macneice boy—might do something —I talked to Bertie Wells about him. Eliot's a sham. Sassoon's mediaeval—chivalry and slop. Romantics, really, the whole lot of them—too much Browning cluttering up the unconscious. It's a new age. We want new verse—verse that does something, gets you somewhere. What we've got to do is to make a Clean Cut. Get hold of these young men, brace them up, turn their unconsciouses upside down and give them a Good Shake-out.' "

Michael said softly:

> *"And all that Milton, all that Donne e'er gave,*
> *Awaits alike Paucrine's Redeeming Power*
> *Who disembowels the Art she hopes to save."*

" 'That man Gray—spittle and bunkum! Bourgeois! Atavistic poppycock!' "

" 'Have your unconscious cleaned, turned and pressed by Madame Paucrine!' "

" 'Let *us* put the New into your Neurosis!' "

" 'Send all your bitches to Tonie et Compagnie to be clipped, stripped and prepared for showing!' "

They went on hand in hand, laughing like young children, past St Martin's Steps and through the scrimmage of Trafalgar Square.

"I wouldn't mind," Tonie said with a sudden constraint, "if it wasn't for Mother being all mixed up with that crowd. She is so frightfully tired."

"But—do they tire her?"

"No, it's Mickett Lane that tires her—Mickett Lane and everything that means. She goes to the B.B.S. for relief, and that's the sort of relief she gets. Mother's worth something better than that."

From every Whitehall building a rivulet of umbrellas and raincoats came to swell the current flowing swiftly northwards along the wide pavement. Here in the shadow of the War Office voices were sedate and confident, '... obviously Legal Branch...' '... Finance wouldn't play...' impervious to minor concerns; while every smaller sound was flushed by the fizzle of tyres on the streaming road.

"It's terribly hurting," she said. "She's so madly disappointed that I don't want to go with her and take some interest, back her up. And I can't, I just positively can't. I belong to the other side, I don't want to be sane and sterilized, I want to love people and God." She was almost crying. "Michael, tell me—do tell me, honestly—ought I to pretend? Just to make her a bit less unhappy. I'll try and do it if you say so. Ought I to tell her I've grown out of loving and believing, tell her I see now that all that dreary chat about being freed from theistic emotionalism is perfectly right?"

"You can't!" he answered with the swift assurance of his sex and his three extra years. "You can't make people happy by pretending to accept a lot of bilge you don't believe in at all."

"But I can't let Mother go on like this! I can't bear her being completely alone. It makes me so desperately unhappy."

"You know," he said, with the irrelevance she was so used to, "it was just here that Charles walked out to the scaffold." And as if that picture had taken possession of him she saw his lean face hardening, his mouth sardonically tightened, as they went on past the Cenotaph. From a taxi taking him to the House, held up for a moment in Parliament Street, Raymond caught sight of a tall young man, soaked in his shirt, striding along the kerb like one who sees his objective far ahead and London as a paltry encumbrance, while the girl beside him was almost running to keep pace. He called to them, but neither heard and the taxi moved on into Parliament Square.

"We weren't meant to be happy," Michael said when they turned into Bridge Street, "we were born at the wrong time."

The crowd hurrying for the shelter of the station parted them, but he was easy to pick up again with his height and his pale-blue shirt. A procession of trams was turning on to the Embankment; she said, as they waited to cross: "I suppose it doesn't really matter whether we're happy or not. But if we can't be and no one else can I don't quite see the point of it. Being here, I mean—being alive. Is it just to breed people for a future that's going to work out better?"

"The future? That's just a gag which the old use to get more work out of the young: the gorgeous future with aeroplanes doing a thousand miles an hour and a radiogram in every home and free vitamins for everyone on Boxing Day—only the Paucrines get a kick out of that."

"But we've got to believe in *some* sort of future."

"Have we? I did when I was a child. All these War Memorials, they were just about the same to me as Pevensey Castle—they were there to remind me of old, unhappy, far-off things. I used to hear men gassing about what they saw and did in the war—masters at school—and I always thought, 'Well, that's what the human race was like just before it grew up.' Setting fire to a house with a sniper in it and then shooting him up as he bolted—'Rather pretty sport,' old Chiddimore said it was—that seemed to me as much in the past as the Battle of Troy. Well, it doesn't look like that now. There may be some sort of future for *les autres*. Mine's on the other side of the memorial at school —there's a space they thoughtfully left blank for it."

"Then there isn't anything?" she demanded. "Nothing worth bothering or even thinking about?"

He stopped and leant on the balustrade. "There's this," he said, staring with sombre eyes at the ghostly arena hedged by the reflected curve of Embankment lamps and a flaring torch which travelled slowly over Hungerford Bridge. *"Moi, le triste instinct m'y' ramène. Rien n'a changé là que le temps."* Sliding curtains of rain with fringes stroking the water blew coldly into their faces, the hiss of rain and wind blunted the footsteps of people passing behind them, they seemed to be perfectly alone. He said: "We've got the past. They can't deny us that."

"But didn't you say the past was all a cruel stupidity?"

"Not all."

A tram passing like the tail of a storm hid his voice, and then she heard:

> *"While yet a boy I sought for ghosts, and sped*
> *Through many a listening chamber, cave and ruin,*
> *And starlight wood, with fearful steps pursuing*
> *Hopes of high talk with the departed dead.*

No, it's not a case of just breeding future generations. We were meant to bequeath something more than our blood. Everything men have learnt of beauty and understanding—we were to be the living channel for all those riches to flow to men who are still to come."

"We? Us?"

"Because our minds are turned to values and others' aren't. And now we shan't even grow old enough to accept our heritage, let alone bequeath it. I shan't. Those people in that car, they're the sort who are going to grow old. And what do they understand, what do they think about—are they capable of anything you could even call thought? Tell me, what does the past mean to them? Do you think their blood would run any faster if they heard the very voice of Socrates or Lincoln? Have they once in their lives got up to watch a sunrise? Do they look at anything except the picture papers? Do they ever shed tears? I tell you, I know them all. I've seen them standing in front of Raphael's *Transfiguration* and telling each other it was 'rather muddy'. They go to hear Druzzini and they complain that she's fat. They know nothing, they feel nothing, they take everything that's brought to them and suck it down without tasting it into their great brutish bellies. And those are the people who are going to side-step all the mess that's coming and propagate their kind. *Ave Imperatores! Morituri vos salutant!*"

He stared at the dark shape of a launch moving down-river, leaving a dance of green and silver shreds on the kilted surface of the tide; in the hard light of the nearest lamp his young Athenian profile was bitter and smiling, his hands, tightened on the coping, were white. He has forgotten I am here, Antonia thought. He had given her no word of comfort; and yet she found courage in his lithic presence, and the fierceness and stature of his grief already diminished hers. Still gazing at the river he said, suddenly:

"You've got to keep things for us both. Nothing's safe with me—just one odd bit of shrapnel and everything will be gone."

"Michael—what things?"

"Everything you or I have been fond of. You know—the smell of trains. Watching the squirrels at Burnham. Making jokes about pompous people in the bus. And you remember that day we got lost in the fog and then had to wait for hours and hours in an icy station? And we were so horribly hungry and we only had elevenpence left and then you told me all about the earliest things you remembered at Weald Street? That belongs to me now, only you've got to keep it for me—ever so carefully. And the things I've told you about that happened at school—old Mohrlüder being suddenly human and thanking me for getting a credit in German as if I'd done him a personal favour. I want that sort of thing to be kept, it's too good to be chucked away." He caught hold of her arm and led her on past the County Hall and under the railway bridge. "I could write some of it down, but it wouldn't mean anything, I can only give it to you. The excitement of it, possessing so much, the craft of Sumer and the learning of Babylon, all the freight of the human mind which seedy caravans and ragged underpaid soldiers brought to the West across the deserts—we inherit that treasure, we can feel and smell it, it lives again in us. The wisdom of Hellas and the splendour of Byzantium, it's all free and open to the hawkers of Camden Town, only there's hardly any fertile soil for it. Hardly anyone sees the magnificence of being a human being. Michelangelo lying on his back for four whole years, all by himself, to do the Sistine ceiling; Livingstone setting out again from Unyanyembe when he was nothing but rotted flesh and bone—they were creatures with minds and bodies formed like ours, we can look at them from inside as well as out—those of us who've got just that amount of curiosity. I don't mind being smashed up—just for myself, I'm a fairly useless person, I don't know how to make anything, I can't even add up accounts properly. I'm hopelessly shy, I goggle and blither at people. But I enjoy things. Thousands of people can read about Xenophon's Ten Thousand, but I can hear that great shout, 'Thalassa! Thalassa!'—I heard it when I was climbing Cader Idris very early on a December morning, I could see the soldiers staggering up through the mist, I saw them falling on each other's necks and weeping, I could smell their sweat with the smell of the sea. I loathe to think of all that magic being snuffed like a candle before I've given it to my sons." Through a gap between the buses they ran together across St George's Circus; he still held her arm as if he were afraid of her escaping. "You must, my dear, you must hang on to everything we've found and gathered, it must go to your children if it can't go to mine."

They took the cut through St Kentigern's Yard, where the earthy smell of printer's ink blew warmly from Romney Agates' open windows and the clamour of the rotary presses crushed all speech like the fall of rock. The rain had slackened. Pilchard Row, lit broadly by the arc lamps of the bus depot, was thronged with railway-men and cleaners hurrying across to Abie's coffee-stall or stopping to joke with the knife-voiced girls who stood in the employees' entrance to MacDougal's Supper Room. There was strident laughter as they passed, the tall, patrician boy in his braces and the slender, bedraggled girl whom he held as if he had caught her picking his pocket; he smiled in shy response, like a young prince acknowledging the cheers of the crowd, while she, walking as if in a trance, seemed to hear and see nothing. They went on up Juror's Steps and turned into the dank gloom of Iddesleigh Road. It was Michael who suddenly asked:

"Where are we? Are we going all right?"

She answered abstractedly: "Yes, we go left at the end. Then home through Bidault's Place."

"Of course!" he said. "Yes, of course, you never make a mistake."

"Well, I ought to know when we're only half-a-mile from Mickett Lane."

"Only half-a-mile? Yes, I suppose so. I wish it was a thousand miles."

"Don't you like Mickett Lane?"

"It's the best home I've ever had," he answered simply. "Only it's not good enough for you."

"There's nothing wrong with it," she said. "Except that it frightens me."

Surprised, he said anxiously: "Frightens you! What frightens you?"

"I don't know. Mother being so tired."

He halted. "Tonie, I can't have that—I can't have you living in a place where you're frightened. I'll take you away somewhere, I'll get a job, I'm not too big a fool to load trucks or something."

"That would only hurt them both," she said calmly. She was grown-up now, he the child. "They like talking to me sometimes. Even Mother does—it's rather awful, some of the things she says, but she's got to say it to someone and it doesn't matter with me. And Daddy can tell me things he wants Mother to know and sometimes I can make her understand. Only just a bit, of course."

They went on again, slowly, and at the corner he turned to look at her in the light from a tobacconist's window as if he were seeing her for the first time. He said reflectively:

"So you really do mean something to them?"

She answered, "Well, I suppose you always mean something to your parents. At my age you don't to anyone else. Not really." They were walking a foot apart now. "Michael, it was awfully sweet of you to say that, about taking me away. But I'm not really unhappy. Only sometimes."

"No, it wasn't kind of me," he said gravely. "You see, nothing that happens is any use to me when you're not about. Well, no, that isn't quite true. I can enjoy things sometimes by thinking about telling you afterwards. Or sometimes I can by imagining you there. There's a place at Dillys Court, a natural grotto—I go there whenever I can't stand Father and that Hilda person any longer—and I picture you sitting in a kind of chair there is cut out of the rock. It's quite easy, because everything in the grotto is perfect as far as it goes—there are the ferns hanging down over the rock, and the water trickling, and a floor of short turf—it's all so obviously a place that must have you to complete it." He spoke haltingly, as an old man would play solitaire with the help of a childhood memory; starting sentences and throwing them away. "Yes, whenever I see beautiful things you're there automatically. You have to be. I can't walk through a wood without seeing you against the trees, and I can't look at a lovely vase without imagining that your hands are holding it. But it's much more difficult to find you when I need you most. You know, sometimes, when I'm having a gargantuan dinner with Father and I think of the sort of meal Mother's having, and Trevon being ill so often—well, it just feels as if life isn't bearable at all, the whole of creation seems to be just a crazy blunder. Then I can only save myself from going mad by remembering that creation includes you. Of course it's difficult—in that ghastly dining-room—it's hard to make you quite real. I can always see a picture of you, but I have to concentrate to make it solid. I can't get it all together, the smell of your hair and the shape your mouth goes into just before you laugh, the way your hands move, like a pianist's hands. And then of course there's a lot I can't get at all when you're not actually there—it's a kind of alteration in the feeling of any room you come into, it's like something a real artist does to a pupil's painting which brings all the tones into harmony. I can never capture that, I can only remember that it happens." He had taken one of her hands with both of his, he was feeling each finger in a serious way as if he were a blind modeller who had been set to copy it, while they walked rather raggedly, she on the kerb and he in the gutter, and the vans rolling towards Southwark Yards spattered them with mud. "But that's enough, in a way. It's enough to make me glad I was born instead of being angry and resentful. It—for me—it just justifies everything. I think, 'Well, if the Creator has made just one being as perfect and glorious as that there can't have been anything fundamentally wrong with His intentions.' I wish I could put it better than that. I—well, you see—the whole point of existence is just knowing that *you* exist. I knew that even when you were quite small—when I first saw you. You've always changed everything. Everything you touch or look at turns into music. Sometimes you make life almost more beautiful than I can bear."

Behind the four-inch walls of Bidault's Place men and women argued with a dreary, sing-song petulance; mingled with the sedative Portland voice deploying the day's violences there were voices of children whimpering, a man who sang in Polish as he shaved. Moving like sleep-walkers through belts of shadow left by the sickly lamps they stumbled against prowling cats and refuse bins, a door was slammed and a gust of tearing laughter resounded between the sprawling houses, a woman yelled, "It serve the bugger right, by Christ it does!" and a tipsy stevedore lay sobbing at their feet. Here the sickening, compound stench had been softened by the rain, which had left a rustle and patter of water pouring from broken pipes, and from where a drain was blocked a widening stream, scummed with cabbage leaves and cartons, flowed sinuously between islands of empty tins; in the strip of sky which roofed this grey ravine there were still no stars. She held his arm, which was stiff as a guardsman's, while he marched ahead like a courageous man condemned to be hanged.

She said seriously, fluttering only a little: "I'm not like that, Michael. I'll try to be. All my life—I'll try."

In the angle by Zadolski's they stopped, and with their hands on each other's shoulders kissed each other, her lips pressing his, his lips hers, with a great and equal gentleness; and after a few moments they went on slowly, a little stunned by the goodness of living, through the Coronation passage and into Mickett Lane.

Gordon called from the kitchen door: "Well, if it isn't Mike and Tone, both arrived at the same time! The odd things that do happen, who ever would believe!"

They gravely smiled, hardly noticing him; but they could not equally ignore Armorel, when she came to the top of the stairs and gazed down on them with her serious, distant eyes: she stood so still, and looked so tall there, wearing a little of Edith Cepinnier's presence; so slender and so ill, with the light from the passage lamp thrown too intensely on the whiteness of her skin, on the perfect throat and forearms left bare against the darkness of the old velvet dinner-dress. They came to a stop, as if she had called 'Stay there!'

She said almost tonelessly: "What has happened? Antonia, why are you like this?"

"Like what, Mother?" Tonie asked, and then looked down at her soaking skirt.

Michael vaguely smiled. "We missed some buses," he said.

There was nothing in this remark to amuse a woman who had expected her daughter at least an hour earlier and had arranged a meal for that time. Armorel said:

"I thought you told your mother you were off to Windsor for the evening?"

"Yes, Aunt Rellie. Only I changed my mind."

"Does it matter, Mother?" Tonie asked quietly.

Armorel turned and went to the door of the Grists' room. Elizabeth, coming to answer her knock, peered out uncertainly.

"Oh, is that Rellie? Do come in!"

"Oh, Elizabeth dear, I just thought you'd like to know that Michael's back. Apparently it was a mistake about his going to Windsor."

Passing Michael without another glance, Armorel led Tonie to their own room and leant against the bed watching her take off her wet clothes. Curiously, she was smiling now. She said reflectively:

"He's very capricious about his plans. He gets that from his father, poor boy."

Absorbed, Tonie said: "I thought his father was a dreary old business man. I didn't think he was erratic."

"You mean Henry Kinfowell?—he's not Michael's real father. It was a man called Aquillard."

They heard the sound of nasal giggling outside the door, and then Gian's angry voice: "Ain't you got nothink better to do, Gordon, than stand there listenin' at keyholes!"

"I'm afraid I've got to be out tonight," Armorel said, "I had to say I'd take the chair at a meeting instead of Mrs Vestige. I was hoping you'd have a nice evening with your father, but he says he'd rather be at that affa'r of Trevon's in Three Tuns."

Sitting on the floor with one stocking half pulled-off, Tonie remained as still as if she had been seized by cramp. She said, "Michael's never told me that. I suppose he doesn't know."

"He only tells people what he wants to," Armorel said, turning towards her dressing-table. "At his age he must know why his mother was divorced. Of course, he doesn't mean to be deceptive."

Still motionless, Tonie asked: "What kind of man was he, this—Aquillard?"

"Oh, he's just a sort of school-teacher who's always made a muddle of things. Not entirely right in the head, poor fellow. I used to know him quite well, I tried to help him, only it wasn't any use." Still faintly smiling, she bent her head to fasten the necklace which had come to her from Gertrude. "Of course, you'll probably get quite a different account from other people. You'll have to listen to anything they tell you—it's dishonest not to listen to every side of a question. People who are jealous get together and twist things so as to influence others—you'll understand when you're older—but I should be silly if I asked you to believe in me just because I'm your mother."

In the mirror of the gimcrack dressing-table her face showed like a work of Praxiteles, perfected and final; still, not with repose but from inurement: her hands, skilfully touching the hair at her neck, revealed scarcely a sign of the work they did all day. While she was putting on her coat her eyes were closed, and it looked as if she could never bear through a public evening the weight of fatigue betrayed by the slackened muscles of her eyelids and mouth. But her movements were swift and certain as she straightened the counterpane where she had been leaning, put a pair of shoes together, closed her wardrobe; her body was wholly within her command when she stooped gracefully to kiss Antonia's forehead, there was an artist's ease in the way she managed her skirt as she turned to open the door, which always stuck a little in winter, as she moved with her gentle and matchless dignity over the worn linoleum, down the narrow and shabby stairs.

37

*I*T WAS in that month that Raymond saw her, was alarmed by her appearance, and begged her to come to his home for at least a few days' rest and change. She was grateful but refused: she had several engagements ahead in connection with her B.B.S. work, her absence would mean letting people down. Spring seemed to renew her vitality, and when he saw her in July she was looking better than he had seen her for a long time.

She did fall ill in September, and was in bed for nearly three weeks. There appeared to be some pain in the region of the mastoid process, but no one knew exactly what was wrong. Gian, acting on Trevon's advice, got hold of that very able doctor Stanhope Ewell, but she discovered that he had been a medical missionary and would not let him examine her. (She had lately adhered to Miss Sessabeeke's theory that the taint of supernaturalism runs all through the medical profession and that doctors use their privileged access for implanting superstitution where mental resistance has been lowered by disease.) When Elizabeth took her temperature it proved to be only a little above normal. She lay all day under a yoke of lassitude, eating very little, seldom sleeping, gazing patiently at the brown brick and the grubby window of Matilda Empire's room on the other side of the street.

She was difficult to nurse, for the presence of anyone in the room seemed to worry her. In his off-hours Gian was constantly peeping into the room, and she always seemed to know he was there. "Is there anything you want, Gian?" He would cautiously insert himself and try in his clumsy way to straighten things. "Thought you could do with some fresh water, Sue," and he would hurry off to re-fill the tumbler; he would plant it gingerly beside her and stand like a retriever, a foot from her bed, smiling anxiously at her face. Then she would say: "That's—very kind. Only—if you don't mind—it rather—I mean, I just want to be quite alone for a bit." She responded to Tonie's attentions in much the same way. Only Gordon, who went in now and then in a businesslike fashion to draw the curtains or give her a clean pillow-slip, did not seem to get on her nerves at all.

Elizabeth had not much time to help. She was spending every morning at the Pearson School in Woburn Place being trained as a telephone operator, and the running of her home, small as it was, had become a laborious business now that she could only tell a fork from a spoon by peering at it closely; she had not yet learnt to work entirely by touch. But she did slip into Armorel's room as often as she could, to open or close a window, to sponge her face, or to make those small shifts of pillow and undersheet which change a sickbed from a stony grave into a gentle embrace. On several afternoons she found half-an-hour to sit knitting beside her bed.

She could not tell whether Armorel liked to have her there, for as a rule hardly any speech passed between them; but to one who had spent so many hours sitting in silence with Matilda this did not matter.

The sick, she thought, generally valued your presence in the way that people living alone like to have a cat or a canary about them, something which does not call for much attention but is a little more sentient than the rest of the familiar furniture, something which breathes and stirs. It was always rather dark in this room, which the sun reached only in the earliest morning. They were like tired travellers, strangers in a railway carriage which moves somnolently through the endless suburbs of an industrial city; awake, but perhaps hardly more conscious of each other than of the stir in neighbouring houses, the persistent mewl of wireless, the enclosing wall of sound from the main road.

Often, when Armorel spoke at all, she seemed merely to be thinking aloud, as prisoners in solitary confinement do. She would say without any introduction: "For Tonie, yes, I could cut it down for her, it would make her a nice little petticoat. But then, you see, she doesn't want it. All that work I've done, all these years, making her nice things. She doesn't like the things I do for her. You don't, do you, Tonie? You don't really." And late on a grey afternoon, when the sounds of bickering in the kitchen had dwindled into silence, they had a conversation which was to remain in Elizabeth's memory like those rare dreams which hover on the mind's margin all day and return when the head sinks into the pillow next night. In her soft and sensible voice, Armorel said abruptly:

"Of course he loved Chrissie. Much more than me."

"Who did, dear?"

"You could see from the way he kissed her. Of course she always ran to meet him, she had very long legs, she always got there first and jumped up and hugged him. Well, of course, I was older. When you're older you don't do that sort of thing."

"Of course not. Rellie, would you like me to get you some tea?"

"You see, she hadn't any brains, Chrissie never had any brains, she was always nearly at the bottom of her form, so of course she couldn't understand what Mother told us. Just couldn't understand. Didn't try to understand. I mean, that wasn't my fault."

"I expect you won all the prizes at school?"

"But she could have tried to understand. She could have pretended. Then it would have been all right. Well, you couldn't blame Mother for being so cross when Chrissie just didn't try, when she just grinned like that and ran away. I don't think Mother was really being beastly, I think it was just because Chrissie treated her as if she thought she was silly. I think Chrissie always *knew* she'd make Mother cross, I think she did it on purpose, so that then Daddy would feel sorry for her."

"You know," Elizabeth said, "I do want to meet Christine again. I've only seen her once or twice, I don't feel I know her at all."

Armorel turned her head a little way, so that Elizabeth's face came just within her view.

"Chrissie? You want to meet Chrissie?"

"Well, of course I want to know her. Just because she's your sister."

Like a commentator filling the last few moments before a procession starts, Armorel said: "Chrissie? She married a stockbroker. They've got heaps of money. It spoils her clothes, coming here." The tired head turned slowly back to where it was before. "He always wanted to be sweet to everybody. That was the trouble. Mother explained it all to me, Mother thought things out so clearly, that was why I always understood her and no one else could. I suppose that was what Father didn't like."

"Don't you think you ought to go to sleep for a bit, if you can? Your voice sounds rather tired."

"You see, they got at him, all those people. The Bible-thumpers—that's what Mother called them. All the holy people. They get hold of unpractical people who always want to be kind and never think things out—Mother explained it all—they got hold of him and taught him to hate her, her and me."

"Oh, but, Rellie dear, surely you're forgetting things! You told me once, you were terribly fond of him."

"Fond of him? Fond of who?"

"Your father. You told me he was the dearest man who ever lived."

Armorel said uncertainly: "They all got hold of him, Chrissie used to run and jump up to get hugged. I'm most awfully sorry, but it does tire me rather when you keep on talking. You don't mind, do you? It's rather awful when people are talking and talking. You see, they keep trying to prove that I'm wrong, but it isn't any good, because I know I can think more clearly than anyone. That's what counts in the end. They said I couldn't do anything because people weren't fond of me, they said I couldn't do anything about Gian. Well, I did, I married him."

It was a tired voice, but not one that Elizabeth recognized as belonging to delirium. It was gentle and clear, a little monotonous, like the voice of those who, relating some dreadful experience, try at once to disguise emotion and to hide the strain of disguising it. When it had stopped, and a minute's silence had passed, Elizabeth stood up cautiously and leaned across the bed till her eyes were near enough to discern the separate features of Armorel's face.

The eyes were open, but resting upon a landscape of their own they were left unstirred by Elizabeth's gaze; and in the small circle margined with shadow which her enfeebled sight left open she could study this still face as boldly as you may study the face of the dead: tissue stretched upon a padded frame, palely tinted, puckered where the frame was recessed, impaired by roughness and by tiny stains. She thought, as you think about dead faces, This is the same face whose loveliness enthralled me when I first saw it, which has been illumined and warmed for me by many varying lights of sympathy, which I have never ceased to love. And like all dead, loved faces it yielded nothing to quicken those memories, it made no greater impact on the spirit than a tablet of stone which says 'This is humanity without its decorations, this is all there is.'

And yet it was not lifeless. Though the eyes were like still pools below a clouded sky the muscles about them were perceptibly moving, the lips worked as if with a conscious life of their own. As she watched those tiny movements, listened with painful fascination to the laboured, irregular breathing, her contemplation of the Armorel she had known slackened. Seen so large, losing all familiarity, the features had become unreal. But underneath this palaestra of small agitations there must be something else beside the dead machinery which caused it, the kick of exhausted nerves, mechanic afterplay of mental impulse sprung from passions that have died. There is a prisoner here, she thought, a total stranger to me, one whom I can never know, and yet in some way the image of myself.

As real and separate as myself; as lonely as I was before Trevon found me. The air in this room was weighted with the breath of illness, her mind slid drowsily to the night when the shock of meeting Empire's customer had torn the bandage from her own wounds: for a moment she lived again the bitterness of seeing herself as in a mirror, paltry and virtueless, exiled without friends or hope. Then the long silence was cut, and the voice she heard was her own, whispering desperately:

"I know, I know! I've been there myself."

She could not expect an answer, she had not even intended to speak. But an answer of a kind came almost at once, in the same small, calm voice that Armorel had used before:

"I can't even have Tonie. Gian won't let her love me, he's poisoning her love."

So sudden, so typographically clear, these words released Elizabeth from the paralysis which had crept upon her mind. When she spoke again it was with the voice she had used years before with young medical officers who thought they understood nursing better than she:

"Rellie! Rellie, I want you to wake up—you're talking very foolishly. Listen! Rellie, listen! You know Tonie loves you, you know she's devoted to you, and so is Gian. You mustn't say such stupid things, you'll start believing them. Listen, you don't realize what love is. Trevon could tell you. It isn't only emotion, it's something more than you or I understand. Rellie, listen, you've got to let me help!"

She had scarcely hoped that any pitch of voice could reach a mind so clouded by its own effluvium; she was surprised when the eyes which had been so frigid took on the warmth of life again and turned towards her own in sure regard. The twitches stopped, the mask softened and relaxed like the face of a lost child when he comes upon someone he knows. It was, just then, a child's face; the face of Armorel herself, but younger still than the Armorel whom Elizabeth had first known, more innocent, not yet remoulded by the needs of courage or pretension. She had never seen Armorel weep. But she found it natural that this younger, gentler Armorel should crumple and give way to the surge of tears; she was ready for the struggling cry which came:

"They don't, they can't, I've always been like that, I'm someone that can't be loved."

Ready: but not armed against her own emotion, the heat of compassion which filled her own eyes with tears, which made her stretch out recklessly to hold and fasten Armorel's shaking body against hers, to press her forehead into Armorel's hair, repeating "I've always loved you! Rellie—my darling—always, always!" It seemed natural, it seemed to be what they had always wanted, that she should hold her close until the sobbing at last grew feeble, and that when she had laid the exhausted body back in the pillows she should continue to hold and chafe her fingers, letting the strong current of her tenderness flow through their hands, tenderly smiling towards the eyes which at last had closed.

It was only when she heard Trevon's voice calling her, the voice of his bad days with a hint of childish tears in it, that she let the hand go. Only then that Armorel seemed to recover her self-possession, brusquely wiping her face with the sleeve of her night-gown, tightening her lips, saying collectedly: "I think I hear your husband calling. Do go to him, please. Yes, really I prefer to be by myself, Gordon will be in to give me anything I need."

A few nights later, hearing unusual noises in the small hours, Trevon went downstairs and found her moving about the kitchen, barefoot, in the thin, laced night-gown which Gian had given her; she was rather feverishly pushing things into cupboards and fretting over the room's untidiness, while Mrs Inch, on the little bed she always made up close to the stove, watched her with frightened eyes. When he told her that there was no need to bother about the kitchen now, that he would tidy it himself in the morning, she answered austerely: "I know Elizabetn doesn't mind a hugger-mugger, she can keep her own part of the house just as she likes, but I'm not going to have a pigsty here." But as soon as he told her firmly to go back to bed she obeyed him without a word.

They found her looking better next morning, and two days afterwards she was down for breakfast. She fell immediately into her normal, packed routine, her quickness and competence seemed to return in a matter of hours. Everyone marvelled at the physical resource which produced such swift recuperation. When Raymond saw her again, on the day of Maria's funeral, she appeared to be, if not the Rellie of his old sentimental fondness, at any rate a healthy woman, with all her splendid faculties awake and absorbed.

38

*F*OR SEVERAL WEEKS Maria had shown some slackening of her nervous forces. Her laugh was less flagellant, she fretted a little, complaining that Simon refused to take her back to Italy; sometimes when Mrs Oestermann or Lizzie Bentlock was talking she fell fast asleep.

Relying for funds on the weekly contribution from Gian, she became more casual than before about her shop-keeping: when the shop door was opened she often called out from the back room, telling the customer to take what she wanted and leave the money, or would merely shout, *"Andarsene,* chop close, gose avay!" Dishes were never washed now until they were needed again, nothing was tidied or cleaned except when Armorel made one of her alarming visits to put things straight. For a year or more Maria's only exercise had been to shuffle as far as the back yard and feed the poultry, and now it became increasingly difficult, at bedtime, to get her tremendous bulk up the dozen stairs to the room which Armorel and Gian had once occupied: she surmounted two steps, with Simon stooping and valiantly thrusting his shoulders against her mountainous afterpart, and then paused for a minute or more, wheezing and giggling, before she panted "Avanti, piccino—uppasanosser!" Despite her repeated assurance that she had 'senice gay stomaco likese yong donzella' Simon was faintly disturbed.

The first frosty night set her grumbling with something of her old vigour, and next day she stayed in bed, having a little trouble with her breathing. It was not—she explained to Simon—that she had anything wrong with her lungs: merely that the air of England was dirty and also cold, she refused to get it inside her by walking about, he must take her at once to Genoa where all the air was pure and *cortese* and warm. Simon spent the day washing her clothes and preparing a stew for her, which she pushed away with silent, convulsive mockery.

She seemed to be sleeping peacefully that night, but a little after one o'clock in the morning she wakened Simon to tell him that the air had got worse and was hurting her chest severely: he saw for himself that her breathing had become extremely painful. Would she like a nice cup of tea? he asked. No, but she would like to look at one of her hens, she thought they must all be suffering from the cold, she must have one of them up here to see. Sleepy and anxious, Simon stumbled out to the poultry shed, seized the first bird his hands found and carried it flapping and squawking up to her room. By now she was sitting upright, heaving with the pain, which was sharply increased when the sight of the cockerel he had got hold of sent her into ecstatic laughter. Weeping with agony and mirth she gasped out, "Ahi—Simon—mio selovly pazzo! I tellim givmitse gallina, tsehen I say, an' he givmitse gennelman hen!" and he was obliged to repeat the laborious journey, leaving the cockerel behind. By the time he reappeared she had decided to review all her hens, and he had to travel back and forth, carrying one or two at a time, until there were frightened and miserable fowls all over the room. She was breathing a little more easily now, and for a few minutes she seemed content, watching the lively confusion, while Simon stood and shivered beside her. Then she wanted a particular hen to cuddle for its warmth, and soon she was imperiously demanding a knife to kill it with, because, she said, it was a lonely hen, too *gentile* for the others, and would be happier in the splendour and repose of death. If the English air suffocated her, she added, she would like to have her dear hen at her side for the journey to the purgatorio. After that she became quite calm again and Simon, thinking that she would sleep, got back into his side of the bed.

He fell asleep but she woke him once more, saying rather feebly that she could not go to the purgatorio before she had seen a priest. He protested sleepily that he could not possibly wake up a priest at that hour. Very well, he must read the Mass to her himself. Perhaps she would like to see a doctor? No, the English doctors were no use, the only thing that would do her good was to hear the Mass. Once more he went downstairs, and after much hunting found the torn and soiled remains of a missal below an old cookery book in one of the kitchen drawers. "Read it me vereverevere quick!" she said.

Sitting on the end of the bed with the counterpane round his shoulders, twisting the missal to get the light on it and repeatedly pushing back the spectacles which slipped down his nose, Simon stumbled through the Asperges and the Vidi Aquam as best he could. With this Maria seemed to be content. She lay peacefully, clutching the warm dead hen against her neck, she smiled and occasionally nodded, breathing very quickly like an exhausted runner but apparently no longer in pain. Presently she said abruptly:

"Tsatissenoff! Tsatiss veregood, tsatiss ol-right, verol-right. Now, kiss-kiss-kiss!"

Simon bent over her and she clutched his face against hers fiercely, as a shipwrecked man clutches a piece of wreckage which may keep him afloat, while his spectacles fell into the mess beside the pillow. Releasing him, she laughed, weakly but with all the old joy and bravado in her eyes. She whispered, "He issa *silly* man, mio Simono, verevere silly man! But he issa verevereverevere lovly man," and she hugged him once more. That effort ended in a sharp fit of coughing and she did not move again.

She needed a cup of tea, Simon thought. He went downstairs, put a kettle on the gas and washed out a mug. Tea, milk, and sugar had all to be hunted for among the litter on the table and dresser, the whole business took a long time and when he returned to the bedroom Maria appeared to be asleep; her head had fallen face downwards into the pool of blood from the hen. It cost him some effort to lift it up and get her into a more comfortable position, and while he was doing this the mug, which he had put down on the bed, fell over and poured its contents across the quilt; so that the general disorder of the bed, the state of Maria's face with the blood smeared all over her smiling mouth and chin, began to worry him a great deal; but he could not think where to start putting things straight. The chickens huddled under the washstand had been roused again, two of them started to fly about the room and their panic added to his own confusion. He no longer dared to look at Maria's face, for her eyes were open, staring towards the door as if she expected some visitor, and her grin unnerved him.

He realized that she was dead, for the shape of death had been familiar to him in his seafaring days, but he would not quite admit it. People were dead, he had always thought, either through some accident such as being drowned or after a period of illness; and although Maria had never conformed with the ordinary rules he did not see how she could be so full of life one minute and empty of it the next. Chiefly, however, he objected to the notion of her being dead because he could not conjure that of living without her. Lately the work of the house— or that part of it which had been attempted—had fallen largely on his own shoulders; but in this he had seen himself merely as a limb directed by her intelligence: he could not imagine himself deciding what food he ought to buy, or even to buy any at all. Without Maria, what reason could there be for buying it? The object of his life for several years had been to provide what Maria required: a little money and some casual labour, scraps of gossip from the street, warmth at night; a target for her coaxing and commands, her mockery and petulance, her damp and gusty embrace. With that object removed he would be like the blinded horse which works the mill.

At any rate he must get a doctor: one of these clever London doctors might know some dodge for warming her blood again, and perhaps, if such a man advised it, he would borrow some money and take her to Genoa, where the sunshine she had once been used to would set her on her feet.

But when he got as far as the kitchen it occurred to him that no proper doctor would come inside a house as untidy as this, where the underclothes Maria had washed two days before were all mixed up with poultry food and cooking utensils, where a rusty bicycle leant against the three-legged sofa and there were dishes stained with gravy on every chair. Weeping a little, he began to collect the crockery and pile it on the sofa and in the sink, intending to wash at least a few of the things; but he could not find the clout, and when he called up to ask Maria where it was there was no reply. His eye caught a pair of Maria's boots, which were very dirty, and he spent some time contentedly scraping the mud off with a table-knife, while his thoughts wandered to his grand-daughter and the delicious way she had thanked him for the last birthday present he had given her. Then, as he hunted for boot-polish, he came across a small bottle of cooking brandy, and the new vitality this gave him recalled his mind to the main task in hand. He must get the doctor quickly! He put his bare feet into a pair of sea-boots, and as his own overcoat was not to be found he donned the short moleskin coat that Maria had got at a jumble sale some years before; his cap also was missing but he found a bowler hat which had belonged to Ed. Thus attired, he finished the brandy and was about depart when a new anxiety arose: he felt it was not quite safe, when Maria prized them so dearly, to leave her poultry in the house alone: so having laboriously cleared a tea-chest which he found in the shop he carried it upstairs, and keeping his eyes away from Maria's face he set about capturing the seven live fowls, which again ran in terror all over the room. It was not an easy task for a tired old man: the earliest captures escaped while he chased the others, they ran between his legs and rocketed over his shoulders in a way that got on his nerves, while the cockerel upset him by perching on Maria's head and defiantly crowing: but in twenty minutes he had them all inside and had fastened a pillowcase over the top to keep them in. With his eyes shut he kissed Maria's forehead, whispering, "They'll be all right with me, pretty-sweet—I won't be long." Then he struggled downstairs with the box, got it up on the cross-bar of the bicycle and manoeuvred it out through the shop.

He did not know where to go for a doctor, but Gian would tell him, and he set off a little unsteadily, wheeling the top-heavy bicycle, towards Mickett Lane; the idea of guarding Maria's fowls so carefully, of making this resolute foray to get the doctor who would save her life, inspired him with a sense of heroism; and though the windy streets were cold for his legs where the vast gap between coat and boots left only his pyjamas to protect them, his heart felt brave and warm.

Tonie was away. It was Armorel who was wakened by his knock and who went downstairs to open the door. Simon stumbled in with the tea-chest and put it down in the passage, loosening the makeshift cover as he did so. The cockerel immediately flew out and went halfway up the stairs.

Armorel asked gently: "What have you come for, Papa Simon?"

He couldn't answer for a time, he just stood shivering and weeping. Then he mumbled that he only wanted to have a word with Gian.

"But, Simon dear, do tell me what the trouble is!"

Trouble? He wouldn't give her any trouble. "See the way it is, Miss Susie, I wouldn't want to trouble nobody, it being late like it is. Only I don't have any call to go on to doctors—not for some years back —only Gian, you see, he'd tell me where to go. I wouldn't want to be any trouble."

"Is there something wrong with Madre?"

"Well, if I could just have a word with Gian," he repeated.

The kitchen door had opened and Mrs Inch in her curious wrappings stood gazing with interest and some alarm at the unusual scene: at Armorel, collected, grave and beautiful in her crimson dressing-gown, the old man with his bowler hat and spectacles at opposite slants who was shaking and blubbering beside her, the scattered audience of bewildered fowls. She called huskily:

"They don't go on like that in decent houses. Not in the sort of houses I've been in."

"I don't want to give no one any trouble," Simon said again.

Armorel ignored the old woman. "You're cold, Papa Simon!" she said. She took him by the arm, led him upstairs and coaxed him into her own warm bed. "You must leave everything to me," she told him, "everything will be quite all right." She sat beside the bed and delicately stroked his cold cheek with her soft, warm fingers until he was fast asleep.

Childlike, in the days that followed, he submitted to all the plans that Armorel made for him. He was to eat this, to drink that, to sit in the kitchen till she had made him a fire in the front room? Of course, yes! Yes, at once—he didn't want to be any trouble. He was to live, presently, on the other side of the road, above Mr Heald's shop? Certainly, yes—only he didn't want to be a trouble. In the little room next to Mrs Empire's, yes! And Miss Susie would bring some of his things from Contessa Street, yes, yes, of course, just as she pleased, he wouldn't give any trouble at all. On the day of the funeral he let Gian dress him in his best clothes and then sat in the front room awaiting fresh orders, smiling in a shy fashion and rubbing his hands. Only at the last moment did he express a wish of his own: to take one of Maria's hens to the funeral with him. "Maria, you see, she's always been fond of them birds, in a manner of speaking. She'd think it funny if there wasn't one of them." And since he was not to be dissuaded, Tonie put one in a small hat-box for him, with little holes to give it air and a view.

In the car he sat beside Gian with the box on his knees, worried but still intermittently and modestly smiling, like a newly elected mayor. The sun was out, and it seemed to please him when people on the busy pavements stopped to stare and a man here and there lifted his hat.

It was Raymond's car: Raymond was always ready to show some kindness which would not put him to any great expense: he was driving himself, wearing the dark suit and the gravely sympathetic face he kept for funerals, a little worried about the amount of petrol this low-gear work involved, enjoying the autumn sun when it found its way between the roofs and listening indolently to the stream of low-voiced talk from Armorel, who sat beside him.

". . . make these people realize that a purely negative view of ethics gets us nowhere . . . calling it 'A Synthesis of Humanism'. I know that may sound *vieux jeu,* but I believe I'm really doing something that hasn't exactly been done before. It's something for the man in the street who doesn't want a whole lot of complicated reasoning, it gives him just the essentials of what the greatest thinkers and teachers have contributed to progressive morality—with brief explanations, of course. There are passages from Buddha, Confucius, Jesus of Nazareth, Marcus Aurelius, Montaigne, Bertrand Russell—of course I haven't included any part of their work which shows the influence of the superstitions prevailing in their time. It takes a good deal of donkey-work, I get up early now and put in an hour's research before breakfast."

"Extraordinarily interesting!" Raymond said, nudging towards the kerb to let a tram pass him.

The black wool dress she wore in deference to Simon's feelings enhanced her slenderness and her colouring, Raymond had seldom seen her looking so well. It was only her way of talking which made him faintly uneasy; it seemed to him unnaturally rapid, a little forced, like the talk at railway stations of people who have another minute to get through before the guard's whistle parts them. Yes, and the feeling her voice gave him, the suggestion of painful self-mastery, was reflected just perceptibly in her gestures and behaviour. She had greeted him with an embrace which seemed a trifle less spontaneous than of old, she had made a rather needless fuss about getting Simon into the car and snapped at Gian for lighting a cigarette while he was waiting. Of course, one expected a certain nerviness in a woman who overworked herself so recklessly for the comfort of others; and a moment after the cigarette incident she had been as gentle and composed as usual. But when a halt at traffic lights allowed him to glance at her face he fancied he could see, behind the surface of calm, the signs of an intolerable strain. Those eyes, he reflected, were not the eyes of Arthur Cepinnier, as he had sometimes imagined; the frontal architecture and the orbits reminded him now of Gertrude, but the pupils themselves were not like those of any Truggett he had known, they had the strength but not the eagerness, the valiance but not the passion. Such calm eyes now, but so desperately tired.

"I think they want us to move on," she said. "The cars behind are hooting rather."

"What? Of course, yes—I didn't notice, these lights are always changing—much better in the old days when they had a policeman."

A lorry had got between him and the hearse, but he wasn't going to worry. The engine was beautifully quiet today, even in middle gear, it was delicious to purr along so sedately with a handsome woman beside him. Even the ugliness of this main road, the endless procession of seedy shop-fronts, banal advertisements in senseless agglomeration, had for him the subtle virtue of familiarity. The sounds and smells might have altered, the cabs and drays had gone, but this was the very road he had once travelled, in one of Thompson's brakes, on his way to play cricket at Burgh Heath; the plaiting of meanness and flamboyance, the glum parade of independent and robust vulgarities, these seemed as aboriginal as the soil they hid, and the fates would surely spare a settlement so aged and hideous as this. A boy narrowly escaping his wheels spat adroitly at the radiator, calling, "Off t'bury the one you knock over *last* week, eh, cock!" and Raymond smiled in response. On a day when he had lunched so well he liked to hear his fellow citizens exercising their freedom of speech. Indeed, he felt benevolent towards everyone on the busy pavements, chattering girls in their bright cheap clothes, dowdy and overburdened matrons, because they expressed the town's stability. They were troubled, these folk, about the price of tea and the whims of their men; deaf to the jeremiads and alarms of the newspaper headlines; and if so rational a people could remain unmoved by impending disasters, taking it for granted that their own world was stablished fast for ever, he could surely bury his own anxieties in the same way. He saw in the driving mirror that he was faintly smiling; and a snatch of Gian's voice just audible through the stream of Armorel's, ". . . don't go there so much now, she don't really fancy me goin'," made him bring his face to attention.

"Are you all right, Gian—is your father quite warm? . . . Are you quite comfortable, my dear?"

"Yes, thank-you, Raymond. Only shouldn't we have gone left at the last turning? The hearse went that way."

"I'll take the next," he answered rather irritably. "We can easily get round."

When they came to the brand-new, anxiously Italian church, where the mourners were eddying confusedly about the portico, it was she who took command again. She whispered rapidly: "Go on, will you, Raymond—pull in just beyond that coal-cart—I don't want him to see more of it than he must . . . Gian, just wait a moment—I think it will be best if you let all those people go in first, and then Papa can sit somewhere near the back. Raymond, be a dear, slip along and tell those people to go inside, and tell Trevon if you can see him to keep two places fairly far back. Oh, and send Tonie to me, I want her to take her grandfather's other arm." She helped Simon out of the car and stood holding his hand and smiling kindly. "Yes, you can leave the box with me, it will be quite all right. Tell Tonie to get a service book and find the place for you—there's nothing to worry about, there won't be anything else for you to do."

Simon's eyes were wet now, and he seemed rather reluctant to leave the hen behind; but he still smiled patiently, like a nervous bridegroom. "Don't want to be a trouble to anyone!" was all he said. He looked contented, if slightly confused, when Gian and Tonie led him towards the church door.

"Of course I'm not going in," Armorel said to Raymond, "but you go if you want to, I shall be quite all right sitting here. Oh, well, that's very sweet of you! . . . I suppose it can be argued that this sort of thing has its psychological value—it localizes morbid sentimentalities. The Catholics are intelligent in their own way. Bad for Simon, though— all that flummery will upset him. He's borne up very well so far." She leant back and closed her eyes. "Yes, I shall be glad when we've got this business over. Of course I meant Milligan to do it—he's the most reliable undertaker I know—but he had four other funerals fixed for today and Gian let him farm out the work to this man Orfit, who's tiresome and thoroughly dishonest. I believe he's got certain business connections with Ed Hugg, and that doesn't say—"

She stopped abruptly. Raymond, filling the gap, asked:

"How's Gordon getting on with him? I suppose he'll be going on to work for some rather more settled firm before long?"

"Gordon? Oh, yes—yes, I suppose he will."

"You hadn't thought about the army, I suppose? I mean, he's a strong, healthy-looking chap—"

She laughed a little. "You mean, because he was in trouble when he was hardly more than a baby! Yes, Raymond dear, I know you do— it's what men like you always say. You say, 'That fellow's a bit too much to handle, dammit! The army's the place for him—get the corners rubbed off him!'"

"Rellie, I may be a very old man, but I was not alive with Sheridan and I do not say 'dammit'. By the way, where is he—Gordon? I haven't seen him today."

"He's away."

"What, on holiday?"

"Well, yes, I think so. He went off on some business for Ed, and then I think he decided to stay there for a bit."

"Stay where?"

"I don't exactly know. He's not the sort of boy who writes letters. Does it matter?"

"No, only—he's a bit young, isn't he, to be going off by himself without your knowing where he's going? What is he—fifteen?"

She sighed. "Yes, I know everyone thinks I'm very incompetent—"

"—My dear, I never said anything of the sort!"

"Well, anyway, I'm tired of people giving me advice about Gordon. I happen to know Gordon in a way that nobody else does—

because I'm his mother and I've studied him scientifically—and I trust him absolutely. He's not without his faults, of course. He may be canny with people who can only think of him as a boy who got into trouble in early infancy. With me he's absolutely open and straightforward—which is more than I can say about a lot of other people."

"I'm sorry!" he said helplessly.

Her eyes had closed again. "It doesn't matter. I mean, there's nothing to be sorry about."

He was bitterly grieved. Once or twice he had seen Rellie in a spasm of impatience such as the gentlest of women will suffer in the long nervous strain of marriage and motherhood; but never before had she spoken like that to him. He knew he was a blunderer and a bore, but surely he had always deserved her confidence, surely she realized that what he said to her, however gauche, came from the humblest sort of kindness. This breeze could not be left to blow itself out; and all at once he realized that here was the occasion he had waited for so timorously and so long.

The street was a quiet one. A pair of workmen were loitering on the other side of the road, engrossed in their own talk; apart from them, Armorel and he were quite alone. He had to be firm now, whatever it cost him. He had to tell her bluntly that she was overworking and must give herself a rest, for the sake of others besides herself; he must put it in the plainest possible language that she had acquired an exaggerated notion of her own capacities, that she expected at once too much and too little from other people, that as mistress of a family she was trying to achieve by regulation what could, in fact, only be won by—by?—he hadn't the word. Tact? Intuition? Neither of those was right. He turned to stare at the appalling structure of the church, because he could not look at Rellie's face without emotion. He was never, never able to regard her with the same eyes as anyone else. In days that were precious to his memory he had seen her sitting on her father's shoulders—Arthur's shoulders, Arthur, the most brave and lovable of all men, for ever tortured by some fresh discovery that others were not as selfless as he—he had watched the smile of unfulfilled maternity in Georgie's face when she had held the little girl, the softness that had come even to the stoic, puritan face of Edith. To him, Rellie was still a child, the whole apparatus of her maturity was nothing more intrinsic than the velvet gowns she had used for dressing-up in the nursery at Hayward's Heath; and because he saw her as a child he, knowing himself too stupid to follow the workings of another mind, could yet feel that he grasped the shape of hers. I know her, he thought, all but aloud. Not in the way that other people do, not as Mrs Ardree, the capable manager of a difficult household, not as the grand panjandrum of some intellectual society, nor even as a sensible and forceful woman, but as herself, another human with a spirit essentially so like my own that the difference of sex and age is almost irrelevant; a being as much the centre of its own reality as I am of mine. There is nothing to separate her from my understanding except the loneliness which has thickened about her spirit till it has become another skin; that, too, is something I am specially made to understand. I have only to call to her in the voice of our old familiarity—now, now, quickly, before it's too late—and the child I know so well will hear and find her way to me.

But that voice was not at his command. Perhaps he had never possessed it, perhaps the only voice he had ever used was the one so like his clothes, fitting perfectly a man of the middle shape, sedulously avoiding any tone which might suggest some sentiment, taste or pretension different from those of other Englishmen of the collared rank. He cleared his throat and it remained completely clear. He buttoned and unbuttoned his dark-grey gloves. A worrying, un-English smell came to his nose: the door of the church had opened and they were beginning to come out. Heavens, what a lot of friends that old woman had had, how terribly gregarious she must have been! That was surely old what's-his-name—Olleroyd—in the appalling hat, and weeping like a child . . . Surprisingly, and in a watery fashion, his voice started to work:

"I say, Rellie! Rellie, my dearest, there's just one thing—I mean, you know we've been friends for ever so long, and I was awfully fond of your father, you know. It's just that if you want any help any time—anything special, you know what I mean. I'm not one of these psychoanalytical people you get nowadays, I'm—well, I suppose I'm a great deal stupider than most of your friends—only I've always been terribly fond of you, I suppose really you mean more to me than you do to anyone else except Gian—"

"Gian?" she broke in, quite quietly. "I don't mean anything at all to Gian. He doesn't tell me anything, not even when he goes and kills someone."

"Rellie!" he said sharply. "You're talking in a very foolish way! I don't even think it's at all certain—"

"Well, that's a subject I've got rather tired of." She opened the door of the car. "You know," she said over her shoulder, "I really am grateful to you for coming and helping me with the transport like this. Ah, there they are!"

Simon was coming along very slowly, supported now by Gian and his old friend Izzy Brooks. The change in him was that he had lost the patient smile and his face was now devoid of expression. I have only seen very drunk men, and once a Russian criminal condemned to execution, looking as he looked then. Armorel, swiftly taking Izzy's place, said: "Come along, Papa, and we'll make you comfy in the car again. Do you know, there's going to be a specially lovely tea for you when it's all over and we get back home."

" 'And some there be which have no memorial,' " Trevon said softly and angrily. "May I be one of them!"

In a long, scalene triangle between the football ground and the railway embankment there were jammed as tightly as possible the strange devices by which the living would glorify their dead: the dun brick vaults, tables of granite and Carrara marble, truncated pillars, giant four-posters held down by canopic jars or peevish seraphim. The sun was covered now, the day seemed to have fallen dead. Veering north, the wind had cleared the haze and given the place a chilled, metallic feel, sharpening sounds, the feel of winter mornings in barrack squares; it stirred what little grass there was, and blew a fine dust along the cinder paths; from the massif of smoked houses crammed against the cycle works it brought a ciderish smell and more faintly the smell of laundry soap. An exultant cheer came from the football ground as the Rolls hearse which Orfit had hired to bear Maria's remains crawled down the slope from the canal bridge and made the awkward turn through the iron gates.

Holding the wreath she had made herself, Tonie stood apart from the others in an angle of the Gothic entrance lodge: she had come on from the church in Raymond's car, he had taken another wrong turning and arrived a long time before the hearse. She showed no emotion and felt none: here there was not even the feel of Sunday, the sadness veined with triumph that she had looked for was flattened into boredom by the monochrome of the scene. As she prayed, 'O God, let me cry a little, just for Grandfather to see,' she heard Raymond's low, despondent voice, ". . . memorized the route most carefully from the little atlas I've got. Simply can't imagine where I went wrong."

The car which James Ardree had hired for himself and the Huggs had confidently followed Raymond's and was standing behind it just outside the gates. Crippled but vigorous, sniffing loudly and casting his valuer's eyes to right and left, James advanced upon Simon with half his weight on a rubber-ferruled stick and half on his great-niece Evangeline's arm. "Merciful release!" he shouted. "That's the way you want to look at it, Simon boy. Merciful release!" Rosie hobbled behind him on her varicose legs, where the bandages showed in high relief through the black silk stockings; the black and shapeless hat she wore hid most of her face, whose remaining prettiness had been washed out by the tears she had shed in church, her thin black coat only just buttoned across her dilating front. She called feebly, "Wait Vangie, I want your other arm!" Ed, who had stopped to light a cigarette, went past her, giving his hat a backward tilt, and made for Gian, who stood dejectedly on the edge of the drive with his friend Terence Hubbitt beside him. "Sad occasion!" he said succinctly. "Of course, you've got to think of it, the old girl was getting on a bit, like it or not. Sad, all the same. Only really it's what you might call a merciful release."

"You won't remember me," James said heartily to Raymond, "—Mr Ardree is the name—only I remember you—never forget a face! You're the gent who's got that nice little place over the other side of London, place I thought might make into a nice little business proposition. Now listen, I'm sixty-nine. Started out in the world without a halfpenny to my name . . ."

"Heard from that Gordon yet?" Ed asked.

Gian said: "No."

Armorel joined them. "Were you asking about Gordon? I haven't had a letter yet—of course he doesn't ever do much writing—"

"I'll say he doesn't!"

"But I'm sure he'll make up if he's overstayed the leave you've given him."

"Didn't give him any—but that's not the question, Mrs Sue! Question is, can he make up the eighteen quid four-an-a-kiss he's got owing to two of my customers? I only just ask because the cops have been round my place inquiring."

"But, Ed, there must be some mistake. Of course I know Gordon's careless—"

Ed nodded, whistling gently with his teeth, as if the more he considered her remark the more interesting it became. In the silence that followed they caught the voice of Raymond, saying miserably, "But I'm not sure that I really *want* to make any brass."

"See here," muttered Gian, suddenly taut with rage, "I'm not goin' to have nobody sayin' things about my son."

"Careless, yes!" Ed said thoughtfully, keeping his voice small and ignoring Gian altogether. "Forgets things. Seems to have quite forgot about the kid I have in my shop doing the typing—forgot he given her a Woolworth ring. Got her ma come round moaning at me—says the kid's three months gone. Not that I want to say anything to spoil a nice good-class funeral like this."

The hearse had come to a halt a few yards down the main drive.

Headed by Olleroyd, with Mrs Inch trotting gamely at his heels, the rest of the mourners were straggling along from the bus stop in Pennard Road. They were oddly decked with whatever bits of black clothing they had managed to find in damp-locked drawers, and they moved without much order or grace, only with certain exhaustless obduracy, like soldiers who have marched for a great distance. And indeed, most of them had travelled far, and not over easy country. Daise, stumping along by herself, almost hidden by her twenty-five-shilling wreath, was perhaps thirty years younger than any of the others, and even Miss Toble looked juvenile with the white-haired and shrivelled Lizzie Bentlock limping fiercely beside her. Flock himself was becoming an old man; he marched at attention, scolding Slimey under his breath, "Head up, Slimey lad, chest out, swing those arms—it's not you that's got to be put underground!" but his legs were giving a little at the knees in a way he would have mastered three years before; while Bet Oestermann, advancing slowly and shakily like the wind-worn statue of an empress being moved to a new site, was uttering little whimpers of distress. It was slightly painful for more than one of them, even this bare quarter of a mile, for their legs had been much abused by steep staircases and the coldness of kitchen floors; painful for little Mrs Diddus with her sciatica and for Lofty Chiffop's corns. But their faces showed little of what their bodies were suffering, and not much curiosity about the unfamiliar scene, for they were people accustomed to bodies that worked painfully and as Londoners they took the whole of the physical world without expectancy or surprise. For an instant, as they passed between the grandiose pillars of the gateway, one or two looked self-conscious; they possessed no title to such splendours except that they were friends of Maria, who evidently had rights within this place; but seeing people they knew, Maria's strange son and the grandchild with her friendly smile, they relaxed into the dour apathy of those who realize that every job of work is uniformly dull. The hearse moved on again. The bearers were on foot now, Orfit and Tiny Bates in the awkward grandeur of hired morning dress, Clip Starkie and his friend with black coats over their working clothes. Maria's family fell in behind. Between the wistful angels and marble scrolls, the many sonorous eulogia on those who had arrived before, the promiscuous company of Maria's friends which plodded along the asphalt, stoic faces in tune with wilted clothes, appeared to restore to death the dignity of common speech.

"I beg of you one favour," Trevon muttered. "Don't bury me here. Have me cremated and chuck the ashes away. I loathe all this childishness—trying to decorate a mystery with little dingy flags."

"If you were dead," Elizabeth answered quietly, "I couldn't decide that sort of thing. I shouldn't be really alive myself."

They were a little way behind the others; a curious pair, Raymond thought, glancing back: he in the very coat, patched and turned, which he had worn at Armorel's wedding, the wreck of a formidable man, a barbarian image dug out and cleaned to show the rough nobility of its head; she, fragile as Sèvres, wearing her old grey suit with so serene a carriage that it seemed a part of her body's elegance. She looked ill today, but in Raymond's eyes she had never been more beautiful, with her pale flesh appearing to be translucent, the sweetness which laughter had given to her mouth perfected now in its still repose. She held tightly to Trevon's arm, and a close observer could see that she placed her feet cautiously. Yet you could not be sure that she was being led, and not leading him, for while he appeared to drag himself along in several pieces her walk was purposeful and even. It was she who brought them both to a halt.

"Dearest, I don't want to go too near. We don't really belong."

He stood with his weight on one leg and stared vacantly after the crowd, working his mouth as if a seed had stuck between his lower teeth. "You'll get cold," he said irritably. "You shouldn't have sold that fur thing."

"I'm not cold when I'm with you," she replied.

The hearse had stopped again. Not without competence, even a rough dignity, Orfit and his ill-matched men were taking out the peculiarly shaped coffin, which, with its load of white flowers, rather resembled a giant Christmas cake. Fidgeting morosely, Trevon shifted his weight to the other leg.

"She was a very dirty old woman," he said, "and her house always stank."

"But these people loved her."

Behind them, the silt of cloud above the grandstand had broken once again. Where a surplice fluttered a strong and gentle voice said, "Eternal rest grant unto her, O Lord!" and the answering murmur, ". ... shine upon her!" reached them faintly through the rustle of leaves blowing across the path. A goods train which seemed to have no end was labouring along the embankment, an express came screaming down the centre track and a twisting sash of smoke lay across the high walls of Valiant's Brewery and the jumbled roofs of Haythorn Hill. It lifted slowly; and beyond the line, in the slanting yellow light, a row of sycamores showed for an instant like a fountain of new gold against the blackened coaling sheds.

"Do you see that?" Trevon said in sudden excitement. "Those trees?"

"Trees?"

"I'm sorry—I forgot." He turned to look with anguish at her eyes. He said: "I forgot. I've stolen all that. I've stolen everything you had."

"I see everything with your eyes," she answered simply. "I like things that way—yours have always been better than mine."

Borne awkwardly upon uneven shoulders, Maria's coffin bobbed and lurched through the granite jungle. *And let perpetual light shine upon her!* The dark stream of Maria's friends, turned from its course, was flooding through the several channels which twisted between the graves, adding a new untidiness to the desolation.

The pain of his face became a smile. "Yes," he said, "I suppose they loved her, or else they wouldn't be here. Do you think they love her now?"

She did not understand. "I suppose it's her memory they love."

"Just that?" He searched her face again, uncertain in these days how much she could see of his own. He took her other hand, which was cold, and started chafing it. "You know," he said falteringly, "I simply can't believe that, it doesn't make sense—loving something so nebulous and abstract as a memory. Those faces—no, you couldn't see them in the church as I did, they must have looked to you quite ordinary faces.

I mean, it seems so strange, to love just the memory of an old woman like that."

"Perhaps that isn't what I mean."

"I don't know what love is," he pursued, still fumbling for words, still warming her hand, "but I know it joins one person to another, it depends on them both. And yet when one of them is put away under the ground like this it still goes on. If you were dead, my love for you wouldn't stop—a hundred years wouldn't make any difference to it. And one can't love something that's ceased to exist."

She found an answer. "But I think that's what I meant. I suppose I should go on living within your mind, as part of yourself."

"No!" he said soberly, but almost in a whisper, as if he were struggling not to weep. "No, nothing so perfect could exist within me, any more than it could come to an end." His mouth smiled again; he was drawing out his thoughts as one unravels a tangle of string. "I can think of myself finishing, not you. You see, you never alter. I've given you nothing, no comforts, so little understanding, nothing a woman ought to be given. I've only destroyed your sight. And you're still the same to me, God himself could scarcely ask for the love I get from you. Can anyone imagine all that goodness, all that splendour, is just the result of nerves and cells—that it's over when the heart stops pumping!"

In his agitation he had started to walk on again; they turned from the main path and he led her very carefully between the graves towards the place where the mourners were hiving. She whispered, tightly holding his arm and moving with the same sad dignity:

"I don't know—there's nothing I understand. It's only—my life seems to be all in you. It's all I need, having you and your love. I can't think of afterwards."

Beside the grave, the bearers were threading slings through the coffin's handles. The rumble of another train had subsided, and in the quietness which followed a new burst of cheering from the football ground the priest's voice sounded like the unfurling of a flag: ". . . that Thou deliver it not into the hands of the enemy, nor forget it unto the end; but bid it to be received by Thy holy Angels and conducted into Paradise, its true country." Rigid, flinching a little from the pain that was coming on, Trevon crossed himself. He looked along the skirt of the crowd to where Rosie stood apart from the rest, crying bitterly, and he saw Gian slip back to put his arm in a stolid and awkward fashion round her shoulders. Among these shabby followers who peered with a kind of expectation towards the grave, among the dull, devoted, the old and tired faces, he caught sight of Tonie's, brave and solemn in adolescence, as she stood at attention holding her grandfather's hand; beyond her, the scraggy, pocked, contemptuous face of Lizzie Bentlock, who, while he watched, suddenly knelt down in the grey slime. He began to shiver, not from the cold: one of his worst attacks was starting, and he wondered whether he would get home before he had made himself an exhibition. But now the endurance of these worn faces restored his own: some pain was worth the suffering, to be among this woman's friends. With his eyes wandering across the chaos of masonry, over to the sooted factory windows, back to the trees, he said with a soft finality, "No, this isn't the end!" tightening his grip on Elizabeth's arm.

A new and stronger gust of wind had rain in it, but the business would be over soon, Raymond supposed. The wretchedness of the day had surpassed his fears. He had expected to be ill at ease, as he always was among the Ardrees and their friends; to feel as if he was something peculiar and rather contemptible, like a gentleman of the chorus in musical comedy. He had realized that the venue would be dismal and the weather cold. But that strange and rather disturbing outburst of Rellie's, his own humiliating mistakes about the route, the sudden appearance of that alarming brother of Simon's, these had all reduced him to abject misery and jumping nerves. Worse still, the blatant emotion of Rosie and others had infected him with an unimagined sentimentality. The shape of the coffin reminded him of Maria too well. A dreadful person, he had always thought her, with her billowing fat and cacophonous laughter: yet now, remembering how narrow and jejune the surroundings of her life had been, how little she had demanded in comfort or admiration, he felt sad that so much magnificence had been kept to honour her remains. His eyes kept turning to Daise's enormous wreath and the coarse stockings which showed below it, now to the weeping Olleroyd's threadbare suit and the bunch of Michaelmas daisies in his big flabby hand. "At thy coming may the Martyrs receive thee," the virile and tender voice besought, "and bring thee into the holy city, Jerusalem. May the choir of Angels receive thee, and with Lazarus, once a beggar, mayest thou have eternal rest." As the coffin started to go down he found that his own eyes were obscured by tears.

It will soon be finished, he silently repeated, staring at his shoes. This is always the worst part—it will all be over soon. But when he looked up again one end of the coffin still showed. He heard the voice of Mrs Diddus, low and mournful but quite distinct:

"They do say it bring you bad luck if your coffin jam."

The hubbub from the football ground had vexed him; now he longed for it to start again. The priest had lost his place, and in the fearful hush the whispers of the bearers were plainly audible twenty yards away. " 'Ere, pull it up again—not you—Clip, your end . . . All right—hold it! Where's the diggin' bloke?" ". . . Well, three-foot-four-a-half shoulder is what they tell me, I got it written down. Two-foot-one at the narrer end . . . Think I don't check up with the plumb!" " 'Old on, Tiny, for cri—'ere, give that one to me!" And now the thin, ferocious whisper of Sergeant Flock, "Fumin' civvy job! Lor love a bleedin' duck, can't even shove the ole perisher two foot under the ground!" Scorched and almost paralysed with shame, Raymond just retained enough of his meagre wits to realize the greatest danger of all.

"Rellie," he said behind his glove, "you must get your father-in-law away from here—somehow!"

She did not even move. "I told Gian," she answered softly, "I said he was merely asking for trouble if he employed these men. He never does anything I say."

But Simon, in fact, was unaware that matters at the grave were wrong. The string by which he had been holding the hat-box had broken, the hen had fluttered away and he was giving chase.

Another gust of wind brought a heavier load of rain. The spectators stood motionless, as the English do; solemn, tolerant of mischance, preserving even their studied reverence; and it seemed to Raymond that he bore the whole moral weight of these shameful happenings alone. The whispered altercation was increasing in violence. Orfit had obviously lost his head and the whole pack of them, he thought, would presently come to blows. Surely the priest should exercise some authority! But that young and unpretentious man was never equal to such a situation as this, and after one more attempt to continue the prayers he stood in frozen silence with a face almost as distraught as Raymond's own, while the wind sent his surplice thrashing about his waist and the rain poured mercilessly onto his book. Now, in anguish, Raymond saw that the hen was rushing towards him, with Simon in brave pursuit.

Instinctively he stooped to field the bird as it passed his feet, and actually caught it by one leg; but the horror of being, as it were, in church with a creature flapping and squealing in his hands was more than he could bear. He let it go, and without hesitation Simon resumed the chase, fruitlessly coaxing, grabbing, stumbling, as the frightened creature dashed towards Mrs Inch, swerved, cannoned against the priest's legs, darted between Bet Oestermann's, turned again and flew with vociferous cries towards the grave. Mercifully, Flock had now taken command. The priest, a little reassured, was starting to read again, and interwoven with the august, the slightly faltering sentences, a voice of absolute certainty, no longer subdued, was bringing the hideous confusion within control. "Now you—Clip—you hold on 'ere —jump to it! (Someone wring the neck of that perishin' fowl!) Now then—wait for the cautionary word . . ." Responding to that authority the bearers were once more working like a team, in a few moments they had the coffin back on terra firma and the sides of the grave were being scraped with a spade. A sense of relief spread through the little crowd. True, the rattled and exhausted Bates had still to pay out his sling too fast, the coffin had yet to go into a dive and stick once more, head down, before it finally dropped with a sickening crash to the grave's floor. But when Raymond opened his eyes again the unnerving rite was at an end, the men were mopping their faces and the mourners rather gratefully moving away.

"Pity the rain come on like this!" he heard Mrs Inch say. "But it's been a lovely funeral, reely, all the same."

As he followed the rest he turned round once to glance at the empty stage where Maria's temporal career had come to its close: at the flowers spread on the grey soil, where the rain was already battering the petals and obliterating the little cards; at the mud-stained planks, the digger surreptitiously filling his pipe. He saw Trevon looking the same way, while Elizabeth tried to hurry him on; he joined them and they walked together towards the gate. Ahead of them Simon was chattering, laughing and sobbing in turn, while Tonie walked gravely beside him with the hen under her arm.

It was generally agreed that the old man had come through the ordeal very well; and back at Mickett Lane he seemed to be pleased with the special tea which Armorel had promised him. He sat by the fire in the arm-chair she had told him to regard as his own, filling his mouth with crumpet and chattering to Olleroyd about the good times he had once enjoyed with Izzy and Lofty, happily ignoring the butter which trickled onto his knees. Once or twice, looking at his watch, he said: "I can't think what's happening to my old girl." But Armorel was always at hand with a fresh cup of tea, which appeared to wash the trouble away.

The curtains were not yet drawn; the last, grey daylight showed the street palely behind the room's reflection and the rain thrown like sand against the glass sharpened the sense of cosiness within. Raymond had departed, and with him that restraint which an elegant woman will bring upon a public bar. Side by side on the settee, Gian and Tonie talked in low voices, avoiding laughter, as if Maria's spirit might still be disturbed; but their tired faces had the contentment of sailors who have brought their craft through dangerous seas.

"Poor Evangeline—she does look *rather* funny somehow in black."

"Hh! No need to get her up that fashion, not at her age, not as far as I can see. That Ed, he just don't know what to do with his money."

"What was Uncle Ed going on and on about at the cemetery, just before we went to the grave?"

"Ed? Oh, just his nonsense! No good takin' notice of anything Ed says."

Armorel was kneeling on the hearth-rug, pouring fresh hot water into the tea. She said coolly, but with a suddenness that surprised them:

"I don't want to be fussy, but if you two have got to say things you don't want me to hear I wish you'd go to another room. I suppose it's stupid, but I've got a bit of a head and I really find it rather tiresome, having to keep my ears closed all the time."

They were too much startled to reply. And as women do, with their instinctive fear of losing momentum, she continued the attack:

"I do realize that you're both of one mind about Gordon. You'd both like him to stay away."

"But, Mother, we weren't talking—"

"—I can only say that *I* wanted him to go through with the course Dr Liedke-Urban advised. It was you, Gian, who insisted on going right against that advice. If Gordon had only—Yes, Elizabeth, is there something you want?"

Elizabeth was feeling her way forward from the door, screwing her eyes to identify the several faces in the room. She said:

"Oh, I hope I'm not interrupting—did I hear you say you'd had some news of Gordon?"

"Which Gordon?"

"Why—yours! I only thought—"

Without raising her voice, but speaking a trifle faster than usual, a little more metallically, Armorel said:

"Well, if you really want to hear all the gossip about Gordon you'd better ask Gian's brother-in-law. I don't know that I'd recommend him as a paragon of truthfulness, but that may be personal prejudice. You'll be able to get it from Antonia, anyway, since she spends half her time with you. I expect—"

Almost dumbfounded, Elizabeth said: "But, Rellie, I—really, I didn't in the least mean to be inquisitive. I just—I only came in to ask if Tonie would do something for me—"

Tonie said: "Of course—!"

"—It's just to go round to Bishops' and get a prescription made up. Trevon's had rather a nasty turn—"

Armorel said swiftly: "Well, it's not my business, but I personally shouldn't have let him go to that cemetery, his health being what it is nowadays. However, he's your husband, not mine. I'm afraid Tonie's got prep to do. I—"

Gian was on his feet. "Bit of a walk do me good—"

"No!" Armorel interrupted. "I'm sorry, but Gian's been wet through once today already, and he gets these fearful colds. I—"

"—Here now, Sue, you're talkin' silly—"

"—I'll take it round myself as soon as I've done the washing-up. I suppose that will be time enough?—"

"—Mother, I've only got—"

"—Now see here, Susie—"

"Please—" Armorel said—"I've got a headache and I don't feel like arguing. Give me that prescription, please—I'll go in ten minutes."

Elizabeth was already retreating. "I'm terribly sorry, I really didn't mean to be a nuisance. I can go myself, easily." And had her sight been normal those words would have taken her out of the room. But she had to move carefully, feeling for obstructions, and the delay gave Armorel time to say, in her normal voice and without a trace of excitement:

"Oh, as you are here, Elizabeth—I was going to speak to you—I don't want Michael to come here any more. I'm sorry, but I can't allow it."

Elizabeth turned round.

"But, Rellie—I don't understand! Michael not come here? Why?"

"I hoped you wouldn't ask me. I don't in the least want to make any accusations—it's just that I've found money disappearing from my room every time Michael's been here, and I simply can't afford those losses, that's all. I suppose I ought to lock things up, but I can't get used to living in that fashion, and I don't intend to. So I'm afraid Michael will have to stay away."

Tonie said: "Mother!"

It took Elizabeth a moment or two to find her voice, and when it came it sounded like the voice of one just returning to consciousness after an accident.

"But—but this is Michael's home. He hasn't anywhere else."

No longer facing her, Armorel said: "I imagine his father has an establishment. His legal father, I mean."

Elizabeth's voice remained so quiet that it sounded unreal.

"Michael's home is with me. And this is the only home I've got."

"You have it on a monthly sub-tenancy, as far as I remember."

"You can't get cheap rooms nowadays," Elizabeth said with a great simplicity. "We've nowhere else to go."

"That's very unfortunate," Armorel answered, with the air of one quietly gathering her skirts. "I only wish things hadn't turned out like this."

Was Gian to blame for his silence then? He knew, he must have known, that it was his business as a man to intervene: a very few words, spoken quietly but with absolute firmness, would surely have brought his wife to her senses or at least unarmed her: he had merely to say that he was master in this house, that most of the money came from his earnings, that he would not see gross injustice done to people who were not only satisfactory sub-tenants but also devoted friends. It is equally certain, however, that he would not have said anything of the kind even if minutes instead of seconds had been allowed for the plodding machinery of his mind and tongue to work. He was not the master; in all his married life he had no more dreamed of being so than an able boy of colour would think to lord it over his fellows in an English school; and if moments of crisis move nervous men to desperate courage, it is seldom courage of that kind. He said nothing; and his mouth, which mercifully no one saw, fell into a senseless grin. Antonia was not even trying to speak; for she felt just then exactly as if she herself had struck Elizabeth in the face, and the effort of not crying gagged her as effectively as a hand grasping her throat. To her, emotionally tired, and sixteen years of age, what happened was not a melancholy quarrel, a grave embarrassment; it was something final, an outrage at once upon her heart and understanding, a humiliation so sharp and sudden that it seemed to have cut through the roots of her existence, letting all the sweetness of life drain away. Afraid to meet Elizabeth's eyes or her mother's, she stared at a swan-shaped patch of damp above the piano; hearing as if from outside time the laboured mumble of Simon telling Olly some story all over again, the dismal sounds of the drenched street. Surely Mother would go now, surely she would go away to her own room, and then they could at least say something to re-start the springs of kindness! But Armorel was not given to actions which might suggest theatricality: it was Elizabeth who went away.

In her competent, unhurried fashion, Armorel put the tea-things together, drew the curtains, made up the fire; trying—as she always did—to give warmth and pleasantness to their unpretentious room. Her lips were parted a little by a smile which seemed to hang from her remoter thoughts: she evidently did not notice the painful looks that followed her, did not hear Elizabeth feeling her way downstairs again or the street door being slammed full open by the wind.

"I've been wondering," she said to Tonie, "whether we ought to think about getting you into one of the younger universities. Possibly Birmingham. I feel they're less narrow and academic than the older ones, they think rather more about tomorrow and less about the Chaldeans and soothsayers. I mean, if you're going to take up a position of leadership in the modern world you've got to know what the world is like . . ."

39

R AYMOND WROTE:

My dear Edith: I was with Armorel yesterday at the funeral of old Mrs Ardree (a most shamefully mismanaged affair—not Armorel's fault, I'm certain). Frankly, I did not feel happy about her, although I should have said from her *appearance* that she had recovered completely from the recent illness, which from what the Grists tell me was in the nature of nervous disorder. It is hard to describe what I think is wrong with her now. Although tired, she has plenty of physical energy, and seems as clear-headed and competent as ever. But I cannot get away from the impression that she is still dangerously overburdened by various anxieties. I think that Gordon is probably a good deal to do with it. She is so proud of that handsome scalawag, and he is completely undisciplined—he acts according to her wishes just when it happens to suit him, and for the rest according to his own wayward inclinations. (His moral inheritance is palpably from someone on his father's side, or else from Armorel's mother.) And then she seems to be no longer capable of maintaining a really satisfactory relationship with Gian. I do not mean that they are actually at loggerheads—it is simply that he seems to be on her nerves all the time, although he is obviously most anxious to treat her as a husband should—indeed, I should say that in spite of everything he is still devoted to her in his own way. Here the root of the whole trouble is, of course, the affair of five years ago. As I see it, Gian threw that very unwholesome fellow down the stairs in the course of a scuffling quarrel, probably not meaning to kill him. By good fortune he was acquitted, and that, as far as he is concerned, was the end of it. (You will hardly realize, my dear Edith, how little weight is attached to such happenings by people who have a much rougher background than ours, and among whom occasional violence is almost a commonplace.) Armorel, naturally, does not view the matter in at all the same light, and the fact that Gian has not been clothed in sackcloth and ashes ever since is—if I interpret the business rightly—a permanent affront to her moral sense. She simply cannot see how one can live in terms of close friendship with a man who has not only committed an appalling crime but is obviously quite complacent about it. There, of course, I have the greatest sympathy with Armorel's point of view—I mean, of course, it is entirely the right point of view, the only possible one for a civilized person—and incidentally it shows how thoroughly sound was the moral training which you and Gertrude gave her. And yet—while I am anything but an expert on any sort of religious question—I should have thought that a Christian wife had duties vis-à-vis her husband somewhat different from those of anyone else. If family life counts for anything I do not really see how it is to be managed if the wife conducts herself in strict accordance with the regulations issued to the early Semites by Elijah or some personage of that kind. However, that is your province, not mine.

The reason I write is this. If ever I had any influence with Rellie it has gone. She has always realized that I am very far from being a clever man, and now she has come to regard me as a clumsily interfering one. Your own position is different. I know that you and she have been estranged for a long time. But I also know, from odd remarks which I have heard from Rellie herself, that through all the estrangement she has retained a high respect for your integrity and—forgive so awkward a phrase—your solid sense. You are more closely related to her than I. And in what I take to be the hopeless moral confusion in which she exists at present I do believe that you are the one person alive who might, if the estrangement were brought to an end, so influence her that she would regain her equilibrium.

Is such a reconciliation really impossible? I ask nothing as a favour to myself, but I do beg you, for the sake of Arthur whom you and I both loved, to consider whether by any means and at any cost you can come to the rescue now. I use those words most seriously. I am more than unhappy about Rellie, I am very gravely alarmed . . .

Edith's answer wakened in him a strange echo of the voice of her mother:

. . . I can assure you, Raymond, that you have no need to use any eloquence in making such an appeal to me. If God does open any way for my friendship with Rellie to be restored, no weakness of my own (and I am a woman of many weaknesses) shall stand in the way. I am even ready, at some cost to my conscience, to tell Rellie that on matters where she and I disagreed (when she was little more than a child) I was in the wrong. But would such an admission—true or false—have any effect upon her now? Rightly or wrongly I opposed her unconventional marriage. (In a sense, wrongly, since much that Georgina has told me about Rellie's husband proves to me that my conception of him was considerably mistaken: and with regard to the criminal charge brought against him some time ago I see no reason why you, my dear Raymond, should consider your verdict more certain than that of an honourable jury guided by one of the King's judges.) It would be quite possible for me to tell Rellie, now, that my judgement was wholly at fault and to ask her forgiveness for so wrongly opposing her in a matter which was for her alone to decide. (As you know, I am by no means without personal vanity, but I recognize that as a weakness which must be overcome.) The question I ask myself is, Would such an admission carry the weight of sincerity when the marriage has proved, as you tell me, by no means a happy one? I am only a person of very average intelligence—as I think you point out in your letter—but to me the answer to that question is hardly in doubt. I believe that Rellie would think me either deficient in candour or else an imbecile; and seriously I cannot see what advantage would be gained by her holding either view. When you have very carefully examined my reasoning I shall be glad to hear of any errors you may find in it—in my day women were not, of course, trained as logicians.

I am afraid that I have aged a good deal in body and mind since we were last in correspondence, and I now have to regard myself as an old—indeed, an ancient—woman. Georgina, whom you have lately seen, has withstood the years much more robustly than I. I was able to continue my parish visiting nearly to the end of last year, but it cost me not inconsiderable pain and Dr Jacquelin at length forbade it absolutely. Since April, I have lived almost entirely in one room, where my meals are brought to me, and where Georgina has to assist me in dressing, etc: Father Bensitt is very good in administering the Sacrament to me here. I can be lifted downstairs on special occasions, though the operation induces a certain muscular pain of which Jacquelin disapproves. (One must not, of course, quarrel with the professional pride which these men take in keeping useless people alive as long as possible.) In spite of these handicaps I am very willing to make a journey into London if anything is to be gained by my doing so. (Jacquelin will be on holiday shortly, and his partner is a much younger man whom I can easily defy.) I only wait to be persuaded that Armorel will pay any attention at all to anything I may say. At present I am not so persuaded.

Raymond dear, I hope that you will believe at least in my sincerity. In these days, when I am a prisoner of my useless limbs and do not sleep well, I have more time than I really want for reflection, and I suffer rather painfully from the thought of how few people I have made to care for me, how many have been alienated by my stupidities and my lack of that warmth which a Christian should surely be able to show to all her fellow-men. If by any means at all I could feel that what harm I have done to Armorel has been a little repaired—if in any way I could make her know that I still love her with a strength which far surpasses ordinary sentiment—then I should undertake to do so at every possible cost. Therefore let me know, dear Raymond, if she can be persuaded at least to see me. If she will, then I shall go to her, in spite of any opposition from Georgina. And if the results of such a journey should be—as others would say—disastrous to myself, then God will have dealt with me with abundant mercy . . .

40

*T*HE PROSCRIPTION of Michael was waived almost as casually as it had been imposed.

While Armorel was dusting the front room Trevon arrived with a trench-coat over his pyjamas and sat on the piano stool, gripping the sides as if he were on a switchback railway. Startled to see him there, she said:

"I thought you were ill—I thought you were supposed to be in bed."

He did not answer that. He watched her for a few moments, and then he said wearily, looking out the window:

"I'm going to hunt about as soon as I'm fit. For somewhere else to live. Someone at the Club may know where to look. Elizabeth's got too much to do—this telephone training, it gives her no time for house-hunting. I'll hunt about myself—as soon as I've got rid of this damned thing in my inside."

"You mean, you want more space?"

"No. No, we're perfectly all right here. Only we've got to have Michael with us. That's definite. We're not complete without him. I should think that's fairly obvious."

"But I always let you have that top room for Michael."

"You told Elizabeth he wasn't to come."

"Did I? Oh, yes. Yes, I was feeling tired, I felt there were too many people in this wretched house."

She turned to go on with her work.

"I should have thought," he said, "that someone else might go. Mrs Inch, for example—she's nothing but a sponger—"

"Yes," Armorel retorted, "you religious people talk a great deal about charity. When you find someone practicing it—"

"Yes," he said, "yes, I suppose you're right. So Michael can come home as usual?"

"Oh, yes, I suppose so."

He continued to sit on the stool as if he were chained there.

"Is there anything else?" she asked.

"A lot else. Only I'm not really in very good form."

"I'm afraid there's nothing I can do about that. I shouldn't like to interfere with Elizabeth's job."

"No, of course not."

"And I suppose that when a disease comes from things that have happened in the past there's nothing much that anyone can do."

"No, there isn't."

"Except to be sympathetic. And that's rather easier for Elizabeth because she—well, she understands about—well, promiscuity."

It took him a little time to answer this observation, time in which he seemed to be making a long and painful journey.

"I see what you mean," he said at length. Then: "Susie, I wish I wasn't in this state—can't quite trust myself, you see—wish I wasn't in this state, because I might be some use. Some help. To you, I mean."

"Well, I don't think I really need any help."

"You see," he persisted, speaking slowly and with something like a drunkard's cautious enunciation, "we've always loved you, Elizabeth and me. Only Elizabeth can't help you, however much she wants to, because she's—well, she's such a good person. You must know that, really—you do, don't you? And such very good people seem so far away from us." He was frowning at her overall (exactly as he had often frowned in their Hollysian House days) and now suddenly he looked at her face, faintly smiling. "Don't you feel like that, really?"

"No," she answered woodenly, "I don't feel at all like that. I'm sorry," she added, "if you find Elizabeth's goodness such a worry to you. Perhaps you should have chosen someone more ordinary."

"That isn't what I mean. Look here, Susie, I'm not trying to get at you, not in any way. I'm past that, don't you see, I'm past wanting to get the better of people in an argument, wanting to be a smart guy." He was on his feet, and the wave of resurgent energy brought a little colour to his face. "It's the one good thing about being what I am now —practically burnt out—you don't try to impress people any more.

You don't even try to impress yourself. Susie—listen—I'm sorry if—"

"I'm afraid I can't quite see what this has to do with me."

"Nothing," he answered, "nothing whatever if you're perfectly happy."

That was just such a remark as he would have made in the old days. Then the voice would have been edged with sarcasm; and to be certain, now, that no trace of bitterness was left she needed to look at his eyes. Had she brought herself to do that, she would have seen a face not only blanched with physical pain but sublimated by a peculiar humility. Illness hid none of its blemishes; together with its brusque masculinity the coarseness of skin and features showed more crudely since the muscles had fallen slack and the fount of blood become so feeble. But all the petulance had gone, the niggling contempt. And to the eyes which were watching her so patiently there had come a tenderness that seemed too powerful to spring from a wasted body like this. He held on to the back of a chair, a spectacle to pity, the gaunt and broken frame of the man shaking like a tree when its roots have been loosened by frost. Yet pity would have faded against the strong and steady light of his own compassion. He said with simplicity:

"I can't bear you being so lonely—I've been through it, I realize what it's like. You know, I know what you feel about us. I think I should too. Only it's hopeless if you keep nursing that sort of feeling. God knows I'm not the person to preach to you—except that bad people are better preachers than good, because they know what they're talking about. You see, so long as you go on telling yourself that everyone else is the cause of all your troubles, trying to believe there's nothing shoddy in yourself . . . You see, it hurts me like a cancer, seeing you so unhappy. It would, even if I wasn't so terribly fond of you. If you—"

"Trevon," she said without harshness, busy at the mantelshelf, "I don't want to be rude—especially when you're unwell—but I really have got rather a lot to do. I've got a great many friends and they all expect me to give them some of their time. You came to ask me whether I minded Elizabeth's boy coming here in the holidays. I've told you that I don't mind. Oh, and nowadays I don't much care for sentimentalities. In fact, you may remember that I never did."

That was their last conversation until they met on the stairs some weeks later (when in defiance of his doctor's advice he was setting off to the Club) and exchanged a few conventional remarks. Michael did not come home in the Christmas holidays after all. It was understood that Henry Kinfowell wanted him in Scotland. He sent letters to Antonia from there.

For those letters Antonia lived; throughout that curious winter it was the escape which they provided, even more than her natural resilience, which kept her calm and gentle-tempered in a house where nearly all the confidence and understandings of home had petered out. She could no longer talk with spontaneous gaiety, when her mother gave her only forced attention and her father kept a constant, nervous eye on his wife's face. But while Gian fumbled through his hours at home in a swaddle of anxiety, Antonia did maintain at least a semblance of normal behaviour. She teased Ollie as she had always done, was thoughtful for Elizabeth and Trevon, kind to Daise. To them, and sometimes even to herself, she tried to pretend that nothing had changed and that Mother was only tired; while in chance encounters, sidelong glances, the reflection seen for a moment in the mirror of Mother's dressing-table, she watched for some chink through which their former understanding, however tenuous, might be restored.

She grew accustomed, as the young may do, to the dulled and fidgety pattern, to the strained silences, the sense of performing in a theatre where the audience has caught the whiff of fire. There were still the jokes she could share in the kitchen, always her father's small, shy gestures of devotion. Sometimes she loathed this meagre house, where you found neither privacy nor the solaces of communal living, its strait routine of tedious duties and unconvivial meals, the deadening familiarity of pictures soiled by damp, tea-cloths patched to last till the January sales, bath water running cold because the boiler was always going wrong. But in the way that the centre of a soldier's life is generally the home he has left, the barrack-room merely a place of business, Antonia's centre had shifted from Mickett Lane. In the letters which brought her Michael's warm, low voice, his peculiar smile, his indignations and his gentleness, she possessed a world which made immediate realites seem to be nothing more than the discomforts of a season's campaign.

The envelopes that came in the Christmas holidays were postmarked 'Inverurie'. They might—Armorel thought—have been sent first to some friend of Michael's for posting in that town. The letters themselves disappeared after Tonie had read them, and Armorel did not find them in any of Tonie's drawers, even the one which was kept locked (but for which she had found a key to fit). Naturally she did not ask Tonie if she might see the letters, or question her about them, except to say, "Do you hear from Michael at all? Is he all right?" She found a loose board in the floor near Tonie's bed and searched beneath that, but without result.

She was likewise discreet about Tonie's movements, realizing that in these days a girl of sixteen expected a large measure of freedom. "If you're going to be in later than ten," she said, "I'd like to have some idea where you are, so that you can be fetched if the weather's very bad or anything. You see, your father's inclined to get worried . . ." But apart from that she was too sensible to make stipulations or to ask directly where Tonie was going or had been. She did, as a rule, get at the information by indirect questions. ("Was the fog very thick where you were last night, darling? Heald was telling me the buses had a fearful time down in the Hammersmith direction . . .") And as far as possible she verified any information that came. If, for instance Tonie was supposed to be going to the Queen's Hall, she would make sure from the *Telegraph* that the concert mentioned was in fact being given on that evening; later, having learnt one or two details of the programme from some member of the B.B.S. who had attended it, she was ready to slip in a few casual questions which Tonie wouldn't be able to answer if she had really been somewhere else. These stratagems yielded nothing. And because they yielded nothing her assiduity increased. It was certain that at some time Tonie and Michael would secretly arrange to meet, and she must contrive to know about that meeting in advance. To forbid their seeing each other was out of the question, and if she asked to be told about their plans she would merely drive them further into secrecy. The only course, then, was to be secret herself, to know as much as possible, to use but never to disclose her knowledge. If it was disagreeable to act in that way, she must remember that it was for Tonie's own sake. Tonie was young, inexperienced: a boy of pleasant appearance and manners would easily charm and might very well seduce her: useless to try and persuade so impressionable, so immature a creature that a youth who talked with an engaging vivacity, who carried the romantic air of hidden sadnesses, was endowed with a double heritage of treachery and deceit.

There was Gian to be watched as well. Mentally child-like, it was natural that he should be on terms of childish intimacy with Tonie, to whom he showed a sentimental devotion altogether unlimited by reason. What more likely than that Tonie shared her secrets with him, that in obedience to the nursery laws of honour—as well as his own back-street taste for petty conspiracy—he guarded those secrets as obstinately as his own. He might even be the guardian of Michael's letters: at any rate it would be worth Armorel's while to make a thorough search of his room. But it was still more probable (she thought as time went on) that the hiding-place was somewhere in the Grists' part of the house, which Tonie visited often. If anyone understood the minor technique of duplicity it was Elizabeth, who would do anything in Michael's interest. And what a culminating triumph for Elizabeth, one day, to claim Armorel's daughter for her son!

The savage wind which arrived with the new year, alternately cold and tasselled with rain, continued nearly to the end of the month: in the streets it dragged at your clothes, spattered stockings with mud, wetted your wrists and neck. Indoors the windows never stopped rattling. The patch of damp on the ceiling above the stairs steadily grew, drawers stuck, everything you touched was moist and the chilly airs which blew about the house smelt like a conservatory when the pipes are cold. These minor but continuing discomforts were such as anyone can tolerate with a very little fortitude if he has his friends about him, to share the grumbling and to keep his mind alight. Here, such friends were not at hand. The women Armorel met on committees were mostly wives and daughters of men on the director level, impossible to entertain in a house like this. Duffy was in Malta, Christine too lazy to come. Of course, Armorel was never alone in the house: Daise was generally rattling her tools in one of the rooms, at any hour the mournful face of Simon would diffidently appear beside the umbrella-stand, the querulous, discordant voices in the kitchen rumbled like the noise of a factory all day long. But these presences only increased her isolation, she had nothing to share with people of that kind. In this grey, apprehensive midwinter the view from the windows was like a faded film seen over and over again; the day's changeless routine—breakfast things, beds, front room, list for Heald—left her vigorous mind to run like an engine without load, senses feebly occupied by dust on wainscots were sharp for little sights and sounds which might have more significance than they immediately betrayed. The picture woven by the shuttle of her thoughts became more elaborate: the picture of how people would behave if Gian had set them to spy on her movements. And by degrees she saw how the actuality seemed to coincide.

She took precautions now. Before going through Tonie's drawers she always locked the door and put a handkerchief to cover the keyhole; from time to time she listened intently to make sure that no one had crept up outside, and she was careful to replace all Tonie's things exactly as they had been before.

A certain lethargy which came on in the mornings, and which she thought was due to some digestive disorder, was at last sufficiently troublesome to make her visit a doctor. She considered his advice unsound, and the presence of a huge family Bible in his consulting room convinced her that the man was a fool; but a sentence of his, "Of course this kind of thing is sometimes partly due to overwork—you get it with students cramming for examinations," reminded her of another resource. She called on Liedke-Urban, ostensibly to see whether he could advise any new line of remedial action if Gordon reappeared, and mentioned that the strain of her committee work, which conscience forbade her to give up, seemed to be affecting her general health. Liedke-Urban was sympathetic, and suggested that a few further conversations might enable him to help her. She arranged to spend an hour with him on three mornings a week.

It was far from easy to fit this into her crowded programme, but the effort seemed to be worth-while. The room that Liedke-Urban used looked on to Regent's Park, its modern furniture designed by Gesquin Scarp was in perfect harmony with its eighteenth-century proportions, the flowers were beautifully arranged. When Liedke-Urban spoke, his gentle, slightly foreign voice had a comfort of its own. ". . . I understand . . . I understand . . . Tell me, I should like to know—but only if you wish . . ." His silences, attentive, infinitely patient, breathed a tranquillity in which the rubs and tangles of the day were all submerged.

At home, the kindness of her actions increased; for now that everyone was against her it was important to make them see she bore no malice in return. However early Gian rose she was downstairs before him, and despite his embarrassed protests she had the kitchen fire and the boots done before he arrived. She seized so quickly on Tonie's mending that Tonie found hardly any to do herself. When Elizabeth came back from the training school or from one of her visits to Matilda she found more than once that her room had been swept and fresh flowers arranged on the table.

At the same time she became more acquiescent to their own ideas. It was without a trace of bitterness, now, that she said to Gian: "I expect you'll be helping Trevon tonight? Or would you rather stay at home?" She even tried to show some kind of sympathy with Tonie's taste for religion, asking, "Was it an interesting sermon? And I expect the singing is very well done? Your grandfather was always rather interested in that sort of thing." Her smiles, then, were like those of the very ill, pale fruits of unremitting struggle, and she would quickly turn to some busyness of her own, hardly waiting for an answer. But however much they were perplexed by these approaches they could never deny (she thought) that the smoke of hostility came from their own fires. . . . No, there was no single charge they could bring against her. Her society, her interest, her goodwill were all at their disposal, and if they would not respond with their confidence it could only mean they had privacies of which they were ashamed. So she had to be circumspect. She listened for doors opening. If Tonie upon some excuse went into the Grists' room she noted to the minute how long she was there. She had the impression that when she came into the sitting-room father and daughter habitually let their voices trail off into silence: she would say, smiling, "I'm sorry—was I interrupting?" and in the hours she spent alone, next day, would draw together the conjectures which had risen like wreathing smoke from their taciturnity.

Through the newspapers, in those months, ran a current of dismay and foreboding which flashes of blustering optimism did less and less to interrupt. In humble streets the tickle of fear, caught from echoes in the shops and bars, reached people who had seemed too obscure to be concerned. Inhabitants of a place like Weald Street were accustomed to relieve such apprehension by shouting their views, enriched with splendid blasphemies, from one window to the next but three. In Mickett Lane, a little nearer to the trunk roads, vocally quieter from its fumbling pretensions towards respectability, the channel of fear was monotony: the clink of milk-bottles at the same time every day, kitchen smells, a faint pattern thrown by tinted lozenges on polished linoleum, the whine of a door swinging.

Your mind might breathe in such a climate harmlessly, so long as it had normal exercise by which the tainted air could be expelled. Here there was conversation of the kind which people use with shy partners at a formal dinner, deliberate choice of subjects, assiduous prompting and response; but the sturdier kind where random thoughts are allowed to dance and tumble like children at a party, the kind which belongs to home, was not at Armorel's call. A little mockery would have sweetened the stale atmosphere; or she could have freshened it by asking some small favours for herself; but the soil was already too far impoverished for such pleasantness to flower. She would not even be thanked for her own kindnesses: it seemed to offend her that anyone noticed them. Elizabeth, venturing just inside the sitting-room door one evening, said humbly: "It was awfully good of you to wash those tea-cloths—I had no idea you'd think of such a thing"; and the reply which came was short and flat as a rebuke: "Oh, I had some of my own to do." When Gian told her with timid gratitude that he could not let her go on doing the boots she answered dryly that she preferred to have them properly done. Plainly, that was not the behaviour of one who does helpful things simply from policy—to score a point, to get something in return. Was it, then, in the spirit of people who, living selfish lives, will yet give freely to charities by way of appeasing the fates? *'I have refused to be nominated for the Jubilee Organization Committee,'* she wrote to Daphne at that time, *'although it would bring me in contact with interesting people, because I want more leisure to help Tonie with her school work . . . I do try to give my family everything they expect of me, and a bit more. Household chores probably occupy about eleven hours of my day. What more can I do?'* Was that pure selfishness in disguise? Search, if your light is strong enough, through the many strata of the self you know, and see whether you find a thick seam of virtue or only veins appearing here and there in matter of quite another kind. In those dank winter months when she worked herself so remorselessly, when she lived in that busy and crowded house as if entirely alone, nothing she did for others could with certainty be called purely virtuous. Yet surely there may have been an element of virtue even in so crude a service. And can even a little virtue be thought of as something casual and autonomous, like the smudge of lichen which appears on the stem of a tree? Can it exist with no tap-root of its own?

What more can I do? The despairing question tossed at her friend may have been tritely rhetorical. But a group photograph taken during the later part of that winter shows her with the eyes of a Magdalene, unhappy and self-searching eyes. And there are in Raymond's possession four significant letters (or versions of a letter) which she wrote at that period to Michael Kinfowell.

None of these was ever posted: they were found by Antonia, much later, tucked into one of the account books which her mother kept, and through her they came into Raymond's hands. The earliest was dated the 5th December:

> Dear Michael: Your mother may have told you that I thought it would be impossible for you to come here in the Christmas holidays, since the room I generally lend her for you to use was to be occupied by someone else. I write to let you know that the other guest is now unable to come, so the room will be available after all. Yours sincerely, Armorel Ardree.

This was written in ink. It was crossed out by one stroke of a pencil, and underneath appears—in pencil—an entirely different draft:

> My dear Michael: Your mother may have told you about something which gave me a certain amount of worry last holidays. There were three pound notes on the table by the window one morning when you were in the sitting-room talking to Antonia, afterwards they were nowhere to be found and I thought it was just possible you might have carelessly picked them up—as one does fumble with things in absent-minded moments—and put them in your pocket. I meant to ask you about it, but forgot. I thought you would just like to know that the missing notes have now been found—they were right underneath the piano, where the wind must have blown them! I expect Antonia is looking forward to seeing you in the holidays—so many of the young men she knows are to be out of London at Christmas-time.

This one, too, is crossed out, and the word 'NO' is written violently in the margin. The third attempt, on a separate piece of paper, shows evidence of having been done at several sittings. Originally it opened:

> My dear Michael: I think there may be some advantage in my writing myself to tell you of an unfortunate misunderstanding which occurred in connection with your stay here last holidays. I must admit that I made an error in judgement.

That passage, written closely and carefully with a fountain pen, is almost smothered by carets and erasures in copying pencil, which make it finally read thus:

> I feel bound to write myself to tell you of an error in judgement which I made during your stay here last holidays. I hope you will understand how the mistake arose.

There follows a passage taken, with a few alterations, from the earlier draft. This stops in the middle of a sentence, and a new opening, written with a steel pen, begins underneath:

> I really do not quite know how to explain the most regrettable misunderstanding which occurred last holidays.

The words '*most regrettable misunderstanding*' etc. are crossed out and the phrase 'very stupid mistake I made' substituted. That phrase is again replaced (in pencil) by 'my unforgivable misjudgement.' Now comes a long passage, bedevilled with corrections, in which the mechanics of the mistake about the three pounds are explained and interlarded with small excuses, diffident apologies. A fresh paragraph begins:

> I hope that however cross you may feel with me you will not feel less friendly towards Antonia, who of course had nothing to do with all this and does not know about it [the last six words crossed out] and very much enjoys your companionship.

This version ends with 'Yours affectionately', changed to 'Yours very sincerely', and even a memorandum in the margin 'get address from Tonie' is altered, 'Tonie' giving place to 'Elizabeth'.

The last version on a new piece of paper and again in pencil, differs so much from the others that it might almost have been written by another hand. Except for the heading, it is free from corrections, but there are many mistakes, words omitted or written twice. The writing is large and bold but towards the end it sprawls, the lines curving downwards, and words are so joined or broken that it becomes very hard to read. At the head is written 'Weald Street'; this is crossed out and underneath, rather oddly, is 'Cromer Lane, S.E. Thursday March 14'. (March 14 in that year was not a Thursday.) The text reads:

> I have been trying for a long time to write this letter, I don't know how to do it now, I am very tired, but I can't be happy till it's done. Michael dear, you know me pretty well, I am old friend on your mothers—who is one of the sweetest women ever made—but you may not have realized that I am a very stupid woman and also I am afraid a dishonest one. Elizabeth will have told you you that I accused you to her some time ago of stealing money from my room. I had really no grounds for my suspicions—no, I

must tell you the whole truth, it was just a fabrication from start to finish. I can't tell you why tell you why I such a wicked thing, I'm not sure if I quite know myself, I can only say I am bitterly ashamed of such meanness and ask very humbly your forgiveness. I have been very tired, it is rather late at night, but that is not an excuse. It has made Tonie very unhappy and and I have got to ask her to forgive me too. Things are not easy, it is hard to know what everyone in this house in doing, but I do ask you to forgive me. I did not really not really wanto hurt you or Tonie, Gordon has gone away and you know she is the mos precious being in the world to me. You must forgive me for mistakes in this letter, it is very late, I think it is past two o'clock. You must not think, Michael, that I have anything against you. You have always seemed to me to be worthy of your mother, and I cannot pay you a greater compliment than that. There have been reasons why your friendship with Tonie hurt me, I can't explain, but I have put that all behind me now, I only want Tonie to be happy and if you do anything to make her happy I shall always be grateful to you and try to show my grateful show my gratitude. Michael dear do forgive me and make Tonie forgive me if you can it would mean everything to me I am so terrible I amso am so terribly lonely and unhappy.

A matching envelope was found with that letter, stamped and addressed. No doubt when she read it over with a comparatively fresh mind she saw that it needed to be re-written, and that is presumably why it was not posted next day. The letter she actually sent to Michael was not written till some six months afterwards.

'I think it is past two o'clock': when Antonia came to read those words she remembered vividly the night when they must have been written. Waking to find her mother's bed still empty, she had gone downstairs and seen a light showing under the sitting-room door, which was locked. She had called softly, "Mother, are you all right?" but received no reply.

Elizabeth remembered that night as well: how the sound of anxious voices, Tonie's and Gian's, had brought her out to the passage, where she had shivered in her thin dressing gown; how she had seemed to see every line of Gian's distracted face while they three whispered together in the darkness that would continue, for her, into the day. She remembered Tonie's tearful voice, "Isn't there something we ought to do! I can't let her be like that, all by herself!" Gian's despairing answer, "Y'see, it ain't no good, no matter what I say it only put me in the wrong!" and a little afterwards the very quiet, painful voice of Trevon as he led her back to the bedroom, "It's no good any of us going to her—she's got to come to us before we can be any use." Those recollections, vivid, shadow-edged, had their place in the continuity of time, loosely joined to prosaic happenings of the day before. But the last of that night's memories, balanced between wakefulness and sleep, seemed to stand a little outside time and outside reality: footsteps dragging past the door, sobs which penetrated the curtain of sleep to fall like physical blows upon her own heart.

It appeared strange to Raymond, when Elizabeth came to tell him of those recollections, that a creature of human understanding, human affections, should have been struggling in utter loneliness at the very hour when such fullness of love was so near at hand. Yet he seemed to see faintly why the stream never reached the parched ground. It was love, he thought, blended with pity, and until the soil's crust is finally broken it will hold against pity as a film of wax resists the acid bath. He got down Sarah Goodwin's book and read again the passage from Dorothea Truggett's journal where that archetype of sanity and resolution recounts her long fight against the Colliery Manager at Ailsthwaite: 'I knew that my accusations were not true in every respect, but throughout those two years I refused to withdraw one jot or tittle of them, because I thought it would show moral weakness to do so. At the end of that time I told him that everything I had said about him personally was stupid and unjust. He capitulated that very day, gave me all I had demanded for the men, and became my life-long friend . . . I have made the same mistake over and over again, I have spent seventy years learning and re-learning that I am neither wiser nor more morally sound than Him who said "Blessed are the Meek" . . . Conquest is easy, it is surrender which is so desperately hard and which a weak human creature like myself cannot achieve alone.'

*

41

*T*HE LONG LETTER written by Liedke-Urban was also dated 14th March. It is not unlikely that it reached Armorel on the morning after she had made her fourth attempt to compose a letter to Michael; it is safe, at least, to suppose that she received it not more than two or three days after that attempt. It was faultlessly typed on hand-made paper (stamped *Mr Liedke-Urban London* in Madonna Ronda) with very wide margins.

PRIVATE AND CONFIDENTIAL.
My dear Mrs Ardree:
   You asked me if I could send you a brief summary of what our consultations have yielded up to the present time. This is against my usual practice, since there is always a danger that the Consultor may be over-influenced by conclusions based upon an incomplete inquiry and therefore subject to modification. With you, however, I feel that that danger is almost non-existent, since your knowledge of my analytical methods, acquired in a long period of what I might almost call professional association, will enable you to detect for yourself any points in my interim analysis which are likely to require revision when we have explored portions of the ground more minutely.
   May I say, here, that our conversations have been the source of great pleasure to me. Much of my work is done for people who, however much they may wish to be honest with me, are quite unable to overcome for themselves that instinctive reticence which stands as a barrier between them and the help I have to offer. This makes the remedial process slow, laborious, and often exhausting. It has been so refreshing to work with a Consultor who comes to me not only with complete sincerity but also with the strength and suppleness of the trained mind, and whom, therefore, I am able to regard rather as a colleague than as a patient. I would add, if I may, that my admiration for your intellectual gifts has constantly increased in the course of our discussions.
   You have, I think, already become fully aware of what I shall here call the Secondary Causation of that disequilibrium of which you are periodically conscious and which has led you to seek my opinion. This Secondary Causation consists, in the simplest terms, in a sense of frustration due to a lack of scope for your special talents. The mental power to which I have already referred would have found fulfilment in one of the intellectual professions—most probably, in my judgement, in university teaching. Failing that, it could almost equally have been satisfied by social and domestic life if you had been granted a milieu appropriate to your attainments; particularly, if you had married a man who was your equal in intellectual range and subtlety, one to whom you could talk in the

language of scholarship and of refined perceptions; one, moreover, who had the means to take you into your own kind of society. You have lacked all these outlets; and the very fact that you have borne the deprivation so courageously and without any complaint must necessarily have intensified its effect.

In a large measure, however, I think that the necessary compensation is already on its way. In your work with the Bradlaugh Society you have at least some scope for your peculiar energies and capacities; you are enabled to associate with people of similar intellectual distinction; and as your reputation in that, and in wider spheres, increases, you will, I believe, find the sense of frustration proportionately relieved and diminished. My advice, then, would be on no account to forgo or even reduce these activities, even if they occupy time which would otherwise be devoted to the necessary but circumscribed activities of your home; for the latter will only suffer if your personality and powers are being unnaturally confined, just as a man's muscles, if given no work to match their strength, will presently become useless for work of any kind.

Your very clear presentation of the data convinces me that you have already in large measure appreciated the nature of this Secondary Causation, and will be in sympathy with my own approach. If you find it less easy to follow sympathetically my analysis of the more difficult Primary Causation, I am sure that you will, none the less, bring to it a care in study and a perceptiveness in judgement equal to those which I have done my best to exercise in its preparation. I have, incidentally, kept my analysis as free as possible from technical terminology, since I think you agree with me that such terminology often tends to obscure what we call the Ground Plan.

You have told me, with admirable candour and with a truly scientific attention to detail, that your philosophical outlook is almost diametrically opposed to that of your father, whose was the primary influence in your early philosophic education. This is, of course, a fairly common situation, particularly with a generation which has largely broken free from certain atavistic concepts which have governed and inhibited the human reason for many centuries. Now, the fact that you detached yourself rationally from the concepts given to you by your father does not necessarily imply that the influence of such concepts was finally broken. Indeed, the very fact that you have so courageously abandoned them, to follow the path illumined by your own reason, may actually have increased the security of those concepts within what I call (using,

I think you agree, a more accurate term than that employed by more old-fashioned Consultants) the Residual Self. The most important of these concepts, implanted by the early Influence, is the Guilt Concept.

You have told me that in your earliest years you were not often punished for 'faults', but that the idea of being guilty (of some mischief normal among children) was frequently impressed upon you; that the 'guilt' was associated not necessarily with the damage or inconvenience which the mischievous act had done to others, but with the notion of an absolute evil. Simultaneously you were given the further concept of expiation, the idea that the guilt could be negatived by certain simple forms of naïve totemism—mystic formulae spoken at the parent's knee, etc: children of average intellectual calibre often accept such totemism, are satisfied by it, and thus suffer little harm from the guilt concept; but a child of higher mental potential instinctively rejects the expiation concept, even when his reasoning power is altogether undeveloped, and what is left is the Guilt Concept alone; which, as the reason develops, is necessarily relegated to the Residual Self.

There, in some cases, it remains quiescent and causes no injury to the Subject. But with you, a particular mechanism has been set up whereby the submerged concept is able to operate noxiously. You held your father in great affection. His death, violent and premature, occurred before you had reached full maturity. As a natural consequence, your affection, violently severed from his person, attached itself to the concept which was particularly associated with him and elevated that concept, despite the unflinching opposition of your reason, to a position of paramountcy. In recent years (I deduce from my study of the data of your dream-life) this phenomenon has been intensified by anxiety about your son, whom the Residual Self identifies with your father, and whose flight the Residual Self interprets as being a new demand made by your father for your guilt to be expiated. In that outline analysis you have, I believe, the Directional Index of the Prime Causation.

Now this Guilt Concept, before it can act upon the near-conscious, demands to be associated with some particular experience. Your very great patience has enabled me, I believe, to identify that experience. You have told me that a few years ago your husband was indicted on a criminal charge. He was acquitted. You have confided to me that although he has always maintained his innocence you yourself are fully persuaded that he did, in fact, commit the crime for which he was indicted. My knowledge of reactions persuades me that this situation has affected your near-conscious in a special way. Although your husband has not been able to make the response to your intellectuality which you (or, I should say, which a less unselfish woman) would have desired, you are, by reason of the strength and singleness of your personality, attached to him by an invincible loyalty. This loyalty, conjoined with the need of the Guilt Concept to attach itself to actual experience, has caused you, near-consciously, to assume responsibility for your husband's crime as if it were your own and to feel a violent remorse for it. In support of this, I would remind you of the incident which you recounted to me in our eighth conversation; how, at the age of four years, you were sharply rebuked by your father for catching and destroying a butterfly. Such an incident sufficiently accounts for the later attachment of the Guilt Concept to the notion of taking life; one might say, in broad terms, that you have unconsciously expected to take life, that you now feel that you have taken it, and that the Guilt Concept has flowed into this channel as the electricity discharged in a storm flows to a lone tree.

You will fully realize that at this stage it is impossible for me to give full advice as to the mental strategy whereby this Prime Causation is to be attacked. But I think that I can safely indicate certain lines of procedure which will be helpful to you.

First of all, I ask you to scrutinize my analysis (as far as it at present goes) with the most careful attention, devoting to it that capacity for logical reasoning with which you are so fortunately endowed. Examine it, if possible, with a hostile mind, as a lawyer examines his opponent's case, seeking some logical flaw which will give him the means to attack and destroy it. I ask this for two reasons: first, because I should like to satisfy myself that this work of mine will withstand the most searching and intelligent criticism; secondly, because the analysis will be of no use to you until it fully persuades your reason—until you have made it your own.

Next, I would suggest that you devote as much time and mental energy as you can find to re-examining your own conscious thoughts about 'guilt.' I have found that many of my most rational Consultors, some of them men and women of brilliant intellect, have been so immersed during the formative years in archaic beliefs about 'guilt' that they have never really escaped from them, and this is largely because, accepting readily the new and rational view, they have never troubled thoroughly to dissect the old. You yourself know well that when we talk of a man being 'guilty' what we really mean is that he has acted in such a way as to cause pain or inconvenience to others; nothing else. The causes of such action may be found in heredity, environment, race, sex, etc. etc. and can be proved to lie outside what metaphysicians call 'the volition'; to talk of 'guilt' as of some mystical entity which, belonging to a man by his own wish, should lower him in our esteem, is palpably absurd. Yet that insidious absurdity does so possess the near-conscious of many otherwise rational people that their actions are sometimes hardly to be distinguished from those of theological moralists of the old school. All this, I repeat, is well known to you; but I believe that you will not be wasting your time if you go over the ground once again, forcing your conscious mind to concentrate upon the fact that 'guilt', as understood by the non-rational, is a nonsensical figment and that the notion of taking over responsibility for the 'guilt' of another person is one without any meaning at all. Here you may find that some simple form of mental exercise is helpful. You might repeat to yourself—particularly in the last moments before sleep—the simple phrases, "There is no such thing as Guilt, Guilt does not exist, No one is guilty, I am not guilty." Practised with determination over a long period, this kind of exercise, elementary as it may seem, has often proved more powerful in its operation upon toxins of the Residual Self than more elaborate and ambitious methods of treatment.

With diffidence, I have at this stage a further suggestion to make. (I do so only because you have been good enough to place the greatest confidence in me as friend and professional consultant, and I therefore feel it my duty to turn such confidence to your greatest advantage.) You have told me that subsequent to your husband's indictment intimacy has been discontinued. (This, one may readily see, has been due to the mechanism for expiation set up by the Residual Self, and thus serves to reinforce the Guilt Concept.) My view is that if it can at any time be resumed, such resumption would be most desirable.

I look forward, as I hope I may, to the pleasure of seeing you at your usual time next Tuesday; or rather, if it be just as convenient to you, a few minutes earlier, since Lady Hilda, who as usual will be following you, will have a train to catch for Scotland.

Meanwhile, believe me, my dear Mrs Ardree,
Most sincerely yours,
Gustav Liedke-Urban.

That letter, as Raymond afterwards ascertained, was written when Liedke-Urban had not seen a medical report, called for one, or thought of doing so.

Its effect was remarkable.

The year was, of course, moving forward into spring, which makes its power felt not less where men have done their best to exclude it. Even in narrow streets where houses stand hard against the roadway the earlier light and the parting of clouds bring some feeling of release; bedraggled shrubs by the Unitarian chapel in Frith Street show points of green, it is possible to find wrens nesting not many yards from the Elephant, and in the morning, before the traffic reaches its full fury, you may distinguish the songs of half-a-dozen birds in Borough Road itself. You would think that where so many lively smells jostle for precedence the whole year round there would be no room for the freshness which, in Cumberland or Dorset, March will bring like a salute from the waking soil. But you do know as you come out of the tube that something has altered, that what people describe as the smell of pavement has changed dramatically, sending your thoughts perhaps to Sussex woods, as if the whole weight of brick and bustle were too slight a load to hinder the breathing of the earth below. This sense derived from altered light, from the air's sharper taste, will penetrate to the girl selling cigarettes in the dark depths of St Pancras Station, to men in the fusty offices of shipping firms: often it affects those who would deny they felt it, aged and sullen caretakers in Hanbury Street, first-class travellers sheathed in impeccable serge who read the *Financial Times* for fun. Tim Heald felt it in Mickett Lane, and he told both Simon and Matilda that he could see from their faces how "this spring got right in the guts of 83." But the new vitality which came upon Armorel was something more than a response to the quickening of the year.

She came, in the common phrase, 'out of herself'. This did not mean that the barriers in the house were instantly broken, all the tension eased; for outside the cinema the intricate texture of a contented home is not produced or repaired by a conjuring trick, it is a matter of years, not hours. She was still separated from the others as a friendly foreigner is by limitations of speech. But Antonia, at least, no longer felt that her mother was living in the deepest shadow of hostility and self-defence.

Outwardly, the change was like that in a born actress who suddenly takes courage to leave the text-books behind. She had served them well before, but the flavour of martyrdom had soured all her kindnesses, making them feel there was a bill to pay in some currency they did not possess. Now the look of weariness had lifted, and what she gave them no longer seemed to come from a dwindling resource. Her movements appeared to cost her less effort, the modulations in her voice became warmer, her eyes less shy and strained.

"I reckon she been frettin' over Gordon," Gian said to his father. "I reckon she's gettin' over it a bit—made up her mind there ain't nothink she or me can do, an' that's all there is to it."

And slowly, as a child bowled over by a wave ventures again into the sea, he responded to the easing of her temper. He ceased to move and to shut doors with the desperate care of a schoolboy in the headmaster's house, at meals he talked a little, of the job he was on, the men who worked with him, and instead of staring down at the table he looked about him, sometimes even turning towards Armorel herself. When she was not about he whistled, and began in a small way to swagger again, giving his old imitation of Pittock the blind boxer, poking sidelong fun at Olleroyd for his supposed romance with Mrs Inch. His confidence varied from day to day, as Susie's mood depressed or encouraged him. There were times when she seemed as remote as before, lagging in response to what he said, like a busy adult striving to interest herself in the children's play: the smile he occasionally won from her never looked to be quite home-made. But now that she no longer appeared to find his presence a burden he supposed she would go on to recover all her old equanimity. The sunshine of late April made him optimistic. In Peckham Rye, where he was working on the new Borough Estate, the wind blowing between the brick stacks was fresh and sweet; at home the daffodils which Tonie bought drew in the season's gentleness like a salve for the cramp and wrinkles of the house. Yes, before the summer was over Susie would be herself again, and he did not ask for more than that.

He bought some pink distemper and with the help of three boys from Apostles' Court he did the whole of the upper passage one Saturday afternoon when she was out. When she returned and went upstairs he waited for her in the sitting-room, standing by the window and pretending to read the paper, shaking with nervous excitement. "Gian, you —you have worked hard!" she said when she found him there. "It's really—it's quite astonishing what you've done!" "Posh the ole place up a bit!" he responded gruffly; and as he eyed her over his shoulder, sniffing noisily, cleaning his gums, trying not to grin, he inhaled such a breath of happiness as had come to him once or twice, eighteen years before, at the North View Hotel.

He was troubled again when she began to talk about Gordon, whose name had been tacitly excluded since the day of Maria's funeral.

"Daise and I are going to spring-clean your room, I want it to be spick and span for when Gordon comes home."

That remark, uttered quite casually at supper, affected his faculties like a stroke. The only hint of news about Gordon was a paragraph which Ed had shown him in a Sunday paper and which he had paid Ed ten shillings not to let Armorel see: it reported a case of larceny and attempted rape at Carlisle, and certain particulars in the description of the guilty youth had made it appear to correspond with his son's. He remained completely dumb, with his eyes towards the door, and as usual it was Tonie who had to fill the gap.

"Yes," said Tonie smoothly, "it will be nice to have Gordon back."

The subject was dropped then. But at intervals it came up again until hardly a day passed without Susie mentioning him. "I think I'll try to get Gordon on some sort of technical course when he comes back. I must see what Gustav says . . . It's really very lazy of Gordon not to write. I suppose he's in some sort of trouble, it's a nuisance that boys have to go through this business of sowing their wild oats. It takes up so much time . . ." He found a formula for these occasions (as he had found one for so many of the awkwardnesses of married life): "Well, I reckon we'll be gettin' a letter from Gordon any day now." But they continued to disturb him in the way that small, irregular noises from a machine that otherwise runs smoothly will disturb the engineer in charge.

He had another talk with Trevon at Hollysian House, where they were safe from Susie's interruption, and begged him to write again to a friend he had in the Carlisle police.

"You know," Trevon said, "there's one thing—I think that whatever happens Gordon ought not to come back here. Not as things are now. I'm certain you could do something with him if you were left to get on with it. But you wouldn't be. And Susie couldn't help him—in fact, she'd probably do him a lot of harm, the way she is at present. You don't mind my saying that?"

Gian protested: "Well, y'know, I reckon she's got over whatever she had wrong. Quite different, she's been, since the weather change an' that. You ask your missis, she'll tell you the same."

Trevon stared at his thumbs.

"Susie's not right yet."

"Well, I reckon it would likely put her right, suppose we get Gordon home."

"I wish I thought that," Trevon said, "I just don't." And a man who knew him less well than Gian did would not have doubted the sincerity of his tired voice, of the weakened eyes gazing through the walls of this place he had created towards some country he had seen and been denied. "You see, I know what it feels like, the sort of thing that Susie's got. I've been through it—pretty often."

"You don't think you could tell her anything? Mean t'say, have a bit of a talk—now she's not so awkward like she was—get her out of herself, see what I mean?"

"Out of herself? I'm not certain if that's what she needs." He let his forehead fall on his hands; half-a-dozen boys were noisily waiting for him outside the door, all with problems to which they expected complete solutions, and in these days Trevon could only just get through an evening's work. "Listen, Gian, you know I'd do anything I could. Only at present I just don't believe it can be done. You see, it isn't herself that she's showing us—not the Susie you and I know. And you can't do anything with someone who's pretending to be someone else. No, there's nothing I can do—not yet."

But it looked as if Gian's judgement of Armorel's case was better than his, for through the summer her strangely recovered confidence seemed to be bringing their relationship towards its old tranquillity. If she still appeared to watch them at a little distance, the place she watched from was no longer heavily curtained with distrust. Her response grew more rapid, till she could leave her own thoughts almost instantly to say: "The boys? Oh, yes, the boys at Apostles' Court, yes, it must be interesting, I suppose you can teach things even to boys like that." And with her nerves less harshly taxed, her physical strength increased. She had built up the reserve she needed before the day—it was early in September—when Gian came home looking grey and old; when, staring at her waist and almost in tears, he blurted out, "Paid off! Packin' up the job, the firm are—no warnin' or nothink. Jus' turn us off, see, put us on the fumin' dole, the whole fumin' lot!"

42

She was kind to him then, perhaps kinder than she had ever been before, spontaneously and ungrudgingly kind.

What did it matter! she said. They would be on short commons for a time, but that would do them no harm. A tradesman of his skill could not be out of a job for long, she would write to all her friends and see what was offering. (Never a word about the excellent chance she had once got for him to become a partner in a Hatfield firm, which he had flatly turned down.) Meanwhile she would get a loan from Raymond for Tonie's school fees, she could probably find work herself as she had done in the early days of their marriage. A holiday would actually do him good . . . And when he continued to sneak about the house like a whipped dog, to sit in a corner and fidget maddeningly with the evening paper, she changed to a sympathetic silence, perfumed with small, confiding smiles.

They must have a little treat, she pronounced next morning, when the odd sensation of not having a bus to catch intensified his gloom: it would take their minds off this troublesome affair.

She sent Tonie across to Heald's to phone the chairman of the Development Committee and say she could not attend that evening. At the back of the hanging cupboard she found a green and yellow frock which had not been worn since Christine's summer party two years before and which could be freshened in ten minutes with an iron, and the old evening-shoes in which she was keeping the nucleus of her Fox Tie Fund yielded nearly three pounds ten. The country, she thought: they must get away from bricks, they must breathe clean air with the smell of hay in it. But she remembered almost instantly that the treat was not for herself and that Londoners are scared and depressed by the country's solitude. "We'll go to the sea," she said. "Somewhere with lots of people. Brighton—no, that's full of rich people. We'll go to Southend.

"I think your father would like it better," she said to Tonie, "if he and I went by ourselves—it would give him more of a honeymoon feeling. You don't mind, do you! I expect you can have your meals with Elizabeth—no, look, I'll ring up Aunt Chrissie and ask if she can give you dinner and perhaps keep you there for the night."

But it was plain that Gian, if he had to go on the excursion, wanted

Simon to be included; and when Olleroyd spoke wistfully of not having seen the sea for thirty years she felt she must take him as well. The usual trouble arose with Mrs Inch, who followed them in tears all the way to the bus stop, complaining in her specious fashion that her Mr Ollie was off to amuse himself with daughters of joy while she was left to starve alone. The sky was overcast, the day hot and close, with thunder threatening. Before they reached Southend, in the Silver Swallow Coach, Simon had been slightly sick.

The three men were acquiescent to all her suggestions, contributing not much themselves. Would they like to have tea here, at the Victory Café? Yes, that would do very nice. Or along there at Macpherson's Astoria, where there seemed to be a wireless going? Yes, that would do all right. They kept half a pace in rear as she led them along the promenade: Gian darkly respectable, Ollie incongruously festive in the fawn and blue-checked cap on which he had spent a week's Lloyd George money, Simon collarless, wrapped up in suspicion and fatigue: they talked among themselves in low tones, as if they were swapping cribs under the teacher's nose. Would they like to go on the pier? she asked. Well, yes, if she wanted to go on the pier they didn't mind. Or would they rather sit on the beach? Well, that would be quite all right. They hired deck chairs and sat on the beach.

"Take it very kind of Mrs Ardree," Olleroyd confided to Simon, wiping his forehead and staring sombrely at the crowded foreshore. "Thirty year it is since I seen the sea."

"Different thing," Gian was mumbling to Olleroyd, "if they sack you for somethink you done, or somethink you ain't done. Mean t'say, if a bloke's not up to his job, out he goes, sense enough."

Olleroyd nodded understandingly.

"Same in the fur trade. Fur nailer, I used to be. Now, that's a skilled trade. Twelve years it takes to make a good nailer. Well, now, I was working with Linnenkohl's—count among the best people in the trade—"

The excursion steamer back from Margate was coming towards the pier. Armorel turned to Simon.

"Does this make you feel you'd like to be at sea again?"

Simon said: "They don't get no air in those buses, see. That's what it is. Can't breathe properly when they don't give you no air, see."

"Eighteen years, I been with them," Gian continued. "I ain't never been a high-paid man, that I grant—not like clurks and such, office blokes, banks and such—never did come to me, stool work, as you might say. Still, I know my trade as well as the next, there ain't never been a week what I didn't bring back the money. You got a home to keep you got to make money the best way you can, see. Well, I always bring back my money every week, ever since I got married, see."

"Same with the fur trade," Olleroyd agreed.

It became unnaturally dark. A breeze which seemed to move only at ground level blew bits of newspaper, ice-cream cartons and a torn bathing-cap about their feet.

"We ought to get somewhere under cover before it rains," Armorel said. "There's a show called the *Folly-wood Fancies*, it might be quite amusing, do you think you'd enjoy that?"

Olleroyd said it would be very kind.

The trams were full, so they had to walk the whole length of Marshall Street. He hadn't realized it was to be a walking excursion, Simon said. There was just one seat in the second row of the three-and-sixes, the girl at the guichet said fretfully, and three seats immediately behind.

Gian sat with his bowler on his knees, sucking a dead cigarette. He whispered to Simon: "I tell her before we got married, I said, 'Well, granted I don't add up to much, I can always do a job of work,' I said. I said, 'You won't find me idlin' about at home,' I said, 'nor yet queuein' up at the Poor Law,' I said. I said, 'I'll keep you supported, an' any kids what may come,' I said. 'May not amount to much,' I said, 'but I'll bring back somethink every week, come wet or fine,' I said."

Simon nodded, noisily drawing a clot of phlegm back into his nose. "You see what it is," he muttered, with his eyes fixed balefully on the five plump girls who were stamping and bouncing on the stage, "they ain't got the deckin' fixed right. Prentice job! Stage that size, you got to have a middle joist—cog him in snug on the members both ends. You want a proper tradesman on a job like that."

Armorel turned round to speak to Gian. "Do you think your father would see better if he had my seat? . . . What about you, Ollie, can you see all right?"

Olleroyd woke with a start.

"Thank-you, Mrs Gian, very kind, I'm sure, very kind indeed."

"See how it is," said Gian, "blokes see me walkin' round the streets, 'Look at that great fat idle b——,' they say, 'got a family to keep and don't do nothink about it, jus' bums along an' picks up the fumin' dole!'"

"Would you mind not talking!" the woman next to Simon hissed. "I can't hardly hear a word the lady's trying to sing."

"Ay, muggy it is!" Simon said in response. "Been muggy all day —put a vomit on me sittin' in the bus."

The soprano gave way to a lightning artist, the artist to a Bermondsey man in a very tight striped blazer who said he came from Lancashire and had a terrible cold. Southend, he said, was all right if you were 'strog eduff to stad the zubber'. His landlady had turned him out for complaining about his bed and board—he wasn't certain which was which. He had sent a postcard to Adolf Hitler, 'Dear Adolf,' he had written, 'if it's right what they tell me you're looking for Colonies, you'd better come to Southend and start looking in my bed.' Talking of Hitler, the man in the blazer said, he had a friend called Isaac MacIsaacs, nice bloke, always lend you a half a dollar if you give him a quid deposit; a great pal of Hitler's, Isaac MacIsaacs was; Isaac MacIsaacs had been to see Hitler the week before, and Hitler had said, "Isaac, I'm having trouble with Hurr Gurbles." "Hur what?" Isaac MacIsaacs had said. "Oh, you mean there's Something in the Wind!" Isaac had said, "Well, you might try her on Syrup of Figs." Almost before the guffaws had ceased the Folly-wood Radi-oh-Five, having changed from bright green to bright mauve knickers, began to stamp and bounce again. They were followed by a plethoric youth in tails who, lurching about the stage and waving a whisky bottle, sang a topical ballad of some length with the refrain, *I'm Gaiety Gussie, the Auxfahd Blue, I've buckets of boodle and damn-all to do, So long as I'm healthy— now don't tell a soul—I'll shirk all the work and* (hiccough) *I'll pocket the dole!* The spot-light changed to amber and blue, the soprano, now crinolined and parasoled, sang *Loving's What They Love in Alabama*, and the funny man appeared again in a mountainous female hat. The air in the iron-roofed hall, reeking of vinegar and tired excursionists, had become insufferably close; in the shafts from the top-lights the smoke of four hundred cigarettes showed like a blue fog. He was sorry about the hat, the funny man said, he had picked it up by accident, leaving his girl-friend's room in a hurry—no one had told him commercial travellers sometimes came home on Thursday nights. Simon murmured to Ollie that he wanted to be sick again, but Ollie was once more asleep.

"The girl had quite a good voice, really," Armorel said as they went back to the Victory Café for supper. "It wants to be trained, of course, and she should be given something decent to sing. Didn't you think it was quite a nice voice, Papa Simon?"

"Muggy it was in there!" Simon replied.

Olleroyd said tactfully: "Still, it was nice to see Mrs Gian enjoying herself. And paying the bus and all—very kind, I'm sure!"

They gave Simon a thimbleful of brandy to strengthen him for the journey home; it went immediately to his legs, so that Armorel and Gian had to support him on either side as they hurried to catch their coach, whilst Olleroyd came panting behind. Really the day had already been too much for Simon, it was not surprising that children yelled 'Penny for the Guy!' as the pair dragged him, damp, grey and hanging disjointedly in his undistinguished clothes, along the fiercely lighted street; but he had enough mettle left for bursts of wavering song, "I'll chuck Audrey Work and I'll—*pocket* the dole!" It was only in the last hundred yards that he altogether lost his self-command, weeping on Armorel's neck, crying to passers-by that the angels had taken his little wife and left him nothing but this baby lass to fill her place. He slept all the way back to Charing Cross, kneeling on the floor of the coach with his face in Armorel's lap; while in the seat behind, Olleroyd, his head against the window and his cap pulled over his eyes, was snoring with the noise of a choked drain. But Gian, who sat beside him and hardly turned his gaze from the back of Armorel's head, continued talking to him as if he were still awake:

"I mean, what's the good, I mean, if you lose y'job same as you might lose a tanner out of a hole in your coat! I mean, I ain't done nothing wrong, I ain't allowed no bad workmanship in any job I been foreman on. Late jus' one time—that was when the bus got held up in the fog—more than two years back, that was. Mean t'say, y' can't do more than know your trade. Got no money, see, same as you might have a bloke got money off his dad or that—I jus' got my trade. Well, what's a bloke do when he wants to work and they tell him there ain't no work he can have—tell him he ain't no fumin' use, that's what it work out at. Might as well pack in—a bloke ain't no use if they won't give him no fumin' job . . ."

They were home a little after midnight.

When Armorel was ready for bed she put on her dressing-gown and went across to Gian's room, which she found empty. His jacket, waistcoat, collar and tie were lying on his bed. She went on to the door of the Grists' room, and standing there she heard Gian's voice, and Elizabeth's, but could not quite make out what they were saying. She returned to Gian's room and waited for him there.

When he came she said: "Gian dear, I'm sorry, I'm afraid it wasn't a very successful day."

There was no obvious answer for a man like Gian to make to that. He said diffidently:

"I reckon it cost a bit. S'pose we do better keep off that kind of outin'—no proper money comin' in."

"I don't want you to worry about money," she said with a quiet assurance. "You must let me do the worrying."

He did not reply.

"You know Tonie's away tonight?" she asked.

"Uh-huh."

"I've been thinking, it seems rather silly, doesn't it, you and I having to have two rooms."

He bent to fiddle with a shoe-lace. He mumbled:

"I thought that was how you wanted."

"I had a sort of stupid idea," she said. "It was after that business —you know, Empire and all that. I just—well, I had a stupid idea about that."

He looked up at her nervously.

"You mean, someone been telling you that wasn't aught to do with me?"

She smiled faintly, but not at him. She did not meet his eyes.

"I've come to think about these things in rather a different way."

"Uh?"

She said with a very slight tremor: "I'm going to feel awfully lonely in that room, with no Tonie."

"Uh?"

"I'd love it if you felt like keeping me company."

He glanced at her face again, in time to see what might be a smile: but not a smile that could be understood by a man like him, since her eyes still avoided his. Unable to deal with it, he returned to his shoelace, which in his confusion he had carefully re-tied.

Armorel went back to her own room, where she left her door a few inches open. She fixed an old silk scarf round the electric lamp, so that the light thrown on the bed became gentle and warm.

It was only when she got into bed that she found a note which Antonia had tucked into the opening of the pillow-slip. It said.

> Darling Mother, I decided not to go to Aunt Chrissie after all, because Arthur Augustus would be there and I do find him such a bore, I hope you don't mind. I rang up Aunt Chrissie and made quite a good excuse and she didn't seem to mind at all. I am going to Marigold's, you know I did say I'd go there a long time ago and she's been writing to ask if I've forgotten her now we're not still at school together. Back tomorrow about dinner time. Love, Tonie.

Having read that almost at one glance she screwed the paper and tucked it under the pillow. She lay very still.

Twenty minutes, half-an-hour passed. She could not know that Gian, still only half-undressed, was sitting on the edge of his bed, exhausted in spirit, actually trembling from the stress of a conjuncture in which reason refused to guide and instinct to impel him.

Extreme weariness seems to remove certain loads which act as a brake upon the mind's swift course. Lying there, waiting with dwindling expectation, she thought she saw in a light of growing intensity how small happenings were connected. The purpose of Gian's visit to the Grists' room became clear.

She brought out Tonie's note and smoothed it again. An expert had once told her how it was possible to find out whether handwriting that looked hasty and casual were really so; she had forgotten the details of his method, but she felt certain that the carelessness of this note was studied and false. Why should Tonie suddenly decide to recover her friendship with Marigold, who, though gay and warm-hearted, was a quite uninteresting girl! No: today had given Tonie the very chance she had been waiting for all these weeks; she had readily assented to the Christine proposal, and even while that arrangement was being made she had been working out her own plans, including the Marigold screen. Probably Elizabeth had taken a hand in the business and—yes —had passed the word to Gian when he came in. At any rate Tonie was with Michael now.

There were pin-heads of sweat on her forehead. The storm had not come and the air felt as if the room were heated by steam. Her eyes had closed; when she reopened them the coloured light from the shaded lamp made all the familiar objects in the room seem strange to her, as when you wake in a hotel. And the sounds from outside, a lorry grinding somewhere towards the river, footsteps along the pavement, were strange, as from a city to which she did not belong. For an instant she thought of going to Elizabeth and asking her, perhaps with tears, at least to restore her Tonie; but Elizabeth, she knew, would only hide herself behind some fresh veil of deception. They were all deceiving her and she was quite alone, always, always alone. Unless Gian . . .

She raised her head; she had heard the noise of Gian moving in his room.

The sound that followed was the click of his light being switched off and then there was silence. Presently she put her night-gown on again. She did not turn out her own light or try to go to sleep.

Elizabeth was wakened rather (she thought later) by instinct than by any sound; but when she opened the door someone was coming along the passage in bare feet. She said softly, "Is that Gian? Are you still worrying—can't you get to sleep?" but there was no reply. Someone went swiftly past her towards the stairs, and she knew from the sound of silk rubbing, the faint odour of a Dubarry shampoo, that it was Armorel.

Downstairs, at the little desk which Dorothea Truggett had once given to her daughter Gertrude, Armorel wrote one more letter to Michael. This time there were no hesitations or afterthoughts: she wrote as if at someone's steady dictation; or as if the letter had been mentally composed, rehearsed and perfected some time before.

Dear Michael
I want to take you into my confidence and explain something which must have perplexed you. I expect you have often felt that I have not altogether approved of your friendship with Antonia. Actually I should have been glad to see you so happy together, especially as your mother is an old and close friend of mine. But there is one reason why I have not wanted you and Antonia to become too much attached to each other. It is a very difficult thing for me to tell you, but now that you are a little older I feel bound to do so. I have no doubt that your mother has told you most of what there is to be told about your real father, and you probably know that about the time when you were born he was engaged to me. But

there is something else that your mother does not know, and no one else does either. He was an entirely unscrupulous man, and at the time of my marriage I was a young, foolish and extremely susceptible girl. He visited me very shortly after my marriage, on an occasion when my husband was away from home, he was in a very miserable state, I felt very sorry for him and he took advantage of my pity. That was how Antonia came to be born, and I do not think I need say any more about the relationship between her and yourself. I am afraid this information may come as a shock to you. I hope you will act wisely.

I need not emphasize that I have written this in the strictest confidence. You will see how much distress it would cause to my husband and to Antonia herself if it were known to them.

Yours very sincerely
Armorel C. Ardree.

She addressed this letter care of Henry Kinfowell; put on some clothes and went out to post it before she returned to bed.

43

OLLEROYD, following Gian into the passage, touched his arm and whispered: "Something wrong with your Tonie. Upstairs. I don't know what it is."

Gian said: "Tonie? Uh. Where's the missis, d'y'know?"

"She's gone out."

"Uh."

He went slowly upstairs.

He had been to Leytonstone on another fool's errand, having learnt that a firm wanted bricklayers there; as it proved, they had wanted three, and twenty-six had applied. He had walked from there to Stoke Newington and on to Finsbury Park, then out to Highgate, fruitlessly. He was now very tired.

Tonie! Something wrong with Tonie! A headache, a cold perhaps, nothing serious, there couldn't be anything seriously wrong with a girl like Tonie, compact with warmth and humour, so easy and gentle, so calm. And then he thought, At least it's not my fault, not this. All my fault—stand to reason—Susie getting back like she was before—should have realized—thought she wanted me in with her just to kind-of compensate, bit of a titbit for me, me being down over the job. Should have realized, she may have wanted it for herself, might be like that, judging by what some blokes tell me about the way it is with women, only you can't tell. She'd taken him wrong, one way or the other, and he couldn't put it right now. Like a stupid tune the cogitations with which his mind had laboured through the long, brown North London streets took hold of him again, repeating and repeating their action as a captive beast patrols its cage, almost excluding any fresh anxiety. Tonie—there couldn't be anything wrong with Tonie, not seriously wrong!

He knocked at her door, and after a little time, in which he heard sounds of drawers being opened and shut, she called, "Come in!" Entering, he stood by the door holding his cap, just as if Susie were there.

" 'Lo, Tonie! Olleroyd down there tell me you're feelin' bad."

"What, Ollie? Oh, I had a bit of a head."

She gave him the semblance of a smile and turned away, pretending she had something to do at the chest of drawers where she kept her things. She said:

"I'll be down in a moment—in five minutes. I'll get your supper. You must be awfully tired. Mother's left something. She told me; it's fish, I think. I—I'll try and make it nice."

But he was not blind. Her voice, carefully controlled, was hardly different from the voice he knew; she stood quite straight, and gracefully—the way she stood and moved was always a wonder and joy to him. But her light was out.

He said painfully, very quietly: "It don't matter about me."

Because they were peculiarly his, those five words broke her control. She turned and dropped across the end of her bed, burying her face.

He sat beside her, not attempting to say a word: just then he was physically incapable of speech. But as nervously as a boy in love he slipped one hand into her armpit, while the fingers of the other, strong and sensitive from his crafts, passed through her hair and down to the nape of her neck. Presently he lifted and moved her so that her breast lay on his thighs, and then he found a faint comfort in feeling how the violence of her sobs, cushioned by his own body, gradually diminished. At last he said:

"Aw, tell me, Tonie! You can tell me, surely—it don't matter anythink you tell t'me!"

When she had stopped crying she was still unable to speak. She sat beside him and held his hand, drawing clonic breaths as you open a jammed drawer, only glancing at his face like a candidate who scarcely dares to meet his examiner's eyes. But after a while she seemed to arrive at a decision; from the band of her skirt she took out Michael's letter, which she put folded into his hand.

"You can read it," she managed to say.

Then she kissed him, and went to wash her face, and on downstairs.

He took it to the light, and made his way through the unfamiliar kind of handwriting as a townsman steers himself through a coppice.

Darling darling darling Tonie, I shan't be coming home as I said, I shall be going straight from here to Oxford, or I may not go to Oxford at all, I may go abroad instead. Tonie my darling my only beloved darling I won't be seeing you now and perhaps not again. I love you more than anyone ever loved anyone before, I love you love you love you love you, but I think we've got not to see each other any more. In fact we absolutely mustn't. I can't explain. Only you must trust me, you must must trust me that there's a reason why I can't explain which isn't my fault or anything to do with me. I'll try and say something more, I don't think it matters my writing, only just now I can't, my brain's absolutely flat, life doesn't seem to mean anything, it's just filthy and sordid and stupid and meaningless, I'm just flat and ill with loving you and wanting you so absolutely desperately and not being able ever to see you again. You mustn't come here, it would lead to everything being worse for us both. All this doesn't make any really final difference, it only means that we have got to be unhappy all our lives, it doesn't make any difference to my loving you, always and always throughout every moment of my whole life, and perhaps after we are dead we can be together. Darling darling do just try to think of just that. I want to write something else, something that would make you feel less awful, but I can't, my brain's absolutely flat, all I can do is to tell you that you are the most dear and wonderful person who was ever born and that I shall always always always go on loving you. Your own for always and always your own Michael.

He read it three times and then went slowly downstairs, twisting it in his hand. He met Tonie carrying the supper things along the front passage and followed her into the sitting-room, where she quietly took the letter from him.

"I don't make head nor tail of it," he said.

She got out the table-cloth, unfolded and spread it almost without moving her feet. "No," she said evenly, "I don't think I do either. It's very strange." For a moment she stared at the tray she had just brought in as if it were some curiosity, then she began to set the table. "Mother said she might be in but if you came first we were not to wait. I think I'll lay three places in case she does."

He would have helped her, but he could not fit in with her speed, and he was left to stand like a dummy, marvelling; for her face, except in its pallor, showed scarcely a trace of the storm, and the movements with which she set the knives and forks, took out the tumblers from the corner cupboard, placed the serving spoons beside the condiments, were precise and dignified, those of a young woman only interested in the exact performance of domestic rites.

He found his voice again to say: "I reckon it can't be some other girl. Not by what he says, it can't."

"No," she answered, "no, it doesn't look like that. I suppose—well, I suppose the only thing is to leave it where it is. I mean, I shall have to write to him. Write to him and say I—well, say I sort-of understand. And—say good-bye. I suppose I'd better do that." Then she said: "I—I'm sorry I was making such a fearful fuss."

She should not have spoken those last words; for at once they trebled his need to give an answer, and finally destroyed his power of answering. She saw that. And she went on at once, gravely:

"Only, you see, it's made it all different, having you in it with me. I had to do that. There's no need—no need to talk about it any more. I think I'd rather not, really. Only I shall know all the time that you know. It's—you know—it's marvellous having someone who doesn't think he's got to talk about everything. It's so much better, for me." She picked up the empty tray. "I'd better see what's happening to the fish. I left Ollie in charge of it."

He was still in the same position, leaning against the piano and staring at the table, when he heard the front door opening. Armorel came into the room.

She asked: "Where's Antonia? I told her to get on with supper and not wait."

"She's gettin' it now," he answered, "she's in the kitchen."

"Oh."

She would have gone on upstairs but he stopped her.

"Here, Sue, half a tick!"

Surprised, "Yes?"

"Tonie's bad."

"Bad? What's wrong with her?"

"Well—well, I don't rightly know. She's kind-of bad in herself."

Armorel pulled off her second glove by the fingers, folded it with its fellow and pushed back her rings. She said a little impatiently:

"Yes, I think I know. It's some sort of a boy-and-girl affair that's gone wrong. I believe she's had some letter. Girls of her age are always breaking their hearts over one young man or another—it never amounts to anything really. I must slip up and change, I've got to go out again afterwards."

But he caught her by the sleeve.

"Tonie ain't that kind!" he said. "You got no right to talk like it don't matter, Tonie being like that. No matter if you're feelin' low in your own self or what. You can't go treatin' Tonie like that."

"Oh, nonsense, Gian!" she answered crisply, and jerked her arm away.

Alone again, he scanned the three places laid for supper as if they formed an intricate problem for him to solve. After a few moments' irresolution he went off, hatless, to the end of the street and got on a bus for Three Tuns.

44

THEY ALL KNEW at Apostles' Court that something was wrong with the Boss.

Not that he altered his routine. Before it was dark he had made his tour of the Pan, sniffing and nodding with satisfaction at the dahlias, criticizing the work of the path squad. He was in the workshop for half-an-hour, squaring up the cupboard door which Red East had on the bench, finishing a bookshelf for McCaffrey, with his usual patter of comment and advice. "Like coal hammers, them fingers o'yourn—you treat this here timber like as if you got a grudge on him. Got a sort of feelin', this timber has, you got to codger him up the way you want, see, not go at him like a bleedin' heavyweight . . . No, that ain't so bad, that ain't so bad at all. The way you're goin' on, you might make a joiner, shouldn't wonder, some day before they put y' underground. Only you got to learn that ain't no manner of holdin' on to a bull-nose plane, not like you're doin' it now, same as if you was workin' a compressor-drill . . ." The noise that went on all the time, the lachrymose voice of Radio Luxembourg enmeshed with fifty shrill and riotous voices, the incessant stamp of feet and slamming of doors, was varied a little by the sounds which always came when the Owner was on board: his orders bellowed from the top landing, the corporate, hilarious roar from the upper games-room when some puny child had thrashed him at bagatelle. But they saw a difference in him all the same. Tonight he was calling them by the wrong names, and the grin they were used to—that rather foolish, rather endearing grin—was constantly fading as electric lights do when there is something wrong at the power-house. They saw him stop, as he went from one room to another, as if he had lost his way.

A few knew the reason, or thought so, and before the evening was over it had gone the round. "You heard?—the Boss been sacked! Naaw, not from this joint, sacked off his fumin' job—Tishy got it off a bloke that go to the Hollies Club . . . Course he does—does a job o' work the same as any other bloke . . . Naaw, it weren't for anythink he done, they jus' pack up an' run 'im on the fumin' dole, firm what employ him. Same as any other firm—get sick 'n' tired of employin' blokes, can't afford the fumin' luxury . . ." Such news, one had said, could scarcely show effect on creatures in whose lives misfortune ran as regularly as the trams, whose own fathers were as often out of work as in; but as it spread it curiously dulled the uproar, in the way that the news of sudden death or defeat does. Long before closing time someone turned off the wireless. And the standard jokes which should have greeted his entrance to any room ("Cor, it's the Owner—give me quite a turn—thought it was somethink escaped from the circus!") were left unmade.

He found Terence Hubbitt in the corner of the reading-room, shielded by a book-stack, which served as office. "Goin' all right?" he asked as usual, and Terence, with the yawn he kept to hide his tireless industry, answered, "Yep, everything hottesy-tot!"

Gian sat on the table. "It don't feel the same," he said.

"What you mean," Terence said, pitching him a cigarette, "is you don't feel the same y'self."

"Well, I d'know."

Terence nodded. "I heard about it. Bleedin' shame. Fumin' scandal, if you ask me."

"You heard about what?"

"Them givin' you the quick-march. Fumin' scandal. Bloke give 'em all he got, twenty year or more, than all they got to say is 'You jus' nip off—don't want y' any more. You jus' b—— off and get on the fumin' dole!'"

"It ain't that," Gian said.

"Uh?"

"It's Tonie—you know, my kid. Chap turn her off. Do' know why—gone crazy or somethink, sounds like to me. Broke her heart, that's just about what he's gone an' done."

Terence could only say, viciously, "There's some fumin' t——s around, no doubt about it!"

Apparently Gian did not hear that. Watching the smoke of his cigarette he said, almost as if to himself: "I reckon it's all chalk up on my board, the way it go on. Don't get anythin' come in right. I reckon it's all on account of what I done to your dad—ain't had nothin' go right since I done that."

Terence said awkwardly: "He don't hold no grudge, my ole bloke don't. He reckon it come in like one of the risks of the trade, same as it might do a runnin' horse, or somethink drop on his nap."

They had been through this in the same embarrassed fashion more than once before; and Gian gloomily nodded. "Ye'! Ye', I reckon you don't get better men than your ole dad. That's just how it is—he don't come on to me for no pay-off, as you might say, so it jus' gets chalk up on my board."

He lingered for a while, faintly enjoying the cigarette and the sympathy in Terence's familiar, silent companionship. From this mooring he dreaded a little to go back into the stream, for tonight the Club had come to feel as it had felt on his first visit after the trial; no longer a background in which he merged as easily as the boys themselves, but a place where his oddity showed as starkly as in Mickett Lane. Still, he wasn't here to sit on his arse, moaning for young Hubbitt to come and nurse him. The run-away from one of the basins in the cloak-room was blocked, he'd noticed it the week before and sent a message for old Slimey to get on to the job, but Slimey as likely as not was still turning it over in his wobbly mind. He grunted, stubbed out the cigarette and went downstairs again.

Yes, the magic of the place was gone: nearly all the ingredients were there; familiar smells, windows he had made himself and notices he had signed, the comfort of a patterned disorder; but they no longer held together. On any other evening the exercise of his skill in working at the choked pipe with a length of iron wire, delivering his sarcasms on brainless plumbing to the admiring specators, would have filled him with a contentment in which his other lives were forgotten. Tonight the enamelled basin, distempered walls, the grubby faces of the boys themselves, were screens on which he saw again and again the shape of Tonie's face; not the face of Tonie weeping, but the white, brave face which she had conjured when he followed her into the sitting-room. Beneath his own voice, pattering with the quiet assurance that Apostles' Court had given him, he continually caught the shadow of Tonie's: *I suppose the only thing is to leave it where it is:* until he found that those stoic words were sounding into silence, that his sight was blurred and the boys were staring at him in bewilderment.

He turned away, leaving the tools where they happened to be lying.

"Have another go—some other time."

Some other time: but it was dawning on him that he would not be here again. He was useless now, he thought; and though he could not have told the reason he realized intuitively that he had nothing more to give away. Among these children he had passed for a happy man, with his mild prosperity; the watch-chain, the house they had heard of with carpets and a piano; and from a man who had managed to move from their world into one of pleasantness and security they had taken what orders and homely advice he had to give. Now the last of these pretensions had gone. His sympathy was not enough: these creatures were starved of happiness, and how much of that could he impart when his own precarious stock had finally given out!

He returned slowly towards the games-room, stopping to fidget with a bracket which supported the hand-rail. (He must get Slimey on to that; or better still do it himself, have the thing clean out, make good and re-plug the wall.) But what would he do with himself if he didn't come here? Outside working hours there were two situations in which he had always felt at ease, being here or being alone with Tonie.

The room he slept in, with its tasteful curtains that Susie had chosen, its chest of drawers kept free of ornaments and photos because Susie disliked them, had never belonged to him as this place did; at home he could gossip a bit with Daise or Olleroyd, but always with the faint sense of sacrilege and danger which a schoolboy feels reading shockers under the lid of his desk, he could never clear his guts in the sitting-room or use the whole of his chest to bawl at Mrs Inch for leaving the back door open. A place where people accepted him as normal, liked and admired him a little; a place to which he had given a little of his own breath, where he could see his personality reflected as he sometimes saw it—the expression of his old pugnacity, the shrug done with the eyebrows—in Tonie's face and gestures: that was what he needed, and never more than now.

The door of the games-room was ajar; hands in pockets, he opened it with his knee, summoned his grin and went inside. The voices and the laughter went out like candles in a draught.

"Well, now, what's goin' on in here?" he asked expansively. "No cheatin', I hope! You kids got to learn to play by the rules, else they'll never have y' in the Arsenal!"

At this witticism, which he had made every week for years, one of the two boys playing ping-pong put down his bat and the ball rolled away under the bagatelle table. The other player tittered awkwardly.

"Stuff y' bleedin' noise!" an older boy said sharply. "Don't see nothin' comic in what Mr Ardree tell y', do y'!"

A child whose narrow body was screwed like the blade of a fan shyly pushed forward the chair he had been sitting on. "Take this f' yer arse, Mr Ardree. Get y' down, this joint, hangin' around," and another voice said, "Cor, yes, bellyachin' chore, run a fumin' outfit like this 'ere."

But Gian picked up one of the bats.

"Play y', Mike Emmie—give y' a pastin'!"

Most evenings it went for a good knockout turn, the Boss at ping-pong. The big hand which controlled a chisel so precisely could do nothing with a bat, he was always hitting the table, the net, even his own elbow, everything except the ball. Tonight the pixies were in charge. His bat found the ball every time, the ball instead of flying to the ceiling shot like a dart to the table's rim, the cross-eyed Mike—expert in the leisurely, lobbing games he played with little Fu Shui—

had no defence at all. Each lucky stroke was applauded. "Cor, pretty shot . . . Coo, love-*lee,* put 'em down a treat, see the way he time the bocker, ain't half got an eye on 'im!" As in a dream, he glanced along the pinched and dirty faces, looking for the twist of impudence in their mouths, the satire in attentive eyes, which would have brought the scene to reality. There was none. The childish innocence within these beings of grown-up attitudes and experienced regard, the part of them he was friends with, was nowhere to be seen; tonight they were mature, anxious, studying him with an adult comprehension. And because he found no opening for the remarks he generally used ("Do' know what's wrong with me t'night, reckon the bat got a twist in him") he could only respond to their applause with a grin which hung on his face like the flag on a ship becalmed. He struck wildly, and the ball only went faster to the proper place. Once again he heard Mike's sad, respectful murmur, "Cew, got me bockered!" and he was ready to weep.

When the game finished O'Neil, leader of every rebellion, sardonic and shifty-eyed, brought him a mug of tea. No one seized the bats to start another game, they hung about the room like men at their first levee and talked to each other in undertones or with strenuous courtesy to him. "Beautiful ply, Mr Ardree, do me good to watch y'! Puttin'm down a masterpiece, an' no mistake!" He looked about once more for someone in the mood of everyday, someone to put up a moan or give him a bit of sauce. But the child Schlichten had a shy, paternal air, the smeared puck face of Tisher from Bundle Court was grave with chivalry. He turned to Fishy Reynold, thrice expelled for pilfering, in the hope that a burst of argument would loosen the air. " 'Ere, Fishy, what you done about them spots o' yourn? Wha'didy'do with the tanner I give y' to get the ointment for 'em?" A sixpenny-bit came out of a repulsive trouser pocket and was placed on the table like a tip, the scabbed face of 'Bitchey' Reynold's son frowned at the wall. "Get it t'night, Jeezer truth—don't want the tanner—Mum's new bloke got a chore." Gian turned about and went to the door.

"Find me up in the office, anythink anyone want to know."

He did not get back to the office, however. Where the passage turned, an undersized twelve-year-old, all stomach and forehead, was wandering with his eyes on the floor and Gian all but knocked him down. Startled into a burst of temper he stopped, clenched his fists and cursed the boy.

". . . Tell y' once, tell y' a thousan' bloody times! Roamin' round, don't use y' nap, don't even y' bloody eyes! Bloody danger, that's what you are!"

The child stood quite still. It was evident that he would have cried had that been within his capacity, but this over-used face was not supple enough for crying, it had not been tearful even when Gian had found him two years before in a corner of Spain Yard, with three weals showing through his torn jersey and blood oozing into the snow. All he did now was to stare up with his feeble and watery eyes, and to draw quick, flinching breaths as if he were bathing in a cold sea; and this nervous reflex he presently brought under control. He sucked his teeth in an ugly, mannish way, blew sharply through his nose and swept the mucus away from his furred lip with the back of his thumb.

"Mistardery?" he said, as if meeting a stranger. Then, "I heard. Tom—see?—Tom Oles, he tell me." He looked away, grimacing, and something like a laugh leaked out. "Mistardery—Tom what tell'n—Mistardery got the push. Fumin' firm—Tom Oles what tell'n—firm give 'n the fumin' push. Kids 'n' all. Nothink only fumin' dole."

His right hand, the one that was like a lobster's claw with only two broad fingers, was searching in the lining of his jacket, and now it came out pinching a sticky canteen bun. Ludicrously, like a toddler feeding an elephant, he held it up towards the Boss's face.

"Like y' t' have it!"

Gian took it but said nothing; after a second or two he did not try. He went downstairs and straight out of the Club.

As far as the Carpenter the darkness of the ill-lit street was a comfortable wrapping, like a warmed bed to a man stricken in fever, and even in Three Tuns Road, thronged and vociferous from the emptying Ritz, he enjoyed a sense of solitude. Still holding the sticky bun, he crossed the tram lines and slouched on through the Hauling into Breadalbane Street, where little lighted shops gave place to the gaunt Masonic Institute and friendly dockland smells were stifled by the locked fumes of cars. The buses going his way were half-empty, but he did not think of going aboard. It did not matter whether he was here or somewhere else, there was no imaginable reason for haste.

He was back at Mickett Lane a little after half-past twelve. He saw a light in the Grists' room.

On the fringe of sleep, Elizabeth knew that Trevon had gone into their sitting-room, but she did not stir. She had learnt that these vigils, when he leaned on the table or wandered about the small room for half-an-hour, for perhaps two hours, were among his necessities. Earlier in their life together she had supposed that she could help him, if only by being there to listen while he squeezed the bitterness of his thoughts—the affliction he had brought to her, the sum of his life's missed opportunities and failures—into half-coherent sentences. But she had come to realize that in those hours he needed to be alone in body as in mind; that no comfort of hers could penetrate the shadow in which he deliberately journeyed then; that if the voyage left his body exhausted the morning would find his spirit sweetened and refreshed.

But a second voice gradually roused her, and after a while she got up and opened the communicating door.

Yes, the voice was Gian's: ". . . Mean to say, it won't make no difference, anythink I say to her. Jus' broke her heart, that's what it seem like to me. Mean to say, it don't seem no good goin' on livin', havin' Tonie that way. Don't matter about me—all right so long as Tonie's all right. Only y' see she got in a state like I don't know what to say. See her that way—well, it get me in the stomach, see, the way I can't stand it, see . . ."

Elizabeth reached for the edge of the table, and from there found her way to Gian's side as readily as if she could see him. She said quickly, "What is it, Gian, what's happened to Tonie?" But intuition and circumstance gave her most of the answer before he did: yesterday Michael's weekly letter had not arrived, and he had scarcely ever failed before. She asked, "Is it something to do with Michael?"

It was Trevon who answered. "Yes, I'm afraid so."

"See how it is," Gian began. "Your Michael, y' see, might be he didn't know just how it was with Tonie. Got gone on him, y' see, the way a girl do—"

"You mean, Michael has—thrown her over?"

"Well, she got a letter off him, letter tellin' her he ain't goin' to see her any more."

She wished that the darkness would hide her as it hid them. Her thoughts moved like a searchlight's beam, to her last dim view of Michael's face, to Gordon Aquillard in his mood of cynical despair. She found nothing to say.

Trevon's arm came round her and he put her into the basket chair. He said quietly and composedly (though she knew he was in physical pain): "It's difficult to understand. Michael says he's still in love with her, he doesn't give any reason why they're not to see each other."

"I must see him," she said with decision. "I must go there tomorrow."

"To Dillys Court?"

She hesitated again. "I might possibly get him to meet me in town —I don't see how Henry could object to him coming up—"

"Only he might not come," Trevon said. "Listen, why can't Gian and I go? Michael—well, he's not frightened of me. I think we understand each other."

"But, darling, you're not up to a journey like that!"

"I'm up to things that are worth doing. I've put in twenty-five hours at the Club since Sunday."

She stretched up to feel his face, the cold cheeks, the moist forehead. But you could not tell: all his body seemed to be so shrunk and wasted now that you could not understand how he moved and worked at all. Only his eyes would have told her what she wanted to know.

"Gian, tell me!" she said softly. "Tell me what he looks like. Is he fit to go to Leicester?"

But no one could have looked elsewhere while she sat with her face turned up to him, sightless and yet appearing to see, her mouth seeming to be lit with the anxious and tender light to which her eyes were now opaque; so thin and frail a woman in the cotton dressing-gown, so much aged, with the hair at her temples grey, the syenite veins standing from almost translucent skin; and yet so potent in her stillness.

"You see," she said, "both of them mean everything to me."

"What I mean, I wouldn't want to be no trouble," Gian said. "Only it's Tonie, y' see. If Mr Trevon was to speak to your Michael— tell him the way it is with Tonie—"

Trevon, with his hands on Elizabeth's forehead, said: "It's Michael who matters, not me. It's so little to do for you—so little I can ever do. I've got to go. Gian, you'll come?"

It is easy to blame Trevon for the hideous untidiness of the meeting with Michael. He did manage things badly. He could so easily have telephoned from Leicester station and persuaded Michael to come into the town, where they could have talked comfortably in a corner of some hotel. But he did not think of that, he thought only about finding a bus to take him and Gian somewhere near Dillys Court. The evident fact is that he had not, just then, any reasoning power to spare. From St Pancras he had been struggling to focus his mind, so that its weakened and diffracted light should illumine clearly one problem only, what he should say to Michael when they met; he forgot, as such people do, that this would not be like the special interviews which Flock stage-managed at Hollysian House.

The court, built for a manufacturing hosier, was one of Nellerdine's abortions, successful in eschewing all comfort, unsuccessful in its aspiration to dignity. Perhaps they would like to wait in the drawing-room, the servant said, deciding from Trevon's voice that this one was gentry rather than village, whatever the other one might be; Mr Michael, he explained, was just finishing his lunch.

And then, of course, the message to the dining-room went astray, and it was Hilda Kinfowell who found them. She was not at all disturbed, for her experience of life had been that things which proved inconvenient were presently removed, as bath water goes down the drain. They had come to see Michael? Oh, he would be here in a minute. They would find him not at his best, he was evidently nervous about going up to Oxford, he had been working too hard, really the boy was over-conscientious. They had come from London? At this time of the year, frankly, she found London a bore. And really country life was so amusing, the people were so quaint.

"These are friends of Michael's," she said to Henry when he came, "they've come to see him."

"That's grand," said Henry, "grand! Are we going to have some coffee, my dear? You'll have some coffee, won't you! Grand, grand! You'll find Michael a little below the mark—I'd say he's been working too hard, the lad's over-conscientious in his studying, maybe. Well, well! I'm afraid I didn't quite catch the name—"

"My name's Grist. This is Mr Ardree. I'm Elizabeth's husband."

"Oh, fancy!" Hilda said. "How is darling Elizabeth?"

"Well, you know of course that she's lost her sight."

"Ay," said Henry, "that's a great misfortune. Indeed, yes, a very great misfortune! But men of science tell us that nature provides her own compensation for those who suffer that terrible affliction. They become wonderfully sensitive in the touch, wonderfully sensitive. Ay, the ways of Providence are not for creatures like ourselves to understand. Now I'll tell you a curious tale—"

But then Michael came in.

For a moment, standing between the Doric pillars which for no reason flanked the door, the boy looked as an actor might who has made his entrance at the wrong time. But a face so numb as his could not wear surprise for long. He came unsmiling across the parquet, shook hands with the visitors almost as if they were strangers, and then resumed the part he always played at that hour; set the occasional tables, took the coffee-cups as Hilda filled them, went round again with the sugar and milk. Henry watched him with kindness.

"I was saying to Mr Grist, it's a great misfortune about your mother's eyesight. I was saying, the ways of Providence are hard to understand."

"Yes," Michael said.

"Henry was telling Mr Grist that you've been working too hard," said Hilda. "He was saying that you're over-conscientious."

"Oh."

So oddly shaped a party might not have been successful. But it wore, at least for the Kinfowells, the appearance of success. For Hilda's mental needs were not extravagant, and Henry, who often described himself as 'a homely fellow', was at his most contented when surrounded by things of his own. Yes, he and Lady Kinfowell loved the country, he said: the simplicity, the sense of being close to nature. A stack of beech logs blazed in the huge Jacobean fire-place, through the five tall French windows the late September sun came with the force of limelight upon crimson wall-paper, the gilded cornices, the Khorassan rugs. Yes, he said, he really preferred this house to Easterhatch, it was more convenient for getting to town, and it had more room for the odds and ends he had collected. Perhaps they would care to look at the T'ang screen he had bought in New York, which was said to be superior to the similiar specimen in the Leipzig Museum. They would see it best if they stood just over here. Ah, now this was a good piece, a desk in the Adam style, his agent had bought it after a stiff battle at Sotheby's; and this old chest, he had paid a tidy sum for it, it showed grand workmanship. That cabinet standing beside it, that was French, Louis Quinze, his agent had secured it at the selling-up of an old château, and the china inside was Dresden-Meissen, said to be better than a similar set at Chatsworth. His guests, standing side by side in their heavy boots, nodded gravely at his face, at each new piece of costly bric-à-brac, and the inarticulateness of their praise in no wise troubled him: it was a day they would remember, he thought, the opportunity of seeing so many rare things: and from them his genial smile travelled the whole length of the room to fix upon his wife who, in her Fifth Avenue country suit, sat contentedly upon the high fender, just showing her silken knees. The contents of this room, he confided to Gian, were separately insured for nineteen thousand. Over by the door which led to the Florentine loggia Michael sat in total silence, staring out the window, like a child travelling to his first boarding-school.

"Indeed?" Trevon repeated. "Yes, remarkable."

The journey had brought on prematurely the pain in loins and forehead which he had to expect every few days. He had learnt to deal with this; not by struggling to detach himself, but by yielding to it as to a friend, letting it absorb his mind as well as his senses. Only, today, he had to reserve enough of clarity for the task ahead. In such half-consciousness, where the sense of time was stilled and the hours preceding this were blotted out, his sight and hearing worked with abnormal intensity. The florid blazon carved in the mantel, Hilda's complacent face, were unnaturally close, all the objects ranged about this vast and vulgar room appeared to be over-solid and over-sized: beneath the rolling tide of his host's voice he could hear distinctly the tap of Michael's heel drumming on the floor, and when he spoke himself he found his words coming back to him a fraction late, and foreign to him, as a man unpractised in oratory hears his own voice in a public speech. It seemed, that alien voice, to be saying what was required; and the part of him which acted in this monstrous unreality, where Michael and where Gian were nothing but stage properties, appeared to know its rôle as well as if it had been rehearsed. He waited, waited, with the patience of the sick, for the long, fantastic play to end.

". . . cosier for them here . . ."

". . . letters to sign . . ."

". . . promised the bishop's wife I'd be there for tea."

In the great mirror behind the chiffonier he saw a wan and shabby man get up, stand for a minute shifting his weight, obsequiously smile, shake hands: and realized it was Trevon Grist. He heard himself say to the varnished clod whom Elizabeth had lived with all those years, "So good of you!" and to the woman who had supplanted her ". . . been so very nice!" Presently the great door swung, sighing through its vacuum closer, and shut with a tiny click. The Kinfowells had gone, and like early daylight through the curtains of a banqueting hall reality was creeping in.

Sitting back in the deep chair, with his eyes shut, he presently heard Michael's colourless voice:

"I don't quite see why you couldn't let me know you were coming."

And a little afterwards, the voice of Gian, vibrating with a stifled anger he had never heard in it before:

"You know you got no right to lead her on that way! Don't give no reason, neither. Think it jus' don't matter, treatin' her like that, breakin' her heart. Jus' because you're an edgecated young gent you think you can do what you fumin' please with my girl—!"

Then Michael again, flat and far away:

"Yes, everything you say is perfectly right. There is a reason, but I can't tell you what it is, so there isn't anything worth saying. If you want to beat me up I really don't mind."

It seemed to Trevon, at this moment when he needed all the power he had saved, that it was running out of him as water escapes from a paper bag. He had mapped a dozen lines of approach for use according to Michael's mood, he had prepared whole sentences in advance; and now, with the pain reaching its climax, his mind was like a smooth-tyred wheel revolving uselessly in liquid mud. The force of long experience at Hollysian House might have enabled him to deal with an angry and defiant Michael: no man in his condition could handle a Michael locked in apathy such as this.

He stood up, and the pain sank a little way, releasing its tight hold on his forehead. He said, as if to himself:

"It's awfully stuffy. I'd like to see the garden—Michael, won't you show me?"

He found that he was walking at Michael's side on a gravel path fenced with shrubs. They turned through a wrought-iron gate into a terraced garden where the overlay of cornucopiae and dolphins, of French gazebos and blue Korean vases, had failed to obliterate the virtuosity of Paxton's original design.

"This is supposed to be the best part," Michael said. "Is there anything else you'd like to see?"

Trevon sat down on the rim of the fountain.

"No, I don't think so. I wanted to talk, really. It's weeks and weeks since I've seen you."

"If there was anything to say I'd say it," Michael answered. "I suppose it's no good trying to convince you or anyone else, but what you've come about happens to be my own affair, and that's all there is to it."

Following them, Gian had stopped at the gate. Trevon, looking that way, saw him fidgeting nervously with a cigarette. The air was very still here, sweet with verbena and marjoram, the purr of a mower on the lawn beside the house sounded very far away.

With his forehead in his hands, Trevon said: "Yes, I see how it is—I thought it would be like that. There are some hells one has to go through alone—I know, because I lived in one of them till a few years ago."

"But you don't now?"

"No."

"Well, mine isn't a temporary affair."

"I know. The difference is that I made my own. You haven't, it's just come to you."

"How do you know?"

"I know your mother. I know what kind of things could not happen to her son. It's conceivable that you might do stupid things, or wrong things. You couldn't do anything utterly selfish. I just know that, and the rest follows." He had not once looked at Michael's face, and his tone was such as an engineer might use in discussing a technical problem. He said presently: "I'll tell Elizabeth that I found you all right but rather tired. Overworked and all that. More or less what that ass (what's his name?—Kinfowell), more or less what he said. I think that story'll do as well as any other. You see, I've got to tell her something—that's my particular problem."

"Yes, I suppose so."

"You see, I've got very little left in me now, and what I have got has to be used for her. You see what I mean—anything that could possibly spare her any unhappiness."

"Oh—yes."

"Only most of her happiness is wrapped up in you—of course you realize that. So if there's anything you want me to do—to prepare the way before you see her, anything to make things easier—well, you've only got to tell me."

"I would," Michael said, "if I could think of anything." And then: "This business about me and Tonie, I want her to forget it, that's all."

"She can't because you can't."

"Well, then, there's nothing anyone can do."

"Well—there are things to avoid doing."

"What things?"

"Committing suicide."

"You don't think I'm as mad as that!"

"You don't need to be mad. I can remember very clearly the time I nearly did, and I was perfectly sane. I'd simply decided that I had more on me than any human being could tolerate. Of course I shouldn't have been like that if I'd had Elizabeth then. As it was, there seemed to be no one alive who could help me—because there was no one I trusted enough to talk to. When you're in that position the thing simply builds up until you don't feel you can stand it. That isn't the same thing as madness."

"No, I suppose not." Michael was looking at Trevon's face now. "Look here, hadn't you better come back to the house? You—you're looking so damned ill. I could get you some tea or whisky or something."

Trevon said: "Michael, do for God's sake tell someone. Some outsider, if you can't tell Elizabeth—a priest or someone, someone you can trust. I know I'm no use, to you I'm just an interloper—"

Turning round, Michael saw that Gian was still on the far side of the gate, looking at the sculptured yews with a Londoner's contemptuous indifference. He said abruptly, "There isn't anyone I'd trust more than you," and in a moment the letter which had been in his breast pocket was transferred to Trevon's. "You might wait till you're quite by yourself before you read that. Then—well, I'd rather you decided if Elizabeth ought to see it. Nobody ought to, really. Only I'm finished—I'm tired of trying to see what I ought to do."

He led his visitors back to the house, and when they had declined to eat or drink anything he got a car for them. He made an effort to say something to Gian, but it wouldn't come; before the car moved forward, and without even a gesture of farewell, he had disappeared indoors.

In a lavatory at the station Trevon read the letter from Armorel which Michael had given him.

Jammed against him in the crowded carriage, Gian studied Trevon's grey face with curiosity: the eyes open but expressionless, the taut lips restless, as if they were rehearsing an actor's lines. He had known several kinds of illness, he had seen his friend in such a case as this before; but he felt, now, that something new had happened, that Trevon had moved, as so rare a person might, into a region where he could not follow. It would have eased his feelings to do what a woman would, put something to make the sick man's head more comfortable, speak a word of gentleness; but that (which he would have done for any of the Apostles' Court boys) was outside his present range. He could only gaze at these features of an old friendship as people stare through a shop window at a piece of furniture which was once their own.

The train shook on the Glendon points and Trevon stirred. His voice came to Gian as if on a poor telephone line: "We've got to be terribly patient. He's overworked, you see, he's not himself at all. We've got to be frightfully patient, we must wait till his mother can see him. I've got to arrange that—she can't go to that place—I don't know how but I'll arrange it somehow. You must tell Tonie—you must tell her he's overworked, tell her she's got to be terribly patient. Elizabeth—I expect Elizabeth'll talk to her. Elizabeth will know what to do."

At Wellingborough the rest got out and the elderly couple who took their place fell into a doze as soon as the train started. Trevon moved into a corner seat, his head slid back against the window and presently he too was asleep.

It was then that Gian noticed the piece of paper just protruding from his breast pocket. Standing by the wrought-iron gate he had tried, inevitably, to hear what the other two were saying: no word had reached him, but eyes accustomed to pick up details in one glance across a building site had not failed to notice something like a white handkerchief passing from one man to the other. He looked, now, to make sure that their fellow-travellers were still nodding; and then it was easy, and natural, for him to slip the letter out and unfold it.

He read it just as he had read Michael's letter to Tonie, line by line, almost as slowly as a fourth-form boy construing Ovid. When he had been all through it twice he put it in his own pocket and then sat perfectly still, sucking his long-dead cigarette, with his comatose eyes turned towards the drifting trees and flat, brown fields, the Bedford houses cramming towards the line and scattering again, the blue swell of the Chilterns, lights from distant windows which flecked the greying scarf as the train gathered fresh power to pelt through Borehamwood.

45

*E*VENTS TRAIL shadows larger than themselves, and much that Mickett Lane people afterwards said about those days came from springs of imagination almost free from the pollution of fact. As example, Mrs Inch told Dora Webbel that "I see Mr Ardree the night he come back from his day out with Mr Grist, he come into my kitchen with his eyes all wild like a wild beast." Actually, Gian did not return to No. 83 that night at all; he stayed with his father over at Heald's. Even the less mercurial Olleroyd afterwards stated that "Mr Grist, he went bounding up the stairs hollering for Mrs Grist"—a feat that was plainly beyond Trevon's physical capacity at that time. On the other hand, the account given by Tim Heald of what he saw and heard that evening was palpably reliable; for Heald was accustomed to observe intelligently any unusual happening in his narrow world, and his native wits had long absorbed the principle that most facts are more interesting naked than in home-made fancy dress. From his recollections it was easy to establish the sequence of the evening's main events.

It was not long after he had shut-up shop that Daise came downstairs to say that her mother had 'come over very bad.' His first action was to telephone for a doctor, the next to go across to 83, where his knock was answered by Armorel. Might he speak to Mrs Grist? he asked. She demurred: she could take a message, perhaps; her manner was as frigid as if he had been a total stranger, but he was not surprised by this because for several days he had seen her in what he described as 'one of her old moods', stiff and detached. No, he said, he would prefer to see Mrs Grist himself; and having the great advantage of the uncultured, a skin like galvanized iron, he prevailed. He took Elizabeth back with him and she went straight up to Matilda's room.

About half-an-hour after this Gian came into the back room, for what Heald took to be one of his ordinary evening visits, and sat down beside his father, who had fallen asleep over the *Evening News*. Heald told him that Matilda was in a bad way and had the doctor with her, besides Daise and Elizabeth, but he did not seem to hear; he looked to Heald extremely tired and 'like as if he'd had a gun let off right behind his ear-'ole.' He drank most of the cup of tea Heald made for him, but would eat nothing.

Trevon arrived five minutes later, greatly excited—light-headed even—and announcing that he must see his wife immediately. He would, in fact, have blundered on up to Matilda's room, but Heald wisely stopped him, saying that he would get Mrs Grist down as quickly as he could. As Heald started up the stairs he heard Trevon saying feverishly: "You must be patient, old chap—don't get excited, don't let it get on top of you! I'm going to talk to Elizabeth—I think it's all a cock-and-bull story, I'm almost certain it is!"

Heald's memory of those happenings was no doubt the sharper because they happened on the night when Matilda died. The death of an old woman, long bedridden, was not an occurrence by which a man like him was shocked or awed; but it was an occasion, and in the way that the birth or death of royalty does it underlined the events surrounding it. His recollection of the few minutes which immediately followed her death was far less precise. In this familiar room there had often been untidy traffic, friends dropping in and staying late, the gentle hubbub of gossip and artless ribaldries, but all that life had been roughly patterned with its centre in himself, whose personality was always ripe enough to command it. The confusion of circumstances which started now was so far outside his control that he felt as if the very framework of experience had been pulled out of shape.

It was like a play written by someone with no understanding of the theatre and produced by another ignoramus who has not even studied the script: a scene in which no two elements fitted together so that it seemed to be more untidy than life itself. Under the stress of emotion, Elizabeth had failed to grasp Heald's message, and she had for the present only one idea, something she wanted to say to Gian. She knew when she entered the room that Gian was there, because she heard his cough; she did not know that Trevon was there too, and he, relapsed after the extra effort he had made to cross the road (when he had trusted that the day's fatigue would end in his own room), could not immediately find strength to get hold of her and take her aside. Daise, who followed Elizabeth into the room, was admirably calm, and if dignity could ever be ascribed to a being so cruelly afflicted by nature she had it then. It was she who caught the words, uttered in scarcely more than a whisper, which Trevon had meant for Elizabeth, "I must speak to you, do come here!" and she, therefore, who went and stood in front of his chair, gravely waiting for what he should have to say; while the doctor, coming in just behind her, a young man new to the district, went straight to Heald, naturally supposing that he was the husband of the woman who had just died.

Elizabeth, when she had felt her way to Gian, spoke to him very quietly and collectedly so that her words were among the few which remained like an engraving upon Heald's memory of that hour: "Gian, I think you ought to know, Matilda told us what really happened about her husband—she told us how she came up behind him on the landing and pushed him. The doctor was there and he heard it all, so did Daise. I know you'll be glad she told us that. You understand, don't you? She wanted to tell us before she died."

But Gian apparently could make nothing of that: all he answered was, "Matilda? Died?" as if even the name was strange to him. And she could only say despairingly: "Where's Mr Heald? Tim, where are you, you must tell him, you must make him understand!"

Meanwhile Trevon, finding Daise in front of him, and awaking to the reason for her damp eyes, had struggled to collect his faculties for yet another task. He took her hand, he said: "I'm sorry—Daise, I'm most terribly sorry. You won't be all alone—you belong to all of us—we won't let you be lonely." That was all he could manage; and because this crude condolence was so warm with sincerity it overcame her thin, brave defences. She broke into fresh tears, turned away and shrank into the corner by the shop door; where Elizabeth, hearing her sobs, came stumbling against chairs and packing-cases to find and comfort her.

By then the doctor, realizing at last that Heald was not Matilda's husband, had inferred that Simon must be, and with admirable gentleness was telling him that he must have someone to lay out the body: a Mrs Forbes, he suggested, who lived in Piggold Street only ten minutes away, would probably perform that office. It appeared that Simon did not understand what was meant by laying-out, and the doctor began patiently to explain.

Gian, at last, had been stirred a little from his apathy. Slowly and confusedly, like one wakened in the small hours, he rose and went across to the corner where Elizabeth stood with her arm round Daise's shoulder. For a time he merely watched them, and then he said something to Daise which no one but she heard. The effect of that was curious, so foreign to anything in Heald's experience that it found a steady place within the tumult of those memories: the dwarf seemed suddenly to smile—you could never be sure, with that dreadful mouth of hers—she stretched to catch hold of Gian's enormous hand, clutched it to her and voraciously kissed it. Over by the fireplace Simon was asthmatically laughing.

"Listen," Trevon was saying in the tremulous voice of a frustrated child, "Tim, listen! I've got to get hold of my wife, I simply must get her alone, I've got to talk to her!"

But if Trevon Grist—one of the few men he respected as a superior—was helpless, Heald himself could only remain passive in a situation which precluded his laughter, acerbity, or ordinary kindness. He watched with cataleptic eyes as Elizabeth felt her way along the farther wall, as Daise, still at Gian's side, continued to weep convulsively, while at the other end of the room, between bursts of throaty laughter, Simon was squealing, "Eh—couldn't do that! They couldn't do all that to my ole girl—not *now!*" Overhead the door of Matilda's room, which had always been kept carefully closed, was swinging and thumping in the wind.

That was how Heald remembered the scene, and that was how Armorel found it, when she came round by the yard and knocked at the outside door.

She said, standing in the doorway: "Excuse me, Mr Heald, is my husband here? Oh, Gian, there you are! I do wish you'd come and have your supper."

Her voice brought the room to absolute stillness. From her strange, utter solitude she asked:

"There's nothing wrong, is there?"

But no one stirred, there was no answer, no sound except Matilda's door banging and banging.

A little before midnight, when the room was empty except for himself and Gian, Heald set off for bed. Gian could doss down with his father, he suggested with kindness, since he was evidently disinclined to go home; or else bring down blankets and make himself a bed by the fire.

But he was only half-way upstairs when he heard the yard door opening once more, and then Trevon's voice. With no more than the ordinary curiosity of mankind he went quietly down again, and with his head against the door he heard most of the conversation which ensued.

". . . invention from start to finish. Yes. Elizabeth's certain, absolutely certain. You see, she remembers quite clearly that that man Aquillard was still in America for several months after you were married—after Tonie started coming. He was writing to her from America at the time. There isn't any doubt about it at all. Elizabeth's absolutely certain. Listen—Gian—you do believe what Elizabeth says, don't you!"

"Don't see it. Don't see why Susie want to think up a humbug like that. Don't see how anyone can think up a thing like that."

"But she did—that's the point, she did think it all up. I don't know why. At least, I do, in a way. It's very difficult, it's almost impossible to explain that sort of thing. You see, the human heart is a very strange thing, you get a very little poison in it and the results are sometimes much more queer and frightening than when the body's poisoned. I can't explain everything just now—"

"She better explain herself, I reckon. If that's a fack what she put in that letter she better say herself, not go writin' to Michael. An' if it's not a fack—"

"—It isn't, Gian, there isn't a word of truth in it, I absolutely promise you that—"

"—An' if it's not a fack she better come 'n' tell me the reason why. I don't want no explanations, I jus' want to know why she put that in that letter, makin' out she was actin' worse than a punkie, tellink all that to that Michael an' settin' him wrong with Tonie, gettin' Tonie like she might break her heart. That's all I want to know, and she better tell me, see. I don't want no explanation from no one—it's all on her, see, an' she got to do the explainin'."

Trevon said desperately: "She will, in time. You've got to be patient, she's ill at present, she's not right in her mind."

"I don't care what anyone says, she got to explain," Gian repeated. "She got to make it right with Michael an' Tonie. An' me too, come to that—"

"—Gian, listen! Elizabeth's going to have another talk with her in the morning. Listen, you're perfectly right, we want Susie to talk to Michael herself, it's the only way she can undo all the harm she's done. Only we've got to be patient—"

"Patient? I reckon I been patient! Goin' on that way, actin' like a misery, actin' like it was all because of me! Why don't she come over now, say what she mean? Do she reckon I'm not good enough to be Tonie's dad? We was married, wasn't we, church an' all—not on any notion of mine neither, she didn't have to give herself to me nor any other bloke that wasn't fit for her. She got a tongue, ain't she? She's edgecated, she know how to say what she want to say. Why don't she come an' say what she mean? Story like that—so be it *is* a story—"

"Now, Gian, wait! I know everything you're thinking and feeling, and I should be exactly the same. But listen: this is the one time in your life when you can show the sort of man you really are—and you're a bloke with a better heart and a better mind than almost anyone I know. I mean that. There's only one person alive who can get Susie out of her present state—"

"I reckon she's always been in that state. I reckon she's no more'n a fumin' lyin' bitch an' never has been . . ."

Heald grew tired of listening to this. He did not know what it was all about and he had heard long before now the kind of conversation when two people, one wearily patient and the other raging, went on and on for world without end amen. Some stew, it seemed, between that decent, luckless runt of an Ardrce and his fancy-acting squaw: he supposed it would all come out in the wash. He yawned and went off to bed.

Much later, through the thin wall which divided his bedroom from Simon's, he heard Gian's voice again; a voice now slithering on tears:

". . . doin' that to Tonie! Done it on purpose, the way it look to me—broke her heart, that's what she done, she jus' turn against the best kid any woman ever had an' broke her heart. She got no right to live, a bitch like that—turn against her own flesh 'n' blood an' break her heart . . ."

But this was not much disturbance to old Heald, who had passed his whole life within the sound of London's insistent voice, its thousand anxious, infiltrating voices. In a few moments he was again asleep.

46

*I*N THE FIRST NIGGARD LIGHT the Elephant was an abandoned fortress, the jangle of a lorry coming up Walworth Road echoed like gun-shots against wooded hills and the tram moaning past shuttered shops was a barbarous intruder in a city as desolate as Ur. Very early it was cold, and the river lay under a quilt of mist; but as the sun came higher above the jumbled outworks of St Paul's the cloud over Westminster thinned, and the day which came with the last breaths of a wind from Battersea was an aftermath of summer.

"Give me a paper!" he said.

The old cripple early on his stand to catch the custom of the workmen's trams looked sleepily across the Embankment, where a scavenger with a wide brush was sweeping yesterday's dust and tickets with a sprinkling of yellow leaves in a haycock against the kerb.

" *'Spress* or *Mail?*"

"Paper, I said!"

"All right, chum, all right!" He pushed out a *Mail*. Dago by the looks of him, he thought, and with transient curiosity his eyes followed the squat figure slouching off up Villiers Street. Dope, he supposed: eyes like that, at this hour. That went with dagoes.

'*Skilled joiner, for finishing. Household and Horticultural Accessories. Apply Wks Manager, Kingfisher Works, West Willesden.*'

The paper slipped off his knees and fluttered under the seat. The sun shone warmly now; and as the stir of the square increased, buses like giant cattle thrusting against the traffic lights, the chequered ribbon from the tube thickening, the pace of the weaving and breaking threads growing faster, there was pleasure of a kind in being free from the government of time. Relaxing, watching the pigeons that pecked and strutted near his feet, he could feel his anger subsiding from its silver violence into a clot of heaviness which, lodged between stomach and chest, sent a steady current of orange flame into his head.

The birds, as if to test their power, rose fussily in a narrow scroll and returned to the very patch they had left. One scrambled into the air again and a score gave chase, they made a lariat above the fountains, wheeled high towards the picture place where Susie had once taken him and scattered down towards St Martin's Steps. He dozed, and in the brushing of a dream, carried past yellow fields with Tonie troubled and estranged beside him, he whispered: "I done it, sweet, it's all all right, she can't do nothink now!" But as his eyes fell open the pain of actuality returned with double force: his wasted rage had become a beast which dragged but would not carry him, and the task was still to be done.

Above the Marble Arch the sky was a Norwegian blue, so perfect and so high a roof that the Bayswater buildings looked small in scale, like those of a coastal town observed from the sea; its limpid light, reflected by plate-glass windows and the shining bonnets of cars, gave to the scene the quickened, ethereal air which comes upon wet sandy beaches in late afternoon. Here the summer frocks were out again, like flowers that grow in a stony waste, girls hatless and bare-legged swung finical bags or steered their little dogs between the hawkers and the bustling clerks. This was a women's town. Men steered the buses sweeping into Edgware Road, men disciplined the torrent of cars to filter past men who held in leash the ferocious power of vacuum drills, high above the pavement the new skeleton of steel was being fashioned by men; but the man-wrought precipice of brick and concrete came down to windows frivolous with taffeta and cretonne, a diadem of perfume flasks, a ballet-fantasque of pouncing legs and bakelite breasts; against the Great Western shunting yards gigantic posters flamed with women deified by toilet soap, along the dingy Harrow Road the wistful dreams of girls were mirrored violently in hairdressers' shops, in the covers of rapturous magazines. A town that laboured for women's delight: but where the bright frocks passed through a band of sun he caught no answering gleam. In the hungry look of a little, bustling Jewess, a young wife's anxious eyes, in the weary faces of a group of laundry girls, he saw repeated as if on an endless band the grief of Tonie's dead, denatured face.

At night, he thought again—he could only do it at night. For the girl who had just gone by was carrying her child, and before he could snatch his glance away he had seen in the line of her mouth something which recalled to him how Susie had looked in the hour of Tonie's birth. "Kingfisher Works?" he asked a man at the corner, and he sauntered on through Freeborn Lane, pausing to clear scraps of litter off the path as he did in the Pan, to peer at passers-by as a man from the Brazilian jungle would.

"It said it in the paper I got."

"I know," the clerk in the timekeeper's office said, taking off his spectacles, "I've told you, that was a repeat, we meant to get it stopped."

He stared with a casual curiosity at this latest applicant. Allowing he might be a foreigner of sorts, there were things that didn't fit together, the watch-chain with the stubbled face, the dirty cap and lack of collar with the respectable blue serge.

"Sorry, but there it is!"

The applicant nodded but did not move. He seemed to be listening like a ship's engineer to the pulse of machinery beyond the breeze partition, the distant whine of saws; sniffing, he smiled faintly, as if the odour of resin and dust took him back to a country of his own.

"Been foreman, see—builder's foreman. Only I done joinery, see —done it at night school. Had five carpenters workin' under me direct, job the firm done over at Lee Green."

"I know, I know—but I've told you, the job went yesterday."

"Got the girl at school, see. Can't take her away, not the way it is now, she's got to have something to take her mind off, see. Cost money, see."

"I know, I know, it's hard times, but that's the way it is. I'm telling you, the job went yesterday."

"Got to pay her schooling, see. The way it is, her mother, see—"

"See here," the clerk said, "how much did it put you back, coming out here?" His hand was already in his trouser pocket. "Come from somewhere the other end, Stepney is it, bob for your bus fare, would it be?" He put half a crown on the counter, screwed his left eye. "Kingfisher's best regards!"

The long domestic street, almost deserted at this hour, was held in a peculiar stillness by the brilliance of the light; it seemed as if the empty day would never advance. He saw at the end a line of pollard trees; there, freed from the pressure of these tall houses, he would feel clean air on his face and the ravel of perplexities which dragged upon his forehead might be loosened out. That hope was frustrated. The worn turf where the trees and the goalposts stood was defended by a rack of steel, the electric trains went by like thunderbolts, he turned at the Infirmary and went on past a long iron fence where the bills cried *Racing Tonight, Racing Tonight*. If Susie were gone, he thought, the thing she had said would be blotted out as well. It might, it might not mean that Tonie would once more belong to him; but surely that look of grey despair would leave her when its cause had been silenced for evermore. Among those causes and results there was some loose fit, as with a tenon and mortise clumsily tooled; but the things which squeezed against his brain, a factory's high wall and the rattle of trains, would not allow him to fiddle it out. It must be enough, he thought, that he meant to act for Tonie the best he could; while the movement of the town, a jostle of prams and shopping-bags, vans raising hollow echoes beneath the railway bridge, was tightening its hold again.

Pretty, he thought it was, a shaft of sunlight on the brightly coloured demijohns, ruby, azure and lemon-green.

He asked, fingering the tin of Rat-O-Cide, "Would it do for a dog?"

"Pardon?" the girl in the white overall said.

"Would it do for a dog?" he repeated. The girl's hair reminded him of Susie's and he kept his eyes away from her face. "Mean to say, would it finish off a dog?"

"Oh! You mean, a big dog?"

"Hh!—lady dog."

"Well, I couldn't say, I'm sure. I mean, I really couldn't say."

"It don't do for a dog?"

"Well, I'm sure I couldn't say."

"A lady dog, I mean."

"Mr Smeet might know."

"Dog?" Mr Smeet said firmly, "no, my friend, you can't use that on a dog." He was shiny-domed and spectacled, he vaguely seemed to be the man whom Gian had met already at the Kingfisher Works. "What sort of dog?"

"Sort of lady dog."

"Well, you'd best get someone to do the job for you. There's an R.S.P.C.A. in Seymour Road, they might do it for nothing there. Or bring her here if you like, I could do it for you here."

"Can't bring her here."

"I mean to say, it's not right to poison a dog. That would be cruel, no matter what you did it with. You don't want your dog to suffer, do you now?"

"No. No, she don't want to suffer. That's what I'm saying, I don't want to see her suffer."

Mr Smeet leaned over the counter,

"Listen now—have you got a friend with a sporting gun? That's the best way of all. Take it out in a field somewhere, give it a juicy bone, let it get down to it. Then give it a shot just behind the ear. Blow its brains out—it won't feel anything at all."

"See how it is, I don't want to have her suffer."

"Well, that's what I'm saying. You might get a friend to do it for you. I know how it is with an animal you've grown fond of."

"Fond of?"

"Well, you know what I mean."

"Nice eyes he's got," the girl said to Mr Smeet as they watched the sack of serge moving across the road like a cork in a stream. "Funny, you know, only rather nice."

"Loopy," Mr Smeet said, "that's what he looks like to me."

Among the horse-brasses and the rivetted willow plates, Buddhas, ikons and bottled ships, a few old firing pieces were displayed in the dusty window. Inside, the shop was a dark labyrinth of vast Victorian wardrobes, deal dressers, gate-legged tables and commodes.

"Gun?" said the little man below the dusty bowler. He burrowed into some dark recess and returned wiping the cobwebs from a Martini-Henry. "This now, this would be a gun "

"Do for a dog?"

"Dog? What sort of dog?"

"Lady dog."

"Well, mean to say, they can train some dogs to go after any sort of gun." The little man held the rifle to catch a narrow shaft of light and gazed at the barrel with damp, distrustful eyes. "It's a nice gun," he said without conviction. "All that rust there, that'd come off, see. Bit o' sandpaper. Drop of paraffin."

"You got the bullets?"

"No, don't keep bullets. Sport shop, that's where you want to go for bullets. Tivvles in Marsh Street, they'd keep bullets, shouldn't wonder. It's a nice gun, see, good workmanship. Hang up in a gentleman's hall, might be."

"You can't fire a gun without bullets in it."

"Well, you'd want to be careful, firing this sort of gun. Only that's good workmanship."

"You got the instruction book?"

"No. See what I mean, there wouldn't be an instruction book. Not with this gun."

"What's it work out at, hirin' this sort of gun?"

"Well, mean to say, it ain't for hirin', this gun. Take it away for three quid. It's a nice gun, good workmanship, see. Go on it with a drop of paraffin."

"I don't want to buy a gun."

"Uh? You don't want to buy it?"

"I tell you, I don't want to buy a gun."

"Got a barrow-meter over here. Nice workmanship. Look nice, hung up in somebody's hall."

"You can't do in a dog with a barrow-meter."

"No, I'm not saying it'd do for doin' in a dog. Show you a nice clock, that one over there."

"Fumin' clock ain't the same as a gun."

"No, I'm not sayin' it's the same thing as a gun."

"Well, that's what I said!"

The huddling shops with wares that overflowed to the pavement gave place to a tidy row, to chromium facia boards, a fish shop like a rich man's bathroom, a lush display of lamp shades and radios. Walking eastwards at the same loose pace he was hardly conscious of hunger or fatigue; but the distances confused him, a girl with a head like Tonie's proved when he crossed the road to be only paper and ink, the outlines of things close at hand grew blurred and waved a little, like objects seen through inferior glass.

They had the look of proud, white sailing ships, the women in curious headdress who had just got off the bus. He did not realize at once where he had seen her, the younger and darker of those two, he only felt that he had known those gentle eyes, the young and serious mouth which so narrowly avoided a smile. He increased his pace to overtake them, fell back for a little way and then caught up with them again, turning to peer with increasing boldness at the young girl's mouth until, after anxious whispering, the pair stopped and faced him. With manufactured calm the elder Sister asked:

"Is there anything we can do for you? Is there something you want?"

His courage was not equal to hers: she was tall and her pale face was like a statue's looking down. "You," he said, glancing at her companion and away again, "—thought I'd seen you somewhere—beg y' pardon."

"Oh—oh, I don't think so."

"Long time ago."

"I'm afraid we have to be getting on," the elder woman said.

He persisted: "I thought I'd seen you. You wouldn't remember, that was a long time ago—Genoa, that was. You know, Genoa—in Italy that was."

The elder Sister said gravely, "Oh, no, we don't go abroad, we haven't been abroad at all."

She would have led her companion away, but the younger woman turned again.

"Excuse me—we wondered—are you in need of money?"

"Money?"

"We thought you might—we thought you looked rather unwell."

"It's not me," he said thickly, "it's Tonie."

"Oh, your little boy is ill?"

"No, m'm, she's not a little boy."

Like flotsam which a gentle current pulls away from the river bank they were moving again: a curious formation to witness in the busy street, the taller Sister urging forward with anxious majesty, the dark one lagging half a pace behind, her compassionate eyes continually turning to the seedy pugilist who lolloped at her heels and answered her glances with an intense and frightening stare. In a shapeless undertone he was explaining and explaining: he had had a dream, he had dreamed of killing Susie—that was the girl who'd married him, a long time ago—it was all because of Tonie who couldn't go on like she was now. It might not all be true, he said, but it was wrong whichever way you looked at it, Susie having another father for Tonie instead of him. There were clouds now, spoiling the brilliance of the day. In the same formation, as if they were joined by crooked towing-bars, the awkward trio crossed at the traffic lights and tacked along Prince Edward Road.

The house they led him to was new, the high, pitch-pine room where they asked him to wait smelt faintly of a church and somewhere near by a bell was jangling. He sat, a wax model of apathy, on a hard chair beside the table.

His eyes led him past the line of meaningless symbols, the time-tables, the calendar and roster-board, to a rocky valley which he had seen somewhere before; and he found it faintly comforting, this construction of many darknesses, the dark cypresses against a livid sky, the brown hills massing darkly upon the dark-blue semi-lune of shrubs. Here was quietness. In the accessible grandeur of these heights and distances the confusion which lay behind, the dream, the shapes and voices of the street, was calmed, and as he came slowly down the one grey shaft of light to the figure kneeling beside a rock the calmness closed upon his labouring mind. Here there was no need to struggle with dragging thoughts: in the agony of this patient face his own was stilled. None of his senses slept. He could feel the pain in his temples as a horse feels the tug of the bit, the sound of leaves blown across the gravel outside, of distant trams, was as clear as on a frosty night. But like the country he had seen from the train this fabric of sensation had no connection with the lingering moment in which he lived. When the door opened he did not move, and when a man addressed him from close at hand the words hovered in his mind, a mere pattern of sound, before they took shape in his understanding.

"You like that picture?"

He answered presently, in an undertone: "Sì, signore!"

"You know who that is?"

"Yes."

He must leave his valley now, the tranquil darknesses, the face that he all but understood. He got up, turning his head.

"No, do sit down, please!"

The man was dressed like a *parroco*, but he was solidly English, with the furred, dawdling voice which that cousin of Susie's had. Behind him, the girl with the feeling eyes was putting a tray of food on the table, tea, biscuits and bread-and-cheese. The girl smiled very faintly and went away.

The parroco sat down and lit a cigarette. "You'll have some tea?—I'll pour it for you. Or beer if you'd rather? I'm glad you've come, I like seeing people. Would you rather sit on that sofa?—you look awfully tired. All right, just as you like! I thought possibly I could do something—Sister Margaret says you've got some sort of trouble on your hands." The voice was warm but not intrusive; free from jauntiness or patronage. It did not insist on any reply.

With his eyes drifting between the door and the table, Gian sipped his tea. Against his desire to respond to this friendly voice there lay the weight of his weariness, and the thoughts stampeding like a frightened herd could never be brought to the narrow path of speech. Only a word or two came like a bubble to the surface.

" 'S on account of Susie, see."

"Susie? That's your wife? Is Susie ill?"

"Do' know. Well, she don't look like that."

"Well, now, what's wrong with Susie? Or is it something you don't want to tell anybody?"

"Uh? Well, there ain't nothink wrong. Only she don't act right."

"You mean, she doesn't do her work—doesn't get your meals properly?"

"Uh? She do her work all right. You can't say that, no one can't say she don't do her job right."

"But she's—done something you think's wrong?"

"Uh?"

"Has she been—going about with someone else?"

Gian turned the cup in the saucer; it worried him that owing to the cloudiness of his eyes he could not make the pattern fit.

"Well, you can't say. Well, I reckon that might be what she done."

"And you can't get her back?"

"I don't want her back."

"But you do love her, don't you? Otherwise you wouldn't mind so much about what she's done."

"I don't want her any more. I reckon she done harm enough. I reckon she want to be finish off."

"I see." The voice did not alter. "But then, you *did* love her?"

"Uh?"

"You loved her when she was just what you wanted her to be. You did, surely!"

"Uh?"

"When you married her you must have been in love."

"Uh? She wasn't like she is now."

"No, in some ways she wasn't." The quiet, uninsistent voice was sinewed with utter certainty. "I'll tell you how it is. You know, they say that love is blind. It isn't—real love isn't. It's what makes us see the truth in people, the best part—the part that's very often hidden by all the complications and the mess we live in. What love sees is the reality—not somebody imaginary—and because it's reality it goes on, even when the person you love seems to have changed. Look, I'll try and make it clear what I mean—"

Gian said suddenly: "You can't do no lovink on her sort. She don't love no one or nothink. She don't care what she do. I done everythink I can, been doin' it year in year out. That sort, she jus' muck things up no matter what it is, jus' for the sake, she muck her own kid up, break her heart, she don't want no lovin' or nothink, never did!"

The parroco nodded slowly.

"You say you don't feel you can love her any more?"

"You can't talk about lovin', not with that sort."

And again the parroco nodded.

"Look," he said reflectively, "I want to ask you a question. I'm not trying to catch you or anything. Tell me, which do you think's better, loving someone nice who pleases me or someone who treats me badly all the time? Which is—well, which is the nobler thing to do?"

The answer came at once:

"You can't—not anybody what treats you like that. There's no lovin' about it. Nobody can."

With a slight, off-hand gesture, the parroco pointed towards the picture.

"He could."

"That's not the same."

"Not the same—how?"

"Well, that was God, sort-of."

"You mean, only God can do that sort of thing—loving people who aren't fit to be loved?"

"Ye', I reckon he could."

"You don't think he can make us do it?"

"Sue says there ain't a God."

"How does she know?"

"Well, she's had a college schoolin', got it pat, the whole set-up."

"She's a clever woman? Cleverer than me?"

"No. I reckon it don't go into skirts like it do men."

With Gian's eyes on his face, the parroco gravely nodded once more. He said with a touch of shyness: "I don't know. But look—would you believe me if I told you that that man in the picture—God, I mean—if I told you he was just as much alive to me as you are?"

"Well, I d'know. They do talk that way. Good-livin' blokes. Mr Grist think that way."

"I don't just think that way," the parroco said, and as his voice fell to a new quietness its vigor was curiously increased. "I *know*. Look—I'm a selfish and very irritable creature, I always want to get my own back on people who treat me badly. And yet I can love those very people, I honestly can. And that can't come out of myself, can it? I know that it just doesn't. It's a power I've got to send for every time, I have to get the whole of my mind fixed on that man in the picture there. It's his love I've got to borrow, and I couldn't if he wasn't someone alive. Do you see what I mean—doesn't it make sense?"

Gian said: "It don't make sense with Susie. You can't do nothing with her."

"And God can't either? Not if you want him to?"

"No one don't take any notice of what I want."

Bending to light a new cigarette, the parroco asked: "You've never said any prayers?"

"Well, times I do like Mr Grist tell me. But that ain't my trade."

"But it is mine. You wouldn't object to me praying for you and your Susie?"

"Uh? I got no call to be takin' up anyone's time."

"Oh, but I don't agree! You see, it's what I'm paid for, I'm paid to be a sort of servant to people like you, people who've been mucked up . . . Yes?"

Someone at the door said: "I'm sorry, Father, the matron's rung up from the hospital, they'd like you to come. It's Brigid O'Donagh."

"Oh—very well." The parroco got up, pinched out his cigarette and tucked it away in his cassock. "Look, I probably won't be more than half-an-hour. Just stay and make yourself comfortable—have some more tea and finish up that cheese." A sudden, lopsided smile made the old man's face as droll as a schoolboy's. "You will stay, won't you! Then we can go on talking. I—I like having people like you—I have to spend so much of my time with absolute bitches of dear old ladies. You'll quite like me when you've got used to my silly voice."

The door closed, an ancient bicycle rattled down the drive.

It was as if the sun had penetrated the fog for a few moments on a November afternoon and then given up. In the emptiness Tonie's face returned, Tonie's voice, *I suppose the only thing is to leave it where it is.* And he thought, in what felt like a moment of triumph, That's what they don't understand—about Tonie: they're all so smart but they don't understand.

Released from the strange compulsion of the parroco's voice, he saw by degrees that he had been led towards a trap. He had known all along that there was a soft and easy solution: to do nothing, let things take their course as he had always done, get on with Sue as best he could: and that was the solution this voice had offered, so artfully got up in fancy words that it sounded like something brave and new. Yes, he could let things slide, feeling generous and good: Susie would settle down as she had done before, keep the place nice, hardly ever worry him. And Tonie—would she become her old self again?

Would she lose the memory of Michael's smile? Could he pretend to her that Michael's letter was nothing out of the way, that boys were always apt to change, that one was as good as the next? Could he go on talking as if her mother was good and kind and only a little out of health?

Keeping his eyes away from the picture, he began to walk about the room, as if by physical effort he could shake off the parroco's gentleness. That voice, lulling a man's sense of duty, had merely quickened the old uncertainties; while what he needed was new fuel for his anger, to make it blaze so high that it would dim the smaller flames of an ancient tenderness, of pity and fear. He knew it was 'wrong', the course on which he was all but resolved, that the punishment might go on through an after-life which had no end. For Tonie's sake he would take that as it came. Only the moment itself through which he had lived already a hundred times, a glimpse in imperfect darkness of the heart-known face, the cry of pain, this possessed him with a terror against which courage was too feeble a defence.

There was a threepenny piece in one of his waistcoat pockets: that was the railway price for a cup of tea, and in an access of dignity he put it on the tray. The staircase and hall were empty; he thought he heard someone calling after him as he went down the drive, but there was no pursuit.

They looked as permanent as the furniture of the antique shop, the bandaged youth devouring *Boy Detective,* men with splints and crutches, the row of old women huddled forlornly on a bench against the wall. Above their heads a notice said *NO Smoking or Musical Instruments. ALL Bottles given to outpatients MUST be returned.* By the end of an hour and a quarter he had moved up to the place next the door.

"Next!"

He followed the ginger-headed boy along the corridor and through the door marked O-P 2, where the smell of disinfectant suddenly increased. The very young, tired doctor stood in a corner washing his hands.

"Got the blue card?"

"First time come," the boy said.

The doctor dried his hands and turned round.

"Well, what's your trouble?"

"Well, it's not my trouble, see what I mean."

"?"

"See what I mean, it's a thing you got to have a doctor tell you, you can't get it off anyone else."

"I'm afraid I don't quite follow. Something you want to ask about? Someone ill at your home?"

"Well, it's not my home, as you might say. Well, it's a person I know, it's a lady, see. Sort of an auntie."

"Oh. And she's—what's wrong with her?"

"Well, she got her neck cut with a knife, see."

"What, badly?"

"Well, y' see, what I wanted to know about, I wanted to know about whether that hurt, whether it hurt really bad, I mean."

"Wait—I don't understand. You say some woman you know has been injured—is she being attended?"

"Well, she was—she was cuttin' some bread, see—or cuttin' meat, it might have been, an' she sort of slipped and got her neck cut—"

"—Yes, but when did this happen? Where?"

"Well, it was—well, last week that would have been—"

"Somewhere near here?"

"No, it was—it weren't anywhere near here. Leicester, it would have been. What I wanted to know about—ask a doctor, see—I wanted to know if it give her a lot of pain, gettin' a knife in her that way."

"Depends how far it went. Is she—is she recovering?"

"No, she got finished off. Peg out."

"Oh. Oh, I'm sorry. Well, it's—it's not an easy question to answer. I mean, if the wound was very deep—if certain arteries were severed—she must have died very quickly, she wouldn't have had time to suffer very much. On the other hand it's possible, of course, for a wound to be fatal but less deep, and then the patient may retain consciousness for some little time. In that case—well, of course, there must be very severe suffering. One has to hope that your friend—the lady you're interested in—one hopes that the accident caused almost immediate death. It's quite possible that it did. I—I'm sorry. It must have been very distressing news for you. I think it's quite reasonable to hope that she didn't suffer very much."

It was queer, the doctor thought (though half the people who came in here were queer, one way or another) that a tough like this should exhibit that kind of tenderness, so nice a curiosity about physical pain. The fellow looked as if he had actually been weeping. What was he, a stoker or something? Not with a suit like that, good enough for a chapel elder, an indefinable respectability which ended abruptly at the top of the waistcoat. And what was he standing like that for, as if he'd lost the use of his limbs?

The gingerhead had returned. He said jauntily:

"One more customer—five minutes to closing time."

"Not 'customer', Wicken—I'm tired of telling you. 'Patient.'"

"Not what *I'd* call him," the boy said under his breath.

The present Case remained motionless.

"Is there—anything more?" the doctor asked.

"Well, what I wanted to know, see, I wanted to know if you can get done-in that way an' not feel any pain. With a knife, I mean."

"But I think I've told you, haven't I? If the knife made a big, deep wound the patient would lose consciousness—well, almost immediately."

"A big wound? Like as if you got a strong bloke doin' it?"

"Cor, f— me!" the boy said.

"Hold your tongue, Wicken—clear out! . . . You know, I really think you'd better try to forget about your friend who had the accident. Forget about the accident, I mean. It doesn't do to brood over that sort of thing."

"Ye'. Only y' see, I wouldn't want to have her suffer no pain, see."

"No, no, of course not."

"It got to be a deep wound, that's what you said?"

"Yes—now listen, I've got another patient to see and he's been waiting a long time. I think you'd better try to forget about the accident as quickly as you can. *Wicken!* Wicken, fetch the next cust—fetch the next patient . . . Good-evening!"

Lights were on in Marylebone Road, but the day was turning back. Above the Town Hall the clouds which had been silting up all afternoon parted again, and from an aureole of smoke and sun which no one stopped to see, a yellow radiance, subtle as moonshine, re-lit the taxi-roofs and pavements and the faces pressing upon Baker Street. The re-quickened air smelt of autumn, you could not tell if it was evening or dawn. This strangeness of the unexpected and unregarded light gave an air of falsity to the business of the town; the solidity of the buildings looked false; and within the mystery and gentleness of all sensation it seemed unreal that men should cry the evening papers, that fat, bedizened women should dart between the hounding cabs to get at a milliner's shop before it shut.

As with every ordeal postponed, the delay of nightfall at once relieved and tormented him. He was glad that the sham summer of this morning was over, he had longed all day for the concealment and the narrowing of space which darkness would bring. But the night which hovered now would prove as counterfeit as the day had been, darkness without sleep or rest, no salve for the hours gone by but an infection of those to come: for these who hurried past him a blessed interval, for himself a wakeful agony which would never be enshrouded in the past. He began, as he walked slowly eastwards, to stop one person after another and ask the time; receiving no impression of what they said, earnestly thanking them, and in fifty yards or so asking again.

But at least, as night subdued the complexity of all sensation, his nerves were falling into quietness. Above the flowing stream of light the parade of buildings, losing outline, became one grey blockade against a sky streaked vividly with green and rose. That majesty overrode the fret of objects close at hand, a jeweller's daylit window, the twinkle of advertisements; and with the freshened air, with the noise of wheels and voices lowered by darkness to a steady diapason, his sick fatigue and the pain from a nail in his shoe were turned to an opiate calm. Here, with comforting tears, he could gather a picture of Tonie's face in childhood, their walks together in Kennington Park, her smiling confidence. Here, detached from the people hurrying past him on their smaller purposes, he felt the besieging darkness, the bloody stain on a sullen and tranquil sky, as companion and master of his own. The task was outside his choice, his duty was to her, its foulness to be measured against the cancer brought upon her innocence: for a while, in the dark harmony between the captured earth and his intention, his misery was transmuted by the dreadful splendour of soldierhood.

" 'Scuse me, can you tell me the time? . . . Tell me the time, please? . . . Give me the time?"

"I'm sorry, I've no watch."

"Sorry, chum."

"Look up there, mate—that's a clock, ain't it, bang in front of your eyes!"

They realized, he thought, that he was different from themselves, these people who had done a day's work and were going home to sleep in warm beds: perhaps they saw in his face what his own night's work was to be and were afraid that even his glance would befoul them. Yes, it was like a sombre dream recurring, this change in people's faces as they turned to his; this was how everyone had looked when they thought he was the man who had taken Empire's life. And now it would be for always, never again would anyone smile at him, talk to him, as if he were the same kind of creature as themselves.

With this knowledge his need for intercourse increased. From a shabby hawker on the station steps he bought a rubber duck which opened its beak and squawked. Would it do for a little girl? he asked. Yes, it would do all right for a girl. Only his little girl, he said, was nearly grown-up now. Pity, the hawker said. Had the hawker a little girl of his own? He had his stock to clear, the hawker replied, and would he mind getting out of the fuming light. A tired young woman of his own kind was struggling up the steps with a heavy case. "I'll carry that," he said, "I won't charge y'," and when she showed reluctance he took it from her almost by force. He had a girl belonging to him, he told her as they went into the station; or at least, she had belonged to him when she was small; she was nearly grown-up now, she'd had some trouble, trouble about a boy. "How old are you?" he asked. "You got a boy-friend?" But she would not say a word, as soon as the chance came she recovered her bag and hurried away. Everyone was hurrying, they bumped against him, some saying 'Sorry' and some cursing him, as he stood in the middle of the stream and peered about for someone who would be shabby, desolate and brave enough to endure a minute of his company.

"Look here," the booking-clerk said, "you've been here before! I've told you, we don't sell tickets for Italy. Book you to Preston if you like. Book you to Glasgow. Book you to *Stornoway*. But Genoa—not, *non, nein, nil*. Got that?"

"Jus' thought you might give me a sort of idea what it cost, see."

"Victoria's where you want to go."

"No, Genoa."

"Oh, for God's sake!" the passenger behind said.

Gian turned round. "Give me the time, please?"

"You've pinched about an hour of mine," the man answered grimly. "You can get the rest from someone else . . . Third-return Carlisle."

But a woman further back told him it was just on ten o'clock.

Ten o'clock? He had decided during the morning that he would start walking back to Mickett Lane at half-past twelve: that would get him home at some time after one, the house would all be dark then and Sue asleep. So this must last for two and a half hours. He stopped a porter.

"Tell me the time, please?"

"Clock over there, mate."

Beside the departure-board a child sprawled on a trunk, tired out, bewildered and apparently alone. He approached her cautiously and held out the rubber duck.

"It squeak, see. I'll show y'—only don't you be frightened, mind. It ain't real, see. There!"

The little girl stared fearfully, curiously, and at last smiled.

"Like to keep it? It belong to Tonie, only she don't need it any more. There y' are! Yes, you can keep it."

A woman hurried up. "Maur-een! What you doin', Maureen? You give that back at once!"

"I give it her," he explained.

"At once!" the woman repeated. "I've told you before, you're not to go bothering strangers."

"Tell me the time, m'm?"

"I don't know, I'm sure. Now you come on and keep close to me, Maureen."

A girl he followed as far as the tube entrance darted away when he spoke to her. He stood still for a time, idly squeaking the duck, watching the people who came past him from out of the lift. "—insists on playing every part as if it was a lead—" "—after all, a tanner's a tanner whichever way you look at it—" "—I told her, I said, You won't make him do it just nagging at him like that. If he doesn't want to, I said, Well, I said—" "—After all, Bertie, I said, it is your home—" "—flat four per cent and stop worrying. Can't have it both ways—" "—point is, I can't drop three hundred quid twice in one month and nothing to show for it—" "—why *not* put him out on the wing and bring Stevens in—" "—Well, Mr Carter, you know as well as I do, I said, the rule Mr Nicholson laid down is they've got to be on his desk by nine o'clock on Thursdays—" "—So I took her little vest, and her little nighties, and I went and washed them and hung them out before I went up to make the beds—" " 'Scuse me, can you tell me the time? . . . Give me the time? . . ." Over where steam showed against lighted windows a kitchenmaid whose walk was rather like Tonie's emerged with cups on a tray, he pursued her past the revolving doors which brought cigar smoke and the faint sound of music, she made her way swiftly through the stream which flowed towards the Edinburgh train, dodged off among stacks of crates and in the obscurity beyond them disappeared. In the tongue of darkness between circling taxi-lamps and the heaped confusion of the loading bay, where gang-men with their baskets passed like shadows against the wall, where the hollow voice announcing trains sounded curiously close, he grew cold and afraid: of the time passing, of falling asleep; frightened at once of forgetting what he had to do and of letting his mind revolve it till the old doubts and evasions gathered again. Shivering, unconsciously weeping, he limped back to the circus of rustle and clangour and yellow twilight; to stand in the shadow by a closed tobacco stall, watching the meaningless change of names on the great board, the clock which stared at him like a full and fatuous moon, the cold, contented faces passing through a dusty shaft of light towards the train; again and again asking the time.

The porter said, "If you *can't* see for yourself, it's just gone one."
"One? Morning?"
"Well, chum, if you think it *looks* like dinner time you can have it your own way."
"Uh!"

As soldiers do, he felt, crossing the Euston Road into the near-darkness of Judd Street, that the body obedient to this dreadful duty was separate from himself; that he who had loved the pageant of tulips in the Park, and familiar voices and the quietness of Weald Street Sundays, who had proudly watched the houses shaping to plans, whose voice or laugh would quiet the uproar at Apostles' Court, was merely a dumb rider tied to this creature's back. Even the pain from his heel, which bored up into his leg now, seemed to belong to someone else. He moved very slowly, clutching onto railings, keeping to the darker side.

A linotype mechanic afterwards remembered how, on his way home through Theobald's Road, he had seen a broad-backed runt of a man emerge from Lamb's Conduit Street nursing a toy of some sort and squeaking it as he went along. This drunk (as he supposed), after falling headlong at the edge of the kerb and scrambling up again, had crossed the road a yard in front of him; the mechanic had heard him muttering, ". . . don't come on Tonie, see. God 'n' Jes'-Christ, Holy Mary. All on me, see, nothin' on Tonie . . ." and had stopped to watch him limping on with a jerky resolution, 'like a tin being kicked by a schoolboy', into Bedford Row.

47

*T*HE LETTER which Edith had sent to Christine the morning before is shakily written: it must be one of the last she wrote with her own hand.

> Georgina has given me your telephone message. I have had a similar message from Raymond Hutchinson—that very kind and helpful woman Mrs Grist has been in touch with him as well. Incidentally, our cousin Raymond, who often has excellent intentions, never seems to remember that he was in great•part responsible for the marriage which has led to the present state of affairs.

(This—let me say with all respect to Edith Cepinnier's memory— was a gross travesty of the facts. At the time when Armorel told me of her engagement I had taken great pains to stress the folly, as I regarded it, of such a match; only when she had made it clear that she would accept no one's advice but her own did I agree to make the arrangements for her wedding which she desired.)

> I am very glad indeed that you have Antonia staying with you. I hope that it may be possible for you to keep her until there is news that Armorel's peculiar state of mind has altered.
> I have written to Rellie herself at some length with all the wisdom and forbearance I can find, and not without seeking God's guidance. At present, I see nothing more that I can do. I have, as you know, been a total invalid for some time past . . .

Yet when the hired car drew up in Mickett Lane—that museum-piece of a car which Heald had occasionally seen arriving a year or two before—he caught a glimpse of a second old woman sitting beside the one he knew. Neither got out. The senile driver was sent to knock at the door.

Heald looked at his watch: he thought it late for old ladies to be paying a call—on towards eight o'clock.

He saw Daise come out and stand talking for some time at the window of the car, first bovine and then tearful. (She was in a bad way, Daise: she had blubbered a good deal this morning when he told her that Gian had gone off in the night.) Presently, after Daise had returned indoors, Mrs Grist appeared and the old ladies had some conversation with her. Then the car was turned and driven away.

With many cushions wedged behind her back, Edith sat almost upright, looking with absolute indifference at the paralysing beauty of the smoky river lit by the afterglow, at once-familiar streets, at the crowd on the pavement.

"Ask Mr Bates," she said, "if he can drive a little faster. We're not at a funeral."

"But, Edie, I specially told him to go as slowly as he could. I didn't want him to shake you. It might—it might be dangerous."

"That doesn't matter at all."

"Faster, Mr Bates!" Georgina called through the partition, and a sense of excitement, girlish and wicked, passed over her again. Suppressing it, she sat back, red and faintly smiling.

"Some joke?" Edith inquired.

"Joke? No, I don't think so. No, I'm certain . . . Edie, I can't help feeling—I do really think we should have waited for Rellie to come back as Mrs Grist said."

"She might not go home till very late. Then I shouldn't have been fit to see her when she did come."

"I mean, we don't really know what kind of meeting this is that she's attending—"

"—By what Mrs Grist told us, it's merely a small group of female atheists—"

"—And I mean, it being in a hotel, and there may be lots of people—in the hotel, I mean—and it might upset Rellie. I suppose our clothes aren't what people are wearing nowadays."

"Well, Georgie, if you really want to, you can stop and buy a pair of boy's trousers—I believe that's the fashionable thing for women to wear now. I hadn't realized you had that kind of ambition."

"No, but I do think everything would have been much easier in that little house of Rellie's. You see, we don't often go to hotels at all."

Edith, struggling with atrocious pain, said thinly: "Georgie, I'm sorry, but I cannot bear all this fuss. Our grandfather *owned* the St Pancras Hotel. If you're too frightened to go in and find Rellie you can stay in the motor. I'll go in myself."

"Oh, no, Edie, you couldn't possibly! It's going to be hard enough getting you out of the car when we get home."

The car had stopped. The driver opened the door.

"This is the hotel. You want to go in, m'm?"

Edith said: "Miss Georgina will go in."

Georgina was suddenly terrified.

"But, Edie, what am I to say? What shall I tell her?"

"You needn't say anything. I've written a note—here—just give her this and ask her to read it."

The note (which Georgina never saw) was in the kind of envelope used at Cromer's Ride for at least twenty-five years. Containing only a dozen words, it was totally different from any other letter which Edith ever wrote: *'Darling, darling Rellie. Do please, please come and see your loving old aunt Edie.'*

The driver helped Georgina on to the pavement.

"And you'll stay where you are, Miss Edith?"

"I—yes, I think so. Yes, I—yes."

Absurdly, the entrance lounge possessed Georgina with an intense delight. She knew that this, of all occasions, was one for anxiety and grief. She knew—a mirror told her—that her appearance here was grotesque. Yet the size of the place and the warm light which flooded it, the wealthy smells, the saccharine air that a string quartette was playing beyond the banked hydrangeas, these enclosed her like a virgin's dream. Such worldliness! But the thought came: Could heaven perhaps be deliciously like this? Blinking, panting from the effort of mounting the steps and negotiating the revolving door, she stood in the middle of the gangway, greatly ashamed of her reflections, and giggled like a girl.

A waiter returning from the coffee tables offered to assist.

"What a lovely hotel!" she said.

The waiter believed so. "You are meeting someone, madame?"

"Meeting someone? Oh! Oh, I should like to see Rellie—Armorel."

"Your who, madame? . . . Mrs Ardree? She is staying in the hotel?"

"Well, Mrs Grist didn't say so."

"She is with Mrs Paucrine's party, perhaps?"

"Oh, perhaps."

"That's in the Liverpool Room."

A boy to whom she was entrusted led her through a greater length of corridors than she had thought possible in one building. Such carpets! Heaven could surely have nothing *softer* for your feet. But if heaven was suitable for Edie—which no one could doubt—it would never be so luxurious as this.

"In here, m'm."

The child opened a door. Terrified, she went inside.

A screen mercifully hid her as she stood only a yard from the door, nerveless and longing to be at home. Beyond the screen some woman was speaking on a rather high note; between her sentences came flutters of applause, and the smothered noise, which sounded curious here, of locomotives discharging steam. It was a little time before Georgina recognized that public voice as belonging to Armorel herself.

". . . In my daily life—in the poorer part of London where I live—I am always meeting cases of needless misery due to people being haunted with a sense of having done *wrong*, instead of realizing that they've simply acted without intelligence. That's what makes me feel that it's worth-while giving my time, giving everything I've got to give, to fighting against this bogey, this mediaeval notion of guilt as a kind of microbe which attacks everybody and yet everybody's got to be ashamed of. And that's why I mean to go on fighting against it till my dying day. I must say again, I think it's really wonderful of you to have given me this beautiful vase. I shall always treasure it gratefully as a souvenir of many friendships which I value more than I say."

Before the clapping had stopped chairs were scraping and a buzz of many voices began. Georgina peeped round the screen.

Armorel caught sight of her almost at once. She excused herself from the blue-caparisoned woman who was talking into her face and came smiling across the room. She looked happy, Georgina thought in that moment, and very beautiful; perhaps a little pale in the dark chiffon dress—and naturally the speech making would have strained her—but alight with excitement and zest.

"Georgie—what a surprise—how lovely of you—how did you know where to find me?"

The cigarette smoke had got into Georgina's eyes. She said, accepting Armorel's kiss: "It was Edie, it was all Edie's idea. I'm ever so sorry. These clothes—I didn't think of coming here—you needn't say I'm anything to do with you—"

"I think they're perfect! . . . Audrey, do come and meet my favourite aunt—Georgie, this is Miss Owesson, and Mrs Bestwell-Deakin, and Mrs Fuce—my aunt, Miss Cepinnier. Georgie, wait one minute, I've left my bag on the table."

"Wasn't it a perfect little speech!" Mrs Fuce said. "You must feel terribly proud of your niece! You *will* have a glass of sherry, or would you rather tea? It's her sincerity which makes her such a wonderful speaker, I always say. She makes me feel that I've been lifted up into a higher realm of thought. Don't you feel like that, Ursula?"

"Born organizer! Better than a man!"

"And yet, you know, so wonderfully modest about it all."

"Works like a Trojan."

"You will have some coffee?"

"Miss Spinner ought to come to one of our big do's. You've no idea how exhilarating they are. Really wonderful speakers, we get sometimes. Really vital minds. They really do make you feel that you're getting right down to grips with the real problems."

"But you know, Letitia, I find a small friendly meeting like to-night is a very real help. You get thoughts that you can carry away with you. You feel that it clarifies your mind—it's very hard to put it into words—sometimes you hear something which is like a great light shining and clearing away all the old cobwebs of obscurantism and superstition."

"Wasn't Mrs Ardree wonderful!"

"My dear, what wouldn't I give for a mind like hers!"

Armorel had got her bag and was slowly picking her way back through the thicket of her friends.

"Darling, you were wonderful!"

"It was a lovely speech, dear, really it was! It was so exactly right for the occasion, and yet it wasn't just a complimentary speech, it had real thought in it. There was something for every one of us to take away."

"Oh, that's terribly kind of you. Do come and meet my aunt—Georgie, this is a colleague of mine, Stella Jegg. Stella really does all my work for me and I get all the credit."

Someone had found Georgina a chair, someone a cup of tea. And she had given up hope. Beneath the thresh of high, incisive voices, the bewilderment of tinctured faces which appeared close to hers and faded into the nightmare dance, even her vision of Edith sitting in pain and fury outside became too faint to have effect. Rellie: she was there to fetch little Rellie: but the handsome, regnant woman that Rellie had become was part of this intricacy of shapes and tearing sound, no more at call than the strident personage now roaring in her ear, "I would never kowtow to my constituents—would you!" She threw a whisper:

"Rellie!"

"Aunt Georgie, this is another very good friend of mine, Mrs Rowland Wicknell."

"Oh, how do you do!"

"Isn't it a lovely party! Wasn't she marvellous!"

"I do hope you're going to join the Movement, Miss Spinner? We do want every shoulder to the pump in these days, young and old alike."

"Such a sweet dress!"

"Do give Miss Pinner some more tea."

"If only some of those bishops could have heard her!"

"Couldn't stand up to it, my dear. No mental guts."

"Or one of these sandwiches, they're rather duck."

She tried again: "Rellie! Rellie, I should like—could I talk to you, just a moment or two—"

"But of course, Georgie! . . . Hilda, I'll be back in a moment, my aunt's finding it rather stuffy—"

Georgina was back in the corridor, her head swimming, Rellie holding her arm.

"Georgie darling, you are naughty—you shouldn't have come into that stuffy room—all that noise. How stupid of the hotel people, they could easily have fetched me down—"

"Oh, but, Rellie, it was wonderful. You making a speech—all those people—they all thought it was so splendid, they all seemed so fond of you. Of course Edie would say it was wrong—"

"It's really just a bore," Armorel said, "all that bouquet-throwing." And already the flame of her excitement was out, leaving only the pallor and a weariness in the eyes that made them look like an old woman's. "You get nothing done at that sort of meeting, it's the committee work that really counts . . . There's—nothing wrong, is there?"

Committee work, Georgina thought: that was what Edie had always talked about in the old days. What did they mean? There was something about Minutes and Points of Order . . . And Edie waiting out there all this time . . . They were moving slowly along the passage. She said:

"What? Oh, no, nothing wrong. Only there was a message—Edie had a message from Christine. On the telephone. Edie's nurse took it—she may have got it all wrong—"

"About Tonie? Tonie isn't ill or anything?"

"Ill? Oh, there was a note. Edie gave it me to give to you. She's in the car."

Armorel took the note but did not open it.

"In the car? Where?"

"Where you go into the hotel. Oh, Rellie, it was funny, those roundabout doors—"

Armorel came to a halt.

"Aunt Edie? *Here?*"

In fact, Edith was nearer than Georgina had said. They had turned a corner; along the shorter corridor where they now stood the boy who had conducted Georgina was sauntering towards them, whistling softly as if he were taking a walk in the country; and then, at the far end, they saw Edith herself.

When Edith caught sight of them she stopped, as if the very little momentum which carried her forward had petered out. She had one hand against the wall, and she was bent like a bow in tension, but she stood with perfect steadiness, with a frightening immobility of body and of face. Georgina started towards her and then wavered. The sight of Edie on her feet, and rigid like that, deprived her of power to move or speak. But worse followed. Her sister's features moved, stiffly, to form what was meant to be a smile.

Mastering herself, Georgina ran, yes, ran, to her sister's support. But with her free hand Edith motioned her aside. She called in a voice that was very small but clear and gentle:

"Rellie! Rellie, do come to me."

As if compelled, Armorel came slowly to where she could have touched Edith by putting out her hand.

Georgina, lost and useless, stared fearfully at Edith's bloodless face, and perceived that the smile was altering. It moved from the dry, faintly moustached mouth to the eyes, where, incredulously, she saw the coming of tears. Her frightened glance slipped round to Armorel. In her face surely, oh, surely, there would be an answering light. And she did for an instant see the damp of pity in those burdened eyes, she did see such a shy and fleeting smile as Rellie had once used to greet her in the panelled hall at Hayward's Heath.

That smile was lost, like an early snowflake which comes on unwelcoming soil. Looking at Edith's face, but not at her eyes, Armorel said with the touchy solicitude of elderly nurses: "Aunt Edith—surely it's—it's foolish, coming out like this!"

Edith worked for breath. "Yes. Yes, we are both—rather foolish women. But I—I wanted to see you. I heard—I heard you were unhappy. I—you know—I'm often unhappy."

Armorel said quickly: "No, Aunt Edith, that isn't true, I'm not unhappy, you can't be unhappy if you always know your own mind as I do."

There was silence, and Edith's next attempt to speak gave out, as when an engine is asked to move too great a load. To Georgina, herself scarcely able to go on standing, it seemed that not even Edith's will could summon the force to keep her upright and to let her speak again.

Not far away there were voices and laughter. Someone called: "Where *has* Armorel got to?"

"You can't—you mustn't keep standing!" Armorel said, looking about her like a trapped creature. "Page!"—the boy was still lurking inquisitively at the end of the passage—"Page, go and get someone, some man. Be quick!" She had moved to support Edith by the arm. She said distractedly, her eyes following the page: "It was very good of you to come."

Edith was not smiling any more: with most of her weight on Armorel's arm, with the muscles of her face fallen slack, she hardly looked like a living woman. But when she spoke again her whispering voice was steadier than before:

"You see, I just thought you might be ready. Ready to come to me again. You see—Rellie—people need love. God's love and other people's. And I've got so much for you."

The porter who came, with one of the waiters, was efficient and kind. Yes, straight to the car, Georgina said, and they took Edith there, so swiftly (and yet with gentleness) that people in the entrance lounge hardly noticed anything unusual occurring. Armorel followed them, and when Edith had been settled in the car she stood by the rear window. She said again, rather breathlessly and with an undirected smile that seemed to be weighed down with the evening's weariness: "I

—it was very good of you to come." Then she went back into the hotel and got her coat, ignoring the civilities of the friends she passed in the corridor, and left by the station exit, and got on the tube to go home.

48

SHE FOUND Mrs Inch creeping about in the front passage as she often did, and asked casually:

"Has Mr Ardree come home, do you know?"

"From what I been told," the old woman said, "he's not *likely* to come home. From what his pa tell me, over with Tim Heald there—"

Armorel said, "That isn't what I asked you," and went on upstairs.

There was a light under the Grists' door, and from the little room at the turn of the passage she could hear Olleroyd's leonine snore. Yet the house felt empty, and damp, as if it had not been lived in for some time. She looked into Gian's room and saw the bed just as she had made it the day before.

What was it Tonie had said just before she went to Christine? It didn't matter, the child was in an emotional stage, normal in middle puberty. What was it, though? Oh, it couldn't matter.

She opened a drawer of Tonie's chest, took out some of the clothes and felt them carefully. Yes, everything was slightly damp. She would hang these out tomorrow and tell Mrs Inch to take them in if it rained —not that Mrs Inch would remember. What was on tomorrow? No, it would be better to hang them in the kitchen. Not tomorrow (What was on tomorrow?) but later on, just before Tonie came back. (When was Tonie coming back? What had she said?) Then they might still feel cosy when Tonie put them on. Perhaps Tonie really ought to have a room to herself—it could be done if she made one more effort to get Olleroyd into some home for old men—and yet she would rather keep Tonie in here. This room might be made to feel more as if it belonged to Tonie: she could give her a free hand to alter pictures and hangings. After all, there was nothing here that she cared about for herself. The bedroom at Weald Street had possessed some character, perhaps because she had made it out of such a pigsty; this one was an assembly of furniture and nothing more. Perhaps the best thing would be to move to another house, and let Tonie arrange the rooms as she wished: with so good an instinct for her own clothes, Tonie might stumble on a way of grouping things so that the feel of a room, its lights and smell, would have the gentleness which had never been wakened here.

That was, if Tonie would come. She was handling a crêpe de chine petticoat of Tonie's and she held it against her cheek. Yes, if it was fine tomorrow she would hang everything outside.

She began to undress in the idle way that children use, lounging on the side of the bed and leaving the clothes where they fell; letting a dimly coloured film of Weald Street pass hurtfully before her mind's strained eyes while her body's were shut. She was ready for bed when she noticed a tray of tea-things with a plate of clumsy sandwiches on a chair by the door. That, of course, was Elizabeth's work, as the unmatched cup and saucer would alone have witnessed. Apparently it gratified some histrionic vanity of Elizabeth's to perform these needless services, but there was something ridiculous and faintly offensive in the practice when, as now, they two were estranged. If she resolutely ignored such benefactions they would probably cease.

But the need for someone, anyone, to exchange a few words with had suddenly increased in vehemence. Tomorrow she would wake to emptiness, she would breakfast reading the paper and Daise—if she had returned to normal—would bring flat gossip about people along the street . . . The tonelessness into which this room had fallen, the silence which it caught like an infection from the house's creeping silences, were too much for a tired woman to endure alone. She put on her dressing-gown and went into the passage, where she called: "Elizabeth! I'd like to speak to you."

Lying back on her bed with the petticoat against her face, wondering if Elizabeth would come, she felt her mind starting to drag once more at the question of Michael, as a tearful child tries to straighten a piece of knitting which has gone all wrong. Was that what Tonie really demanded, would she never again warm the house with her voice and smile unless Michael were restored? But then, could Armorel restore him? What exactly had she written in her letter, that confused, unreal night—was it something that by any means could be reversed? In America, Elizabeth had said: Gordon had been in America all the time. Was that another of Elizabeth's inventions? It was hard to remember things after this evening's strains and disturbances. Suppose

Elizabeth died—now, quite soon: if Elizabeth were dead, she mused, she could study the problem of Michael from fresh points of view. Michael himself: she could find no harm in him. Perhaps, if she could talk to Tonie again . . .

Elizabeth's tired voice at the open door: "Did you call me?"

As she saw in one glance Elizabeth's draggling hair, her face flaccid and colourless, the brown linen dress which had lost all its shape, the reflection came: No reason to prolong the struggle with this woman who stands in the doorway like a lazy chambermaid. With the one Elizabeth had been, lovely and secret, for ever usurping life's quintessences, yes. Not with a spent creature like this.

Unless the sick exhaustion were just one more device.

She said: "There's a chair just beside you—to your left. I only wanted to say, it was kind of you to make those sandwiches, but I don't eat anything at night."

"I just thought—"

"Oh, and I wondered just why you sent my aunts on to the hotel. I suppose that was you? I thought I'd made it clear—I left the address just in case Gian came in and wanted to know where I was."

"But didn't you want to see them? They'd come all the way from Streatham."

"Well, as a matter of fact I'm not thinking of what I wanted. It was much too great a strain for an old woman like Edith—they shouldn't have ventured out at all. It was all—well—very upsetting. Still, I suppose you didn't realize. Well, good-night."

She let her eyes close, but when she opened them again Elizabeth was still there. And now she found her presence intolerable. The blind, with their still and empty eyes, seemed always to be hunting you from a screen of safety. She asked, with a tremor:

"Is there something you want?"

And then she said more pacifically:

"I'm sorry about Trevon. I hear the journey—that trip he made to Leicester—I hear it was rather too much for him."

Elizabeth did not answer that. "You saw the paper?" she asked. "That paper I put on the tray?"

"No. What is it, a letter?"

"No." Elizabeth was feeling out for the tray. "No, it's a paper for you to sign. There may be mistakes—I typed it myself—but I think it's more or less all right."

Armorel went and took the paper which Elizabeth's fingers had found. She read, in the clumsy typescript: 'By this I acknowledge that the statement I made in my letter to Michael Kinfowell about Antonia Ardree's parentage was completely untrue. Signed . . .' She put the paper down on the bed.

"Elizabeth, is this some sort of joke?"

Elizabeth said: "I want that to send to Michael first of all. And to show Gian. Of course, nothing can undo all the harm that's been done, but that will help."

That voice, was it really Elizabeth's? Had the loss of sight corrupted her speech as well? Armorel said:

"You don't really think I'd sign a thing like this? Just because you asked me?"

"You've got to."

"Got to?"

"Otherwise I'll give that letter to Gordon Aquillard, that letter you wrote to Michael."

"You can't. You don't know where he is now."

"I can send it through Duffy. And I can ask him to bring an action, for my sake."

Armorel said suddenly: "I want to see it—that letter—I can't remember what I said."

"You do remember."

"Where is it?"

"I haven't got it. Trevon's still got it."

"Well, then, I must get it from him—"

Elizabeth had her back against the door.

"No!" she said. "He's ill—he's very ill. You're not going anywhere near him."

"Then *you* must get it."

"No!"

In the close, expectant calm, Armorel watched through half-closed eyes the image of Elizabeth receding and approaching; now oddly clear; the stain on the brown dress like a child's drawing of a swan, pale runnels serpenting from the soiled creases below the eyes. A little colour had returned. It was the same Elizabeth, beautiful even now, for ever to be loved, for ever demanding love's subservience. She said impassively:

"I'll talk about that tomorrow. I'll talk to Gian."

"To Gian? Do you think he's coming back?"

Armorel said, still patiently: "You know, I've had rather a stiff evening. I should have thought you could see I'm fairly tired—"

"I can't see," Elizabeth said. "I'm glad, really. If I could see you I'd start pitying you and loving you again. Now I can only see you as you are really."

"Will you please go away!"

"I've been persuading myself—all these years—I've been telling myself there must be something inside you to make you look so lovely and gentle. I thought I could see it sometimes. I've thought how things would look from where you are—I'm a woman, I've got my own confusions and feebleness—I thought you were merely scared and lonely, I thought if I tried hard enough I could find my way to some reality, something human—"

"—I'm not listening. Will you go away—"

"—but there isn't anything. I know now. Nothing but greedy selfishness. Nothing but cheap little envies and infantile conceits."

Armorel moved towards the door. "I'm going to see Trevon. I want that letter. And I'm going to tell him to keep you under control."

She seized the handle of the door and jerked it open. Elizabeth, thrown off her balance by this unexpected violence, fell on one knee. In an instant she was up again, grabbed wildly and caught hold of Armorel's arm.

"You're not to go—he's ill!"

"Let go!"

"You're not—"

As Elizabeth felt it, the blow might have been struck with a weighted thong. It was actually the ring on Armorel's left hand which caught her on the bone of her cheek, lighting so fierce a pain that for a moment she was stupefied; and she found herself whimpering, as a child would, while she groped for the doorway, which was clear. As she steered herself along the passage wall she heard Armorel's voice behind her, subdued and broken, "All right—go to him—go—!" followed by the bang of her door, and then, faintly, what sounded like a tempest of stifled laughter, submerged by degrees in the shallow, continuous stream of noises from the street.

She went to sponge her face, and waited for her breathing to become normal again, before she returned to her own room.

This was like a hideous journey ending in summer. Here, while the warmth of anger stayed in her blood, its hurt had ceased; here the current of experience, split and tumbled by a jagged reef, gathered to flow calmly again. With the smell of the room, the roughness of the tablecloth, its colours returned; warmer than those she had once seen, glowing orange on soft and ruddy shades of umber, liquid crimson and shadowed purple merging in stygian blue. Sitting still, she took in the closely remembered objects one by one: the Dürer engraving by the door, a little walnut desk she had been allowed to bring from Easterhatch, the polychrome of books on a shelf beneath the window: (the flowers beside the sewing-machine, would they have faded since Friday—would Trevon have told her?); delighting in their nearness, seeking from their permanence some small security to outlast this hour.

As a child delays opening the best of his birthday parcels, the tour brought her slowly to Trevon's chair: the old wicker chair, with its smell of bleach and its worn upholstery of faded blue. Blue? Or greeny-grey?—it did not matter, she had it as a whole. And the soiled burberry he wore for a dressing-gown, pocked with little burns, she had the look of that as if she could see it now. She would keep that coat, a thing her fingers could examine again and again, she would always have it close to her at night; for to feel it would be a little like feeling his rough skin, a little of his smell might stay in its folds, its very dilapidation would open springs of peculiar sweetness in her memory. He was all untidiness, she thought, breathing gently the faint tobacco smell in the comfortable darkness: patron of cheap barbers and dealers in shoddy clothes, a man of infinite hesitations, whose sternness had been wrapped in bluster and whose gentler virtues were screened by graceless foible: and never had a legion of imperfections been knit to form a creature so whole in sympathy, so perfect to possess. It would seem in years to come (not many, she prayed, not many of those) that her life with him had been only a fleeting interval between the unreality before and the emptiness which followed. But could happiness so profound and so resplendent be shrunk with the time in which it was borne! The darkness was tightening a little, grey clouds blown before grey curtains, the warm throbbing of the pain in her cheek lulled her towards sleep. Flowers, she thought, tomorrow I must buy new flowers, Olleroyd will take me to Wherry Lane where I can get them cheaper from the barrows. Dahlias? He liked red flowers.

Since her return his chair had not creaked. She listened for the sound of his breathing, usually stertorous at this hour, and heard nothing. Suddenly frightened, she whispered:

"Trevon! Are you asleep?"

"Asleep?" he said. "No, not now."

She went to grasp his hand, which was cold.

"What have you been doing?"

"Watching you smile."

"Your hand's cold," she said. "I'll get the fire going. Or shall I get you into bed now?"

"No, I don't feel cold. I thought Flock would come—I want to see Flock, I don't know what's happening at the Club. I'll go round tomorrow—I don't care what that fellow Bautz says, he's only a child, he doesn't know anything."

"We'll see how you feel tomorrow."

"When did I last go to the Club?"

"Oh, about a week ago—I can't quite remember. Your hands are terribly cold."

"I don't feel them, I only feel yours. Yours are beautiful. I don't feel things now."

He broke unexpectedly into laughter, his old, gusty laugh, but narrowed so that it sounded like an over-used recording: enough to bring his face to her in high relief, the peculiar folding of his mouth, the way the flesh drew tight on one side while the other broke in deep and forking crevices. And his voice, so low it would not have been audible on the other side of the room, came crinkling with gaiety.

"Call himself a doctor—Bautz—ordering me about! First time I met that fellow he was piddling on the steps of the County Hall. Little bastard to deal with, always. Put Flock on him—you remember Flock? I said, 'That fellow Bautz, he wants a hiding.' He wouldn't at first. 'Bloke got no father nor mother, sir.' Sentimental old possum! I told him, 'That's why you've got to thrash him.' Then Bautz came to me—next morning, it was. 'What's wrong, Bautz?' 'Very sorry, Mr Grist, had a knock-up with the sergeant, hurt him pretty bad, reckon I might've killed him, Mr Grist!' Chap like that ordering me about, talking like a medical dictionary, telling me I can't go to the Club!"

"He does his best," she said.

"He does more than his best. Bautz? There's nothing wrong with Bautz, he's bloody fine. Got himself through Guy's, absolutely nothing behind him except his own guts. Fellow like that—"

He caught his breath, she knew he was in pain again.

"Darling, it's hurting you, talking—"

"Those boys," he whispered, "you know, they're bloody queer. Never break a promise. Not one of them—all the time—not one of them's ever broken a promise he made to me personally. I can't see why. You get a person like me, and you get them. I get the thing all mucked up and they never do. I don't see where their virtue comes from, I don't see *why* they're so brave and so bloody unselfish. I went to see that fellow—you know, the old cop—Hubbitt. That fellow smashed him up, you know. Ardree. He said to me—old Hubbitt—he said, 'Well, if I can do anything to help the lad you've only got to say.' I mean, a fellow like that, he makes you feel like something on the ape level. I sometimes wish to God they wouldn't be so bloody kind. Where's that book—my little book? I made a note, didn't I? Ardree. I've got to look him up, see what sort of place he lives in. Used to come to the Club. Cuddish was talking about him."

"Darling, I think I ought to get you to bed now. Otherwise you'll get that pain again."

"Pain? It doesn't matter, I don't mind it now. Elizabeth! Elizabeth, listen—have I been stupid again? Have I been saying something silly, something to hurt you? I don't want to hurt you—I couldn't, I couldn't hurt anything so precious as you. I've hurt you so much, I—"

"You've never hurt me," she said. "You're tired, you're a bit muddly."

"You're tired, too," he said gravely. "You oughtn't to do things. We might get Slimey." His voice changed, like that of a man shaking himself clear of sleep. "Muddly? No, I'm not muddly, I'm clear, I've never been so clear as I am now."

She said as a mother would: "Oh, I'm glad!"

"So clear," he repeated firmly. "It's a special clearness, it makes you ridiculously happy. You see, I never let myself enjoy any happiness before. I wanted—do you see?—I wanted to buy my own release by not being happy. I thought there must be some trick, it didn't seem possible, it wasn't right, those boys, one lot after another, all doing things for me, all treating me as if I was just as good as themselves. And then you came, and it seemed more impossible than ever. You accepting me like that. And oh, God, what you've had to pay—"

"—No!" she said. "No!—"

"—And I thought—it wasn't thinking, it was just feeling—I

thought, if I could only make myself less happy there wouldn't be so much for her to pay."

"I know," she said, "but, Trevon darling—"

"But it's gone!" he said quietly. "I accept everything now, I just accept it. Your love and all your goodness, I just accept that I was meant to have it—I can't think why—I take it and all the happiness that comes with it, the perfect happiness. I wish I could tell you how it feels."

She could hear that the effort of speaking had become more painful, but she did not try to stop him again.

"You see, I always had the idea that God was demanding payment from me for what I'd done. It's the idea pagans have. I knew in theory that Christ didn't, but I didn't believe it. You can't grasp an idea like that, the idea of love being so powerful, love cancelling what's gone already, Christ's love obliterating the anger of God. I mean, *I* couldn't. Not till I got like this—so clear. I suppose you taught me, you've taught me everything—"

In less than a whisper, "Me?" she said.

"Your love." He was speaking as a child fits the pieces of a puzzle he has done before. "I thought of love as only something you feel. All gentleness. I never saw it was made from self-defeat. I didn't realize it could sweat and fight, with nothing fit to command it."

The noises of the street had perceptibly fallen, the air in the room had the chill of middle night. So close that it might have been a flutter in her own resilient nerves, the sound which she always dreaded and which he did not seem to notice had begun again: a scraping in his chest that was like a separate voice. She ought to be stirring, to be putting on a kettle, getting the medicine. But the warmth restrained her, the coloured warmth of the softly folding darkness, the feel of his bony, hirsute wrist against her cheek, a stillness like the afterwave of music. In a little while, when the splendour had cooled, perhaps when the sound of footsteps or a boy whistling told her it was morning, she would try again to overtake the arrears of routine: slowly tidying, fumbling for brushes, scissors, clean pillow-slips, pondering how long the tea-cloth had been in use. Till then, the stronger voice commanded her to rest: not to question or to understand, simply to hold this moment's preciousness in so steady, so delicate a grasp that it might not ever recede. At least she would wait until he slept.

Perhaps he was asleep already: often, in illness, when he spoke most wakefully he would fall into a doze with a sentence unfinished. But when she moved a little to listen more closely to his breathing he spoke again, and his voice was stronger than before.

"You've hurt yourself—your face! What have you done?"

"It isn't anything," she answered, "I can hardly feel it now. I was stupid, I knocked it against the side of Rellie's door."

"Door? Yes," he said, finding his way back, "yes, I remember, Susie was calling, you went to see her. Susie—is she all right?"

"Yes, she's all right."

"Yes," he repeated, "I remember. I want to see Gian, I must see him, it's terribly important. He'll do something silly if I don't see him. Gian—is he there, has he come back?"

"No, I don't think so. Darling, don't worry now, I'll try and get him for you in the morning."

He seemed to accept that. But presently he said:

"And she's all alone, poor Susie! It's so much worse for a creature like her. I mean, you can live inside yourself if it isn't a self you loathe and detest."

She said quietly: "She doesn't. Trevon, she doesn't, she thinks she's never been wrong, she thinks there's nothing in her to be ashamed of."

"I ought to see her," he insisted. "You see, she's lonely now—"

"—She doesn't mind! She's always lived like that—"

"—She's lonely, I think she'd talk to me, people sometimes talk to you when they're lonely."

"But, darling, she's gone to bed now, she's probably asleep. I'll ask her tomorrow."

"Asleep? No. No, when people are like that they don't sleep."

Elizabeth said patiently: "She was just getting to bed when I saw her. I'm sure she must be asleep."

But even then she heard someone moving in the passage. She released his hand, went by way of the table-edge to the door and turned the key.

The step passed and re-passed; of someone treading softly, as if guiltily; along the passage and back again, along and back again. At last they heard a tap on the door, and Armorel's voice:

"Can I come in?"

At once Elizabeth answered:

"No! He's ill. You can't."

The handle was turned and the door pushed sharply against the lock. Then the steps receded.

Elizabeth returned to the chair, stooped and got her wrists into his armpits. "Darling, I'm going to get you into bed now." But tonight he made no move to help. He asked:

"Beloved, why can't she come?"

"You've done enough for today," she said quickly, "you've been up much too long—"

He still resisted.

"You'll let her come and see me when I'm in bed?"

Elizabeth stopped trying to lift him. She said, distraught:

"You can't—you're not fit for it! You're ill—you must realize that—you're not fit to talk to people, it's a strain, it's too much for you. Don't make me, darling—I can't, I can't let her. She's done enough, trying to poison everyone's lives because she's too cheap and selfish to manage her own. I can't—we've got so little left, so little time."

He echoed: "Yes, so little time—and so little I've done, so little that was any use. If only—"

"Trevon, she's dangerous!" she said frantically. "This bruise you saw, she gave me that. She doesn't know what she's doing or saying. I can't protect you, not if she gets in here. She might do the same thing to you. Trevon, don't make me—please—please don't make me!"

He got hold of her hand and placed it, in a way he had, under his chin. He said with a patient simplicity:

"She's all alone. And we've got so much."

After a while Elizabeth went to unlock the door; and when, a few moments later, they heard Armorel's voice again, calling strangely, "I've got to come in!" she answered,

"Yes, come in!"

For some time the lamp shade had been torn, and the light which fell towards the fire-place was full and harsh. It displayed to Armorel, as she came from the semi-darkness of the passage, the room's detailed penuries, chipped paint, the Woolworth fire-irons; it showed frayed edges that she herself would quickly have rebound, the hearth stained with spilt cocoa, segments on the mantelshelf which the duster had missed: the aroma less of genteel distress than of barren insensibility. This was the place towards which some virulent curiosity had driven her, and this was all: a room wilted from neglect, the ruin of a man with a dirty raincoat slumped in a basket chair, a woman whose looks had gone for ever sitting on the floor with her neck against his thigh. Nothing but that. There were unwashed cups on the table and the curtains had not been drawn.

(Could Elizabeth know he had got to look like this, his skin like cardboard ash, his bright, wet eyes sunk far into their livid cavities, the lips shrivelled to show hideously his gums and teeth? 'He's very ill,' Elizabeth had said; but did she realize this?)

Trevon said, "Susie, come and sit down!" and she looked for a chair. "No, here!" he said.

In tired obedience she sat on the stool table close to the left arm of his chair.

But how little her presence matters, Elizabeth thought, feeling faintly the new warmth brought by Armorel's breath, smelling her hair, while the fluttered folds of her own tranquillity fell back into place, while the echoes which had stopped began to sound once more. He had wanted this, and the most he wanted in this hour was too little for her to give. Perhaps her own possession had never been complete, perhaps there had always been some need in him, as once in poor distracted Gordon, which only Rellie could have satisfied. Strangely, the touch of that surmise provoked no bitterness, no pain. His body, she thought, has belonged to me, its power and feebleness, its need to be comforted; in his mind I have found dark places, but no doors locked, his spirit's warmth has been for me alone and the beauties there which pudency has hidden from all others have been unveiled for me. Tonight, when the last stone of our union has seemed to be laid in place, possession has lost significance. Already I can feel his state is changing, as the state of substance changes under heat, and as life within the womb is not enough for the foetus grown animate, so the world of voice and touch, thoughts and emotions interchanged, has become too narrow for his metamorphosis. What we have possessed together and secretly is complete, no one can damage or take it away. The rest does not belong to any creature, and if strangers see the light in his face which I see, it is their possession as well as mine.

His body stirred. What was the time? The city's voice was all but silent, surely she had meant an hour ago to put him to bed. No, someone had come in, someone she knew well and who had hurt her: Rellie, who had written that letter to Michael, Rellie was here. She felt no excitement, only an exhausted anger, for surely the subterranean war, unwanted and undeclared, had come to its end. She said sleepily, across the long silence:

"Rellie wants that letter she wrote to Michael. You've got it, haven't you?"

And when seconds had passed, she heard Armorel saying: "No, I don't want it now."

The voice was small but composed. "I've decided," Armorel said, "I shall write to him again. I shall tell him I was unwell when I sent that other letter—I was suffering from some interference with memory."

"Yes?"

"I don't think you quite realize, I've been living under rather a strain. I mean, when one's husband—well, you know what Gian is, and you know what he was supposed to have done—what everyone thought he'd done, whatever the Court said."

"Yes."

"You see, I have to take a long-term view of things. It's nice for Tonie and Michael to be friends, but that doesn't necessarily mean that they're suited to each other as partners for life. Michael's used to a lot of money, and moneyed people. Tonie's been brought up to realize that she's got to make her own way. She's very strong-willed—when Michael got older he might find her very different from what she seemed as a child. These things develop faster than you think if you're not wide awake."

Elizabeth asked, without acerbity: "Rellie, is it any use talking about all that?"

"I want you to realize that I'm not so unreasonable as you think. I know I made a mistake, when I was under a great strain—"

"It doesn't matter," Elizabeth said wearily. "It really doesn't matter, how you talk about things. If you want to call it 'making a mistake' —well, it doesn't matter."

Armorel's voice was losing its steadiness.

"Well, what do you want to call it? I'm only trying to put an end to this stupid quarrel—"

"It doesn't matter. Not now. It doesn't do any good, describing things."

"Listen, you called me conceited and selfish—"

"I'm sorry, I'll take it back. I don't want to go on with this—"

"I want to know just what you mean. I want to think clearly, even if you don't. I've always tried to think clearly—"

Like that of a stranger who has entered unawares, it was Trevon's diminished voice, certain, detached, which cut her short:

"Susie dear, you haven't. You've always steered your thoughts to give you the answer you wanted, you've started by saying you've never done anything wrong—"

"—You think the same as she does?"

"Yes. Yes, I think you're utterly selfish and viciously cruel."

She said distractedly: "If that was true it wouldn't be my fault. I can't help what I'm made like!"

"You can," he answered evenly. "I know, because I know how I was made."

"That's cant! It's nothing but cant!"

In tears, Elizabeth said: "Why can't she go away! Why can't she go!"

"Go? Go where? Who can I go to! What am I to do?"

Trevon said: "You've got to start by losing sight of yourself. Enough to begin loving someone."

And that was spoken gently; but as if his voice had flashed with anger hers broke into flame, "Loving!" and crumpled and sank as when flame passes: "How can a thing like me do that! Who is there left for me to love?"

Men powerless to interfere have stood quite still while they watch a friend burning alive: still, and apparently calm, though the fire be so close that it scorches their own skin. For their reason is protected then by a kind of incredulity; the torture they see will not be contained in the imagination, and so imagination rejects it altogether. Hearing that cry, the known voice with its surface peeled away, hearing it shrivel and die, Elizabeth stayed motionless. Only when moments had passed, slowly, as time falters in disaster, did she feel the dried spring of compassion starting to flow again, to gather urgency, to swell, until the flood of it released her from her impotence. An instant from the past came back, as to a shell-shocked man recovering memory. She turned, and reaching over, felt about for Armorel's hand to bring it to her mouth, she caught her by the other arm and pulled her down to clasp her between Trevon's body and her own. Here, broken and quivering, was the being she had sought for through the twisted corridors in which men hide themselves, had seen for a moment once, and altogether lost, believing that glimpse to have been illusion: here, with a certainty outstripping knowledge, she perceived the ultimate reality, the essence beneath the last disguise, such a creature as she could find by searching intently within herself: and as love's daylight dims the lamp of compassion she knew she was bound to her by love, that when others' need of it had ceased her love would find its labour and solace here. As if from a long way off, she heard Trevon's voice: ". . . Wasted? But there's always some part of us we've got to waste—some gangrenous part that's got to be cut away. . . . You've come to the beginning—don't you see?—the burning of the gates, it's the start of freedom. The journey you're meant for is still ahead—you'll come with us, you'll come?" She felt his cold fingers creeping like shy children to her neck and up into her hair, Rellie's hand tightening in hers and the gusts in her breathing dying into calm. The curled edge of the hearth-rug hurt her knees, the tiredness of these days hung like a chain on her shoulders and the tasks ahead—meals to be found and cooked, the losing struggle against squalor, the hundred little things to be done for Trevon—were like noises of the stirring camp which penetrate a soldier's dreams. Somewhere towards the Thames a clock was striking, and tomorrow she might find herself alone. But as happiness accepts the sweetened streams which flow to join it from sunlit hills, so, she thought, listening, listening to the way he breathed, when its channel is through salted land it will absorb the bitter waters in its wide and deepening course.

At some time after eleven Armorel was in Heald's back room. What Heald took to be 'a long petticoat' showed some inches below the overcoat she wore, and she had old shoes, with the laces trailing, on her bare feet. Her face, according to the account which Heald gave afterwards, was 'queer'; he could not describe it, but when he was asked if she had looked worried, he replied: "No, that's what was queer, if you see what I mean—first time for days I seen her *not* looking in a worry. Sad, yes, but she didn't look like she had anything to worry her, not like she usually did. That was what I thought was queer." Had she seemed rather—well—scattered, rather wild? No, nothing like that about her, you couldn't have had a woman look more calm than she did that night.

She apologized to Heald for intruding at that hour, and then went to Simon, who was sitting over the fire. Had he seen Gian, she asked, had Gian come back? He did not answer or even stir: his face showed that he had been crying, and he now appeared to be in the kind of coma which had seized him on the day after Maria's death. Heald pointed to the empty tumbler at Simon's feet and said with a significant glance that the old man was suffering from a chill. They had not seen young Mr Ardree, he told her, since the night before.

After a moment or two of uncertainty she approached Simon again. With her hands on his shoulders, she said restrainedly:

"Papa Simon, if Gian comes here, will you tell him, please, that I'd like to see him. Will you ask him very specially—will you give him my love and say I want him very badly."

His answer was to twist his shoulders free as a man shakes off the clutch of a bramble.

"He's upset about him," Heald told her laconically. "He don't altogether like what's going on. Got on his mind."

She nodded reflectively.

"Will you tell Gian if he comes? Tell him I need him so very badly."

"I'll tell him," Heald said, "only—well, I'll tell him if he come."

Elizabeth, wakened by the street door closing and hearing Armorel return along the passage, had to struggle for a minute or two before her will overcame the weight of her body's resistance. Then she forced herself out of bed and went once more to Armorel's room. "Was he there?" she asked softly, but got no answer. Hearing from Armorel's bed the sound of deep breathing, the peaceful breathing of one who sleeps as happy children do, she went back to her own.

49

SHORTLY AFTER Armorel had left, Heald, whose exceptional patience had been exhausted by Simon's morose and histrionic behaviour, told him that he ought to go to bed. Simon took no notice. Heald made no attempt to persuade him, for his general notion of liberty was that no one should be persuaded to do anything. (He was wont to say that if all the politicians, parsons, schoolmasters, and newspaper writers were locked up in Wormwood Scrubs the world would be a better place, except for the other poor bastards in Wormwood Scrubs.) He went to bed himself.

As he was falling asleep he heard Simon go out to the yard. There was nothing unusual in that, because three of Maria's hens were still kept there and Simon often went out at night to count them, or merely to chat to them, saying apologetically that his wife was busy and would visit them later on.

Simon went round into the lane, where he met a man he knew, one Teddy Small, coming home late from a Buffalo celebration. Small told him that he ought not to be out of doors without coat or shoes. Simon replied that he was as hot as hell, and they chatted agreeably for a minute or two about the prospects of war. Small said it would do his little business no good if they had a lot of bombs smashing the place up and frightening the womenfolk. Simon said it was all on account of the Government not cutting the throat of every fuming Hun there was in 1918, man, woman and child. That would have been a bit of a job for someone, Small said, and Simon answered: "It only want nerve—you got to have nerve, that's all." He seemed to Small to be in a cheerful mood, though a little abstracted.

When Small had left him he crossed the road and went up the side street to the back door of 83. His walk was not abnormal, but all his movements were slow and careful, like those of a man in an early stage of intoxication; he had, in fact, drunk about a third of a pint of cheap Californian brandy with half that volume of water—not enough to affect a younger man of normal constitution. He knocked boldly on the door and after a while Mrs Inch came and opened it a few inches; whereupon he pushed his way inside and went to the front of the house.

The account given afterwards by Mrs Inch was: ". . . A great big man push the door right in my face. Tread right on my foot an' never say he was sorry or nothing. I thought it might be Mr Jenkins. I didn't put on no light because I got my skirt off after being in bed, what wasn't nice with a fellow looking. I ask him what he want in here and he say, 'You keep quiet!' he said, so then I could tell by the way he spoke he was Mrs Ardree's husband and I went back to my bed."

Simon went into the front room and switched on the light. The curtains were undrawn, and the light shone right across the street. From its place above the mantelshelf he took the knife which he had always claimed as his own, and leaving the light on went upstairs to the lavatory and then to Gian's room, where for about five minutes he sat on Gian's bed, talking to himself as if he were instructing a rather difficult child. Then he went across to Armorel's room.

Armorel, half-waking, and discerning a figure beside the bed, said: "Gian! Is that Gian?"

Simon said: "You can't have him no more—he tell me what you done. He tell me everything. You gone on treatin' him like muck—it's you that's muck, see. You ain't goin' to do no more, no matter what."

Armorel said: "Simon, listen! Listen, Simon, I love him—I know it's all true what you say, but—"

"I done listening to your talk," he said. "Think it don't matter what kind of tale you tell to me! You done enough, see!"

The curtains were slightly parted at the top and enough light came from outside to show him where her head was. With something like a hedger's action with a billhook he struck twice at her neck, then seized the bed-clothes and rammed them down on her face.

At a Putney theatre where he worked for a time he had listened night after night to the curtain line in *Nimrod's Justice:* 'Yes, little heart, my operation was successful. A man whose breath made flowers wither has died.' These words had been in his head all day, and as he went downstairs he declaimed them softly in the very tone, as he remembered it, which Seton Warner had used: *A man whose breath made flowers wither—has died!* A few steps and he stopped with his arm on the rail, his head a little to one side, smiling, as Warner had smiled, towards the frightened girl he could picture standing close to the footlights: . . . *made flowers wither—has died!* And again, further down, letting his head turn more slowly, making the smile more enigmatic, *A man whose breath made flowers wither—has died!* That had been genius, the poise, the perfect control of body, expression and voice; something he could never aspire to; and yet at this moment the splendour of the words seemed to belong to him . . . *Made flowers wither—has died!* He had reached the bottom of the stairs when he realized that he had left the knife behind. That was a matter of importance, for although he was sure it belonged to him he did not want

Gian to suppose he had filched it. So he returned to Armorel's room and found the knife on the floor close to the bed. Having wiped it on the side of the bed, just as he wiped his razor every Saturday evening, he went downstairs once more, still murmuring, *"Yes, little heart, a man whose breath made flowers wither—has died."*

The attention of a man named Samuel Carter, deputy foreman of a bakery in Snow's Fields, was attracted by the light shining broadly across the lane, and he paused beside Heald's shop to stare at the window it came from. He saw a man come into the empty room, cross to the far side and do something on the wall over the fire-place. This exhausted his curiosity, and being already rather late for his shift he hurried on. He could not afterwards describe the man he had seen, except to say that he was "on the tall side, I should reckon, only a bit bent over." He was quite certain, he told the police, that it had not been Gian Ardree, whom he happened to have known well, for they had once worked together at the Hibbage Lane depot; but since he had not met him, as far as he could remember, for at least ten years, this asseveration was considered to have no great value. Likewise his statement, "When I had gone on a few yards I heard a door opening. That made me look back and I saw someone come out of one of the houses—it might have been the house where I'd seen the light showing," was obviously too vague to be of much use.

Equally little attention was paid to the confused statement of the puritanical old tailor-hand who lived on the ground floor of No. 68. She had been wakened—at what hour of the night she could not say—by the noise of someone being sick on the pavement outside her window. Presuming that it was one of the Coronation Building people going home drunk, she had put up the window and called out ('not angry, only solemn'), "Woe unto them that rise up early in the morning that they may follow strong drink!" to which the old man who was standing on the kerb had answered, "The little heart who made the flowers wither has died." When she told him that the Lord would pursue after him and punish his sins he had answered ('very sad') that the Lord would know he had meant no harm. Then he had run off towards Mr Heald's shop, 'as if he had a wild beast behind him,' and crying like a young child.

50

*T*HE PAIN was like glittering silver wire and like a high shrill note on the violin. Then it was crimson steam, one cloud advancing through another, until a darkness like infinity rolled down upon them all. Out of the darkness it returned as a burning scarf bound tightly about her throat.

They seemed by their gentleness to know that the scarf prevented her from responding: Christine, grubby and gay, running beside her along the road to Turvin's farm, Tonie with her music-case, anxiously peering back from a little way ahead; they smiled to see her taking Michael's arm, "As if he was my son!" she said, and though her voice came soundless they nodded as if they understood.

The pain was like a magnetic darkness which drew her again and again into its wedge. Now her eyes were free to see above it, now the whole of her was occupied in serving its demand for endurance. When it released her for a little while she ran from group to group in the cold gymnasium, asking by signs if anyone knew where Gian might be, and occasionally she caught a glimpse of his face, the face she had seen on the night when Tonie was born; but the faces of the rest she knew, the coarse, the laughing, eager faces, were always crowding in to hide him. She came to Trevon's office and entering humbly found her father there. He, at least, could see what she needed, and with his arm about her shoulders to keep her from slipping further into pain he led her past the sweet shop, through the kissing-gate and along by the hedge which smelt of honeysuckle towards Barrow Wood. Across the stable yard they caught a glimpse of Gian in Poulter's blue shirt and gaiters, busy planing a board while a circle of children stood admiring his skill; without looking up he called in a shy and frightened way that she mustn't come near, her clothes would scare his boys. "Gian!" she cried, "Gian, I've something to give you, I've had it for you all this time!" but the dress she was trying to take off had caught across her face. "He'll wait for you, Rellikin," her father said, speaking with Trevon's gentlest voice, "you've only to go that little way, there's nothing in between." Then pain like a giant wrestler threw her down, and she saw with anguish that the country lit by spring, the room warmed with the odour of men's evening weariness and by voices laughing in tune with hers, the garden where Gian paused in his work to send her his diffident, tender smile, were drawing further from her reach.

In this familiar street the faint persistence of the town's conglomerate noise, a hollow reverberation from a train on Hungerford Bridge, the mutter of armoured earth too weary from flagellation to sleep, seemed to intensify the stillness; and together, now, with the day's load of vision—the tangle of lights and lettering, a grey repetition of windowed walls, the traffic of faces passing and passing—the long war of inward voices had been subdued to a single blur upon his mind. Weariness such as he suffered now could not be relieved by sleep, only by action; and against the need for that relief neither his bodily fatigue nor the last whispers of doubt were strong enough to offer resistance.

He did stop at the corner to replace his shoe, which he had been carrying to ease the pain in his heel; and while he stood in shadow on the steps of the Savings Bank a man passed him whose face, in the light of a street-lamp, he instantly recognized, though he could not remember what he was called: years before, they had worked together in the depot at Hibbage Lane. Instinctively he moved to accost him, and then drew back, remembering he had lost his title to be anyone's friend. While he watched him crossing the tram lines he heard a woman's voice from the other direction, and the sound, he thought, of vomiting; but these made only a small impression on his exhausted senses. As soon as the man's footsteps had ceased to echo in the empty street he found his stiff legs moving him, with the ponderous momentum of a dragged cartwheel, on the last stage of the journey which seemed to have started in a forgotten land.

One problem which had slightly vexed him was solved: the front door was open. Inside, he put his cap down on the little table, and then, because Susie had often complained of that untidiness, removed it to a peg. In the front room he drew the curtains and sat down at Susie's desk.

The letter he wrote is curiously free from any important mistake, and although the lines waver the writing is in a respectable childish hand.

> Dear Tonie I am writing this because I expec they will not let me see you after. It is jus to give you All my love. You will think what I have done is wrong and that is right for you to think, I do not want you to ever think of doing such a terrible thing, which

you would not, because Trevon and them have learned you to love God and be a Cristian girl and that is the only thing for a sweet girl like you are to be. Only I am not the same, I am only an uneducate working man (foreman) & partly I-Tie, and I can not see people being crule and let them be, though I no that is not same as a Cristian man would, I am not good enough for that. Dear Tonie she has been a wicked woman she has tole lies and been immorel and she has done all that to make you unhapy. When she is gone there will be nobody tell you you are not to be with Michael, he is a good boy like his mum who has been good friend to me. So that is all I can do and I hope you will forgive me if it hurt to know and I hope it will not hurt Sue (Mum), the doctor tell me it dont hurt much, and I hope she will be all right where you go afterwards, I would like you to do a (mass) for mum if your clergiman do that for when they are dead. Dear Tonie I love you very very bad, you have been wonderful dauhter to me. Your loving GIAN ARDREE (Daddy) X X X X X X X X X X X X

He folded that across, wrote 'Tonie' on the back and placed it so that it stuck out from the closed flap of the desk. With his eyes on a photograph of Tonie which stood on the mantelshelf he reached for the knife, hanging in its usual place, and put it in the hip pocket of his trousers. There his fingers came upon a crumpled cigarette, which he lit and smoked for a few moments, wandering about the room; but when only half an inch had gone he pinched it out, put it tidily in the ash-tray which stood on the piano and turned to go upstairs.

The sound of the front door shutting had disturbed Olleroyd, who slept only fitfully in the small hours, and he came by degrees to wakefulness with the feeling that someone had broken into the house. He got out of bed, put a jacket over his night-shirt and switched on the light. Deliberate footsteps sounded on the stairs and he opened his door a few inches to see who it was.

The narrow shaft of light showed him, a few feet away, Gian's face: the face of an exhausted man, unshaven, filthy with the city's grime and the stains of dried sweat. But that was not what he afterwards recalled. The face he was to remember, and describe in his own fashion when closely questioned, was one which lacked both sadness and exaltation. It had, in the Caesarean lips and concentrated eyes, the look of experienced soldiers returning to the line, the tortured resolution in which all fears are solved, the dignity that martyrs have worn. For just a moment those prospecting eyes looked straight at his, but with no more recognition than you would discover in the eyes of the blind; and so strange was the experience of seeing that familiar face with a look that was not its own, of being scanned but apparently not observed, that he came to wonder whether it had been reality or a vivid and peculiar dream.

It was partly the light of a crescent moon, reflected by slate roofs, which came through the aperture between the curtains; partly a street-lamp's penumbral light. It caught a tumbler on the washstand, it outlined dimly the heap of her clothes on a chair and the shape like rolling downland of her bed. He closed the door behind him and stood quite still, drawing deep breaths. There was a new smell in the room, but beside it the old, emotive smell.

If I am very quick, he thought, the devices which always deceived me, the sweetness of her mouth, her body's fragility, will have no time to work. Only a moment more, while I silence the rebellious voices, and then the power which has brought me here will take me in charge again, the intended thing will happen, and then I can rest. But minutes passed and his body stayed motionless and slack.

A sound came from the bed, very small, like that which a child makes when troubled by dreams. Curiosity, working alone, moved him to her side.

He put both thumbs between his teeth, trying to control the fit of violent shivering which had seized him. Bending, he heard her voice, "Gian! . . . Gian, please let me come!"

He asked, "What's wrong?"—the voice belonged to a man he had been long ago, "What is it, Sue, what's wrong?" He discerned her hand emerging like a separate, small creature, he slipped his own beneath and cautiously enclosed it, as if the slightest roughness might stop its breath. There was dampness where his wrist lay, but his mind had no spare force to wonder what it was. "Sue! Is it something wrong? Are you ill, Sue?"

"He hurt me," she said. "It doesn't matter now."

He said, "I'll get something, I'll get y' a cup o' tea—" but she answered, "No—stay here, stay with me, Gian, don't go away!"

His shivering had stopped; as one who has passed the crisis of fever he felt himself enclosed by a shawl of weariness, and the tears flooding to mouth and eyes were like the cool-warm sponge in a gentle nurse's hand. He let his head fall beside hers, his free arm slid beneath her neck, and now, for the first time, he lay beside her with no tinge of self-reproach, no fear at all. He said, weeping, "I never meant y' to have no pain." "You've come," was all she said, "it's all right now you've come."

Sleep, so long refused, gained only a portion of him now. His eyes were shut, his body rested, the questioning part of his mind lay still; and yet he knew where he was, and could feel with heightened sensitivity the fine, soft hair pressing against his cheek; through his drowsiness he did not cease to experience the overwhelming gratitude of one awaked from a dreadful dream. As the grief of a dream will continue into wakefulness, his, with the banks broken, flowed widely on; but like the mysterious sorrows of children this torrent was grief's fulfilment and its healing. His need to explain, to be forgiven, was almost satisfied by her body's slight weight and warmth. The words would come, and till then he was content to lie still at her side.

They came as if of themselves: "I reckon I gone all wrong, see, goin' off—Tonie 'n' all, got on me mind, see—treated you bad. I'll make it up, see. Get some sort of a job—I'll make it up, see." And later on: "I better tell you—I got it in mind to do you wrong. Worse I could, see. You better know. Got m' feelin's all wrong. I reckon I woulden be that way never again. Only I reckon you oughter know. Might have hurt you bad, see."

She said clearly, after a while, "You couldn't ever hurt me. It wouldn't hurt if it was you."

And when she spoke again her voice was still quite clear, controlled, although so slenderly spun that he only heard it because his ear was close to her lips.

"Listen, Gian, listen—can you hear me? Gian, I didn't know, I never knew what you were like—how good you are. I only saw you through myself, you can't see anything like that. I wouldn't let you in, I didn't want you or anyone to see me inside. Gian, do you see, do you understand? I hated it, I was ashamed, you see, I was ashamed of needing people. I thought I'd find it by myself, I thought I'd always find my way."

He did not understand what she was saying; only some quality in the trembling voice awoke in him a terrible pity and remorse. He said, with his words muted to match the fragility of hers:

"I'll get it the way you want. I'll find some place—"

"Gian, don't," she whispered, "Gian, don't be unselfish any more. Not to me, please not to me. I can't bear you to be so good."

And now the voice had changed. It was still her own, her 'sensible' voice, reasoning and persuasive, the one she had always used to make him fall in with her plans; but in the personality which belongs to each of one man's several voices it was different from anything Gian had heard before. In physical distance it seemed to come from far away; yet as that distance lengthened, its nearness to his understanding increased. It was naked now, relaxed, as the face of royalty relaxes when the door shuts and only the closest friends are left inside.

"My darling—Gian, can you hear?—Gian, my darling, I only want one thing. I want you to think of me as I am now. You can't forgive me everything, I don't want that. Only—can you hear me, darling, can you hear?—only when you think of what I've been, all that selfishness, so cruel and blind—darling, can you hear?—when you think of that, will you, will you try to think there was someone else—someone different—all the time? Wanting—can you hear me? Darling, can you hear? —wanting and wanting to love you, only I was so small, so blind."

He struggled to say: "We'll get it all right, Sue. We'll make it all right."

"Yes. Yes, you and Tonie. Loving people—you and Tonie—you can do that, you've always known how to love." Her voice was ebbing again. "I want you to have a garden. Those children—you showed me— those children with peeky faces, the ones you look after, I want you to have them all the time. All the time. If I was there—Gian, if I was there I'd do what you wanted. Everything. Everything you told me. If I could go on now, if I could be with you, I'd make myself so you could love me."

His hold became at once more vehement and more tender. He said with the quietness of absolute certainty:

"It don't alter, the way I reckon. I couldn't be lovin' you more 'n' what I do, nor any bloke do any girl. I reckon it been like that all the time, only you bein' tired, see, you havin' things on your mind, same as any woman do—"

The ghost of her voice broke out: "I didn't know! Oh my darling, I didn't know!"

Those words were sealed by a gasp in which her whole body was shaken; and then came a cry, small and remote, but shaped like the cry of labour. In a whisper of terror and anguish, Gian called:

"Sue! Sue! Have you got the pain? Is it bad—Sue, is it bad?"

Quietening, "Such pain!" she said, "I can't—" And then, "It's beautiful—the pain—O beloved, it's beautiful, it's all wrapped up in love."

Strangely, he understood those words more clearly than anything she had ever said. They were, of course, spoken close to his ear, and the nervous impulse which framed and projected them could be felt in his own body, to which hers was closely bound; but the nearness from which they came exceeded that. It was perhaps extreme exhaustion which altered in him the mechanism by which one hears and understands, as when a motor, run hotly for some time, seems to acquire a power too fluent to come from the complex labour of pistons and valves. He felt, as she lay against him like a part of his own body, peacefully, still gently warm, her breathing grown so quiet he could scarcely feel its movement, that they had stumbled upon a common speech: a speech available to all humanity and yet peculiarly theirs. The things he would explain to her were simple now; for as she had opened her doors to him, and her hiding-place had seemed as easy for him to walk in as a familiar street, so he could yield to her the place where he himself had been ashamed and alone. He knew that the words he wanted would not come. But his need of them had passed; the touch of her fingers still just moving to stroke his hand was enough, he knew that no such artifice as speech could hold them apart when their very weakness, the weakness both knew and understood, gave them freehold of this country they had not imagined before.

They lay side by side, their arms enfolded, while the nightlong murmur of the town was quickened to the noise of reveille; as aged soldiers listen from high windows to the sound of hoarse commands and stamping feet he heard the moan of trams, distant sirens hooting, the orchestra of small and busy sounds rising to possess the day. As the light grew he saw by degrees how pale she was, matching her flesh's coldness, and how the dampness he had felt had spread to cover her breast like a broad scarf of rusty brown. He did not move, for she had begged him not to leave her alone; content to caress with his hand the softness of her cheek and forehead, to hear her voice returning and returning like a melody to the ear of his mind, he lay waiting for someone to come.

It was Daise who came; and who, betraying no horror or fear, seeming to enclose the scene in some understanding of her own, sat quietly by the bed on Gian's side; looking only at his face with the intensity of the simple in spirit, timidly stroking the arm of his coat.

51

He turned the car and placed it close to the gates; he could stay there (the policeman said) for up to a quarter of an hour. From a man who passed he bought an *Evening News,* to look at rather than to read.

'*Appeal Fails* . . . learns that a new, last-minute appeal on the ground of insanity will be made to the Home Secretary . . .' The rest, an inflammatory speech at Frankfurt, new instructions on air-raid precautions, was news which changed so little that one accepted it as Eskimos accept the onset of arctic night: meaning almost everything to him, it meant, at this moment, nothing at all. He turned the page and his eyes, in a dilatory excursion of their own, came upon a fill-up in a left-hand column: 'The body of an aged man who had applied at several shipping offices for employment as a steward was found early this morning hanged from a bollard in Greenland Dock': and because the smaller happenings were nearer to his present mood than large ones, that sentence penetrated a little below the surface of his mind. Did it matter, when the stage was being set so zealously for the death of millions? Yet it seemed a pitiful fact that no one had found any use for that old man.

Half-an-hour passed and then she reappeared, walking rather quickly; entirely self-possessed; with her mother's dignity, in the light-grey coat and skirt which Rellie had once worn.

From a group of people standing opposite the gates a man with a camera suddenly came across the street. In an instant Michael was out of the car and standing in front of him. "Just take one photograph," Michael said with extreme quietness, "and I shall knock you down and smash that thing to bits." The man went away.

She sat in the car and he closed the door as if the smallest noise might damage her. They drove off without speaking and turned eastward on the road leading into town.

She asked, as the houses crowded more closely upon the road, as the clamour and confusion thickened: "Where are we going?"

"I thought—back to the Liskes'. I thought you'd want to rest."

When they had travelled another half-mile she said: "I suppose Elizabeth's expecting you back?"

"Not till this evening. She's out at Raymond's place."

"You could phone her, later on?"

"Yes."

"Could we go the other way—Sussex? Would it be an awful bother?"

"Nothing would be."

And at the roundabout he went off to the right, on the Teddington road.

"There's a place," she said, "I forget what it's called, I saw it going to the funeral. I think it was somewhere near Handcross."

"We'll look."

"There was a pub with a chestnut outside, just where the road got very narrow. The church was on a little hill, all by itself. Very small. Very old."

"I saw it," he said. "Saxon, part of it."

"I thought you would have."

"I can find that."

In sunlight hazed by the smoke of factories they crossed the Kingston By-Pass and went on towards Ewell and Burgh Heath.

She said: "I thought I'd like to be there till it's over. I mean, in the church. It's so on its own."

"You mean, all night?"

"Yes. Would they let me?"

"I don't see why not."

The grip of the interminable town slowly relaxed. Nearing Reigate, he said: "I'd like to be there as well. Not close, I don't mean. I mean, just somewhere near by. In the porch, I mean, in case you wanted anything."

She answered: "Yes. Yes, please."

Tired of the lorry fumes, he turned off the main road and followed the lanes through Norwood Hill. A breeze from the west brought into the open car the smell of earth released from snow. In the banks a few primroses showed.

She said: "It was funny, he thought I was Mother part of the time. I'm glad. Because he was so grateful. Grateful and loving. I'm glad."

"Yes."

He took his left hand from the wheel and put it beside him so that hers, if she wished, could rest on it.

"Then afterwards he knew," she said. "Knew it was me. He was quite clear then. He knew everything. The time it was to be—they'd told him. He was perfectly clear."

They twisted through Charlwood.

"He's happy. Absolutely happy," she said.

Farther on, he stopped the car. Now that the sun was lower the air was cold; the silence was like that of winter and it seemed as if the gentleness of the afternoon light had been only counterfeit. But the soil's breath, moist and sweet, had the potence and vitality of spring. Her toes had gone to sleep, she told him. Bending down, he took off her suède shoe and very carefully rubbed her foot.

He said: "One thing—you'll keep that rug round you, in the night?"

"Yes. But you—? Is there another rug?"

"I'll be all right."

He put the shoe on again and tied the lace.

He said, "If you want anything, in the night, you'll only have to call. You might possibly feel faint or something. I'll come then. Only I won't come unless you call. I won't be where I can actually see you."

He started to work on her other foot.

"You see, you'll want to use the whole of yourself. I can see that. Anyone else would be—well, taking something that ought to go to him. Him and her. You see?"

She whispered: "Yes, I do see."

"I know you'd let me share, if I asked you. Later on," he said, "sometime, we'll go back to it. Then I'll share as much as I can. I'll know most of what it was like. The pain. Not the sacredness. I won't try to share that. You see, I'm small, comparatively. I understand it. But it's all your own. You see what I mean?"

"Yes."

He put back the second shoe. She asked:

"What time is it now?"

"Just after six."

"Fourteen hours."

"Yes."

She asked, "Do you think he'll sleep?"

He answered slowly: "Yes. I mean, from what you've told me—his being happy. But I don't know if it matters. I think from what you told me before he understands everything. All that matters is to understand."

"Yes." She had his wrist in both her hands, she was studying it intently, fingering the hairs and the veins, as a collector appreciates a figurine of immeasurable worth. "Yes, Michael, yes!"

Without moving his wrist he restarted the engine and slipped-in the gear with his right hand. The darkening sky was still free from cloud, tomorrow there would be clear sunlight again. They went on slowly into Crawley, friendly with lights in cottage windows, where with the calm faces of people who know their business, they rejoined the traffic in the main road.

He did sleep, with only comfortable dreams. Early in the morning they brought him tea and things to eat and a cigarette. He smoked a little, but the cigarette kept going out and he threw it away. They brought, too, the paper and pencil he had asked for, and he wrote to Terence Hubbitt:

> Dear Tery There is a job I diden finish off, it is the 2nd basin in clokroom, the pipe was block behind. I have got it free but it want a new section of piping which Slimey mus put in, I think the 7/8 spaner is still on the windesill what he will want. You better tell Sargent Flock to send Slimey or he will never come. All the best yours truely G. Ardree PS Please tell them I am sorry I will not see them again.

He appeared much relieved to have got that done; he smiled warmly at the man who had promised to get the note delivered, and thanked him again and again. After that he fell into a kind of bashfulness like that of a shy boy who will soon have to appear in public to be presented with a prize. He was listening all the time, and he seemed to be a little reassured when some fragment of London sound, the noise of buses and of lorries grinding towards the Basingstoke road, came faintly to his ears.

Yes, it is today, eight o'clock, they said, it must be that soon. "Can you tell me the time? Give me time, please? Tell me the time?" I suppose it don't hurt long, bad but not very long, only it'd be better if you knew before what sort of hurt it was. And then nothing after that, only it might not be nothing, depend if what they say is right. Not what Sue said, because I know she didn't mean what she said. You can't think of there being nothing after that. Tonie said she'd be all right. Tonie'll be all right. It's all right if Tonie's all right. This here wasn't done by a proper joiner, kid at the Apostles' make a better job of it than that. Young East, he'd make a better job of it than that. Yes, it'll be bad but it won't go on long, like it did with Sue, and she put up with that, didn't cry or nothing. See East again, ask how his mum gone on in hospital. No, no time now. "Tell me the time, please? Give me the time?" Just plain ignorance, using nails instead of screws. Sort of a kid's job. Young East do it better than that. You can't think of it, just nothing going on and on. "Sì, signore!" Tired he look, look half-asleep, shame to get the ole gent up this time in the morning. "Sì, signore!" And not got his collar fixed right, bit of shirt or what showing in between. Only how do you fix a collar like that? Can't have a thing at the front else it would show. Only you want something so as not to have the shirt showing like that, it wouldn't pass by Susie, not for Sunday, not having something showing what oughtn't to be showing like that. "Sì, signore! Tell me the time, please?" Well, of course it hurt. Only not long, can't go on long. Not like it done with Sue. "Well, no, I reckon there ain't nothing I got to say. I never done it, see, only that don't make no difference, 'cause I would've done it, see, so it's all the same as if I did. You don't have to tell me, see—I reckon it got to come on me just the same as if I done it." Sinned? All have sinned? "Well, I s'pose that's right, only that don't mean the same, not the same as doin' what I had in mind, only someone else done it." May be the black thing underneath not been fixed right. Want someone like Sue, put in a stitch in a half a jiff, fix it on the shirt. Quick with her needle, wouldn't find a better hand with a needle and thread. 'Loved the world?' No sense in it, you can't love a thing like the world. 'Everlasting life.' Everlasting life! Everlasting life! Just going on and on and on. You can't think of a thing like that. Everlasting life. Without Tonie or Sue. Only if so, Susie begun on it. Might see Susie. All right with Susie. Susie understands, nothing Sue don't understand. Sue! "Beg pardon, yes, I'm listenin'. No, it don't mean much. Yes, it do mean somethink. Like y' to go on with that. Like y' to stay, see. Yep, I heard somethink of that kind—lambs an' that. Lady called Pieta, she talk that way. No, you wouldn't know, that's a long way back, back where I was born, see. Only I reckon it don't apply, not when you do someone in, someone like Sue. Got her wrong, see—not much edgecation—only she understand, she tole me she understand. I reckon I can't do with that, not everlasting life, jus' goin' on an' on. I reckon I got to go through it, see, take it the way it come, gettin' punish by God, see, only not on an' on. It don't say it go on an' on an' never stop? Lovin'? I don't see. Yes, she tell me she love me, that's honest she did, she tell me after she had that done. I reckon it was all right then, her an' me. Only God ain't like a human bein', see. Give me the time, please? Reckon I oughtn't to keep y hangin' about. Yes, I'd believe that if I knew how. Yes, I'll say it after you—only m'voice ain't much good, not much edgecation, see, somethin' wrong with m'voice, see." Reckon he'll get it fix up when he get back home. Someone like Sue, fix it up with a bit o' thread. Tonie said she'd be O.K. She look all right. She look as if she was happy in herself, all excep' on account of me. She got a headpiece, Tonie, she'll do all right. Mrs Liz see to it she's O.K. "Got punished instead. Punish himself? You say it don't go on? He don't want to punish nobody? Well, that's the same as what Trevon tell me. Tell me the time, please—give me the time? Certain? You mean you know that? Me? Love me? Same as I love Sue an' Tonie? You quite certain? Didn't ought to keep y'—time goin' on. Yes, I'll say that. Yes, I'll keep on sayin' that. Well, yes, I reckon I'd like that, if it ain't takin' up too much of your time." No, this ain't it, this can't be it, they can't be goin' to do it now. Not a day like this, they can't do it a day like this, decent blokes, they can't do it a day like this. Exercise, it is. Mornin' exercise. Can't be nothin' else. Not a day like this. Decent blokes. They can't do that, not a day like this. Loved the world. 'He loves you.' Loves me. 'Yes, same as you love Sue an' Tonie.' Got to think. Just a bit o' time, bit more time to think. Might see how it work, just a bit more time. 'Loves you.' Same as me lovin' Sue an' Tonie. Dark. Gone all dark. "Wait! I got something to say! Wait! *Wait!* Let me go, let go my arms, let me out. *I got something to say! Got something to say! Let me out!*" They can't do that. Sort of a joke. Dream. Sort of a joke. Not really. Won't happen. Somethin' go wrong. Won't really happen. Some as lovin' Sue an' Tonie. Same as lovin' Sue. Sue! Sue! Jes's Chris'. Jes's Chris'. Jes's Chris'. Love me. Sake amen. Now. Stop them, don't let them! *Let me out!* Love me. Jes's Chris'. Jes's Chris'. . . . Terror, naked, the endless moment of terror like sky splitting, like a sword of ice driven upward from bowels to throat. Pain like mountains falling together upon one small creature. *Love me— Jes' Chris'!* The terror and the pain, the pain and the darkness, darkness and peace. The peace, the Peace.

Crondall, Hampshire
Designed 1940
Written 1945-48

Continued from page viii

'STUMPER' BEAD, a master bricklayer.
MR PEGLETT, builder's foreman.
MR COOD
MR DUCKETT } Night School teachers.
MR BENFELLOW
MR JOHNSON, alias of Charlie Empire.
MRS EUSTACE
MR BRODIE } Permanent residents at 16A, Weald Street.
MONACA PIETA, a Nun of Genoa, remembered by Gian.
ELIZA BENTLOCK
BET OESTERMANN
MARY TOBLE } Friends of Maria Ardree.
MRS DIDDUS
DR HAHMIED
DR WAINSEL } Physicians.
DR JACQUELIN
AUSTIN and HILDA NICHOLEDD
NORAH CHILCOTT } Friends of Henry Kinfowell.
RHODA, wife of Gordon Aquillard.
FRANK HUGHES, a friend of Trevon Grist.
MR LIEDKE-URBAN, practitioner in psychiatry.
LUCY, servant of Elizabeth.
GUY and NED FILLIARD, children of Duffy.
ARTHUR AUGUSTUS LISKE, son of Christine.
ALICE and MURIEL DERBY
ELSIE BODWIN } Guests at Antonia's birthday party.
TOMMIE EDE
EVANGELINE HUGG, daughter of Rosie.
MARIGOLD
AUDREY HUBBITT

Mr Justice Swift ⎫
Mr St Anscar, barrister-at-law, ⎬ at the Central Criminal Court.

Mrs Elm, previous tenant of 83, Mickett Lane.

Ted Orfit ⎫
Tiny Bates ⎬ Removal men and undertakers.
Clip Starkie ⎭

Miss Paulidge, from the Queen's Road House of Eventide.

Mr Hoven, solicitor. (Mentioned)

Mr Lionel C. Sture, barrister-at-law. ⎫
Mr Bertram Silkinson of the London ⎬ Friends of Raymond.
  County Council. ⎭

Dr Synvenor, practitioner in remedial psychiatry. (Mentioned)

Boys at Apostles' Court; members of the Belgrave Bradlaugh Society and other Free Philosophers; residents in Weald Street and Mickett Lane; Priests and Nuns; workmen, shopkeepers, drivers, porters, policemen, gaolers; a Prison Chaplain; a press-photographer; and some others.